"SUPERB AND MAGNIFICENT—
A CLIFFHANGER OF THE SOUL."
—John Gunther

"A *cri de cœur* by a major novelist in the great
tradition of Russian literature. Systematically, he
lays bare for us all the circles of Stalin's Inferno,
writing with power, insight, savage sarcasm and
even occasional humor."

—John Barkham,
Saturday Review Syndicate

"FOR ITS SARDONIC AND TEN-
DER REVELATION OF HUMAN
NATURE UNDER STRESS, THIS
BOOK IS A MILESTONE."
—Edward Weeks,
The Atlantic

THE FIRST CIRCLE "ESTABLISHES
[SOLZHENITSYN] AS ONE OF THE CLAS-
SIC WRITERS OF CONTEMPORARY
EUROPEAN LITERATURE...AS MOR-
ALLY EARNEST AND LINGUISTICALLY
SKILLFUL AS TOLSTOY."

F. D. Reeve,
Book World

ABOUT THE AUTHOR

Aleksandr I. Solzhenitsyn, Nobel prize laureate and Russia's most celebrated living writer, was born December 11, 1918, in Kislovodsk. In February 1945, as a young captain in the Russian army, he was arrested by Soviet counterintelligence, who had discovered in his letters derogatory remarks about Stalin. Solzhenitsyn spent eight years in concentration camps and three years in exile for his offense—an experience that provided the raw material for *One Day in the Life of Ivan Denisovich* and *The First Circle*. In 1954 he underwent radiation therapy for treatment of cancer, which became the catalyst for his novel *Cancer Ward*, published in the late 1960s. In 1962, protected by Khrushchev's anti-Stalin campaign, *One Day in the Life of Ivan Denisovich* was published in the Soviet Union. It remains the only one of his works published in his native land. Solzhenitsyn was awarded the Nobel prize for literature in 1970 but was unable to attend the Nobel ceremony in Sweden for fear that he would be barred from returning to his family. In 1972, despite government sponsored ostracism and the loss of most of the privileges afforded other Soviet writers, Solzhenitsyn produced *August 1914*—a masterful account of World War I—and the following year, in defiance of Soviet law, authorized the Western publication of *The Gulag Archipelago, 1918–1956*. This so outraged the Soviet authorities that after waging a campaign of vilification against him, they stripped Solzhenitsyn of his citizenship and on February 13, 1974, expelled him from Russia. He now lives with his family in Vermont and has since published his autobiography, *The Oak and the Calf* (1975), the acclaimed *Lenin in Zurich* (1975), and the next two volumes in *The Gulag Archipelago* canon (in 1974 and 1976).

The
First
Circle

Aleksandr I. Solzhenitsyn

Translated from the Russian by
Thomas P. Whitney

BANTAM BOOKS
TORONTO • NEW YORK • LONDON • SYDNEY • AUCKLAND

THE FIRST CIRCLE
*A Bantam Book / published by arrangement with
Harper & Row, Publishers*

PRINTING HISTORY
Harper & Row edition published September 1968
2nd printing ... October 1968   3rd printing .. December 1968
4th printing . . . . . January 1969
Condensation appeared in
THE SATURDAY EVENING POST *October 1968*

Book-of-the-Month Club edition published October 1968

*Bantam edition / September 1969
16 printings through September 1976*

*Bantam Windstone edition / March 1981
18th printing . . . . . July 1982*

Windstone and accompanying logo of a stylized **W**
are trademarks of Bantam Books, Inc.

ISBN 0-553-22904-4

Published simultaneously in the United States and Canada

PRINTED IN THE UNITED STATES OF AMERICA

H   27 26 25 24 23 22 21 20 19

CONTENTS

"I don't have to do anything for anyone, remember that!

TRANSLATOR'S NOTE

The word "sharashka" as it occurs in this story derives from
a Soviet slang expression meaning "a sinister enterprise based
on bluff or deceit." By 1949, the time of the novel, it meant,
particularly, a special scientific or technical institute staffed
with prisoners—or, in Soviet slang, "zeks." The sharashka
in which much of the action of this novel takes place is located on the outskirts of Moscow. It is called the Mavrino
Institute, and the 281 zeks who are employed there are inmates of the Mavrino Special Prison, which is housed in the
same complex of buildings.

The Soviet State Security organ charged with the functions
of security and counterintelligence—in other words, the
Soviet secret police—has had various names since it was established in 1917, and has been known in different periods
by the Russian initials of its contemporary official title.

From December 1917 until 1922 it was the Cheka (with
the accent on the last syllable), from two of the initials of
"All-Russian Extraordinary Commission for the Struggle
Against Counterrevolution and Sabotage."

The Cheka contributed the name "Chekist" to Soviet secret police officers and employees, a label which has lasted
right up to the present time. In 1922 the Cheka was renamed and reorganized as the GPU (pronounced *Gay-Pay-
Oo*), from the initial letters of the Russian words for "State
Political Administration." That same year the GPU became
the OGPU (*Oh-Gay-Pay-Oo*), when the Russian word for
"consolidated" or "unified" was added to its name, but both
names were used almost interchangeably until 1934.

In that year the OGPU was merged into the NKVD

(*En-Kay-Vay-Day*), Peoples' Commissariat for Internal Affairs. This administrative entity had supervision over the ordinary police as well as the secret police, and it was the organization which, under the direction of Commissar Yezhov, carried out the horrendous purge of 1937–1938, known also as the *Yezhovshchina*.

Shortly before World War II, with Lavrenty Beria now in charge of secret police affairs (following Yezhov's execution), the secret police functions were taken from the NKVD and turned over to the smaller NKGB (*En-Kay-Gay-Bay*), Peoples' Commissariat of State Security, as its exclusive responsibility.

In 1946 the NKGB was renamed the MGB (*Em-Gay-Bay*), Ministry of State Security. And in that same year Victor S. Abakumov was named Minister of State Security. This, then, was the organization exercising supervision over the Mavrino sharashka in December 1949, the period of this novel. Abakumov, whom we meet in these pages, was removed from office some time in 1951 or 1952 by Stalin and arrested, apparently on charges of malfeasance. He was shot—or at any rate his execution was announced—in December 1954, more than a year and a half after Stalin's death, on charges of having framed a group of Soviet leaders in the "Leningrad Case" of 1949 and 1950.

There are two other Soviet agencies concerned with police work whose names are found frequently in the text. The MVD (*Em-Vay-Day*) was the Ministry of Internal Affairs, which existed from 1946 on and was the linear descendant of the NKVD. It supervised the ordinary, as distinct from the secret, police, but sometimes performed State Security functions, particularly in the area of prison and camp administration. SMERSH was the wartime Soviet counterintelligence agency operating with the army at and behind the front, and its name was derived from the Russian words meaning "Death to Spies!"

All the zeks of the Mavrino sharashka belonged, though they were not at the time in hard-labor camps, to the realm of GULAG—the Chief Administration for Corrective Labor Camps. This organization kept its identity through all the rechristenings of its parent organization. It ruled most of the Soviet northland and Siberia, and it had more inhabitants behind its barbed wire and "zones" than some of the prosperous middle-sized European countries.

T.P.W.

CHARACTERS

Victor Semyonovich Abakumov: Minister of State Security.

Grigory Borisovich Adamson: A zek engineer, serving his second term.

Bobynin: Zek boss of Laboratory Number Seven at Mavrino.

Vladimir Erastovich Chelnov: Professor of mathematics, a "transient zek," serving his eighteenth year of imprisonment.

Rostislav (Ruska) Vadimich Doronin: A zek mechanic, 23.

Ivan Selivanovich Dyrsin: A zek engineer.

Larisa Nikolayevna Emina: A free employee in the Design Office at Mavrino.

Dinera Galakhov: Daughter of the prosecutor Makarygin, wife of Nikolai Galakhov.

Nikolai (Kolya) Arkadevich Galakhov: A popular writer.

Illarion Pavlovich Gerasimovich: A zek physicist specializing in optics, a relative newcomer to Mavrino.

Natalya Pavlovna Gerasimovich: His wife.

Isaak Moiseyevich Kagan: Zek "director of the battery room."

Ilya Terentevich Khorobrov: A zek radio engineer, imprisoned for defacing his election ballot.

Lieutenant Colonel Ilya Terentevich Klimentiev: Head of the Mavrino Special Prison.

LIEUTENANT KLYKACHEV: Director of the Decoding Laboratory and assistant to Party Secretary Stepanov at Mavrino.

HIPPOLYTE MIKHAILICH KONDRASHEV-IVANOV: Resident zek painter at Mavrino, age 50.

ALEXEI LANSKY: A young literary critic.

CLARA PETROVNA MAKARYGIN: Youngest daughter of the prosecutor Makarygin, a free employee at Mavrino.

MAJOR GENERAL PYOTR AFANASYEVICH MAKARYGIN: A prosecutor, father of Dinera, Dotnara, and Clara.

YAKOV IVANOVICH MAMURIN: "The Iron Mask," now a zek, formerly Beria's Chief of Special Communications.

MAJOR MYSHIN: The Mavrino Prison security officer.

JUNIOR LIEUTENANT NADELASHIN: A Mavrino Prison guard.

GLEB VIKENTYEVICH NERZHIN: A zek mathematician, age 31.

NADYA NERZHIN: His wife.

FOMA GURYANOVICH OSKOLUPOV: Head of the Special Equipment Section of the Ministry of State Security.

LIEUTENANT GENERAL ALEKSANDR NIKOLAYEVICH POSKREBYSHEV: Chief of Stalin's personal secretariat.

ANDREI ANDREYEVICH POTAPOV: A zek electrical engineer, 45, one of the designers of the Dnieper Hydroelectric Power Station; a former POW in Germany.

VALENTINE (VALENTULYA) MARTYNICH PRYANCHIKOV: A zek radio engineer, 31, also a former German POW.

DUSHAN RADOVICH: An orthodox Marxist Serb, former member of the Comintern.

MAJOR ADAM VENIAMINOVICH ROITMAN: Deputy to Yakonov at Mavrino.

LEV GRIGORYEVICH RUBIN: A zek philologist and teacher, 36, a Communist from youth.

MIKHAIL DMITRIYEVICH RYUMIN: A senior interrogator in the MGB for important political cases.

SEVASTYANOV: Deputy Minister of State Security, in charge of communications and precision technology.

CAPTAIN SHCHAGOV: Ex-soldier friend of Lansky.

MAJOR SHIKIN: The Mavrino Institute security officer.

LIEUTENANT SHUSTERMAN: A Mavrino Prison guard.

ARTHUR SIROMAKHA: A zek mechanic in Number Seven.

LIEUTENANT SMOLOSIDOV: An MGB officer on the Mavrino Institute staff.

DMITRI ALEKSANDROVICH SOLOGDIN: A zek designer, 36, a survivor of the northern camps now serving his second term.

IOSIF STALIN: Real name Iosif Vissarionovich Djugashvili, sometimes called "The Plowman."

BORIS SERGEYEVICH STEPANOV: Communist Party secretary at Mavrino.

SERAFIMA (SIMOCHKA) VITALYEVNA: An MGB lieutenant in the Acoustics Laboratory at Mavrino.

DOTNARA (DOTTY) VOLODIN: Daughter of prosecutor Makarygin, wife of Innokenty Volodin.

INNOKENTY ARTEMYEVICH VOLODIN: State Counselor in the Ministry of Foreign Affairs, age 30.

ANTON NIKOLAYEVICH YAKONOV: Colonel of Engineers of the State Security Service, chief of operations at the Mavrino Institute.

SPIRIDON DANILOVICH YEGOROV: The zek janitor at Mavrino, age 50.

LIEUTENANT ZHVAKUN: A Mavrino Prison guard.

1

AND WHO ARE YOU?

The fretwork hands stood at five past four.

In the dying light of the December day the bronze face of the clock on the shelf looked black.

The double panes of the tall window looked down on the busy street and the janitors shoveling dirty brown snow, newly fallen but already soggy, from under the feet of the pedestrians.

Staring at all this without seeing it, State Counselor Second Rank Innokenty Volodin leaned against the edge of the window and whistled a thin, drawn-out note. His fingertips leafed through the glossy, bright-colored pages of a foreign magazine. But he saw none of it.

State Counselor Second Rank Innokenty Volodin, whose rank in the diplomatic service was equivalent to that of lieutenant colonel in the army, was tall and narrowly built. Dressed not in uniform but in a worsted suit, he looked more like a young gentleman of leisure than an executive in the Ministry of Foreign Affairs.

It was time either to turn on the lights in the office, which he did not do, or else to go home. He made no move to do that, either.

Four o'clock did not mean the end of the working day but of its daytime, or lesser, part; everyone would now go home to have dinner and take a nap, and then, from ten o'clock on, thousands of windows in sixty-five Moscow ministries would light up again. There was only one person, behind a dozen fortress walls, who could not sleep at night, and he had taught all official Moscow to keep vigil with him until three or four in the morning. Knowing the nocturnal habits of the Sovereign, the three score ministers sat up like schoolboys in expectation of a summons. So as not to get sleepy they called out their deputies, and the deputies harassed their section heads; reference librarians on stepladders pored over their card catalogues, filing clerks dashed down corridors, secretaries broke pencil points.

And even today, on the eve of Western Christmas, when for two days all the embassies had been quiet, frozen up, their phones still, and people were probably right this minute sitting down around their Christmas trees, there would still be night work in their own ministries. Some would play chess and others would tell stories and still others doze on couches—but there would be work.

Volodin's nervous fingers swiftly and aimlessly leafed through the magazine. And all the time within him the pang of fear now rose and burned a little, then subsided and chilled.

How well Innokenty remembered from childhood the name of Dr. Dobroumov! At that time he had not yet become such a luminary. They did not send him abroad with delegations. He was not even known as a scientist, but simply as a medical doctor, and he went out to make house calls. Innokenty's mother was often indisposed, and she always tried to get hold of Dobroumov. She had faith in him. The moment he arrived and took off his sealskin cap in the entry, the whole place would be filled with an atmosphere of good feeling, calm, assurance. He never stayed less than half an hour by the bedside. He asked about every complaint; and then, as though it gave him great satisfaction, he examined the patient and expounded the prescribed cure. On his way out, he never passed the boy without asking him a question, and he would stop to listen to the reply, as if he seriously expected to hear something intelligent. The doctor was graying even then. What would he look like now?

Innokenty flung down the magazine and, tense and preoccupied, paced the room.

Should he telephone or not?

If all this had involved some other professor of medicine whom he didn't know personally, Innokenty would never have thought twice about trying to warn him. But Dobroumov!

Could there possibly be a way of identifying a person

speaking over a public telephone—if one wasted no time and hung up and left quickly? Could they recognize a voice over the phone? Surely there was no technique for that.

He went to his desk. In the twilight he could still make out the top sheet of the instructions covering his new assignment. He was to leave before New Year's Day, on Wednesday or Thursday.

It was more logical to wait. It was more reasonable to wait.

Oh, God! A shudder gripped his shoulders, so unaccustomed to such burdens. It would have been better if he had never learned about it. If he knew nothing about it, had never learned . . .

He took the instructions and everything else off the desk and carried them all to the safe.

How, indeed, could anyone condemn what Dobroumov had promised? It showed the generosity of a talented man. Talent is always conscious of its own abundance and does not object to sharing.

But Innokenty's uneasiness grew stronger and stronger. He leaned against the safe; his head drooped, and he rested there with his eyes closed.

Then suddenly, as if he had been letting a last chance slip by, without phoning the garage for his car, without closing the inkwell, Innokenty went out of his office and shut the door, handed his key to the duty officer at the end of the corridor, put on his plain overcoat, and rushed down the staircase almost at a run, passing the permanent staff of the building in their gold braid and gold embroidery. And he ran out into the raw twilight, finding relief in action.

His French-style shoes plunged into the dirty wet snow.

Passing the Vorovsky monument in the half-enclosed court of the ministry, Innokenty looked up and trembled. He sensed a new meaning in the new building of the Bolshaya Lubyanka which faced on Furkasovsky Lane, and he shuddered. This nine-storied gray-black hulk was a battleship, and the eighteen pilasters hung on its starboard side like eighteen gun turrets. Solitary and frail, Innokenty was drawn toward it, across the little square, under the prow of the heavy, swift ship.

He turned away, as if to save himself—to the right, down Kuznestsky Most. There, tight up against the curb, a taxi was preparing to pull away. Innokenty got in and ordered the driver to proceed along Kuznestsky Most and turn left beneath the just-lit street lights on Petrovka.

He was still hesitating—wondering where he could phone without having someone outside the booth rap the glass with a coin. But to hunt for a quiet, isolated booth—that would be even more obvious. Wouldn't it be better to find one somewhere right in the middle of the maelstrom, provided it was up against a wall? He decided, too, that it was stupid to be wandering around with the taxi driver as a witness. He dug into his pocket for a fifteen-kopeck piece.

But all this didn't matter any more. In the past few minutes Innokenty had felt a calm descending on him; he realized clearly that he had no other choice. It might be dangerous, but if he didn't do it . . .

If one is forever cautious, can one remain a human being?

At the traffic light on Okhotny Ryad his fingers found two fifteen-kopeck pieces—a good omen!

They passed the university building, and Innokenty motioned the driver to the right. They sped onto the Arbat; Innokenty gave the driver two bills without asking for change and walked across the square, attempting to keep his pace measured and slow.

The Arbat was already lit up. Lines of customers in front of the cinema were waiting to see *The Love of a Ballerina*. The red letter "M" on the metro station was almost hidden by the gray mist. A gypsy-like woman was selling sprigs of yellow mimosa.

Try to do it as quickly as possible! Say it as briefly as possible—and hang up. Then the danger will be minimal.

Innokenty went straight ahead. A passing girl glanced at him.

And another.

One of the wooden phone booths outside the metro station was empty, but Innokenty avoided it and went inside the station.

Here were four more, sunk in the wall—all taken. But on the left a fellow a bit in his cups was already hanging up. As soon as he left, Innokenty entered quickly, carefully pulling shut the thick glass door and holding it closed with one hand, while with his other, trembling, without taking off his glove, he inserted the coin and dialed the number.

After several long rings the phone at the other end was lifted.

"Yes?" said a woman's voice which sounded either over-solicitous or irritated.

"Is this the residence of Professor Dobroumov?" he asked, trying to change his voice.

"Yes."

"Please ask him to come to the phone."

"Who wants to talk to him?" The woman's voice was heavy and lazy. She was probably lolling on her couch and she was in no hurry.

"Well, you see . . . you don't know me. . . . Look, that's not really important. But for me it's very urgent. Please ask the professor to come to the phone!"

Too many unnecessary words—and all because of his damned politeness!

"But the professor simply can't be bothered to talk to every unknown person who calls," said the woman, taking offense.

She sounded as if she might hang up then and there.

Outside the thick glass, people were rushing past the row of booths, hurrying, catching up with one another. Someone was already waiting outside Innokenty's booth.

"Who are you? Why can't you give your name?"

"I'm a friend. I have important news for the professor!"

"And so? Why are you afraid to give me your name?"

It was time for him to hang up. People ought not to have stupid wives.

"And who are you? Are you his wife?"

"Why must I answer you first?" the woman protested. "You tell me."

He should cut off the conversation at once! But the professor wasn't the only one involved. . . . By this time, Innokenty was in a rage and no longer trying to disguise his voice or to speak quietly. He began to plead excitedly with the phone: "Listen to me! Listen! I have to warn him about a danger!"

"About a danger?" The woman's voice dropped, then broke off. But she didn't summon her husband—not at all. "All the more reason I can't call him. Maybe it's all untrue. How can you prove you're telling the truth?"

The floor was burning beneath Innokenty's feet, and the

black receiver on its heavy steel chain was swimming in his hand.

"Listen to me, listen!" he cried in desperation. "When the professor was in Paris on his recent trip, he promised his French colleagues he would give them something! Some kind of medicine. And he's supposed to give it to them in a few days. To foreigners! Do you understand? He must not do it! He must not give the foreigners anything! It could be used as a provoca—"

"But—" There was a dull click and then total silence, without the usual buzzing or ringing on the line.

Someone had broken the connection.

2

DANTE'S IDEA

"New ones!"

"They've brought in new ones!"

The prisoners from the camps filed into the main corridor. A group of Mavrino zeks, some on their way to dinner, others who had eaten on the first shift, crowded around them.

"Where from, comrades?"

"Friends, where are you from?"

"And what have you all got on your chests and your caps—patches of some kind?"

"That's where our numbers were," said one of the newcomers. "On our backs too, and our knees. When they sent us away from camp, they ripped them off our clothes."

"What do you mean, numbers?"

"Gentlemen," said Valentine Pryanchikov, "may I ask what age we are living in?" He turned to his friend, Lev Rubin. "Numbers on human beings? Lev Grigorich, let me ask you, is that what you call progressive?"

"Valentulya, don't put on a show," said Rubin. "Go get your dinner."

"But how can I possibly eat if human beings are going

around somewhere with numbers on their caps? It's the Apocalypse!"

"Friends!" said another Mavrino zek. "They're giving nine packs of Belomors for the second half of December. You're in luck."

"You mean Belomor-Yavas or Belomor-Dukats?"

"Half of each."

"The bastards—choking us with Dukats. I'm going to complain to the minister, I swear I am."

"And what kind of outfits are those?" asked the newcomer who had spoken first. "Why are all of you dressed like parachutists?"

"It's the uniform they make us wear now. The stinking bastards are tightening up on us. They used to issue woolen suits and overcoats."

More Mavrino zeks came in from the dining hall.

"Look, new ones!"

"They've brought new ones."

"Come on, you hot shots! Stop acting like you'd never seen live prisoners before. You've jammed the whole corridor!"

"Say! Who do I see! Dof-Dneprovsky! Where have you been all this time, Dof? I looked all over Vienna for you in '45, over the whole damn place!"

"All in rags and unshaven! From what camp, friends?"

"Different ones. From Rechlag—"

"—Dubrovlag—"

"How come I've been doing time for more than eight years and haven't heard of them?"

"They're new camps, Special Camps. They were only set up last year, in '48. There was a directive from Stalin on strengthening the rear—"

"Whose rear?"

"Right at the entrance to the Vienna Prater they picked me up and—into the police wagon."

"Wait a minute, Mitenka, let's listen to the new ones."

"No, out for our walk, out for our walk! Out in the fresh air! It's the schedule—even during earthquakes! Lev will question the new ones, don't worry."

"Second shift! To dinner!"

"Ozerlag, Luglag, Steplag, Peschanlag—"

"You'd think there was some great unrecognized Pushkin in the MVD. He doesn't bother about long poems or even verses; he just gives poetic names to concentration camps."

"Ha, ha, ha! That's amusing, gentlemen, very amusing," said Pryanchikov. "What age are we living in?"

"Quiet, Valentulya!"

"Pardon me," a newcomer asked Rubin, "what is your name?"

"Lev Grigorich."

"Are you an engineer, too?"

"No, I'm not an engineer, I'm a philologist."

"Philologist? They even keep philologists here?"

"You might better ask whom they don't keep here in the sharashka," Rubin said. "We have mathematicians, physicists, chemists, radio engineers, telephonic engineers, artists, translators, bookbinders, architects, designers, and even a geologist who got in by mistake."

"And what does he do?"

"He doesn't do badly—he got himself a spot in the photo lab."

"Lev! You claim to be a materialist, but you keep cramming people with spiritual stuff," Valentine Pryanchikov said. "Listen here, friends! When they take you to the dining hall, we'll have thirty plates set out at the last table by the window. Fill up your bellies—just don't burst!"

"Thanks very much, but why deprive yourselves?"

"It's nothing. Who eats Mezen herring and millet grits nowadays? It's vulgar!"

"What? Millet grits vulgar? I haven't seen millet grits in five years!"

"It's probably not millet; it's probably *magara!*"

"*Magara*—you're crazy! Just let them try to give us *magara!* We'd throw it in their faces!"

"And how is the food in the transit camps these days?"

"At the Chelyabinsk transit camp—"

"Chelyabinsk new or Chelyabinsk old?"

"Your question indicates a connoisseur. At the new one—"

"How is it there nowdays? Do they still forbid you to use the toilets and make you use latrine buckets and carry them down from the third floor?"

"Still."

"You said 'sharashka.' What does 'sharashka' mean?"

"And how much bread do they give you here?"

"Who hasn't had dinner yet? Second shift!"

"White bread—fourteen ounces, and the black bread is out on the table."

"Pardon me, what do you mean—out on the table?"

"Just that: out on the table. Sliced. You want it, you take it; you don't want it, you don't take it."

"Yes, but for that butter and that pack of Belomors we have to break our backs for twelve and fourteen hours a day."

"That's not breaking your back! You're not breaking your back if you're sitting at a desk. The one who breaks his back is the guy who swings a pick."

"The hell with that! We sit in this sharashka as if we were in a swamp—we're cut off from life. Do you hear, gentlemen? They say they've clamped down on thieves and pickpockets, and that even in Krasnaya Presnya they don't fool around any more."

"The butter allotment for professors is one and a half ounces and for engineers three-quarters of an ounce. From each according to his abilities, to each according to his possibilities."

"So you worked at Dneprostroi?"

"Yes, I worked with Winter. And I'm serving time because of Dneproges."

"What do you mean?"

"Well, you see it was like this—I sold it to the Germans."

"Dneproges? But it was blown up!"

"So what? I sold it to them blown up."

"Honest to God, it's like a fresh wind! Transit camps! Stolypin cars! Camps! Activity! Oh, just to roll off to Sovetskaya Gavan!"

"And back, Valentulya, and back!"

"Yes, you're right! And back even faster, of course!"

"You know, Lev Grigorich," a newcomer was saying to Rubin, "my head is spinning from this sudden change. I've lived fifty-two years, I've recovered from fatal illnesses, I've been married to pretty women, I've had sons, I've received academic prizes—but never have I been so blessedly happy as I am today! Where have I landed? They won't be driving me out into icy water tomorrow! An ounce and a half of butter! Black bread—*out on the table*! They don't forbid books! You can shave yourself! The guards don't beat the zeks. What kind of great day is this? What kind of gleaming summit? Maybe I've died? Maybe this is a dream? Perhaps I'm in heaven."

"No, dear sir," said Rubin, "you are, just as you were previously, in hell. But you have risen to its best and highest circle—the first circle. You ask what a sharashka

is? Let's say the concept of a sharashka was thought up by
Dante. Remember that Dante tore his hair trying to decide
where to put the wise men of ancient times. It was a Christian's duty to toss those pagans into hell. But the Renaissance conscience couldn't reconcile itself to the idea of enlightened men being packed in with all sorts of sinners and
condemned to physical torture. So Dante thought up a
special place for them in hell. If you'll allow me . . . It's in
the Fourth Canto and goes about like this:

> "At last
> we reached the base of a great Citadel . . .

Look around at the old arches here!

>   . . . circled by seven towering battlements
>   and by a sweet brook flowing round them all. . . .

You came here in the Black Maria, so you didn't see the
gates—

>   . . . I saw four mighty presences come toward us
>   with neither joy nor sorrow in their bearing.
>   '. . . What souls are those whose merit lights their way
>   even in Hell? What joy sets them apart?' "

"Ah, Lev Grigorich, you're too much of a poet," said
Valentine Pryanchikov. "I shall explain to the comrade what
a sharashka is much more clearly. You need only remember
the newspaper piece that said: 'It has been proved that a
high yield of wool from sheep depends on the animals' care
and feeding.' "

3

A PROTESTANT CHRISTMAS

Their Christmas tree was a sprig of pine wedged into a
crack in the stool. A braid of small, low-voltage, colored

lights on milky plastic-covered wires wound around it twice and dropped to a battery on the floor.

The stool stood in a corner of the room, between double bunks, and one of the upper mattresses shielded the whole corner and the tiny Christmas tree from the glare of the ceiling lights.

Six men in thick, dark-blue parachutists' coveralls stood together near the Christmas tree and listened, heads bowed, while one of them, swarthy, thin-faced Max Richtman, recited a Protestant Christmas prayer.

There was no one else in the big room, which was crowded with double bunks with welded frames. After dinner and an hour's walk everyone had gone to night work.

Max finished the prayer, and the six sat down. Five of them were filled with bittersweet recollections of their homeland—their beloved, well-ordered Germany, beneath whose slate roofs this most important holiday of the year was so bright and affecting. The sixth among them was a great hulk of a man with the thick black beard of a Biblical prophet— he was a Jew and a Communist.

Lev Rubin's fate had been intertwined with Germany in both peace and war.

In peacetime he was a philologist specializing in Germanic languages, who conversed in faultless *Hochdeutsch* and could, when the occasion demanded, switch to the dialects of Middle High or Old High German. He could recall any German writer who had ever been published as if he had been a personal acquaintance. He could talk about minor cities on the Rhine as if he had often walked their well-watered, shaded lanes.

But he had only been in Prussia—and then only on the front.

He had been a Soviet major in the "Section for Disintegration of Enemy Armed Forces." From the POW camps he picked Germans who were willing to help him. He took them out of the camps and provided them with decent maintenance in a special school. Some he passed through the front with TNT, false reichsmarks, false discharge papers, and army identification papers. They could blow up bridges and wander home to enjoy themselves until they were caught. With others he discussed Goethe and Schiller —and propaganda leaflets; and provided them with sound

trucks from which to persuade their fellow soldiers to turn
their guns against Hitler. With still others he crossed the
front and, by sheer force of persuasion, took strongpoints,
saving Soviet battalions.

But he had not been able to convert Germans without
becoming one of them, without coming to love them, and,
from the day of their defeat, without pitying them. For this,
Rubin had been arrested. Enemies in his own administration
accused him of agitating, after the January 1945 offensive,
against "blood for blood and death for death."

The charges were correct, and he did not recant. Yet the
situation was immeasurably more complicated than it appeared in the newspapers or in his final indictment.

Two night tables were pushed against the stool on which
the lighted Christmas tree stood, to form a dining table.
They began regaling themselves with canned goods from
the Gastronome (sharashka zeks were allowed to order
from fancy food stores in Moscow with funds from their
bank accounts) and with cold coffee and a homemade cake.
A formal discussion started. Max guided it firmly toward
peaceful themes: old folk customs, moving stories of Christmas night. Alfred, who wore glasses—a Vienna physics
student who had not been able to complete his studies—
talked very entertainingly in his Austrian accent. Gustav, a
young man from the Hitlerjugend who had been taken
prisoner a week after the war ended, sat there round-
cheeked, his rosy ears translucent, staring wide-eyed at the
Christmas lights, hardly daring to participate in the older
men's conversation.

Nevertheless the conversation turned to the war. Someone
remembered Christmas in 1944, five years before, when
every German took pride in the Ardennes offensive, and,
as in antiquity, the vanquished were pursuing the victors.
They remembered how on that Christmas Eve Germany
had listened to Goebbels.

Rubin, plucking at the bristles of his stiff, black beard,
confirmed this. He remembered that speech. It had been
effective. Goebbels had spoken with deep anguish, as if he
had personally assumed the burdens which were crushing
Germany. It was as if he had had a premonition of his own
end.

SS Obersturmbannführer Reinhold Zimmel, whose long
body scarcely found room between the table and the double

bunk, did not appreciate Rubin's refined civility. It was unbearable to think that this Jew should dare pass judgment
on Goebbels. He never would have deigned to sit at the
same table had he the strength of will to renounce spending
Christmas Eve with his compatriots. But the other Germans
had all insisted that Rubin be there. For the tiny German
colony, borne by fate into the golden cage of the sharashka
in the heart of this wild, cold country, the only comprehensible person at hand was this major from the enemy army
who had spent the whole war spreading discord and destruction among them. Only he could interpret for them the
manners and customs of the people here, advise them how
to behave, and translate fresh international news from Russian.

In an effort to say something as irritating as possible to
Rubin, Zimmel declared that there had been hundreds of
fiery orators all over the Reich. It would be interesting to
know, he added, why Bolsheviks preferred to read only
those speeches which were prepared and approved in advance.

The accusation was all the more wounding for being just.
And one really could not explain the historical reasons for it
to this enemy and murderer. Toward Zimmel, Rubin felt an
unwavering revulsion. He remembered him as he had arrived
at the sharashka after many years in Butyrskaya Prison,
wearing a crackling leather jacket that still showed traces of
its civilian SS insignia—the civilian SS having been the
worst branch. Even prison could not soften the expression
of relentless cruelty on Zimmel's face. The mark of the executioner had been stamped there. Zimmel's presence had
made it unpleasant for Rubin to attend this dinner, but all
the rest had insisted on his coming, and he was sorry for
them, lonely and lost here, and he found he could not cloud
their holiday with a refusal.

Suppressing his rage, Rubin quoted, in German, Pushkin's
advice to certain people not to attempt to deliver judgments
higher than their boot tops.

Max, alarmed, hastened to break up the impending conflict. It was Max who under Lev's guidance was already reading Pushkin in Russian, syllable by syllable. Why, he demanded, had Reinhold taken cake without whipped cream?
And where had Lev been that Christmas Eve?

Reinhold took some whipped cream. And Lev recollected

that he had been in his bunker at the Narew bridgehead near Rozan.

And as the five Germans were remembering their torn and trampled Germany, adorning it with the richest colors, so, too, Rubin suddenly remembered the Narew bridgehead and the wet forests around Lake Ilmen.

The little colored lights shone in the six men's eyes.

Rubin was asked about today's news. But he was ashamed to review what had happened in December. After all, he could not behave like a non-Communist and abandon the hope of indoctrinating these people. And he could not try to explain to them, either, that in our complex age Socialist truth sometimes progresses in a roundabout, distorted way. Therefore he had to choose for them—for the sake of history, just as subconsciously he made such selections for himself—only those current events which indicated the main road, neglecting those which obscured it.

But that particular December, except for the Soviet-Chinese talks, which had been dragging on, and the seventieth birthday of the Leader of the Peoples, nothing positive had taken place. And to tell the Germans about the trial of Traicho Kostov, where the whole courtroom farce had been so crudely staged, where correspondents had been handed, after a delay, a false confession allegedly written by Kostov in his death cell—that would have been shameful and would hardly have served the purposes of indoctrination.

So today Rubin dwelt mostly on the historical triumph of the Chinese Communists.

Max listened to Rubin and nodded agreement. His brown, olive-shaped eyes were innocent. He was devoted to Rubin, but since the Berlin blockade he had had his doubts about the information Rubin gave them. Rubin did not know that Max would risk his neck in the microwave laboratory where he worked to assemble, listen to, and then dismantle a miniature receiver which did not look at all like a receiver. With it he could listen to Cologne and to the BBC in German, and he knew not only about Traicho Kostov, and how he had denounced in open court those false confessions forced out of him during his interrogation, but also about plans for the North Atlantic Alliance and the economic news of Western Germany. All of this, of course, he passed on to the other Germans.

And all of them were nodding at Rubin approvingly.

In any case, it was long past time for Rubin to go. He had not, after all, been excused from night work. Rubin praised the cake, and the Vienna student, flattered, acknowledged the compliment. Rubin excused himself. The Germans insisted on his staying as long as politeness required, then let him go. Then they prepared to sing Christmas carols in muffled voices.

Rubin went out into the corridor carrying a Mongolian-Finnish dictionary and a volume of Hemingway in English.

The corridor was broad, with a rough temporary wooden floor. It had no windows and was lit by electricity day and night. It was the same corridor in which Rubin, together with the other inquisitive inmates, had, an hour before, during the animated dinner intermission, interviewed the new zeks from the camps. A door from the inner staircase opened on this corridor, as well as the doors of several room-cells. They were rooms because they had no locks, and they were cells because there were peepholes in the doors, little glass windows. These peepholes were never used by the guards here, but they had been installed, as they always were in real prisons, in accordance with prison statutes, because in official papers the sharashka was labeled a "special prison."

Through one of these peepholes another Christmas Eve celebration could have been seen: a goup of Latvians who had also asked to be let off for the holiday.

The rest of the zeks were all at work, and Rubin was afraid that he might be detained and taken to Major Shikin to explain his absence.

Large double doors stood at each end of the corridor. One pair was wood-paneled and led through an arch into what used to be the enclosure above the altar of the country-house chapel. It, too, was now a room-cell. The other pair was locked and faced from top to bottom with sheet iron—and this was called by the inmates "the Holy Door."

Rubin went up to this iron door and knocked at the little window in it. From the other side the attentive, immobile face of the guard pressed up against the glass.

The key turned quietly in the lock. This guard happened to be easygoing.

Rubin emerged at the top of the main staircase of the old building, its two flights of stairs curving apart and then joining again. He walked across the marble landing past

two antique fretwork lanterns which no longer worked. On
this floor he entered the laboratory corridor and pushed
open a door with the sign: ACOUSTICS.

4

BOOGIE-WOOGIE

The Acoustics Laboratory was a wide, high-ceilinged room
with several windows. It was disorderly and crowded with
electronic instruments on plank shelves, shiny aluminum
counters, assembly benches, new plywood cabinets from a
Moscow factory, snug writing desks that had been war
booty.

Large overhead bulbs in frosted globes cast a pleasant,
dispersed white light.

In a far corner of the room stood a sound-insulated
acoustical booth. It looked only partially completed. On the
outside, plain sacking had been tacked over straw. Its two-
foot-thick solid door was open at the moment, and the
woolen curtain over it had been thrown back to air the
booth. Next to the booth, rows of brass plugs gleamed on
the black bakelite face of the main switchboard.

At a desk by the booth, her back to it, her narrow
shoulders barely covered by a shawl, sat a tiny, frail girl
with a stern face.

All the other people in the room, ten or so, were men,
all dressed in the same dark-blue coveralls. Lit by the overhead lights and by additional spots of light from flexible
desk lamps, they tinkered, walked about, hammered, sold-
ered, and sat at the assembly benches and writing desks.

From different places in the room three different radio
receivers, cabinetless and put together on whatever aluminum
chassis had come to hand, broadcast the conflicting rhythms
of jazz, a piano concert, and folk songs of the East.

Rubin walked slowly through the laboratory to his desk,
still holding his Mongolian-Finnish dictionary and his Hem-

ingway. There were white pastry crumbs on his curly black beard.

Though the coveralls issued to the prisoners were all identically made, they were worn in different ways. On Rubin's, one button had been ripped off, the belt was loosened, and folds of cloth hung at his stomach. On the other hand, a young fellow with flowing chestnut hair, who was at the moment blocking Rubin's way, wore the very same dark-blue coveralls like a dandy. His cloth belt was cinched tight around his thin waist, and he wore a blue silk shirt which, though faded from frequent washing, was closed with a bright necktie. This young man entirely blocked the side passage Rubin was trying to get through. In his right hand he brandished a hot soldering iron, and he had placed his left foot on a chair. Leaning on his knee, he concentrated on a radio diagram in a copy of the magazine *Wireless Engineer*, and sang at the same time:

> "Boogie-woogie, boogie-woogie.
> Samba! Samba!
> Boogie-woogie, boogie-woogie.
> Samba! Samba!"

Rubin could not get past him, and he stood there for a moment with a mock expression of meekness. The young man did not appear to notice him.

"Valentulya," Rubin said, "couldn't you move your hind foot a bit?"

Valentine, not looking up, answered in a strong clipped voice, "Lev Grigorich! You're interrupting. You're wasting time. Why come here nights? What is there for you to do here?" He now looked at Rubin with bright young eyes full of surprise. "What the hell do we need philologists for! Ha, ha, ha!" he said ironically. "After all, you're no engineer! For shame!"

Pursing his fleshy lips in a childlike pout and opening his eyes unbelievably wide, Rubin said, "My boy! There are all kinds of engineers. Some of them here have built successful careers selling soda water."

"Not me! I'm a first-class engineer! Take that into consideration, little man!" Valentine retorted sharply, placing the soldering iron in a wire stand and standing erect.

He had the clean look of youth. Life had not stained his face. His movements were boyish. It was hard to believe that he had graduated from an institute before the war, survived German POW camps, been in Europe, and was now serving his fifth year of imprisonment in his own country.

Rubin sighed. "Without duly attested references from Belgium the administration cannot—"

"What references are you talking about?" Pryanchikov's brows flew up. "Ha, ha, ha! Just forget it! Consider—I love women madly!"

The stern young woman near them could not control her smile.

Another inmate, at a window near the passageway Rubin was trying to get through, put down his work and listened to Valentine with approval.

"Only theoretically, it would appear," answered Rubin with a bored, meditative expression.

"And I love spending money!"

"But you don't have any."

"Well, then how can I be a bad engineer? Just think: in order to love women—and different ones—all the time, I need a lot of money! And in order to have a lot of money I have to earn it! And to do that as an engineer I have to be brilliant in my field. And how can I do that if I'm not genuinely fascinated by it? Ha, ha! You look pale!"

Wholehearted conviction shone in Valentine's face, raised challengingly to Rubin.

"Ah-ha!" cried the zek next to the window, whose writing desk faced the young woman's. "Lev, come and hear how well I've caught Valentulya's voice! It has a bell-like quality! That's what I'm going to write in my report. Bell-like. You can recognize a voice like that on any phone. No matter how much interference there is."

And he opened a big sheet ruled off in squares, on which there were columns of names followed by tree-shaped voice classifications.

"What kind of nonsense is that?" Valentine said, brushing the remark aside. He took up his soldering iron, and rosin began to smoke.

The passageway opened up, and Rubin, on his way to his chair, paused to bend over the sheet of voice classifications.

He and his friend Gleb Nerzhin looked at it together in silence.

"We've made some real progress, Gleb," he said. "Used together with voice prints, it will make a good tool. Soon we'll be able to understand what a telephone voice depends on." He gave a start. "What's that on the radio?"

The jazz was louder in the room, but a lilting, bubbling piano piece came through his own homemade receiver on the window sill, with a single melodic line which kept gleaming and disappearing.

Nerzhin replied, "It's a miracle. That's Beethoven's Seventeenth Sonata in D Minor. For some reason it's never—listen, listen."

They both bent closer to the receiver, but the jazz interfered badly.

"Valentine," said Gleb. "Please, let us listen! Show a little consideration!"

"I've already shown a little consideration," Valentine said. "I knocked your receiver together. Now I'm going to unsolder your coil and you'll never find it."

The young woman raised her severe brows and said, "Valentine Martynich! Really, it's impossible to listen to three radios at once. Turn yours off as you've been asked."

Valentine's radio at this point was playing a slow fox trot, and the young woman secretly liked it very much.

"Serafima Vitalyevna! That's monstrous!" He seized the back of a chair and gesticulated as if he were speaking from a platform. "How can a normal, healthy person not enjoy energetic, invigorating jazz? You're all being corrupted by all kinds of old trash! Have you really never danced the 'Blue Tango'? Have you never seen the skits of Arkady Raikin? You just don't know the best that man has created! Worse than that—you've never been to Europe. Where could you possibly have learned how to live? I advise you very, very seriously: you must fall in love with someone." He delivered this oratory from behind the chair, not noticing the bitter set of the young woman's lips. "Anyone—*ça dépend de vous!* Lights twinkling in the night. The rustle of stylish clothes."

"He's gone out of phase again!" Rubin said with concern. "So we have to use force."

And behind Valentine's back he turned off the jazz himself.

Valentine turned around, stung. "Lev Grigorich, who gave you the right to do that?"

He frowned and tried to look menacing. The free-flowing
strains of the Seventeenth Sonata rose in all their purity,
competing now only with the crude song from the third
radio around the corner.

Rubin's face slackened, showing yielding black eyes and
a beard dotted with cake crumbs.

"Engineer Pryanchikov! Are you still worrying about the
Atlantic Charter? Have you written your will? Whom will
you refuse to leave your bedroom slippers to?"

Pryanchikov's face suddenly grew serious. He looked
brightly into Rubin's eyes and said quietly, "Listen, what
the hell! You're driving me crazy. A person at least ought
to have some freedom in prison."

He was called away by one of the assembly workers, and
he left in a state of gloom.

Rubin settled silently into his armchair, back to back with
Gleb, and prepared to listen to the music. But the soothing,
plunging melody broke off unexpectedly, like a speech cut
off in the middle of a word. And that was the uncere-
monious end of the Seventeenth Sonata.

Rubin delivered himself of a string of oaths, comprehensible to Gleb alone.

"Spell it out. I can't hear you," Gleb said, his back still
turned.

"That's my luck, I tell you," said Rubin hoarsely, not
turning around either. "There you are—I missed the sonata
and I've never heard it."

"Because you're disorganized. How many times have I
pounded it into you?" his friend declared. Just a minute before, when he was recording Pryanchikov's voice, he had
been full of enthusiasm, and now he was listless and sad
again. "And the sonata was very, very good. Why doesn't it
have a name like the others? 'The Shining Sonata,' wouldn't
that be right? Everything in it flashes, shines—good and
bad, sad and merry, the way it does in life. And there's no
ending . . . just like life. That's what it should be called—
the *Ut in Vita* Sonata. And where have you been?"

"With the Germans. We were seeing Christmas in," Rubin
said, grinning ironically.

They talked without seeing each other, the backs of their
heads almost touching.

"Good man," Gleb thought, then aloud: "I like your attitude toward them. You spend hours teaching Max Russian. Yet you have every reason to hate them."

"Hate? No, but my former love for them, of course, has been a bit tarnished. Even nonpolitical Max—doesn't he, too, share some responsibility with the executioners? After all, he didn't do anything to stop them."

"Just as we, right now, are not doing anything to stop Abakumov or Shishkin-Myshkin."

"Listen, Gleb, once and for all, I am no more a Jew than I am a Russian. And I am no more a Russian than I am a citizen of the world!"

"Well said! Citizens of the world! It sounds pure and bloodless."

"In other words, cosmopolites. They were right to put us in prison."

"Of course they were right. Even though you are always trying to prove the contrary to the Supreme Soviet."

The radio on the window sill promised the "Daily List of Production Competitions" in thirty seconds.

In the course of those thirty seconds, Gleb Nerzhin reached for the radio knob with calm deliberation and cut off the announcer's hoarse croak. His tired face was grayish.

Valentine Pryanchikov was at this moment absorbed in a new problem. Calculating what series of amplifications to use, he sang to himself in a loud, carefree voice:

> "Boogie-woogie, boogie-woogie.
> Samba! Samba!"

5

A PEACEFUL EXISTENCE

Nerzhin was the same age as Valentine Pryanchikov, but he looked older. His reddish hair was neither thin nor gray, but there were already many deep wrinkles in his drawn face—whole wreaths of them around his eyes, at the corners

of his lips, long furrows on his forehead. His skin looked
faded because of the lack of fresh air. But it was most of
all his economy of movement that made him seem old—that
wise economy with which nature husbands a prisoner's
strength against the drain of a concentration-camp regime.
True, in the relative freedom of the sharashka, where the
diet included meat and energy wasn't burned up in physical
labor, there was no real need for economy of movement;
but Nerzhin understood the uncertain nature of his prison
sentence, and practiced that restriction of effort to ensure
its becoming a permanent habit.

Whole barricades of books and file folders were piled on
his large desk, and even the working space left in the middle
was taken over by file folders, typewritten texts, Russian
and foreign books and magazines—all of them spread out
open. Any unsuspecting person would see in this chaos the
aftermath of a hurricane of scientific thought.

But, in fact, it was all a false front. Nerzhin set things
up every evening just in case the bosses happened in.

Actually, he wasn't looking at what lay in front of him.
He had pulled aside the bright silk curtain and was looking
out the window into the darkness. Beyond the depths of the
night, the variegated lights of Moscow began, and the whole
city, hidden behind a hill, shone like a huge pillar of pale,
diffused light which turned the sky dark brown.

Nerzhin's special chair, with a spring back which yielded
comfortably to his every movement, his special roll-top desk
of a kind not manufactured in the Soviet Union, and his
comfortable spot at the south window—all would have indicated to anyone acquainted with the history of Mavrino
sharashka that Nerzhin was one of its founding members.

The sharashka took its name from the nearby village of
Mavrino, which had long been absorbed into the Moscow
city limits. The sharashka had been established on a July
evening a little more than three years ago. Some fifteen
zeks had been brought in from concentration camps and
delivered to an old manor house in the Moscow suburb, encircled for the occasion by barbed wire. At the sharashka
those early days were now referred to as the "Krylov"
period and were remembered as a pastoral era. At that time
one could walk freely at evening in what had since become
the forbidden "zone," lie on the dewy grass which, against
all prison regulations, had not been cut (grass was supposed

to be cut to the roots so that zeks would not creep silently up to the barbed wire), and observe either the eternal stars or the ephemeral sweating of Zhvakun, the MVD master sergeant on night duty, as he stole logs from the restoration site and rolled them under the barbed wire to take home for firewood.

No one in the sharashka at that time knew what its field of scientific endeavor would be. They were kept busy unpacking a vast number of crates delivered by two freight trains . . . rounding up comfortable chairs and desks . . . sorting out-of-date and broken equipment—for telephony, ultra-high-frequency radio communication, and acoustics. It turned out that the best apparatus and the papers documenting the newest scientific research had been stolen or destroyed by the Germans while the MVD captain who had been sent to pack the German equipment for shipment to Russia had been combing the environs of Berlin to furnish his own Moscow apartment and those of his superiors. (He understood furniture very well but knew nothing about the German language or radio.)

Since then the grass had been cut. The gates to the yard where the zeks took their exercise were open only at the ringing of a bell. The sharashka had passed from Beria's jurisdiction to Abakumov's and had been put to work on secret telephonic communications. The assignment was to have taken one year, but it had already stretched to two, becoming larger, confused, and encompassing more and more related projects. And here, on Rubin's and Nerzhin's desks, it had reached the stage of identifying voices on the telephone, and discovering what makes a human voice unique.

No one, it appeared, had undertaken this study before. In any case, they were unable to find any monographs on the subject. They had been allotted half a year for the work, and then another half-year, but they had made little progress, and now time was pressing.

Conscious of this urgency, Rubin complained over his shoulder, "For some reason I haven't the slightest desire to work today."

"That's amazing," barked Nerzhin. "Can it be that after fighting for only four years and spending only five in prison you're already tired? Get yourself a paid vacation in the Crimea."

They fell silent.

"Are you busy with something of your own?" Rubin asked quietly.

"Uh-huh."

"And who is going to do the work on voices?"

"To tell you the truth, I was counting on you."

"What a coincidence! I was counting on you."

"You have no conscience. How much material have you taken out of the Lenin Library with that work as a pretext? Speeches of famous lawyers, *The Memoirs of Koni*, Stanislavsky's *An Actor Prepares*. And you finally lost all shame with your research on *Princess Turandot*. What other zek in the land of GULAG can boast of a selection of books like that?"

Rubin pushed out his thick lips in a pout, which always made his face look comically foolish. "That's funny. I read all those books, even *Princess Turandot*, with somebody else, and during working hours, too. Wasn't it you?"

"Yes, it was me. And I should be working. And I'd be working today unstintingly. But two things have knocked me off my stride. In the first place I am very troubled by the thought of parquet floors."

"What parquet floors?"

"At the Kaluga Gates, in the MVD apartment house, the rounded one with the tower. Our camp was building it in 1945, and I was working as an apprentice, laying parquet floors. And I learned just today that Roitman is living in that very apartment house. So I've been worrying every since about my workmanship, or, if you prefer, my prestige. Do my floors squeak or don't they? After all, if they squeak, that means it was jerry-built flooring. And here I am, unable to correct it!"

"Yes, that could get to be a nightmare."

"Exactly. And the second thing: Isn't it bad form to work on Saturday night when you know that Sunday will be a day off for the free employees only?"

Rubin sighed. "Even at this moment the free employees have gone out to places of amusement. Of course, that's a very obvious dirty trick."

"But do they choose the right places? Do they get more satisfaction out of life than we do? That's the real question." With the habitual caution of prisoners they were speaking quietly so that even Serafima Vitalyevna, who was seated opposite Nerzhin, could not overhear them.

Now they half-turned, with their backs to the rest of the room. They faced the window and the lights in the forbidden zone, the watchtower whose presence could only be guessed in the darkness, the separate lights of the distant green-houses, and the faintly visible, whitish pillar of light from Moscow.

Nerzhin, though a mathematician, was no stranger to linguistics, and from the time the sounds of Russian speech had become a research project at the Mavrino Scientific Research Institute he had paired off with the only philologist there, Rubin. For two years they had been sitting back to back twelve hours a day. At the very beginning of their acquaintance they had discovered that they had both been front-line soldiers, that they had been together on the North-west Front and on the Belorussian Front and both had a proper collection of war decorations, that they had both been arrested at the front in the same month and by the same SMERSH unit and under the provisions of the same *universally applicable* tenth point—in other words, not restricted by education, property qualifications, or material situation. And both had received a ten-year term. (As a matter of fact, nearly everyone received the same.) There was a difference of only six years between them and one step in military rank—for Nerzhin had been a captain. It turned out, in addition, that before the war Nerzhin might even have attended one of Assistant Professor Rubin's lectures.

They looked out into the darkness.

Rubin said sadly, "Anyway, you're intellectually deprived. That worries me."

"But I'm not trying to understand things; there's a lot of intelligence in the world, but not much that's any good."

"Here's a good book for you to read."

"Hemingway? Is this another one about the poor mixed-up bulls?"

"No."

"Persecuted lions?"

"Not at all!"

"Listen, I can't make sense out of people—why should I bother about bulls?"

"You *have* to read it!"

"I don't *have* to do anything for anyone, remember that! I've already paid off my debts, as our friend Spiridon says."

"Read it! It's one of the best books of the twentieth century!"

"And will it really reveal to me what everyone needs to understand? Has he really worked out what's got people confused?"

"An intelligent, morally good, boundlessly honest writer, a soldier, hunter, fisherman, drunkard and lover of women, quietly and frankly despising all falsehood, simple, very human, with the innocence of a genius—"

"Oh, come off it!" Nerzhin laughed. "I've lived for thirty years without Hemingway, and I'll manage to get through a few more. First you tried to force Capek on me, then Fallada. As it is, my life has been torn apart. Let me stop spreading myself so thin! Let me at least find some direction."

And he turned back to his desk.

Rubin sighed. He was still not in the mood to work.

He looked at the map of China that was propped against the shelf of the desk. He had cut this map out of a newspaper and pasted it on cardboard. The whole past year he had marked in red pencil the advance of the Communist armies; now, after their total victory, he had left it in front of him so that in moments of depression and fatigue it would lift his spirits.

But today sadness gnawed at Rubin, and even the big red mass of victorious China could not overcome it.

Nerzhin, occasionally sucking thoughtfully on the sharp end of a plastic pen, wrote in a needle-fine hand on a tiny sheet buried in his camouflage of books and file folders:

I remember a passage in Marx (if I could only find it) where he says that perhaps the victorious proletariat can get along without expropriating the prosperous peasants. That means he saw some economic way of including *all* the peasants in the new social system. The Plowman, of course, did not seek such paths in 1929. And when did he ever seek anything worthwhile or intelligent? Why should a butcher try to be a therapist?

The large Acoustics Laboratory hummed with its own peaceful everyday existence. The motor on the lathe droned. Orders were shouted: "Turn that on!" "Turn that off!" Sentimental trash was coming over the radio. Someone was calling loudly for a 6K7 tube.

Taking advantage of a moment when no one was looking at her, Serafima Vitalyevna looked attentively at Nerzhin, who was still writing in his microscopic handwriting.

Security Officer Major Shikin had ordered her to keep an eye on that prisoner.

6

A WOMAN'S HEART

Serafima Vitalyevna was so tiny that it was difficult not to call her "Simochka." She was dressed in a cambric blouse, wore a warm shawl around her shoulders, and was a lieutenant in the MGB, the Ministry of State Security.

All the free employees in this building were MGB officers.

The free employees, in accordance with the Stalinist Constitution of the U.S.S.R., had a great many rights, among them the right to work. However, this right was limited to eight hours a day and also by the fact that their work was not creative but consisted of surveillance over the zeks. The zeks, to compensate for being deprived of all other rights, enjoyed a broader right to work—for twelve hours a day. The free employees rotated duty periods in each of the laboratories so that the zeks would be supervised at all times, including the dinner break, from 6 to 11 P.M.

Now Simochka was on night duty. In the Acoustics Lab this birdlike woman was the only representative of authority, the only executive present.

According to regulations, she was supposed to see that the zeks worked and did not loaf, that they did not use the lab to make weapons or to mine the premises or to tunnel out, and that they did not use the multitude of radio parts at their disposal to set up two-way communication with the White House. At ten minutes to eleven she was supposed to collect all supersecret documents and place them in the large safe and then seal the door of the laboratory.

It was only a half-year since Simochka had completed the course at the Institute of Communications Engineers and been assigned, because of her crystal-clear security form, to this highly secret scientific research institute, which for security reasons was christened with a number but which the prisoners, in their irreverent lingo, called the sharashka. The free employees accepted here were immediately commissioned and paid wages higher than those of an ordinary engineer. They were paid for their rank, paid for their uniform, and all that was demanded of them, essentially, was devotion and vigilance.

The fact that no one made demands on her knowledge in her special field was lucky for Simochka. Not only she but many of her girl friends had graduated from the institute without any such knowledge. There were many reasons for this. The young girls had come from high schools with very little grounding in mathematics and physics. They had learned in the upper grades that at faculty council meetings the school director had scolded the teachers for giving out failing marks, and that even if a pupil didn't study at all he received a diploma. In the institute, when they found time to sit down to study, they made their way through the mathematics and radio-technology as through a dense pine forest. But more often there was no time at all. Every fall for a month or more the students were taken to collective farms to harvest potatoes. For this reason, they had to attend lectures for eight and ten hours a day all the rest of the year, leaving no time to study their course work. On Monday evenings there was political indoctrination. Once a week a meeting of some kind was obligatory. Then one had to do socially useful work, too: issue bulletins, organize concerts, and it was also necessary to help at home, to shop, to wash, to dress. And what about the movies? And the theater? And the club? If a girl didn't have some fun and dance a bit during her student years, when would she do so afterward? For their examinations Simochka and her girl friends wrote many cribs, which they hid in those sections of female clothing denied to males, and at the exams they pulled out the one they needed, smoothed it out, and turned it in as a work sheet. The examiners, of course, could have easily discovered the women students' ignorance, but they themselves were overburdened with committee meetings, assemblies, a variety of plans and reports to the dean's office and to the rector. It was hard on them to have to give an examination a second time. Besides, when their students failed, the examiners were reprimanded as if the failures were spoiled goods in a production process—according to the well-known theory that there are no bad pupils, only bad teachers. Therefore the examiners did not try to trip the students up but, in fact, attempted to get them through the examination with as good results as possible.

As their courses neared their ends, Simochka and her friends realized with a feeling of despondency that they did not like their profession and, in fact, found it a bore. But by then it was too late. Simochka trembled at the thought of actually working at it.

Then she had turned up at Mavrino. She was glad that they did not assign her any independent research. But even someone less small and frail than she would have found it awesome to cross the forbidden zone of this isolated Moscow castle, where a special guard and supervisory staff kept watch over important state criminals.

All ten graduates of the Institute of Communications were given their instructions together. They were told that on this assignment it was worse than being at war, that they had come to a snake pit where one careless move would confront them with destruction. They were told that they would encounter here the dregs of the human race, people unworthy of speaking the Russian language. They were warned that these people were particularly dangerous because they did not openly show their wolf fangs but constantly wore a mask of courtesy and good breeding. If one were to ask them about their crimes—which was categorically forbidden—they would try with clever lies to portray themselves as innocent victims. It was pointed out that the girls, as Komsomol members, must not pour out their hate on these vipers, but must show them outward politeness—without entering into any discussions unrelated to the work, without doing any errands for them outside—and that at the first violation, suspicion of violation, or possibility of suspicion of any violation of these regulations they must hurry with a confession to the security officer, Major Shikin.

Major Shikin was a short, swarthy, self-important man with a big head, a graying crew cut, and small feet on which he wore boy-sized shoes. It occurred to him, he said on this occasion, that, while to him, as to other experienced people, the reptilian inner nature of these malefactors was perfectly clear, there might among such inexperienced young women as these new arrivals be one whose humanitarian heart would waver; and that she might be guilty of some infraction, such as, for instance, giving a prisoner a book from the free employees' library. He would not even mention mailing a letter outside. (For any letter, no matter to what Marya or Tanya it was addressed, was obviously being sent to some foreign espionage center.) If any of the young women were to witness the fall of one of her friends, she was to give her comradely help—that is, report what had taken place to Major Shikin.

Finally, the major did not conceal the fact that liaison with prisoners would be punished under the Criminal Code, and that the Criminal Code, as everyone knew, was elastic. It could mean twenty-five years of hard labor.

It was impossible not to tremble as they pictured the dark future awaiting them. Certain girls even found tears coming to their eyes. But mistrust had already been sown among them. Leaving the instruction session, they did not talk about what they had just heard.

Neither alive nor dead, Simochka had followed Engineer Major Roitman into the Acoustics Lab, and for the first minute she felt as though she were going to faint.

Half a year had passed since then, and something dreadful had happened to Simochka. Not that her conviction about the black plots of imperialism had wavered. She still found it easy to believe that the prisoners who worked in all the other rooms were bloodstained criminals. But every day, as she met the dozen zeks in the Acoustics Lab—grim and indifferent to freedom, to their own fate, to their terms of ten and twenty-five years, all of them, scientists, engineers and technicians, concerned only with the work, even though it was not their own, meant nothing to them, and brought them not a cent of wages nor a grain of glory—she tried in vain to see in them those desperate international bandits so easily identified in the movies, so skillfully trapped by counterintelligence.

Among them Simochka felt no fear. She could not feel any hate for them. These people aroused in her only unqualified respect, and their varied skills and knowledge, their steadfastness in bearing misfortune. And though her sense of duty cried out, though her love for her country demanded that she report to the security officer all the inmates' sins of commission and omission, Simochka for reasons she did not understand began to find that duty loathsome and impossible.

It was particularly impossible in the case of her closest neighbor and coworker, Gleb Nerzhin, who sat facing her across their desks.

For some time past Simochka had been working closely with him, under his direction, in carrying out experiments in speech articulation. At the Mavrino sharashka it was often necessary to evaluate the fidelity with which speech characteristics were transmitted by various telephone circuits. Even with all the new instruments, there was still no meter which could measure the quality of speech transmission. An evaluation of the distortions could be arrived at only if one person read individual syllables, words, and phrases into a mouthpiece at one end of the circuit, and a listener at the other end tried to gauge the percentage of errors in the transmission. Such experiments were called experiments in articulation.

Nerzhin occupied himself with the mathematical programing of these experiments. They proceeded successfully, and Nerzhin had even produced a three-volume monograph on their methodology. When he and Simochka were overwhelmed by too much to do at once, Nerzhin formulated precisely the sequence of work which was immediately necessary and the work which could be postponed, determining all this with great assurance. At such times his face grew young. And Simochka, imagining the war as she'd seen it in motion pictures, visualized Nerzhin in a captain's uniform, reddish hair flying, amid the smoke of explosions, shouting the order to fire.

But Nerzhin felt compelled to work swiftly so that, having done his assigned work, he could disengage himself from all activity. He had once said to Simochka, "I am active because I hate activity." "And what do you like?" she had asked shyly. "Contemplation," he had replied. And indeed when the squall of work passed, he would sit for hours hardly changing his position. The skin of his face would turn gray and old and the wrinkles would appear. Where had his self-assurance gone? He became slow and indecisive. He would think a long time before writing down a few of those needle-small notes which Simochka, even today, saw on his desk among the pile of reference works and monographs.

She even noticed that he slipped them somewhere at the left of his desk, not in the drawer. Simochka burned with curiosity to know what he was writing and for whom. Nerzhin, without knowing it, had become for her an object of sympathy and admiration.

Simochka's life as a woman had so far turned out very unhappily. She was not pretty. Her face was spoiled by a nose which was too long. Her hair was thin and was gathered together at the back of her head in a damp little knot. She was not just small—which enhances a woman—but excessively small; she was more like a seventh-grade schoolgirl than a grown woman. Moreover, she was strait-laced and not inclined to fun or casual play; and this, too, made her unattractive to young people. So at twenty-five no one had paid court to her, no one had embraced her, no one had kissed her.

But not long ago, just a month earlier, something had gone wrong with the microphone in the booth, and Nerzhin had called Simochka to fix it. She came in with a screw driver in her hand, and in the soundless, stifling booth, small, crowded, with hardly room for two, she bent toward the microphone which Nerzhin was examining, and before she realized it her cheek was touching his. She touched him and nearly died on the spot. What would happen now? She should have drawn away, but she continued looking foolishly at the microphone. There passed the longest and most terrifying minute of her life—their cheeks burned, united, and he did not move away! Suddenly he seized her head and kissed her on the lips. Simochka's whole body melted in joyous weakness. She said nothing in that instant about Komsomols or country, but only: "The door's not closed!"

A thin dark-blue curtain, swinging back and forth, separated them from the noisy day beyond, from people walking around and talking who could have pulled aside the curtain at any moment. The prisoner Nerzhin risked nothing more than ten days in the punishment cell. The young woman risked her whole security clearance, her career, perhaps even freedom itself. But she had no strength to draw away from the hands which held her head.

For the first time in her life a man had kissed her.

Thus it could be said that a cunningly wrought steel chain broke at the link which had been forged from the heart of a woman.

7

"OH, MOMENT, STAY!"

"Whose bald head is that behind me?"

"My boy, I'm in a poetic mood, no less. Let's have a chat."

"In principle I'm busy."

"Busy—nonsense! I'm in a state, Gleb. I was sitting by that makeshift German Christmas tree and I said something about my dugout at the bridgehead north of Pulutsk, and suddenly I was at the front again! The whole front came back to me, so vivid, so poignant. Listen—even war can turn into a good memory, can't it?"

"You shouldn't let it. The Taoist ethic says, 'Arms are the instruments of unhappiness, not of nobility. The wise man conquers unwillingly.' "

"What's this? You've switched from skepticism to Taoism?"

"Nothing final yet."

"First I remembered the best of my Krauts—how we made up captions for the leaflets together: the mother embracing her children, and our blond Margaret in tears—that was our masterpiece. It had a text in verse."

"I know. I picked one of them up."

"I remembered how on quiet evenings we used to go out on sound trucks to the front lines."

"And between the touching tangos they'd try to persuade their brother soldiers to turn their guns against Hitler. We used to climb out of the dugouts and listen, too. But your appeals were somewhat simple-minded."

"What do you mean? After all, we did take Graudenz and Elbing without firing a shot."

"But that was already 1945."

"Little drops of water wear down big stones! Did I ever tell you about Milka? She was a student at the Institute of Foreign Languages, graduated in 1941, and was sent immediately to our section as a translator. A little snub-nosed girl; all her movements were quick."

"Wait, was she the one who went along with you to accept the surrender of a fortress?"

"Yes. She was terribly vain, and she loved to be praised for her work (God help you if you dared to reprimand her!), and she liked being recommended for decorations. Do you remember the Northwest Front right beyond the Lovat River, between Rakhlits and Novo-Svinukhovo, south of Podtsepochiya? There's a forest there."

"There's more than one forest there. The far side of the Redya River or the near side?"

"The near side."

"Yes, I know it."

"Well, she and I spent a whole day roaming around that forest. It was springtime—not even springtime, still March. We sloshed through the puddles in our felt boots, our fur hats sopping with sweat. That eternal smell of awakening springtime. We wandered around like people in love for the first time, like newlyweds. Why is it that with a new woman you experience the whole thing right from the beginning, just like a kid? That endless forest! The smoke from scattered shelters where a battery of seventy-sixes stood in a clearing. We kept away from them. We roamed around like that till twilight, soaking-wet and flushed with happiness. She drove me crazy the whole day; then after dark we found an empty gun emplacement."

"Aboveground?"

"You remember? Sure. A lot of them were built there that year, like shelters for wild animals."

"Wet ground there. You couldn't dig in."

"Yes. Inside there were pine needles on the floor, the smell of resin from the logs, smoke from the fire—no stove; you had to warm yourself at an open fire. There was a hole through the roof. No light at all, of course. The fire cast shadows on the beams. How about it, Gleb? Some life!"

"I've always noticed that if there's an innocent girl in a prison story, everyone—including me—ardently hopes that by the end of the story she won't be innocent any more. For zeks that is the main point of a story. There's a search for world justice in that, don't you think? A blind man has to get reassurance from those who can see that the sky is still blue and the grass green. A zek has to believe that there are still real, live, adorable women in the world and that they give themselves to fellows with luck. That's the night you remember—a lover in a smoky shelter, and nobody shooting at you. War, hell! That same night your wife was turning in her sugar coupons—for stuffed candies, all stuck together and mashed up and mixed with paper, and wondering how to divide them between your daughters so that they'd last a whole month. And in Butyrskaya Prison, in Cell 73—"

"On the second floor, on a narrow corridor—"

"Exactly. The young Moscow history professor, Razvodovsky, who had just been arrested and had never of course been at the front, was proving intelligently, convincingly, and with great enthusiasm, through the use of social, historical, and ethical precepts, that there is a good side to war. And there were desperate young guys in that cell who had fought everywhere and in every army—they almost ate that professor alive. They were furious and said, no, there's not a single damn crumb of good in war. I listened and kept my mouth shut. Razvodovsky had some pretty good arguments. At times I thought he was right. And then sometimes my own memories were good. But I didn't dare argue with the soldiers. Whatever basis I had for agreeing with that civilian professor was the very same thing that distinguished me—an artillery officer with the reinforcements attached to the High Command—from the infantry. Lev, after all, at the front, except for taking those fortresses, you were a complete goldbrick. After all, you never had to stay put in a line of battle you could retreat from only at the cost of your head! I was partly a goldbrick, too, because I didn't take part in an attack myself and didn't send men in to attack. And then our memory plays tricks on us and conceals what was terrible—"

"Yes, I'm not saying—"

"Whatever was pleasant floats to the surface. But when the Junker dive bombers almost tore me apart near Orel—I can't recall any particular inner satisfaction there. No, Lev, the only good war is a war that is over and done."

"Well, I'm not saying it's good, but that what you remember is good."

"Sure, and we'll have good memories of the camps someday. Even of the transit camps."

"The transit camps? Gorky? Kirov? No!"

"That's because headquarters took your things away, and you can't be objective. But some people were well off even there—the ones who checked food packages and the bath attendants; there were some who could even shack up with the female prisoners, and they'll go around telling everyone there's no better place on earth than a transit prison. After all, the very concept of happiness is conditional, a fiction."

"'The transitory nature and unreality of the concept are implicit in the word itself. The word 'happiness' is derived from the word that means this hour, this moment."

"No, dear Professor, pardon me. Read Vladimir Dahl. 'Happiness' comes from a word that means one's fate, one's lot, what one has managed to hold on to in life. The wisdom of etymology gives us a very mean version of happiness."

"Just a minute! My explanation comes from Dahl, too."

"Amazing. So does mine."

"The word ought to be researched in all languages. I'll make a note of it!"

"Maniac!"

"Never mind! Let me tell you something about comparative philology—"

"You mean the way everything is derived from the word 'hand'—as Marr would say?"

"Go to hell. Listen—have you read the second part of *Faust?*"

"You'd better ask whether I've read the first part. Everyone says it is a work of genius, but no one reads it. Or else they only know it through Gounod."

"No, the first part is not difficult at all:

> I've nothing to say of the sun and world,
> I see only the torments of man."

"Now I do like that!"

"Or:

> What we need we do not know,
> And what we know we do not need."

"Great!"

"The second part is on the heavy side, I admit. But even so, what an idea there is there! You know the contracts between Faust and Mephistopheles. Mephistopheles will receive Faust's soul only when Faust cries out, 'Oh, moment, stay! You are so fair.' But no matter what Mephistopheles offers Faust—the return of his youth, the love of Marguerite, easy victory over his rival, limitless wealth, knowledge of the secrets of existence—nothing can force the ultimate exclamation from Faust's breast. Years pass. Mephistopheles himself has grown weary of pursuing this insatiable being. He sees it's impossible to make a human being happy, and he wants to give up the fruitless attempt. Faust, who has by now aged a second time and grown blind, orders Mephistopheles to gather thousands of workers to dig canals and drain the swamps. In his twice-aged brain, which seems to the cynical Mephistopheles to be clouded and insane, a great idea has been kindled: to make humanity happy. At Mephistopheles' signal the servants of hell appear—the lemurs—and begin to dig Faust's grave. Mephistopheles wants only to bury him and be rid of him, no longer hoping for his soul. Faust hears the sound of many spades digging. 'What is that?' he asks. Mephistopheles remains true to his spirit of mockery. He tells Faust the swamps are being drained. Our critics love to interpret this moment in a socially optimistic sense: because he believes he has done humanity a great service and because this thought brings him his greatest happiness, Faust can now exclaim, 'Oh, moment, stay! You are so fair!' But if one analyzes it, wasn't Goethe laughing at the illusions that underlie human happiness? In actual fact, there wasn't any service to humanity at all. Faust pronounces the long-awaited sacramental phrase one step from the grave, utterly deceived, and perhaps truly crazy. And the lemurs immediately shove him into the pit. What is that, a hymn to happiness or a mockery of it?"

"Oh, Lev, my friend, I love you the way you are right now, when you argue from your heart and talk intelligently and don't try to pin abusive labels on things."

"Wretched descendant of Pyrrho! I never knew I gave you pleasure. But listen: At one of my prewar lectures—and they were damned bold for the times—on the basis of that quotation from *Faust* I developed the melancholy notion that there is no such thing as happiness, that it is either unattainable or illusory. And then a student handed up a note written on a piece of graph paper torn from a tiny notebook: 'But I am in love—and I am *happy!* How do you answer that?' "

"What did you answer?"

"What can you answer?"

8

THE FIFTH YEAR IN HARNESS

They became so absorbed in their conversation they no longer heard the noises in the laboratory or the intrusive radio in the far corner. Once again Nerzhin swiveled in his chair so that his back was to the lab. Rubin turned around in his armchair and rested his beard on his crossed arms.

Nerzhin was speaking fervently, like a man imparting long-matured thoughts:

"When I was free and used to read books in which wise men pondered the meaning of life or the nature of happiness, I understood very little of those passages. I gave them their due: wise men are supposed to think. It's their profession. But the meaning of life? We live—that's the meaning. Happiness? When things are going very well, that's happiness, everyone knows that. Thank God for prison! It gave me the chance to think. In order to understand the nature of happiness we first have to analyze satiety. Remember the Lubyanka and counterintelligence? Remember that thin, watery barley or the oatmeal porridge without a single drop of fat? Can you say that you *eat* it? No. You commune with it, you take it like a sacrament! Like the prana of the yogis. You eat it slowly; you eat it from the tip of the wooden spoon; you eat it absorbed entirely in the process of eating, in thinking about eating—and it spreads through your body like nectar. You tremble at the sweetness released from those overcooked little grains and the murky liquid they float in. And then—with hardly any nourishment—you go on living six months, twelve months. Can you really compare the crude devouring of a steak with this?"

Rubin could never bear listening to others for long. In every conversation, he was the one to impart the treasures of inspiration he had unearthed. Now he was trying to interrupt, but Nerzhin seized him by his coveralls and shook him to prevent his speaking.

"So in our own poor hides and from our miserable comrades we learn the nature of satiety. Satiety depends not at all on *how much* we eat, but on *how* we eat. It's the same way with happiness, the very same. Lev, friend, happiness doesn't depend on how many external blessings we have snatched from life. It depends only on our attitude toward them. There's a saying about it in the Taoist ethic: 'Whoever is capable of contentment will always be satisfied.' "

Rubin grinned ironically. "You're an eclectic. You pluck bright feathers from everywhere."

Nerzhin shook his head. His hair hung down over his forehead. The discussion interested him, and at that moment he looked like an eighteen-year-old.

"Don't try to mix things up, Lev. That's not how it is at all. I draw my conclusions not from the philosophy I've read but from stories about real people that I've heard in prison. And afterward, when I have to formulate my own conclusions, why should I discover America all over again? On the planet of philosophy all lands have long since been discovered. I leaf through the ancient philosophers and find my newest discoveries there. Don't interrupt! I was about to give an example. If in camp—and even more so in the sharashka—there should be a miracle like a free, nonworking Sunday, then in the course of that day the soul unfreezes. And even though nothing in my external situation has changed for the better, still the yoke of prison has let up on me a bit, and I have a real conversation or read an honest page and I'm on the crest of a wave. I haven't had any real life for many years, but I've forgotten about that. I'm weightless, suspended, disembodied. I lie there on my upper bunk and stare at the ceiling. It is very close, it's bare, the plasterwork is bad—and I tremble with the utter joy of existence! I fall asleep in perfect bliss. No president, no prime minister can fall asleep so satisfied with his Sunday."

Rubin grinned benignly. In that grin there was both acquiescence and a shade of condescension toward his deluded younger friend.

"And what do the great books of the Veda have to say about that?" he asked, his lips set in a humorous pout.

"I don't know about the books of the Veda," countered Nerzhin firmly, "but the books of the Sankhya say: 'For those who understand, human happiness is suffering.' "

"You certainly have everything worked out," Rubin muttered into his beard. "Did you get it from Sologdin?"

"Maybe. Idealism? Metaphysics? Yes? Go ahead and paste

on the labels, shaggy beard! Listen! The happiness of incessant victory, the happiness of fulfilled desire, the happiness
of success and of total satiety—*that* is suffering! That is
spiritual death, a sort of unending moral pain. It isn't the philosophers of the Vedanta or the Sankhya, but I personally,
Gleb Nerzhin, a prisoner in harness for the fifth year, who
has risen to that stage of development where the bad begins
to appear the good. And I personally hold the view that
people don't know what they are striving for. They waste
themselves in senseless thrashing around for the sake of a
handful of goods and die without realizing their spiritual
wealth. When Lev Tolstoi dreamed of being imprisoned, he
was reasoning like a truly perceptive person with a healthy
spiritual life."

Rubin laughed. He often laughed when he categorically
rejected his opponent's views in an argument.

"Take heed, youngster! There speaks in you the immaturity
of a youthful mind. You prefer your personal experience
to the collective experience of humanity. You're poisoned
by the stink of prison-latrine talk—and you want to see the
world through that haze. Just because our lives have been
wrecked, because our destinies have not worked out, why
should men change their convictions?"

"And you're proud to hold to your convictions?"

"Yes! *Hier stehe ich! Ich kann nicht anders.*"

"Pigheaded fellow! That's what metaphysics is! Instead of
learning here in prison, instead of learning from our real
life—"

"What life? The bitter poison of failure?"

"—you've willfully put a blindfold over your eyes, plugged
up your ears, assumed a pose, and you call that intelligence? According to you, intelligence is the refusal to
grow!"

"Intelligence is objectivity."

"You—objective?"

"Absolutely!" Rubin declared with dignity.

"I've never in my life known a person as lacking in objectivity as you."

"Get your head out of the sand! Look at things in their
historical perspective. I shouldn't quote myself, I know, but:

A moth's life lasts but a moment,
An oak flowers a hundred years.

Natural law—do you understand the meaning of that term? Inevitable, conditioned, natural law? Everything follows its inevitable course. And it's useless to root around for some kind of rotten skepticism."

"Don't think for a moment, Lev, that skepticism comes easily. Perhaps for me it's a shed by the roadside where I can sit out the bad weather. But skepticism is a way of freeing the dogmatic mind, and that's where its value lies."

"Dogmatic? You are a blockhead! How could I be a dogmatist?" Rubin's big warm eyes stared with reproach. "I'm the same kind of prisoner as you—from the *draft* of 1945. And four years at the front, a shell fragment in my side, and five years of prison. So I see things just as well as you. What must be, must be. The state can't exist without a well-organized penal system."

"I won't listen to that. I don't accept it."

"Of course. There goes skepticism! Sound the fife and drum! What kind of a Sextus Empiricus have we here! Why are you so upset? Is that the way to be a proper skeptic? A skeptic is supposed to withhold judgment. A skeptic is supposed to be imperturbable."

"Yes, you're right," Gleb said in despair. "I dream of being restrained. I try to have only . . . lofty thoughts. But circumstances overcome me and I get dizzy; I fight back in outrage."

"Lofty thoughts! And you're at my throat because in Dzhezkazgan there's not enough drinking water."

"You should be sent there yourself, you bastard! You're the only one of us who thinks the Plowman is right, that his methods are normal and necessary. You should be sent off to Dzhezkazgan—you'd soon be singing another song."

"Listen, listen!" Now it was Rubin who grabbed Nerzhin by his coveralls. "He's the greatest! Someday you will understand. He's the Robespierre and Napoleon of our Revolution wrapped up in one. He is wise. He is really wise. He sees far beyond what we can possibly see!"

"You should believe your own eyes," Nerzhin interrupted. "Listen, when I was a little boy, I started to read his books after reading Lenin's, and I couldn't get through them. After a style that was direct, ardent, precise, suddenly there was a sort of mush. Every one of his thoughts is crude and stupid—he doesn't even realize that he always misses what's important."

"You discovered all that as a boy?"

"When I was in the upper grades. You don't believe me? Well neither did the interrogator who put together the case against me. All that pretentiousness, the didactic condescension of his proclamations, drives me mad. He seriously believes that he's more intelligent than any Russian—"

"But he is!"

"—and that he makes us happy just by letting us admire him."

Carried away by their argument, the friends became careless, and their conversation could now be overheard by Simochka, who for some time had been glancing disapprovingly at Nerzhin. She was hurt that he not only didn't think of taking advantage of the fact that she was on duty but didn't even look in her direction.

"You're all wrong—particularly because you are meddling in matters you know nothing about! You're a mathematician, and you have no real knowledge of history or philosophy— so how dare you hand down such a verdict?"

"Listen here, enough of these legends about people who discovered the neutrino and weighed Beta Sirius without ever having seen them being so infantile they can't orient themselves in the simple problems of human existence. We have no choice. If you historians no longer concern yourselves with history, what is left for us mathematicians and technicians to do? I see who wins the prizes and who gets the academic salaries. They don't write history; they just lick a certain well-known spot. So we, the scientific intelligentsia, have to study history ourselves."

"Oh, come on! How dreadful you make it sound!"

"And in addition our approach is technical, and mathematical methods aren't so bad. History wouldn't suffer from a little of them."

At the unoccupied desk of Engineer Major Roitman, the head of the Acoustics Laboratory, the institute intercom telephone rang. Simochka got up to answer it.

". . . Yes! And so the pretrial investigator didn't believe that my study of dialectical materialism was what led to my indictment under Section 58, Paragraph 10. I had never known real life; admittedly, I'd always been immersed in books; but I compared those two styles again and again, those two methods of argument, and in the texts—"

"Gleb Vikentich!"

"—in the texts I discovered errors, distortions, crude oversimplifications—and so here I am!"

"Gleb Vikentich!"

"Yes?" said Nerzhin, realizing he was being called. He turned away from Rubin.

"Didn't you hear? The telephone rang." Simochka addressed him sternly. She was standing at her desk, frowning, her arms crossed, her brown shawl pulled around her shoulders. "Anton Nikolayevich wants to see you in his office."

"Oh, yes?" On Nerzhin's face the enthusiasm of argument faded and the wrinkles returned. "Very well, thank you, Serafima Vitalyevna. You hear, Lev? It's Yakonov. Why?"

A summons to the office of the chief of the institute at ten o'clock on Saturday night was an extraordinary event. Though Simochka tried to maintain an appearance of official indifference, her glance, as Nerzhin realized, expressed alarm.

Then it was as if there never had been any flare-up of bitterness. Rubin looked at his friend with concern. When his eyes were not transformed by the heat of argument, they were almost feminine in their softness.

"I don't like it when top management takes an interest in us," he declared. " 'Don't build your house near the prince's palace.' "

"But we aren't. Our job is a minor one: voices."

"And now Anton is going to be after us. We'll catch hell for the memoirs of Stanislavsky and the book of lawyers' speeches." Rubin laughed. "Or maybe it's about articulation in Number Seven?"

"Well, the project results have already been turned in, and there's no backing out. Just in case, if I don't come back—"

"Don't be silly."

"What do you mean, silly? That's how life goes. Burn that, you know where." He closed his roll-top desk, gave Rubin the key, and went off with the leisurely stride of a prisoner in his fifth year in harness who never hurries because he expects only worse from what lies ahead.

9

THE ROSICRUCIANS

Nerzhin climbed the broad, red-carpeted stairway, beneath the brass sconces and molded plaster ceiling. At that late hour it was deserted. He forced himself to walk with an appearance of unconcern as he passed the duty officer at the outside phones and knocked at the door of the chief of the institute, Colonel of Engineers of the State Security Service, Anton Nikolayevich Yakonov. The office was spacious, furnished with rugs, armchairs, couches. In the center of the room stood a long conference table covered with a bright blue cloth. In the far corner curved the brown bentwood forms of Yakonov's desk and armchair. Nerzhin had been exposed to this grandeur only a few times before, more often at meetings than alone.

Colonel of Engineers Yakonov was over fifty but still in his prime. He was tall; his face was slightly powdered after shaving; he wore a gold pince-nez; and there was about him the soft portliness of a princely Obolensky or Dolgorukov. His majestically assured movements distinguished him from the other dignitaries in the ministry.

"Be seated, Gleb Vikentich," he said expansively, sitting back in his oversized armchair as he toyed with a thick colored pencil on the brown surface of his desk.

The use of Nerzhin's first name and patronymic indicated courtesy and goodwill, yet cost the colonel of engineers no effort, since under the glass on his desk lay a list of all the prisoners with their first names and patronymics. (Anyone who did not know about this was astonished by Yakonov's memory.) Nerzhin greeted him silently, without standing at attention; and, watchfully, he sat down at a small varnished table. Yakonov's voice had a resonance like an actor's. One wondered why this aristocrat did not roll his "r's" in the manner of the old nobility.

"You know, Gleb Vikentich, half an hour ago I had reason to be reminded of you, and I was wondering what really brought you to the Acoustics Laboratory, to—Roitman?"

Yakonov pronounced the name in a deliberately contemptuous manner, not bothering to call him Major even in front of a subordinate. The bad relations between the chief of the institute and his first deputy had reached the point where it was not considered necessary to conceal them.

Nerzhin became tense. He sensed that the interview had already taken a bad turn. There had been the same irony on Yakonov's lips when he had said to Nerzhin, several days before, that though he, Nerzhin, might be objective about the results of the work on articulation, his attitude toward Number Seven was one of active indifference. Number Seven was the horse Yakonov was betting on, but the work there was going badly.

". . . of course I value highly your personal accomplishments in the techniques of articulation—"

(He was mocking him.)

"—and I am terribly sorry that your original monograph was printed in a small classified edition, depriving you of the glory of being recognized as a Russian George Fletcher—"

(He was mocking him brazenly.)

"—However, I would like to derive more 'profit,' as the Anglo-Saxons put it, from your work. After all, you know that for all my esteem for abstract science I am a practical man of affairs."

Colonel of Engineers Yakonov held a high rank, but he was not so close to the Leader of Nations that he had to disguise his intelligence or abstain from holding personal opinions.

"Well, anyway, let me ask you frankly: what are you doing in the Acoustics Laboratory right now?"

He could not have hit upon a more merciless question! Yakonov simply hadn't the time to go into everything—otherwise he would have known the answer well enough.

"Why the devil are you bothering with that parroting business—'cheese,' 'choice'? You, a mathematician, a university man. Turn around."

Nerzhin turned around, then stood up. There was a third person in the office. A modest-looking man in black civilian clothes got up from the couch and approached Nerzhin. His bright round spectacles gleamed. In the generous light from overhead, Nerzhin recognized Pyotr Trofimovich Verenyov, before the war an assistant professor in his own university. However, in keeping with the habit he had formed in prison, Nerzhin said nothing, made no movement. He assumed that the person facing him was a prisoner, too, and he was afraid to harm him by a hasty sign of recognition. Verenyov smiled, but he, too, seemed embarrassed.

Yakonov rumbled on reassuringly: "Really, there's an enviable display of restraint among you mathematicians. All my life I have thought of mathematicians as Rosicrucians of some kind, and I always regretted that I never had the opportunity of being initiated into their secrets. Please feel at ease. Shake hands and make yourselves quite at home. I shall leave you for half an hour to your fond reminiscing and also to allow Professor Verenyov to tell you about the tasks that have been set for us."

Yakonov raised himself from his oversized armchair—his silver-and-blue shoulder boards emphasized the imposing mass of his heavy body—and moved swiftly and easily to the door. When Verenyov and Nerzhin met to shake hands, they were alone.

This pale man, whose glasses glittered with reflected light, seemed to the prisoner Nerzhin a ghost unlawfully returned from a forgotten world. Between that world and the world of today there had been the forests below Lake Ilmen, the hills and ravines of Orel, the sands and marshes of Belorussia, the fat Polish farms, the tile roofs of German cities. In the nine-year period that separated them there had been the glaring, bare cells, the "boxes," of the Bolshaya Lubyanka; gray, stinking transit prisons; stifling compartments of "Stolypin" transports; the cutting wind of the steppe. All this made it impossible to recover the feelings that had been his when he had written out the functions of an independent variable on the yielding surface of a linoleum blackboard.

Nerzhin felt uneasy.

Both men lit cigarettes and sat down, separated by the small varnished table.

This was not Verenyov's first meeting with one of his former students at Moscow University or at R—— University, where before the war, during the struggle between theoretical schools, he had been sent to put the hard line into effect. But for him, too, there were unusual elements in today's meeting: the isolation of this institution in the suburbs of Moscow, surrounded by a haze of secrecy and girdled by barbed wire; the strange dark-blue coveralls instead of ordinary clothes.

Unaccountably, Nerzhin, the younger of the two men, the failure with no academic title, asked the questions, the creases around his mouth sharply drawn. And the older man answered as if he were ashamed of his unpretentious personal history as a scientist: evacuation in wartime, re-evacuation, three years of work with K——, a doctoral dissertation in mathematical topology. Nerzhin, who had become inattentive to the point of discourtesy, did not even ask Verenyov the subject of his dissertation in that dry science in which he himself had once taken a course. He was suddenly sorry for Verenyov. Quantities solved, quantities not solved, quantities unknown—topology! The stratosphere of human thought! In the twenty-fourth century it might possibly be of use to someone, but as for now . . .

> I've nothing to say of the sun and world,
> I see only the torments of man.

How had Verenyov gotten into this organization? Why had he left the university? Well, he had been assigned to it. Couldn't he have gotten out of it? Yes, he could have refused, but the salaries were double. Any children? Four.

For some reason they began to review the list of students in Nerzhin's class who had taken their finals, as he had, on the day the war started. The more talented had been shell-shocked or killed. They were the sort who were always pushing ahead, who didn't stop to look out for themselves. And those from whom nothing could have been expected were now either completing their postgraduate work or already held appointments as lecturers in higher-educational institutions. And what about our pride and joy, Dmitri Dmitrich Goryainov-Shakhovsky?

Goryainov-Shakhovsky! The little old man, slovenly in his great age, would sometimes smear his black corduroy jacket with chalk, at other times would pocket the blackboard rag instead of his handkerchief. He was a living legend, made up of a multitude of "absent-minded professor" jokes. He had been the soul of the Warsaw Imperial University,

having moved to industrial R— in 1915, as one might
move to a cemetery. Half a century of scientific work
brought congratulatory cables from Milwaukee, Capetown,
Yokohama. And then he was purged in the interests of "freshening up" the staff. He went to Moscow, and returned with a
note from Kalinin: "Don't touch this old man!" It was
rumored that Kalinin's father had been a serf of the professor's father's.

So they did not touch him. They did not touch him in a
way that was awesome. He might write a research paper in
the natural sciences containing a mathematical proof of the
existence of God. Or at a public lecture on his beloved
Newton he might wheeze from behind his yellow mustaches:
"Someone just passed me a note: 'Marx wrote that Newton was a materialist, and you say he was an idealist.' I
reply: Marx was wrong. Newton believed in God, like every
other great scientist."

Trying to take notes on his lectures was frightening. The
stenographers would be driven to despair. Because his legs
were weak, he sat right at the blackboard, facing it, his back
to the auditorium, and wrote with his right hand while eras-
ing with his left, muttering to himself all the while. It was
absolutely impossible to understand his ideas while listening
to his lectures, but when Nerzhin, working together with
one of his comrades, succeeded in actually taking down what
he had said and figuring it out overnight, they were inwardly
moved as by the twinkling of starry heavens.

Well, what had happened to him? When R— was bombed, the old man had been shell-shocked and had been evacuated to Kirghizia half-alive. Then he had returned, but he
was apparently no longer at the university but at the Peda-
gogical Institute. So he was alive? Yes, alive. Amazing.
Time flies and, then again, it doesn't. . . .

But why, after all, had Nerzhin been arrested?

Nerzhin laughed. "Why 'after all'? For my turn of mind,
Pyotr Trofimovich. In Japan they have a law under which a
person can be tried for his unexpressed thoughts."

"In Japan! But we have no such law."

"Indeed we do, and it's called Section 58, Paragraph 10."

Nerzhin only half-heard Verenyov's explanation of Yakonov's purpose in bringing them together. Verenyov had been
sent to Mavrino to intensify and systematize the cryptography work. They needed mathematicians, many mathema-

ticians, and Verenyov was delighted to learn that right at hand was his own student, whose prospects had been so bright.

Nerzhin abstractedly asked the appropriate questions. Pyotr Trofimovich, who was warming with mathematical fervor, explained the problem and told him what tests were to be made, what formulas gone over. But Nerzhin was thinking about those little sheets of paper he had covered with his tiny handwriting, those notes he had been able to write so serenely behind his stage props, under the guarded armorous glances of Simochka, with Rubin's good-natured muttering in his ears. These little sheets of paper were his first coming of age in all his thirty years.

Of course, it would have been more desirable to achieve maturity in his own field. Why, one might ask, should he stick his head into those gaping jaws from which historians themselves had fled into safe eras of the distant past? What compulsion drove him to grapple with the riddle of the inflated, gloomy giant who had only to flutter his eyelashes for Nerzhin's head to fly off? As they say: *why do you have to stick your neck out?* And, more than anything, *what are you looking for?*

Was he, then, to surrender to the tentacles of cryptography—fourteen hours a day, no days off and no breaks, his head crammed with theories of probability, theories of numbers, theories of error, a dead brain, a dried-out soul? What would be left to think with? What would be left for learning about life?

Yet there was the sharashka. It was not a camp. Meat at dinner. Butter in the morning. Hands not flayed with work. Fingers not frozen. No lying down on boards, dead as a log in dirty hemp sandals. At the sharashka you lay down in a bed under a white sheet, with a feeling of contentment.

But why live a whole life? Just to be living? Just to keep the body going? Precious comfort! What do we need it for if there's nothing else?

And good sense said, "Yes," but the heart said, "Get thee behind me, Satan!"

"Pyotr Trofimovich, do you know how to make shoes?"

"What did you say?"

"I asked: Will you teach me how to make shoes?"

"Pardon? I don't understand."

"Pyotr Trofimovich, you're living in a shell. I, after all,

will finish my sentence and go off to the remote taiga, to permanent exile. I don't know how to work with my hands, so how will I live? It's full of bears. Out there we won't need the Euler functions for three more geological eras."

"What are you talking about, Nerzhin! As a cryptographer, if the work is successful, you'll be freed ahead of your term, the conviction will be removed from your record, and you will be given an apartment in Moscow."

"They'll remove the conviction from my record!" Nerzhin cried angrily, his eyes narrowing. "Where did you get the idea that I want that little gift? 'You've worked well, so we'll free you, forgive you.' No, Pyotr Trofimovich!" And with his forefinger he stabbed at the varnished surface of the little table. "You're beginning at the wrong end. Let them admit first that it's not right to put people in prison for their way of thinking, and then *we* will decide whether we will forgive *them*."

The door opened to admit the portly dignitary with the gold pince-nez on his fat nose.

"Well, my Rosicrucians, have you come to an agreement?"

Nerzhin did not rise but looked steadily into Yakonov's eyes as he answered, "It's up to you, Anton Nikolayevich, but I consider that my task in the Acoustics Laboratory is unfinished."

Yakonov was now standing behind his desk. Only those who knew him could have recognized that he was angry. He said, "Articulation—against mathematics! You have traded the nectar of the Gods for lentil soup. Goodbye."

And with his thick colored pencil he wrote on his desk pad: "Nerzhin to be sent away."

10

THE ENCHANTED CASTLE

For many years—during the war and after—Yakonov had been secure in his position as Chief Engineer of the Special Equipment Section. He wore with dignity the silver shoulder boards with sky-blue edging and the three large stars which his knowledge had earned him. His post was such that he could exercise over-all direction at a considerable remove, occasionally reading an erudite report before high-ranking listeners, occasionally talking intelligently and colorfully with an engineer about his finished model. On the whole he maintained the reputation of being an expert without being responsible for anything, and every month he received quite a few thousand rubles. Yakonov presided at the birth of all the section's technical undertakings, absented himself in the difficult period of their growing pains and coming of age, and reappeared to officiate over their black coffins or to crown them with a hero's golden crown.

Anton Nikolayevich was neither so young nor so self-confident as to pursue the deceptive glitter of a Gold Star or a Stalin Prize, or grab every chance to take on a project assigned by the ministry or even by the Boss himself. Anton Nikolayevich was both experienced enough and old enough to want to avoid the whole complex of emotions, alarms, and intense ambition.

Maintaining these views, he led a rather comfortable existence until January 1948. That January someone suggested to the Father of Western and Eastern Peoples the idea of creating a special secret telephone intended for his use only —an instrument so constructed that no one could understand his telephone conversations even if they were monitored. With his august finger, the nail of which was yellowed by nicotine, the Father of Peoples pointed on the map to the Mavrino unit, which until then had been used to create portable transceivers for the police. His historic words on this occasion were: "What do I need those transceivers for? To catch burglars? Who cares?"

He announced a time limit: the first of January, 1949. Then he reflected a moment and said, "All right, you can have till May first."

The assignment had top importance and priority and a particularly tight time limit. In the ministry they considered the matter and selected Yakonov to see it through personally. Yakonov strove in vain to prove that he was overloaded with work and could not conceivably do two jobs at once. The head of the section, Foma Guryanovich Oskolupov, stared at Yakonov with his green, feline eyes—and Yakonov remembered the stain on his official security record. He

himself had been in prison for six years. So he kept his
mouth shut.

Since then—almost two years ago—the chief engineer's
office in the ministry building had been vacant. The chief
engineer spent day and night at the suburban institute, which
was crowned by a hexagonal tower rising above the dome
over the site of the chapel altar.

At first it had been pleasant to direct things himself: to
slam the door of his personally assigned Pobeda car with a
weary gesture, to be rocked in it as it sped to Mavrino, to
pass the saluting guard at the gates wound with barbed wire.
It was good in the springtime, when everything was so young
and green, to walk among the century-old lindens of the
Mavrino grove surrounded by a suite of captains and majors.
His superiors had not demanded anything of Yakonov yet—
only endless drafts of plans and the promises of "Socialist
obligations" to be fulfilled. And the horn of plenty had
emptied its bounty on the Mavrino Institute: imported and
Soviet-made radio parts, equipment, furniture, a technical
library of thirty thousand items, prisoner specialists pulled
out of camps, the very best security officers and file super-
visors (always cocks-of-the-walk on a secret project), and
finally a special, iron-hard corps of guards. It was necessary to repair the old building and build new ones, for the
staff headquarters of the special prison, for experimental
machine shops. And by the time the lindens were in yellow
flower and sweet with fragrance, the mournful talk of shift-
less German POWs in their lizard-like tunics could be heard
in the shade of the ancient giants.

These lazy Fascists in their fourth year of postwar imprisonment had no desire whatever to work. To the Russian eye it was unbearable to watch them unload bricks
from the trucks—slowly, carefully, as if the bricks were
made of glass, passing each one from hand to hand until it
was stacked on the pile. While they installed radiators at the
windows and refloored the rotten floors, the Germans wandered around the supersecret rooms and looked sullenly at the
German and English markings on the equipment. Any German schoolboy could have guessed what type of laboratory
it was. Rubin set forth all this in a report to the colonel of
engineers, and his report was perfectly accurate. But it was
also very inconvenient for the head security officers, Shikin
and Myshin (known among the prisoners, collectively, as

Shishkin-Myshkin), for what could be done about it now?
Were they to report their own carelessness to higher authority? And it was too late to correct matters anyway, because
the POWs had been sent back to their homeland, and those
who went to West Germany could, if one really stopped to
think, report the location of the institute and the disposi-
tion of individual laboratories to anyone who was interested.
Therefore, without sending on Rubin's report, Major Shikin
insisted that no workroom in the institute should know the
secrets of any other, any more than it should know the news
of the marketplace on the island of Madagascar. If officers
in other divisions of the same ministry sought out the colonel
of engineers on ministry business, he was not allowed to
divulge the address of his institute; to preserve this inviolate
secrecy he met them at the Lubyanka.

When the Germans were sent back to their homes, they
brought in zeks to replace them, just like those in the sharashka except that their clothes were dirty and torn, and
they didn't get white bread. Now beneath the lindens was
heard the sound of good camp cursing, sometimes justified
and sometimes not, which reminded the sharashka zeks of
their staunch Motherland and their own implacable fate.
Storms of bricks flew from the trucks so that hardly a one
was left whole. With a shout of "One, two, three—heave!"
the zeks hoisted a plywood hood on the back of the truck.
They climbed under it and were locked inside and driven off
through the streets of Moscow, meanwhile making joyful
passes at the cursing girls among them. Thus, each night,
they were taken back to their camp.

And so, at this enchanted castle, set apart from the capital and its uninformed inhabitants by a magic no-man's land,
these lemurs in their black-quilted jackets wrought fabulous
changes: a water supply, a sewage disposal system, central
heating and flower beds.

Meanwhile this favored institution was growing and ex-
panding. The Mavrino Institute took under its wing still
another research institute, with a full staff, which had been
engaged in similar work. This institute came complete with
desks, tables, cabinets, file folders and rolls of documents,
equipment of the kind which becomes obsolete not in years
but in months, and its chief, Major of Engineers Roitman,
became Yakonov's deputy. Alas, the creator, inspirer, and
protector of the newly arrived institute, Colonel Yakov Ivan-

ovich Mamurin, the Chief of Special Communications and one of the most important government officials, had disappeared earlier under tragic circumstances.

It happened that the Leader of All Progressive Humanity once talked with Yenan Province and was dissatisfied with the squeals and static on the telephone. He called in Beria and said in Georgian: "Lavrenty! What kind of an idiot have you got as head of communications? Get rid of him."

So they got rid of Mamurin; that is, they imprisoned him in the Lubyanka. They got rid of him, but they did not know what to do with him next. There were none of the customary subsequent directives; no instructions on whether to sentence him, and, if so, for what and what prison term to give him. Had he not been one of their own, they would have given him "a quarter and five on the horns," as they said—twenty-five years and five additional years of deprivation of civil rights—and sent him off to Norilsk. But, mindful of the saying, "It's you today, me tomorrow," his former colleagues stood by Mamurin. When they were convinced that Stalin had forgotten him, they sent him without interrogation and without sentence to the suburban country house at Mavrino.

So, on a summer evening in 1948, they brought a new zek to the sharashka. Everything about this arrival was unusual: the fact that he was brought in a passenger car and not in the Black Maria, that he was accompanied by the head of the Prison Section himself, and, finally, that he was served his first dinner, covered by a cloth, in the office of the head of the special prison.

They heard (zeks were supposed to hear nothing, but they heard everything) how the arriving prisoner had said that he did not "care for sausage," and how the head of the Prison Section politely urged him to eat. A zek on his way to the doctor for medication heard that over a partition. Discussing such exciting news, the indigenous population of the sharashka reached the conclusion that the new arrival was nevertheless a zek, and went to sleep satisfied.

The historians of the sharashka never established where the newcomer slept that first night. Early the next morning, on the broad marble landing where prisoners were henceforth not allowed, one rough-and-ready zek, a clumsy lathe operator, ran into him face to face.

"Well, brother," he said, pushing him in the chest, "where're you from? How'd you get burned? Sit down, let's have a smoke."

But the newcomer stepped back from the lathe operator in disdainful horror. The lathe operator glared at his whitish eyes, his light, balding hair, and said angrily, "All right, you snake-in-the-grass! You're sure as hell going to talk to us after you've been locked up with us for a night!"

But the "snake-in-the-grass" was not shut up in the general prison. Off the laboratory corridor on the third floor they found him a little room which had formerly been used as a photographic darkroom, and they pushed in a cot, a table, a wardrobe, a house plant, and an electric hot plate. They tore off the cardboard covering the barred window, which looked not into God's light but onto a back-stair landing. The stairs were on the north side, so even in the daytime the light barely reached the privileged prisoner's cell. Of course, the bars could have been taken off the window, but the prison administration, after some hesitation, decided, after all, to leave them. Even those in authority did not understand this puzzling affair and could not settle on a correct line of action.

It was then that the new arrival was christened "The Man in the Iron Mask." For a long time no one knew his name. No one could talk with him. Through the window the zeks could see him sitting in his solitary cell with his head bowed, or wandering like a pale shadow among the lindens at hours when other zeks were not allowed outside. Iron Mask was as sallow and thin as a zek ordinarily gets after a good two-year investigation. However, his irrational refusal of sausage denied this interpretation.

Much later, when Iron Mask had begun to work in Number Seven, the zeks learned from the free employees that he was the same Colonel Mamurin who, as head of Special Communications, had forbidden anyone to put his heels down when going past his office—they had to walk on tiptoe. Otherwise he dashed out in a rage through his secretary's anteroom and screamed, "Whose office do you think you're tramping past, lout? What's your name?"

Still later it became clear that Mamurin's suffering at the sharashka was on a moral plane. The world of the free rejected him, and he would have nothing to do with the world of the zeks. At first in his solitude he read books all the time—such immortal works as Panferov's *Struggle for Peace* and Babayevsky's *Cavalier of the Golden Star*. He read Sobolev, Nikulin, and then he read the verses of Prokofiev and Gribachev. And within him a miraculous transfor-

mation took place: he began to write poetry himself. It is
well known that unhappiness and torment of the soul give
birth to poets, and Mamurin's torments were more acute
than those of any other prisoner. In prison for two years,
without investigation or trial, he lived as he had lived previously, solely according to the latest Party directives and,
as before, he deified the Wise Teacher. Mamurin confessed
to Rubin that it was not the prison food that was so awful
(his was prepared specially); nor was it the pain of being
parted from his family (once a month they took him secretly
to his own apartment, where he spent the night); it was not
so much his primitive animal needs—but it was bitter to have
lost the confidence of Iosif Vissarionovich; it was painful to
find himself no longer a colonel, but discharged and dis-
graced. That was why people such as Rubin and he found it
immeasurably more difficult to bear confinement than did
the unprincipled bastards around them.

Rubin was a Communist. But after hearing the avowals
of his presumably orthodox and like-minded colleague, and
after reading his poetry, Rubin began to avoid Mamurin,
even hide from him, and he spent his time with the men
who attacked him unfairly but who shared his lot.

As for Mamurin, he was driven by the desire, as insistent
as a toothache, to justify himself through work. Alas, his
entire acquaintance with communications, even though he
had been a high official in the field, began and ended with
holding a telephone. Therefore he, personally, was unable
to work; he could only direct. But management, if the
project to be managed was obviously ill-starred, would
never put him back in the good graces of the Best Friend
of Communications Workers. He had to manage a project
with some promise.

By this time, two such promising projects were taking
shape at the Mavrino Institute: the vocoder and Number
Seven.

For some deep-rooted, illogical reason, people either do or
do not get along with each other from the first glance.
Yakonov and his deputy Roitman did not get along. Every
month each became more and more intolerable to the other;
being harnessed to the same chariot by a heavier hand than
theirs, they could not break away, but they did pull in
different directions. When secret telephony began to be approached through two separate experimental schemes, Roit-

man gathered up everyone he could to work in the Acoustics Laboratory on the vocoder, which in Russian was called the "artificial-speech device." In retaliation, Yakonov picked through all the other groups and gathered all the most skillful engineers and the best imported equipment into Number Seven—that is, into Laboratory Seven. Tentative starts on other solutions to the problem were wiped out in the unequal battle.

Mamurin picked Number Seven for himself because he could not become the subordinate of his own former subordinate, Roitman, and also because the ministry deemed it wise to have a fiery and vigilant eye glaring over the shoulder of the non-Party and slightly tainted Yakonov.

From that day on, Yakonov might be at the institute at night or not, as he pleased. The discharged MVD colonel, the lone prisoner with feverish white eyes, hideously sunken cheeks, refusing food and drink, suppressing his new-found passion for poetry, slaved until two in the morning putting Number Seven on a fifteen-hour working day. Such a convenient working schedule could exist only in Number Seven because the free employees did not have to stand special night duty since there was no need for a security watch over Mamurin.

When Yakonov left Verenyov and Nerzhin in his office, he had gone directly to Number Seven.

11

NUMBER SEVEN

No one ever tells ordinary soldiers what the generals are planning, but they always know perfectly well whether they have been deployed in the main line of advance or on a flank. In the same way, the three hundred zeks of the Mavrino sharashka were correct in assuming that Number Seven was the crucial sector.

No one in the institute was supposed to know the true name of Number Seven, but everyone did know it. It was the "Clipped Speech Laboratory." "Clipped Speech" had been taken from English, and not only the engineers and translators, but also the assembly and installation men, the lathe operators, and perhaps even the hard-of-hearing carpenter knew that the piece of equipment in question was being built along the lines of American models. But it was accepted practice to pretend it was all of native origin. Therefore the American radio magazines with diagrams and articles on the theory of "clipping," which were sold in New York on counters outside secondhand-book shops, were here numbered, bound with string, classified, and sealed up in fireproof safes, out of reach of American spies.

Clipping, damping, amplitude compression, electronic differentiation and integration of normal human speech were engineering desecrations comparable to the dismemberment of a southern resort area like Novy Afon or Gurzuf into little fragments of matter, stuffing them into a billion matchboxes, mixing them all up, flying them to Nerchinsk, sorting them out and reassembling them in their new location so that the result could not be distinguished from the original— a re-creation of the subtropics, the sound of waves on the shore, the southern air and moonlight.

The same thing, using little packets of electrical impulses, was to be done with speech, and in such a way that not only would everything be comprehensible but so that the Boss would be able to recognize by voice the person he was speaking to.

In the sharashkas, those cushiony institutions where the snarl of the camp struggle for existence was not heard, it had long since been the established rule that those zeks most involved in the successful solution of a problem received everything—liberty, a clean passport, an apartment in Moscow; while the rest received nothing, not a single day off their term, nor three ounces of vodka in honor of the victors.

There was no in-between.

Therefore the prisoners who had been able to acquire that camp tenacity thanks to which a zek could apparently cling by his fingernails to the surface of a vertical mirror, the most tenacious prisoners tried to get into Number Seven in order to leap from there to freedom.

That was how the brutal engineer Markushev got there, his pimply face panting with eagerness to die for the ideas of Colonel of Engineers Yakonov. And others of the same sort got there that way, too.

But the perspicacious Yakonov also picked men for Number Seven who did not try to get there. That was the case with Engineer Amantai Bulatov, a Tatar from Kazan who wore big horn-rimmed glasses, a straightforward person with a deafening laugh, sentenced to ten years for having been captured by the Germans and associating with the enemy of the people Musa Djalil. It was also true of Andrei Andreyevich Potapov, a specialist in ultra-high voltages and the construction of electric power stations. He got to the sharashka at Mavrino through the mistake of an ignorant clerk who handled the cards in the GULAG card file. But being an authentic engineer and a wholehearted worker, Potapov quickly found his place in Mavrino and became irreplaceable in work that involved precise and complex radio-frequency measuring equipment.

Another member of the group was Engineer Khorobrov, a great radio expert. He had been assigned to Number Seven from the very beginning, when it was an ordinary unit. More recently he had grown weary of Number Seven and did not join in its furious pace. And Mamurin had grown weary of Khorobrov.

Finally, "getting people and horses in a lather," there arrived from a strict-regime work brigade of a hard-labor camp at the infamous construction project Number 501, near the settlement of Salekhard, the gloomy engineering genius Bobynin. He was immediately put over everyone else. He had been snatched from the gates of death, and in the event of success he would be the first candidate for freedom. So he stayed up and worked after midnight, but he worked with such contemptuous dignity that Mamurin was afraid of him. Bobynin was the only one in the whole group he avoided rebuking.

Number Seven was a room similar to the Acoustics Laboratory on the floor below. It was equipped and furnished like the other except that it had no acoustical booth.

Yakonov visited Number Seven several times a day, and for that reason his appearance there didn't create the flurry of a visit from the big boss. Only Markushev and the other toadies pushed to the fore and bustled about more eagerly than ever. As for Potapov, he set a frequency meter in the one open spot on the high, instrument-filled shelves which

fenced him off from the rest of the laboratory. He did his
work quickly, without frantic spurts of effort, and at this
moment he was making a cigarette case out of transparent
red plastic, planning to present it as a gift the next morning.

Mamurin rose to greet Yakonov as an equal. He was not
wearing the dark-blue coveralls of ordinary zeks but an expensive wool suit, yet it did nothing to enhance his emaciated
face and bony figure.

What appeared at this moment on his lemon-hued forehead and bloodless, deathly lips was interpreted by Yakonov
as pleasure: "Anton Nikolaich! We've readjusted to every
sixteenth impulse, and it's much better. Here, listen, I'll
read to you."

"Reading and "listening" were the customary test of the
quality of a phone circuit. The circuit was altered several
times a day, by the addition or the removal or replacement
of some unit or other, and to set up a formal articulation-
index test each time was a cumbersome procedure, too slow
to keep pace with each new design idea dreamed up by the
engineers. Moreover, there was no point in getting discourag-
ing figures from a system which had once been objective but
had lately been taken over by Roitman's protégé Nerzhin.

Dominated as usual by a single thought, without asking
anything or explaining anything, Mamurin retired to a far
corner of the room and there, turning his back and pressing
the telephone to his cheek, he began to read a newspaper
into the transmitter. At the other end of the circuit, Yakonov
put on a pair of earphones and listened. Something dreadful
was happening in the earphones: the sound of Mamurin's
voice was interrupted by bursts of crackling, roaring, and
screeching. But, as a mother gazes lovingly at her ugly offspring, Yakonov not only did not tear the phones from his
assaulted ears but listened all the more closely and concluded that the dreadful noise seemed less dreadful than the
previous dreadful noise, which he had heard before dinner.
Mamurin's reading was not the swift, elided speech of conversation but was measured and intentionally precise. Moreover, he was reading a piece about the insolence of the
Yugoslav border guards and the self-indulgence of Yugoslavia's bloody executioner, Rankovich, who had transformed
a peace-loving country into a mass torture chamber. Therefore Yakonov easily guessed at what he did not hear, un-

derstood that he had guessed it, forgot that he had guessed it, and was all the more assured that the reception was better than it had been before dinner.

He wanted, too, an exchange of views with Bobynin. The latter sat nearby, massive, broad-shouldered, with his hair cropped like a convict's, even though haircuts of every style were permitted at the sharashka. He had not turned around when Yakonov entered the laboratory; bent over the long band of photo-oscillogram film, he was measuring something with the points of his calipers.

This Bobynin was one of the insects of creation, an insignificant zek, a member of the lowest class. And Yakonov was a dignitary. Yet Yakonov could not bring himself to interrupt Bobynin no matter how much he wanted to.

One can build the Empire State Building, discipline the Prussian Army, elevate the state hierarchy above the throne of the Almighty, but one cannot get past the unaccountable spiritual superiority of certain people.

Some soldiers are feared by their company commanders. There are laborers who intimidate their foremen, prisoners who make their prosecutors tremble.

Bobynin knew this and made use of this power in his dealings with authority.

Every time Yakonov talked with him he caught himself in the craven desire to play up to this zek, to avoid irritating him. He was angry at himself for feeling this way, but he noticed that everyone else reacted similarly to Bobynin.

Taking off the earphones, Yakonov interrupted Mamurin: "It's better, Yakov Ivanich, definitely better! I'd like to have Rubin listen to it. He has a good ear."

Someone who had been gratified by an opinion of Rubin's had once said he had a "good ear." Unconsciously this premise was seized upon and believed. Rubin had gotten to the sharashka by accident, and he had managed to hang on there by doing translations. His left ear was as good as anyone else's, but his right ear had been deafened by concussion on the Northwest Front——a fact he had had to conceal after he had been praised for his "good ear." The reputation of having a "good ear" had made his position firm, until he made it even firmer with his magnum opus in three volumes: *The Audio-Synthetic and Electro-Acoustical Aspect of Russian Speech.*

So they phoned the Acoustics Laboratory for Rubin. While

they waited, they listened again themselves for the tenth time. Markushev, with knitted brows and eyes strained in concentration, held the phone a moment and declared firmly that it was better, that it was very much better. (The idea of readjusting it on a sixteen-impulse basis was his; therefore even before the readjustment was made he had known there would be an improvement.) Dyrsin smiled reluctantly, apologetically, and nodded. Bulatov shouted across the whole laboratory that they should get together with the code experts and readjust to a basis of thirty-two. Two accommodating electricians, pulling the earphones in opposite directions as each listened with one ear, immediately confirmed with joyous exuberance that it had indeed become clearer.

Bobynin continued to measure the oscillogram without looking up.

The black hand of the big electric wall clock jumped to 10:30. Soon work would end in all the laboratories except Number Seven, classified magazines would be locked in safes, zeks would go back to their quarters to sleep, and the free employees would run to the bus stop, where fewer buses passed in the late hours.

Ilya Terentevich Khorobrov, in the rear of the laboratory and out of sight of the chiefs, walked with heavy tread behind the wall of shelves to Potapov. Khorobrov was from Vyatka, and from its most remote area, near Kai, beyond which, through forests and swamps, a realm vastly bigger than France stretched for hundreds of miles, the land of GULAG. He saw and understood more than many, but the necessity of always hiding his thoughts and suppressing his sense of justice had bent his body, given him an unpleasant look, etched hard lines at his lips. Finally, in the first postwar elections, he could stand it no longer and on his ballot wrote crude peasant curses directed against the Greatest Genius of Geniuses. It was a time when ruined houses were not being rebuilt and fields were not being sown because of the shortage of workers. But for a whole month several young detectives studied the handwriting of every voter in the district and Khorobrov was arrested. He went off to camp with a simple-hearted feeling of gladness—at least there he could speak out as he pleased. But the ordinary camps did not work that way. Informers showered denunciations on Khorobrov, and he had to shut up.

At the sharashka good sense demanded that he lose himself in the activity of Number Seven and assure himself, if not of liberation, at least of a decent existence. But nausea at all the injustices aside from his own case rose inside him until he had reached the point where a man no longer wants to live.

Going behind Potapov's wall of shelves, he bent over the desk and proposed quietly, "Andreich. Time to quit. It's Saturday."

Potapov had just fitted a rose-colored catch to the transparent red cigarette case. He cocked his head to one side, admiring his handiwork, and asked, "How about it, Terentich—the color matches, doesn't it?"

Receiving neither approval nor disapproval, Potapov looked at Khorobrov with grandmotherly interest over the plain metal frames of his glasses. "Why tempt fate?" he said. "Time is working with us. Anton will leave and then we'll vanish into thin air *im-mediately*."

He had a way of dividing a word into syllables and lingering over each one.

By this time Rubin was in the laboratory. Now, at eleven o'clock at night, the working day over, Rubin, who had been in a lyrical mood the whole evening anyway, wanted only to get back to the dormitory and continue reading Hemingway. However, pretending to show great interest in the quality of Number Seven's new circuit, he asked Markushev to read, since his high voice with a basic tone of 160 cycles per second ought to transmit poorly. (By this approach he at once established himself as a specialist.) Putting on the earphones, Rubin listened and several times gave Markushev orders to read louder, or more quietly, to repeat the phrases "The fat pheasants fell forward" and "He looked, he leaped, he conquered"—phrases thought up by Rubin for the verification of individual sound combinations which were well known to everyone in the sharashka. Finally, he delivered the verdict that there was a general tendency toward improvement: the vowel sounds were being transmitted quite remarkably well, the voiceless dentals somewhat worse; he was still bothered by the formant of the letter "zh"; and the consonant formation so prevalent in Slavic languages, "vsp," was not being transmitted at all and required work.

There was a chorus of voices, expressing delight that the circuit was better. Bobynin looked up from the oscillogram and in a derisive, dense bass said, "Idiocy! One step forward, two steps back. There's no point in feeling it out by guess-work. You have to find a method."

Everyone fell silent under his firm, unwavering stare.

Behind his shelves Potapov glued the rose catch to the cigarette case, using pear essence. Potapov had spent three years in German camps and survived principally because of his superhuman ability to make attractive cigarette lighters, cigarette cases, and cigarette holders out of refuse, without using any tools.

No one hurried to leave work, although it was the eve of a "stolen" Sunday.

Khorobrov straightened up. Putting his classified material on Potapov's desk to be turned in and locked in the safe, he marched out from behind the shelves and headed for the exit, passing on the way all those crowded around the voice clipper.

Mamurin, pale, glared at his back and called out, "Ilya Terentich. Why don't you listen to it? In fact, where are you going?"

Khorobrov turned about unhurriedly and with a crooked smile answered distinctly, "I would rather have avoided men-tioning it aloud. But if you insist: at this particular moment I am going to the toilet—or, if you prefer, to the can. If everything goes well there, I'll continue on to the prison and lie down to sleep."

In the ensuing silence Bobynin, who hardly ever smiled, shook with deep laughter.

It was mutiny.

Mamurin stepped forward as if to hit Khorobrov and de-manded shrilly, "What do you mean, sleep? Everyone else is working and you're going to sleep?"

With his hand on the door handle Khorobrov answered, almost at the limit of his self-control, "Yes, just that—*sleep!* I have worked the twelve hours the Constitution demands—and that's enough."

He was about to burst out with something further, which would have been irreparable, but the door swung open and the duty officer announced: "Anton Nikolaich! You are wanted urgently on the city phone."

Yakonov hurriedly rose and went out ahead of Khorobrov.

Soon Potapov, too, turned out his desk lamp, placed his and Khorobrov's classified documents on Bulatov's desk and limped inoffensively toward the exit. He favored his right leg because of a motorcycle accident he had had before the war.

Yakonov's phone call was from Deputy Minister Sevastyanov. He was to be at the ministry by midnight.

Yakonov returned to his office, to Verenyov and Nerzhin, dismissed the latter and invited Verenyov to accompany him in his car. He then put on his coat and gloves, returned to his desk, and under the notation "Nerzhin to be sent away" he added: "Khorobrov, too."

12

HE SHOULD HAVE LIED

When Nerzhin, vaguely sensing that what he had done could not be mended but not yet fully realizing it, returned to the Acoustics Laboratory, Rubin was gone. The others were all still there. Valentulya, puttering in the passageway with a panel on which dozens of radio tubes were mounted, turned his lively eyes on him.

"Easy, young man!" he said, stopping Nerzhin with his raised palm, like a policeman halting a car. "Why is there no current in my third stage? Do you know?" Then he remembered: "Oh, yes, why did they call you out? *Qu'est-ce que c'est que c'est passé?*"

"Don't be crude, Valentine," said Nerzhin, sullenly evading the question. He could not admit to this priest of his own science that he had just repudiated mathematics.

"If you have troubles," Valentine declared, "I can give you a piece of advice: turn on dance music. Have you read the thing in what's his name? You know, the poet with the cigarette in his teeth. Doesn't wield a shovel, calls on others.

> My police
> Protect me!
> In the restricted zone
> How good it is!

In fact, what else besides dance music could we ask for?"

Then Valentine, not waiting for an answer, but already preoccupied with a new thought, called out: "Vadkal Plug in the oscillograph."

As he approached his desk, Nerzhin noticed that Simochka was in a state of alarm. She looked at him openly, and her thin brows twitched.

"Where's The Beard, Serafima Vitalyevna?"

"Anton Nikolayevich summoned him to Number Seven, too," Simochka answered loudly. And still more loudly, so that everyone could hear, she said, "Gleb Vikentich, let's check the new word lists. We still have half an hour."

Simochka was one of the announcers in articulation exercises. The enunciation of all the announcers was evaluated against a standard of distinctness.

"Where can I check you in all this noise?"

"Uh—let's go into the booth." She gave Nerzhin a meaningful look, took the list of words written in India ink on drawing paper, and entered the booth.

Nerzhin followed her. He shut the two-foot-thick door behind him and bolted it, then squeezed through the small second door, shut it too, and pulled down the shade. Simochka hung on his neck, standing on tiptoe, and kissed him on the lips.

In the constricted space, he lifted this frail little girl ~~his arms and set~~

The amplifier's not turned on? We won't be broadcasting over the loudspeaker?"

"What happened?"

"Why do you think something happened?"

"I felt it immediately when they called. And I see it in your face."

"How many times have I asked you not to use that formal 'you'?"

"But if I find it hard not to?"

"But if I want you to?"

"What went wrong?"

He felt the warmth of her light body on his knees; his cheek was pressed against hers. A very unusual feeling for a prisoner. How many years had it been since he'd been so close to a woman?

Simochka was astonishingly light, as if her bones were full

of air, as if she were made of wax. She seemed ridiculously weightless, like a feathery bird.

"Well, little one . . . it seems I'll be leaving soon."

She twisted around in his arms and pressed her small hands against his temples, letting her shawl fall from her shoulders.

"Where to?"

"What do you mean, where to? We come from an abyss. We go back to where we came from—camp."

"My darling, why?"

Nerzhin looked closely, uncomprehendingly, into the widened eyes of this plain-looking girl whose love he had so unexpectedly earned. She was moved by his fate more than he was himself.

"I could have stayed," he said sadly. "But in another laboratory. We wouldn't have been together anyway."

With all her little body she pressed herself against him, kissed him, asked him whether he loved her.

These past weeks, after the first kiss, why had he spared Simochka? Why had he taken pity on her, keeping in mind her illusory future happiness? She was hardly likely to find anyone to marry her; she would fall into somebody's hands. The girl came into your arms by herself, holding herself close to you with such frightening readiness. Why deny ourself and her? Before plunging into camp, where there uld certainly be no chance for this for many years.

Gleb said in agitation, "I'll be sorry to leave like this. I'd like to take with me a memory of your—your—I mean— to leave you with a child."

She immediately hid her shamed face and resisted his fingers, which tried to raise her head again.

"Little one, please don't hide. Lift your head. Why don't you say something? Don't you want that?"

She lifted her head and from deep within herself said, "I'll wait for you! You have five years left? I'll wait the five years for you. And when you are freed, you'll come back to me?"

He had not told her that. She had twisted things around, as if he had no wife. She was determined to be married— the dear little long-nosed girl!

Gleb's wife lived out there, somewhere in Moscow. Somewhere in Moscow, but she might as well have been on Mars.

And besides Simochka on his knees and besides his wife

on Mars, there were also, buried in his writing desk, the abstracts which had cost him so much labor, his own first notes on the post-Lenin period, the first formulations which contained his finest thoughts.

If he was sent off on a prison transport, all those notes would be destined for the flames.

He should have lied to her and said he would come back to her. A lie, a promise, as everyone always promises. Then when he did go away, he could leave what he had written in her safekeeping.

But he could not find the strength to lie to those eyes, which were looking at him so hopefully.

Avoiding them, he kissed the angular little shoulders his hands had uncovered from beneath her blouse.

A moment later he said hesitatingly, "You once asked me what I'm writing all the time."

"Yes, what are you writing?" Simochka asked with avid curiosity, using the familiar form of address for the first time.

If she had not interrupted him, had not pressed him so eagerly, he probably would have told her something right then and there. But she had asked with an insistence that put him on his guard. He had lived so many years in a world where ingenious and invisibly fine trigger wires were attached to mines, trip wires to explosives.

These trusting, loving eyes—they might very well be working for the security officer.

After all, how had it begun between them? The first time it was she who had touched her cheek to his, not he hers. It might have been a trap.

"It's something historical," he said. "Historical in a general way from the time of Peter. But it means a great deal to me. Yes, I'll go on writing until Yakonov throws me out. But where will I leave it all when I go?"

Suspiciously his eyes searched the depths of hers.

Simochka smiled calmly. "Why do you have to ask? Give it to me. I'll keep it. Go on writing, darling." And then, seeking out in him what she wanted to know, she said, "Tell me, is your wife very beautiful?"

The telephone which connected the booth with the laboratory rang. Simochka picked it up without putting it near her mouth and pressed the "talk" button so that she could be heard on the other end of the line. Sitting there blushing, her clothes in disarray, she began to read the articulation list in a dull measured voice: "*Dop, fskop, shtap.* Yes? What, Valentine Martynich, a dual diode-triode? We don't have a 6G7, but I think we have a 6G2. I'll finish the word list right away and come out. *Droot, moot, shoot.*" She released the "talk" button and brushed her head lightly against Gleb's. "I have to go. It's becoming obvious. Well—let me go. Please . . ."

But there was no determination in her voice.

He embraced her, pressing her whole body even more tightly to his.

"You're not going anywhere! I want—I—"

"Don't! They're waiting for me. I have to close the laboratory."

"Right now! Here!" he demanded. And he kissed her.

"Not today."

"When?"

She looked at him obediently. "On Monday. I'll be duty officer again. In place of Lyra. Come here during the dinner break. We'll be alone for the whole hour. If only that crazy Valentulya doesn't come here to work."

While Gleb unlocked and opened the doors, Simochka succeeded in buttoning herself up and combing her hair, and she went out ahead of him haughty and cold.

13

THE BLUE LIGHT

"I'm going to heave my shoe at that blue light bulb one of these days. It gets on my nerves."

"You'll miss."

"At five yards? How could I miss? I'll bet you tomorrow's stewed fruit I can hit it."

"Take off your shoes on the lower bunk. That's a yard farther."

"So, at six yards. The monsters—what won't they think

up next just to make a zek miserable? It presses on my eyes all night."

"The blue light?"

"Yes, the blue light. Light exerts pressure. Lebedev discovered that. Aristip Ivanich, are you asleep? Do me a favor—hand me one of my shoes."

"I can give you one of your shoes, Vyacheslav Petrovich, but first tell me what is it about the blue light that bothers you?"

"For one thing it has a short wave length and therefore more quanta. And the quanta keep hitting my eyes."

"It gives a soft light, and it reminds me personally of the blue icon lamp my mother used to light at night when I was a child."

"Mama! In sky-blue shoulder boards! There you are—I ask you: how can you grant people democracy? I've noticed that in any cell the most trifling question—about washing bowls or sweeping the floor—stirs up every possible shade of conflicting opinion. Freedom would be the end of mankind. Alas, only the bludgeon can show them the truth."

"Yes, but it wouldn't be a bad idea to put an icon light here. It used to be an altar."

"Not an altar, the dome above the altar. They added a ~~v~~ in between."

"~~~tri~~ Aleksandrovich, what are you doing? Opening a ~~window~~ in December! Enough of that!"

"Gentlemen, it's oxygen that makes a zek immortal. There ~~_____~~ side. I'm only opening it one volume of Ehrenburg."

"Make it more! It's stifling up here!"

"An Ehrenburg-wide or an Ehrenburg-tall?"

"An Ehrenburg-tall, of course. It fits the frame perfectly."

"A guy can go crazy here! Where's my camp jacket?"

"I'd send all these oxygen addicts to Oimyakon. For general work. At sixty degrees below zero twelve hours a day, they'd crawl into a goat shed to get out of the cold."

"On principle I'm not against oxygen, but why does it always have to be cold oxygen instead of warm oxygen?"

"What the hell's going on here? Why is it dark in the room? Why have they put the white light out so soon?"

"Valentulya, you're acting like an innocent. You'd still be wandering about till one. What light do you need at midnight?"

"And you're a slave to fashion.

> "In dark-blue coveralls
> I've got a fashion plate over me
> In prison.
> How wonderful!"

"You've got the place all smoked up again? Why do you all smoke? Phooey, what a stink! And the teapot's cold, too."

"Where is Lev?"

"Why? Isn't he in his bed?"

"There are a couple of dozen books, but no Lev."

"No doubt he's over by the toilet."

"Why?"

"They've screwed in a white bulb there, and the kitchen makes the wall warm. He's probably reading. I'm going to wash up. What shall I tell him?"

". . . Yes, well, it was like this: she made up a pallet on the floor for me, and she was up there on the bed. What a juicy piece, juicy!"

"Friends, please. Talk about something else, not women. With our meat diet, that's a socially dangerous subject."

"Come on, you birds, cut it out! The lights-out bell rang a long time ago."

"Yes, but there's still a lot of music in here."

"You want to sleep, you'll sleep."

". . . In Africa I served with Rommel. The bad thing was that it was very hot there and there wasn't any water."

". . . In the Arctic Ocean there's an island called Makhotkin. Makhotkin was a pilot in the Arctic. Now he's in prison for anti-Soviet propaganda."

"Mikhail Kuzmich, what are you rolling around for?"

"I have the right to turn over, don't I?"

"You do, but remember that every small turn down there is felt up here with enormous amplification."

"Ivan Ivanovich, you missed out on the camps. If someone climbs into a bunk for four there, three men get rocked. And then someone on the bottom bunk hangs up a curtain, brings in a woman, and goes to work. It's an earthquake. But people sleep anyway."

"Grigory Borisovich, when did you first get into a sharashka?"

"I was thinking about putting a pentode there and a small rheostat."

"He was an independent, careful person. When he took his shoes off at night, he didn't leave them on the floor, he put them under his head."

"In those years you didn't leave anything on the floor!"

"I was in Auschwitz. In Auschwitz it was awful: they led you to the crematorium right from the station, with music playing."

"The fishing there was wonderful, that's one thing, and another was the hunting. In autumn you could go out for an hour and you'd have pheasants slung all over you. If you went into the reeds, there were boars, and out in the fields, rabbits."

"All these sharashkas were started in 1930 when they sentenced the engineers of the 'Promparty' on the charge of conspiring with the British, and then decided to see how much work they'd produce in prison. The leading engineer of the first sharashka was Leonid Konstantinovich Ramzin. The experiment was successful. Outside prison it was impossible to have two big engineers or two major scientists in one design group. They would fight over who would get the name, the fame, the Stalin Prize, and one would invariably force out the other. That's why outside prison all design offices consist of a colorless group around one brilliant head. But in a sharashka? Neither money nor fame threatens anyone. Nikolai Nikolaich gets half a glass of sour cream and Pyotr Petrovich gets the same ration. A dozen academic lions live together peacefully in one den because they've nowhere else to go. It's a bore to play chess or smoke. What about inventing something? Let's. A lot has been created that way. That's the basic idea of the sharashka."

"Tell me, then, where'd Bobynin has been taken off somewhere."

"Valentulya, stop whining or I'll choke you with my pillow!"

"Where, Valentulya?"

"How did they take him away?"

"The junior lieutenant came; told him to put on his overcoat and cap."

"With his gear?"

"Without his gear."

"He's probably been called to the big boys."

"To Oskolupov?"

"Oskolupov would have come here himself. Try higher."

"The tea is cold, what a dirty deal!"

"Valentulya, you're always clicking your spoon on your glass after taps and I'm sick of it."

"How do you expect me to dissolve the sugar?"

"Silently."

"Only celestial catastrophes take place silently because sound is not transmitted in outer space. If a new star should burst behind our backs, we wouldn't even hear it. Ruska, your blanket is falling off, why are you hanging over the edge? Are you asleep? Do you know that our sun is a new star, and that the earth is condemned to perish in the near future?"

"I don't want to believe it. I'm young and I want to live."

"Ha, ha, how primitive! *C'est le mot!* He wants to live. What cold tea!"

"Valentulya, where did they take Bobynin?"

"How do I know. Maybe to Stalin."

"And what would you do, Valentulya, if they took you to Stalin?"

"Me? Ho, ho! I'd tell him all my complaints from A to Z."

"For instance, which?"

"Well, all of them, all of them. *Par exemple,* why do we have to live without women? It limits our creative possibilities."

"Pryanchikov, shut up! Everyone has gone to sleep long ago. What are you hollering about?"

"But if I don't want to sleep?"

"Friends, who's smoking? Hide your cigarette. The junior lieutenant is coming."

"What's that bastard doing here? Don't trip, Citizen Junior Lieutenant, you might bust your big nose."

"Pryanchikov!"

"What?"

"Where are you? Are you asleep yet?"

"Yes, I'm asleep."

"Get dressed, come on, get dressed, put on your overcoat and cap!"

"With my gear?"

"Without. Quick. The car is waiting."

"I'm going with Bobynin?"

"He's already gone. There's another car for you."

"What kind of a car, Junior Lieutenant, a Black Maria?"

"Quicker, quicker. No, it's a Pobeda."

"Who's asking for me?"

"Come on, Pryanchikov, why should I explain everything to you? I don't know myself. Faster."

"Valentulya, you tell them over there."

"Tell them about our visiting privileges. Why the hell are Section 58 prisoners allowed visits only once a year?"

"Tell them about our taking walks outside."

"And letters."

"And about our clothing issue."

"*Rot front*, boys! Ha, ha! Adieu!"

"Comrade Junior Lieutenant! Where is Pryanchikov?"

"He's coming, Comrade Major! Here he is!"

"Hit them up for everything, Valentulya, don't be bashful."

"There's a hell of a lot of running around tonight."

"What happened?"

"This never happened before."

"Maybe there's a war on. They're hauling them out to be shot."

"Don't be a fool! Who'd bother about us in ones and twos? If there was a war, they'd mow us down all at once or infect our kasha with plague."

"All right, friends, time to sleep! We'll find out about it tomorrow."

". . . It used to happen in 1939, and in 1940 Beria summoned Boris Sergeyevich Stechkin from the sharashka. He wasn't the kind to come back empty-handed. Either the head of the prison would be changed or they'd allow more time for outdoor walks. Stechkin could never stand that system of graft, those different ration categories, when an academician gets eggs and sour cream, a professor an ounce and a half of butter, and ordinary work horses half that much. He was a good man, Boris Sergeyevich—may heaven be his home—"

"He died?"

"No, they let him out. They gave him a Stalin Prize."

14

EVERY MAN NEEDS A GIRL!

Then the weary, measured voice of the second-termer Adamson fell silent. He had been in sharashkas during his first term, too. Here and there an unfinished story was still being whispered. Someone was snoring loudly and, at moments, explosively.

The blue bulb set into the round arch above the double doors cast its dim light on a dozen two-decker bunks placed fanwise in the big semicircular room. This room, undoubtedly the only one of its kind in Moscow, was a good thirty-six feet in diameter. Above was a spacious dome, surmounted by a hexagonal tower, and in the dome were five graceful circular windows. The windows in the outside wall were barred but not boarded, and in the daytime one could see across the highway to an untended, forest-like park. From there on summer evenings one heard the exciting, disturbing songs of the manless girls of the Moscow suburbs.

Lying on his upper bunk beside the central window, Nerzhin was not asleep, was not even trying to sleep. Below him Engineer Potapov had long been sleeping the serene slumber of a hard-working man. On the upper bunks near him were, to his left across the passageway, the round-faced vacuum specialist Zemelya, sprawled trustingly and breathing heavily; on his right, on the bunk tight up against his own, Ruska Doronin, one of the youngest zeks in the sharashka, tossing sleeplessly. Beneath Zemelya, Pryanchikov's bunk was empty.

Now, when he could reflect on the conversation in Yakonov's office, Nerzhin understood everything more clearly. His refusal to participate in the cryptographic group was not a mere incident but a turning point in his life. It was certain to result, perhaps very soon, in a long and arduous journey to Siberia or the Arctic, to death or to a hard victory over death.

He wanted to think about this sudden break in his life. What had he managed to do during this three-year respite in the sharashka? Had he sufficiently tempered his character before this new leap into the abyss of camp?

It so happened that the next day would be Gleb's thirty-first birthday. (He had, of course, no heart to remind his friends of the date.) Was this the middle of his life, almost the end of it, or only the beginning?

His thoughts became muddled. He could not keep his mind on essentials. On one hand, a feeling of weakness overcame him; after all, it was not too late to correct matters, to agree to join Cryptography. He felt again the pain of the long months without a glimpse of his wife. It had been nearly a year since he had been allowed a visit. Would he be allowed one before he left?

And finally within him stirred the sharp, quick, tough fellow who had been born long ago in the young boy standing in line at bread stores during the First Five-Year Plan. This tenacious inner self was already prepared for the countless body searches that awaited him—on leaving Mavrino; at the reception center in Butyrskaya; at Krasnaya Presnya—and figuring out how to hide pieces of broken pencil lead in his padded jacket, how to smuggle his old work clothes out of the sharashka—since for a working zek every extra layer was precious—how to prove that the aluminum teaspoon he had kept with him throughout his term was his own and not stolen from the sharashka, which had almost the same kind.

He itched to get up and, in the light of the blue bulb, begin getting ready, repacking, preparing his hiding places.

Meanwhile Ruska Doronin kept changing his position abruptly. He lay first on his stomach with his head under the pillow and pulled the blanket up and off his feet. Then he turned over on his back, throwing off his blanket, leaving the white upper sheet and the darkish lower sheet exposed. (After every bath they changed one of the two sheets, but in December the sharashka had overdrawn its soap quota, and all baths had been held up.) Suddenly he sat up and pushed himself and the pillow backward against the iron bed. On the edge of the mattress he opened a volume of Mommsen's *History of Rome*. Noticing that Nerzhin was not asleep but staring straight at the lamp, Ruska asked in a hoarse whisper, "Gleb! Do you have a cigarette? Give me one."

Ruska normally did not smoke. Nerzhin reached into the pocket of his coveralls, which were hung on the back of the bunk, pulled out two cigarettes, and they lit up.

Ruska smoked with concentration, without turning toward Nerzhin. Beneath a loose cloud of tawny hair, his face was attractive even in the deathlike light of the blue lamp. It was always changing: sometimes simplehearted and boyish, sometimes the face of an inspired confidence man.

"Use this," said Nerzhin, giving him an empty Belomor package to use as an ashtray.

They began to drop their ashes in it.

Ruska had been at the sharashka since summer, and Nerzhin had liked him at first glance. Ruska aroused his protective instincts.

But it turned out that even though Ruska was only twenty-three (and they had given him a full twenty-five-year sentence), he did not need protection in the least. Both his character and his outlook on the world had been formed in a short but stormy life—not so much by his two weeks at Moscow University or his two weeks at Leningrad University as by his two years of living on forged passports while he was on the all-Union list of wanted criminals (Gleb had been told this carefully kept secret), followed by two years of imprisonment. With instant understanding, he had mastered the jungle laws of GULAG, was always on guard, spoke candidly to very few, and impressed everyone else as being childishly frank. Beyond that, he was energetic and tried to get a lot done in a short time; reading was also one of his occupations.

Gleb, dissatisfied with his disordered, petty thoughts and feeling no inclination to sleep, whispered in the silence of the room: "Listen. How is your theory of cycles coming along?"

They had discussed this theory not long ago, and Ruska had been looking for confirmation in Mommsen.

Ruska turned at the whisper but looked at him uncomprehendingly. His brow wrinkled in his effort to understand what he was being asked.

"I said, how's your theory of cyclical change?"

Ruska sighed deeply and the strain left his face, along with the restless thought which had absorbed him when he was smoking. He slipped down onto one elbow, dropped the dead butt in the empty packet Nerzhin had given him, and said listlessly, "Everything bores me. Books and theories both."

Again they fell silent. Nerzhin wanted to turn over on his other side when suddenly Ruska laughed and began to whisper, gradually getting carried away and speaking more rapidly.

"History is so monotonous it's repulsive to read. The nobler and more honest a man is, the more despicably his compatriots treat him. The Roman Consul Spurius Cassius Vecellinus wanted to give the common people land, and the common people condemned him to death. Spurius Maelius wanted to feed the hungry, and he was executed for allegedly seeking the throne. The Consul Marcus Manlius, who awoke at the cackling of the legendary geese and saved the Capitol, was executed as a traitor. So?" He laughed. "And the great

Hannibal, without whom we would never have known the name of Carthage, was exiled by that insignificant Carthage, had his property confiscated and his house leveled to the ground. It has all happened before. They put Gnaeus Naevius in prison to make him stop writing free and courageous plays. And the Aetolians declared a false amnesty to lure émigrés back and murder them. Even in Roman days they discovered the truth, afterward forgotten, that it is uneconomical to let a slave go hungry, that one has to feed him. All history is one continuous pestilence. There is no truth and there is no illusion. There is nowhere to appeal and nowhere to go."

In the deathly blue light the quiver of skepticism on such young lips was particularly disturbing.

Nerzhin himself had planted these thoughts in Ruska, but now, as Ruska uttered them, he felt a desire to protest. Among his older comrades Gleb was used to being the iconoclast, but he felt a responsibility toward the younger prisoner.

"I want to warn you, Ruska," Nerzhin replied very softly, leaning closer to his neighbor's ear. "No matter how clever and absolute the systems of skepticism or agnosticism or pessimism, you must understand that by their very nature they doom us to a loss of will. They can't really influence human behavior because people cannot stand still. And that means they can't renounce systems wh ͧ which summon them to advance in som

"Even if it's into a swamp? Jus͏ ͚o slog along?" Ruska asked angrily.

"Even that. Who the hell knows?" Gleb wavered. "Look, I personally believe that people seriously need skepticism. It's needed to split the rockheads. To choke fanatical voices. But skepticism can never provide firm ground under a man's feet. And perhaps, after all, we need firm ground."

"Give me another cigarette," said Ruska. He smoked nervously. "What a good thing it was that the MGB didn't give me a chance to study," he said in a clear, rather loud whisper. "I would have finished at the university and perhaps even gone on to a graduate degree, the whole idiotic process. I might have become a scientist. I might have written a big thick book. I might have done research on the early administrative districts of Novgorod from some eighty-third point of view, or on Caesar's war with the Helvetians. How many cultures there are in the world! And languages and countries. How many intelligent people there are in every country, and even more intelligent books—and what fool is going to read all of them? How did you put it: 'Whatever great minds think up, at the cost of great effort, eventually appears to still greater minds as something phantasmal'? Was that it?"

"All right!" Nerzhin replied accusingly. "You're losing sight of everything solid, of every goal. One can certainly doubt, one is obliged to doubt. But isn't it also necessary to love something?"

"Yes, yes, to love something!" Ruska took him up in a triumphant, hoarse whisper. "To love something—not history and not theory, but a woman!" He leaned over on Nerzhin's bunk and grasped him by the elbow. "What have they really deprived us of, tell me? The right to go to meetings or to subscribe to state bonds? The one way the Plowman could really hurt us was to deprive us of women. And he did it. For twenty-five years! The bastard! Who can imagine —" and he struck his fist against his chest—"what a woman means to a prisoner?"

"Watch out you don't end up insane!" said Nerzhin, trying to defend himself, but a sudden wave flooded through him at the thought of Simochka and her promise for Monday evening. "Get rid of that notion," he said. "It'll black out your brain. A Freudian simplex or complex—what the hell do they call it? Sublimation's the answer. Shift your energy into other areas. Concentrate on philosophy—you won't need bread or water or a woman's caresses for that."

(But Monday! What happily married couples take for granted arouses the pangs of lust in a prisoner.)

"My brain is already blacked out. I won't sleep till morning. A girl! Everyone needs a girl! To have her tremble in your arms. To—oh, what the hell!" Ruska tossed his still-burning cigarette on the blanket without noticing it and abruptly turned away, flopped down on his stomach and pulled the blanket over his head.

Nerzhin managed to grab the cigarette as it was about to roll off the bunk onto Potapov below, and he put it out. Yes! Only two more days to live through, and then Simochka. All at once he imagined in detail how everything would be the day after tomorrow; then with a shudder he put out of his mind the piercingly sweet thought that dulled his reason. He bent over to Ruska's ear.

"Ruska, how about you? Do you have someone?"

"Yes! I do!" Ruska whispered in torment, turning on his back and embracing his pillow. He breathed into it, and the warmth of the pillow, and all the ardor of his youth, tricked into sterility and withering away in prison—everything heated the young, caged body that begged for release and found none. He had said, "I do," and he wanted to believe that there was a girl, but what had happened was only elusive. There had been no kiss, not even a promise. It was only that a girl had listened to him that evening with a look of sympathy and delight while he told her about himself, and in this girl's glance Ruska had for the first time seen himself as a hero whose story was extraordinary. Nothing had taken place between them yet, and at the same time something had taken place which gave him the right to say that *he had a girl*.

"Who is she?" Gleb demanded.

Raising the blanket just a crack, Ruska answered from the darkness, "Shhh . . . Clara—"

"Clara? The prosecutor's daughter?"

15

THE TROIKA OF LIARS

The head of Section Zero-One was completing his report to Minister Abakumov.

Tall, with black hair combed straight back, wearing the three-star shoulder boards of a general commissar of the second rank, Abakumov authoritatively trod his great desk with his elbows. He was hefty but not fat—he knew the value of a fine figure and even played tennis. His eyes were those of a man who is nobody's fool; they revealed agility, suspicion, quick wit. Where necessary he corrected the head of the section and the latter hastened to make notes.

Abakumov's office, though not vast, was no ordinary room.

There was a marble fireplace left from earlier times, which was not used, and a tall wall mirror. The ceiling was high, with a sculptured plaster molding, a chandelier, and a painting of cupids and nymphs pursuing one another. (The minister had left the painting as it was except for the green, which had been painted out because it was a color he could not stand.) There was a balcony door, nailed shut winter and summer, and big windows which were never opened looked out on the square. There were clocks: a grandfather clock with a beautiful case, a mantel clock with a little figurine that struck the hours, an electric railway station clock on the wall. These clocks showed different times, but Abakumov always knew what time it was because he had, in addition, two gold watches on his person, a wristwatch on his hairy wrist and a pocket watch in his pocket.

The offices in this building increased in size according to the rank of their occupants. The desks grew larger. The conference tables with their velvet tablecloths grew larger. But the portraits of the Great Generalissimo grew largest and fastest of all. Even in the offices of ordinary interrogators his portrait showed him far larger than life size. And in Abakumov's office the Most Brilliant Strategist of All Times and Peoples was portrayed on a canvas fifteen feet tall, full length from his boots to his visored marshal's cap, in the glitter of all his orders and decorations. (In fact, he never wore these honors, many of which he had awarded to himself, or received from foreign presidents and potentates.) Only the Yugoslav decorations had been carefully painted out.

However, as if to acknowledge the insufficiency of this fifteen-foot-high portrait, and recognizing the need to be inspired at every moment by the sight of the Best Friend of Counterintelligence Operatives, Abakumov also kept a portrait of Stalin on his desk.

On another wall hung a good-sized square portrait of a saccharine person in pince-nez who was Abakumov's direct superior—Beria.

When the head of Zero-One Section had left, Deputy Minister Sevastyanov, Major General Oskolupov, the head of the Special Technical Section, and the chief engineer of that section, Colonel of Engineers Yakonov, appeared at the door. Demonstrating their respect for the proprietor of the office, they advanced Indian-file, in order of seniority, down

the pattern of the carpet, almost on each other's heels—and
only Sevastyanov's steps were audible.

A spare old man in a gray suit, whose short-cropped hair
showed mingled shades of gray, Sevastyanov alone of the
minister's ten deputies was a civilian. His responsibility was
neither operational nor investigatory; he was in charge of
communications and other precision technology. Therefore
he suffered less from the minister's wrath at meetings and in
the orders he received, and he was less tense in that office.
He sat down at once in a thickly upholstered armchair in
front of the desk.

Oskolupov was then at the head of the file. Yakonov stood
directly behind him as if to conceal his portliness.

Abakumov looked at Oskolupov—whom he had seen perhaps three times in his life—and sensed something likable
in him. Oskolupov, too, was disposed to corpulence. His
neck was bursting out of his tunic, and his chin, now ob-
sequiously pulled in, was double. His oaken face was the
simple, honest face of a man of action, not the abstruse face
of a self-assured intellectual.

Squinting over Oskolupov's shoulder at Yakonov, Abakumov asked, using the familiar pronoun, "Who are you?"

"Me?" Oskolupov bent forward, distressed at not being
recognized.

"Me?" Yakonov pushed forward a bit, too. As well as he
could, he held in his defiant stomach, which grew and grew
despite all his efforts, and not a solitary thought showed in
his big blue eyes.

"You and you!" puffed the minister affirmatively. "You're
the Mavrino project, aren't you? All right, sit down."

They sat down.

The minister picked up a paper cutter made of ruby-
colored plastic, scratched behind his ear with it and said, "All
right. How long have you been fooling around with me?
Two years? According to plan you had fifteen months.
When will the phones be ready?" And he added threateningly: "Don't lie. I don't like lies."

This was the very question for which the three high-ranking liars had been preparing themselves since the moment
they learned they were all being summoned together. Oskolupov began, as they had agreed. He spoke as if his squared
shoulders were thrusting forth his words, and he looked
triumphantly into the omnipotent minister's eyes: "Comrade

Minister! Comrade Colonel General! Let me assure you that the personnel of the section will spare no effort—"

Abakumov's face expressed surprise. "Where do you think we are? At a meeting? What am I supposed to do with your efforts—wrap them around my backside? I'm asking you: what date?"

And he took up his gold-tipped fountain pen and pointed at his weekly appointment calendar.

At that moment, as agreed, Yakonov spoke out, his very tone and his low voice underscoring the fact that he was speaking as a technical specialist and not as an administrator. "Comrade Minister, in the frequency range up to 2,400 cycles, given an average transmission level of zero point nine—"

"Cycles, cycles! Zero point cycle zero—that's exactly what you're producing! Zero point my ass! I want the telephone—two complete units. When will I have it? Well?"

Now it was Sevastyanov's turn to speak—slowly, running his hand through his short grayish hair: "Please, let us know what you have in mind, Victor Semyonovich. Two-way conversations when we still don't have absolute encoding—"

"Why are you trying to make an idiot out of me? What do you mean, absolute encoding?" The minister looked at him sharply.

Fifteen years before, when neither Abakumov nor anyone else could have dreamed he would become a minister, when he was an NKVD courier, a strapping, husky young fellow, long-legged and long-armed, four years of primary education had been enough for him. He "advanced himself" only through jujitsu, and his only formal training was in the gymnasium of the Dynamo Sports Club.

Then, during the years that saw the replacement and expansion of investigative personnel, it turned out that Abakumov conducted interrogations effectively; his long arms were an asset when it came to smashing people in the face. His great career was on its way. After seven years he became head of the counterintelligence agency SMERSH, and now he was a minister. And not once in all this long climb had he ever felt any deficiencies in his own education. He managed himself in such a way, even in this top post, that his subordinates could not make a fool of him.

At that instant Abakumov got angry and raised his clenched fist like a cobblestone over the desk. As he did, the tall doors opened, and a short little cherub of a man, with a pleasant, rosy color in his cheeks, came into the room without knocking—Mikhail Dmitriyevich Ryumin. The entire ministry called him "Minka"—but very seldom to his face.

He moved as silently as a cat. As he approached, he took in at a glance the men who were seated there. He shook hands with Sevastyanov, who rose; he went to the end of Abakumov's desk and, bending close to the minister, his fat little hands stroking the edge of the desk, purred thoughtfully, "Listen, Victor Semyonovich. If we're going to take up such problems, we should turn them over to Sevastyanov. Why should we feed them for nothing? Can't they really identify a voice from a magnetic tape? Kick them out if they can't."

And he smiled as sweetly as if he were treating a little girl to chocolate candy. He looked at all three of the section representatives caressingly.

For many years Ryumin had lived completely unknown— the accountant for the Union of Consumers' Cooperatives in Archangel Province. Pink-cheeked and plump, with thin, indignant lips, he harassed his bookkeepers with as many nasty remarks as he could think of, sucked on the hard sugar drops he would share with the forwarding agent, talked diplomatically with chauffeurs, arrogantly with draymen, and put accurate documents on the chairman's desk on time.

During the war they took him into the navy and made him a Special Section interroga[...] [...]ed the work, and soon he was framing a case ag[...] [...]ly innocent journalist with the Northern Fleet. But he put the case together so crudely and so brazenly that the prosecutor's office, which did not normally interfere in the work of the security organs, reported the matter to Abakumov. The little SMERSH interrogator of the Northern Fleet was called to Abakumov for a reprimand. He stepped timidly into the office expecting the worst. The door closed. When it opened an hour later, Ryumin emerged with an air of importance—having just been appointed to the central apparatus of SMERSH as a senior interrogator for special cases. From that time on, his star had risen steadily.

"I'll take care of them, Mikhail Dmitriyevich, believe me. I'll take such care of them that no one will be able to collect their bones!" Abakumov answered, looking threateningly at all three.

The three guiltily lowered their eyes.

"I'll give them the tape of the conversation. They can play it over and compare it."

"Oh!—did you arrest anyone?"

"Of course." Ryumin smiled sweetly. "We grabbed four suspects right near the Arbat metro station."

But a shadow crossed his face. He knew the suspects had been grabbed too late, that they were the wrong ones. Yet, having once been arrested, they would not be released. In fact, it might just be necessary to pin the case on one of them—so that it would not remain unsolved.

Annoyance grated in Ryumin's insinuating voice: "I can get half the Ministry of Foreign Affairs on tape for them, if you like. But that's not necessary. Only six or seven people have to be picked up—the only ones in the ministry who could have known about it."

"Well, arrest them all, the dogs. Why fool around?" Abakumov demanded indignantly. "Seven people! We have a big country—they won't be missed!"

"You can't do that, Victor Semyonovich," Ryumin objected. "It's a ministry, not the food-processing industry; and we'd lose every trace that way. In this case we have to find out exactly who it was. And as quickly as possible."

"Hmm," Abakumov thought aloud. "Comparing one tape with another. Yes, someday we'll have to master that technology, too. Sevastyanov, can you do it?"

"I still don't understand what it's all about, Victor Semyonovich."

"What's there to understand? Nothing at all. Some bastard, some swine—probably a diplomat, otherwise how would he have known about it—telephoned some professor today. I can't remember his name—"

"Dobroumov," prompted Ryumin.

"Yes, Dobroumov. A doctor. Well, in brief, he'd just returned from a trip to France, and while he was there he promised to send them one of his new medicines—a matter of exchanging experience, the bastard said. He never even gave a thought to the priority of Russian discoveries! And we wanted him actually to give them that medicine, and to catch him in the act and then make a big political case out of it—toadying to foreign powers. So some filthy swine phones the professor and tells him not to give them the medicine. We'll arrest the professor and work up our case against him anyway, but it's partly spoiled. Well, what about it? Find out who it was and you'll be very popular."

Sevastyanov looked past Oskolupov at Yakonov, who met his glance, raising his brows slightly. He was trying to say that this was a new art, the research hadn't been corroborated, and they had trouble enough without taking this on, too. Sevastyanov was sufficiently clever to understand both the movement of Yakonov's brows and the entire situation. He was prepared to take the question out in the woods and lose it.

But Foma Guryanovich Oskolupov had his own ideas about his own job. He had no desire to be a mere figurehead as head of the section. Ever since he had been appointed, he had been filled with a sense of his own value and fully believed he was the master of all problems and could solve them better than anyone else—otherwise they would never have appointed him. And though in his time he had not even completed seven years of school, now he would not admit that some of his subordinates might understand the work better than he—except of course in the details, in the diagrams, where it was a matter of taking an actual hand. Not long before, he had been staying at a certain first-class resort, in mufti, and he had introduced himself as a professor of electronics. There he met a very well-known writer, and the writer could not take his eyes off Foma Guryanovich, kept jotting down notes in his notebook and declaring he would base the portrait of a contemporary scientist on him. After that, Foma knew once and for all that he was a scientist.

Suddenly he grasped the problem and jerked ahead in his traces. "Comrade Minister! We can do it!"

Sevastyanov looked at him in amazement. "Where? In what laboratory?"

"The telephone laboratory at Mavrino, of course. They talked on the telephone, didn't they?"

"But Mavrino is busy with another, more important problem."

"That doesn't matter. We'll find the people! We have three hundred people there, why can't we find them?"

And he gazed at the minister with a look of readiness.

Abakumov did not quite smile, but once again his face expressed a sort of liking for the general. This was the way he himself had been when he was on his way up—wholeheartedly willing to cut to ribbons anyone he was told to. A younger person who resembles oneself is always likable.

"Good for you," he said. "That's the way to talk: the interests of the state first and all the rest later. Right?"

"Exactly right, Comrade Minister! Just exactly, Comrade Colonel General!"

Ryumin, it appeared, was not at all surprised, nor did he seem to be appreciating Oskolupov's selfless dedication. Looking at Sevastyanov, he said, "You'll be contacted in the morning."

He exchanged glances with Abakumov and went out silently.

The minister picked at his teeth with a fingernail, trying to get at a piece of meat struck there since dinner.

"So then—when? You've kept stringing me along—August 1, then the November holidays, then New Year's. Well?"

He settled his eyes on Yakonov, forcing him to reply.

Yakonov seemed to be bothered by the position of his neck. He moved it a little to the right, then a little to the left, looked up at the minister with his cold blue gaze and looked down again.

Yakonov knew he was very talented. Yakonov knew that people even more talented than he, concentrating on their work fourteen hours a day, without one day off in the entire year, were also sweating over that cursed apparatus. And foreign scientists, who published the details of their inventions in easily available journals, were also engaged in working on the device. Yakonov knew, too, the thousands of difficulties that had been overcome and yet were only the beginning, through which, like swimmers in the sea, his engineers were pushing their way. In six days the last deadline would run out, the last of all the last deadlines they had begged from this piece of meat in uniform. But they had been stuck with this succession of idiotic deadlines because the Coryphaeus of Sciences had from the start set a one-year time limit on a ten-year task.

In Sevastyanov's office they had agreed to ask for a ten-day postponement. To promise two telephones by the tenth of January, that was what the deputy minister insisted on. That was what Oskolupov wanted. They calculated they could produce something which, though imperfect, would at least be freshly painted. And while the whole thing went through tests of its absolute-encoding capacity, the laboratory work would continue and they could then ask for more time to complete and perfect it.

But Yakonov knew that inanimate objects do not obey human deadlines, that even by January 10 the apparatus would not be emitting human speech but only mush. And what had happened to Mamurin would inevitably happen to Yakonov. The Boss would call Beria and ask him, "What fool delivered this machine? *Get rid* of him!" And Yakonov would become at the very best an Iron Mask, and perhaps just an ordinary zek again.

Under the minister's gaze, feeling the noose tightening around his neck, Yakonov overcame his wretched fear and, as involuntarily as one draws air into his lungs, said in a hoarse voice, "Give us one more month! One more month! Till the first of February!"

He looked at Abakumov with the beseeching eyes of a dog.

Talented people are sometimes unjust to others. Abakumov was smarter than Yakonov thought, but through long disuse the minister's mind had become worthless to him. Throughout his whole career he had lost out whenever he tried to think and won when he acted out of zeal. So Abakumov burdened his mind as little as possible.

He could understand that neither six days nor a month would help when two years had already gone by. But in his eyes this troika of liars was to blame—Sevastyanov, Oskolupov, and Yakonov were personally to blame. If it was so difficult, then why, when they took on the assignment twenty-three months before, had they agreed to one year? Why hadn't they asked for three? (He had by now forgotten that he had hurried them just as unmercifully then.) If they had held out against Abakumov at the start, he would have held out against Stalin and bargained for a two-year time limit, and then stretched it out to three years.

But so great was the fear instilled in them by their long years of subordination that not one of them, then or now, would have had the courage to hold out against his superiors. Abakumov himself followed the well-known practice of leaving some leeway, and in his dealings with Stalin he always added a couple of extra months as a reserve. That was how matters stood now. Stalin had been promised one telephone by March 1. So, if the worse came to the worst, he could give them one more month—as long as it was really a month.

Again taking up his fountain pen, Abakumov said, "What kind of a month do you mean? An honest month or are you lying again?"

"Exactly a month! Exactly!" Oskolupov beamed, gladdened by the happy turn of events, obviously eager to go straight from the office to Mavrino and personally take up a soldering iron.

With a flourish of his pen, Abakumov wrote on his desk calendar.

"There. Make it January 21, the anniversary of Lenin's death, and you'll all receive a Stalin Prize. Sevastyanov, will it be ready?"

"Yes! It will!"

"Oskolupov! I'll have your head! Will it be ready?"

"Yes, Comrade General Commissar. All that needs to be done is—"

"And you? Do you know what you're risking? Will it be ready?"

Maintaining his courage, Yakonov persisted, "One month! The first of February!"

"And if it's not ready by the first? Colonel, weigh your words—you're lying."

Of course, Yakonov was lying. And, of course, he should have asked for two months. But it was already out in the open.

"It will be, Comrade General Commissar," he promised sadly.

"Well, just remember, I didn't make you say it. I can forgive everything but deceit! You may go."

Relieved, they went out, still in single file, one after the other, lowering their eyes before the fifteen-foot-high portrait of Stalin.

But they were rejoicing too soon. They did not know that the minister had set a trap for them.

No sooner had they gone out than another person was announced.

"Engineer Pryanchikov."

16

NO BOILING WATER FOR TEA

That night on Abakumov's order, conveyed by Sevastyanov, Yakonov had been summoned. Later on, two secret messages were phoned to the Mavrino Institute at intervals of fifteen minutes, ordering first the prisoner Bobynin and then the prisoner Pryanchikov to be brought to the ministry. Bobynin and Pryanchikov were brought in separate cars and left to wait in different rooms, to prevent any collusion between them.

It was unlikely, however, that Pryanchikov would have been capable of collusion because of his unnatural sincerity, which many sober sons of the age regarded as a psychic abnormality. At the sharashka they would say, "Valentulya is out of phase."

Least of all could he have brought off a deal or any other ulterior scheme now. His whole soul was stirred by the bright lights of Moscow, twinkling and glittering outside the windows of the Pobeda. Leaving the dark suburban section around Mavrino, it was all the more amazing to emerge onto the big gleaming avenues, into the cheerful bustle of a railway station plaza, and past neon-lit store windows. Pryanchikov forgot all about the driver and his two escorts in civilian clothes, and it seemed as if not air but flame were entering and leaving his lungs. He did not take his eyes from the window. They had never brought him through Moscow even in the daytime, and not a single zek had seen nighttime Moscow in the whole history of the sharashka.

Just before the Sretenka Gates the car had to stop for a crowd coming out of a movie theater and then wait for the traffic light to change.

Prisoners in their millions tended to feel that life in freedom had, without them, come to a stop; that there were no men left; that lonely women wore sackcloth and ashes out of an excess of love and fidelity. And here before Pryanchikov was the well-fed, animated, urban crowd—hats, veils, silver fox furs—and the perfume of passing women overwhelmed his trembling senses, through the frost, through the impenetrable body of the car, like a series of blows. He could dimly hear conversation, but the words were not distinct; he wanted to smash his head through the unyielding glass and shout to the women that he was young, that he was overcome with longing, that he had been locked up in prison for no reason. After the monastic loneliness of the sharashka this was a fairy play, a sort of *Midsummer Night's Dream*, a fragment of that elegant life which he had never had the chance to live, first because of his student poverty, then because he was a POW, then because of prison.

Later, in the waiting room, Pryanchikov could scarcely distinguish the chairs and tables standing there; the feelings and impressions which had overcome him did not relinquish their hold easily.

A polished young lieutenant colonel asked him to follow him. Pryanchikov, with his frail neck and thin wrists, narrow-shouldered, thin-legged, had never looked so unimpressive as when he stepped into the office at the threshold of which the accompanying officer left him.

It was so spacious Pryanchikov did not even realize at once that it was an office, nor that the individual with gold shoulder boards at the far end was its owner. Nor did he notice the fifteen-foot-tall Stalin behind his back. Moscow and the women of the night still floated before his eyes. It was as if he were drunk. He found it hard to imagine why he was in this hall, what kind of a hall it was. Yet it was still more curious that somewhere in a semicircular room crowded with bunks and lit by a blue bulb—though the war had ended five years earlier—an unfinished glass of cold tea awaited his return.

His feet moved across the vast carpet. It was soft, with a heavy nap, and he wanted to roll on it. Along the right side of the hall ran great windows, and on the left side hung a floor-length mirror.

People on the outside do not realize the value of things. For a zek who gets along with a cheap little mirror smaller than the palm of his hand and who doesn't always have that, it's a whole adventure to look at himself in a big mirror.

Pryanchikov, as if drawn by a magnet, stopped in front of the mirror. He went up very close to it and examined with satisfaction his clean, fresh face. He adjusted his necktie and the collar of his blue shirt. Then he began to move back slowly, his eyes fixed on himself *en face*, then at three-quarters, then in profile. After a moment of this he made a kind of half-dancing movement, went up to the mirror again and studied himself very closely. Deciding that, despite his blue coveralls, he was quite well proportioned and elegant, feeling then in an excellent state of mind, he moved on, not because a business conversation awaited him—for Pryanchikov had completely forgotten about that—but because he intended to continue his inspection of the room.

The man who could put anyone in half the world in prison, the omnipotent minister before whom generals and marshals turned pale, was now looking at this puny blue zek with curiosity. It had been a long time since he had seen close up any of the millions of people he had arrested and sentenced.

With the gait of a dandy on promenade, Pryanchikov approached the minister and looked questioningly at him, as if he had not expected to find him there.

"You are Engineer Pryanchikov?" Abakumov said, milling among his papers.

"Yes," Valentine answered absent-mindedly. "Yes."

"You are the leading engineer of the group—" and again he looked in his notes— "working on the artificial-speech apparatus."

"What artificial-speech apparatus?" Pryanchikov said, brushing the question aside. "What nonsense! No one in our shop calls it that. They gave it that name in the struggle against toadyism to foreign cultures. We call it the vo-co-der. V*oice coder*. Encoded voice."

"But you are the leading engineer."

"In general, yes. Why?" Pryanchikov was suddenly on guard.

"Sit down."

Pryanchikov sat down willingly, pulling up the pressed trouser legs of his coveralls.

"I want you to speak with absolute frankness, without fear of getting into trouble with your superiors. When will the vocoder be ready? Speak frankly. Will it be ready in one month? Or maybe two? Tell me, don't be afraid."

"The vocoder? Ready? Ha, ha, ha, ha!" Pryanchikov roared, with a ringing, youthful laugh that had never before echoed in these surroundings. He fell back against the soft leather and threw up his hands. "What are you saying? What can you be thinking? You obviously don't understand what the vocoder is. I will explain it to you!"

He jumped supplely from the springy armchair and rushed to Abakumov's desk.

"Do you have a piece of paper? Yes, here is some!" He tore a sheet from a clean pad on the desk, grabbed the minister's pen, which was the color of red meat, and began hurriedly and clumsily drawing a sinusoid wave.

Abakumov was not frightened—there was so much child-like sincerity and spontaneity in the strange engineer's voice and in all his movements that he endured this assault and stared at Pryanchikov without listening to what he was saying.

"I must tell you that a human voice consists of many harmonics." Pryanchikov was almost choking in his urgent desire to say everything as quickly as possible. "And the idea of the vocoder is to reproduce artificially the human voice—damn it! How can you write with such a lousy pen?—to reproduce it by simulating, if not all, at least the basic harmonics, each sent by an individual transmitter. Well, you're acquainted, of course, with Cartesian coordinates—every schoolboy knows about them—and the Fourier series?"

"Wait a minute," Abakumov said, collecting himself. "Just tell me one thing: *when* will it be ready? When?"

"Ready? Hmm—I hadn't thought much about that." Now Pryanchikov was no longer being carried forward by his impressions of the nighttime capital but by his enthusiasm for his beloved work, and once again it was difficult for him to stop. "The thing is: the problem is made easier if we are willing to coarsen the timbre of the voice. In that case the number of units—"

"Yes, but by what date? What date? The first of March? The first of April?"

"Good heavens, what are you talking about! April? Not counting the cryptography work, we'll be ready in, say, four, five months, no sooner. And what effect will the enciphering and deciphering of the impulses have? After all, that introduces more distortion. Oh, let's not try to guess," he urged Abakumov, tugging at his sleeve. "I'll explain the whole thing to you now. You'll understand then and agree that in the interests of the work itself it shouldn't be rushed!"

But Abakumov, with his gaze fixed on the meaningless

wavy lines of the drawing, had already found the bell button
in the desk.

The same polished lieutenant colonel appeared and invited
Pryanchikov to leave.

Pryanchikov obeyed with a confused expression, his mouth
half open. He was especially disappointed because he had not
finished explaining everything. Then, when he was already
on the way out, suddenly realizing whom he had been talking
with, he made an effort. He remembered that the boys had
asked him to complain, to try to get something. . . . At the
door, he turned abruptly and started back.

"Yes! Listen! I completely forgot to tell you—"

But the lieutenant colonel blocked his way and forced
him back; the man at the desk was not listening to him. In
that brief awkward moment, all the illegalities, all the prison
abuses perversely flew out of Pryanchikov's mind, now occupied by nothing but radio diagrams, and he remembered
one thing only and shouted, "Listen! About the boiling water
for tea. We come back late in the evening from work and
there's no boiling water! We can't have tea."

"No boiling water?" the man, a general of some sort, was
asking. "All right. We'll do something about it."

17

"OH, WONDER-WORKING STEED"

Bobynin came in dressed in the same blue coveralls. He was
a big man, his red hair cut short in convict style.

He showed about as much interest in the office furnishings
as if he came here a hundred times a day. He walked directly in and sat down without greeting the minister. He sat
in one of the comfortable armchairs not far from the minister's desk and blew his nose with deliberation in the not-so-
white handkerchief he had washed himself in the course of
his last bath.

Abakumov, who had been somewhat put off by Pryanchikov's frivolity, was pleased that Bobynin looked more im-

pressive. He did not shout at him, "Stand up!" Instead, supposing that he did not understand differences in rank and that he had not guessed from the enfilade of doors where he was, he asked him almost peaceably, "Why did you sit down without permission?"

Bobynin, looking slightly sideways at the minister, kept on cleaning his nose with the help of his handkerchief and replied in a casual voice, "Well, you see, there's a Chinese proverb: 'It's better to stand than to walk, it's better to sit than to stand, and the best of all is to lie down.'"

"But do you understand who I am?"

Comfortably leaning his elbows on the arms of his chosen chair, Bobynin now looked directly at Abakumov and ventured a lazy guess: "Well, who? Someone like Marshal Goering?"

"Like who?"

"Marshal Goering. Once he visited the aircraft factory near Halle, where I had to work. The local generals there all walked on tiptoe, but I didn't even glance in his direction. He looked and he looked and then he moved on."

Something like a smile wavered on Abakumov's face, but then he frowned at the unbelievably impudent prisoner. He blinked from tension and asked, "What's this? You don't see any difference between us?"

"Between you and him? Or between *us*?" There was a ring of steel in Bobynin's voice. "Between *us* I see it very clearly: you need me and I don't need you."

Abakumov, too, had a voice that could roll like thunder, and he knew how to use it to intimidate people. But at that moment he felt it would be useless and undignified to shout. He understood that this prisoner was a difficult one.

He only warned, "Listen, prisoner. Just because I'm easy on you, don't forget yourself—"

"And if you were rude to me, I wouldn't even talk to you, Citizen Minister. Shout at your colonels and generals. They have too much in life they're afraid of losing."

"We would make you talk."

"You are wrong, Citizen Minister!" Bobynin's strong eyes shone with hate. "I have nothing, you understand—not a thing! You can't get your hands on my wife and child—a bomb got them first. My parents are already dead. My entire property on earth is my handkerchief; my coveralls and my underwear that has no buttons—" he demonstrated by baring his chest—"are government issue. You took my freedom away long ago, and you don't have the power to return it because you don't have it yourself. I am forty-two years old, and you've dished me out a twenty-five-year term. I've already been at hard labor, gone around with a number on, in handcuffs, with police dogs, and in a strict-regime work brigade. What else is there you can threaten me with? What can you deprive me of? My work as an engineer? You'll lose more than I will. I'm going to have a smoke."

Abakumov opened a box of special-issue Troikas and pushed it toward Bobynin. "Here, take these."

"Thanks, but I don't change brands. Those make me cough." And he took a Belomor from his homemade cigarette case. "Just understand one thing and pass it along to anyone at the top who still doesn't know that you are strong only as long as you don't deprive people of *everything*. For a person you've taken *everything* from is no longer in your power. He's free all over again."

Bobynin fell silent, concentrating on his smoking. He enjoyed baiting the minister and sitting back in such a comfortable armchair. His only regret was that for the sake of effect he had declined the luxurious cigarettes.

The minister checked his papers. "Engineer Bobynin! You are the leading engineer of the speech clipper?"

"Yes."

"I am asking you to answer with absolute precision: when will it be ready for use?"

Bobynin raised his heavy, dark brows.

"That's something new! Isn't there anyone senior to me to put the question to?"

"I want to find out from you personally. Will it be ready by February?"

"By February? Are you joking? If it's a question of slapping something together in a hurry and regretting it later, well then—in half a year. As for absolute encoding—I haven't the least idea. Maybe a year."

Abakumov was crushed. He remembered the angry, impatient tremor of the Boss's mustache, and he felt sick when he remembered the promises he had made, based on what Sevastyanov had said. He had the sinking feeling of a person who had come to be cured of a head cold and discovers he has cancer of the nasopharynx.

The minister said in a constrained voice, "Bobynin, I'm

asking you to weigh your words carefully. If it can be done faster, then tell me: what has to be done?"

"Faster? It won't work."

"But why? What's the reason? Who's to blame? Tell me, don't be afraid! Tell me who's to blame, and no matter what their rank I'll rip off their shoulder boards."

Bobynin threw back his head and stared up at the ceiling where the nymphs of the "Russia" insurance company were gamboling.

"After all, that adds up to two and a half or three years!" the minister raged. "And you were given a time limit of one year!"

Bobynin exploded. "What do you mean, given a time limit? How do you picture science to yourself? 'Oh, wonder-working steed, build me a palace by morning,' and by morning there is a palace? And what if the problem has been incorrectly stated in the first place? And what if new phenomena turn up? A time limit! Don't you suppose that in addition to giving orders you need calm, well-nourished, free people to do the work? And without all this atmosphere of suspicion. You know, we were hauling a small lathe from one place to another, and, whether it happened while it was in our hands or later, the bedplate got broken. God only knows why it broke. But it would cost thirty rubles to weld. Yes, and that lathe is a piece of shit, one hundred and fifty years old, with no motor, a pulley under an open belt-drive—and because of that crack Major Shikin, the security officer, has been dragging everyone in and questioning them *for two weeks*, looking for someone to pin a second term for sabotage on. That's the security officer in the institute, a parasite, and there's another one in the prison and all he knows how to do is get on people's nerves with reports and problems. What the hell do you need all these security officers for? After all, everyone says we are working on a secret telephone for Stalin, that Stalin personally is pressing for it. Yet even in an operation like that you can't assure us a supply of material. Either we need condensers we don't have, or the tubes are the wrong kind, or we don't have enough oscillographs. Poverty! It's shameful! 'Who is to blame?' And have you thought about the people? They all work for you twelve, even sixteen hours a day, and you feed only the leading engineers with meat and the rest get bones. Why don't you allow Section 58 prisoners visits with their relatives? We're

supposed to have them once a month, and you allow them
once a year. Does that help morale? Maybe you don't have
enough Black Marias to carry the prisoners around? Or
money to pay the guards for working on their days off? The
regime! The regime gives you a headache, the regime can
drive you out of your mind. On Sundays we used to be allowed to go for an all-day walk; now it's forbidden. Why? So
we'll work more? What do you think you're doing—putting
sour cream on shit? Making people stifle without fresh air
won't make things go faster. Oh, what's the use of talking?
Here you are—why did you summon me at night? Isn't
there enough time during the day? After all, I have to work
tomorrow. I need sleep."

Bobynin stood up straight, wrathful, big.

Abakumov, breathing heavily, pressed against the edge of
the desk.

It was twenty past one. In an hour, at half-past two, Abakumov was to present a report to Stalin at his house at
Kuntsevo.

If this engineer was right, how could he worm his way
out of the mess?

Stalin never forgave.

Right then, as he let Bobynin go, he remembered that
troika of liars from the Special Technical Section. A black
rage stung his eyes.

He sent for them.

18

THE BIRTHDAY HERO

The room was small and low. There were two doors and no
windows, but the air was fresh and pleasant. A special engineer was responsible for its circulation and purity. Much
of the room was taken up by a low, dark ottoman with
flower-patterned pillows. Twin light bulbs with light-rose
glass shades burned on the wall above it.

On the ottoman reclined the man whose likeness had been

sculpted in stone; painted in oil, water colors, gouache, sepia; drawn in charcoal and chalk; formed out of wayside pebbles, sea shells, glazed tiles, grains of wheat, and soy beans; carved from ivory, grown in grass, woven into rugs, pictured in the sky by squadrons of planes in formation, and photographed on motion picture film . . . like no other likeness during the three billion years of the earth's crust.

He lay there with his feet up, wearing soft Caucasian boots which were like heavy stockings. He wore a service jacket with four large pockets, two on the chest, two on the sides—old, well worn, one of several service jackets he had been used to wearing since the Civil War and which he changed for a marshal's uniform only after Stalingrad.

This man's name filled the world's newspapers, was uttered by thousands of announcers in hundreds of languages, cried out by speakers at the beginning and the end of speeches, sung by the tender young voices of Pioneers, and proclaimed by bishops. This man's name was baked on the lips of dying prisoners of war, on the swollen gums of camp prisoners. It had been given to a multitude of cities and squares, streets and boulevards, palaces, universities, schools, sanatoriums, mountain ranges, canals, factories, mines, state and collective farms, battleships, icebreakers, fishing boats, shoemakers' artels, nursery schools—and a group of Moscow journalists had proposed that it be given also to the Volga and to the moon.

And he was only a little old man with a desiccated double chin which was never shown in his portraits, a mouth permeated with the smell of Turkish leaf tobacco, and fat fingers which left their traces on books. He had not been feeling too well yesterday or today. Even in the warm air he felt a chill on his back and shoulders, and he had covered himself with a brown camel's-hair shawl.

He was in no hurry to go anywhere, and he leafed with satisfaction through a small book in a brown binding. He looked at the photographs with interest and here and there read the text, which he knew almost by heart, then went on turning the pages. The little book was all the more convenient because it could fit into an overcoat pocket. It could accompany people everywhere in their lives. It contained two hundred and fifty pages, but it was printed in large stout type so that even a person who was old or only partly literate could read it without strain. Its title was stamped on the binding in gold: *Iosif Vissarionovich Stalin: A Short Biography.*

The elemental, honest words of this book acted on the human heart with serene inevitability. His strategic genius. His wise foresight. His powerful will. His iron will. From 1918 on he had for all practical purposes become Lenin's deputy. (Yes, yes, that was the way it had been.) The Commander of the Revolution found at the front a rout, confusion; Stalin's instructions were the basis for Frunze's plan of operations. (True, true.) It was our great good fortune that in the difficult days of the Great War of the Fatherland we were led by a wise and experienced leader—the Great Stalin. (Indeed, the people were fortunate.) All know the crushing might of Stalin's logic, the crystal clarity of his mind. (Without false modesty, it was all true.) His love for the people. His sensitivity to others. His surprising modesty. (Modesty—yes, that was very true.)

Very good. And they said it was selling well. Five million copies of this second edition had been printed. For such a country that was too few. The third edition should be ten million, perhaps twenty. It should be sold directly to factories, schools, collective farms.

He felt a touch of nausea. He put the book aside, took a peeled feijoa fruit from the round table and bit into it. If he sucked it, his nausea would go away and a pleasant aftertaste with a trace of iodine would remain in his mouth.

He noticed, but was afraid to admit it, that his health was getting worse and worse every month. He had lapses of memory. He was tormented by nausea. He felt no specific pain, but hours of disagreeable weakness riveted him to his couch. Even sleep didn't help; he awoke just as unrefreshed, as exhausted, with the same pressure in his head, as when he lay down; and he had no desire to move around.

In the Caucasus a man of seventy was still a young fellow! Up the mountain, up on a horse, up on a woman. And he had been so healthy! He had been sure of living to ninety! But what had happened? For the past year Stalin could no longer enjoy his greatest pleasure in life—good food. Orange juice made his tongue smart, caviar stuck to his teeth, and he ate with torpid indifference even the spicy Georgian lamb soup, kharcho, which he wasn't supposed to eat at all. Nor did he derive the old, clear enjoyment from wine—his hangovers ended in dull headaches. Even the thought of a woman was repulsive.

Having set himself the goal of living to ninety, Stalin thought sadly of the fact that these years would bring him no personal joy, that he simply had to suffer another twenty years for the sake of humanity.

One doctor had warned him that—(but he had, it seemed, been shot subsequently). Stethoscopes trembled in the hands of the most famous men in Moscow medicine. They never prescribed injections for him. (He himself had ordered all injections stopped.) High-frequency electrotherapy and "more fruit." Trying to tell a man from the Caucasus about fruit!

He bit again, squinting.

Three days ago had been his glorious seventieth birthday. They had celebrated it in sequence: on the evening of the twentieth Traicho Kostov had been beaten to death. Only after the cur's eyes had turned glassy could the real festivities begin. On the twenty-first there had been a ceremonial celebration in the Bolshoi Theater, and Mao Tse-tung and Ibarruri and other comrades had made speeches. Then there had been a big banquet. And after that a small banquet. They had drunk old wines from Spanish wine cellars. He had had to drink with caution, and all the time he was searching out the cunning in the reddened faces around him. And afterward he and Lavrenty had drunk Kakhetinskoye wine and sung Georgian songs. On the twenty-second there was a big diplomatic reception. On the twenty-third he had watched himself portrayed on the screen in the second part of Virta's *The Battle of Stalingrad* and in Vishnevsky's *Unforgettable 1919*.

Although they tired him, he liked both these works very much. (A Stalin Prize for both of them.) Nowadays his role in the Civil War as well as in the Great War of the Fatherland was being depicted more and more accurately. It was becoming clear what a big man he had been then. His own memory told him how often he had warned and corrected the rash and too easily trusting Lenin. And Vishnevsky had done well to have him say: "Every worker has the right to speak his mind. Someday we'll put such a paragraph in the Constitution." What did that mean? It meant that while defending Petrograd from Yudenich, Stalin was already thinking about a future democratic constitution. Of course, it was called "the dictatorship of the proletariat" then—but that didn't matter, it was true, it was strong!

And in Virta's scenario that nighttime scene with the Friend was well written. Even though no such loyal, big Friend was left to Stalin because of people's perfidy and constant insincerity. (Indeed, never in his whole life had there been such a Friend! That was the way things had worked out, there never had been.) But watching Virta's scene on the screen Stalin had felt a tightness in his throat and tears in his eyes (now that was an artist for you!) and longed for such an upright, unselfish friend, to whom he could tell the things he thought about all night long.

Never mind. The simple ordinary people love their Leader, understand him and love him—that was true. That much he could see from the newspapers, and from the movies, and from the display of gifts. His birthday had become a national holiday, and that was good to know. How many messages there had been! From institutions, organizations, factories, individual citizens. *Pravda* had asked permission to print two columns of them in every issue. Well, they would have to run for several years, and all right, it wasn't a bad idea.

And the gifts had overflowed ten halls of the Museum of the Revolution. So as not to keep Muscovites from going to see them in the daytime, Stalin had gone to see them at night. The work of thousands upon thousands of master craftsmen, the finest gifts of the earth, stood, lay, and hung before him. But there, too, he felt that same indifference, that same fading of interest. What good were all those gifts to him? He had quickly become bored. And then the place itself awoke something unpleasant in his memory, yet, as happened so often lately, he could not track it down, he could not grasp it, and all that he was aware of was a disagreeable feeling. He had gone through three halls and not selected anything. He stood before the big TV set with the engraved words "To the Great Stalin from the Chekists." (Made at Mavrino, it was unique—the biggest television set ever made in the U.S.S.R.) And then he had turned and left.

That was how the remarkable holiday had passed, but there had been no feeling of fulfillment in the celebration.

There was a certain sensation in his chest which troubled Stalin, and it had to do with the museum, but he could not quite grasp what it was.

The people loved him, yes, but the people themselves swarmed with shortcomings. How could these be corrected? And how much quicker Communism could be built if it were not for the soulless bureaucrats. If it were not for the conceited big shots. If it were not for the organizational weakness of indoctrination efforts among the masses. For the "drifting" in Party education. For the slackened pace of construction, the delays in production, the output of low-quality goods, the bad planning, the apathy toward the introduction of new technology and equipment, the refusal of young people to pioneer distant areas, the loss of grain in the fields, overexpenditure by bookkeepers, thievery at warehouses, swindling by managers, sabotage by prisoners, liberalism in the police, abuse of public housing, insolent speculators, greedy housewives, spoiled children, chatterboxes on streetcars, petty-minded "criticism" in literature, liberal tendencies in cinematography.

No, the people still had too many shortcomings.

And in '41, what made them retreat? After all, the people had been ordered to stand to the death. Why hadn't they? Who had retreated then if not the people?

But in remembering 1941 Stalin did not evade the recollection of his own weakness—his hurried and unnecessary departure from Moscow in October. Of course, it wasn't running away. For when he went, Stalin left responsible people in charge, and gave them firm orders to defend the capital to the last drop of blood. But unfortunately those very comrades faltered, and he had had to return again, come back to the capital himself and defend it.

He thereupon sent to prison every single person who remembered that panic on October 16. But he punished himself, too—he stood in review at the November military parade. This moment in his life was like the time he had fallen into an ice hole during his exile in Turukhansk: ice and despair, but out of ice and despair had come strength. It was no laughing matter—a military parade with the enemy at the walls.

But how could it be easy to be the Greatest of All the Great?

Exhausted by inaction, Stalin involuntarily gave in to oppressive thoughts. He did not fix his weary attention on anything at this particular moment. He closed his eyes tight and lay there, while disconnected memories from his long life stole into his head. Yet for some reason what he remembered was not the good but the bad and vexing. If he recalled his birthplace, Gori, it was not the pretty green hillocks, nor the meanderings of the Medzhuda and Liakhva rivers, but what had been hateful there, what had kept him from returning, even for an hour, to his childhood home. If his thoughts turned to 1917, it was to remember how Lenin had appeared, with his opinionated doctrines, and overturned what had already been done, and how they had laughed when Stalin proposed forming a legal party and living at peace with the Provisional Government. They had laughed at him more than once—but why had it been accepted practice to dump everything that was difficult and unrewarding on him? They laughed at him, but on July 6 it was he, not someone else, whom they sent from the Kshesinskaya Palace to the Petropavlovsk Fortress to convince the sailors to surrender the fortress to Kerensky and retreat to Kronstadt. Grisha Zinoviev would have been stoned by the sailors. One has to know how to talk to the Russian people. He remembered 1920 and, again, how Tukhachevsky, his lips twisted, had cried out that it was Stalin's fault he had not taken Warsaw. He had shouted himself right into that one, the fool!

All his life things had never worked out. They had never worked out because there were always people who interfered. And when one had been removed, someone else always turned up to take his place.

He heard four light knocks at the door, not even knocks, but four soft strokings, as if a dog were brushing against it.

Stalin turned the switch beside his couch, the remote-control bolt clicked back, and the uncurtained door opened slightly. It was not covered by a portiere because Stalin did not like bed curtains, drapes, or recesses where anyone could hide. It opened just far enough, indeed, to admit a dog; but instead there appeared the young balding head of Poskrebyshev, with his permanent expression of honest devotion and absolute compliance.

Concerned for the Boss's health, he observed that Stalin was lying half covered by a camel's-hair shawl, but he did not ask about his health directly. (It was assumed to be excellent.) He said quietly, "Yos Sarionich, Abakumov will be here at two-thirty. Will you receive him? Perhaps not?"

Iosif Vissarionovich unbuttoned his breast pocket and pulled out his watch and chain. (Like all old-fashioned people, he could not abide wristwatches.)

It wasn't yet two in the morning.

He did not feel like changing his clothes and going into his office. But he could never loosen the bonds of discipline either. If he let up on the reins even the slightest bit, they would be aware of it right away.

"We'll see," Stalin answered wearily and blinked. "I don't know."

"Well, let him come. He can wait!" said Poskrebyshev and nodded three extra times. (By emphasizing his apparent boyishness he made his position much firmer.) And then he froze again, looking at the Boss with fixed attention. "What are your orders, Yo Sarionich?"

Stalin looked sadly on this creature who, alas, could not be a friend either, because of his utter subservience.

"Run along for now, Sasha," he said from under his mustaches.

Poskrebyshev nodded once more, withdrew his head, and shut the door tight.

Iosif Vissarionovich set the remote-control bolt in place and, holding his shawl around him, turned over on his other side.

Then he noticed on the low table beside the ottoman a book in a cheap paperback edition with a red-and-black cover.

Immediately he remembered what had caught in his chest, what had burned, what had spoiled his birthday: the person who still interfered with him today and had not been removed—Tito! Tito!

How had it happened? How could he have mistaken that scorpion soul? The years 1936 and 1937 had been so glorious! So many heads hitherto untouched had fallen that year, but he had let Tito slip out of his hands.

With a groan Stalin let his legs down from the couch. He sat up and raised his hands to his reddish, graying head on which a bald spot could be seen. Frustration and a vexation past relieving took hold of him. Like a legendary hero, Stalin had all his life been cutting off the hydra's ever-sprouting heads. He had disposed of a whole mountain of enemies in his lifetime. And he had tripped on a root.

Iosif had tripped over Iosif.

Kerensky, who was still alive somewhere, did not disturb Stalin in the least. For that matter, as far as Stalin was concerned, Nicholas II or Kolchak could come back from the grave—he felt no personal enmity toward them: they were open enemies, they didn't dodge around offering some new, better socialism of their own.

Better socialism? In *some other way* than Stalin's? Snot! Who could build socialism *without Stalin?*

It was not a question of Tito's succeeding. Nothing could come of what he was doing anyway! Stalin looked on Tito the way an old country doctor, who has ripped open countless stomachs, cut off an endless number of limbs in chimneyless huts, or on planks along the roadside, looks on some little intern in a white gown.

The collected works of Lenin had been changed three times and those of the Founders twice. Everyone was long since asleep who had disagreed, who had been mentioned in the old footnotes, who had thought of building socialism *in some other way.* And then, when even in the northern forests neither criticism nor doubts could be heard, Tito had crawled out of the woodwork with his dogmatist-theologist Kardel and declared that things ought to be done *differently.*

Then and there Stalin noticed that his heart was beating harder, that his vision had fogged, that he felt unpleasant spasms throughout his body.

He altered his rate of breathing. He stroked his face and his mustache. He couldn't give in. If he did, Tito would steal his last peace, his last appetite, his last slumber.

When his eyes cleared, he was once more aware of the red-and-black book. The book had not been to blame. Stalin reached for it with satisfaction, put his pillow behind him, and again half-reclined for several minutes.

It was a copy of the multimillion edition prepared in ten European languages of *Tito, the Traitors' Marshal* by Renaud de Jouvenel. (It was a good thing that the author apparently stood outside the argument, an objective Frenchman, yes, and with an aristocratic name, too.) Stalin had already read the book carefully several days before, but, as with every pleasant book, he did not want to part with it. How many eyes it would open to this self-adoring, cruel, cowardly, perfidious, evil tyrant! This loathsome traitor! This hopeless blockhead! Even Communists in the West had gotten mixed up. That old fool of a Frenchman André

Marty—even he would have to be thrown out of the Communist Party for defending Tito.

He leafed through the book. Yes, here it was! Now people could not keep on glorifying Tito as a hero: out of cowardice he had twice wanted to surrender to the Germans, but the Chief of Staff, Arso Jovanovich, had *compelled* him to remain as Commander in Chief. Noble Arso had been killed, and Petrichevich, too: "Killed only because he loved Stalin." Someone was always killing the best people, and the worst were left for Stalin to finish off.

Everything was here, everything—that Tito was apparently a British spy; how proud he was of his undershorts with the royal crown embroidered on them; how physically repulsive he was, like Goering; how festooned he was with orders and decorations, his fingers covered with big diamond signet rings. (What kind of pathetic vanity was this in someone with no gift for military leadership?)

An objective, principled book. Didn't Tito have certain sexual aberrations? That would have to be written about, too.

"The Yugoslav Communist Party is in the clutches of murderers and spies." "Tito could only take over the leadership because Béla Kun and Traicho Kostov supported him."

Kostov! How that name irked Stalin! Rage flooded his head, and he kicked out hard with his boot—into Traicho's bloody snout! And Stalin's gray eyelids trembled from a satisfied feeling of justice.

That accursed Kostov, the dirty bastard!

Surprising how, in retrospect, the intrigues of these scoundrels became clear! How cleverly they had disguised themselves! At least he had slammed down on Béla Kun in 1937; but just ten days ago Kostov had defamed a Socialist court. How many successful trials Stalin had conducted, how many enemies he had compelled to abase themselves and confess to any despicable crime—yet he had failed in Kostov's case! A disgrace throughout the world! What black resourcefulness, to deceive the experienced interrogators, to crawl at their feet—and then in the public session, in the presence of foreign correspondents, to repudiate everything! What had become of decency? And the Party conscience? And proletarian solidarity? All right, die, but die so that you're some use to us!

Stalin tossed the book aside. No, he could not just relax and lie here. The struggle called.

A carefree country can sleep, but not its Father. He stood up, but did not straighten up all the way. He unlocked the other door in the room (not the one through which Poskrebyshev had entered), then locked it behind him. Barely shuffling in his soft boots, he went down a low, narrow, twisting, windowless corridor, under a skylight, past one-way mirrors through which he could see the entrance hall. He went on into his bedroom, low-ceilinged, too, small, windowless, air-conditioned. There was armor plate behind the oak paneling of the bedroom walls and, on the outside, stone.

With the little key he wore on his belt Stalin unlocked the metal top of a decanter, poured a glass of his favorite, invigorating liqueur, drank it down and relocked the top.

He moved to the mirror. His eyes looked clear and incorruptibly stern. Even prime ministers could not stand up to those eyes. His appearance was severe, simple, soldierly.

He summoned his Georgian orderly to dress him.

Even to those close to him he appeared as he would to history.

His iron will. His inflexible will.

19

LANGUAGE IS A TOOL OF PRODUCTION

Night was Stalin's most fruitful time.

His mistrustful mind unwound slowly in the morning. With his gloomy morning mind he removed people from their positions, cut back expenditures, ordered two or three ministries merged into one. With his sharp and supple nighttime mind he decided how to increase the number of ministries by dividing them up, and what to call the new ones; he signed new budgets and confirmed new appointments.

All his best ideas were born between midnight and 4 A.M.:

the way to exchange old bonds for new ones to avoid paying the bondholders; what the sentences should be for absenteeism from work; how to stretch the working day and the work week; how to bind laborers and other employees permanently to their jobs; the edict concerning hard labor and the gallows; the dissolution of the Third International; the exile of traitor populations to Siberia.

The exile of whole nationalities was both his major theoretical contribution and his boldest experiment, but now nothing else remained to be done. All his life he had undoubtedly been the Party's foremost specialist in the question of Soviet nationalities.

There had been many other remarkable edicts. However, he still found one weak spot in the whole architectonic system, and gradually an important new edict was ripening in his mind. He had everything nailed down for good, all motion stopped, all outlets plugged, all 200 million knew their place—only the collective farm youths were escaping.

Of course, things were going very well on the collective farms. Stalin was certain of this after seeing *Cossacks of the Kuban* and reading *Cavalier of the Golden Star*. Both authors had visited collective farms. They had seen everything and reported what they had seen, and it was obviously good. And Stalin himself had talked with collective farmers in presidiums.

But as a profound and self-critical statesman, Stalin probed even more deeply than these writers. One of the provincial Party secretaries (he had evidently been shot later) had blurted out to him that there was a dark side to things: the old men and old women registered in the collective farms since 1930 were working with enthusiasm, but the young people (not all of them, of course, just certain unconscientious individuals) were trying, as soon as they finished school, to get passports by deceit and go chasing off to the city. Stalin heard this, and within him the invisible corrective process began.

Education! This whole business of universal seven-year education, universal ten-year education, with the children of cooks going on to universities, had produced a mess. Lenin had been confused on this point, but it was still too early to tell the people that. Every cook, every housewife should be able to run the state! Just how did he picture that concretely? That cooks should not cook on Fridays but go off to meetings of the provincial executive committee? A cook is a cook, and her job is to prepare dinner. As for governing people, that's a high calling; it can be entrusted only to specially picked personnel, tried and true, who have been tested over a period of many years. And the management of this personnel can only be in one pair of hands, the practiced hands of the Leader.

The statutes of the collective farms should provide that, just as the land belongs to them in perpetuity, so every person born in a given village automatically becomes, from the day of his birth, a member of the collective farm. It should be presented as an honorific right. And only the presidium of the local district executive committee could then authorize anyone's departure from the collective farm.

Then an immediate propaganda campaign, a series of newspaper articles: "The Young Heirs of the Collective Farm Granary," "An Important Step in the Construction of the New Village." Certainly the writers would find ways to express it.

Indeed, it seemed as if someone from among the *rightists* had warned that this problem would arise. (Such "rightists" never really existed—Stalin himself grouped certain people together under this label so as to get at them all the more conveniently.)

For some reason it always happened that annihilated opponents turned out to have been right about something. Fascinated by their hostile thoughts, Stalin listened warily to their voices from beyond the grave.

But even though that edict was urgent, and even though other edicts, also urgent, had matured in his mind, on entering his office Stalin today had felt drawn toward something loftier.

On the threshold of his eighth decade he had no right to put it off any longer.

It would seem that everything possible had already been done to assure his immortality.

But to Stalin it appeared that his contemporaries, though they called him the Wisest of the Wise, still did not admire him as much as he deserved, that their raptures were superficial, that they did not yet understand the profundity of his genius.

One thought had been eating at him lately: to achieve yet one more scientific feat, to make his indelible contribution to a science other than philosophy and history. Of course, he could have made such a contribution to biology, but he had entrusted that job to Lysenko, that honest, energetic man of the people. Besides, mathematics, or at least physics, was more attractive to Stalin. He could never read without envy the discussion about zero and minus-one-squared in *The Dialectics of Nature*.

But no matter how often he leafed through Kiselev's textbook, *Algebra*, and Sokolov's *Physics* for advanced classes, he could not find an appropriate inspiration anywhere.

He had, in fact, chanced upon just such a felicitous concept in a completely different field, in linguistics, in connection with the recent case of Professor Chikobava of Tiflis. Chikobava had written some apparently anti-Marxist heresy to the effect that language is not a superstructure at all but simply language, that it is neither bourgeois nor proletarian, but simply national speech—and he had dared to cast aspersions openly on the name of Marr himself.

Since both Marr and Chikobava were Georgians, there was an immediate response in the Georgian University journal, a gray, unbound copy of which, printed in the characteristic Georgian alphabet, lay at this moment in front of Stalin. Several linguistic disciples of Marr had attacked the insolent scholar. In the wake of their accusations he could only sit and wait for the midnight knock of the MGB. It had already been hinted that Chikobava was an agent of American imperialism.

Nothing could have saved Chikobava if Stalin had not picked up the phone and let him live. He would let him live —and would himself give the man's simple, provincial thoughts an immortal exposition and a brilliant development.

True, it would have been more impressive to refute the counterrevolutionary theory of relativity, for example, or the theory of wave mechanics, but because of affairs of state he simply did not have the time. Philology, however, was the next thing to grammar, and, in respect to difficulty, Stalin had always put grammar on a level with mathematics.

He could write this vividly, expressively (he was already sitting down and writing): "Whatever language of the Soviet nations we take: Russian, Ukrainian, Belorussian, Uzbek, Kazak, Georgian, Armenian, Estonian, Latvian, Lithuanian, Moldavian, Tatar, Azerbaidzhanian, Bashkir, Turkoman—"

(Damn it! With the years it had become harder and harder
to stop enumerating things. But why shouldn't he? That way
it sank into the reader's head more effectively and weakened
the impulse to object.) "—it is clear to everyone that—"
Well then, put down something or other that's clear to
everyone.

But what is clear? Nothing is clear. As they say, "It's piled
seven miles to heaven and it's forest all the way."

Economics—that's the basis. Social phenomena—that's
the superstructure. And there is no third element. Yet with
his experience of life Stalin recognized that you can't get
anywhere without a third element. For example, you can
have neutral countries, can't you? (But not neutral people,
of course.) And suppose in the twenties you had said from
the speaker's platform: "Whoever is not with us is not necessarily against us"? They'd have chased you off the podium
and out of the Party. But it turns out that way. That's
dialectics.

It was the same thing now. Stalin had thought about
Chikobava's essay, struck by an idea that had never occurred
to him: if language is a superstructure, why doesn't it change
with every epoch? If it is not a superstructure, what is it?
A basis? A mode of production?

Properly speaking, it's like this: modes of production
consist of productive forces and productive relationships. To
call language a *relationship* is impossible. So does that mean
language is a productive force? But productive forces include the instruments of production, the means of production, and people. But even though people speak language,
language is not people. The devil himself doesn't know—he
was at a dead end.

To be really honest, one would have to recognize that
language is an instrument of production like—well, like
lathes, railroads, the mail. It, too, is communications, after
all.

But if you put the thesis that way, declaring that language
is an instrument of production, everyone will start snicker-
ing. Not in our country, of course.

And there was no one to ask advice from; he alone on
earth was a true philosopher. If only someone like Kant
were still alive, or Spinoza, even though he was bourgeois
. . . Should he phone Beria? But Beria didn't understand
anything at all.

Well, he could put it more cautiously: "In this respect language, which differs in principle from superstructure, is not distinguishable, however, from instruments of production, from machines, let us say, which are as indifferent to class as language is."

"Indifferent to class"—that, too, could never have been said before.

He placed a period after the sentence. He put his hands behind his head, yawned and stretched. He had not got very far, but he was already tired.

Stalin stood up and walked around the small room, his favorite nighttime office. He approached a tiny window in which two sheets of yellowish bulletproof glass with a vacuum between them had been substituted for ordinary glass. Outside was a small fenced-in garden where, mornings only, the gardener went about under the eyes of a guard. For days no one else set foot there.

Beyond the bulletproof glass there was mist in the garden. Neither the earth nor the universe was visible.

However, half the universe was enclosed in his own breast, and that half was harmonious and clear. It was only the second half—objective reality—which cowered in global mist.

But here, in his guarded and fortified night office, Stalin did not fear that second half in the least; he felt in himself the power to warp it, to bend it as he pleased. Only when he was obliged to step into that objective reality—when, for example, he had to go to a big banquet at the Hall of Columns, cross the frightening space between the automobile and the door, climb the stairway himself, and cross the too-large foyer between two ranks of rapt and reverent but nevertheless too numerous guests—at these moments Stalin would feel ill, totally undefended, would not even know how to use his hands, long since worthless for any real defense. He would place them on his stomach and smile. They thought the Omnipotent was smiling to favor them, but he was smiling because he was afraid.

He himself had described space as the basic condition for material existence. But having made himself master of one-sixth of terrestrial matter, he had begun to be afraid of space. That was what was good about his night office: there was no *space*.

Stalin closed the steel shutter and slowly returned to the

desk. It was late even for the Great Coryphaeus to be at work, but he swallowed a pill and sat down again.

Things had never worked out for him, yet he had to keep on toiling. Coming generations would appreciate him.

How had it happened that there was an oppressive, an Arakcheyev regime in philology? Everyone was afraid to say a word against Marr. How strange and timid people were! You could try to teach them democracy, you could even chew things up for them so that all they had to do was swallow—and they would turn their heads away.

Everything depended on him, on Stalin; here, too, it all depended on him. Inspired, he wrote down several phrases:

"The superstructure was created by the basis *for the purpose of* . . ."

"Language was created *for the purpose of* . . ."

His brownish-gray, smallpox-pitted face, with its great plow of a nose, bent low over the sheet of paper, and he did not see the angel of medieval teleology smiling over his shoulder.

That Lafargue—all those theoreticians were the same. His speaking of "a sudden revolution in language between 1789 and 1794." What revolution was that! It had been the French language before, and it stayed the French language.

"In general one must say for the benefit of those comrades who are fascinated by explosions that the law of transition by explosion from an old quality to a new quality is not only inapplicable to the history of linguistic development, but is also rarely applicable to other social phenomena."

Stalin leaned back and reread it. It had turned out well. The propagandists would have to elucidate the point thoroughly: that all revolutions come to a stop at a certain moment and further development proceeds only by evolution. And it might even be that quantity does not develop into quality. But this he would save for another time.

"Rarely?" No; that could still be embarrassing.

Stalin crossed out "rarely" and wrote in "not always."

What would be a nice example?

"We moved from a bourgeois, individual-peasant structure" (a new term had turned up and a good one!) "to the socialist collective farm."

And having at last put a period to his sentence, he thought further and added the word "structure." This was his favorite style, one more blow on a nail already driven in. The repetition of all its words made any sentence more comprehensible. Inspired, his pen wrote on:

"And it was possible to do this successfully because it was a revolution *from above, because* the revolution was carried out on the initiative of the existing authority."

Stalin frowned. Stop. This had turned out poorly. Didn't that make it appear that the initiative for collectivization had not come from the collective farmers?

A soft stroking was heard at the door. Stalin pressed the button which released the latch. In the doorway appeared Sasha with his clown's face, battered and glad to be battered.

"Yos Sarionich!" he asked almost in a whisper. "Do you want me to send Abakumov home or do you want him to wait some more?"

"Oh, yes, Abakumov." Carried away by his creative work, Stalin had completely forgotten about him.

He yawned. He was tired now. The passion for inquiry had burned in him briefly and had gone out; besides, his last sentences had not been successful.

"All right. Call him."

And from his desk he got out another metal-topped decanter, unlocked it with the key from his belt, and drank a glass.

He must be a mountain eagle always.

20

GIVE US BACK CAPITAL PUNISHMENT, IOSIF VISSARIONOVICH

There was hardly anyone who dared dream of calling him Sasha instead of Aleksandr Nikolayevich, much less say it to his face. "Poskrebyshev called" meant *"He called." "Poskrebyshev ordered"* meant *"He ordered."* Aleksandr Nikolayevich Poskrebyshev had been chief of Stalin's personal

secretariat for more than fifteen years. That was a very long
time, and anyone who hadn't studied him close up might
well be surprised that his head was still on his shoulders.
But the secret was simple. In his soul this veterinarian from
Penza was an orderly, and it was this plain fact that assured
his safety. Even after he had been made a lieutenant general,
a member of the Central Committee, and Chief of the Special Section for Keeping Members of the Central Committee
under Clandestine Observation, he still considered himself
a nonentity before the Boss, tittering boastfully whenever
they clinked glasses in a toast to his native village of Soplaki.
Stalin's intuition never detected doubt or opposition in
Poskrebyshev. His surname, which meant bread baked from
scraps of dough, was justified: it was as though they had not
scraped up enough qualities of mind and character when they
baked him.

But when he dealt with subordinates, this balding courtier
with the air of a simpleton acquired enormous self-impor-
tance. To those of inferior rank he spoke on the phone in a
barely audible voice; one had to jam one's head against the
receiver to understand him. Now and then one could joke
with him about trifles, but one could never ask him casually,
"How is everything over there today?" (Even the Boss's
own daughter could not find out *how everything was*. When
she phoned, she was told only: "There is movement" or
"There is no movement," depending on whether the Boss's
steps could be heard.)

Tonight Poskrebyshev told Abakumov, "Iosif Vissarionovich is working. He may receive you. He said you should
wait."

He had taken Abakumov's briefcase, led him into the
reception room, and left.

So Abakumov did not ask what he wanted most of all
to know: what was the Boss's mood today? He remained
alone in the reception room, his heart pounding heavily.

This strong, husky, decisive man stood rigid with fright
each time he went to report to Stalin, just as citizens during
the waves of arrests had quaked when they heard the tramp of
steps on the stairs. His ears first turned icy-cold from fear,
and then began to burn—and each time Abakumov grew
even more afraid that his persistently fiery ears would arouse
the Boss's suspicion. Stalin was suspicious of the smallest
thing. For example, he didn't like anyone to put his hand in

an inside pocket in his presence. Therefore Abakumov transferred from his inner pocket to his outer breast pocket all three fountain pens, which he had ready for writing down instructions.

The day-to-day direction of State Security came through Beria, from whom Abakumov received most of his orders. But once a month the Absolute Ruler himself wanted to feel out the personality of the man to whom he had entrusted the safekeeping of the system he led.

These hour-long appointments were a heavy price to pay for all the power, all the might Abakumov wielded. He lived and enjoyed himself only from appointment to appointment. As the time drew near, everything inside him sank, his ears grew icy; he would hand over his briefcase before going in without knowing whether he would get it back; he would bow his bull-like head at the office door not knowing whether he would be straightening up again in another hour.

Stalin was terrifying because one mistake in his presence could be that one mistake in life which set off an explosion, irreversible in effect. Stalin was terrifying because he did not listen to excuses, made no accusations; his yellow tiger eyes simply brightened balefully, his lower lids closed up a bit—and there, inside him, sentence had been passed, and the condemned man didn't know: he left in peace, was arrested at night, and shot by morning.

The silence and that squint of the lower lids were worst of all. If Stalin threw something heavy or sharp at you, if he stamped on your foot, spat on you, or blew a burning coal from his pipe in your face, that anger was not the ultimate anger, that anger passed. If Stalin was crude and cursed, even using the worst profanity, Abakumov rejoiced: it meant that the Boss still hoped to straighten him out and go on working with him.

Of course, Abakumov understood by now that in his zealous enthusiasm he had climbed too high. To have stayed lower would have been less dangerous. Stalin spoke pleasantly, good-naturedly, with those well removed from him. But there was no retreat once one had become an *intimate*.

The only thing left was to wait for death. One's own. Or . . .

And things happened so inexorably that in Stalin's presence Abakumov always dreaded that something had been discovered.

Before today he had often trembled with fear that word

of his enriching himself in Germany might have reached Stalin's ears.

At the end of the war Abakumov had been head of the all-Union SMERSH, and the counterintelligence services of all active fronts, and the entire army, were under his direction. That had been a period of unrestricted plunder, which had lasted only briefly. To assure an effective final blow against Germany, Stalin adopted from Hitler the practice of permitting booty to be sent home from the front. The decision was based on his understanding of a soldier's nature, on what he himself would have felt had he been a soldier: it was fine to fight for the country's honor—and even better to fight for Stalin—but to risk one's life at that most tantalizing time, when the end of the war was at hand, a powerful incentive was needed—specifically, he allowed each soldier to send home ten pounds of booty a month, each officer twenty, and a general thirty. This arrangement was just, because a soldier's knapsack should not be too heavy when he attacked, and a general always had his automobile. SMERSH was in a still better position, out of reach of enemy shells, not a target for enemy planes. It was always in an area behind the lines where the Ministry of Finance inspectors had not yet arrived. Its officers were enveloped in a cloud of secrecy. No one dared verify what they sealed in freight cars, what they removed from confiscated property guarded by SMERSH guards. Trucks, trains, and planes carried back the wealth of SMERSH officers. Lieutenants, if they were not fools, could get out with thousands, colonels with hundreds of thousands, Abakumov with millions.

True, he could not imagine how he could be saved by gold, even gold deposited in a Swiss bank, if he fell from his post as minister. It seemed quite clear that wealth would not help a minister who had been beheaded. Yet he could not bear watching his subordinates getting rich while he took nothing himself. So he sent one special detachment after another on treasure hunts. He could not even turn down two suitcases full of suspenders. He plundered in a somnambulistic trance.

But his Nibelungen treasure was useless to Abakumov and gave rise to the constant fear of exposure. No one who knew about it would have dared report the omnipotent minister, but at the same time any accident could bring it all to light and destroy him. He had been foolish to take it, but it was too late now.

He had come at 2:30; at 3:10 he was still pacing back and forth in the reception room, holding his large, fresh notebook and feeling weak inside from fear; his ears had started to burn. Above everything, he would have been glad if Stalin had gone on working and not received him at all today. Abakumov dreaded being called to account about the secret telephony. He did not know what lie to tell just now.

But the heavy door opened, halfway. Poskrebyshev came out quietly, almost on tiptoe, and beckoned him silently. Abakumov followed, trying not to put all his weight on his feet. He scraped through the next door, which was also half open, keeping hold of its polished bronze handles so that it would not open wider. On the threshold he said, "Good evening, Iosif Vissarionovich! May I come in?"

He had blundered, had failed to clear his throat in time, and his voice had sounded hoarse, not sufficiently loyal.

Stalin, wearing a tunic with gilt buttons and several rows of medal ribbons, but no shoulder boards, was writing at his desk. He finished his sentence and only then looked up with owl-like malice at the visitor.

And he said nothing.

A very bad sign! He had not said a word.

He began writing again.

Abakumov closed the door behind him but did not dare advance farther without a nod or a gesture of invitation. He stood leaning slightly forward, long arms at his sides, with a respectful smile of greeting on his meaty lips. His ears were afire.

Abakumov had been in both the Leader's offices—his official daytime office and this small night one.

In the big daytime office, on an upper floor, it was sunny and there were ordinary windows. In the bookcases the whole parade of human thought and culture was assembled, packaged in colored bindings. On the high, spacious walls hung favorite portraits of the Leader, in the winter uniform of the Generalissimo, in a marshal's summer outfit. There were divans, armchairs, many other chairs, for the reception of foreign delegations, for conferences. That was where Stalin was photographed.

Here in the night office, close to the earth, there were neither paintings nor decorations, and the windows were small. Four low bookcases stood against the oak-paneled walls, and a desk stood out from one wall. There was also a radio-phonograph in one corner; next to it was a book-stand holding records. Stalin loved to listen to his old speeches at night.

Abakumov bent forward submissively and waited.

Stalin kept on writing. He wrote in the consciousness that his every word straightaway belonged to history. His desk lamp lit only the paper; the indirect upper light was dim. He didn't write all the time. He would turn away, squinting off to one side, toward the floor, or look unpleasantly at Abakumov, as if he were listening to something, though there was no sound in the room.

How had this commanding manner, the weighty import of each small movement, developed? Had not the young Koba—as Stalin had been called in the Caucasus—moved his fingers, his hands, raised his brows, and stared in exactly the same way? But at that time no one was frightened, no one inferred from these gestures their awful meaning. It was only after the number of bullet-torn heads had reached a certain figure that people began to see in these same small gestures a hint, a warning, a command. And noticing what others noticed, Stalin began to observe himself; and he, too, saw in his gestures and glances that threatening inner mean-ing, and he began consciously to work them up; and they got to be even better and affected people around him even more positively.

At last Stalin looked severely at Abakumov and, gesturing with his pipe, indicated where he was to sit.

Abakumov trembled with relief, walked across the room, and sat down—but only on the edge of the seat, so that he could get up again more easily.

"Well?" demanded Stalin, searching among his papers.

The moment had arrived! Now he had to seize the initia-tive and not lose it. Abakumov cleared his throat and spoke out hurriedly, in a ceremonious tone. (Later he cursed him-self for his garrulous servility in Stalin's office, and for his immoderate promises, but somehow it always turned out that the more hostile the attitude of the Omnipotent, the more unrestrained was Abakumov in his assurances, and he kept getting in deeper and deeper.)

The invariable ornament of Abakumov's nighttime reports, the thing which attracted Stalin to them, was the revelation of some very important and widespread hostile group. Without such a group to identify and thwart—a new one each time—Abakumov did not make reports. Today he had prepared a case against a group in the Frunze Military Academy, and he could spend a long time on its details.

But he began by reporting successful developments—and he did not himself know whether they were real or illusory—in the plot to assassinate Tito. He announced that a delayed-action bomb would be put on board Tito's yacht before it sailed for the island of Brioni.

Stalin raised his head, put his dead pipe in his mouth, and puffed at it once or twice. He made no other movement, showed no interest at all; but Abakumov, who had come to fathom his chief a little, felt nonetheless that he had hit the spot.

"And Rankovich?" asked Stalin.

"Oh, yes! The moment will be chosen so that Rankovich and Kardel and Mosa Pijade—the whole clique—will be blown into the air together! We estimate it will take place not later than this spring." (The whole crew of the yacht was supposed to perish in the explosion, too, but the minister did not mention that detail, and the Best Friend of Sailors did not question him about it.)

But what was he thinking, puffing on his cold pipe, looking blankly at the minister over his pendulous nose?

He was not, of course, thinking of the fact that the Party he led had at its inception repudiated individual acts of terror. Nor that he had resorted to terror himself. As he sucked his pipe and looked at this red-cheeked, well-nourished, bold young fellow with the burning ears, Stalin was thinking what he always thought when he saw his eager, ingratiating subordinates.

His first thought always was: how far can this person be trusted? And his second: has not the moment come for this person to be liquidated?

Stalin knew all about Abakumov's secret wealth. But he was in no hurry to punish him. Stalin liked the fact that Abakumov was that kind of person. Self-seeking people are easier to understand and easier to manage. Most of all, Stalin was wary of people committed to staying poor, like Bukharin. He did not understand their motives.

But he could not trust even this understandable Abakumov. Mistrust was Iosif Djugashvili's determining trait. Mistrust was his world view.

He had not trusted his mother. And he had not trusted
that God before whom he had bowed his head to the stone
floor for eleven years of his youth. Later, he did not trust
his own fellow Party members, especially those who spoke
well. He did not trust his fellow exiles. He did not trust the
peasants to sow grain and reap harvests unless they were
coerced and their work was regularly checked on. He did not
trust workers to work unless production norms were set for
them. He did not trust members of the intelligentsia not to
commit sabotage. He did not trust soldiers and generals to
fight without the threat of penalty regiments and machine
guns in their rear. He did not trust his intimates. He did not
trust his wives and mistresses. He did not trust his children.
And he always turned out to be right.

He had trusted one person, one only, in a life filled with
mistrust, a person as decisive in friendship as in enmity.
Alone among Stalin's enemies, while the whole world
watched, he had turned around and offered Stalin his friendship.

And Stalin had trusted him.

That man was Adolf Hitler.

Stalin had watched with malicious delight as Hitler sub-
dued Poland, France, and Belgium, as his planes darkened
the skies over England. Molotov came back from Berlin
frightened. His intelligence officers reported that Hitler was
gathering his forces for war in the East. Hess flew off to
England. Churchill warned Stalin of an attack. All the jack-
daws in the Belorussian aspens and the Galician poplars
screamed of war. All the women in all the marketplaces
predicted war from day to day. Stalin alone remained un-
ruffled and carefree.

He had believed Hitler.

It had almost—but not quite—cost him his neck.

So now, once and for all, he mistrusted everyone.

Abakumov could have responded bitterly to this mistrust,
but he did not dare. It had been wrong for Stalin to wander
off the track, to have summoned that blockhead Petro Popi-
vod, for instance, and talk about newspaper articles attacking Tito. He should never have turned down, just on
the basis of their security questionnaires, those fine fellows

Abakumov had handpicked to hunt down the bear. He should have talked with them and come to trust them. Now, of course, the devil himself couldn't tell what would come of the assassination plan. All this loss of effectiveness angered Abakumov.

But he knew his Boss. One must never work full force for Stalin, never go all out. He did not tolerate the flat failure to carry out his orders, but he hated thoroughly successful performance because he saw in it a diminution of his own uniqueness. No one but himself must be able to do anything flawlessly.

So even when he seemed to be straining in harness, Abakumov was pulling at half-strength—and so was everyone else.

Just as King Midas turned everything to gold, Stalin turned everything to mediocrity.

But today it seemed to Abakumov, as he went on with his report, that Stalin's face was brightening. And when he had explained the details of the proposed explosion, the minister hastily reported on the Frunze Academy, then moved quickly on to the Theological Academy, and went on and on, avoiding the question of the telephone and trying not to look at the desk phone so as not to call the Leader's attention to it.

But Stalin was remembering! At this very moment he was remembering something, and it might be the telephone. His forehead gathered in heavy wrinkles and the cartilage of his big nose strained. He fixed his stubborn gaze on Abakumov (the minister tried to assume a forthright, honest look), but he could not remember! The evanescent thought slipped away. The wrinkles on his gray forehead faded helplessly.

Stalin sighed, packed his pipe and lighted it.

"Oh, yes," he said into the smoke of the first puff, recalling something else, not the main thought which had eluded him. "Has Gomulka been arrested?"

Gomulka had recently been removed from all his official posts, and had instantly fallen into the abyss.

"He has!" Abakumov said with relief, half-rising from his chair. (And the fact had already been reported to Stalin.) Arresting people was the easiest job his ministry had to handle.

Pressing a button on his desk, Stalin turned up the lights. The wall lamps blazed. He got up from his desk and, with his pipe trailing smoke, he began to walk. Abakumov understood that his report had been completed, that instructions would now be dictated. He opened the big notebook on his knees, took out a fountain pen, and prepared to write. The Leader liked to have his words written down.

But Stalin walked to the radio-phonograph and back, smoking and not saying a word, as if he had completely forgotten Abakumov. His gray, pockmarked face frowned in a tortured effort of recollection. As he passed Abakumov, the minister saw that the Leader's shoulders were hunched forward, making him appear even shorter, very small. And—though he usually forbade himself such reflections here, lest they be read by some kind of instrument hidden in the walls—Abakumov thought that the Little Father was not going to live another ten years, that he would die. Abakumov wanted it to happen soon. It seemed to all the intimates that when he did die, an easy, free life would begin.

Stalin was depressed by this new lapse of memory. His brain was refusing to serve him. Coming from the bedroom he had thought of what he wanted to ask Abakumov, and now he had forgotten it. In his impotence, he did not know which part of his brain to command to remember.

Suddenly he raised his head and stared at the wall. Something else had come to mind, not what he wanted to remember now but something he had been unable to recall two days before, in the Museum of the Revolution, something very unpleasant.

It had been 1937, the twentieth anniversary of the Revolution, when there was so much reinterpretation of history. He had decided to look over the museum exhibits to be sure they hadn't got something wrong. In one of the halls—the same one in which the enormous TV set now stood—he had seen as he entered two large portraits high on the opposite wall. The faces of Zhelyabov and Perovskaya were open, fearless, and they cried out to all who entered: "'Kill the tyrant!'"

Stalin, struck by their twin stares as by two shots, drew back, wheezed, coughed. His finger shook, pointing at the portraits.

They were removed immediately.

At the same time, the first relics of the Revolution—the fragments of Alexander II's carriage—were removed from the Kshesinskaya Palace.

From that very day, Stalin had ordered shelters and apartments to be built for him in various places. He lost his taste for dense city surroundings, and settled in this house in the suburbs, this low-ceilinged night office near the duty room of his personal guard.

And the more people's lives he took, the more he was oppressed by constant terror for his own. He contrived many improvements in the guard system, such as announcing who was to be on duty only an hour before the men were to take their posts, and mixing soldiers from different barracks in each detail. That way, they met for the first time when they came on duty, and for one day only, and thus had no chance to plot. He built his house like a labyrinth mousetrap, with three circles of fencing, and gates that weren't lined up with each other. And he had several bedrooms, and ordered which bed was to be made up just before he retired.

These arrangements did not seem to him signs of cowardice but merely the reasonable things to do. His person was priceless. Others, however, might not realize this. So as not to be conspicuous, he prescribed similar measures for all the *little* leaders in the capital and the provinces: he forbade them to go to the toilet unaccompanied by bodyguards, ordered them to travel in one of three identical automobiles moving in file.

In the night office, remembering the portraits, he stopped in the middle of the room, turned to Abakumov and said, waving his pipe in the air, "And what are you doing about security for Party executives?"

Cocking his head far to one side, he glared malevolently at his minister.

With his open notebook, Abakumov sat erect in his chair, facing the Leader—he did not stand, knowing that Stalin appreciated immobility in those he was talking to—and with complete readiness he began to speak of things he had never intended to mention. An immediate response was essential in a meeting with Stalin; he interpreted any kind of hesitation as a confirmation of his evil thoughts.

"Iosif Vissarionovich," began Abakumov in a voice trembling with injured feelings. "That's why we exist, our whole ministry, so that you, Iosif Vissarionovich, can work undisturbed, can think and guide the country."

Stalin had said "security for Party executives," but Abakumov knew that he wanted an answer only about himself.

"Every day I conduct checks, make arrests, investigate cases."

With his head still cocked like a crow with a wrung neck, Stalin watched him closely.

"Listen," he asked, "what about it? Are there still instances of terrorism? They haven't stopped?"

Abakumov sighed bitterly. "I would like to say that there are no cases of terrorism, but there are. We turn them up even in stinking back kitchens, even in the marketplace."

Stalin closed one eye; satisfaction was visible in the other. "That's good," he nodded. "So you're working."

"But, Iosif Vissarionovich," Abakumov said, unable to remain seated any longer before his Leader. He rose without fully straightening his legs. "But, Iosif Vissarionovich, we don't let those cases reach the stage of actual preparation. We catch them at the moment of inception, of intention, using Section 19."

"Good, good," Stalin said, and with a pacifying gesture he instructed Abakumov to be seated. (All he needed was to have such a carcass towering over him.) "So you believe there is still dissatisfaction among the people?"

Again Abakumov sighed and replied regretfully, "Yes, Iosif Vissarionovich. There is still a certain percentage . . ."

(It would have been a fine thing to say there was none! Why in that case should his ministry exist?)

"You are right," Stalin agreed. "And that means you have a job to do in State Security. Some people tell me no one is dissatisfied any more, that everyone who votes 'yes' in the elections is satisfied." Stalin smiled ironically. "That's political blindness! The enemy may vote 'yes,' but they have gone into hiding and they are still dissatisfied! Five percent, would you say? Or perhaps eight?"

Stalin was particularly proud of this insight of his, this capacity for self-criticism, this immunity to praise.

"Yes, Iosif Vissarionovich," Abakumov confirmed, "that's exactly right. Five percent, perhaps seven."

Stalin continued on his trajectory through the office and circled the desk.

"That's a fault of mine, Iosif Vissarionovich," Abakumov added, growing bold now that his ears were cool again. "I just can't be complacent."

Stalin lightly knocked his pipe on the ashtray. "And what about the mood of the young people?"

Question followed question like knives, and all it took was one mistake. If you were to answer "Good," that would be political blindness. If you said "Bad," you did not believe in the future. Abakumov gestured expressively with his hands and said nothing.

Stalin did not wait for a reply. He said with conviction, tapping his pipe, "We must pay more attention to the young people. We must be particularly intolerant toward the faults of the young people."

Abakumov caught himself and began to write.

Stalin was fascinated by his own thought; his eyes burned with a tiger-like gleam. He filled his pipe once more, lit it, and once again, more intently, paced the room.

"We must intensify our watch over the moods of the students! We must uproot not only individuals but entire groups! And we must take advantage of the full measure of punishment the law allows us—twenty-five years, not ten! Ten years—that's like school, not prison. You can give school-children ten. But anyone who has hair on his face— twenty-five! They're young, they'll survive."

Abakumov wrote assiduously. The first in a long series of gears had begun to turn.

"And it's time to put a stop to the vacation-resort conditions in political prisons! Beria told me that food parcels are still allowed in political prisons. Is that right?"

"We'll stop them! We'll forbid them!" Abakumov said with pain in his voice, continuing to write. "It's our mistake, Iosif Vissarionovich. Forgive us." (It really was an oversight! He could have figured that one out for himself.)

"How many times do I have to explain things to you? It's about time you understood once and for all."

He spoke without anger. In his softened eyes there was confidence in Abakumov—he would understand, he would learn. Abakumov could not remember when Stalin had spoken to him so simply and so benignly. The feeling of fear left him completely, and his brain worked like that of an ordinary person under ordinary conditions. And the problem which had long been troubling him, like a bone caught in his throat, now found expression.

His face enlivened, Abakumov said, "We understand, Iosif Vissarionovich!" He said, speaking for the whole ministry, "We understand: the class struggle is going to intensify! All the more reason, Iosif Vissarionovich, for you to see our situation—how our hands are tied by the abolition of the death penalty! We've been beating our heads against that wall for two and a half years. Now there is no legal way of processing the people we are going to shoot. It means the sentence has to be written out in two different versions. And then when we pay the executioners—there's no way to clear their fees through our accounting department, and the accounts get messed up. Then there's nothing to scare them with in the camps. How we need capital punishment! *Give us back capital punishment, Iosif Vissarionovich!*" Abakumov pleaded with all his heart, putting his hand to his chest and looking hopefully at the swarthy-faced Leader.

And it seemed that Stalin smiled, barely smiled. His coarse mustache quavered slightly.

"I know," he said quietly, understandingly. "I've thought about it."

Amazing! He knew about everything! He thought about everything! Even before he was asked. Like a reigning deity, he anticipated people's thoughts.

"One day soon I will give you back capital punishment," he said thoughtfully, looking outward, as if he were seeing years into the future. "It will be a good educational measure."

How could he help but think about that measure! More than anyone else he had suffered during the last two years for having yielded to the impulse to brag to the West, tricking himself into the belief that people were not totally depraved.

This had always been his distinctive trait as a statesman and military leader: neither dismissal, not ostracism, nor the insane asylum, nor life imprisonment, nor exile seemed to him sufficient punishment for a person he recognized as dangerous. *Death* was the only reliable means of settling accounts in full. And when his lower lids squinted, the sentence which shone in his eyes was always *death*.

On his scale, there was no lesser punishment.

From the bright distance into which he had just been staring, Stalin shifted his eyes to Abakumov, and suddenly they narrowed craftily.

"Aren't you afraid you'll be the first one we shoot?"

He hardly said "shoot" aloud, letting it hang on the fall of his voice like something to be guessed.

But the word tore into Abakumov like a winter frost. The Nearest and Dearest stood over him just out of Abakumov's reach and watched the minister's every feature to see how he was taking the joke.

Daring neither to stand up nor remain seated, Abakumov half-stood on his strained legs, which were trembling from tension.

"Iosif Vissarionovich! If I deserve it . . . If it's necessary . . ."

Stalin gazed wisely, penetratingly. At this moment he was silently debating his obligatory second thought about an intimate: had not the time come to get rid of him? He had long since toyed with that ancient key to popularity: first to encourage the executioners and then, in good time, to repudiate their immoderate zeal. He had done this many times and always successfully. Inevitably the moment would come when it would be necessary to throw Abakumov into the same pit.

"Correct!" Stalin said with a smile of goodwill, as if to approve his quickness of wit. "When you deserve it, we will shoot you."

He motioned to Abakumov to sit down again, thought for a moment, and then spoke more warmly than the Minister of State Security had ever heard him speak: "You will have a great deal of work soon, Abakumov. We are going to carry out the same measures as in 1937. Before a big war a big purge is necessary."

"But, Iosif Vissarionovich," Abakumov dared contradict, "do you think we aren't arresting people now?"

"You call that arresting—you'll see! And when the war comes, we'll be arresting still more people in other places. Strengthen the organizations! Staff, pay—I'll refuse you nothing."

Then he let him go in peace: "All right, go along."

Abakumov did not know whether he walked or flew through the reception room to pick up his briefcase from Poskrebyshev. Not only could he live another month, but wasn't this the beginning of a whole new era in his relations with the Boss?

True, there had been the threat that he would be shot— but that, after all, was a joke.

21

OLD AGE

The Immortal, stirred by great thoughts, paced his night office. A kind of inner music surged in him, a kind of enormous orchestra provided marching music for him.

Dissatisfied people? All right. There were always dissatisfied people and there always would be.

But reviewing in his mind the not-so-complex history of the world, Stalin knew that with time people would forgive everything bad, even forget it, even remember it as something good. Entire peoples were like Lady Anne, the widow in Shakespeare's *Richard III*. Their wrath was short-lived, their will not steadfast, their memory weak—they would always be glad to surrender themselves wholly to the victor.

That was why he had to live to ninety—because the battle was not yet finished, the building not completed, and there was no one to replace him.

To wage and win the last world war. To exterminate like gophers the Western social democrats and then all the others in the world who were still unbeaten. Then, of course, to raise the productivity of labor, solve the various economic problems. Only he, Stalin, knew the path by which to lead humanity to happiness, how to shove its face into happiness like a blind puppy's into a bowl of milk—"There, drink up!"

And afterward?

There was a real man—Bonaparte. He paid no attention to the yelping of the Jacobins, he declared himself emperor—and that was that.

There was nothing bad in the word "emperor." It simply meant "commander," "chief."

How would that sound, Emperor of the Planet? Emperor of the Earth!

There was not the least contradiction here with the idea of world Communism.

He paced and paced, and the orchestra played on.

And then perhaps they would find a medicine, some

means of making him, at least, immortal? No, they wouldn't be able to do it in time.

How could he leave humanity? In whose care? They'd make a mess of everything.

Well, all right. He would have more monuments to himself constructed, more and bigger ones. By that time technology would be able to help—what might be called indoctrination through monuments. Put a monument on the peak of Mount Kazbek and another on Mount Elbrus—so that his head would always be above the clouds. And then, all right, he could die—the Greatest of all the Great, without equal in the history of the earth.

Suddenly he stopped.

And up there? Higher? He had no equals, of course, but if there, up there . . .

Again he paced back and forth, but slowly.

Now and again that one unresolved question crept into Stalin's mind.

There was, in fact, nothing vague about it. Everything necessary had long since been proved, and what stood in the way had been disproved. It had been proved that matter cannot be destroyed and is not created. It had been proved that the universe is infinite. It had been proved that life began effortlessly in the warm ocean. It had been proved that it was impossible to prove that Christ had existed. It had been proved that all miraculous cures, spirits, prophecies, and thought transference were old wives' tales.

But the fabric of our soul, what we love and what we have grown accustomed to, is created in our youth, not afterward. Memories of childhood had recently come powerfully to life in Iosif.

Until the age of nineteen he had grown up on the Old and New Testaments, on the lives of the saints and church history. He helped celebrate the liturgies, he sang in the choir, and he used to love to sing Strokin's "Now You Are Forgiven." Even now he could sing it without missing a note. And how many times in the course of eleven years in school and in the seminary had he drawn near the icons and looked into their mysterious eyes! He wanted that photograph included even in his anniversary biography: graduate-of-the-church-school Djugashvili in a gray cassock with a closed collar; the dull, adolescent oval face exhausted from praying; the hair worn long, severely parted, in preparation for the priesthood, humbly smeared with lamp oil and combed down to his ears; only the eyes and strained brows giving any clue that this obedient pupil might become a metropolitan.

That very church inspector, Abakadze, who expelled Djugashvili from the seminary, had been left untouched on Stalin's orders. Let the old man live out his life.

And when on the third of July, 1941, in front of the microphone, his parched throat tightening with fear and tearful self-pity (for there is no heart entirely immune to pity), it was not by chance that the word "brethren" burst from his lips. Neither Lenin nor any other leader would have thought of saying it.

His lips said what they had learned to say in his youth.

Yes, and in those July days he had perhaps even prayed inside himself, just as certain other atheists crossed themselves involuntarily when the bombs were falling.

In recent years it was quite gratifying to him that the church in its prayers proclaimed him the Leader Elected of God. That was why he supported the center of the Russian Orthodox Church at Zagorsk with Kremlin funds. Stalin greeted no prime minister of a great power the way he greeted his own docile, decrepit Patriarch. He went to meet him at the outer doors, and he led him to the table by the arm. He had thought about finding a little estate for him somewhere, a country seat, and presenting it to him as a gift. The way they used to give, for the good of one's soul.

In general Stalin noticed in himself a predisposition not only toward Orthodoxy but toward other elements and words associated with the old world—that world from which he had come and which, as a matter of duty, he had been destroying for forty years.

In the thirties, for the sake of politics alone, he had resurrected the forgotten word "homeland," which had not been used for fifteen years and which had seemed almost a disgraceful term. Yet, with the years, he himself had come actually to enjoy pronouncing "Russia" and "homeland." He had come to like the Russian people very much—this people which never betrayed him, which went hungry for so many years, for as long as it was necessary, which had calmly gone forth to war, to the camps, into all kinds of hardship, and had never rebelled. After the victory Stalin had said with complete sincerity that the Russian people possess a clear mind, a staunch character, and patience.

With the years, Stalin himself had more and more come to wish that he, too, were recognized as a Russian.

He found something pleasing even in the words that evoked the old world: there should not be "heads of schools" but "directors"; not "commanding staff" but "the officer corps"; not the All-Russian Central Executive Committee but the Supreme Soviet ("Supreme" was a very fine word). Officers had to have "orderlies." High school girls were to study separately from boys, and wear pinafores, and pay tuition. The Soviet people should have a day of rest, like all Christians, on Sunday and not on impersonal numbered days. Only legal marriage should be recognized, as had been the case under the czar, even though he had had a hard time with it in his day. It did not matter what Engels thought about it in the depths of the sea.

It was right here in his night office that for the first time he had tried on in front of the mirror the old Russian shoulder boards—and felt real satisfaction.

In the final analysis, there was nothing shameful even in a crown, the highest sign of distinction. After everything had been said, it had still been a staunch world which had held firm for three hundred years. Why not borrow the best of it?

Although the surrender of Port Arthur could only gladden him when he was an exile escaping from Irkutsk Province, still he was not wrong when he said after Japan's surrender in 1945 that Port Arthur had been a stain on his pride and that of other older Russians.

Yes, yes, the old Russians! Stalin sometimes fell to thinking that, after all, it was not a matter of chance that he had established himself as head of this country, that he had won over its heart—he and not all those famous, protesting, goateed Talmudists, kinless, rootless, with nothing positive about them.

Here they were, right here, on these shelves—choked, shot, ground into manure in the camps, poisoned, burned, killed in automobile accidents or by their own hand. Eradicated, given over to anathema, apocryphal people by now— here they were all lined up! Every night they offered him their pages, they shook their little beards, they wrung their hands, they spat on him, they wheezed, they cried out to him from the shelves: "We warned you! You should have done it another way!" That was why Stalin had collected them all right here, so that he could be more spiteful at nighttime when he made decisions.

The invisible inner orchestra to which he marched was no longer keeping time; it had fallen silent.

His legs began to ache; he felt as if he were about to lose the use of them. His legs, from the waist down, had begun to fail him sometimes.

The master of half the world, dressed in the tunic of a generalissimo, slowly ran his finger along the shelves, passing his enemies in review.

And as he turned from the last shelf, he saw the telephone on his desk.

Something which had been evading him all night slipped from his memory again like the tip of a snake's tail.

He had wanted to ask Abakumov something. Had Gomulka been arrested?

He had it! Shuffling in his boots, he made his way to the writing desk, took the pen, and wrote on his calendar: "Secret telephony."

They had told him they had assembled the best people, that they had all the necessary equipment, that everyone was enthusiastic, that there were deadlines—so why wasn't it finished? Abakumov, the brazen fellow, had sat there a good hour, the dog, without saying one single word about it!

That was the way they all were, in all the organizations— every one of them tried to deceive the Leader! How can you trust them? How can you *not* work at night?

He staggered and sat down, not in his own armchair but on a small chair next to the desk.

The left side of his head seemed to be tightening at the temple and pulling in that direction. His chain of thoughts disintegrated. With an empty stare he circled the room, hardly seeing the walls.

Growing old like a dog. An old age without friends. An old age without love. An old age without faith. An old age without desire.

He did not even need his beloved daughter any longer, and she was permitted to see him only on holidays.

That sensation of fading memory, of failing mind, of loneliness advancing on him like a paralysis, filled him with helpless terror.

Death had already made its nest in him, and he refused to believe it.

22

THE PIT BECKONS AGAIN

When Colonel of Engineers Yakonov left the ministry by the side entrance on Dzherzhinsky Street and circled the black marble prow of the building beneath the pillars on Furkasovsky Lane, he did not recognize his own Pobeda right away and was about to open someone else's and get in.

The whole past night had been densely foggy. The snow which had begun falling in the early evening had melted at once and then stopped. Right now, just before dawn, the mist lay on the ground, and the water from the thaw was thinly covered by a fragile layer of ice.

It was turning cold.

Though it was almost 5 A.M., the skies were still pitch-black.

A first-year university student, who had been standing with his girl in an entryway all night, looked enviously at Yakonov as he got into the car. The student sighed, wondering whether he would live long enough to have a car. Not only had he never taken his girl out in one, but the only time he had driven anywhere was on the back of a truck going out to harvest on a collective farm.

But he did not know the man he was envying.

Yakonov's driver asked, "Home?"

Yakonov stared at him with a wild look. He held his pocket watch in his palm, but he did not see what time it showed.

"What? No."

"To Mavrino?" the driver inquired, surprised. Even though he had been waiting in a sheepskin coat and hood, he was shivering and wanted to go to sleep.

"No," answered the colonel of engineers, placing his hand over his heart.

The driver turned and looked at the boss's face in the faint light from the street lamps which penetrated the fogged window.

It was not the same man. Yakonov's lips—always so haughty and tightly pressed—were quivering helplessly.

He still held his watch in his palm, uncomprehending.

And although the driver had been waiting since midnight, and was angry at the colonel, swearing great oaths into his sheepskin collar and remembering all Yakonov's nasty actions during the past two years, he started off at random without asking any more questions. Slowly his rage left him.

It was so late that it was already early in the morning. Now and then they encountered a solitary automobile on the deserted streets of the capital. There were no police, no passers-by, and no robbers to steal the clothes off their backs. Soon the trolley-buses would start running.

The driver kept glancing back at the colonel; he had to decide where to go, after all. He had already driven to the Myasnitsky Gates and along Sretensky and Rozhdestvensky boulevards to Trubny Square, then turned onto Neglinnaya. But he couldn't drive around like this till morning.

Yakonov stared straight ahead, with a completely senseless, immobile look, seeing nothing.

He lived on Bolshaya Serpukhovka. The driver, calculating that the sight of the nearby streets would suggest to the colonel that he should go home, decided to cross the river to Zamoskvarechye. He went down Okhotny Ryad, turned at the Manège, and drove back across bleak, empty Red Square.

The crenelations of the Kremlin walls and the tops of the spruces beside them were touched with frost. The asphalt was gray and slippery. The mist seemed to be trying to disappear beneath their wheels.

They were about 200 yards away from the wall, from the wall's teeth, from the guard behind whom—as they might have imagined—the Greatest Man on Earth was ending his night. But they passed without even thinking about him.

When they had driven past St. Basil's Cathedral and turned left onto the Moscow River embankment, the driver slowed down and asked, "Would you like to go home, Comrade Colonel?"

That was precisely where he should be going. He probably had left fewer nights at home than fingers on his hands. But as a dog goes off to die by itself, Yakonov had to go anywhere but home to his family.

The Pobeda stopped. Gathering up the skirts of his thick

leather coat as he got out, he said to the driver, "You, brother, go on home and sleep. I'll get home by myself."

He sometimes called the driver "brother," but there was such grief in his voice it was as though he were saying good-bye forever.

A blanket of mist covered the Moscow River to the top of the embankment.

Without buttoning his coat, and with his colonel's high-peaked fur hat tipped a bit to one side, Yakonov, slipping a little, made his way along the embankment.

The driver wanted to call out to him, to drive along beside him, but then he thought to himself, "With a rank like that they probably don't go drowning themselves." He turned around and went home.

Yakonov walked down a long stretch of the embankment where there were no intersecting streets, a sort of endless wooden fence to his left, the river to his right. He walked in the middle of the asphalt, staring ahead at the distant street lights.

When he had gone a certain distance, he felt that this funereal walk all alone was giving him a simple satisfaction that he hadn't experienced in a long time.

When they had been summoned to the minister the second time, the situation was beyond remedy. It felt as though the universe had come crashing down. Abakumov had raged like a mad beast. He had stamped on their feet, chased them around the office, cursed at them, spat, barely missing them, and, with every intention of inflicting pain, he had punched Yakonov on his soft white nose, which had begun to bleed.

He had declared that Sevastyanov would be broken in rank to lieutenant and sent off to the Arctic forests. He had demoted Oskolupov to ordinary guard again, to serve at Butyrskaya Prison, where he had begun his career in 1925. And Yakonov, for deceiving him and for "second-offense sabotage," would be arrested and sent in dark-blue cover-alls to Number Seven, under Bobynin, to work on the speech clipper with his own two hands.

Then he had caught his breath and given them one more chance, the last deadline: January 22, the day of mourning for Lenin.

The big, tasteless office had rocked before Yakonov's eyes. He had tried to dry his nose with his handkerchief. He had stood there defenselessly before Abakumov, and thought

about the three human beings with whom he spent no more
than one hour a day, but on whose account he squirmed
and struggled and played the dictator during all the rest of
his waking hours: his two small children, eight and nine, and
his wife, Varyusha, all the dearer to him because he had
married her so late in life. He had married at the age of
thirty-six, just after leaving the very place to which the
minister's iron fist was now driving him back.

Then Sevastyanov took Oskolupov and Yakonov to his
office and threatened to put them both behind bars; he
would not tolerate being reduced in rank and sent to the
Arctic.

After that Oskolupov had taken Yakonov to his office and
stated with perfect frankness that he had come finally to
connect Yakonov's prison past with his present sabotage.

Yakonov approached the high concrete bridge which led
to the right, across the Moscow River. He did not attempt
to go around and climb up to it, but walked beneath it,
through a viaduct where a policeman was patrolling.

The policeman suspiciously watched the strange drunk
with the pince-nez and the colonel's tall fur hat.

This was where the Yauza River flowed into the Moscow
River. Yakonov crossed the short bridge, still not trying to
figure out where he was.

Yes, a deadly game had been going on, and its end was
near. Yakonov knew, he already felt, that insensate, unbearable pressure of hurry when people are tied hand and foot
by arbitrary, impossible, crippling time limits. It was a
squeeze, a wringing out . . . faster . . . more, still more . . .
an honorary extra shift . . . a competitive duty . . . fulfillment
of goal ahead of schedule . . . even further ahead of schedule. . . . When things were done this way, houses did not
stand, bridges broke down, construction collapsed, harvests
rotted or the seed did not come up at all. But until the great
truth dawned that one cannot demand the superhuman
from a human being, those trapped in this vortex had no
other way out except to get sick, to get caught in the gears
and injured, to have an accident—and then wait it out in a
hospital or sanatorium.

Always up to now Yakonov had managed to jump nimbly
out of situations which were being irrevocably wrecked by
hurry and into others which were either calmer and more
settled or still in the early stages.

But this once, this one time, he felt he could not get out of it. He could not save the speech-clipper project that quickly. He could not go anywhere else.

And he could not get out of it by getting sick.

He stood at the parapet of the embankment and looked down. The mist lay on the ice, not concealing it, and directly below, where it had melted, Yakonov could see a black hole of moving water.

The black pit of the past—prison—again opened before him, again called him to return.

Yakonov considered the six years he had spent there a foul disgrace, a plague, the greatest failure of his life.

He had been imprisoned in 1932 when he was a young radio engineer, who had by then been sent on foreign assignments twice (it was because of those foreign assignments that he had been arrested). He had been among the first zeks who, in accordance with Dante's concept, had made up one of the first sharashkas.

How he wanted to forget his prison past! And to have others forget it, too. And to have fate forget it. How he kept away from those who reminded him of that unhappy time, who had known him as a prisoner.

Abruptly he stepped back from the parapet, cut across the embankment boulevard, and started to climb steeply uphill. A well-trampled path skirted the fence of still another construction project; it was coated with ice, but it was not very slippery.

Only the MGB's central card file knew that now and then former zeks hid in MGB uniforms.

Two, in addition to Yakonov, had been at Mavrino.

Yakonov had carefully avoided them, tried never to have any conversation with them except in the line of work, and never stayed alone in the office with them, so that no one would get the wrong idea.

One of them—Knyazhetsky, a seventy-year-old chemistry professor, a favorite student of Mendeleyev, had completed his ten-year term. Then, in view of a long list of scientific accomplishments, he had been sent to Mavrino as a free employee and had worked there for three years after the war, until the lash of the Decree on Strengthening the Rear struck him down. One noon he was summoned to the ministry by phone and did not return. Yakonov remembered how he had gone down the red-carpeted stairs of the institute, shaking his silvery head, still not understanding why they were summoning him for "half an hour." And behind him, on the upper landing of the staircase, Security Officer Shikin was already using his pen knife to clip the professor's photograph from the honor lists on the bulletin board.

The second was Altynov. He had not been a famous scientist, but simply a businesslike worker. After his first term he had been reticent, suspicious, with the canny distrust of a member of the prison tribe. And as soon as the Decree on Strengthening the Rear began to make its first sweeps around the boulevards ringing the capital, Altynov simulated heart trouble and was admitted to a heart clinic. He simulated it so effectively and for such a long time that by now the doctors had no hopes of saving him. His friends had stopped their whispering, understanding that his heart, worn out by so many years of shifts and dodges, had simply not held up.

So Yakonov, doomed the previous year for being a former zek, was now doubly doomed as a saboteur.

The pit was calling its children back.

Yakonov made his way up the vacant lot, not noticing where he was going, not noticing the rise. Finally, shortness of breath brought him to a stop. His legs were tired, his ankles strained from the unevenness of the ground.

And then, from the high spot he had climbed to, he looked around him with eyes which now perceived what they saw, and tried to work out where he was.

In the hour since he had left his car, the night had gotten colder; it was almost over. The mist had lifted and disappeared. The ground beneath his feet was strewn with pieces of brick, gravel, broken glass, and there was a crooked wooden shed or booth near him. Below was the fence along which he had walked, surrounding a large area where construction had not yet begun. And, though there was no snow, it all loomed white with hoarfrost.

On that hill so near the center of the capital, which had undergone some strange devastation, white steps rose, about seven of them, then stopped, then, it seemed, began again.

Some dull recollection stirred Yakonov at the sight of those white steps on the hill. He climbed them uncomprehending, and continued up the hard-packed cinder pile above them, and then up more steps. They led to a building, dimly outlined in the darkness, a building of strange form, which appeared to be ruined yet, at the same time, whole.

Were these bomb ruins? But there were no such places left in Moscow. Other forces had visited ruin on this place.

A stone landing separated one flight of steps from the next. And now big stone fragments obstructed his climb. The steps led up to the building in rises, like the entrance to a church.

They ended at broad iron doors, shut tight and piled knee-deep with caked gravel.

Yes, yes! The memory lashed Yakonov. He looked around. The river, a curving line of lights, wound far below, its strangely familiar bend disappearing under the bridge and continuing beyond it, toward the Kremlin.

But the bell tower? It was not there. And those piles of stone—were they all that was left of it?

Yakonov's eyes grew hot. He squinted.

He sat down gently on the stone fragments which littered the church portico.

Twenty-two years before he had stood on this very place with a girl called Agniya.

23

THE CHURCH OF ST. JOHN THE BAPTIST

He pronounced her name aloud—Agniya—and, like a breath of air, completely fresh and long-forgotten sensations stirred in his middle-aged, well-fed body.

He had been twenty-six then and she twenty-one.

The girl was not born of this earth. It was her misfortune to be high-minded and demanding to an incredible degree. Sometimes her eyebrows and nostrils quivered like wings when she spoke. No one had ever spoken so severely to Yakonov, upbraided him so harshly for actions which seemed to him quite ordinary. She, astonishingly, considered them base and mean. And the more faults she found in Yakonov, the more he became attached to her. It was very strange.

One could only argue with her very cautiously. She was so frail she would become exhausted from climbing a hill, from running, even from a spirited conversation. It was easy to offend her.

Nevertheless she found the strength to walk in the woods day after day, though, curiously enough, this city girl never took books along. Books would have been in the way, would have distracted her from the forest. She simply wandered there, and she would sit studying the secrets of the woods. When Yakonov went with her, he was astounded at her observations: why the trunk of a birch was bent toward the ground; how the shades of color in the forest grass change at evening time. He did not notice things of that sort himself; the forest was the forest, the air was lovely, and everything was green. But she even skipped the descriptions of nature in Turgenev; their superficiality offended her.

"Forest Brook"—that was what Yakonov called her in the summer of 1927, which they spent at neighboring houses. They went out together and they came back together and in everyone's eyes they were considered to be engaged.

But things were, in fact, very different.

Agniya was neither pretty nor ugly. Her face changed often: she might show a winning and comely smile, or she might wear a long face, tired and unattractive. She was taller than average, but slender and fragile; her walk was so light she seemed not to touch the earth at all. And although Yakonov was already quite experienced, and valued substantial flesh in a woman's body, something other than her body drew him to Agniya. And because he was attracted to her, he told himself that she also pleased him as a woman, that she would blossom.

But while she was glad to share the long summer days with Yakonov, walking miles with him into the forest depths, lying beside him in grassy glades, only reluctantly would she let him take her arm. When he did, she would ask, "Why that?" and try to free herself. And this wasn't because of embarrassment in front of other people, for when they got near a settlement, as a concession of his vanity she would compliantly walk arm in arm with him.

Telling himself he loved her, Yakonov confessed his love, falling at her feet on the woodland grass. "How sad," she said, "I feel that I'm deceiving you. I can't answer you. I don't feel anything. That's why I don't even want to go on living. You are intelligent and wonderful, and I should be happy, but I don't want to live."

She talked this way, and yet every morning she waited eagerly to see whether there were any changes in his face, in his attitude.

She talked this way, but she would also say: "There are lots of girls in Moscow. In the fall you'll meet one who is beautiful, and you'll stop being in love with me."

She let him embrace and even kiss her, but when she did, her lips and her hands were lifeless. "How difficult it is!" she lamented. "I thought love was the coming of a fiery angel. And here you love me, and I shall never meet anyone better than you, yet it doesn't make me happy, and I don't want to live at all."

There was something backward about her, something childlike. She feared the mysteries which bind a man and a woman in marriage, and with a sinking voice she asked, "Can't we do without that?" And Yakonov answered excitedly, "But that's not the main thing at all! It's only something that goes with spiritual communion." Then for the first time her lips moved weakly in a kiss, and she said, "Thank you. Otherwise, without love, why would anyone want to live? I think I am beginning to love you. I'll certainly try to."

That same fall they were walking one early evening along the side streets off Taganka Square, when Agniya said in her woodsy voice, which was difficult to hear above the city roar, "Would you like me to show you one of the most beautiful places in Moscow?"

She led him up to a fence surrounding a small brick church which was painted white and red, whose sanctuary, with the main altar, backed on a crooked, nameless side street. Inside the fence there was only a narrow pathway circling the tiny church for processions of the Cross, just wide enough for the priest and the deacon to walk side by side. Through the grated windows of the church one could see, deep inside, the peaceful flames of altar candles and colored icon lamps. And at one corner inside the fence grew a large old oak, taller than the church. Its branches, already yellow, overshadowed even the cupola and the side street, making the church seem very tiny indeed.

"That's the church of St. John the Baptist," said Agniya.

"But it's not the most beautiful place in Moscow."

"Just wait."

She led him through the gate posts into the courtyard. The flagstones were covered with yellow and orange oak leaves. In the shadow of the oak stood an ancient, tent-shaped bell tower. The tower and a little house attached to the church blocked the already sinking sun. The iron double doors of the north vestibule were open, and an old pauper woman standing there bowed and crossed herself at the radiant singing of vespers from within.

"*This church was famous for its beauty and its splendor,*" Agniya half-whispered, holding her shoulder close to his.

"What century is it?"

"Why must you know the century? Isn't it lovely?"

"Very pretty, of course, but not—"

"Look!" said Agniya, freeing herself from his arm and drawing him closer to the main portico. They came out of the shadow into a blaze of light from the setting sun, and she sat down on the low stone parapet.

Yakonov drew in his breath. It was as if they had suddenly emerged from the crowded city onto a height with a broad, open view into the distance. A long, white stone stairway fell away from the portico in many flights and landings, down the hill to the Moscow River. The river burned in the sunset. On the left lay the Zamoskvorechye, casting blinding yellow reflections from its windows, and below, almost at one's feet, the black chimneys of the Moscow Electric Power Plant poured smoke into the sunset sky. Into the Moscow River flowed the gleaming Yauza; beyond it to the right stretched the Foundling Hospital; and behind it rose the sharp contours of the Kremlin. Still farther off the five gilded cupolas of the Cathedral of Christ the Saviour flamed in the sun.

And in this golden radiance Agniya, with a yellow shawl around her shoulders and seeming golden, too, sat looking into the sun.

"How well the old Russians chose sites for churches and monasteries!" she said, her voice breaking. "I've been down the Volga River, and down the Oka, too, and everywhere they're built on the most majestic sites."

"Yes, that's Moscow!" Yakonov echoed.

"But it's disappearing, Anton," said Agniya. "Moscow is disappearing!"

"What do you mean, disappearing? That's nonsense."

"They're going to tear this church down," Agniya persisted.

"How do you know they're going to tear it down?" he said, growing angry. "It's an architectural monument; they'll leave it." He looked at the tiny tentlike bell tower, where the oak branches almost touched the bells.

"They'll tear it down!" Agniya predicted with conviction, sitting as immobile as before, in her yellow shawl in the yellow light.

Not only had her family not brought Agniya up to believe in God, but in the past when one had been obliged to go to church her mother and grandmother did not go, did not observe the fasts, did not take Communion, snubbed the priests, and always ridiculed religion because it had accepted serfdom so easily. Her grandmother, mother, and aunt had their own creed: always be on the side of those who were oppressed, arrested, pursued, and persecuted by the authorities. Her grandmother had evidently been known by all the "People's Will" revolutionaries because she gave them refuge in her home and helped them in whatever way she could. Her daughters took after her and hid fugitive Social Revolutionaries and Social Democrats. And little Agniya was always on the side of the rabbit that was being hunted, of the horse that was being whipped. As she grew up, this came to mean, to the surprise of her elders, that she was for the church because it was supposedly being persecuted.

Whether she came thereby to believe in God or forced herself to believe, in any case she insisted that it would now be ignoble to avoid church, and to her mother's and her grandmother's horror she began to attend services and little by little came to care about them.

"How, in your opinion, are they persecuting the church?" Yakonov asked in astonishment. "No one stops them from ringing their bells; they can bake their Communion bread the way they please; they have their processions with the Cross—but they should not have anything to do with civic affairs or education."

"Of course it's persecuted," Agniya objected, as always quietly, softly. "If they speak out against the church, publish whatever they want against it and don't permit it to defend itself, when they inventory religious property and exile priests —isn't that persecution?"

"Where have you seen them being exiled?"

"Not on the streets, that's certain."

"And even if they are persecuted," Yakonov insisted, "that means they've been persecuted for ten years! And how long did the church persecute people—ten centuries?"

"I wasn't alive then," said Agniya shrugging her narrow shoulders. "After all, I'm living now. I see what happens in my own lifetime."

"But you must know your history! Ignorance is no excuse! Have you never wondered how the church managed to survive 250 years of the Tatar yoke?"

"It could mean that faith went deep," she ventured. "Or that Orthodoxy was spiritually stronger than Islam?" she asked, without affirming it.

Yakonov smiled condescendingly.

"You have a wild imagination! Was our country ever Christian in its *soul*? Do you really think that during the thousand years of the church's existence people really forgave the oppressors? Or that they loved those who hated us? Our church lasted because after the invasion Metropolitan Cyril, before any other Russian, went and bowed down before the Khan and requested protection for the clergy. It was with the Tatar sword that the Russian clergy protected its lands, its serfs, and its religious services! And, in fact, Metropolitan Cyril was right, he was a realist in politics. That's just what he should have done. That's the only way to win."

When Agniya was pressed hard, she did not argue. She looked at her fiancé with new bewilderment.

"That's what all those beautiful churches with their splendid sites were built on!" Yakonov thundered. "And on schismatics being burned to death. And on members of dissenting sects being flogged to death. So you've found whom to take pity on—the persecuted church!"

He sat down next to her on the sun-warmed stone of the parapet.

"And in every way you're unjust to the Bolsheviks. You haven't taken the trouble to read their major books. They have great respect for world culture. They believe no person should have arbitrary power over another person, they believe in the realm of reason. The main thing is they are for equality! Imagine it: universal, complete, absolute equality. No one will have privileges others don't have. No one will have an advantage either in income or in status. Could there possibly be anything better than such a society? Isn't it really worth all the sacrifices?"

(Apart from the desirability of this society, Anton's social background made it essential for him to *attach* himself to it as early and as effectively as possible, while it was still not too late.)

"And these affectations are only going to block your path to the institute. And what does your protest amount to anyway? What can you do about it?"

"What can a woman ever do?" She tossed her fine braids—she wore braids at a time when no one did, when everyone had cut them off, and she wore them only out of contrariness even though they did not suit her. One fell down her back, the other on her breast. "A woman can do nothing but keep a man from performing great deeds. Even a woman like Natasha Rostov. That's why I can't bear her."

"Why?" Yakonov asked in surprise.

"Because she didn't let Pierre join the Decembrists!" And her voice broke again.

Well, she was made up of such surprises.

The diaphanous yellow shawl slid down over her shoulders and hung on her arms like a pair of thin, golden wings.

With his two hands Yakonov cupped her elbow as if he feared to break it.

"And you would have let him go?"

"Yes," Agniya said simply.

He himself could not think of any great deed for which he would have needed Agniya's permission. His life was very active. His work was interesting and was leading him higher and higher.

Past them now came late-arriving worshipers who had climbed up from the embankment. They crossed themselves at the open church doors. Entering the churchyard, the men removed their caps. It seemed there were many fewer men than women, and no young people at all.

"Aren't you afraid you'll be seen near a church?" Agniya asked without intending any derision, but sounding derisive nonetheless.

Those were the years when to be noticed near a church by one's fellow employees was actually dangerous. Indeed, Yakonov did feel he was too conspicuous here.

"Take care, Agniya," he cautioned, beginning to be irritated. "One must recognize what is new in time, before it is too late, for whoever fails to do so will fall hopelessly behind. You've been attracted to the church because it encourages your indifference to life. Once and for all, you must wake up and force yourself to be interested in something—if only in the life process itself."

Agniya hung her head, and her hand, wearing Yakonov's gold ring, drooped listlessly. Her childlike body seemed bony and terribly thin.

"Yes, yes," she said in a sinking voice. "I admit that it's sometimes very hard for me to live, I don't want to at all. The world doesn't need people like me."

He felt himself breaking up inside. She was doing everything to kill her attraction for him! The courage to carry out his promise and marry Agniya was weakening.

She glanced up at him with a look of curiosity, unsmiling.

"She *is* plain," Yakonov thought.

"Surely fame and success await you, and lasting prosperity," she said sadly. "But *will you be happy*, Anton? Be careful yourself. People who interest themselves in the *process* of life lose . . . they lose . . . But how can I tell you?" Her fingertips were seeking her words, and the torment of her search showed in the pained little smile on her face. "There— the bell has rung, the sound of singing has died, and it won't come back; yet all the music is there. Do you understand?"

Then she persuaded him to go inside. Under massive arches a gallery whose small windows had gratings in the ancient Russian style ringed the church. A low, open archway under the gallery led to the nave. Through the narrow windows of the cupola the sinking sun filled the church with light, scattering gold over the iconostas and the mosaic image of the Lord of Hosts.

There were few worshipers. Agniya placed a thin candle on the large brass pillar and, barely crossing herself, stood austerely, her hands clenched at her breast, looking straight ahead, entranced. And the scattered light of sunset and the orange glitter of the candles restored life and warmth to her cheeks.

It was two days before the birthday of the Mother of God, and a long litany was sung in praise of her. The litany was infinitely eloquent, the attributes and praises of the Virgin Mary rolled forth in a torrent, and for the first time Yakonov understood the ecstasy and poetry of the prayer. No

soulless church pedant had written that litany, but some
great unknown poet, some prisoner in a monastery; and he
had been moved not by passing lust for a woman's body but
by that higher rapture a woman can draw from us.

. . . Yakonov awoke from his reverie. He was sitting on
the portico of the Church of St. John the Baptist on a
mound of jagged fragments, dirtying his leather coat.

Yes, for no real reason they had wrecked the tent-shaped
bell tower and the stairs descending to the river. It was incredible that this December dawn was breaking on the same
square yards of Moscow earth where they had been that
sunny evening. But the view from the hill was still as distant,
and the bends of the river traced by the lamps were just the
same.

Soon after that evening he had gone on his assignment
abroad. And when he returned, they had given him a newspaper article to write—or, rather, to sign—about the disintegration of the West, its society, its morality, its culture,
about the impoverished condition of the intelligentsia and
the impossibility of science making any progress there. It
was not the complete truth, but it was not exactly a lie
either. The facts existed, though there were other facts, too.
Hesitation on Yakonov's part might have aroused suspicion,
harmed his reputation. And, after all, whom could such an
article hurt?

The article was published.

Agniya sent him back his ring by mail, tying to it a piece
of paper on which she had written: "For Metropolitan Cyril."

And he had felt a sense of relief.

. . . He got up and, standing as tall as he could, peered
through one of the little grated windows of the gallery. It
smelled of raw bricks, chill, and mold. What was inside was
ill-defined: heaps of broken stone and trash.

Yakonov turned from the window; his heartbeat slowed
and he leaned against the stone embrasure of the rusty door
which had not been opened for many years.

Again the icy weight of Abakumov's threat struck him.

Yakonov was at the peak of his visible power. He held
high rank in a powerful ministry. He was intelligent, talented
—and reputed to be intelligent and talented. His loving wife
awaited him at home. His red-cheeked children slept in their

little beds. He had an excellent apartment in an old Moscow building. It had high-ceilinged rooms and a balcony. His monthly salary was measured in the thousands. A Pobeda assigned to him personally awaited his phone call. Yet he stood leaning with his arms against dead stones, and he did not want to live any longer. Everything was so hopeless within him that he had no strength to move.

It was growing light.

There was a sparkling purity in the festive, frosty air. Abundant hoarfrost furred the broad stump of the felled oak, the cornices of the almost-wrecked church, the fretwork gratings on its windows, the electric wiring leading to the next house, and, below, a stretch of the long, circular fence around the construction site of the future skyscraper.

24

SAWING WOOD

It was growing light.

The regal, lavish hoarfrost covered not only the fence posts of the zone and prezone area, but also the barbed wire, twisted into a thousand tiny stars and braided into a score of strands, the sloping roof of the watchtower, and the tall weeds on the vacant land beyond the wire.

Dmitri Sologdin gazed wide-eyed at this miracle and took delight in it. He stood by a saw horse for cutting firewood. He wore a work-camp padded jacket over his blue coveralls; his head was uncovered and his hair showed the first gray streaks. He was an insignificant slave with no rights. He had already been imprisoned twelve years, but because of his second sentence there was no end to prison in sight for him. His wife's youth had withered in fruitless waiting. So as not to be fired from her present job, as she had been fired from others many times, she had lied, saying that her husband did not exist, and she had ceased all correspondence with him. Sologdin had never seen his only son. His wife had been pregnant when he was arrested. Sologdin had survived the forests of Cherdynsk north of the Urals, and the mines of Vorkuta beyond the Arctic Circle, and two interrogations, the first lasting half a year and the second a year. There had been sleeplessness, exhaustion, and loss of body fluids. Long ago his name and his future had been trampled into the mud. His personal property was a used pair of padded cotton pants, now kept in the prisoners' check room in expectation of worse times ahead. For money he received thirty rubles a month, not in cash. He could breathe fresh air only at certain fixed hours permitted by the prison administration.

Yet there was inviolable peace in his soul. His eyes shone like those of a youth. His chest bared to the frost rose with the fullness of life.

His muscles, which had become like dry strings during the course of the interrogations, had again grown solid and begged for action. Therefore, voluntarily and without any compensation, he went out every morning to saw and split firewood for the prison kitchen.

However, the ax and the saw—awesome weapons in the hands of a zek—were not entrusted to him so simply. The prison administration, which was paid to suspect perfidy in the zeks' most innocent acts, judging others by themselves, could simply not believe that a person would willingly agree to work for nothing. Therefore Sologdin was strongly suspected of preparing an escape or an armed uprising. An order was issued to post a guard five yards away from Sologdin while he worked so that the guard could watch every movement he made, and yet stay out of range of the ax. There were people available for this dangerous duty, and the relationship itself—one guard to one worker—did not seem extravagant to an administration indoctrinated in the good moral values of GULAG. But Sologdin got stubborn, thereby only intensifying their suspicions. He declared intemperately that he would not work in the presence of a personal guard. For some time the cutting of firewood stopped altogether. (The head of the prison could not compel the zeks to work—it was not a camp, and the zeks were engaged in cerebral work and were not under his jurisdiction.) The basic problem was that the planning officials and the accounting office had not made provision to have this sort of work done by the kitchen help. Therefore the free women employees who prepared the prisoners' food refused to cut wood be-

cause they were not paid for it. The administration tried to
send off-duty guards to do the job, interrupting their domino
game in the guardroom. They were all young fellows who
had been chosen because of their good health; however, in
the course of their years of service in the guard corps they
had evidently lost their ability to work—their backs began
to ache, and the domino game attracted them. They simply
could not seem to cut as much wood as was needed. And so
the head of the prison had to give in. Sologdin and other
prisoners who came out to work with him—most often
Nerzhin and Rubin—were permitted to cut and saw without a special guard. Anyway, they could all be seen from the
watchtower as though held in the palm of a hand, and the
duty officers were instructed to keep an eye on them from
around corners.

As the darkness scattered and the fading lamplight mingled
with the light of day, the janitor Spiridon appeared around
the building; he was wearing a pea jacket and a fur cap
with big ear flaps which had been issued to him alone. The
janitor was a zek, too, but he was under the orders of the
institute administration and not that of the prison. It was
therefore only to avoid a dispute that he sharpened the saw
and axes for the prison administration. As the janitor approached, Sologdin noticed that he was carrying the saw
which had been missing from its place.

At any hour between reveille and lights-out Spiridon Yegorov walked around in the yard, on which machine guns were
always trained, without any accompanying guard. The administration had decided on this bold step because Spiridon
was totally blind in one eye and had only 30 percent vision
in the other. Though there were supposed to be three
janitors at the sharashka, according to the table of organization, since the yard actually consisted of several connecting yards with a total area of about five acres, Spiridon,
not knowing this, coped with the work alone and was none
the worse for it. The main thing was that he ate a stomach-
ful here, not less than three pounds of black bread a day
because you could eat as much bread as you liked, and the
boys let him have their kasha, too. Spiridon obviously had
put on weight and grown soft since his time at SevUrallag,
since his three winters of timbering and three springs of
timber-rafting when he had nursemaided many thousands of
logs.

"Hey, Spiridon!" shouted Sologdin impatiently.

"What?"

Spiridon's mobile face, with its grayish-red mustache, grayish-red eyebrows and reddish skin, often assumed a ready and willing expression when he was spoken to, as it did now. Sologdin did not know that too great a show of readiness and willingness on Spiridon's part was a sign of derision.

"What do you mean, what? That saw won't cut."

"Why shouldn't it cut?" Spiridon asked in surprise. "How you've complained this winter! Well, let's give it a try."

And he handed him one end of the saw.

They began to saw. Once or twice the blade jumped its groove as if it did not wish to settle in it, then it bit in and caught.

"You're holding it very tight," Spiridon advised cautiously. "Hold the handle with three fingers, like a pen, and pull it where it wants to go, smooth. . . . That's the way. When you pull it toward you, don't jerk it."

Each of them savored his clear superiority over the other —Sologdin because he knew theoretical mechanics, the resistance of materials, and many other scientific matters; Spiridon because all material things were obedient to him. But Sologdin did not conceal his condescension toward the janitor. Spiridon hid his for the engineer.

Even cutting through the center of the thick log the saw did not jam and went zinging along, spitting yellowish pine sawdust on the coveralls of both men.

Sologdin laughed. "You're a miracle worker, Spiridon! You fooled me. You sharpened the saw yesterday, and set it!"

Spiridon, satisfied, chanted in time with the saw: "It eats away, chews it up in little pieces, doesn't swallow it itself, gives it away—"

And, with a shove, he broke off the log before it was completely sawed through.

"I didn't sharpen it at all," he said, showing the engineer the cutting edge of the saw. "Look at the teeth yourself. They're the same as yesterday."

Sologdin examined the teeth and indeed found no fresh marks. But the rogue had done something to the saw.

"Well, Spiridon, let's saw up one more."

"No," said Spiridon, putting his hand to his back. "I'm dead tired. Whatever my grandfathers and great-grandfathers didn't finish they piled on me. And your friends will be coming."

However, the friends did not come.

It had grown quite light. A jubilant frosty morning had burned through. All the ground and even the gutters of the eaves were covered with gray frost, and it crowned the lindens far off in the exercise yard.

"How did you get into the sharashka, Spiridon?" Sologdin asked, peering at the janitor.

He had to talk to someone. In his many camp years Sologdin had associated only with educated people, never supposing there was anything worthwhile to be learned from anyone uncultured.

"Yes," said Spiridon smacking his lips. "They scraped together scientific people like you here, and I came in under the same arch. In the card file my card says I'm a 'glass blower.' Well, I really was a glass blower once—a master glass blower at our factory in Bryansk. That was a long time ago, and now my eyesight has gone, and the kind of work we did there has nothing to do with what's done here. Here they need a skilled glass blower like Ivan. We never had one like that at our factory, ever. But they wrote it on the file card anyway. So when I got here, they looked me over to see what I was, and they wanted to send me back again. But thanks to the commandant they took me on as a janitor."

Nerzhin appeared around the corner, coming from the direction of the exercise yard and the isolated one-story headquarters building of the prison staff. He was wearing a padded jacket over his unbuttoned coveralls, and a government-issue towel so short it was almost square hung around his neck.

"Good morning, friends," he greeted them brusquely, undressing as he walked, throwing off his coveralls and stripping off his undershirt.

"Gleb, have you gone mad? Where do you see any snow?" Sologdin asked, looking at him askance.

"Here," Nerzhin replied gloomily, clambering onto the cellar roof. There was a thin furry layer of what could be either snow or frost, and collecting handfuls of it, Nerzhin began vigorously to rub his chest, back, and sides. All winter he would rub himself with snow down to his waist, though if the guards happened to be near, they stopped him.

"Ah! You're steaming away!" Spiridon said, shaking his head.

"Still no letter, Spiridon Danilich?" Nerzhin asked.

"There certainly is!"

"Why didn't you bring it to me to read to you? Is everything all right?"

"There's a letter, but I can't get it. The Snake has it."

"Myshin? He won't give it to you?" Nerzhin stopped his rubdown.

"He put my name on the mail list, but the commandant made me straighten out the attic in the mail period. So by the time I got down there the Snake had stopped giving out mail. Now I have to wait till Monday."

"The bastards!" growled Nerzhin.

"That's why there's a devil—to judge the priests," Spiridon said with a shrug, looking sideways at Sologdin, whom he didn't know very well. "Well, I'm on my way."

And with the flaps of his fur cap flopping comically on either side, like a mongrel's ears, Spiridon marched off in the direction of the guardhouse, where no other zek was allowed.

"The ax! Spiridon! Where's the ax?" Sologdin called after him.

"The duty officer will bring it," Spiridon answered and disappeared.

"Well," said Nerzhin, energetically wiping his chest and back with the mesh towel, "I haven't exactly pleased Yakonov. It seems my attitude toward Number Seven is that it's 'a drunkard's corpse at the Mavrino fence.' Besides that, yesterday he proposed that I transfer to the cryptographic group, and I refused."

Sologdin cocked his head and smiled ironically—firm, rounded teeth, untouched by decay but thinned out during the ordeal of camp, gleamed between his trim reddish-gray mustache and his beard.

"You're not acting like a 'calculator' but like a 'versifier.'"

Nerzhin was not surprised. This was one of Sologdin's well-known eccentricities—to speak in what he called the Language of Maximum Clarity, making no use of what he called "bird words," or words of foreign derivation. It was impossible to know whether he was playing a game or believed in this fancy. Very energetically, sometimes resourcefully, sometimes clumsily, he twisted and turned, trying to avoid in his speech even such essential words as "engineer" and "metal." In his conversations at work and even with the bosses he tried to follow the same line and sometimes made them wait until he had thought up a word.

This would have been impossible if Sologdin had tried to ingratiate himself with the administration, to get more important work, to receive a better food ration. But it was just the other way around. By every possible means Sologdin avoided the attention of the authorities and spurned their favors.

And so at the sharashka he became a permanent "character" among the zeks, recognized as such by all.

He had many other eccentricities. Sleeping all winter long under a window, he insisted on having the window open no matter how cold it was. And there was that completely unnecessary work of cutting firewood every morning, in which he had involved both Nerzhin and Rubin. But his chief quirk was to utter some nonsensical, utterly wild opinion on every question, such as that prostitution is a moral good or that D'Anthès was in the right in his duel with Pushkin; and he would defend that opinion with inspired enthusiasm and sometimes a certain degree of success, his youthful blue eyes sparkling, his sparse teeth gleaming. And sometimes it was impossible to be sure whether he was being serious or only mocking. When he was accused of absurdity, he laughed heartily. "You lead boring lives, gentlemen! We can't all have the same views and the same standards. What would happen? There would be no more argument, no exchange of opinion. It would bore a dog!"

And he supposedly used the word "gentlemen" instead of "comrades" because, having been away from freedom for twelve years, he did not remember how things were *there*.

Right now Nerzhin, still half naked, was finishing drying himself with the fragment of towel.

"Yes," he said cheerlessly. "Unfortunately, Lev is right— I'll never turn out to be a skeptic. I want to have a hand in events."

He put on the undershirt, which was too small for him, and pushed his arms into his coveralls.

Sologdin stood there, leaning theatrically against the saw horse, his arms crossed on his chest.

"That's good, my friend. Your 'aggravated doubt'—" in

the Language of Maximum Clarity this was the usual phrase for "skepticism"—"had to be abandoned someday. You're no longer a boy." (Nerzhin was five years younger than Sologdin.) "And you ought to find out where you are, spiritually understand the role of good and evil in human life. There's no better place to do it than prison."

Sologdin's words sounded full of elation, but Nerzhin showed no readiness to enter into the great primordial questions of good and evil just then. He had hung the damp, scanty, coarse-woven towel around his neck like a muffler. He pulled on his old officer's cap, a relic of the front that was already coming apart at the seams, put on his padded jacket, and said with a sigh, "All we know is that we don't know anything."

He took up the saw, this disciple of Socrates, and offered the other end to Sologdin.

Now they were getting cold, and they went at the sawing with a will. The saw splashed out the brown powder of the bark. It bit in less deftly than when Spiridon had held it, but easily nonetheless. The friends had sawed together many a morning, and the work went along without mutual recrimination. They sawed with that special energy and zest that come when work isn't a matter of necessity.

As they began on the fourth log, Sologdin, whose face had turned bright red, blurted out, "Don't catch a knot."

After the fourth log Nerzhin muttered, "Yes, it's knotty, the bastard!"

With each stroke of the saw fragrant white and yellow sawdust fell on the woodcutters' trousers and shoes. The measured work brought them peace and reordered their thoughts.

Nerzhin, who had awakened in a bad mood a little while before, was now thinking that only the first year of camp could finish him, that he had achieved a completely different tempo, that he would not try to scramble into the ranks of the goldbrickers, that he would not be afraid of camp labor, but would slowly, with an understanding of life's depths, go out for morning line-up in his padded jacket smeared with plaster or fuel oil and tenaciously drag through the twelve-hour day—and so on, for the whole five years remaining until the end of his term. Five years is not ten. One can last five.

He thought, too, about Sologdin, how he himself had

acquired some of Sologdin's unhurried comprehension of life; how in particular it was Sologdin who had first nudged him into thinking that a person shouldn't regard prison solely as a curse, but also as a blessing.

As he pulled away on the saw, that was how his thoughts ran. He could not have imagined that his partner, pulling the saw toward himself at that moment, was thinking of prison as nothing but an unmitigated curse from which one must surely escape someday.

Sologdin was thinking about the great engineering triumph he had achieved in total secrecy during the last few months and particularly in the past weeks. It promised him freedom. He thought about the verdict on his work that he was to learn after breakfast—he had no doubt what it would be. With a violent sort of pride, Sologdin thought of his brain, exhausted by so many years of interrogation and by so many years of famine in the camps and the resulting phosphorus deficiency, yet able even so to cope with a very important problem. At forty, men sometimes have a fresh burst of vitality, especially when their surplus physical energy is not spent in making children, but is transformed, in some mysterious way, into intellectual force.

Then, too, he thought about Nerzhin's imminent departure from the sharashka, inevitable now that he had spoken rashly to Yakonov.

They sawed away. Their bodies grew hot. Their faces gave off heat. Their padded jackets were tossed up on the logs, and there was a good pile of firewood by the saw horses—but they still did not have an ax.

"Isn't that enough?" asked Nerzhin. "We've cut more than we can split."

"Let's take a rest," Sologdin agreed, dropping the saw with a twang of its bending blade.

Both of them pulled off their caps. Steam rose from Nerzhin's thick hair and from Sologdin's thin hair. They breathed deeply. The air seemed to have penetrated the most stagnant inner corners of their bodies.

"But if they send you off to a camp," asked Sologdin, "what will happen to your work on 'time past'?" (By this he meant, on history.)

"What's the difference? After all, I'm not being spoiled here either. Keeping a single line of what I write makes me liable to the dungeon here just as much as there. I don't have access to a public library, and I will probably never be allowed inside an archive as long as I live. If you're talking about fresh paper, then I can find birch or pine bark in the northern forest. And no spy can ever take away my raw materials: the grief I have felt within me and which I see in others is more than enough to illuminate my speculations about history. What do you think?"

"Mag-ni-fi-cent!!" Sologdin exclaimed, breathing the word thickly. "In that primal sphere in which a thought develops—"

"Sphere is a bird word," Nerzhin reminded him.

"I apologize," Sologdin said. "You see how uninventive I am. In that primal *ball*, thought—" he put his hand to his head—"the initial force of a thought determines the success of any cause! And like a living tree it gives fruit only if allowed to develop naturally. Books and other people's opinions are shears which sever the life of a thought. One must first come upon the thought oneself. Later on one can verify it in a book. You have matured greatly. You have—I simply never expected it."

It had become chilly. Sologdin took his cap off the end of the saw horse and put it on. Nerzhin put his cap on, too. He was flattered, but he tried not to let the flattery go to his head.

Sologdin went on speaking.

"And now, Gleb, since your departure might be quite sudden, I must hasten to share with you certain of my rules. They might turn out to be useful to you. Obviously, I am very hampered by being tongue-tied and simple-minded. . . ."

All this was typical of Sologdin. Before expressing a brilliant idea he first made a point of deprecating himself.

"And your feeble memory," Nerzhin said, helping him out, "and the over-all fact that you are a frail vessel full of errors."

"Yes, yes, that's what I meant to say," Sologdin said, baring his round white teeth in a smile. "So then, aware of my imperfections, I have worked out over the course of many years certain rules which bind the will like an iron hoop. These rules are like a *general survey of the approach* to work." ("Methodology" was the way Nerzhin usually translated this from the Language of Maximum Clarity to the Language of Apparent Clarity.) "These are the paths toward the creation of a working unity: solidarity of purpose, and its implementation, and its mode of operation."

They drew on their padded jackets.

They could see that it would soon be time for them to quit work and go to morning check-up. Far off, in front of the staff headquarters, beneath the grove of magically whitened Mavrino lindens, they could see the prisoners taking their morning walk. Among the half-straightened and stooped figures was the tall, erect body of the fifty-year-old artist Kondrashev-Ivanov. They could see, too, how Lev Rubin, who had overslept, was now trying to get out to the firewood. But the guard would not let him pass; it was too late.

"Look—there's Lev with his tousled beard."

They laughed.

"So if you'd like, every morning I will teach you some of my rules."

"Of course, Dmitri, go on with them right now."

Nerzhin sank down on the pile of firewood. Sologdin sat uncomfortably on the saw horse.

"Well, for example, how to face difficulties."

"Don't lose heart?"

"That's not enough."

Sologdin looked past Nerzhin into the zone, at the thick little clumps of bushes all furry with frost and just touched by the gentle pink of the east. The sun seemed uncertain whether to show itself or not. Sologdin's face, drawn and lean, with his reddish-gray, curly little beard and his short mustache, revealed some ancient Russian quality, and recalled the face of Aleksandr Nevsky.

"How to face difficulties?" he declared again. "In the realm of the unknown, difficulties must be viewed as a *hidden treasure!* Usually, the more difficult, the better. It's not as valuable if your difficulties stem from your own inner struggle. But when difficulties arise out of increasing objective resistance, that's *marvelous!*"

The rosy dawn now shone on the flushed face of Aleksandr Nevsky, as if conveying the radiance of difficulties wonderful as the sun.

"The most rewarding path of investigation is: 'the greatest external resistance in the presence of the least internal resistance.' Failures must be considered the cue for further application of effort and concentration of will power. And if substantial efforts have already been made, the failures are all the more joyous. It means that our crowbar has struck the iron box containing the treasure. Overcoming the increased difficulties is all the more valuable because in failure the *growth of the person performing the task* takes place in proportion to the difficulty encountered!"

"Good! Strong!" Nerzhin responded from the pile of firewood.

The shadows cast by the dawn had moved among the bushes and were now extinguished by heavy gray clouds.

As though lifting his eyes from a page he had been reading aloud, Sologdin looked abstractedly down at Nerzhin.

"And now listen: The rule of the Final Inch! The realm of the Final Inch! In the Language of Maximum Clarity it is immediately clear what that is. The work has been almost completed, the goal almost attained, everything seems completely right and the difficulties overcome. But the quality of the thing is not *quite* right. Finishing touches are needed, maybe still more research. In that moment of fatigue and self-satisfaction it is especially tempting to leave the work without having attained the apex of quality. Work in the area of the Final Inch is very, very complex and also especially valuable, because it is executed by the most perfected means. In fact, the rule of the Final Inch consists in this: not to shirk this crucial work. Not to postpone it, for the thoughts of the person performing the task will then stray from the realm of the Final Inch. And not to mind the time spent on it, knowing that one's purpose lies not in completing things faster but in the attainment of perfection."

"Very good!" Nerzhin whispered.

In a completely different voice, crudely mocking, Sologdin said, "Well, where have you been, Junior Lieutenant? This isn't like you. Why are you bringing the ax so late? There's no time left to split wood."

Moon-faced Junior Lieutenant Nadelashin had been a master sergeant only a short time ago. When he was made an officer, the zeks of the sharashka, who had warm feelings for him, rechristened him "Junior."

Hurrying up with mincing little steps and puffing comically, he handed over the ax with a guilty smile, and replied earnestly: "I implore you, Sologdin, split some firewood! There isn't any in the kitchen at all. There's nothing to cook lunch with. You just don't realize how much work I have to do, not including you."

"Whaaat?" laughed Nerzhin. "Work? Junior Lieutenant, do you think you work?"

The duty officer turned his moon face to Nerzhin. A frown was etched on his forehead as he recited from memory: " 'Work is the overcoming of resistance.' When I walk fast, I overcome the resistance of the air, and therefore I am working then, too." He wanted to remain imperturbable, but a smile lit up his face when Sologdin and Nerzhin burst out in friendly laughter in the frosty air. "So please split some wood."

Turning away, he went mincing off to the staff building of the special prison, where, at that moment, the smartly braced figure of its head, Lieutenant Colonel Klimentiev, appeared, wearing an officer's greatcoat.

"Gleb," Sologdin said, surprised. "Do my eyes deceive me? Klimentiadis? Why Klimentiadis on a Sunday?"

That year the newspapers were writing a lot about political prisoners in Greece who were sending telegrams from their cells to all the parliaments and to the United Nations about their sufferings. At the sharashka, where the prisoners could not send even a post card to their wives, not to mention foreign parliaments, there was a fad of recasting the family names of the prison authorities in Greek form: Myshinopulo, Klimentiadis, Shikinidi, etc.

"Don't you really know? Six men are being allowed visiting privileges."

Reminded of the fact, Nerzhin's spirits, which had brightened so during the morning woodcutting, were again flooded with bitterness. Almost a year had passed since he had last left the prison to visit his wife, and it had been eight months since he had applied for a new permit. There were various reasons for this, but there was one in particular: in order to protect his wife's standing at the university, he did not use her student dormitory address, but addressed his letters to "general delivery." And the authorities did not want to send letters to "general delivery." Nerzhin, because of his intense inner life, was free of envy; neither the wages nor the extra meals of other, more meritorious zeks troubled his calm. But his sense of being unfairly treated in the matter of visiting privileges, the fact that one person would be allowed to visit outside every two months, whereas his slender, vulnerable wife sighed and wandered about in vain under fortress walls—this awareness tormented him.

Besides, today was his birthday.

"They're going?" Sologdin asked with the same bitter envy. "The stool pigeons are allowed visits every month. But I'll never see my Ninochka. . . ."

Sologdin never used the expression "until the end of my term," because he had foreknowledge of the fact that terms might have no end.

He watched as Klimentiev, who had been standing with Nadelashin, entered the staff building.

Suddenly he spoke rapidly: "Gleb! Look here—your wife knows mine. If they allow you a visit, ask Nadya to try to find Ninochka and to tell her just three things from me." He looked up at the sky. "He loves her! He believes in her! He hopes!"

"What are you talking about? They've refused me," Nerzhin said annoyed, trying every which way to split a piece of firewood.

"But look!"

Nerzhin looked around. The junior lieutenant was walking toward him, and while he was still some distance away he beckoned him to come. Dropping the ax and knocking over the saw, which clanged to the ground, Gleb ran like a little boy.

Sologdin watched as the junior lieutenant led Nerzhin into the staff building; then he set the piece of wood up on end and struck it so violently that he not only split it in two but drove the ax into the ground.

The ax, as it happened, was government issue.

25

THE JUNIOR LIEUTENANT'S JOB

The textbook definition of work, as quoted by Junior Lieutenant Nadelashin, did in fact apply to his job. Though he worked only twelve hours in every forty-eight, it was demanding work, involved much running up and down stairs and was highly responsible.

He had had a particularly exacting duty period the previous night. No sooner had he taken charge at 9 P.M., and checked that all 281 prisoners were present and accounted for, dismissed them to their night work, posted the guards (at the stairway landing, in the corridor of the staff building, and in a patrol under the windows of the special prison) and begun feeding and housing the new arrivals, than he was called away by a summons from Major Myshin, the prison security officer, who had not yet gone home.

Nadelashin was an unusual person, not only among jailers—or, as they were now called, "prison workers"—but among his countrymen in general. In a land where every second person had gone through camp or front-line schools of cursing, where foul oaths were commonly used not only by drunks in the presence of children (and by children in children's games), not only in boarding a suburban bus, but sometimes even in heart-to-heart conversation—especially in interrogations—Nadelashin not only did not know how to use the mother oaths, but he did not even use words like "hell" and "bastard." When he was in a temper, he used only one term of condemnation: "Bull-butt you!"—and even that he usually said only to himself.

And so, having said to himself, "Bull-butt you!" he hurried off to the major.

Major Myshin, the prison security officer—whom Bobynin had very unjustly called a parasite—an insalubriously fat, purple-faced man who had stayed on the job that Saturday evening because of extraordinary circumstances, gave Nadelashin his assignments:

"Check whether the German and Latvian Christmas celebrations have begun.

"List, by groups, everyone who has participated in the Christmas celebrations.

"Check personally, and also have the regular guards check on their ten-minute rounds, whether they are drinking wine, whether they are digging escape tunnels, what they are talking about, and—the main thing—whether or not they are conducting anti-Soviet propaganda.

"Wherever possible, find deviations from the prison regime and put a stop to that outrageous religious debauchery."

Nadelashin had not been told, "Put a stop to it," but "*Wherever possible* put a stop to it." A peaceful Christmas celebration was not explicitly forbidden, but Comrade Myshin's heart could not bear the idea.

Junior Lieutenant Nadelashin, his face a placid winter moon, reminded the major that neither German nor Latvian was known to him, much less to his guards. (They did not all know Russian.)

Myshin recollected that in four years' service as commissar of a guard company in a camp of German POWs he himself had learned only three words: "*Halt!*" "*Zurück!*" and "*Weg!*" So he cut short his instructions.

Having heard the orders and saluted awkwardly (from time to time he underwent parade drill), Nadelashin went off to assign places to the newly arrived prisoners—having received a list from the security officer showing whom to put in what room and in which bunk. (Myshin put great stock in the centralized regulation of prison dormitories, throughout which he had planted his informers. He knew that the frankest conversations took place not in the bustle of daytime work but just before sleep, and that even gloomier and bitterer remarks were made in the morning, and that it was therefore particularly useful to eavesdrop on people when they were in bed.)

Nadelashin duly entered each room where Christmas was being celebrated—allegedly to ascertain the wattage of the light bulbs hanging there. Then he sent the guards in once. And he wrote down everyone's name on a list.

Then Major Myshin summoned him again, and Nadelashin gave him the little list. Myshin was particularly interested in the fact that Rubin had been with the Germans. He entered this fact in his file.

By then it was time to change the guards, and to settle an argument between two of them as to which had been on duty longer the last time, and who therefore owed whom more time.

After that came "lights-out," the nightly argument with Pryanchikov about boiling water for tea, an inspection of all the rooms, the turning off of the white light and the turning on of the blue one. Then Major Myshin summoned him once more. He still had not gone home; as a matter of fact, his wife was ill at home and he didn't feel like listening to her complaints all night. Major Myshin was seated in his armchair, and he kept Nadelashin standing while he asked him whom, according to his observations, Rubin went around with, and whether there had not been instances in the past week when Rubin had spoken defiantly about the prison administration or had voiced demands in the name of the people.

Nadelashin occupied a particular place among his colleagues who were in charge of the guard shifts. He got dressed down severely and often. His natural good nature had long been a handicap to him in the security organizations. Had he not managed to adapt himself, he would have been expelled a long time ago or even imprisoned. Nadelashin had never been rude to the prisoners. He smiled upon them with honest goodwill, and he was indulgent in small details whenever he could afford to be. For this the prisoners loved him. They never complained about him. They never crossed him. They did not even hesitate to talk freely in front of him. He was a good observer and listener, and quite literate, and in order to remember everything he wrote it down in a special notebook. He reported the contents of this notebook to his superiors, thus making up for his shortcomings.

And so it went now: he got out his little book and reported to the major that on December 17 the prisoners were crowding through the lower corridor after their lunchtime outing, and he, Nadelashin, had been right behind them. The prisoners were muttering that tomorrow was a Sunday but that you couldn't get a day off from the security chiefs, and Rubin had said to them, "When are you going to understand, boys, that you'll never be able to move those rats to pity?"

"He said that—'those rats'?" Myshin asked, purple.

"That's what he said," moon-faced Nadelashin confirmed with a guileless smile.

Myshin again opened the file and made a note. He also ordered Nadelashin to write down his information in the form of an individual denunciation.

Major Myshin hated Rubin and was collecting defamatory evidence against him. When he had first come to Mavrino and learned that Rubin, a former Communist, had been bragging that he was still a Communist at heart, in spite of prison, Myshin called him in to chat about life in general and about working together in particular. But they did not reach an understanding. Myshin put the question to Rubin in precisely the way it was supposed to be done at instruction sessions:

"If you are a Soviet, then you will help us.

"If you don't help us, then you are not a Soviet.

"If you are not a Soviet, then you are anti-Soviet and deserve an additional term."

But Rubin asked, "How am I supposed to write denunciations, in ink or pencil?"

"Well, ink would be better," Myshin advised.

"Yes, but you see, I have already proved my devotion to Soviet authority in blood, and I don't need to demonstrate it in ink."

In this way Rubin immediately revealed to the major his dishonesty and his hypocrisy.

The major called him in once again. On that occasion Rubin had excused himself by saying—it was obviously a dodge—that political confidence had been withheld from him since he had been imprisoned and while this continued he could not cooperate with the security officer.

From that time on Myshin collected whatever he could against Rubin.

Myshin's conversation with the junior lieutenant was still in progress when a passenger car from the Minister of State Security suddenly arrived for Bobynin. Taking advantage of a circumstance so favorable to his career, Myshin quickly put on his tunic and hovered around the car. He invited the newly arrived officer to come in and get warm, and directed his attention to the fact that he was working nights. He tugged at Nadelashin, giving him meaningless orders, and for good measure asked Bobynin whether he was dressed warmly enough. (Bobynin had deliberately put on not the fine overcoat which had been issued him for the occasion but his ragged padded camp jacket.)

Immediately after Bobynin's departure Pryanchikov had been summoned. Now the major certainly could not go home. While waiting to see whom else they would summon and at what time those already summoned would return, the major checked on how the off-duty guards were spending their time. (They were playing dominoes.) He proceeded to question them on Party history, for he was responsible for their political indoctrination. Although the guards were considered to be on the job then, too, they usually slept at this time. But right now they felt like playing dominoes, so they answered the major's questions with a justifiable lack of interest. Their answers were terrible, too; not only were these warriors confused as to why it was correct to separate after the Second Congress and to merge at the Fourth Congress, but they even said that Plekhanov had been the czarist minister responsible for shooting the Petersburg workers on January 9, 1905. Myshin reprimanded Nadelashin for all this—he had let his shift become demoralized.

At that point Bobynin and Pryanchikov had returned together in the same car and, refusing to tell the major anything, had gone off to bed. Disappointed and, even more, alarmed, the major rode home in the car so as not to have to walk. The buses did not run at this hour.

The guards, freed from their posts, cursed the major and prepared to go to sleep. Nadelashin himself wanted to doze off, but he was not destined to; the telephone rang. The call came from the guardroom of the convoy guards, who were responsible for the watchtowers surrounding the Mavrino Institute. The chief of the watch reported in alarm that the tower guard posted at the southwest corner had phoned in to say that he had clearly seen someone hiding by the woodshed in the thickening mist, who then had crept up to the barbed wire of the prezone area and, frightened by the guard's shout, had run off into the depths of the yard.

The chief of the watch reported that he would immediately ring up the headquarters of his regiment and write a report on this extraordinary occurrence, and in the meantime he asked the duty officer of the special prison to investigate the yard.

Though Nadelashin was firmly convinced that the guard had been seeing things, that the prisoners were safely locked in behind new steel doors and strong old walls four bricks thick, still the very fact that the chief of the watch was writing a report demanded energetic action on his part and a corresponding report. He therefore aroused the dozing guards by ringing the alarm and led them with their flashlights through the big, fog-shrouded yard. After that was done, he went through all the cells again. He did not turn on the white lights—so that there would be no complaints—and because he could not see well enough in the blue light, he hit his knee hard on the corner of someone's bunk. Finally, by checking each prisoner's head with the flashlight beam, he counted up to 281.

He then went to the office and wrote out in a round, clear hand, which expressed the limpidity of his inner being, a report on what had taken place, addressed to Lieutenant Colonel Klimentiev, the head of the special prison.

By that time it was morning. Time to check the kitchen, unlock the cabinets, and sound reveille.

That was the way Junior Lieutenant Nadelashin spent his night, and he had good reason to tell Nerzhin he earned his board and keep.

Nadelashin was well over thirty, though he looked younger because of the freshness of his clean-shaven face.

Nadelashin's father and grandfather had been tailors, not for the luxury trade but for people of modest means. They were willing to turn things inside out, to remake hand-me-downs, and they did it on a while-you-wait basis when requested. They had wanted the boy to follow in their footsteps. From childhood that soft and genteel work had suited him, and he prepared himself for it, watching how things were done and helping. But then the New Economic Policy ended. His father was assessed a tax; he paid it. Two days later they added another tax. His father paid that, too. Two days after that, with total shamelessness, they assessed him once more, a triple tax. His father tore up his license to practice his trade, took down his sign, and went off to work in an artel. The son was soon drafted into the army. And from there he went into the ranks of the MVD armies. Afterward he was made a prison guard.

He had not served brilliantly. In the course of his fourteen years of service other guards, three or four waves of them, had overtaken him one after the other. Some had become captains by now, whereas he had only received his commission and his one star a month ago, and then by the skin of his teeth.

Nadelashin understood much more than he ever talked about. He understood, for instance, that many of these prisoners, who had no rights as human beings, were, in fact, on a much higher plane than he. Beyond that, picturing others in his own image, Nadelashin could not discover in the prisoners the bloody criminals they were described as being in political indoctrination sessions.

Even more precisely than he remembered the definition of work from his night-school physics course, he remembered every bend in the five prison corridors of the Big Lubyanka and the interior of each of its 110 cells. According to Lubyanka rules, the guards changed every two hours, moving from one part of the corridor to another, as a precaution against their getting to know their prisoners, so that they would not be influenced or bribed. (The guards were quite well paid.) Each guard was supposed to look in the peepholes at least once every three minutes. Nadelashin, with his exceptional memory for faces, felt he could remember every single prisoner in his prison service from 1935 to 1947, when he was transferred to Mavrino. Among them were famous leaders, as well as ordinary officers from the front, like Nerzhin. He used to think he could recognize any of them on the street in any sort of dress, except that one never met them on the street. From *that* world there was no return to *this* world. It was only here in Mavrino that he encountered certain of his old charges—obviously without letting them know he recognized them. He remembered them staggering from enforced sleeplessness in the blinding glare of the "boxes," ten square feet in area; cutting their fifteen-ounce ration of wet bread with a string; buried in the beautiful old books in which the prison library abounded; going out in single file for clean-up; with their hands behind their backs when they were called out for questioning; engaged in conversations which grew livelier in the last half-hour before bedtime; lying under the bright light on winter nights, with their hands outside the covers wrapped in towels for warmth—the rules demanded that anyone who hid his hands under his blanket be awakened and forced to take them out.

Best of all, Nadelashin loved to hear the arguments and conversations of all those gray-bearded academicians, priests, Old Bolsheviks, generals, and amusing foreigners. It was his duty to listen in, but he listened also for his own satisfaction. He would have preferred to listen to a story from beginning to end: how someone had lived previously and what he had been arrested for. But because of his duties he never succeeded. He was astonished that in the dread months when their lives were shattered, their fates decided, these people found the courage to talk not about their sufferings but about any subject that came to mind: Italian artists, the habits of bees, wolf-hunting, how someone called Carbusier (or something) was building houses for other people somewhere.

Once Nadelashin happened to hear a conversation which interested him especially. He sat in the rear sentry box of a Black Maria, accompanying two prisoners locked inside. They were being transported from Bolshaya Lubyanka to the Sukhanov "dacha," as it was called—an infinitely evil prison outside Moscow from which many went straight to the grave or the insane asylum, and few returned to the Lubyanka. Nadelashin himself had never worked there, but he had heard that the food was administered with refined torture. The prisoners were not given coarse, heavy food, as they were everywhere else, but were brought tender, savory sanatorium fare. The torture was in the portions. The prisoner was brought half a saucer of bouillon, an eighth of a cutlet, two little strings of fried potato. It didn't feed them—it only reminded them of what they had lost. This was much more agonizing than a bowl of watery soup, and it helped drive them out of their minds.

It happened that the two prisoners in the Black Maria were not isolated but for some reason were being transported together. At first Nadelashin did not hear what they were talking about because of the sound of the motor. But then something went wrong with the motor, and the driver went off somewhere, leaving the officer sitting up front. Nadelashin heard the prisoners' quiet conversation through the grating in the rear door. They were berating the government and the czar—but not the present government, not Stalin. They were berating Peter the Great. What had *he* done to them? Yet there they were, settling accounts with him. One of them criticized him, among other things, for having debased and eliminated Russian national dress and deprived his own people of their individuality. This prisoner enumerated in detail, with an extraordinary knowledge of his subject, what the clothes used to be, how they looked and on what occasions they were worn. He said that even now it was not too late to revive certain elements of that attire, which could be suitably and comfortably combined with contemporary clothing, without blindly copying Paris. The other prisoner had joked that two men would be needed to accomplish that: a brilliant tailor who could put it all together and a fashionable tenor who would be photographed wearing it. Then all Russia would quickly adopt it.

This conversation was particularly interesting to Nadelashin because tailoring was still his secret passion. After his duty periods in corridors supercharged with madness he was calmed by the rustle of cloth, the soft pliability of pleats, the goodness of the work.

He made clothes for his children, sewed dresses for his wife, suits for himself. But he kept it secret.

Tailoring would have been considered a disgraceful occupation for anyone in military service.

26

THE LIEUTENANT COLONEL'S JOB

Lieutenant Colonel Klimentiev had hair like pitch, the shiny black of painted cast iron; it lay flat on his head, divided by a part; his rounded mustache looked pomaded. He had not acquired a pot belly, and at forty-five he carried himself like a young, well-built military man. He never smiled while on duty, and this intensified the dark moroseness of his face.

In spite of its being Sunday he arrived even earlier than usual. He cut across the exercise yard while the prisoners were strolling about, catching violations in half a glance. But since it would have been beneath his rank to interfere, he entered the headquarters building and, still on the march, ordered Nadelashin to summon the prisoner Nerzhin and to come back himself. As he had crossed the yard, the lieutenant colonel had noticed that some prisoners in his path had tried to move ahead faster while others slowed and turned away so as not to have to greet him. Klimentiev observed this coldly, but he was not offended. He knew that it was only prompted in part by contempt for his position, that it was mostly due to embarrassment in front of their comrades, the fear of appearing servile. Almost every one of the prisoners behaved amicably when summoned to his office singly, and some even tried to curry favor. There were different kinds of people behind bars, and they were different in their worth. Klimentiev had understood that long ago. Respecting their right to be proud, he insisted unwaveringly on his own right to be strict. A soldier at heart, he brought to prison, he believed, not a degrading discipline but rational military order.

He opened the office. It was hot, and the radiators gave off an unpleasant stifling odor of baking paint. The lieutenant colonel opened the window vent, took off his overcoat, sat down shackled in his tunic and examined the unlittered surface of his desk. The Saturday sheet of his desk calendar had not yet been turned over; there was a note on it:

"New Year's tree?"

From this half-barren office, in which the only instruments of production were a steel cabinet containing the prisoners' files, a half-dozen chairs, a telephone and a buzzer, Lieutenant Colonel Klimentiev—without any visible clutch, drive, or gear box—supervised the outward course of 281 lives and the services of 50 guards.

Despite the fact that he had come in on a Sunday—in return for which he would have a free day during the week —and had arrived half an hour early, Klimentiev did not lose his customary equanimity and control.

Junior Lieutenant Nadelashin stood before him anxiously. A round red spot appeared on each cheek. He was afraid of the lieutenant colonel, even though Klimentiev had never entered his multitudinous mistakes in his personnel dossier. Nadelashin, round-faced, ridiculous, not at all a military type, endeavored vainly to stand "at ease."

He reported that his night duty had passed in perfect order, that there had been no violations, but that there had been two extraordinary occurrences. One of them he had set forth in a report. He put the report on the corner of the desk; it immediately slid off and glided in an intricate arc under a distant chair. Nadelashin rushed after it and brought it back to the desk. The second extraordinary event had been the summoning of prisoners Bobynin and Pryanchikov to the Minister of State Security.

The lieutenant colonel raised his brows and questioned him in detail about the circumstances of the summons and the prisoners' return. The news was, of course, unpleasant and even alarming. To be the head of this special prison was to be forever sitting on top of a volcano—always right under the minister's nose. This was not some remote forest camp where the officer in command could have a harem and jesters and carry out his own sentences like a feudal lord. Here one had to observe the letter of the law, walk the tight-rope of regulations, and not give way to one drop of personal anger or mercy. But that was the kind of person Klimentiev was anyway. He did not think Bobynin and Pryanchikov had found anything illegal in his actions to complain about last night. As a result of his long experience in the service, he did not fear being slandered by the prisoners. Slander was more likely to come from one's colleagues.

Next he glanced over Nadelashin's report and realized that the whole thing was nonsense. That's why he kept Nadelashin—because he was literate and sensible.

But how many shortcomings he had! The lieutenant colonel proceeded to reprimand him. He remembered in detail what omissions there had been in the course of his past duty period. The morning dismissal of the zeks to work had been two minutes late; many of their bunks had been carelessly made; and Nadelashin had failed to demonstrate the required firmness by calling back the offending prisoners and ordering them to remake their beds. He had been told about it at the time. But no matter how often one spoke to Nadelashin, it was like beating one's head against a stone wall. And what had happened during the morning exercise period? Young Doronin had been standing at the very limit of the exercise area, staring at the zone and the area beyond, off toward the hothouses, and, after all, that was an area of broken ground, with a small ravine, very convenient for an escape. And Doronin's sentence was for twenty-five years; his record included the forging of documents and he had been on the all-Union wanted list for two years! No one from the detachment had told Doronin to move on, to keep walking around in the circle. And where had Gerasimovich been going? He had gone off from everyone else in the direction of the machine shops behind the lindens. And what was Gerasimovich's crime? Gerasimovich was on his second term—and he had been sent up for Section 58, 1A, via Section 19. In other words, intent to commit treason. He had not actually committed treason, but neither had he been able to prove that when he went to Leningrad during the early days of the war it was not to wait for the Germans. Had Nadelashin forgotten that it was obligatory to study and get to know the prisoners, both by direct observation and through their personal files? And finally, what kind of appearance did Nadelashin himself present? His field shirt was not pulled down—Nadelashin jerked it down. The star on his cap was crooked—Nadelashin corrected it. He saluted like an old woman. No wonder the prisoners didn't make their beds right when Nadelashin was on duty. Unmade beds were a dangerous breach of prison discipline. Unmade beds today; tomorrow they would refuse to go to work.

Then the lieutenant colonel proceeded with his orders. Guards assigned to accompany prisoners on today's visits were to be assembled in the third room to receive instructions. Let Nerzhin stand in the corridor for the time being. Nadelashin was dismissed.

He went out feeling badly shattered. He sincerely repented every time he heard his superiors out, acknowledged the justice of all their accusations and corrections, and promised not to repeat his offenses. But his job went on, and once again he would come up against the wills of dozens of prisoners, all pulling him in different directions, everyone wanting some little scrap of freedom, and Nadelashin could not refuse them, and he could only hope that it might pass unnoticed.

Klimentiev took his pen and crossed off the note, "New Year's tree?" on his desk calendar. He had made his decision yesterday.

There had never been New Year's trees in special prisons. Klimentiev could remember no such miracle. But the prisoners, those who carried weight, had persistently demanded that there be a New Year's tree this year. And Klimentiev had begun to think: why, in fact, shouldn't it be allowed? It was obvious that nothing bad could result from a New Year's tree; there wouldn't be a fire—after all, everyone around here was a professor of electrical engineering. And it was very important that on New Year's Eve, when all the free employees had gone off to have a good time in Moscow, there should be a letup here, too. He knew that the eves of holidays were most difficult for the prisoners, that someone might do something desperate or senseless. And so the night before he had phoned the prison administration—to which he was directly subordinate—and had discussed the New Year's tree. There was a prohibition in the prison laws against musical instruments, but they could find nothing about New

Year's trees. Therefore, though they did not approve it officially, neither did they formally prohibit it. Long and faultless service lent constancy and assurance to the actions of Lieutenant Colonel Klimentiev. And Klimentiev had already decided the evening before, on the subway escalator on his way home: all right, let them have their New Year's tree.

Getting on the subway, he had thought about himself with satisfaction; after all, he was essentially an intelligent, businesslike person, not a bureaucratic clod; a kind person, even; but the prisoners would never appreciate that and would never know who wanted to allow them a New Year's tree and who did not.

For some reason Klimentiev felt so good about his decision that he did not push his way into the car with the other Muscovites but got in last, just before the pneumatic doors closed. He did not try to grab a seat but held on to the chrome pole and looked at his courageous reflection in the plate-glass window, behind which the blackness of the tunnel and the endless pipes and cables tore by. Then he shifted his glance to a young woman sitting nearby. She was dressed carefully but not expensively in a black coat of artificial caracul and a cap of the same material. A tightly packed briefcase lay across her knees. Looking at her, Klimentiev thought she had a pleasant face, but tired, and a look unusual in a young woman, a lack of interest in what was going on around her.

At that very moment the woman glanced up at him, and they looked at each other without expression for exactly as long as chance fellow travelers look at one another. And in that time the woman's eyes turned wary, as though an uneasy question had flashed into them. Klimentiev remembered her face as a matter of professional routine; he knew right away who she was, and he was unable to hide the fact that he recognized her. She noticed his hesitation and evidently found her guess confirmed.

She was the wife of the prisoner Nerzhin. Klimentiev had seen her during her visits to the Taganka Prison.

She frowned, shifted her eyes away, then looked at Klimentiev again. He was staring out into the tunnel, but from a corner of his eye he felt she was looking at him. Then she rose with determination and came toward him, and he was forced to face her again.

She had risen decisively, but, having risen, lost all her

resolution, lost all the independence of a self-supporting young woman riding on the subway, and it looked almost as though, with her heavy briefcase, she meant to give up her seat to the lieutenant colonel. Over her hung the unhappy fate of all the wives of political prisoners—the wives, that is, of *enemies of the people*: no matter to whom they appealed, no matter where they might go, once their unfortunate marriages became known, it was as though they dragged behind them their husband's ineffaceable shame. It was as though in everyone's eyes they shared the burden of blame with the black villains to whom they had once carelessly entrusted their fates. And the women began to feel they really were to blame—something that the *enemies of the people* themselves, their husbands, accustomed to their situation, did not feel.

Standing right next to him, so that he could hear her words above the rattle of the train, the woman asked, "Comrade Lieutenant Colonel! Please forgive me! After all, you are . . . my husband's superior? Or am I mistaken?"

During his many years of service as a prison officer all sorts of women had stood before him, and he saw nothing unusual in their timid and dependent appearance. But here in the subway, though she spoke very carefully, in everyone's eyes this pleading woman standing before him looked improper.

"You . . . why did you stand up? Sit down, sit down," he said, embarrassed, trying to take her by the sleeve to lead her back to her seat.

"No, no, that doesn't matter at all," the woman said, pulling away and looking at the lieutenant colonel with an insistent, almost fanatical appeal. "Tell me. Why has there been no visit for a whole year? Why can't I see him? When will I be able to? Tell me!"

It was as if one grain of sand had hit another grain of sand at a distance of forty paces. The week before the prison administration of the MGB had sent permission for the zek Nerzhin, among others, to visit his wife on Sunday, December 25, at Lefortovo Prison. But along with the permission was the notation forbidding the announcement of the visit to be addressed to "general delivery," as the prisoner had requested.

Nerzhin had been called in at that time and asked about his wife's real address. He muttered that he didn't know it. Klimentiev, taught by the prison statutes never to reveal the truth to prisoners, did not assume any greater honesty on their part. Nerzhin, of course, knew the address, but did not want to tell it, and it was clear why he didn't want to—for the same reason the prison administration did not permit "general delivery" addresses. Announcements of forthcoming visits were sent by post card: "You have been permitted a visit with your husband at such and such a prison." It was not enough for the wife's address to be registered with the MGB. The ministry did its best to see to it that as few wives as possible should yearn to receive those post cards; that neighbors should be aware of the wives of enemies of the people; that such wives should be brought out in the open, isolated, and surrounded by a healthy public opinion. Which was precisely what the wives were afraid of. Nerzhin's wife even used a different last name. She was obviously hiding from the MGB. Klimentiev had told Nerzhin at the time that this meant there would be no visit. He did not send the announcement.

And now this woman stood so embarrassingly before him while the people around them watched in silence.

"You're not allowed to use general delivery," he said, just loud enough for her to hear above the roar. "You have to give an address."

"But I'm going away!" The woman's face was transformed with animation. "I'm going away very soon, and I don't have a permanent address." She was obviously lying.

Klimentiev's thought was to get off at the first stop—and, if she followed him, to explain to her, in the subway entrance where there would be fewer people, that such unofficial conversations were inadmissible.

The wife of the enemy of the people seemed to have forgotten her own irreparable guilt. She stared into the lieutenant colonel's eyes with a look which was dry, hot, demanding, outraged. Klimentiev was astonished by such a look. What force, he asked himself, bound her so stubbornly and so hopelessly to a person whom she would not see for years and who could only destroy her whole life?

"I need to very, very much!" she assured him with her widened eyes, which had seen the hesitation in his face.

Klimentiev remembered the paper which lay in the safe in the special prison. This paper, extending "the Decree on Strengthening the Rear," dealt a new blow at relatives who declined to give their addresses. Major Myshin had proposed that the contents of the paper be announced to the prisoners Monday. If this woman were not to see her husband tomorrow, and if she went on refusing to give her address, she would not see him in the future. If he told her about tomorrow's visit now, even though the notification had not been sent formally, and was not registered in the book, she might come to Lefortovo as if by chance.

The train was slowing down.

All these thoughts raced through Lieutenant Colonel Klimentiev's mind. He knew that the prisoners' chief enemy was the prisoners themselves. And he knew that every woman's chief enemy was the woman herself. People cannot keep quiet even for the sake of their own salvation. He had already in the course of his career manifested stupid leniency, permitted something which was prohibited—and no one would ever have known about it had not the very persons who had profited from the leniency somehow managed to let the cat out of the bag.

He could not show any leniency now.

However, as the roar of the train dropped in volume nearing a station, within actual sight of the station and its pale marble, Klimentiev said to the woman: "You have been allowed a visit. Come tomorrow, at 10 A.M.," and he didn't say "Lefortovo Prison" because passengers were already crowding toward the doors and standing all around him. "You know where Lefortovo Rampart is?"

"I know, I know," the woman nodded gladly.

And from nowhere her eyes, dry before, were suddenly filled with tears.

Avoiding those tears, that gratitude, and all such nonsense, Klimentiev got out on the platform in order to change to another train.

He was surprised that he had said what he had, and was annoyed with himself.

The lieutenant colonel left Nerzhin waiting in the corridor of the staff headquarters because in general Nerzhin was an insolent prisoner, always trying to find out what the law was.

The lieutenant colonel's calculation was correct: Nerzhin, after standing in the corridor a long time, had not only given up hope of a visit's being granted, but, accustomed as he was to all kinds of misfortune, expected something bad to happen.

Thus he was all the more surprised to learn that within an hour's time he would be leaving for a visit. In accordance with the prisoners' high ethical code, implanted by them in each other, one could not show gladness or even satisfaction, but must ask indifferently at exactly what time to be ready, and then leave. But the change was so sharp and the happiness so great that Nerzhin could not restrain himself, and, beaming with pleasure, he thanked the lieutenant colonel warmly.

The lieutenant colonel did not move a muscle of his face.

And he went immediately to brief the guards who were assigned to the visit detail.

In the briefing there were a number of points: a reminder of the importance of their institution and the deep secrecy surrounding it; an explanation of the incorrigibility of the state criminals who were going on visits today; their single-minded wish to use this particular visit to transmit state secrets in their possession through their wives directly to the U.S.A. (the guards had not even an approximate idea of what was being worked on inside the laboratory walls, and it was easy to fill them with holy terror that a scrap of paper, transmitted from Mavrino, might destroy the entire country). Then followed a basic list of possible secret hiding places in clothes and footwear and methods of discovering them. (The clothes, incidentally, were issued to them one hour before their visits, and were special clothes, for show only.) A period of questions and answers checked how well the instructions had been mastered. Then, as the last item, various examples were given of the possible turns the conversations might take, how to listen to them and cut off anything except personal and family subjects.

Lieutenant Colonel Klimentiev knew the regulations and liked order.

27

A PUZZLED ROBOT

In his rush to the prison dormitory Nerzhin almost knocked Junior Lieutenant Nadelashin off his feet in the dark corridor. The small, coarse-woven towel was still hanging around his neck under his padded jacket.

In keeping with an astonishing human characteristic, everything had instantly changed inside Nerzhin. Five minutes ago, when he had been standing in the corridor waiting to be called in, his whole thirty-year-old life had seemed a meaningless and painful chain of failures from which he had not had the strength to extricate himself. It seemed to him that the worst of these failures was his departure for the war soon after his marriage, then his arrest, and his long separation from his wife. He clearly saw the love between them as fated, predestined to be trampled.

Then had come the announcement of his visit at noon today—and his thirty-year-old life appeared in the light of a new sun: a life taut as a bowstring; a life full of meaning in both big and small things; a life striding from one bold success to another, in which the most unexpected steps toward his goal were his departure for the war and his arrest, and his long separation from his wife. Seen from the outside it appeared an unhappy one, but Nerzhin was secretly happy in that unhappiness. He drank it down like spring water. Here he got to know people and events about which he could learn nowhere else on earth, certainly not in the quiet, well-fed seclusion of the domestic hearth. From his youth on, Gleb Nerzhin had dreaded more than anything else wallowing in daily living. As the proverb says: *"It's not the sea that drowns you, it's the puddle."*

He would be with his wife again! The bond between them was unbroken after all. A visit! And on his birthday! And especially after his talk with Yakonov yesterday. He would never have another visit, so today it was more important than ever. His thoughts flew like flaming arrows: he must not forget to mention this; he must remember to speak of that, about this, and about that, too!

He ran into the semicircular room where the prisoners were hurrying around noisily, some having just returned from breakfast, some on their way to wash up; and Valentulya Pryanchikov was sitting in his underwear, having thrown off his blanket; his arms spread wide, he was laughingly relating his nocturnal conversation with the official, describing how it later became clear that he was the minister. Nerzhin wanted to listen to Valentulya. But it was that delightful moment in life when one is bursting with song, when a hundred years seem too brief to set things straight. And he couldn't skip breakfast; a prisoner does not always get breakfast. Anyway Valentulya's story was reaching its

inglorious end. The room pronounced its verdict on him:
he was *cheap and petty* because he had not told Abakumov
about the prisoners' essential needs. Then he was trying to
get away and yelling, but five self-appointed executioners
dragged off his underdrawers and amidst general hooting,
shouting, and laughter chased him around the room, slapping
him with their belts and spooning hot tea on him.

On the lower bunk along the passageway to the central
window, below Nerzhin's bunk and across from Valentulya's
empty one, Andrei Andreyevich Potapov was drinking his
morning tea. Observing the general game, he laughed until
tears came to his eyes, wiping them off under his glasses.
Even before reveille, Potapov's bed had been made; it looked
like a rigid rectangular parallelepiped. He was spreading
a very thin layer of butter on his bread; he bought nothing
in the prison store and sent all the money he earned to his
old woman. (By sharashka standards they paid him a great
deal—150 rubles a month, one-third of what the free charwomen, received, because he was an irreplaceable specialist
and was in the good books of the chiefs.)

Nerzhin slipped off his padded jacket on the run, threw
it up on his still unmade bunk and, greeting Potapov but
not waiting for his answer, ran off to breakfast.

Potapov was the engineer who had confessed during his
interrogation, and signed the confession, and confirmed at
his trial that he had personally sold the Germans—and very
cheaply—the ornament of the Stalinist Five-Year Plans, Dneproges, the Dnieper Hydroelectric Power Station—although
it had been demolished when he sold it to them. Thanks only
to the mercy of a humane court, Potapov's sentence for
this incredible and unparalleled crime was only ten years of
imprisonment, to be followed by five years' loss of rights,
which in the prisoners' language was called "ten, plus five on
the horns."

No one who had known Potapov in his youth, and still
less Potapov himself, would have dreamed that at forty he
would be thrown into prison for *politics*. Potapov's friends,
justifiably, called him a robot. Potapov's whole life was his
work, and even the three-day holidays bored him. He had
taken only one vacation in his life, when he got married.
In the years afterward, they could never find anyone to replace him and he willingly gave up his vacations. When there
were shortages of bread, or vegetables, or sugar, he hardly

noticed these external hardships at all. He punched one more hole in his belt, pulled it tighter and continued to concern himself with the only thing in the world that interested him: high-voltage transmission. Indeed, he had a very unclear notion of the rest of humanity, of people who did *not* concern themselves with high-voltage transmission. Those who created nothing with their hands but worked only with their tongues, Potapov did not even regard as people. He had directed all the electrical calculations at Dneprostroi, married at Dneprostroi, and his wife's life, like his own, had fed the insatiable bonfire of those years.

In 1941 they were building another power station. Potapov had an exemption from military service. But learning that Dneproges, the creation of their youth, had been blown up, he said to his wife, "Katya, after all I must go."

And she answered, "Yes, Andryusha, you must."

So Potapov went—in his minus-three-diopter eyeglasses, with an overtightened belt, in a folded and wrinkled field shirt, with his officer's insignia and his empty holster. In the second year of that well-prepared-for war there were still not enough side arms for officers. Below Kastornoye, in the smoke from burning rye and in the July heat, he was taken prisoner. He escaped, but he failed to reach his own lines and was taken prisoner a second time. He escaped a second time, but in an open field under a parachute drop he was taken for the third time. (All three times he had no weapon.)

He went through the cannibalistic camps of Novograd-Volynsk and Chenstokhov, where the prisoners ate bark from the trees, grass, and their dead comrades. From such a camp the Germans suddenly brought him to Berlin, and there a person ("polite, but a bastard") who spoke beautiful Russian asked him whether he could possibly be the same Potapov who had been at Dneprostroi. Could he, to prove it, draw, from instance, the diagram for switching on the generator there?

This diagram had at one time been published, and Potapov, without hesitating, drew it. He told about this himself at his interrogation, though he had not been compelled to.

In his indictment, what he did was described as "turning over the secrets of Dneproges."

However, the case against him did not include a further development: the unknown Russian, who had by this means verified Potapov's identity, proposed that he sign a declaration of readiness to reconstruct Dneproges—and he would immediately be given freedom, food rations, money, and his own beloved work.

As this enticing sheet of paper was placed before him, a deep thought crossed the robot's wrinkled face. Without beating his breast and shouting proud words, and without pretending to exercise his right to become a posthumous hero of the Soviet Union, Potapov modestly replied, "But you understand, I signed an oath. And if I sign this, there's a kind of contradiction, isn't there?"

And so, in a mild, untheatrical way, Potapov chose death over well-being.

"All right, I respect your convictions," replied the unknown Russian and sent Potapov back to the cannibal camps.

The Soviet court did not increase his ten-year sentence in spite of this.

Engineer Markushev, on the other hand, signed a similar declaration and went to work for the Germans. And the court gave him ten years, too. That was Stalin's signature—that magnificent equating of friends and enemies which made him unique in all human history.

Neither did the court increase Potapov's sentence for entering Berlin in 1945, riding on top of a Soviet tank as a parachutist, a machine gun in his hands and wearing those same broken and tied-together spectacles.

So Potapov got off easy with only "ten, and five on the horns."

Nerzhin returned from breakfast, took off his shoes, and climbed up on his bunk, rocking himself and Potapov. He had ahead of him his daily acrobatic feat—making his bed with no lumps while standing on it. But when he tossed aside the pillow, he found underneath it a cigarette case made of dark-red transparent plastic, filled tightly with a single layer of twelve Belomorkanal cigarettes, and they were intertwined with a slip of plain paper on which was written in draftsman's lettering:

> That's how he killed ten years
> Spending the flower of his life.

He could not be wrong. In the whole sharashka only Potapov combined the talent for such workmanship with the total recall of passages from *Evgeni Onegin* which had carried over from his school days.

"Andreich!" said Nerzhin, hanging his head down from the bunk.

Potapov had finished drinking his tea, had opened the newspaper and was reading it sitting up so as not to mess up the bed.

"Well, what is it?" he muttered.

"Is this your handiwork?"

"I wouldn't know. You found it?" he said, trying not to smile.

"Andreich!" Nerzhin drawled. "It's a dream!"

The gentle, crafty creases deepened and multiplied on Potapov's face. Adjusting his glasses, he replied, "When I was in the Lubyanka with Count Esterházy, both of us in one cell, me carrying out the latrine bucket on even days, you see, and he on odd days, me teaching him Russian from the 'Prison Regulations' on the wall, I gave him three buttons I'd found in the bread for his birthday—all his had been cut off, and he swore he'd never received a more timely gift from any Hapsburg."

According to the "voice classification," Potapov's voice was defined as "toneless with a crackle."

Still hanging over the bunk, Nerzhin looked warmly into Potapov's coarsely furrowed face. When he wore his glasses, he seemed no older than his forty-five years and even presented an energetic appearance. But when he took them off, his deep, dark eye cavities were almost like a corpse's.

"But it's embarrassing for me, Andreich. After all, I can't give you anything like that. I don't have hands like yours. How could you remember my birthday?"

"Never mind," Potapov replied. "What other notable dates are left in our lives?"

They both sighed.

"Do you want some tea?" Potapov proposed. "I have a special brew."

"No, Andreich, I don't need tea. I'm going for a visit."

"Wonderful!" Potapov said, pleased. "With your old woman?"

"Yeah."

"Just the thing. Come on, Valentulya, don't shout in my ear."

"What right does one person have to mock another?"

"What's in the paper, Andreich?" asked Nerzhin.

Potapov, squinting with Ukrainian slyness, looked up at Nerzhin, still hanging over the bunk:

"The fables of the British muse
Disturb the maiden's sleep."

More than three years had passed since Nerzhin and
Potapov had met in Butyrskaya Prison in a clamorous, overcrowded cell which even in the July days was half-dark.
There, in the second summer after the war, the lives of many
different people had crossed. Newcomers from Europe passed
through that cell. And stalwart Russian prisoners who had
just succeeded in exchanging German POW imprisonment
for a Russian prison. And battered and crippled camp inmates in transit from GULAG caves to the sharashka oases.
When he had entered the cell, Nerzhin had crawled blindly
under the plank beds. (The plank beds were so low that one
could not get under them on all fours but had to crawl on
stomach and elbows.) There, on the dirty asphalt floor,
with his eyes still unused to the dark, he had asked cheerfully, "Who's last, friends?"

And a toneless cracked voice had answered him, "Here I
am. You're sleeping behind me."

Day after day, as prisoners were taken from the cell for
transport, they moved under the plank beds "from the latrine
bucket to the window," and by the third week they moved
back "from the window to the latrine bucket" but this time
on top of the plank beds. Later on they moved once again
across the wooden beds to the window. That was the way
their friendship had been welded, despite differences of age,
personal histories, and tastes.

It was then, in the endless months of deliberation after his
trial, that Potapov admitted to Nerzhin that he would never
have become concerned with politics if politics itself had not
started tearing him apart.

It was then, under the plank beds of Butyrskaya Prison,
that the robot became puzzled for the first time, something
which, it is well known, is not recommended for robots.
No, he still did not regret having refused German bread,
and he did not regret the three years lost in starving, deadly
POW imprisonment. And he still considered it inadmissible
that foreigners should judge our internal difficulties.

But the spark of doubt had been kindled in him and begun
to smolder. Somehow, he could not understand why they
had jailed people whose only guilt was that they had constructed Dneproges.

28

HOW TO DARN SOCKS

At 8:55 there was an inspection in the rooms of the special prison. This operation, which took hours in the camps, with zeks standing out in the cold, being mustered from place to place, counting off by ones, by fives, by hundreds, sometimes by brigades, took place quietly and painlessly here at the sharashka. The zeks drank tea at their night tables; two duty officers, one going off duty and one coming on, came into the room; the zeks stood up (some did not stand up); the new duty officer intently counted heads; and then announcements were made and complaints reluctantly heard.

The officer on duty today was Senior Lieutenant Shusterman. He was tall, black-haired, and while not exactly morose, he never expressed any human feeling whatever—which was how guards who had had advanced training were supposed to behave. He and Nadelashin had been sent from the Lubyanka to strengthen prison discipline here. Several of the zeks remembered them both from the Lubyanka: at one time they had both served as escort guards with the rank of master sergeant; these were the guards who took charge of a prisoner as he stood facing the wall, and conducted him by the famous worn steps to the landing between the fourth and fifth floors, where a passage had been cut from the prison to the investigation-interrogation building. Through this passage for a third of a century all prisoners of the central prison had been led: Cadets, Social Revolutionaries, anarchists, Octobrists, Mensheviks, Bolsheviks, Savinkov, Yakubovich, Kutepov, Ramzin, Shulgin, Bukharin, Rykov, Tukhachevsky, Professor Pletnev, Academician Vavilov, Field Marshal Paulus, General Krasnov, world-famous scientists and poets who would barely creep out of their shells, first the criminals themselves, then their wives, then their daughters. The prisoners were led up to an equally famous desk, where in the thick book of "Registered Lives" each prisoner who passed signed through a slot in a metal plate, without seeing the name above or below his own. Then he was taken up a stairway on either side of which were stretched nets like those for circus trapeze artists to prevent the prisoners from attempting suicide by jumping. He was led down endless ministry corridors stifling with electric light and chilled by the gold glitter of colonels' insignia.

But no matter how deeply those under interrogation plunged into that first fathomless despair, they soon noticed the difference between the two men: Shusterman—of course they did not know his name then—looked like grim lightning under his thick brows; he seized the prisoner by the elbow as though he had claws, and with brute strength dragged him, gasping for breath, up the stairs; moon-faced Nadelashin, eunuch-like, always walked a little apart from the prisoner, not touching him, and he spoke politely, telling him where to turn.

Shusterman, who was younger, already wore three little stars on his shoulder boards.

Nadelashin announced that those who were going on visits should show up at staff headquarters by 9 A.M. Asked whether there would be a movie that evening, he replied that there would not be. There was a light murmur of dissatisfaction but from a corner Khorobrov answered back: "And don't bother bringing shit like *Cossacks of the Kuban.*"

Shusterman turned sharply, cutting off the speaker, and in doing so he lost count and had to start counting all over again.

In the silence someone spoke out audibly but not so as to be identifiable: "That's it. That goes in your personal file."

Khorobrov, his upper lip twitching in anger, answered, "The hell with them. They've already written so much against me there's no more room in the file."

Engineer Adamson in his big square glasses was sitting on the next bunk. He asked, "Junior Lieutenant! We asked about a New Year's tree. Will there be one or not?"

"Yes, there will be a New Year's tree!" the junior lieutenant replied, obviously happy to announce the pleasant news. "We're going to put it right here in the room."

"And we can make decorations?" Ruska called out cheerfully from an upper bunk. He sat up there, Turkish style, a mirror on his pillow, tying his necktie. In five minutes he was to meet Clara—he had seen from the window that she had already passed the watchtower and gone into the yard.

"We'll find out about that. There are no instructions."

"What instructions do you need?"

"What is a New Year's tree without decorations?"

"Friends, we'll make decorations anyway."

"Calm down, fellow. What about our boiling water?"

"Will the minister do anything about it?"

The room hummed merrily, discussing the prospect of the tree. The duty officers had just turned to leave, but Khorobrov drowned out the din of talk with his loud, abrupt call: "You tell them to keep the tree until Orthodox Christmas, January 7! A tree is for Christmas, not New Year's."

The duty officers acted as if they had not heard him and went out.

Everyone talked at once. Khorobrov still had something on his mind which he had not managed to say to the officers, and now, silently, he was addressing some invisible person, energetically, his face working. He had never celebrated either Christmas or Easter, but out of contrariness he had begun to observe them in prison. At least these holidays were not marked by intensified searches or more severe impositions.

Adamson finished drinking his tea. He wiped off his fogged glasses in their large plastic frames and said to Khorobrov, "Ilya Terentich! You are forgetting the prisoner's second commandment: don't stick your neck out."

Khorobrov looked hard at Adamson. "That's an outdated commandment of your own lost wave of prisoners. You behaved yourselves, and they killed you all off."

The reproach was, as it happened, unjust. It was precisely those men who had been arrested along with Adamson who had organized the strikes at Vorkuta. But they came to the same end anyway. One couldn't explain all that to Khorobrov just then. And the commandment—that had been thought up by later waves of prisoners.

Adamson merely shrugged and said, "If you make a scene, they'll send you away to some hard-labor camp."

"And that, Grigory Borisich, is what I want! If it's hard labor, then hard labor it is, the hell with them; at least I'll get in with a good bunch. Maybe there won't even be informers there."

Rubin, always late for everything, had not even had his tea. He stood with his disheveled beard next to Potapov's and Nerzhin's bunks and spoke affectionately to the occupant of the upper level: "Happy birthday, my young Montaigne, you dumbbell."

"I'm very touched, Lev, my dear friend, but you shouldn't—"

Nerzhin knelt on his upper bunk, holding a desk pad. It was clearly a prisoner's craftwork; that is, the most painstaking work in the world, for prisoners have nowhere to hurry to. There were beautifully placed little pockets in Bordeaux calico, fastenings, buttons and packets of fine paper "liberated" from abroad. All the work on it had been done, of course, on government time.

". . . besides they don't let you do much writing in the sharashka anyway—except denunciations."

"And my wish for you—" Rubin's thick lips protruded in their comical pout— "is that your skeptic-eclectic brain be flooded with the light of truth."

"And what is truth, peasant? Can anyone really know what truth is?" Gleb sighed. His face had grown younger in his previsit rush, but it had settled again into ashen wrinkles. His reddish hair hung down on either side.

On the adjacent upper bunk, above Pryanchikov's, a balding, heavy-set engineer, sedate in years, was using the last seconds of free time to read a newspaper he had got from Potapov. Opening it wide and holding it at arm's length, he sometimes frowned and sometimes moved his lips slightly as he read. When the bell in the corridor sounded, he folded the paper haphazardly.

"What the hell's it all about, damn it? They keep going on and on about world domination."

And he looked around for a convenient place to throw the paper.

The immense Dvoyetyosov, on the other side of the room, whose big clumsy legs hung down from his upper bunk, asked in his bass voice, "And what about you, Zemelya? Hasn't world domination gotten to you? Aren't you longing for it?"

"Me?" Zemelya asked, surprised, as if he took the question seriously. "No, no," he said smiling broadly. "What the hell do I need it for? I don't want it." And groaning he began to climb down.

"Well, in that case let's get going and get to work," Dvoyetyosov said and jumped with his whole weight thudding to the floor.

The bell went on ringing. It summoned the prisoners to Sunday work. Its ringing told them that the inspection was

finished and that the "Holy Door" on the institute stairway
had been opened; the zeks moved swiftly out in a packed
crowd.

Now most of the zeks were out. Doronin had run out
first. Sologdin, who had shut the window while they were
getting up and having tea, now opened it again, wedging in
the volume of Ehrenburg, and then he hurried into the corridor to catch Professor Chelnov as he left his "professor's
cell." As always, Rubin had not managed to get anything
done that morning, and he hurriedly put what he had not
finished eating and drinking into his night table. Something
spilled in it. And he was wrestling with his impossibly lumped
and lacerated bed, vainly trying to make it in such a way
that he wouldn't be called back to remake it later.

Nerzhin was adjusting his "masquerade" clothes. There
had been a time when the zeks of the sharashka went around
every day in good suits and overcoats, and wore them on
visits. Now, they had been outfitted in the dark-blue coveralls—so that the guards on the watchtower could clearly tell
the zeks from the free employees and know whom to shoot.
The prison administration compelled them to change into
ordinary clothes for visits, issuing them used suits and shirts
which had probably been confiscated from the private ward-
robes of people whose property had been seized after they
were sentenced. Some zeks enjoyed seeing themselves well
dressed, even for a short time; others, repelled, would gladly
have avoided putting on the clothes of a corpse, but the
authorities absolutely refused to take them on visits in their
coveralls. They didn't want the prisoners' relatives to get a
bad impression of prison. And there was no one with such
an inflexible spirit as to decline the possibility of seeing the
person he loved. So they changed clothes.

The semicircular room was now almost empty. Twelve
pairs of bunks welded in double tiers remained, made up
hospital fashion with the top sheet turned back and exposed
—so as to collect dust and get dirty faster. This method
could only have been conceived in a bureaucratic, and particularly a male head, and even its inventor's wife would never
have used it at home. However, the regulations of the prison
sanitary commission required it.

In the room a rare silence had settled, which one did not
care to disturb.

There were still four people in the room: Nerzhin, who

was getting dressed, Khorobrov, Adamson, and the bald designer.

The designer was one of those timid zeks who even after years in prison could not acquire the typical prisoner's insolence. He would never have dared stay away from Sunday work, but today he was feeling ill and, having been excused from work by the prison doctor, he had spread out on his bunk a vast number of socks with holes in them, some thread, and a homemade cardboard darning egg; and furrowing his brow, he was trying to decide where to begin his darning.

Grigory Borisovich Adamson, who had "lawfully served" one ten-year sentence already, not to mention six years of exile before that, and who had been sentenced to ten more years in the wave of "second-timers," did not exactly refuse to go to work on Sunday, but he tried his best not to go. There had been a time in his Komsomol days when he couldn't have been dragged by the ears from the company of the comrades who worked on their days off; but it was understood then that these enthusiasts were acting in the spirit of the times—to get the economy in shape: one or two years perhaps and then everything would go beautifully and gardens would flower everywhere. And now Adamson was one of the few there who had already "sat out"—and "oversat"—those full ten years, and he knew that it was no myth, no daydream of the court, no amusing adventure until the first general amnesty—as all the newcomers believed—but that it was a full ten, twelve, or fifteen wasting years of a human life. He had long since learned to economize on every muscular movement, to hoard every minute of rest. And he knew that the best thing to do on a Sunday was to lie motionless in bed in his underwear.

Therefore he removed the book Sologdin had wedged in the window and let the window close, slowly took off his coveralls, got under the blanket, wrapped himself up, wiped his glasses with a special piece of suède, put a sugar candy in his mouth, straightened his pillow, and took from under the mattress a thick book wrapped for safety's sake in a paper cover. Just to see him there was comforting.

Khorobrov, on the contrary, was miserable. In gloomy meditation he lay fully dressed on top of the blanket on his made-up bed, his shoes resting on the bed railing. By temperament he suffered keenly and persistently things that others shrugged off. Every Saturday, in accordance with the well-known principle that everything was done on a voluntary basis, all the prisoners, without being asked, were signed up as volunteers to work on Sunday, and a list was submitted to the prison administration. If the sign-up had actually been voluntary, Khorobrov would always have signed up and willingly spent his free days at his desk. But precisely because the sign-up was an open mockery, Khorobrov had to lie there stupidly in the closed-up prison.

A camp zek can only dream of lying in a warm closed shelter on a Sunday, but the sharashka zek's sacroiliac, after all, doesn't ache.

There was absolutely nothing to do. He had already read all the available newspapers yesterday. On the night table next to his bunk was a pile of books from the special prison library. One of them was a collection of journalistic essays by revered writers. Khorobrov opened to an essay by Alexei Non-Tolstoi, as they derisively called Alexei N. Tolstoi in the sharashka. And under the date June 1941 he read: "German soldiers, driven by terror and insanity, ran into a wall of iron and fire at the border." He put it aside at once. In well-furnished houses near Moscow where even before the war they had electric refrigerators, these intellectual giants were inflated into omnipotent oracles, though they heard nothing but the radio and saw nothing but their flower beds. A half-literate collective farmer knew more about life than they did.

The other books in the pile were belles-lettres, but reading them made Khorobrov sick. One was a new hit, *Far from Us*, which at this moment was being widely read on the outside. But after reading a little of it Khorobrov felt nausea. The book was a meat pie without the meat, an egg with its insides sucked out, a stuffed bird. It talked about a construction project which had actually been carried out by zeks, and about camps, but nowhere were the camps named, nor did it say that the workers were zeks, that they received prison rations and were jailed in punishment cells; instead, they were changed into Komsomols who were well dressed, well shod, and full of enthusiasm. And there the experienced reader sensed that the author himself knew, saw, and touched the truth, that he might even have been a security officer in a camp, but that he was lying with cold, glassy eyes.

The second book was the *Selected Works* of the famous writer Galakhov, whose star was at its literary zenith. Having recognized the name Galakhov and expecting something from him, Khorobrov had already read the book, but he put it down with the feeling that he was being mocked just as he was mocked by the "voluntary" Sunday work list. Even Galakhov, who could write quite well about love, had slipped through some sort of spiritual paralysis into that ever more prevalent manner of writing as if one weren't writing for people but for simpletons of no experience who, in their feeblemindedness, were grateful for any kind of diversion.

Everything that really tore and shook the human heart was absent from their books. If the war had not come, all they could have done was to become professional eulogists. The war opened the way for them to simple, generally comprehensible human feelings. But here, too, they elevated to Hamlet-like heights all sorts of fantastic and impossible conflicts—such as the Komsomol member who blew up dozens of ammunition trains behind enemy lines but, because he wasn't a member in good standing of any Party organization, was torn day and night by uncertainty whether he was a real Komsomol member if he didn't pay dues.

There was another book on the night table, too—*American Tales* by progressive writers. Khorobrov could not verify these stories by comparing them with life, but the selection was surprising. In every story there was some obligatory abomination about America. Venomously assembled, they made up such a nightmarish picture that one could only be amazed that the Americans had not yet fled the country or hanged themselves.

There was nothing to read!

Khorobrov thought about smoking. He pulled out a cigarette and started to roll it between his fingers. In the perfectly silent room the tightly packed cigarette rustled in his fingers. He wanted to smoke right where he was, without going out, without taking his feet off the bed railing. Prisoners who smoke know that the only real satisfaction comes from the cigarette smoked while lying on one's own strip of plank bed, on one's own berth, an unhurried cigarette with one's gaze fixed on the ceiling where pictures of the irretrievable past and the unattainable future float by.

But the bald designer was not a smoker and disliked smoke. And Adamson, though he smoked himself, held the mistaken theory that there must be fresh air in a room. Having firmly mastered the principle that freedom begins with respect for the rights of others, Khorobrov with a sigh dropped his legs to the floor and started toward the exit. As he did, he noticed the fat book in Adamson's hands and knew immediately that there was no such book in the prison library and that it must have come from outside, and no one would ask for a bad book from there.

However, Khorobrov did not lose his composure and ask aloud, like an innocent, "What are you reading?" or "Where did you get that?"—because the designer and Nerzhin would hear Adamson's reply. He went right up to Adamson and said quietly, "Grigory Borisich, let me have a look at the title page."

"All right, look," Adamson said reluctantly.

Khorobrov opened to the title page and read, astonished: *The Count of Monte Cristo.*

He whistled.

"Borisich," he asked caressingly, "is there anyone after you? Have I a chance?"

Adamson took off his glasses thoughtfully and said, "We'll see. Will you cut my hair today?"

The zeks did not like the visiting Stakhanovite barber. Their own self-appointed master barbers cut their hair to satisfy all personal whims and worked slowly because they had long terms ahead of them.

"Who'll get us scissors?"

"I'll get them from Zyablin."

"All right, I'll give you a haircut."

"Good. There's a section up to page 128 that can be taken out and I'll let you have it soon."

Observing that Adamson had read up to page 110, Khorobrov went out into the corridor to smoke in a much better mood.

Gleb was increasingly filled with a tremendous holiday feeling in anticipation of seeing his wife. Somewhere in the students' residence on Stromynka, Nadya, too, was probably nervous in this last hour. At such meetings thoughts scatter, you forget what you wanted to say; it has to be written down on paper, learned by heart, then destroyed, for you can't take a piece of paper with you. And you have to remember eight points, eight: that you may be going away, that sentences do not end with the end of the sentence, that there will still be exile, that . . .

He ran off to the coatroom and ironed his "dickey." The

dickey was an invention of Ruska Doronin, and many others had adopted it. It was a piece of white cloth, from a sheet which had been torn into thirty-two parts—though the supply room did not know that—to which a white collar had been sewn. That piece of cloth was just sufficient to cover the opening at the throat of the coveralls where the undershirt showed with its black stamp "MGB—Special Prison No. ——". And it also had two strings which tied at the back. The dickey helped create that appearance of well-being which was desired by all. Not difficult to wash, it served faithfully on weekdays and holidays, and while wearing it one was not ashamed before the free workers of the institute.

On the staircase, Nerzhin tried vainly to shine his worn-out shoes with someone's dried and crumbly shoe polish. The prison did not issue shoes for the visits since they would be under the table and out of sight.

When he returned to the room to shave (razors, even straight razors, were permitted there, such was the whimsicality of the rules), Khorobrov was already buried in his book. The designer with his multitudinous darning had taken over part of the floor as well as his bunk; he was cutting out and patching, marking his patches with a pencil. From his pillow Adamson looked past his book, squinted and advised him as follows:

"Darning is effective only when done conscientiously. God save us from a formalistic approach. Don't hurry. Put stitch after stitch and cross-stitch everything twice. One of the most common mistakes is to use rotten loops at the edge of a torn hole. Don't economize, don't save bad parts. Cut around the hole. Have you ever heard the name Berkalov?"

"What? Berkalov? No."

"Well, how can that be? Berkalov was an old artillery engineer and the inventor of those BC-3 cannon, you know, wonderful cannon, with a fantastic muzzle velocity. Well, there sat Berkalov, also on a Sunday, also in a sharashka, and he was darning his socks. And the radio was on. 'Berkalov, Lieutenant General, a first degree Stalin Prize,' said the radio. And before his arrest he was only a major general. So what did he do? He kept on darning his socks, and then he started making pancakes on a hot plate. The guard came in, cursed him out, took away his illegal hot plate, and made up a report for the chief of the prison which would have meant three days in the punishment block. And then the chief of the prison himself ran in like a schoolboy shouting, 'Berkalov! Bring your things! The Kremlin! Kalinin is summoning you!' Now there's our Russian destiny for you."

29

SOARING TO THE CEILING

The old Professor of Mathematics, Chelnov, a familiar figure in many sharashkas, who wrote "zek" instead of "Russian" in the space for "nationality" on questionnaires, and who would complete his eighteenth year of imprisonment in 1950, had applied his pencil point to many inventions, from the direct-flow boiler to the jet engine, and he had put his soul into some of them as well.

However, Professor Chelnov maintained that the phrase "to put one's soul into something" must be used with care, because only a zek is certain to have an immortal soul; free people are often denied one because of the vain lives they lead. In a friendly zek chat over a bowl of cold gruel or a glass of steaming chocolate, Chelnov did not deny that he had borrowed this notion from Pierre Bezukhov in *War and Peace*. It is well known that when a French soldier forbade Pierre to cross the road, Pierre roared out laughing, "Ha, ha! The soldier did not let me cross. Who—me? He did not let my immortal soul cross!"

At the Mavrino sharashka Professor Chelnov was the only zek not compelled to wear coveralls. (This question had gone all the way up to Abakumov for his personal decision.) The principal basis for such libertarianism lay in the fact that Chelnov was not a permanent zek of Mavrino sharashka but a transient zek. A Corresponding Member of the Academy of Sciences in the past and a Director of the Mathematics Institute, he was at the special disposal of Beria, and each time he was transferred it was to the sharashka where the most urgent mathematical problem had arisen. Once he had solved it in general outline and demonstrated how to work it out, he was transferred elsewhere.

But Professor Chelnov did not take advantage of his freedom to choose his clothing as a man of ordinary vanity
would. He wore an inexpensive suit; the color of the jacket
and trousers did not match; on his feet he wore felt boots;
over the thin gray hairs of his head, he pulled a knitted wool
cap—it might be a ski cap or a girl's cap; and he was particularly distinguished by the eccentric plaid wool shawl
which he wore wrapped twice around his shoulders and
back, rather like a woman's shawl.

However, Chelnov was able to wear that shawl and that
cap in such a way that his presence was not absurd but
majestic. The long oval of his face, his sharp profile, his
authoritative manner of speaking with the prison adminis-
trators, as well as the faded light blue of his eyes, a color
seen only in those of abstract mind—all this made Chelnov
seem strangely like a Descartes or perhaps some mathematician of the Renaissance.

Chelnov had been sent to the Mavrino sharashka to work
out the mathematical basis of the absolute encoder, the device that could assure by mechanical rotation the operation
of banks of relays which would take the separate impulses
into which speech had been chopped up and so scramble
them that not even hundreds of technicians with hundreds of
decoders could decipher a conversation on the wire.

Similarly, in the Design Office a search was going on for
the design solution for such an encoder. All the designers
were busy with this, except Sologdin.

Sologdin had hardly arrived at the sharashka from Inta in
the far north and looked things over than he announced to
everyone that his memory had suffered from prolonged
starvation, that his capabilities had become dulled, and had
in fact been limited from his birth anyway, and that he was
only in condition to perform auxiliary work. He could play
his hand so boldly because at Inta he had not been engaged
in general work but had a good job as an engineer, and he
was not afraid of being sent back there.

However, they did not send him back, as they well might
have done, but left him in the sharashka on trial. Thus, instead of being in the mainstream of work where tension,
hurry, and nervousness prevailed, Sologdin got into a quiet
side stream. He had no status, but no worries either, was
seldom checked on, had enough free time at his disposal;

and without supervision, secretly, at night, along his own lines, he had begun to work out the design of an absolute encoder.

He considered that great ideas are born only in a single mind.

Indeed, during the past half-year he had found a solution which had eluded ten engineers especially assigned to find it but incessantly driven and harassed. Two days ago Sologdin had given his work to Professor Chelnov to check, also unofficially. And now he was climbing the stairs beside the professor, respectfully supporting him by the arm through the crowd of zeks and awaiting the verdict on his work.

But Chelnov never mixed work and leisure.

In the short distance they had covered through corridors and stairways he had said nothing about the matter so important to Sologdin, but was telling him with a smile about his morning walk with Lev Rubin. After Rubin had been prevented from joining the woodcutters, he had read Chelnov his verses on a Biblical subject. There were one or two failures of rhythm, but there were original rhymes, and Chelnov had to admit that the verses were not bad. The ballad told how Moses had led the Jews through the wilderness for forty years, in deprivation, thirst, and famine, and how the people became delirious and rebelled; but they were wrong and Moses was right, knowing that in the end they would reach the promised land. Rubin had, no doubt, suffered over this poem and had put his heart into it.

Chelnov had opinions on the subject.

Chelnov directed Rubin's attention to the *geography* of Moses' crossing. From the Nile to Jerusalem the Jews had at the most 250 miles to go, and that meant that even if they rested on the Sabbath they could have easily covered the distance in three weeks. Wasn't it necessary therefore to assume that for the remaining forty years Moses did not simply lead them but misled them all over the Arabian desert? Hence the exaggeration.

Professor Chelnov took his room key from the duty officer outside the doors to Yakonov's office. Only he and the Iron Mask among the zeks enjoyed this privilege. (No zek had the right to stay one second in his workroom without the supervision of a free employee because prudence dictated that the prisoner would be bound to use that unsupervised second to break into the steel safe with a lead pencil, photograph its secret documents with a trouser button, explode an atom bomb, and fly to the moon.)

Chelnov worked in a room called the "Brain Trust" where there was nothing but a wardrobe and two plain chairs. It had been decided—with the permission of the ministry, of course—to issue a personal key to Professor Chelnov. Since then his room had become a subject of constant preoccupation to Security Officer Shikin. In hours when the prisoners were shut up in the prison by a doubly barred door, this high-paid comrade whose hours were his own came on his own legs to the professor's room, knocked on the walls, hopped on the floor boards, peered into the dusty gap behind the wardrobe and gloomily shook his head, understanding that from such liberalism nothing good could come.

But it wasn't enough for Chelnov just to get his key. Four or five doors farther along the third-floor corridor was a checkpoint for the Top Secret Section. This checkpoint was a stand with a chair beside it. Seated on the chair was a charwoman, not a simple charwoman who swept floors or heated water for tea—there were others for that—but a charwoman with a special function, a charwoman who checked the passes of those proceeding into the Top Secret Section. The passes, printed in the main typography section of the ministry, were of three kinds: permanent, weekly, and one-time, according to the system worked out by Major Shikin. (It had been his idea to make the blind corridor Top Secret.)

The work at the checkpoint was not easy: people went through only rarely, but both in the regulations displayed there and in the frequent oral directives of Comrade Major Shikin, it was categorically forbidden to knit socks. And the charwomen—there were two who divided the twenty-four hours—struggled in torment against sleep throughout their duty period. This checkpoint was also very inconvenient for Colonel Yakonov; he was interrupted all day long to sign passes.

Nevertheless the post existed. And to cover the pay of these two charwomen, instead of the three janitors provided for in the table of organization they kept only one, namely, Spiridon.

Although Chelnov knew perfectly well that the woman

sitting at the post was called Marya Ivanovna, and although she admitted the gray-haired old man every morning, still she demanded, startled, "Your pass."

Chelnov showed her his cardboard pass, and Sologdin got out his paper pass.

They went on past the checkpoint, then past two more doors, past the boarded-over, chalk-smeared glass door to the Iron Mask's personal room, and unlocked Chelnov's door.

It was a cozy little room with one window, that had a view of the prisoners' exercise yard and the grove of centenarian lindens which fate had not spared but had imprisoned within the zone protected by automatic fire. Abundant frost covered their majestic crowns.

A dull white sky overshadowed the earth.

To the left of the lindens, beyond the zone, was an ancient wooden house, grown gray with time and now turning white. It was two stories high, with a sheet-iron roof in the shape of a ship. Once, the estate owner had lived in it before the brick house had been built. Beyond were the roofs of the little village of Mavrino, and then a field, and farther on, along the railway line, there rose a bright silver plume of steam from a locomotive—although the locomotive itself and the railway cars were barely visible in the dull white morning.

But Sologdin hardly noticed the view spread before him. Though invited, he did not sit down. Lithe and feeling his strong young legs beneath him, he leaned against the side of the window and stared at his roll of papers on Chelnov's desk.

Chelnov sat down in a hard armchair with a high straight back, adjusted his shawl around his shoulders, opened his notebook to a page of notes, picked up a long spearlike pencil, and looked at Sologdin severely. At once the bantering tone of their previous conversation disappeared.

It was as if great wings were beating in the small room. Chelnov spoke for no more than two minutes, but so concisely that one could not catch a breath between his thoughts. This meant that Chelnov had done more than Sologdin asked. He had worked out an estimate of the mathematical possibilities of the design proposed by Sologdin. The design promised a result close to that required, at least until they could switch over to purely electronic equipment. However, it was still necessary to find out how to make it insensitive to low-energy impulses and to estimate precisely the effect of the greatest inertial forces in the mechanism so as to assure the adequacy of the flywheel momentum.

"And then—" Chelnov looked at Sologdin with a twinkle in his eye—"and then don't forget: your encoding is built on the principle of chaos, and that is fine. But chaos once determined, chaos which has cooled off, is already a *system*. It would be still better to perfect a solution by which chaos would be chaotically changed."

Here the professor considered, folded the page in half, and fell silent.

Sologdin closed his eyes, as if blinded by a bright light, and stood there, not seeing.

From the professor's first words, he had felt a wave of inner warmth. Now he leaned hard against the window so as not to soar up to the ceiling from happiness, as he felt he might.

What had he been before his imprisonment? What had he been capable of? Was he a real engineer? He had been a kid concerned more with how he looked than with anything else, and had, in fact, been sentenced to five years because of an enemy's jealousy.

Then there had been Butyrskaya, Presnya, SevUrallag, Ivdellag, Kargopollag. . . .

There had been a central investigation-interrogation prison inside the camp, carved out of the mountain.

There had been his "protector," his "old buddy," Security Officer Senior Lieutenant Kamyshan, who spent eleven months on his catechism for a second term, another ten years. In handing out second terms Kamyshan did not bother with the central administration's quotas. He roped in all those whose sentences were too short, who were being held in camp only on special orders till the end of the war. And he didn't waste time over the charges. Someone said to someone else that the Hermitage had sold a painting to the West—and they both got ten years.

There had been a woman, too—a nurse, a female zek, on whose account Kamyshan, a ruddy, imposing skirt-chaser, was jealous of Sologdin. And for good reason. Even today Sologdin remembered that nurse with such distinct physical gratitude that because of her he wasn't even altogether sorry he had got his extra term.

Kamyshan loved to beat people on the mouth with a stick, so that their teeth fell out, bleeding. If he had ridden to camp on horseback—and he was a good rider—that day he would use his whip handle.

It was wartime. Even on the outside everyone was on rations. And in camp? In the Mountain Cave?

Sologdin, having learned from his first investigation, had signed nothing. But he got ten more anyway. They took him straight from the trial to the hospital. He was dying. His body, destined to disintegrate, refused to take bread, porridge, gruel.

The day came when they put him on a stretcher and carried him into the morgue to knock his head open with a big wooden mallet before hauling him off to the cemetery. But he had moved. . . .

And now to be out of here! The thrill of returning to life! After the years of imprisonment, after the years of work, after the comfortable barracks of the engineering and technical personnel, where had he soared? How had it happened? To whom was this Descartes in his woolen cap speaking such flattering words?

Chelnov folded his sheet of notes in four, then in eight.

"As you see," he said, "there's a great deal of work left to do. But this design will be the best of all those proposed. It will give you freedom. And the annulment of your conviction."

For some reason Chelnov smiled. His smile was sharp and thin, like the whole shape of his face.

His smile was directed at himself. Though he had done much more at various sharashkas at various times than Sologdin was about to, he himself was not threatened with freedom or the annulment of his conviction. There had, in fact, been no conviction at all. Once, long ago, he had expressed himself on the subject of the Wise Father, to the effect that he was a loathsome reptile, and he had got eighteen years of imprisonment, without verdict, sentence, or hope.

Sologdin opened his shining blue eyes, straightened up and said rather theatrically, "Vladimir Erastovich! You give me support and assurance! I cannot find words to thank you for your attention. I am in debt to you!" But a vague smile was already playing about his lips.

Returning the roll of papers to Sologdin, the professor remembered something. "I must apologize to you. You asked me not to show Anton Nikolayevich this diagram. However, he happened to come into my room when I was out and unrolled this, as he would. And of course he immediately understood what it was about. I had to tell him who you were."

Sologdin's smile disappeared from his lips. He frowned.

"Is it that important to you?" Chelnov's surprise was accompanied by a very slight movement of his face. "But why? One day earlier, one day later . . ."

Sologdin himself was puzzled about why it was important. He lowered his eyes. Had not the time come to take his diagram to Yakonov?

"How shall I put it to you, Vladimir Erastovich? Don't you think there may be a certain moral question here? After all, this is not a bridge, a crane, a lathe. There is very little industrial significance in it, but a great deal that relates to the palace. When I think of the *customer* who will pick up our transmitter . . . You see, so far I have done this only to try out my own strength. For myself."

He looked up again.

For himself.

Chelnov knew that kind of work very well. As a rule it was the highest form of research.

"But—under the circumstances—isn't it perhaps too great a luxury for you?" Chelnov looked at him with pale, calm eyes.

Sologdin smiled. "Forgive me, please," he said, correcting himself. "It was nothing. I was only thinking aloud. Don't blame yourself for anything. I am grateful, very grateful."

He respectfully gripped Chelnov's weak and tender hand and left with the roll of papers under his arm.

He had come into this room a free contender. And now he left it as a burdened victor. He was no longer the master of his own time, intentions, or labor.

Chelnov did not lean back in the armchair. He shut his eyes and sat there a long time, erect, thin-faced, in his knitted woolen cap.

30

PENALTY MARKS

Still inwardly rejoicing, Sologdin flung open the door with needless force and entered the Design Office. But instead of the crowd he expected to find in the large room, always a buzz of voices, he found only one substantial female figure by a window.

"You're alone, Larisa Nikolayevna?" Sologdin asked, surprised. He crossed the room with his quick stride.

Larisa Nikolayevna Emina, a woman of thirty, a draftsman, turned from the window where her drawing board stood and smiled over her shoulder at the approaching Sologdin.

"Dmitri Aleksandrovich? And I thought I'd be bored all by myself all day."

Her words seemed to carry a suggestive overtone. Sologdin looked at her attentively, and his swift glance took in her big figure in a bright green wool knit skirt and jacket. With precise step he passed her and went to his desk without answering. Immediately, before sitting down, he made a small vertical line on a sheet of pink paper which lay there. Then, standing with his back to Emina, he fastened a drawing he had brought with him to his adjustable drawing board.

The Design Office was a bright spacious room on the third floor with three large windows facing south. Among the ordinary office desks there were a dozen similar drawing boards, some set almost vertically, some inclined, some completely horizontal. Sologdin's stood near the farthest window, the same one beside which Emina was seated. The drawing board was set perpendicularly and placed so as to shield Sologdin from the chiefs and from the entrance door, but still get the full flood of daylight on the drawing pinned to it.

Finally Sologdin asked dryly, "Why is no one here?"

"I thought I'd find out from you," was her melodious reply.

With a quick movement he turned to her and said, "You

can only find out from me where the four unprivileged zeks
who work in this room are. One of them has been called out
for a visit. Hugo Leonardovich is celebrating Latvian Christmas. I am here. And Ivan Ivanovich requested time off to
darn his socks, which in the past year have reached a total
of twenty pairs. But what I'd like to know is where are the
sixteen free workers, in other words the comrades who are
supposedly more responsible than we?"

He was in profile to Emina, and she could plainly see the
condescending smile between his small, precise mustache
and his neat little French beard. She looked at him with
delight.

"What? You don't know that our major came to an agreement with Anton Nikolayevich last night, and that today the
Design Office has a free day. But of course I had to be the
one assigned to duty."

"A free day? What's the occasion?"

"What do you mean, occasion? It's Sunday."

"Since when is Sunday a free day all of a sudden?"

"But the major said we don't have any urgent work right
now."

Sologdin turned sharply toward Emina.

"We have no urgent work?" he cried almost angrily.
"Well, well! We have no urgent work!" Sologdin's lips trembled with impatience. "And how would you like it if I were
to arrange it so that from tomorrow on all sixteen of you
would sit here copying day and night. Would you like that?"

He almost shouted "all sixteen."

In spite of the horrible prospect of copying day and night,
Emina remained calm, which suited her quiet, large-scale
beauty. Today she had not yet even removed the tracing
paper which covered her slightly tilted board, and she was
leaning comfortably forward on it. The close fit of her
jacket emphasized the fullness of her breasts. She rocked
gently back and forth and looked at Sologdin with big
friendly eyes.

"God save us! Would you be capable of such a thing?"

With a cold look Sologdin asked, "Why do you use the
word 'God'? After all you're the wife of a Chekist."

"What difference does that make?" Emina asked in surprise. "We bake Easter cake at Easter. And what of it?"

"Easter cake!"

"So what?"

Sologdin looked down at the seated Emina. The green of her knit suit was vivid, impertinent. Both her jacket and her skirt clung to and revealed her fleshy body. The jacket was unbuttoned at the neck, and the collar of a cambric blouse lay on top of it.

Sologdin drew another vertical line on the pink sheet and said with hostility, "After all, you said your husband is a lieutenant colonel in the MVD."

"That's my husband. My mother and I are women, after all," Emina said with a disarming smile. Her heavy, light-blond braids were wound around her head in a majestic wreath. She smiled, and then she looked like a village woman, but a village woman played by the actress Emma Tsesarskaya.

Sologdin, not replying, sat sideways at his desk, so as not to see Emina, and began to study the drawing pinned there.

He was still under the spell of Professor Chelnov's praise. He felt a mounting joy, and he did not want to lose the feeling. His brain child's insensitivity to low-energy impulses and the question of flywheel inertia Sologdin considered, intuitively, to be problems that could be solved, though it would obviously be necessary to check over all the calculations and allow an ample margin for safety. But Chelnov's last comment about the question of chaos disturbed him. It didn't mean that his work was faulty, but it did indicate where it differed from the ideal. He sensed vaguely that somewhere in his work was an unperfected "Final Inch," that Chelnov had not perceived and he himself had not caught. It was important right now, in the fortunate Sunday quiet, to determine what it was and proceed to rectify it. Only then could he disclose his work to Yakonov and start battering his way out through these thick walls.

So he made an effort to cut himself off from all thoughts of Emina and to return to the sphere of ideas inspired by Professor Chelnov. Emina had been sitting next to him for half a year, but they had never had a chance to talk for long. And they had never been alone with one another as they were today. Sologdin sometimes joked with her when, in accordance with his planned schedule, he allowed himself a five-minute rest period. Larisa Nikolayevna amused him, in her subordinate position as his draftsman, she being a lady from a higher social level while he was only an educated slave, but it was disturbing to behold her big, blossoming body all the time.

Sologdin looked at his drawing, and Emina, continuing to rock back and forth on her elbows, watched him. Her question came out of the blue: "Dmitri Aleksandrovich, what about you? Who darns your socks?"

Sologdin raised his brows. "My socks?" He went on looking at the drawing. "Ivan Ivanovich wears socks because he's still new, he's only been in prison three years. Socks are nothing but a belch from so-called—" and here he almost choked because he was forced to use a "bird word"—"capitalism. I don't wear socks." And he put a vertical line on a white sheet of paper.

"In that case, what do you wear?"

"You overstep the bounds of modesty, Larisa Nikolayevna," Sologdin said and could not help smiling. "I wear the pride of our Russian attire—foot cloths."

He pronounced these words with relish.

"But after all, soldiers wear them."

"Soldiers and two other groups besides: prisoners and collective farmers."

"But they have to be washed and mended, too."

"You're wrong! Who washes foot cloths nowadays? They're simply worn for a year without being washed and then thrown out and you get new ones from the administration."

"Really? Seriously?" Emina looked almost frightened.

Sologdin roared with carefree youthful laughter.

"At least some people see it that way. Yes, and do you think that on our pittance I would actually buy socks? Now you, you're a draftsman in the MGB, how much do you get a month?"

"Fifteen hundred rubles."

"So!" Sologdin exclaimed triumphantly. "Fifteen hundred rubles! And I as a 'creator,' meaning in the Language of Maximum Clarity an engineer, receive thirty rubles a month. You wouldn't throw money away on socks, would you?"

Sologdin's eyes lit up merrily. What he said had nothing to do with Emina, yet she was blushing.

Larisa Nikolayevna's husband, to put it plainly, was a dullard. To him his family had long since become a soft pillow, and to his wife he was just another piece of furniture in the apartment. When he came home from work, he spent a long time eating his dinner with great pleasure and then went off to sleep. When he came to, he read the papers and fussed with his radio. He was always selling his old radio and buying a new one. The only thing that excited him—and, indeed, aroused his passion—was soccer (because of his service branch he always cheered for the "Dynamo Sports Club"). He was so dull, so monotonous in everything, that he could not excite even a spark of interest in Larisa. And for that matter, the other men she knew took their pleasure in recounting their services to the country, playing cards, drinking until they were purple, and grabbing and pawing when they were drunk.

Sologdin, with his light movements, his quick mind and sharp tongue, his unexpected shifts from severity to derision, pleased her without the slightest effort on his part, and his success meant nothing to him.

He had turned back to his drawing. Larisa Nikolayevna went on looking at his face, at his mustache, his little beard, his moist, full lips. She would have liked to feel his beard rubbing and scratching her face.

"Dmitri Aleksandrovich," she said, again interrupting his silence, "am I disturbing you?"

"Yes, a little," Sologdin replied. The Final Inch demanded unbroken concentration. But his neighbor was indeed disturbing him. He turned from his drawing to his desk, and thereby to Emina as well, and began sorting insignificant papers.

He could hear the quick ticking of her wristwatch.

A group of people was coming down the corridor, talking quietly. From Number Seven next door Mamurin's lisping voice could be heard: "Well, is that transformer going to be ready soon?" And Markushev's irritated cry: "You shouldn't have given it to them, Yakov Ivanich."

Larisa Nikolayevna folded her hands and rested her chin on them; she looked languorously at Sologdin.

He was reading.

"Every hour. Every day," she whispered reverently. "You're in prison and you study like that! You are an unusual person, Dmitri Aleksandrovich!"

But clearly Sologdin was not able to read, for he looked up at once.

"And what if I am in prison, Larisa Nikolayevna? I've been in prison since I was twenty-five, and I'll get out at forty-two. Except I don't believe I will. They'll certainly add more. And the best part of my life will have been spent in camps, all my strength wasted. One can't give in to external conditions, it's degrading."

"With you everything is a system."

"I spent seven of my camp years on gruel and did my mental work without sugar or phosphorus. That forced me into a very strict routine. Freedom or prison—what's the difference? A man must develop unwavering will power subject only to his reason."

With her manicured forefinger, the round nail painted raspberry color, Emina tried carelessly and unsuccessfully to smooth the crumpled corner of the tracing paper. Then she lowered her head on her folded hands so that the steep crown of her thick braids was directed at him, and said thoughtfully, "I owe you an apology, Dmitri Aleksandrovich—"

"For what?"

"Once when I was standing at your desk, I saw you had been writing a letter. Well, you know how it can happen, quite by chance. And then another time—"

"You looked again—quite by chance?"

"And I saw you had again been writing a letter, and it seemed to be the same one."

"So, you could tell it was the same one? And was there a third time? There was, wasn't there?"

"Yes."

"So! Larisa Nikolayevna, if this continues, I shall be forced to dispense with your services as a draftsman. And I'll be sorry—you don't draw badly."

"But that was a long time ago. You haven't written one since then."

"However, you did report it immediately to Major Shikinidi?"

"Why Shikinidi?"

"All right, Shikin. You wrote a denunciation?"

"How could you think that?"

"I don't even have to think! Are you going to tell me Major Shikin didn't instruct you to *spy* on my actions, my words, and even my thoughts?" Sologdin took his pencil and drew a vertical line on the white sheet. "Well, he did, didn't he? Speak honestly!"

"Yes—he did."

"And how many denunciations have you written?"

"Dmitri Aleksandrovich! Do you think I'm capable of that? And against you? On the contrary, I've written the very best recommendations!"

"Hmm. Well, we'll believe you for now. But my warning still stands. This is evidently a noncriminal case of pure female curiosity. I will satisfy it. That was in September. It wasn't three days in a row but five—I was writing a letter to my wife."

"That's what I wanted to ask! You have a wife? She's waiting for you? And you write her such long letters?"

"I have a wife," Sologdin replied slowly and intently, "but it's as if she weren't there. I can't even write her letters any more. When I wrote her—no, I didn't finish the long letters, but I worked over them for a long time. The art of letter writing, Larisa Nikolayevna, is a very difficult art. We often write letters too carelessly, and then we are surprised that we have lost people who were close to us. My wife hasn't seen me for many years, but she has felt my hand upon her. Letters are the only tie I have held her by for twelve years."

Emina suddenly moved forward. She rested her elbows on the edge of Sologdin's desk and pressed her palms to her blushing face.

"Are you sure you can hold her? And why, Dmitri Aleksandrovich, why? Twelve years have passed, and there will be five more—seventeen altogether! You are depriving her of her youth! Why? Let her live!"

Sologdin's voice was solemn: "There is a special class of women, Larisa Nikolayevna. They are the companions of the Vikings, the bright-faced Isoldes with diamond souls. You have been living in vapid prosperity and could not have known them."

"Let her live!" Larisa Nikolayevna repeated. "And as far as possible, live yourself!"

Now one would never have recognized the majestic grande dame who floated through the halls and stairways of the sharashka. She still sat in the same way, leaning on Sologdin's desk, breathing audibly. Her heated face was almost peasant-like.

Sologdin looked away and drew another vertical mark on the pink sheet.

"Dmitri Aleksandrovich, for weeks I've been dying to

know what those marks mean. You make them, and then a few days later you cross them all out. What does it mean?"

"I am afraid that once more you're showing an inclination to curiosity." He held up the white sheet. "You see, every time I use a foreign word in Russian when there is no absolute necessity, I make a mark. The sum of these marks is the measure of my lack of perfection. I didn't think to replace the word 'capitalism' with the word 'big-moneyism' and the word 'spy' with the term 'keep under observation'; so I put down two marks."

"And on the pink sheet?"

"You've noticed I also keep a pink sheet?"

"And you use it even more than the white one. Is that another measure of your lack of perfection?"

"Yes," Sologdin said hesitantly. "On the pink sheet I put down 'fault' marks, which in your language would be 'penalty' marks, and then I punish myself according to the number of them."

"Penalty marks? What for?" she asked softly.

"Why do you want to know?"

"What for?" Larisa repeated, even more quietly.

"Have you noticed *when* I mark them down?"

There was not a sound in the room, and Larisa replied in a voice that was hardly more than a sigh, "Yes, I have noticed."

Sologdin reddened and confessed angrily, "I put a mark on the pink sheet every time I'm unable to stand your closeness, when I—desire you!"

A scarlet flame spread over Larisa's cheeks, ears, and neck. She did not move from the edge of his desk and looked him boldly in the eyes.

Sologdin was indignant. "And now I'm going to put down *three* marks at once! I'll be a long time paying them off! First for your impudent, moist eyes, and the fact that I like them. Second, because your blouse isn't closed and you're leaning forward and I see your breasts. And third because I want to kiss your neck."

"Well, then, kiss it," she said, fascinated.

"You've gone mad! Get out of the room! Leave me!"

She recoiled from Sologdin's desk and rose abruptly. Her chair fell back with a crash.

He turned again to the drawing board.

The obsession he had struggled with during the morning woodcutting was now stifling him.

He stared at the drawing and understood nothing about it. And suddenly he felt a full breast pressing against his shoulder.

"Larisa!" he said sternly, and turning, he touched her.

"What?" she asked breathlessly, very close to him.

"Let me—I'm—I'll lock the door," he said.

Without drawing away she answered, "Yes, lock it."

31

VOICE PRINTS

No one, including the free employees, wanted to work on Sunday.

They came to work dispiritedly, without the usual weekday crush on the bus, and thought about how they could sit it out till six in the evening.

But this Sunday there was more disturbance than on a weekday. About ten in the morning three very long and very streamlined automobiles rolled up to the main gates. The guard at the guardhouse saluted. They passed through the gates and drove along the gravel driveways which had been cleared of snow, past the redheaded janitor Spiridon who stood squinting at them, and up to the main entrance of the institute. High-ranking officers with gleaming gold shoulder boards got out of all three cars, and without waiting to be met they went directly up to Yakonov's office on the third floor. No one had a chance to look them over carefully. Some of the laboratories heard the rumor that Minister Abakumov himself had come with eight generals. In other laboratories people sat calmly, unaware of the threat hanging over them.

The truth was half the rumor. Only Deputy Minister Sevastyanov had come, accompanied by four generals.

But something unheard of had happened. Colonel of Engineers Yakonov was not yet at work. The frightened duty officer quickly shut the desk drawer in which lay a book he was reading clandestinely. He rang up Yakonov at his apartment and then reported to the deputy minister that Colonel Yakonov was home with heart trouble but was nevertheless getting dressed and coming. Meanwhile Yakonov's deputy, Major Roitman, his uniform pinched in at his slender waist, adjusted his ill-fitting shoulder belt and, catching his foot in the carpet runner (he was nearsighted), hurried from the Acoustics Laboratory and presented himself before the visitors. He hurried not merely because regulations required it, but also on behalf of the intra-institute opposition which he headed—Yakonov always tried to keep him out of conversations with their superiors. Having already learned the details of Pryanchikov's nighttime summons, Roitman was hastening to mend the situation and convince the high-ranking committee that the state of the vocoder was not so hopeless as, say, that of the clipper. Though only thirty, Roitman was already a Stalin Prize laureate, and he ardently plunged his laboratory into the whirlwind of troubles connected with the interests of the All-Highest.

As many as ten of those present listened to him. Two of them understood something of the technical heart of the matter, and the rest merely assumed a dignified air. However, when Roitman had finished, sallow Mamurin, who had been summoned by Oskolupov, defended the clipper as being *almost* ready to be released to the world. He was stammering with fury. Soon Yakonov arrived with hollow eyes and a face so white it was almost blue and sank down into a chair next to the wall. The conversation broke up, became confused, and soon no one had the least idea how to salvage the derelict enterprise.

Unfortunately, it so happened that the institute's heart and its conscience, Security Officer Comrade Shikin and Party Organizer Comrade Stepanov, respectively, had on that particular Sunday given in to a perfectly natural weakness. They had decided not to come to work and not to preside at the collective which they directed on weekdays. Their action was all the more pardonable since it is well known that when indoctrination and mass-organizational work have been correctly set up, the further presence of the leaders is unnecessary. Alarm and the awareness of his sudden responsibility gripped the duty officer. At some personal risk, he left the phone and ran through the laboratories, whispering to their chiefs the news of the important guests so that they could redouble their vigilance. But because he was very excited and in a hurry to return to his telephone, he paid no attention to the locked door of the Design Office. He also neglected to run to the Vacuum Laboratory, where Clara Makarygin was on duty alone.

The laboratory chiefs in turn made no general announcement, because one couldn't ask people out loud to act as though they were hard at work because the deputy minister and the generals had suddenly arrived. But they went around to all the desks and in a furtive whisper warned each individual.

The entire institute sat waiting for the dignitaries. Having conferred, they separated, some remaining in Yakonov's office, others going on to Number Seven. Only Sevastyanov and Major Roitman went down to Acoustics; for, in order to get rid of this new headache, Yakonov had recommended Acoustics as a convenient base for carrying out Ryumin's instructions.

"How do you plan to discover this person?" Sevastyanov asked Roitman on the way there.

Roitman could not *think*, since he had learned about the assignment only five minutes earlier; it was Oskolupov who had done the thinking for him the night before, when he had taken on this particular piece of work—without thinking. But in five minutes Roitman had already managed to figure something out.

"Well, you see," he said without any servility, calling the deputy minister by name and patronymic, "we have a visible-speech device—known as VIR—which turns out what is called a 'voice print,' and there is a person here, a certain Rubin, who reads these prints."

"A prisoner?"

"Yes. An assistant professor of philology. Recently I've had him busy looking for individual traits of speech in voice prints. And I hope when we turn that telephone conversation into a voice print and compare it with the voice prints of the suspects—"

"Hmm . . . We'll have to get Abakumov's agreement about this philologist," said Sevastyanov, shaking his head.

"Because of security?"

"Yes."

In Acoustics by this time, though everyone now knew about the arrival of the committee, they were still unable to overcome the tormenting inertia of inaction and were therefore only putting up a front, lazily digging through drawers full of radio tubes, examining diagrams in magazines, yawning out the window. The girls among the free employees had gathered in a little group and were gossiping in whispers. Roitman's assistant chased them away. Simochka, fortunately for her, was not on duty; she had the day off in return for the extra day she had worked; therefore she was spared the anguish of seeing Nerzhin dressed up and beaming in anticipation of his visit with the wife who had more right to him than Simochka.

Nerzhin felt like the guest of honor at a celebration; he had gone to Acoustics for the third time, without having any business there, simply because he was nervous waiting for the Black Maria, which was very late. He sat not in his chair but on the window sill, and inhaled with pleasure the smoke from his Belomor while he listened to Rubin. Rubin, who had not considered Professor Chelnov a worthy audience for his ballad about Moses, was now quietly but fervently reciting it to Gleb Nerzhin. Rubin was not a poet. He had never enough skill in polishing rhymes, in working out rhythms, but he sometimes drafted poems which were heartfelt and intelligent. Right now he was anxious to have Gleb praise him for his ballad.

Rubin could not exist without friends, he suffocated without them. Loneliness was so unbearable to him that he did not allow his thoughts to mature in his head, but finding even half a thought there, he hastened to share it. All his life he had been rich in friends, but in prison it turned out that his friends were not like-minded persons and the like-minded persons were not his friends.

So no one in Acoustics was really working, except for the unremittingly cheerful and industrious Pryanchikov, who had already put his impressions of nighttime Moscow and his mad trip behind him and was thinking about a new improvement in a circuit, and crooning:

> "Bendzi-bendzi-bendzi-bah-*ar*,
> Bendzi-bendzi-bendzi-bah-*ar*."

Just then Sevastyanov came in with Roitman. Roitman was saying, "In these voice prints speech is measured three ways at once: frequency—across the tape; time—along the tape; and amplitude—by the density of the picture. Therefore each sound is depicted so uniquely that it can be recognized easily, and everything that has been said can be read on the tape."

He took Sevastyanov on into the laboratory.

"Here is the apparatus which was designed in our laboratory." (Roitman himself had already forgotten the extent to which it had been borrowed.)

"And here," he said, carefully turning the deputy minister toward the window, "is Candidate of Philological Sciences Rubin, the only person in the Soviet Union who can read visible speech."

Rubin had risen, and now he bowed silently.

When Roitman had first pronounced the word "voice prints" at the door, Rubin and Nerzhin were both startled. Their work—which people had for the most part laughed at until now—had emerged into the light of day. During the forty-five seconds it took for Roitman to bring Sevastyanov to Rubin, Rubin and Nerzhin with the sharp perception and quick reactions characteristic of zeks had already understood that there was to be a demonstration of Rubin's ability to read voice prints, and that the test sentence could only be read into the microphone by one of the "authorized" announcers and that the only authorized announcer present in the room was Nerzhin. They also took account of the fact that, though Rubin really could read voice prints, he might still make a mistake in a test and he could not afford a mistake—for that would mean tumbling from the sharashka into the nether world of the camps.

However, they said not a word about all that, but only looked at one another with understanding.

Rubin whispered, "If it's you, and you say the test sentence, say: 'Voice prints enable deaf people to use the telephone.' "

Nerzhin whispered, "If he says it himself, guess by sounds. If I stroke my hair, you're right; if I fix my necktie, you're wrong."

That was when Rubin stood up and bowed.

Roitman continued in that hesitant and apologetic voice, which, even if one heard it with one's back turned, would always betray him as an intellectual: "And now Lev Grigorich is going to show what he can do. One of the announcers

—well, let's say Gleb Vikentich—will go into the acoustical booth and say a sentence into the microphone, and the VIR will record it, and Lev Grigorich will try to read it."

Standing directly before the deputy minister, Nerzhin fixed his insolent camp gaze on him. "Would you like to think up a sentence?" he asked sternly.

"No, no," Sevastyanov answered politely, averting his eyes. "Make up something yourself."

Nerzhin obediently took a sheet of paper, thought a moment, then, finding inspiration, he wrote something down, and, in the silence which followed, gave it to Sevastyanov in such a way that no one else could read it, not even Roitman: "Voice prints enable deaf people to use the telephone."

"Is that really true?" Sevastyanov asked in amazement.

"Yes."

"Read it, please."

The VIR droned. Nerzhin went into the booth. As he went, he thought to himself how terrible the burlap around it looked (that eternal shortage of material in the warehouse). He shut himself in tight. The machine began to clatter, and a two-yard-long tape mottled with a maze of wet inky stripes and smeared spots was delivered to Rubin's desk.

The whole laboratory stopped "work" and watched tensely. Roitman was visibly nervous. Nerzhin came out of the booth and, from a distance, observed Rubin with careless indifference. Everyone stood around; only Rubin was seated, his bald head gleaming. With mercy for his impatient observers, he made no secret of his priestly wisdom and immediately marked the wet tape with his indelible pencil, which was as always badly sharpened.

"You see, certain sounds can be deciphered without the least difficulty, the accented or sonorous vowels, for example. In the second word the 'r' sound is distinctly visible twice. In the first word the accented sound of 'ee' and in front of it a soft 'v'—for there can't be a hard sound there. Before that is the formant 'a,' but we mustn't forget that in the first, the secondary accented syllable 'o' is also pronounced like 'a.' But the vowel 'oo' or 'u' retains its individuality even when it's far from the accent—right here it has the characteristic low-frequency streak. The third sound of the first word is unquestionably 'u'. And after it follows a palatal explosive consonant, most likely 'k'—and so we have 'ukovi' or 'ukavi.' And here is a hard 'v'—it is clearly distinguished from the soft 'v' for it has no streak higher than 2,300 cycles. 'Vukovi'—and then there is a resounding hard stop and at the very end an attenuated vowel, and these together I can interpret as 'dy.' So we get 'vukovidy'—and we have to guess at the first sound, which is smeared. I could take it for an 's' if it weren't that the sense tells me it's a 'z.' And so the first word is—" and Rubin pronounced the word for "voice prints"—" 'zvukovidy.' "

He continued: "Now, in the second word, as I said, there are two 'r' sounds and, apparently, the regular verb ending 'ayet,' but since it is in the plural it is evidently 'ayut.' Evidently 'razryvayut' or 'razreshayut,' and I'll find out which in a moment. Antonina Valeryanovna, was it you who took the magnifying glass? Could I please have it a moment?"

He had absolutely no need of the magnifying glass, because the VIR gave very broad pictures, but this was done, in the camp tradition, for show, and Nerzhin laughed inwardly, absent-mindedly smoothing down his hair, which was smooth already. Rubin glanced at him and took the magnifying glass which had been brought him. The general tension mounted. No one knew whether Rubin would guess correctly. Sevastyanov, astonished, whispered, "It's amazing. It's amazing."

No one noticed when Senior Lieutenant Shusterman entered the room on tiptoe. He had no right to come in, and so he stopped near the door. Beckoning Nerzhin to leave the room at once, Shusterman did not, however, go out with him, but waited for a chance to summon Rubin. He wanted Rubin in order to have him remake his bunk in the regulation manner. This would not be the first time Shusterman had tormented Rubin with the same task.

Rubin had just guessed "deaf" and was struggling with the next word. Roitman beamed, not only because he shared in the triumph but also because he was honestly pleased by every success in the work.

Then Rubin looked up accidentally and, meeting Shusterman's glowering stare, understood why Shusterman was there. He threw him a malicious answering glance, which said, "Go make it yourself."

"The last phrase is 'on the telephone.' That's a combination we run into so often I recognize it right away. And that's it."

"Amazing!" Sevastyanov repeated. "Forgive me, what is your name and patronymic?"

"Lev Grigorich."

"Now listen, Lev Grigorich, can you distinguish individual voice traits on voice prints?"

"We call that the *individual speech type*. Yes. In fact, that's the subject of our research."

"Very good! I think there is an in-ter-est-ing assignment for you."

Shusterman went out on tiptoe.

32

KISSING IS FORBIDDEN

The engine of the Black Maria which would transport the prisoners going out for visits was not working. There had been a delay as telephone calls went back and forth and arrangements were clarified. About 11 A.M., when Nerzhin, summoned from Acoustics, arrived for the body search, the six others who were going were already there. Some of them were still being searched, and others had already gone through it and were waiting—some slumped at a big table, others pacing the room beyond the search area. Within the area, by the wall, stood Lieutenant Colonel Klimentiev—all spit and polish, erect, sleek, like a career warrior before a parade. A strong smell of eau de cologne arose from his stove-black mustache and his black hair.

Hands folded behind his back, he stood there as if he were not involved, but his presence compelled the guards to search conscientiously.

Within the search zone Nerzhin was met by the outstretched arms of one of the most maliciously fault-finding guards, Krasnogubenky, who immediately asked, "What's in your pockets?"

Nerzhin had long since outgrown that obsequious agitation which new prisoners experience in the presence of guards. He did not trouble to answer or hurry to turn out the pockets of the cheviot suit which was so new to him. He looked at Krasnogubenky sleepily and moved his arms from his sides just slightly, allowing the guard to search his pockets. After five years of prison and after many such searches Nerzhin did not feel, as would a newcomer, that this was brute violence, that dirty fingers were fumbling at his lacerated heart. No, nothing done to his body could cloud his brightening mood.

Krasnogubenky opened the cigarette case Potapov had just given him, looked into the mouthpieces of all the cigarettes to see whether anything was hidden there, looked under the matches in the matchbox, checked the hems of Nerzhin's handkerchief. He found nothing else in the pockets. Then he ran his hands over Nerzhin's entire body, feeling between his undershirt and his jacket in case there was anything underneath the shirt or between the shirt and the dickey. Then he sat on his heels and with a close grip passed his hands up and down one leg and then the other. As Krasnogubenky squatted, Nerzhin had a good view of his fellow prisoner, the engraver, and he guessed why he was so nervous. In prison the engraver had discovered that he had a talent for writing short stories, and he wrote them—about POW experiences in Germany, about encounters in cells, about courts. Through his wife he had already transmitted one or two such stories to the outside, but to whom could they be shown? They had to be hidden. They had to be hidden here, too. And one could never hope to take out anything one had written. But one old fellow, a friend of their family, had read what the engraver had sent out and told him, again through his wife, that such perfection and expressiveness were rarely found even in Chekhov. This reaction greatly encouraged the engraver.

For today's visit he had written another short story which he thought was magnificent. But at the very moment he was being searched he got cold feet in front of the same Krasnogubenky, and, turning away, he swallowed the ball of tracing paper on which he had written his story in microscopic handwriting. Now he was overcome by regret for having devoured it—perhaps he would have succeeded in getting it through.

Krasnogubenky said to Nerzhin, "Take off your shoes."

Nerzhin put his foot on the stool, untied the laces, and kicked his shoe off without looking where it landed. In doing this he revealed a torn sock. Krasnogubenky picked up the shoe and felt inside it and bent the sole. With the same imperturbable face, as though it were an ordinary thing he did every day, Nerzhin kicked off the second shoe and revealed a second tattered sock. Presumably because the socks had big holes in them, Krasnogubenky did not think there would be anything hidden in them and did not ask to have them removed.

Nerzhin put his shoes back on. Krasnogubenky lit a cigarette.

Klimentiev had winced when Nerzhin kicked off his shoes. After all, that was a deliberate insult to his guard. If one did not stand behind the guards, the prisoners would take advantage of the administration. Once again Klimentiev regretted his generosity, and he almost decided to find a reason for canceling the visit of this brazen fellow who was not only not ashamed of his criminal condition but even appeared to revel in it.

"Attention!" he called out sharply, and seven prisoners and seven guards turned in his direction. "You know the rules. You must receive nothing from your relatives. Anything which is to be turned over to you or to them must go through me. In your conversations you are not to mention work, work conditions, living conditions, the daily schedule, the location of the institute. You may not name any names. You may say of yourselves only that everything is all right and that you do not need anything."

"Then what can we talk about?" someone cried out. "Politics?"

Klimentiev did not even deign to answer this, it was so patently absurd.

"Talk about your guilt," one of the prisoners advised somberly. "Talk about your repentance."

"No, you may not speak of your indictment. That is secret," Klimentiev replied without a tremor. "Ask about your family, about your children. One more thing. There is a new rule: from now on, holding hands and kissing are forbidden."

Nerzhin, who had remained indifferent to the search and also to the stupid regulations, which he knew how to get around, felt, at the announcement that kissing was forbidden, a dark flare in his eyes.

"We see each other once a year," he cried out hoarsely at

Klimentiev, and Klimentiev turned gratefully in his direction, expecting Nerzhin to go further.

Nerzhin could almost hear Klimentiev roaring, "I deprive you of your visit!"

He choked and said nothing.

His visit, announced at the last minute, was evidently irregular and it would cost nothing to deprive him of it.

There was always somebody to stop those who might shout out the truth or seek justice.

As an old prisoner, he had to master his rage.

So, meeting no rebellion, Klimentiev precisely and dispassionately added for good measure: "If there's a kiss, handclasp, or other violation, the visit will be terminated immediately."

"But my wife doesn't know! She will kiss me!" the engraver cried out.

"Your relatives will be warned, too!" Klimentiev countered.

"There's never been such a rule."

"There is now."

Stupid people! And their outrage was stupid—they seemed to think he had personally thought up the rule instead of finding it in the new regulations.

"How long will the visit last?"

"If my mother comes, won't they let her in?"

"The visits last thirty minutes. I will admit only the person for whom the notification was made out."

"And my five-year-old daughter?"

"Children up to fifteen are admitted with adults."

"And sixteen?"

"Not admitted! Any other questions? All right, let's go. Outside!"

Amazing! They were not being taken in a Black Maria, as others had been recently, but in a small-model blue city bus.

The bus stood before the door of the headquarters building. Three guards, new ones, in civilian clothes and soft hats, holding pistols in their pockets, got on the bus first and took seats well apart from one another. Two of them looked like retired boxers or gangsters. They wore fine overcoats.

The morning frost had already disappeared, but the cold continued.

Seven prisoners climbed into the bus through the front door and sat down.

Three more guards, in uniform, got on.

The driver slammed the door and stepped on the gas pedal.

Lieutenant Colonel Klimentiev got into a passenger car.

33

PHONOSCOPY

At midday Yakonov was not in the velvet silence and gleaming comfort of his office. He was in Number Seven, busy setting up a "mating" of the clipper and the vocoder. That morning the ambitious engineer Markushev had had the idea of combining these two devices into one, and many people had joined the project, each for his own calculated purpose. The only ones opposed to it were Bobynin, Pryanchikov, and Roitman, but no one listened to them.

But four other people were sitting in Yakonov's office: Sevastyanov, who had already talked with Abakumov on the telephone, General Bulbanyuk, the Mavrino Lieutenant Smolosidov, and the prisoner Rubin.

Lieutenant Smolosidov was a heavy-set man. Even if one believed that there must be something good in every creature, it would have been difficult to find it in his unsmiling face, in the morose compression of his thick lips. His position in his laboratory was a minor one; he hardly ranked above a radio assembler, and his salary was that of the lowest female worker. He did steal another thousand a month from the institute and sold radio parts on the black market, but everyone understood that Smolosidov's situation and income were not limited to these activities.

The free employees at the sharashka were afraid of him, even those who played volleyball with him. His face, which never showed the faintest gleam of sincerity, was frightening. The special trust the highest chiefs had in him was also frightening. Where did he live? Did he even have a home?

A family? He never visited his colleagues at home, nor did he share his leisure time with any of them outside the walls of the institute. Nothing was known about his past, except for the battle decorations on his chest and the reckless boast he once made that a certain famous marshal had not uttered a word during the entire war which he, Smolosidov, had not heard. When asked how that could have happened, he had replied that he was the marshal's personal radio operator.

The question of which free employee was to be entrusted with the tape recorder and the tape from the Very Secret Administration was no sooner asked than General Bulbanyuk, who had brought the tape, gave the order: Smolosidov.

Now Smolosidov was setting up the tape recorder on a small varnished table, while General Bulbanyuk, whose head was like a huge overgrown potato with protuberances for nose and ears, said, "You are a prisoner, Rubin. But you were once a Communist and maybe someday you will be one again."

"I am a Communist now," Rubin wanted to exclaim, but it was humiliating to have to prove this to Bulbanyuk.

"So our organizations have confidence in you. You are about to hear a state secret from this tape recorder. We hope you will help us catch this scoundrel, this accomplice of traitors to our country. They want our important scientific discoveries to pass beyond our frontiers. It goes without saying that the slightest attempt to reveal—"

"Understood," Rubin interrupted him, fearing most of all that he would not be allowed to work on the tape. Having long since lost all hope of personal success, Rubin lived the life of all mankind as if it were his own family life. This tape which he had not yet heard already offended him personally.

Smolosidov pushed the "play" button.

Rubin stared intently at the tape recorder's speaker as if he were searching for the face of his personal enemy. When Rubin looked so fixedly, his face tightened and became cruel. One could never beg mercy from a person with such a face.

In the silence of the office, over a light rustle of static, they heard the dialogue of the excited, hurrying stranger and the old-fashioned, phlegmatic lady.

With every sentence Rubin's face lost its set, cruel expression and became perplexed. My God, it wasn't what he had expected at all. It was some kind of wild, strange—

The tape came to an end.

Rubin was expected to say something, but he had as yet no idea what to say.

He needed a little time to consider it from all angles. He relit the cigarette which had gone out and said, "Play it again."

Smolosidov pushed the "rewind" button.

Rubin looked hopefully at his dark hands with their bluish fingers. After all, Smolosidov might make a mistake and turn on the recording head instead of the playing head. And it would all be erased without a trace. Then there would be nothing for Rubin to decide.

Rubin smoked, crushing the hollow mouthpiece of the cigarette between his teeth.

Everyone was silent.

Smolosidov had made no mistake. He had turned on the right head.

Once again they heard the voice of the young man, nervous, almost desperate, and once again the dissatisfied lady, mumbling and peevish. Rubin had to try hard to imagine the criminal, but he was haunted by that lady whom, it seemed to him, he could very easily see, with luxuriant, dyed hair which was perhaps not even her own.

He dropped his face into his hands. The most barbarous thing was that no reasonable person, with an unmuddled mind, could consider any medical discovery a state secret. Because any medicine which asked the nationality of a patient was not a medicine at all. And the man who had decided to telephone that booby-trapped apartment—he may not have understood the full danger—Rubin liked that reckless fellow.

But *objectively*—objectively that man who had wanted to do what seemed to him the right thing had in fact attacked the positive forces of history. Given the fact that priority in scientific discovery was recognized as important and necessary for strengthening the state, whoever undermined it stood objectively in the way of progress. And had to be swept away.

Then, too, the conversation was not all so simple. That frightened repetition of the word "foreigners." To give them "something." That could mean something other than a medicine. "Medicine" could be a code word. History knew of such cases. How had the Baltic sailors been summoned to an armed uprising? By the words "Send us the regulations!" And that had meant: Send a warship and landing party.

The tape stopped. Rubin lifted his face from his hands, looked at the sullen Smolosidov, at silly, pretentious Bulbanyuk. They were repulsive to him. He did not even want to look at them. But here, at this little crossroads of history, they were the ones who objectively represented its positive forces.

One had to rise above one's personal feelings.

It was such butchers, but in the army Political Section, who had shoved Rubin into prison because they were unable to bear his talent and honesty. It was such butchers, but in the chief military prosecutor's office, who had for four years thrown into the wastebasket dozens of outcries from Rubin protesting his innocence.

One had to rise above one's own wretched fate.

And though *these* two were worthy of being blown up by an antipersonnel grenade there and then, one had to serve them, and one's country, its progressive idea, its banner.

Rubin plunged his cigarette into the ashtray, and trying to look directly at Sevastyanov, who struck him at the moment as a decent person, he said, "Well, all right. We'll try." He caught his breath sharply, then sighed. "But if you have no suspects, I won't be able to find . . . One can't record everyone in Moscow. Whose voice am I to compare it with?"

Bulbanyuk reassured him: "We picked up four right near the pay phone. But it probably wasn't any one of them. We got five names from the ministry. I noted them down here without their ranks, and I'm not showing you their official positions so that you won't be afraid of accusing anyone."

He handed him a page from his notebook. On it were written five names:

1. Petrov
2. Syagovity
3. Volodin
4. Shchevronok
5. Zavarzin

Rubin read it and wanted to keep the list.

"No, no!" Sevastyanov warned him sharply. "Smolosidov will keep the list."

Rubin gave it back. This precaution did not offend him; instead, it amused him. As if those five names had not already been etched into his memory: Petrov, Syagovity, Volodin, Shchevronok, Zavarzin. His long philological studies had become so much a part of him that even now he had noted in passing the etymologies of the names: "*syagovity*" —a person who jumped far; "*shchevronok*"—a skylark.

"I request," he said dryly, "that you record the telephone voices of all five."

"You'll have them tomorrow."

Rubin thought a moment and said, "One more thing. I want the age of each one." He nodded at the tape recorder. "I will need to have that tape without interruption, and I'll need it today."

"Lieutenant Smolosidov will have it. You and he will be allotted a room in the Top Secret Section."

"They're getting it ready now," said Smolosidov.

Experience had taught Rubin to avoid the dangerous word "when?" so as not to be asked the same question himself. He knew that there were one or two weeks' work here and that if he asked the chiefs, "When do you need it?" they would reply, "Tomorrow morning." So he asked, "With whom may I speak about this work?"

Sevastyanov looked at Bulbanyuk and replied, "Only with Major Roitman. With Oskolupov. And with the minister himself."

Bulbanyuk asked, "Do you remember all my warnings? Should I repeat them?"

Rubin stood up without permission and squinted at the general as if he were something small and hard to see.

"I have to go and think about it," he said, not speaking to anyone in particular.

No one objected.

Rubin, deep in thought, went out of the office, past the duty officer and, without noticing anyone, started down the red-carpeted stairway.

He had to get Nerzhin into this new group. How could he work without someone's advice? The problem would be very difficult. Work on voices had only just begun. The first classifications. The first nomenclature.

The thrill of scientific research blazed up in him.

This was a new science—finding a criminal by a print of his voice.

Until now they had been identified by fingerprints. They called it dactyloscopy, study of the finger whorls. It had been worked out over the centuries.

The new science could be called voice study—that was what Sologdin would have called it—or *phonoscopy*. And it all had to be created in a few days.

Petrov, Syagovity, Volodin, Shchevronok, Zavarzin.

34

THE SILENT BELL

Settling back in a cushioned bus seat next to a window, Nerzhin was enjoying the pleasant rocking motion. Beside him sat Illarion Pavlovich Gerasimovich, a physicist specializing in optics, a short, narrow-shouldered man with an emphatically intellectual face, wearing a pince-nez like a spy in a poster.

"You know, I thought I'd got used to everything," said Nerzhin, quietly sharing impressions with him. "I'm quite willing to sit with my bare backside in the snow; and even when people are herded into freight cars or the escort guard smashes my suitcase, nothing bothers me, nothing gets to me. But there's one thing in my heart that is living and not dying—my love for my wife. Where she's concerned I can't bear it. To see her once a year and not be allowed to kiss her? They really spit on you."

Gerasimovich knitted his thin brows. They seemed to be in mourning even when he was only pondering diagrams.

"There is probably only one path to invulnerability," he replied, "to kill within oneself *all* attachments and to renounce *all* desires."

Gerasimovich had been at the Mavrino sharashka only a few months, and Nerzhin had not had time to become closely acquainted with him. But somehow he liked Gerasimovich instinctively.

They did not pursue the conversation but fell silent at once. The journey toward a visit was too great an event in the life of a prisoner. It was a time to revive one's soul, which had been asleep in a burial vault. Recollections stirred which on ordinary days never came through. You accumulated thoughts and feelings the whole year to expend them in those short minutes of being with someone close to you.

The bus stopped at the gate. The sergeant of the watch climbed into the bus and counted the departing prisoners with his eyes, twice. Before that the senior guard at the guardhouse had already signed for seven heads. Then the sergeant clambered underneath the bus, checked that no one was riding on the springs—even a disembodied demon would not have been able to hang on there for more than a minute—and then went back into the guardhouse. Only then did the first gates open, then the second. The bus rolled across the magic line, its merry tires whispering along the frost-covered road past the grove.

It was the deep secrecy of their institute that the Mavrino zeks had to thank for these outings. Visiting relatives were not supposed to know where their living corpses dwelt, whether they were brought from a hundred miles away or from the Kremlin, whether they were brought from an airport or from the other world. They saw only well-fed, well-dressed people with white hands who had lost their former talkativeness and smiled sadly and assured them that they had everything and needed nothing.

These visits were rather like scenes on ancient Greek steles which represent both the dead man and the living relatives who put up the monument to him. But on the steles there is always a small line dividing the other world from this one. The living look fondly at the dead person, who looks toward Hades, neither merry nor sad, with a clear and too knowing gaze. Nerzhin turned his head so as to see from a knoll what he almost never had the chance to see: the building in which they lived and worked, the dark-brick building with the rusty spherical cupola over their semi-circular marvel of a room and, still higher, the ancient hexagonal tower. From the southern façade where Acoustics, Number Seven, the Design Office, and Yakonov's office were located, the even rows of windows, which could not be opened, looked outward, uniform and indifferent; and the suburban residents and Muscovites who came to the grove on Sundays could hardly imagine how many eminent lives, trampled yearnings, soaring passions, and state secrets were collected, packed in, intermingled and heated red-hot in that lonely, ancient, suburban structure. Even inside the building, secrecy permeated the place. One room did not know about the next. One neighbor did not know about another. The security officers did not know about the twenty-two wild, irrational women, free employees, who had been allowed into that somber building. And just as these women did not know about each other—only heaven could know, and eventually history—no one knew that all twenty-two, despite the swords hanging over their heads, had found a secret attachment here, were in love with someone and embraced him in secret, or had taken pity on someone and put him in touch with his family.

Opening his dark-red cigarette case, Gleb Nerzhin lit up with that special satisfaction a cigarette can provide at special times in one's life.

Though his thought of Nadya was the supreme, all-absorbing thought, his body, reveling in the novelty of the journey, wanted only to ride on and on. For time to stop, for the bus to go on forever along that snowy highway with black tire marks, past that park white with the frost that covered the branches of the trees, past the children flashing by, voices Nerzhin had not heard, it seemed, since the beginning of the war. Soldiers and prisoners never hear children's voices.

Nadya and Gleb had lived together for one year, a year of running from place to place carrying bulging briefcases. Both were fifth-year students, writing term papers and taking state examinations.

Then the war had come.

By now some people had funny, short-legged kids running around.

But they did not.

One little boy started to run across the highway. The driver swerved sharply to avoid him. The boy became frightened, stopped, put his little hand in a dark-blue mitten to his reddened face.

Nerzhin, who had not thought about children for years, suddenly understood clearly that Stalin had robbed him and Nadya of their children. Even if his term should end, even if they were together again, his wife would be thirty-six, maybe forty. It would be late for a child. Dozens of children dressed in different colors were skating on the pond.

The bus turned into back streets and rattled over cobble-stones.

Descriptions of prisons have always stressed their horrors. Yet isn't it even more appalling when there are no horrors? When the horror lies in the gray methodology of years? In forgetting that your one and only life on earth has been shattered? And being ready to forgive some pig-snout for it? Your thoughts occupied with how you can grab the heel of the loaf rather than the middle from the prison tray; how you can get untorn underwear that will not be too small at the next bath?

One has to live through it; it cannot be imagined. To write such things as "I sit behind bars, in a prison dank," or "Open the prison gate and give me a black-eyed wench," you don't have to be in prison; all of that is easy to imagine. But that is rudimentary. Only endless, uninterrupted years can bring to fruition the true experience of prison.

Nadya had written in her letter: "When you return . . ." But that was the whole horror: that there would be no *return*. One could not go *back*. After fourteen years at the front and in prison there would probably not be a single cell of his body left from the past. They could only come together all over again. A new, unfamiliar person would walk in bearing the name of her husband, and she would see that the man, her beloved, for whom she had shut herself up to wait for fourteen years, no longer existed, had evaporated, molecule by molecule.

It would be good if in that second life they should once again love one another.

And if not?

They had entered the streets on the outskirts of Moscow. At Mavrino the dispersed glow in the night sky made it seem that Moscow was all agleam, dazzling. But here, one after the other, were one- and two-story houses, long in disrepair, with their stucco falling off, their wooden fences tilting. Indeed, they had not been touched since the beginning of the war, effort being expended in very different areas. But in the country, for instance from Ryazan to Ruzayevka, what kind of roofs would there be? What kind of houses?

The bus bounded into the broad, crowded Station Square and crossed it. Once again: streetcars, trolley-buses, automobiles, people. The police wore new, bright, reddish-purple uniforms which Nerzhin had never seen before.

How incomprehensible it was that Nadya could wait for him so many years! To move among that bustling crowd eternally hurrying to catch up with something, to feel men's eyes on her and never waver in her heart. Nerzhin imagined what it would be like in the opposite case: if Nadya were imprisoned and he were free. He might not even be able to stand it for a year. Never before had he understood that this weak girl had such granite determination. For a long time he had had doubts about her endurance, but now he felt that for Nadya it was no longer difficult to wait.

Even back in the Krasnaya Presnya transit prison, after half a year of interrogation, when he had first received permission to write a letter, Gleb had written Nadya with a stub of pencil on a tattered piece of wrapping paper, folded in a triangle, without a stamp:

> My darling! You waited for me four years of the war—don't be angry at having waited for me in vain; now it will be ten years more. All my life I will remember, like a sun, our short happiness. But now be free from this day on. There's no need for your life to be ruined, too. Marry!

From the whole letter Nadya understood only one thing: "That means you've stopped loving me! How can you turn me over to someone else?"

Women! Even at the front, at the Dnieper bridgehead, she had made her way to him, with a forged Red Army identification, in a man's service shirt that was too big for her, subjected to interrogations and searches. She had come to remain with her husband, if she could, till the end of the war—if he were killed to die with him, if he were to survive to survive herself.

At the bridgehead, which had only recently been a death trap but was now quiet, overgrown with indifferent grass, they snatched the brief days of their stolen happiness.

But the armies awoke, moved in to attack, and Nadya had to go back home, once more in the same awkward service shirt, with the same forged papers. A one-and-a-half-ton truck took her off through an open cut in the forest, and she had waved to him a long time from the back of it.

. . . At bus stops crowds stood in disorderly lines. When a

trolley-bus drew up, some held their places, others elbowed
forward. At Sadovya Boulevard their pale-blue bus, half
empty and inviting, passed the regular bus stop and stopped
at the light. A wild Muscovite ran up to it, jumped on its
running board, and pounded on the door, yelling, "Do you
go to Kotelnychesky Quay? Kotelnychesky Quay?"

"No, no, you can't get on!" shouted one of the guards,
waving him off.

Roaring with laughter, Ivan the glass blower called out,
"Sure it does! That's where it goes. Get on, we'll take you
there." Ivan was a nonpolitical prisoner and was permitted
visits every month. All the zeks laughed. The Muscovite
could not understand what kind of bus this was and why he
was not allowed to board it.

But he was used to such prohibitions and jumped off.

A half-dozen other would-be passengers who had crowded
behind him fell back.

The pale-blue bus turned left on Sadovya Boulevard. That
meant they were not going to Butyrskaya, as usual. Probably to Taganka.

Nerzhin would never have parted from his wife and
would have serenely spent his life on the numerical integration of differential equations if only he had not been born in
Russia, or had been born in other times, or if he had not
been the sort of person he was.

There was a scene in Victor Hugo's *Ninety-three*. Lan-
tenae is sitting on a dune. He can see several bell towers at
once, and every bell is in motion. All the bells are sounding
an alarm, but a gale wind carries the sound away and he
hears nothing.

In that same way, through some strange inward sense,
Nerzhin had since adolescence been hearing a mute bell—
all the groans, cries, shouts of the dying, carried by a steady,
insistent wind away from human ears. He grew up without
reading a single book by Mayne Reid, but at the age of
twelve he had gone through an enormous pile of *Izvestiya*
as tall as he was and he had read about the trial of the
saboteur engineers. From the very first, the boy did not
believe what he read. He did not know why—his reason
could not grasp it—but he could clearly see that it was all a
lie. He knew engineers in his friends' families, and he could
not imagine them committing sabotage.

At thirteen and fourteen Gleb did not run out to play in

the street when he had finished studying, but sat reading the newspapers. He knew the Party leaders by name, their positions, the Soviet military leaders, the Soviet ambassadors in every country, and the foreign ambassadors in the Soviet Union. He read all the speeches made at the congresses, and the memoirs of the Old Bolsheviks, and the shifting history of the Party—there had been several versions and each was different. In school, too, in the fourth grade, they had already been introduced to the elements of political economy, and from the fifth grade on they had social sciences almost every day. He was given *In Memory of Herzen* to read, and again and again he pored over the Lenin volume.

Either because his ear was young or because he read more than there was in the newspapers, he clearly sensed the falsity in the exaggerated, stifling exaltation of one man, always one man! If he was everything, did it not mean that other men were nothing? Out of pure protest Gleb refused to let himself be carried away.

Gleb was only a ninth-grader on the December morning when he looked into a display window where a newspaper was posted and read that Kirov had been killed. And suddenly, like a blinding light, it became clear to him that Stalin and no one else had killed Kirov. Because he was the only one who would profit by his death! A feeling of aching loneliness seized him—the grown men, crowded near him, did not understand that simple truth.

Then the same Old Bolsheviks, who had made the entire Revolution and whose whole life it had been, began by the dozens and the hundreds to drift into nonexistence. Some, not waiting to be arrested, swallowed poison in their apartments; others hanged themselves at their houses outside the city. But most let themselves be arrested and appeared in court and unaccountably confessed, loudly condemned themselves with the worst vilifications, and admitted serving in all the foreign intelligence agencies in the world. It was so overdone, so crude, so excessive, that only a stone ear could fail to hear the lie.

Did people really not hear? Russian writers who dared trace their spiritual inheritance from Pushkin and Tolstoi wrote sickly-sweet eulogies of the tyrant. Russian composers, trained in the Herzen Street conservatory, laid their servile hymns at his pedestal.

For Gleb Nerzhin the mute bell thundered through his entire youth. An inviolable decision took root in him: to learn and understand! To learn and understand! Strolling the boulevards of his native city when it would have been more fitting to sigh over a girl, Gleb went around dreaming of the day he would sort everything out and would, perhaps, even penetrate within the walls where those people, as one, had vilified themselves before they died. Perhaps inside those walls it could be understood.

At the time he did not know the name of that prison, nor that our wishes, if they are truly great, are certain to be fulfilled.

Years passed. Everything was realized and fulfilled in Gleb Nerzhin's life, even though it turned out to be not at all easy or pleasant. He was seized and taken to that very place, and he met those who still survived, who were not surprised by his surmises, and had a hundred times more to tell.

Everything was realized and fulfilled, but Nerzhin was left with neither his work, nor time, nor life—nor his wife. Once a single great passion occupies the soul, it displaces everything else. There is no room in us for two passions.

. . . The bus rattled across the bridge over the Yauza and continued along endless, crooked, hostile streets.

Nerzhin said at last, "So we're not being taken to Taganka? Where are we going? I don't understand."

Gerasimovich, emerging from the same kind of gloomy reflections, answered: "This is Lefortovo Rampart. We're coming to Lefortovo Prison."

Gates opened for the bus. It entered a service court and stopped in front of a two-story wing built against the high prison. Lieutenant Colonel Klimentiev was already standing there, looking young without his tunic or cap.

True, it was less frosty here. Beneath dense, cloudy skies stretched a windless, winter gloom.

At a sign from the lieutenant colonel the guards got out of the bus, lined up in a row, and only the two in the back corners still sat with their pistols in their pockets. The prisoners had no time to observe the main section of the prison. They followed the lieutenant colonel inside. There was a long, narrow corridor, and along it were seven open doors. The lieutenant colonel went ahead and gave his orders de-

cisively, as in battle: "Gerasimovich—here! Lukashenko—
in that one! Nerzhin—in the third!"

One at a time the prisoners turned into the rooms.

Klimentiev assigned one of the seven guards to each of
them. Nerzhin got one of the gangsters.

All the rooms were interrogation offices: the barred windows gave little enough light; the interrogator's armchair
and desk were in front of the windows; there were a little
table and stool for the person being questioned.

Nerzhin moved the armchair closer to the door, putting
it there for his wife. And he took the uncomfortable little
stool with a crack that threatened to pinch him. On just
such a stool, behind just such a table, he had once sat out
six months of interrogation.

The door was left open. Nerzhin heard his wife's light
heels clicking down the corridor, and her dear voice: "In
here?"

And she came in.

35

BE UNFAITHFUL!

When the battered truck, jolting over the bare pine roots
and snarling in the sand, had taken Nadya away from the
front, Gleb stood far away in the open cut, and the cut
swallowed him, becoming ever longer and darker. Who could
have told them then that their separation would not end with
the war and indeed had hardly begun?

It is always hard to wait for a husband to return from
war. But most difficult of all are the last months before the
end. Shell fragments and bullets do not count how long a
man has been fighting.

That was when the letters from Gleb stopped.

Nadya would run out to meet the postman. She wrote her
husband, his friends, his superiors. Everyone was as silent
as the grave.

There was not an evening in the spring of 1945 when artillery salutes did not burst in the air. One city after another was taken: Königsberg, Breslau, Frankfurt, Berlin, Prague.

There were no letters. Her hopes dimmed. She began to feel apathetic. But she could not let herself fall apart. If he was alive and if he returned, he would accuse her of wasting her time. She wore herself to the bone with long days of work, she prepared to begin graduate work in chemistry, she studied foreign languages and dialectical materialism, and she wept only at night.

Suddenly, for the first time, Nadya was not paid her allocation as an officer's wife.

So she thought he had been killed.

Then the four-year war ended. People ran through the streets wild with joy. Some fired pistols in the air. All the loudspeakers of the Soviet Union broadcast victory marches across the hungry and wounded land.

They didn't tell her he had been killed. They said he was missing.

And her heart, which because it was human refused to reconcile itself to something which could not be undone, began to invent fairy tales. Perhaps he had been sent off on an intelligence mission. Perhaps he was carrying out a special assignment. A generation brought up on suspicion and secrecy imagined secrets even where none existed.

The hot southern summer burned on, but not for Nerzhin's widow.

Yet she went on as before, studying chemistry, languages, and dialectical materialism, afraid of displeasing him if he should return.

Four months passed. It was time to admit that this man was no longer alive. Then a tattered triangle of paper arrived from Krasnaya Presnya: "My dearest! Now it will be ten years more!"

Those close to her could not understand her. She had learned that her husband was in prison—and she had brightened and become cheerful. Once again she was not alone on earth. What happiness that it was not fifteen years, not twenty-five years! It is only from the grave that no one returns. People do return from hard labor.

Now, when it was not death, when there was no longer

that awful inner lack of faith, when there were only the burden and the threat, new strength flooded Nadya. He was in Moscow. That meant she had to go to Moscow and save him. She imagined that just to be near him would be enough to save him.

But how to get there? Our descendants will never be able to imagine what it meant to travel anywhere at that time and especially to Moscow. In the first place, just as in the thirties, every citizen had to prove with documents why he should not stay where he was, what state necessity compelled him to burden the transportation facilities with his person. After this he was issued a pass giving him the right to stand in line in the station for a week, to sleep on the spittle-covered floor, or shove a timorous bribe in at the back door of the cashier's booth.

Nadya managed to get virtually unobtainable permission to enroll for graduate work in Moscow. Having paid three times the price of the ticket, she went by plane to Moscow, holding on her knees her textbook-laden briefcase and felt boots for the northern forests which awaited her husband.

This was that miraculous high point in life when good powers help us and we succeed in everything. The most respected graduate school in the country accepted the unknown provincial girl who had no name, no money, no connections, and had pulled no strings.

All that turned out to be easier than arranging to visit the Krasnaya Presnya transit prison. They did not allow visits. Not to anyone. All the channels of GULAG were overstrained. There was a stream of prisoners coming from the West which defied all imagination.

But at the guardhouse hastily built out of rough boards, waiting for a reply to one of her useless petitions, Nadya saw a column of prisoners being led out of the unpainted wooden gates of the prison to a landing on the Moscow River. In a happy flash of intuition Nadya guessed that Gleb was among them.

They took out at least two hundred people. All were in that in-between state in which a person says farewell to his "free" clothing and adopts the grayish-black clothing of a zek. Each of them still retained something that recalled his previous life: a visored military cap with a colored band, but without a strap or insignia, leather boots which had not yet been sold for bread or stolen by the criminal gangs in prison, a silk shirt splitting down the back. All were clipped to the scalp and in one way or another were protecting their heads from the summer sun. All were unshaven and all were thin, some of them near physical collapse.

Nadya did not have to search. She felt where Gleb was and then saw him: he was walking in a woolen field shirt with his collar unbuttoned, the artillery officer's red borders still on his cuffs and on his chest the unfaded strips where his campaign decorations had been. He walked with his arms behind his back like the rest of them. He did not look up at the sunny open spaces on the hill, which one might have thought would have drawn a prisoner's gaze, nor did he look to either side at the women with packages. At the transit prison no one received letters, and he did not know that Nadya was in Moscow. As sallow, as emaciated, as his comrades, his face beamed with approval as he listened with intense appreciation to his neighbor, a stately, gray-bearded old man.

Nadya ran alongside and shouted her husband's name, but because of his conversation and the loud barking of the police dogs, he did not hear her. Out of breath, she kept on running so as not to lose sight of his face. It was such a terrible thing that for months he had rotted in dark and stinking cells. It was such a delight to see him there, alongside her. It was such a source of pride that he had not been broken. It was also painful that he was not grieving, that he had forgotten his wife. For the first time she felt pain for herself—a suspicion that he had not treated her fairly, that the victim was not him but herself.

She felt all that in a single moment. The escort guards shouted at her; the horrible, man-hating dogs strained at their leashes, coiled like springs and barking, and their bloodshot eyes burned crimson. They chased Nadya away. The column stretched along a narrow incline, and there was no room for her to squeeze in beside it. The last escort guards stayed far behind, closing off the forbidden space between them and the prisoners, and, following them, Nadya could not catch up with the column. It had gone down the hill and disappeared behind another solid fence.

At night, when the inhabitants of Krasnaya Presnya could not see them, trains of cattle cars arrived at the transit prison. Detachments of escort guards with lanterns bobbing, dogs barking, and with sporadic shouts, oaths and blows, loaded the prisoners forty to a car and sent them off by the thousands to Pechora, Inta, Vorkuta, Sovetskaya Gavan, Norilsk, to Irkutsk, Chita, Krasnoyarsk, Novosibirsk, Central Asia, Karaganda, Dzhezkazgan, Pribalkhash, Irtysh, Tobolsk, Ural, Saratov, Vyatka, Vologda, Perm, Solvychegodsk, Rybinsk, Potminsk, Sukhobezvodninsk, and many other, nameless smaller camps. Other prisoners in groups of one and two hundred were taken out by day in the beds of trucks to places around Moscow such as Serebryany Bor, Novy Iyerusalim, Pershino, Khovrino, Beskudnikovo, Khimki, Dmitrov, Solnechnogorsk, and by night into Moscow itself, where, behind barriers of wooden fences and braided barbed wire, they built the great modern capital.

Fate sent Nadya an unexpected reward: Gleb was not taken off to the Arctic but unloaded in Moscow at a small camp which was building a huge apartment house for the heads of the MVD, a semicircular building at the Kaluga Gates.

When Nadya, hardly feeling anything, rushed to him there for her first visit, it seemed to her he had already been half freed.

On Bolshaya Kaluzhskaya Street limousines made their way, now and then a diplomatic car among them. The buses and trolley-buses stopped at the Neskuchny Gardens gate, where the guardhouse for the camp was located—like an ordinary entry to a construction project. High up, the construction swarmed with people in dirty, tattered clothing, but construction workers all look like that and none of the passers-by guessed that these were zeks.

Anyone who did guess kept his mouth shut.

This was the time of cheap money and expensive bread. Nadya economized on food, sold things, and took her husband parcels. The authorities always took the parcels. But they did not often allow visits. Gleb was not working his production norm.

On the visits it was impossible to recognize him. As with all self-assertive people, misfortune had a good effect on him. He softened, kissed his wife's hands, and followed the sparks in her eyes. He was no longer in prison then. Camp life exceeds in its ruthlessness anything known of the lives

of cannibals and rats, and it had bowed him. But he had
consciously led himself to that boundary beyond which one
is not sorry for oneself, and sincerely and stubbornly he repeated: "Darling! You don't know what you are taking on
yourself. You will wait for me one year, even three, even
five—but the nearer the end, the more difficult it will be to
wait. The last years will be the least bearable. We have no
children. So don't destroy your youth. Leave me! Marry
again!"

Nadya shook her head sorrowfully. "You want to be free
of me?"

The prisoners lived in the unfinished wing of the apartment
house they were building. When the women bringing parcels
got off the trolley-bus, they saw two or three windows of
the men's dormitory above the fence, and the men crowded
at the windows. Sometimes the camp prostitutes could be
seen, too. One prostitute up there embraced her camp "husband" as they stood by the window and shouted over the
fence to his legal wife: "Enough of your streetwalking, you
whore! Hand over your parcel and scram! If I see you once
more at the guardhouse, I'll scratch your face for you."

The first postwar elections to the Supreme Soviet were
approaching. In Moscow they prepared for them energetically. It was undesirable to keep the Section 58s in Moscow.
Of course, they were good workers. But they could be an
embarrassment. And vigilance was weak. So, to frighten all
of them, some at least had to be sent off. Dread latrine
rumors crawled through the camps that soon there would be
prisoner transports to the north. Prisoners who had potatoes
baked them for the trip.

To protect the voters, all visits in the Moscow camps were
forbidden before the elections. Nadya sent Gleb a towel with
a tiny note sewed into it:

My beloved! No matter how many years pass or how many storms
break over our heads [she loved to express herself in high-flown terms],
your girl will be true to you as long as she lives. They say that your section is being sent away. You will be in a distant region, torn for long
years from our meetings, from our secret glances across the barbed wire.
If any diversions can ease your burden in that hopelessly dismal life—
well, what of it? I consent, darling, I even insist—be unfaithful to me,
see other women. After all, you will be returning to me, won't you?

36

THAT'S FINE TO SAY:
"OFF TO THE TAIGA!"

Without knowing a tenth of Moscow, Nadya did know the dismal geography of Moscow's prisons. The prisons were evenly distributed throughout the capital, so situated that it was not far from any point in the city to one or another of them. In delivering parcels, making inquiries, and going for visits, Nadya gradually learned to recognize the all-Union Big Lubyanka and the provincial Small Lubyanka, discovered there were interrogation prisons called KPZs at every railway station. More than once she had been in Butyrskaya Prison and in Taganka Prison. She knew which streetcars, though the stops were not indicated on their route maps, went to Lefortovo and to Krasnaya Presnya. She now lived near the prison called Sailors' Peace, which had been wrecked in 1917 and then restored and fortified.

Since Gleb had once again returned from a distant camp to Moscow, and not to a camp this time but to some amazing sort of institution, a special prison where the food was excellent and where they were occupied with scientific matters, Nadya had again begun to see her husband from time to time. However, wives were not supposed to know where their husbands were being kept, so for their rare visits the zeks were brought to various Moscow prisons.

The most enjoyable visits were at Taganka. It was a prison not for political prisoners but for thieves, and the rules were lax. Visits took place in the guards' club, where, with accordions, the jailers communed with the muses. The prisoners were driven in an open bus through deserted Kamenshchikov Street. Their wives waited for them on the sidewalk, and even before the official start of the visit each prisoner could embrace his wife, stay near her, say whatever was forbidden by the regulations, and even pass something from hand to hand. The visits themselves were conducted in a free and easy manner. Husband and wife sat

beside each other, and there was only one guard to eavesdrop on the conversations of four couples.

Butyrskaya, which was essentially a soft, happy prison
also, seemed chilling to the wives. Prisoners who came to
Butyrskaya from the Lubyankas were immediately heartened
by the generally slack discipline. There was no blinding light
in the "boxes." One could walk through the corridors without
having to hold one's hands behind one's back. One could
talk in a normal voice in the cells and peer out through the
peephole, lie on the plank beds in the daytime, and sometimes sleep under them. Butyrskaya was more relaxed in
other ways: at night one could keep one's hands underneath one's coat, and they did not take away one's eyeglasses; they permitted matches in the cell and did not
gouge the tobacco out of cigarettes, and they cut the bread
in the food parcels into four pieces only, not into tiny bits.

The wives did not know about all these indulgences. They
saw a fortress wall twenty feet high, stretching for a block
on Novoslobodskaya Street. They saw iron gates between
powerful concrete pillars and other, unusual gates slowly
sliding open, mechanically operated to let the Black Marias
in and out. And when the women were admitted for visits,
they were taken in through masonry two yards thick and
led between high walls circling the frightening Pugachev
Tower.

The ordinary zeks saw their visitors through two gratings.
A guard walked in the aisle between the gratings, as if he
were in a cage. Zeks with a higher status, the sharashka
zeks, met their visitors across a large table, underneath
which a solid panel prevented them from touching feet or
signaling to each other. At the end of the table the guard
sat like a vigilant statue listening to the conversation. But
the most oppressive thing at Butyrskaya was that the husbands seemed to appear from the depths of the prison,
emerge for half an hour out of the thick dank walls, smile
in ghostly fashion, assure their wives that they were living
well, that they did not need anything, and then return into
the walls.

Today was the first time Nadya's visit had taken place in
Lefortovo.

The guardhouse guard put a check mark on his list and
pointed out to Nadya a long one-story building.

In a bare room with two long benches and a long bare

table several women were already waiting. On the table sat wicker baskets and canvas market bags, obviously full of foodstuffs. And even though the sharashka zeks were sufficiently well fed, Nadya, who had brought an unimposing pastry in a bag, was hurt and conscience-stricken that she could not treat her husband to something tasty even once a year. She had baked the pastry early in the morning when the others in her dormitory were asleep—from some white flour she had and leftover butter and sugar. She had not been able to get candies or bakery pastries, and anyway she had very little money left to last her till pay day. This visit fell on her husband's birthday, and she had nothing to bring him as a gift. She wanted to give him a good book, but she could not even do that after the last visit. That time Nadya had brought him a book of Yesenin's verses, which she had managed to get hold of by a miracle. It was the same edition her husband had had at the front, which had disappeared when he was arrested. And so Nadya had written on the title page: "Just like this book, everything you lost will return."

But Lieutenant Colonel Klimentiev had torn out the title page in her presence and returned it to her, saying that no written messages could be included in anything handed to a prisoner—the inscription must go separately, through the censor.

When he learned about this, Gleb told her angrily, "Don't bring me any more books."

Four women sat around the table, one of them a young woman with a three-year-old child. Nadya knew none of them. She greeted them, and they replied, then continued their animated conversation.

At the far wall, a woman of thirty-five or forty in a very old fur coat sat on a small bench apart from the others. She wore a gray scarf tied around her head, a "babushka" from which the nap had been worn away exposing the weave. She sat with her arms folded, and she was staring tensely at the floor in front of her. Her whole bearing expressed the determination to be left alone and not to have to talk with anyone. She held no parcel of any kind, and there was none beside her.

The group was ready to receive Nadya, but Nadya did not want to join them. She, too, cherished her special

mood that morning. Approaching the woman who was
sitting by herself, she asked, "Do you mind?"

The woman looked up. Her eyes were totally colorless.
There was no comprehension in them of what Nadya had
asked. She looked right through Nadya.

Nadya sat down, drawing her artificial-caracul coat
around her. She, too, fell silent.

She wanted at this moment to hear of nothing else, to
think of nothing else, but Gleb, and the conversation they
were about to have; of what was forever disappearing into
the murk of the past and the murk of the future; of what
concerned not him, not her, but the two of them together and
was customarily referred to by the worn word "love."

But she could not help hearing the conversation at the
table. The women were discussing what their husbands got to
eat, what was put on the table mornings and evenings, and
how often their linen was washed. How did they know all
that? Did it mean they spent the golden moments of their
visits talking about such things? They were enumerating
which foods and how many ounces and pounds of each they
had brought with them. It was all part of that tenacious female preoccupation which makes a family a family and
keeps the human race going. But this was not how Nadya
saw it. Instead, she thought: how outrageous, how com-
monplace, how pitiful to turn great moments into triviality!
Had it never occurred to these women that they should consider instead who it was that had dared to imprison their
husbands? After all, their husbands might not have been behind bars and thus in no need of those parcels of food.

They had to wait a long time. The visit had been set for
10 A.M., but by 11 no one had yet appeared.

The seventh visitor, a gray-haired woman, arrived out of
breath, later than the rest. Nadya knew her from a previous
visit. She had been the engraver's first wife, and she had
told her story readily. She had always worshiped her husband and considered him a genius. But he had told her that
he was unhappy with her because of a psychological complex, and he had abandoned her and their child for another
woman. He lived with this redhead for three years and
then went to war. In the war he was immediately taken
prisoner, but in Germany he had lived a free life and there,
too, it seemed, he had found diversions. When he returned
from German imprisonment, he was arrested at the border

and given ten years. From Butyrskaya he informed his red-haired wife that he was in prison and asked for parcels. She said, "It would have been better if he'd betrayed me instead of his country! I could then have forgiven him more easily." So then he asked his first wife to forgive him, and she began bringing him parcels and coming for visits—and now he swore her his eternal love.

Nadya remembered how the engraver's wife had declared bitterly in telling her story that if one's husband is in prison the best thing is to be unfaithful to him, "so that when they get out they will value us. Otherwise they will think that nobody wanted us all that time, that no one would have us."

By now the new arrival had changed the conversation at the table. She was telling about her troubles with lawyers and the judicial center on Nikolsky Street. This consultation center was called a "model" one. Its lawyers took thousands of rubles from their clients and made frequent visits to Moscow restaurants—while the clients' cases remained exactly where they had been, which was nowhere. But somehow, in the end, they went too far. They were all arrested, all given ten years, and the word "model" was removed from the sign on Nikolsky Street. Then, even in the nonmodel consultation center, the new lawyers who had been sent in as replacements began taking thousands of rubles and left the cases of their clients as they were before. The lawyers explained confidentially that the large fees were necessary because they had to split them with others. It was impossible to check up on them. Perhaps they didn't split with anyone in spite of their claims that they did, that the business had to go through many hands. The helpless women walked back and forth before the concrete wall of the law as they walked in front of the twenty-foot-high Butyrskaya wall—they had no wings to fly over it, and they had to bow before every gate that opened. The legal proceedings behind the walls were to them the clandestine turnings of a mighty machine, which—despite the obvious guilt of the accused and the contrast between them and those who had imprisoned them—sometimes, by a miracle, turned up a lucky award. And thus the women paid the lawyers not for these miracles but for their dreams of them.

The engraver's wife believed unwaveringly that she would eventually be successful. From what she said it was evident that she had got together forty thousand rubles from the sale of her room and from relatives, and that she had paid all of it to the lawyers. There had already been four lawyers. Three requests for pardon and five appeals on evidence had been filed. She watched the progress of all these appeals, and she had been promised favorable consideration in many different places. She knew by name all the prosecutors on duty at the three main prosecution offices and had breathed the atmosphere of the reception rooms at the Supreme Court and the Supreme Soviet. Like many trusting people, she exaggerated the value of each hopeful remark and each glance that was not openly hostile.

"You have to write! You have to write to everyone!" she repeated energetically, urging the other women to follow her example. "Our husbands are suffering. Freedom won't come by itself. You have to write!"

This story distracted Nadya from her mood and it also troubled her conscience. Listening to the inspired speech of the engraver's aging wife, one could not help but believe that she had outdistanced them all, that she would certainly get her husband out of prison—and ask oneself, "Why couldn't I do as much? Why have I been a less loyal friend?"

Nadya had only once had dealings with the "model" legal consultation center. She had composed a single request with the assistance of a lawyer, and had paid him 2,500 rubles. Apparently it was too little. He took offense and did nothing.

"Yes," she said quietly, as if to herself, "have we done everything? Are our consciences clear?"

The women talking at the table did not hear her, but her neighbor turned to her suddenly as if Nadya had insulted her.

"And what is there to do?" she demanded in a hostile tone. "It's all a nightmare! Section 58—that means *imprisonment forever*. Section 58 is not for a criminal, but for an *enemy!* You aren't going to buy someone out of 58 even for a million!"

Her face was all wrinkled. In her voice there was the ring of pure unmitigated suffering.

Nadya's heart opened to this old woman. In a tone which apologized for the loftiness of her words she replied, "I meant to say that we don't do everything we could. After all, the wives of the Decembrists left everything and followed their husbands without regrets or second thoughts. Maybe if we can't obtain their freedom, we can get exile for them instead. I'd endure his being sent to the taiga, to any taiga anywhere, in the Arctic, where there's never any sun, and I'd go with him, I'd leave everything."

The woman, who had the face of a grim nun and whose gray dress was threadbare, looked at Nadya with astonishment and respect.

"You still have the strength to go to the taiga? How fortunate you are! I have no strength left for anything. I think I'd marry any prosperous old man who'd agree to take me."

Nadya trembled. "And you could leave him? Behind bars?"

The woman took Nadya by the sleeve of her coat. "My dear! It was easy to love a man in the nineteenth century! The wives of the Decembrists—do you think they performed some kind of heroic feat? Did personnel sections call them in to fill out security questionnaires? Did they have to hide their marriages as if they were a disease? In order to keep their jobs; so that their last five hundred rubles a month wouldn't be taken away from them; so as not to be boycotted in their own apartments; so that when they went to the courtyard to get water people wouldn't hiss at them, calling them 'enemies of the people'? Did their own mothers and sisters bring pressure on them to be reasonable and get a divorce? No, on the contrary! They were followed by a murmur of admiration from the cream of society. They graciously presented to poets the legends of their deeds. Leaving for Siberia in their expensive carriages, they did not lose, along with the right to live in Moscow, their last miserable ten square yards; they did not have to think about dealing with such trifles as black marks on their labor booklet, or the pantry where there would be no pots or pans, no black bread! That's fine to say: 'Off to the taiga!' Apparently you have not been waiting very long!"

Her voice was ready to break. Tears filled Nadya's eyes as she listened to her neighbor's passionate arguments.

"It will soon be five years since my husband's been in prison," she said, justifying herself. "And he was at the front before—"

"Don't count *that*!" the woman objected violently. "Being at the front is not the same thing! Then it's easy to wait! Then everyone is waiting. Then you can speak openly. Read letters! But if one has to wait and, in addition, hide it—well?"

She stopped. She saw she did not have to explain to Nadya.

It was already 11:30. Finally, Lieutenant Colonel Klimentiev entered, and with him a fat, hostile master sergeant. The sergeant began to take the parcels, opening factory-sealed packs of cookies and breaking each home-baked meat pastry in two. He broke up Nadya's pastry as well, looking for a message baked into it, or money, or poison. Klimentiev collected everyone's visiting permit, registered all their names in a big book, and then straightened up in military style and declared in a precise voice:

"Attention! Are you familiar with the rules? The visit lasts thirty minutes. You are not to give anything to the prisoners. You are forbidden to ask the prisoners about their work, about their life, about their schedules. Violation of these rules is punishable under the criminal code. And furthermore, from today's visit on, holding hands and kissing are forbidden. In case of a violation the visit will be terminated immediately."

The submissive women kept silent.

"Gerasimovich, Natalya Pavlovna!" Klimentiev read off the first name.

Nadya's neighbor rose and, treading firmly in her prewar felt overshoes, went out into the corridor.

37

THE VISIT

Though she had cried while she was waiting, Nadya had a holiday feeling when she at last went in.

When she appeared in the doorway, Nerzhin had already risen to meet her and he was smiling. His smile lasted only a moment, but she felt a sudden happiness: he remained just as close. He had not changed toward her.

The bull-necked individual in a soft gray suit, looking like a retired gangster, approached the small table. His presence divided the narrow room, preventing them from touching.

"Oh, come on, let me at least take her by the hand!" Nerzhin said angrily.

"It's against the rules," the guard answered, letting his heavy jaw open just enough for the words to come through.

Nadya smiled vacantly and signaled her husband not to argue. She sat in the armchair he had arranged for her. In places the fiber was sticking out of its leather upholstery. Several generations of interrogators had sat in that armchair, sent hundreds of people to their graves, and soon followed themselves.

"Well, happy birthday!" she said, trying to seem cheerful.

"Thank you."

"Such a coincidence, that it should be today."

"The stars."

They were already accustomed to speaking to each other. Nadya tried to disregard the oppressive presence of the guard watching them. Nerzhin tried to sit in such a way that the rickety stool did not pinch him.

The little table that had stood in front of generations of prisoners under interrogation now stood between husband and wife.

"I just thought I'd mention that I brought you a little something to eat, a pastry. You know how Mama makes them? I'm sorry—there's nothing else."

"Silly, you didn't even have to do that. We have everything."

"But not pastry, do you? And you told me not to bring any more books. Are you reading Yesenin?"

Nerzhin's face darkened. More than a month ago someone had sent a denunciation to Shikin concerning his copy of Yesenin, and Shikin had taken the book away, saying it was forbidden.

"I'm reading it."

With only a half-hour was there any point in going into details?

Although it was not at all hot in the room, but indeed rather chilly, Nadya unbuttoned her coat collar and opened it, for she wanted to show her husband not only her new fur coat—about which he had said nothing—but also her new blouse. She also hoped that the orange blouse would brighten her face. She was afraid she might look sallow in this dim light.

With one embracing glance Nerzhin took in his wife—her face, her throat, and the opening at her bosom. Nadya stirred under this look—the most important event in the visit—and seemed to rise to meet him.

"You have a new blouse. Show me some more."

"And my fur coat?" She made a disappointed face.

"What about the fur coat?"

"It's new."

"So it is," Gleb said finally. "The fur coat is new." He looked at the black curls, not even knowing that it was caracul, or whether it was real or artificial, being the last man on earth able to distinguish a five-hundred-ruble coat from a five-thousand-ruble one.

Now she threw back the coat. He saw her neck, finely molded like a young girl's, as it always had been, and the narrow shoulders he had loved to crush when he embraced her, and, beneath the folds of her blouse, the breasts which had lost their firmness in the course of the years.

His brief reproachful thought that she was getting new clothes, making new acquaintances, was replaced by the awareness that the sides of the gray prison van had crushed her life, too.

"You're thin," he said with sympathy. "You should eat better. Can't you eat better?"

Am I homely? her look asked.

You're just as wonderful as ever! her husband's look replied.

(Although such words were not forbidden by the lieutenant colonel, they could not be spoken in someone else's presence.)

"I eat well," she lied. "It's just that my life is busy, harried."

"How? Tell me."

"No, you first."

"What can I tell?" Nerzhin said, smiling. "Nothing."

"Well, you see—" she began with reticence.

The fleshy guard stood a foot and a half from the table, like a bulldog looking down on the couple with stony contempt.

They had to find just the right tone, the winged language of allusion. Their university background suggested the tone.

"Is the suit yours?" she asked.

Nerzhin made a face and shook his head wryly.

"Mine? No. A Potemkin village situation. For three hours. Don't let the sphinx bother you."

"I can't help it," she said, pouting slightly, like a child, flirting, certain now that he still took pleasure in her.

"We get used to seeing the humorous side of it."

Nadya remembered the conversation with the Gerasimovich woman and sighed. "But we wives don't."

Nerzhin made an effort to touch his wife's knees with his own, but the bar under the table prevented even this contact. The table rocked. Resting on his elbows and leaning nearer his wife, Nerzhin said with disappointment, "That's how it is—obstacles everywhere."

Are you mine? Mine? his look asked.

I am the one you loved. I'm no worse, believe me, her shining gray eyes told him.

"And your work—what problems are you having with it? Tell me. You aren't a graduate student any longer?"

"No."

"Then you've defended your dissertation?"

"No."

"How can that be?"

"Well, it's like this. . . ." She began to speak very quickly, frightened that so much time had already passed. "No one has defended a dissertation in three years. They postpone them. For instance, one student spent two years writing her dissertation on 'Problems of Community Food Distribution,' and then they made her change her subject." (Ah! Why talk about that? It wasn't at all important.) "My own dissertation is ready and printed, but they are holding it up for various changes—" (the "Struggle Against Sycophancy" —but could you talk about that here?) "—and then there's the question of photocopies. And I still don't know about having it bound. It's a lot of trouble."

"But they're paying you your fellowship grant?"

"No."

"What are you living on?"

"My wages."

"So you're working. Where?"

"There, in the university."

"As what?"

"In a temporary, unreal job. Do you understand? My situation is precarious everywhere—I live on sufferance. In the dormitory, too. In fact, I—"

She glanced at the guard. What she wanted to say was that the police had canceled her registration at Stromynka but then, quite by mistake, had renewed it for a half-year. The error could be discovered any day. All the more reason why she could not speak of it in the presence of an MVD sergeant.

She went on: "And I was only allowed today's visit because—here's how it happened. . . ."

Ah, but you couldn't tell all that even in a whole half-hour.

"Wait, tell me that later. I want to ask you: are there problems connected *with me*?"

"Very difficult ones, darling. They are giving me—they want to give me a special subject. I am trying not to accept it."

"What do you mean by 'special subject'?"

She sighed helplessly and glanced again at the guard. His watchful face, looking as if he were suddenly about to bark or snap at her, hung less than a yard from their own.

Nadya raised her hands in a gesture of helplessness. She would have had to explain that in the university there were hardly any unclassified subjects left. And work on a classified subject meant a new, still more detailed security questionnaire about her husband, her husband's relatives, and the relatives of their relatives. If one were to say, "My husband was sentenced under Section 58," they would refuse not only to let her work at the university but also to defend her dissertation. Is she were to lie and say, "My husband was missing in action," then she would still have to give his family name, and all they had to do was check it out in the MVD card file and she would be sentenced for perjury. There was still a third possibility, but under Nerzhin's watchful stare Nadya avoided mentioning it.

She told him animatedly, "You know, I'm in a musical group at the university. They send me to play at concerts all the time. Not long ago I played in the Hall of Columns on the same evening as Yakov Zak—"

Gleb smiled and nodded, as though unwilling to believe it.

"Well, it was a trade-union evening, so it happened quite by accident, but, anyway . . . And you know—what a laugh!—they ruled out my best dress, said it wasn't good enough to perform in. They rang up a theater, brought me another, a wonderful one, down to the ankles."

"You played, then they took it away?"

"Oh, yes. You know, the girls scold me for amusing myself with music. But I tell them, 'It is better to be busy with some*thing* than with some*one*.'"

Nerzhin looked at his wife gratefully. Then he asked with concern, "Just a minute, about the special subject—"

Nadya lowered her eyes.

"I wanted to say—now don't take it to heart, *nicht wahr?* —you once insisted that—we should get a divorce." She said it very quietly.

(That was the third possibility, the one which would open up her life again. Of course, she would not write "divorced," because the security questionnaire would still require the family name of her former husband, and his present address and the names of his relatives, and even their birth dates, occupations, and addresses. Instead, she would write "unmarried.")

Yes, there had been a time when he had insisted. But right now he trembled. Only at that moment did he notice that the wedding ring she had always worn was not on her finger.

"Yes, of course," he agreed with great determination.

"Then you would not be against it—if—I have to—do it?" With a great effort she looked up at him. Her eyes widened. The fine gray rainbows in them were alight with a plea for forgiveness and understanding. "It—would not be real," she added with her breath alone, without voice.

"Good girl. You should have done it long ago!" Nerzhin agreed in a voice of firm conviction, though he felt neither conviction nor firmness—and he put off until after the visit all interpretation of what had happened.

"Maybe I won't have to," she said in a supplicating voice, pulling her coat over her shoulders again. At that moment she looked tired, worn out. "I just wanted—in case—so we agree. Maybe I won't have to."

"No, why not? You're right. Good girl," Nerzhin repeated without feeling, his thoughts already shifting to the main thing he had prepared to say to her. "It's important, my darling, that you should not hope too much for the end of my term!"

Nerzhin was already fully prepared for a second term followed by perpetual imprisonment—it had happened to many of his comrades. He could not mention it in letters, and he had to speak about it now.

An expression of fear appeared on Nadya's face.

"A term is a conditional thing," he explained, speaking hard and fast, accenting his words in the wrong places, so the guard could not follow what he said. "It can spiral on forever. History is full of examples. And even if it should miraculously end, don't imagine you and I will return to our city, to our old way of life. You must understand one thing and never forget it: they don't sell tickets to the past. For instance, what I regret most of all is that I'm not a shoemaker. How useful that skill would be in some North Siberian village, in Krasnoyarsk, in the lower reaches of the Angara. That's the only sort of life to prepare for. Who needs Euler's mathematical formulas there?"

He had been successful: the retired gangster did not stir but only blinked as Nerzhin's thoughts flew past him.

But Nerzhin forgot—no, he did not forget, he did not *understand*, just as they all failed to understand—that persons used to walking the warm, gray earth cannot rise over icy mountain ranges all at once. He did not understand that his wife even now continued, as at the beginning, to count off methodically the days and weeks of his term. For him the term was a bright, cold endlessness, and for her there were 264 weeks, 61 months, slightly more than 5 years, left —much less time than had already passed, because he had gone to war and not been home since.

As Nerzhin spoke, the fear on Nadya's face turned to horror.

"No, no!" she cried out. "Don't say that, darling!" (She had already forgotten about the guard, she was no longer ashamed to show her feelings.) "Don't take my hopes away! I don't want to believe it! It simply can't be! Or did you think I would really leave you?"

Her upper lip trembled, her face was distorted, her eyes expressed loyalty, only loyalty.

"I believe you, I believe you, Nadyushenka!" he said in a changed voice. "I understood it that way."

She fell silent and sank back in the chair.

In the open door of the room stood the dark, dandified lieutenant colonel, vigilantly watching the three people who had been drawn together. He quietly called the guard.

The former gangster, unwillingly, as if he had been called

away from his cranberry pudding, went over to the lieutenant colonel. Four steps behind Nadya's back they exchanged only a couple of words in all; but as they did,
Nerzhin, lowering his voice, managed to ask, "Do you know
Sologdin's wife?"

Adroit at such sudden shifts of conversation, Nadya
managed to reply, "Yes."

"And where she lives?"

"Yes."

"They aren't allowing him any visits. Tell her that he—"
The gangster returned.

"—loves her, believes in her, and hopes!" Gleb pronounced distinctly.

"Loves her, believes in her, and hopes," Nadya repeated
with a sigh. She looked insistently at her husband. She had
studied him for years, but somehow, now, she saw him in a
new aspect.

"It suits you," she said sadly.

"What does?"

"Everything. Here. All of this. Being here," she said,
disguising her meaning with inflections of her voice, so the
guard could not catch it.

But Nerzhin's new aura did not bring him closer to her.

She, too, was postponing everything she was learning, so
that it could be thought about and analyzed later, after the
visit. She did not know what would emerge from all this, but
her heart now sought in him the weaknesses, the illness, the
pleas for help—the appeal a woman could devote the rest
of her life to, even waiting another ten years and going to
him in the taiga.

But he was smiling! He was smiling with the same self-
assurance he had had at Krasnaya Presnya! He was always
self-sufficient. He never needed anyone's sympathy. He even
seemed to be comfortable sitting on the little stool. He
seemed to be looking around the room with satisfaction,
gathering material for his thoughts here, too. He looked
healthy, and his eyes sparkled. Did he really need a woman's
loyalty?

But Nadya had not yet thought all this through.

Nerzhin did not guess what doubts were assailing her.

"It's over!" Klimentiev said in the doorway.

"Already?" Nadya asked in surprise.

Nerzhin frowned, trying to remember the most important

thing still left on the list he had memorized before the visit.

"Yes, don't be surprised if they send me away from here, far away, and if my letters stop entirely."

"Can they do that? Where?" Nadya cried out.

What news! And he was telling her only now!

"Only God knows," he said, shrugging his shoulders meaningfully.

"Don't tell me you've started believing in God?"

They had not talked about anything.

He smiled. "Pascal, Newton, Einstein."

"You were told not to name any names!" the guard barked. "Let's break it up."

Husband and wife rose together, and now, when there was no longer any risk of having the visit cut short, Nerzhin embraced Nadya across the small table, kissed her on the cheek and clung to the soft lips he had completely forgotten. He had no hope of being in Moscow a year later to kiss them again. His voice trembled with tenderness: "In everything do what is best for you. And I . . ." He did not finish.

They looked into each other's eyes.

"What is this!" the guard bellowed and dragged Nerzhin back by the shoulder. "I'm canceling your visit!"

Nerzhin tore himself away.

"Go ahead and cancel it, and the hell with you," Nerzhin muttered under his breath.

Nadya backed toward the door, and with the fingers of her ringless hand she waved good-bye to her husband.

Then she disappeared through the door.

38

ANOTHER VISIT

Gerasimovich and his wife kissed.

Gerasimovich was short, no taller than his wife.

Their guard was a placid, simple lad. He did not care at all if they kissed. He was even embarrassed that he had to

interfere with their seeing each other. He would have turned
to the wall and stood there for the half-hour, but that was
not possible; Lieutenant Colonel Klimentiev had ordered
that the doors of all seven interrogation rooms be left open
so that he could keep watch on the guards from the corridor.

The lieutenant colonel did not care either whether the
prisoners and their wives kissed. He knew that no state
secrets would be revealed as a result. But he was wary of
his own guards and his own prisoners, some of whom were
informers and could tell tales about Klimentiev himself.

Gerasimovich and his wife kissed.

It was not the sort of kiss that would have shaken them
in their youth. This kiss, stolen from the authorities and
from fate, was colorless, tasteless, odorless—the pale kiss
one might exchange with a dead person in a dream.

They sat down, separated by the little table with a warped
plywood top used for prisoners under interrogation.

This crude little table had a story richer than many
human lives. For many years people had sat behind it,
sobbed, shuddered in terror, struggled with devastating
sleeplessness, spoken proud, angry words, or signed scurri-
lous denunciations of those close to them. Ordinarily they
were not given either pencils or pens—only for rare hand-
written statements. But the prisoners had left marks on the
warped surface of the table, strange, wavy or angular graffiti,
which in a mysterious way preserved the subconscious
twistings of the soul.

Gerasimovich looked at his wife.

His first thought was how unattractive she had become.
Her eyes were sunken. There were wrinkles at her eyes and
lips. The skin of her face was flabby, and Natasha seemed
to have given it no care at all. Her coat was prewar and
long ago should have at least been turned. The fur on the
collar lay flat and threadbare, and her scarf was as old as
the ages; he seemed to remember they had bought it with a
requisition coupon long ago in Komsomolsk-on-Amur; and
she had worn it in Leningrad when she went to the Neva
for water.

Gerasimovich suppressed the mean thought, which arose
from the depths of his being, that his wife was homely.
Before him was a woman, the only woman in the world who
was half of himself. Before him was a woman, the woman
who shared his memories. What young girl, attractive and

fresh but an incomprehensible stranger, with her own, different recollections, could mean more to him than his wife?

Natasha had been not quite eighteen when they first met in a house on Srednaya Podyacheskaya, at the Lviny Bridge, on New Year's Day, 1930. Six days from now it would be twenty years ago.

Natasha had been just nineteen when he was arrested the first time. For sabotage.

Gerasimovich began working as an engineer at a time when the word "engineer" was still almost synonymous with the word "enemy," and when it was routine to suspect engineers of being saboteurs. Gerasimovich, who had barely graduated from the institute, wore pince-nez for his near-sightedness, which made him look exactly like the intellectual depicted in spy posters during the thirties. He had nodded to everyone, whether he had to or not, and said "Pardon me, please" in a very gentle voice. At meetings he kept totally silent and sat like a mouse. He did not even understand how much he irritated everyone.

But no matter how hard they tried to prepare a good case against him, they barely managed to stretch his sentence to three years. When he arrived at the Amur River, he was released from surveillance immediately. His fiancée came there to join him and became his wife.

It was a rare night indeed when husband and wife did not dream of Leningrad. And they were getting ready to return there—in 1935. But then new floods of prisoners began coming in their direction. . . .

Natalya Pavlovna also observed her husband closely. There had been a time when she had watched that face change, saw the lips become hard, the eyes turn cold, even cruel, behind his pince-nez. Illarion Pavlovich stopped nodding to people, stopped reciting his "beg your pardons." He was constantly reproached with his past. He would be fired from one place and hired elsewhere for a job unsuited to a person of his education. They moved from place to place, lived in destitution, lost their daughter, lost their son. And, deciding finally to risk everything, they returned to Leningrad. They arrived in June, 1941.

There they found it harder than ever to set themselves up in tolerable circumstances. Her husband's security questionnaire hung over him. Yet the laboratory phantom grew stronger rather than weaker from the heavy physical labor which he undertook for want of anything else. He survived the autumn trench-digging. With the first snow he became a gravedigger.

This sinister profession was the most badly needed and the most profitable in the besieged city. As a final tribute to the dead, the survivors gave the gravedigger their pauper's morsels of bread.

One could not eat this bread without trembling. But Illarion found an excuse for himself: "People wasted precious little pity on us; we won't waste pity on them!"

The couple survived. But even before the end of the blockade, Illarion was arrested for *intent* to betray his country. In Leningrad many were arrested for *intent*. After all, they could not directly accuse people of treason who had not been in occupied territory.

Natalya Pavlovna looked carefully at her husband, but, strangely, she found no traces of the difficult years. His eyes looked with calm intelligence through his pince-nez. His cheeks were not sunken. He had no wrinkles. His suit was an expensive one. His necktie was carefully tied.

One might imagine that she was the one who had been in prison.

And her first ungenerous thought was that he was living very well indeed in that special prison. He was not persecuted, he was busy with his scientific work, he had no thought for his wife's sufferings.

She suppressed that spiteful thought.

She asked in a weak voice, "Well, how are things there?"

As if she had had to wait twelve months for this visit, thinking of her husband for 360 nights in a frosty widow's bed, in order to ask, "Well, how are things there?"

And Gerasimovich, whose life had never unfolded, whose world had been a convict's existence in the taiga and the desert and interrogation cells, and who was now enjoying the well-being of a secret institution, replied, "Not so bad."

They had only a half-hour. The seconds were passing. There were dozens of questions to be asked, and desires and complaints to be uttered. And Natalya Pavlovna asked, "When did you find out about the visit?"

"Day before yesterday. And you?"

"Tuesday. The lieutenant colonel asked me just now whether I wasn't your sister."

"Because we have the same patronymic?"

"Yes."

When they had become engaged, and later when they lived on the Amur, everyone took them for brother and sister. There was about them that happy outward and inner alikeness which makes a couple more than husband and wife.

"How are things at work?"

"Why do you ask?" she asked anxiously. "Do you know?"

"What?"

He knew something, but he did not know whether it was what she meant. He knew that on the outside the prisoners' wives were being persecuted.

But how could he know that last Wednesday his wife had been fired from her job because she was married to him? For the past three days, having already been notified of the approaching visit, she had not looked for new work. She had waited for the meeting as though a miracle might occur and the visit would flood her life with a great light, showing her what to do.

But how could he give her sound advice, he who had been imprisoned for so many years and was completely unaccustomed to civilian ways?

She had to decide something: whether or not to disavow him.

In this gray, poorly heated room, in the dim light from the barred window, the visit and her hope for a miracle were slipping away.

Natalya Pavlovna understood that in this bleak half-hour she could not communicate her loneliness and suffering to her husband, that he was moving on his own track, leading his own established life. He would not understand anything anyway, so why upset him?

The guard moved to the side of the room and examined the plaster on the wall.

"Tell me about yourself," said Illarion Pavlovich, holding his wife's hand across the table. In his eyes glowed that tenderness which had burned for her in the most cruel months of the blockade.

"Larik! Is there any possibility of your getting time off?"

She meant getting his sentence reduced. At the camp near the Amur River each day that he worked counted as two served, and his term had been reduced accordingly.

Illarion shook his head. "How would I get time off my

sentence? They don't do that here, you know that. One has to invent something big here—then they let you out sooner. But the trouble is that the inventions—" and he glanced at the guard's back—"are—well, extremely undesirable."

He could not say it more clearly.

He took his wife's hand and caressed it lightly with his cheek.

In frozen Leningrad he had not shuddered when he accepted burial bread from someone who would need burial himself the next day. But now he could not—

"Are you sad all alone? Are you very sad?" he asked tenderly, still caressing her hand with his cheek.

"Sad?" Now her heart sank because the visit was almost over, and she would soon leave and go out onto Lefortovo Rampart unenriched by anything, into the joyless streets, alone, alone, alone. The stupefying purposelessness of every act and every day! Nothing sweet, nothing sharp, nothing bitter, life like gray cotton.

"Natalochka!" He stroked her hands. "If you count how much of the term has gone by already, after all there's not much left now. Just three years. Only three—"

"Only three!" she interrupted him indignantly, feeling her voice trembling, knowing she was not in control of it. "Only three? For you—*only!* For you, to be freed right away is 'extremely undesirable.' You live among friends! You are busy with your beloved work. You are not pushed around. And I've been fired, I have nothing to live on. They won't take me on anywhere. I can't go on! I have no more strength. I can't survive another month! It would be better for me to die! My neighbors persecute me as much as they please. They threw out my trunk, they tore my shelf down from the wall, they know I won't dare say a word. They know they can have me thrown out of Moscow! I've stopped going to see my sisters, my Aunt Zhenya; they all jeer at me, they say they've never heard of such a fool. They keep urging me to divorce you and remarry. When is all this going to end? Look what's become of me! I'm thirty-seven years old. In three years I'll be an old woman. I come home and I don't cook myself dinner, I don't clean up the room; I'm sick of it. I just fall on the couch and lie there without strength. Larik, my darling, please do something to be freed soon. You have a brilliant mind. Please invent something. Save me. Save me!"

She had not meant to say that at all. Her heart was broken. Shaking with sobs and kissing her husband's hand, she let her head fall against the rough, warped little table, on which many such tears had spilled.

"Please calm yourself," the guard said guiltily, glancing at the open door.

Gerasimovich's face froze. The indecorous sobbing had been heard up and down the corridor. The lieutenant colonel stood menacingly in the doorway, glaring at the woman's back, and he himself shut the door.

The regulations did not specifically forbid tears, but, under a higher interpretation of the law, there was no place for them.

39

AMONG THE YOUNG PEOPLE

"There's nothing complicated about it. You dissolve some bleaching powder and brush it on the passport, just like that. All you have to know is how long to leave it and when to wash it off."

"Well, what then?"

"It dries and there's not a trace, it's clean, brand-new, so you sit down and you scribble in some name. Sidorov or Petrushin, born in the village of Kriushi."

"And you never got caught?"

"For that? Clara Petrovna—or perhaps—would you let me—"

"What?"

"—call you Clara—when no one's listening?"

"You may."

"Well, you see, Clara, the first time they arrested me I was a helpless and innocent young boy. But the second time —ha! I was on the all-Union wanted list, in the tough years from the end of 1945 to the end of 1947. That meant I had to forge not only my passport, with my residence registration in it, but also a work registration, a document for ration coupons, and the document allowing me to buy at a particular store. And besides that I got extra bread coupons, sold them, and made my living off that."

"But that is very bad."

"Who says it was good? They forced me—I didn't think it up."

"But you could simply have worked."

" 'Simply working' won't earn you much. From the work of the just, no stone palaces, you know? And what would I have worked as? They didn't give me a chance to learn a skill or a profession. I didn't get caught, but I made mistakes. In the Crimea, a girl in the passport section there— only don't think I had anything to do with her. She was sympathetic and she let me in on a secret, about the serial number on my passport: certain letters in it were a code to indicate I had been in occupied territory."

"But you weren't!"

"No, I certainly wasn't, but it wasn't my passport either! That's why I had to buy a new one."

"Where?"

"Clara! You lived in Tashkent and you were at the Tezikov bazaar and you ask where! I was going to buy myself an Order of the Red Banner, too, but the fellow wanted two thousand rubles and I had only eighteen hundred, and he was stubborn, insisted on two thousand or nothing."

"But what would you want with a decoration?"

"What would anyone want with a decoration? Very simple, I just wanted to brag a bit, play the front-line soldier. If I had a cool head like you—"

"Where did you get the idea that I have a cool head?"

"Cool, sober, and your look is so . . . intelligent."

"Oh, come on!"

"True. All my life I've dreamed of meeting a girl with a cool head."

"Why?"

"Because I'm impulsive and reckless, and she would stop me from doing silly things."

"All right, go on with your story, please."

"Where was I? Yes, when I got out of the Lubyanka, I was simply dizzy with happiness. But somewhere inside me there was this little watchdog asking: what kind of a miracle

is this? How can it be? After all, they never let anyone out,
I was told about that in the cell: guilty or not guilty, it was
ten years and five on the horns—and off to camp."

"What does that mean, 'on the horns'?"

"Well, a muzzle for five years."

"What does 'muzzle' mean?"

"My God, how uneducated you are. And you the daughter of a prosecutor! Why don't you take an interest in what
your father does? A 'muzzle' means you can't bite. You're
deprived of your civil rights. You can't vote or be elected
to anything."

"Wait a minute, someone is coming."

"Where? Don't be afraid, that's Zemelya. Sit down like
you were before. Please! Don't go away. Open this file
folder. That's right. Study it. And so right away I understood they had let me out so as to keep me under observation, to see which of the boys I'd meet, whether I'd go to
see the Americans at their country house again; and that
would be no life at all. So I fooled them! I said good-bye to
my mother. I left home at night. And I went to an old guy.
He was the one who got me into those forgeries. Then for
two years the all-Union search was on for Rostislav Doronin. I kept moving around under false names—Central Asia,
Lake Issyk-Kul, the Crimea, Moldavia, Armenia, the Far
East. And then I got very homesick for my mother. But I
couldn't go home. I went to Zagorsk and got work there in a
factory as a sort of apprentice for everybody to knock
around, and Mama came to see me on Sundays. I worked
there for a few weeks, then I overslept and was late at work.
They tried me!"

"Were you caught?"

"Not at all! They sentenced me to three months under
my alias. I was in a work colony and the all-Union search
kept whistling away: Rostislav Doronin! Blue eyes, straight
nose, red hair, a birthmark on the left shoulder. It cost them
a pretty penny, that search. I worked off my three months,
got my passport from the head of the place, and scrammed
off to the Caucasus."

"On the run again?"

"Why not?"

"Then how did it happen?"

"How did I get caught? I wanted to study."

"So you see, you wanted to lead an honest life. One ought to study, it's important. It's a fine thing."

"I'm afraid, Clara, it's not always so very fine. I found that out later on in prison, in the camps. If your professor wants to keep his salary and is afraid of losing his job, are you going to learn fine things from him? In the humanities faculties? After all, you studied a technical subject."

"I studied humanities, too."

"But you quit, didn't you? Tell me later. Yes, I should have been patient and waited for the chance to buy a high school graduation certificate. It wouldn't have been hard to get one, but carelessness, that's what does us in! I thought to myself: what kind of fools would be still looking for me, a kid, they'd probably forgotten all about me a long time ago. So I took my own old certificate and applied to the university, but in Leningrad, in the geography department."

"But in Moscow you had been studying history?"

"I got to like geography after all that wandering. It was fascinating as hell. You travel and you look around: mountains, valleys, taiga, the subtropics! All kinds of different people! Well, what happened? I'd been going to the university a week when they grabbed me. And back there again! Now it's twenty-five years! And off to the tundra, where I hadn't been yet—to get practical experience in geography."

"You can talk about that and laugh?"

"What's the use of crying? If I cried about everything, Clara, I wouldn't have enough tears. I'm not the only one. They sent me to Vorkuta—and what a bunch of thugs they have there! They're chiseling out coal! All Vorkuta depends on zeks, the whole Northland. It's the fulfillment of Thomas More's dream."

"Whose dream? I'm sorry, there's so much I don't know."

"Thomas More, the old fellow who wrote *Utopia*. He had the conscience to admit that society would always require various kinds of menial and hard labor. No one would be willing to perform them. Who should? More thought about it and found the solution: obviously there would be people in a socialist society, too, who disobeyed the rules. They would get the menial and especially tough jobs. So the camps were thought up by Thomas More; it's an old idea."

"I don't know what to think. To live this way in our times: to forge passports, to change cities like a leaf before the wind—I've never met anyone like you in my life anywhere."

"Clara, that's not the way I am either! Circumstances can make devils of us. You know that the way we live determines the way we think. I was a quiet boy, obeyed my mother, read Dobrolyubov's *Ray of Light in a Dark Kingdom*. If a policeman shook his finger at me, my heart sank. One grows, falls into all that imperceptibly. But what was there left for me to do? Sit there like a rabbit waiting for them to grab me off a second time?"

"I don't know what you could have done, but what a way to live! I can imagine how awful it is: you are always outside society. You are some kind of superfluous, hunted person."

"Well, sometimes it's awful and sometimes, you know, it's not. Because when you look around the Tezikov bazaar—after all, if a man is selling a brand-new decoration and the blank certificate that goes with it, whom do you think that mercenary person is working with? In what organization? Can you imagine? Listen to this, Clara: I myself am in favor of an honest life, but an honest life for everyone, do you understand, for every last person!"

"But if everyone waits for everyone else, then it will never begin. Everyone must—"

"Everyone should, but not everyone does. Listen, Clara, I'm going to put it very simply. What was the Revolution against? Against *privileges*. What were the Russian people sick of? Privileges: some being dressed in overalls and others in sables, some dragging along on foot while others rode in carriages, some listening for the factory whistle while others were fattening their faces in restaurants. True?"

"Of course."

"Right. Then why is it that people now don't shun privileges but pursue them? What is there to say about me? Do you really think it starts with me? I looked at my elders. I looked at them carefully. I lived in a small city in Kazakhstan. And what did I see? The wives of the local authorities —were they ever in the stores? Never! They sent me personally to deliver a case of macaroni to the First Secretary of the District Committee of the Communist Party. A whole case. Unopened. I could figure out it wasn't just that one box and not just that one day."

"Yes, it's awful! That's always made me sick. Do you believe me?"

"Of course, I believe you. Why shouldn't I believe a

living person sooner than I'd believe a book published in a million copies? And then these privileges—they surround people like the plague. If a man can buy things in a store other than the store that everyone uses, he will never buy anywhere else. If a person can be treated in a special clinic, he will never be treated anywhere else. If a person can ride in a personally assigned car, he won't think of riding any other way. And if there's some particular privileged place to go where people are admitted only with passes, then people will do anything to get that pass."

"It's true and it's awful."

"If a person can build a fence around himself, he is bound to do it. When the bastard was a kid, he used to climb over a merchant's fence and steal apples, and he thought it was the right thing to do. Now he puts up a tall, solid fence no one can look through, because it suits his pleasure. And he thinks that this time he is right, too."

"Rostislav Vadimich—"

"What are you calling me Vadimich for? Just Ruska."

"It's hard for me to call you that."

"Well, in that case I'm getting up and leaving. There's the bell for lunch. It's Ruska to everyone, and you especially— I won't have it any other way."

"Well, all right. Ruska, I'm not completely foolish either. I've thought a great deal myself. We have to struggle against all that! But not the way you do, certainly."

"Well, I've not struggled at all yet. I've simply come to the conclusion that if it's to be equality, then it must be equality for everyone, and if it isn't, then shove it. Oh, I'm sorry, I didn't mean . . . We see all this in our childhood: in school they spout beautiful words, but you can't go a step without pull, you can't get anywhere without greasing a palm. So we grow up crafty and clever—*impudence is its own kind of happiness!*"

"No, no, it can't be that way! There is a great deal that is just in our society. You are overdoing it. It can't be like that! You've seen a great deal and it's true you've suffered a lot, but 'Impudence is its own kind of happiness' is not a philosophy of life. It can't be like that!"

"Ruska! The lunch bell has rung, did you hear?"

"All right, Zemelya, run along, I'll be there in a second. Clara! What I'm saying to you I've thought through carefully, solemnly. With all my heart I would be glad to live differently. But if I only had a friend—with a cool head—a girl friend . . . If we could only plan together. How to work life out the right way. I don't know whether I can say all this to you."

"You can."

"How confidently you said that! Yet it's impossible. With your background. You're from a different society altogether."

"My life wasn't easy, don't think it was. I can understand."

"Yesterday and today you looked at me in such a friendly way that it makes me want to tell you everything, just as I'd tell someone close. . . . Anyway, it's only externally that I am, so to speak, a prisoner sentenced to twenty-five years. I—oh, if I could only tell you what a razor's edge I'm on now! Any normal person would die of a heart attack. But I'll tell you about that later. Clara! I want to say now that I have volcanic energy. Twenty-five years—that's nonsense. It's easy to get out of here. This very morning I worked out how I'd get out of Mavrino. From the day my fiancée said to me, 'Ruska, escape! I'm waiting for you!' I swore that in three months I'd escape. I'd forge a passport. I'd not fail. I'd take her off to Chita, to Odessa, to Veliky Ustyug. And we'd begin a new, honest, intelligent, free life."

"Oh, yes, a fine life indeed!"

"You know how the heroes in Chekhov always say, 'In twenty years! Oh, in thirty years! In two hundred years! Just to work an honest day in a brickyard and come home tired!' What ridiculous dreams they had! No, I'm just joking about that. I am really serious. I am absolutely serious about wanting to study, and I want to work. Only not all alone. Clara! Look how quiet it is. No one is here. Would you like to be in Veliky Ustyug? It's a monument of antiquity. I haven't been there yet."

"What a surprising person you are."

"I looked for her in Leningrad University, but I didn't know where to find her."

"Who?"

"Clara, a woman's hands can sculpt me into anything they want—a great confidence man, a brilliant card player, or a leading specialist on Etruscan vases or on cosmic rays. Whatever you want me to be, I'll become."

"You'll forge a diploma?"

"No, I'll really do it. Whatever you name I'll become.
You are all I need. The way you slowly turn to look at me
when you come into the laboratory . . ."

40

THE CHARWOMAN

Major General Pyotr Afanasyevich Makarygin, possessor of
a graduate degree in jurisprudence, had long served as a
prosecutor for special cases, in other words, cases which it
was best for the public not to know about and which therefore were processed secretly. He was a prosecutor who
though not famous, perhaps, was out of the ordinary run.
He was unwaveringly firm in carrying out his duties.

He had three daughters, all by his first wife, who had been
his girl in the Civil War and who had died when Clara was
born. The daughters were brought up by a stepmother, who
had been what is known as a good mother to them.

The daughters were named Dinera, Dotnara, and Clara.
Dinera was derived from the Russian phrase "child of the
new era." Dotnara was derived from the phrase "daughter
of the laboring people." And Clara was simply called Clara,
the meaning of that name being unknown to anyone in the
family.

The daughters were two years apart in age. The middle
one, Dotnara, had completed ten years of school—high
school—in 1940 and, overtaking Dinera, had been married one month earlier than she, in the spring of 1941. She
was then a lithe girl with blond curls which fell to her
shoulders, and she very much liked having her fiancé take
her to the Hotel Metropole to dance. Her father was angry
that she married early, but he had had to make the best of
it. To be sure, his son-in-law happened to be of the right sort
—a graduate of the Diplomatic School, a brilliant young
man with impressive sponsors, son of a famous father who
had perished in the Civil War. This son-in-law was named
Innokenty Volodin.

The eldest daughter, Dinera—while her mother hurried off to her school to do something about her failing math grades—dangled her legs from the sofa and read and reread all world literature from Homer to Claude Farrère. After finishing school, not without her father's help, she entered the Institute of Cinematography as a student actress, and in her second year she married a well-known director, was evacuated with him to Alma-Ata, played the heroine in his film, then left him because of creative considerations, married a previously married general in the supply services, and went off with him to the front—but to the third echelon, the best zone in wartime, where enemy shells do not fall but where the terrible trials of the home front do not reach either. There she met a writer who had just become fashionable, front-line correspondent Galakhov, and she went with him to gather material on heroism for the newspapers. She surrendered the general to his former wife, and went off with the writer to Moscow. Since then, the writer had gone far. Dinera presided over a literary salon, had the reputation of being one of the most intelligent women in Moscow, and had even had an epigram written about her:

> It is pleasant for me to be silent with you,
> Because one can't get a word in edgewise.

So for eight years Clara was the only child left at home. No one said of Clara that she was beautiful, and she was seldom even called "pretty." But she had a clean, forthright face, with a certain fortitude about it. This firmness seemed to begin somewhere around her temples. There was firmness, too, in the unhurried movements of her hands. She rarely laughed. Nor did she like to say much, but she did like to listen.

Clara had finished her ninth year of school when everything fell on her at once: the marriages of both her sisters, the beginning of the war, her departure with her stepmother for Tashkent. (Her father had sent them off on June 25.) Then, too, there was her father's leaving for the army, as a divisional prosecutor.

They spent three years in Tashkent in the home of an old friend of her father, the deputy of one of the chief prosecutors there. Into their quiet, shuttered, second-floor apartment near the Military District Officers Club, there entered neither the southern heat nor the city's grief. Many men were taken for the army from Tashkent, but ten times as many flooded into the city. Though each of them could prove that his place was there and not at the front, Clara had the uncontrollable feeling that she was immersed in a flow of sewage. Implacably, the eternal law of war functioned: although the people who went to the front went reluctantly, still all the best and most spirited found their way there; and by the same mode of selection most of them perished. The peak of the human spirit and the purity of heroism were three thousand miles away, and Clara was living among unattractive second-raters.

Clara finished school in Tashkent. There were arguments over which higher educational institution she should enter. For some reason nothing attracted her particularly, nothing within her had defined itself. Dinera chose for her. In letters and when she had come to say good-bye before going to the front, she insisted very strongly that Clara ought to specialize in literature.

Adn that was what she did, even though she knew from school that that sort of literature was boring: Gorky was correct but somehow ponderous; Mayakovsky was very correct but somehow awkward; Saltykov-Shchedrin was progressive, but you could die yawning if you tried to read him through; Turgenev was limited to his nobleman's ideals; Goncharov was associated with the beginnings of Russian capitalism; Lev Tolstoi came to favor patriarchal peasantry —and their teacher did not recommend their reading Tolstoi's novels because they were very long and only confused the clear critical essays written about him. And then they reviewed a batch of writers totally unknown to anyone: Dostoyevsky, Stepnyak-Kravchinsky, and Sukhovo-Kobylin. It was true that one did not even have to remember the titles of their works. In all this long procession only Pushkin shone like a sun.

All literature courses in school consisted of an intensive study of what these writers had tried to express, what their positions were, and whose social ideas they advanced. This applied also to Soviet writers and writers of the "brother peoples" of the Soviet Union. To the very end, it remained incomprehensible to Clara and her classmates why these people received so much attention. They were not the most intelligent. Journalists and critics and especially Party lead-

ers were all smarter than they. They often made mistakes,
got mixed up in contradictions which even a pupil could
detect. They fell under foreign influence. And yet one had
to write essays about them and tremble over every mistaken
letter and comma. These vampires of young souls could not
inspire any feeling but detestation.

Now for Dinera literature was something completely different, something keenly felt and gay, and she had promised
that literature would be like that at the institute. For Clara,
however, it did not turn out to be any gayer than at school.
The lectures were about old Slavonic letters, religious say-
ings, the mythological and comparative-historical schools,
and it was all like writing on water. In the literary study
groups they talked about Louis Aragon and Howard Fast
and Gorky's influence on Uzbek literature. Sitting at the lectures and listening to these groups, Clara kept waiting to
hear something important about life, for instance about
Tashkent in wartime.

A brother of a fellow student in the tenth grade, for example, had been killed when he and his friends tried to steal
bread from a moving train. In the institute corridor Clara
happened to throw a half-finished sandwich into the trash
bin, and right away a student in her Aragon study group had
come up and grabbed the sandwich out of the bin and, concealing it clumsily, put it in his pocket. One of the girl students had taken Clara along to advise her about a purchase
at the Tezikov bazaar, the biggest bazaar in Central Asia or,
indeed, in the whole Soviet Union. The crowd covered two
blocks. There were already many cripples from the war—
they limped about on crutches, waved the stumps of their
arms, crawled legless on boards, peddled things, told fortunes, begged and demanded. Clara gave them money, and
her heart broke. Farther on the crowd was thicker. One
could not shoulder one's way through the throng of insolent
speculators, draft-dodging men and women. No one was
surprised at, and everyone accepted, the astronomical prices,
though they were in no way proportionate to what people
earned. The city stores might be empty, but one could get
anything here. Anything to eat, anything to wear, anything
. . . including American chewing gum, pistols, textbooks on
white and black magic.

But at the institute they never mentioned that world, as if
they did not even know it existed. They studied a kind of

literature which dealt with everything on earth except what one could see with one's own eyes.

Realizing that in five years she herself would be going off to a school to assign little girls distasteful essays and to hunt for mistakes in their punctuation and spelling, Clara began to play more and more tennis. There were good courts in Tashkent.

Thus she spent the long warm autumn, but in the middle of winter she fell ill.

She was sick a long time, a whole year. She was in bed in a clinic, then at home, again in the clinic and back home again. She was examined by specialists and professors; they gave her intravenous injections, intramuscular injections; they injected salt solution; they made analyses and brought in consultants.

At this time of uncertainty about her future health, during long, sleepless nights in the dark, during lonely wanderings through hospital corridors when hospital sights and smells had become unbearable, there was nothing for Clara to do but think. She found in herself an inclination, and even a talent, for an important, complicated life in terms of which the entire institute was pitifully insignificant, a lot of empty talk.

She did not have to return to the school of literature. By the time she got well, the front was already in Belorussia. Everyone left Tashkent, and they, too, returned to Moscow.

It was strange. Those seemingly clear thoughts about life which had come to her during her illness now dispersed into the light, into noise and movement; they floated off; and Clara could not even resolve such a simple question as which institute to enter. She simply wanted a place where they talked less and did more, and that meant something technical. Also, she did not want to work with heavy, dirty machinery. That was how she entered the Institute of Communications Engineers.

For lack of advice, she had again made a mistake, but she did not admit it to anyone, having stubbornly decided to finish her studies and work wherever she could. Moreover, she was not the only one in her class who was there by accident. It was a time when everyone was chasing the bluebird of higher education. Those who did not get into the Aviation Institute took their documents to the Veterinary

Institute. Those who were refused at the chemical-techno-
logical institutes became paleontologists.

After the war, Clara's father had a great deal of work to
do in Europe. He was demobilized from the army in the fall
and immediately received a five-room apartment in the new
MVD apartment house at Kaluga Gates. On one of the first
days after his return, he took his wife and daughter to look
at the apartment.

An automobile took them past the iron fence of the Neskuchny Gardens and stopped before crossing the bridge over
the railway which encircled Moscow. It was late morning
on a warm October day of a prolonged Indian summer.
Mother and daughter wore rustling dresses beneath light
coats. The father wore a general's overcoat, unbuttoned at
the chest to reveal many orders and medals.

The apartment house at the Kaluga Gates was being
built in two quarter-circles, eight stories high, divided by
Bolshaya Kaluzhskaya Street. In both units, one wing faced
the railway. A sixteen-story tower was planned, with a so-
larium on the roof and a thirty-five-foot statue of a collective-farm woman. The scaffolding was still on the apartment
house, and much of the masonry work remained to be done.
However, yielding to the impatience of the bosses, the construction office had hurriedly turned over to the owners the
second wing to be completed, which was on the railway side
and consisted of one staircase with apartments opening off
each landing.

The construction work was surrounded, as construction
always is on busy streets, by a solid wooden fence. The
strands of barbed wire on top of the fence and the ugly
watchtowers were not particularly noticeable to the passers-
by, and to those living across the street they had become a
familiar sight and were therefore not remarkable.

The prosecutor's family crossed the square and went
around to the other side of the apartment house. There the
barbed wire had been removed. The second section, now
being occupied, was fenced off from the work zone. Below,
at the main entrance, they were met by a polite construction superintendent. There was also a soldier, to whom Clara
paid no attention. Everything had been completed. The paint
on the banisters had dried. The door handles had been
polished. The apartment numbers had been put on. The

window glass had been scraped, and there was only a dirtily dressed woman washing the stairs.

"Look out there!" the construction superintendent shouted to her. The woman stopped washing and moved to one side, making room for one person at a time to get past her. She did not raise her face from the pail, in which a rag floated.

The prosecutor passed.

The construction superintendent passed.

And with a rustling of her pleated, scented skirt, almost brushing it against the charwoman's face, the prosecutor's wife passed.

The charwoman, who could not bear that silk or that perfume, remained bent over; then she looked up to see whether there were more of them.

Her burning, despising glare turned Clara to ash. Streaked with spashes of dirty water, she had the expressive face of an intellectual.

Clara experienced not only the shame one always feels in passing a woman washing the floor, but, seeing her patched skirt and her padded jacket with cotton wool sticking out of the rents, she felt a still greater shame and horror. She froze there and opened her purse. She wanted to turn it inside out and give it to the woman, but she did not dare to.

"Well, pass!" the woman said angrily.

Holding the skirts of her own stylish dress and her dark-red coat, Clara ran on up the stairs.

In the apartment no one was washing the floors—it was a parquet floor.

They liked the apartment. Clara's mother gave the construction superintendent instructions on alterations. She was particularly displeased that in one of the rooms the parquet floor creaked. The construction superintendent rocked back and forth on two or three of the parquet squares and promised to see that the floor was fixed.

"Who is doing all this work?" Clara asked sharply.

The construction superintendent smiled and said nothing. Her father answered: "Prisoners. Who else?"

When they went down, the woman was no longer there. The soldier outside was gone, too.

In a few days they moved in.

Four years had passed since that incident, and Clara still

could not forget the woman; going up to the apartment, she always used the elevator; when it occasionally happened that she had to go on foot, she always stepped to one side when she passed that place on the staircase, as though afraid she would step on the charwoman. It was strange, yet impossible to overcome.

From the first days of his return, her father could not recognize in the postwar Clara the young girl he had left four years before. He had always regarded his two elder daughters as striking but light-minded, and he had assumed that Clara was thoughtful and serious. But she had turned out to have all kinds of wrong ideas, to be thoughtful but in a contrary way. Somewhere she had collected all sorts of terrible stories which she loved to tell at the table. The stories themselves were not so outrageous as the fact that she had acquired the trick of picking up every kind of *untypical* occurrence. After one such story the old prosecutor slammed the table and left without finishing his meal.

Clara had no one to talk to. Year after year she lived with a growing store of questions.

Once, descending the stairs with her brother-in-law, she could no longer restrain herself. When she led him to one side at the place where she had to avoid the invisible charwoman, Innokenty noticed and asked what she was doing. Clara hesitated, feeling she might seem to be insane. Then she told him.

Always the sophisticate and scoffer, Innokenty listened to her story, but he did not laugh. He took her by both hands, looked at her brightly and said, "Little Clara! So you're beginning to figure things out."

Wishing to prolong this happy moment of frankness, not moving from the step where she had passed the charwoman, Clara put her gloved hands on Innokenty's shoulders and showered him with questions which had long been stored up inside her.

Innokenty was in no hurry to reply. Abandoning his façade of banter, he simply looked at his sister-in-law. And suddenly he said, "And I have a question for you, dear little Clara. Why were you such a little girl before the war? Just imagine how joyously I would have married you!"

Clara blushed, stamped her foot, and took her hands from his shoulders.

They went on down the stairs.

Nevertheless she forced Innokenty to begin answering her questions.

That conversation had taken place the previous summer, at about the same time Clara was filling out questionnaires. Her family background was faultless, her life up to then had been illuminated by the even light of prosperity, unstained by any disgraceful acts. The questionnaires were approved, and she entered the gateway of the guardhouse of the secret institute at Mavrino.

41

THE BLOODHOUNDS
OF IMPERIALISM

Clara and the other girls who had graduated from the Communications Institute went through Major Shikin's frightening indoctrination session.

She learned that she would be working among the most formidable of all spies, *the bloodhounds of world imperialism.*

Clara was assigned to work in the Vacuum Laboratory. This was the laboratory that made a vast quantity of electronic tubes for the other labs. The tubes themselves were first blown in the small glass-blowing shop; then in the Vacuum Laboratory proper, a big dark room facing north, they were emptied of air by three whistling vacuum pumps. The pumps partitioned off the room. Even in the daytime the electric lights were kept on. The floor was made of stone slabs, and there was a constant resonance from people walking by, from chairs being moved around. At each pump a zek vacuum specialist worked. Elsewhere other zeks sat at desks. There were only two other free employees: a girl named Tamara and the head of the laboratory, who wore his captain's uniform.

Clara was introduced to her chief in Yakonov's office. He was a plump, elderly Jew with a certain air of indifference.

Without any further warning about the dangers awaiting her, he motioned her to follow him. On the stairs he said, "You don't know anything and you can't do anything, is that right? I'm referring to your profession."

Clara replied indistinctly. All she needed on top of being afraid was to be humiliated. They would expose her now, reveal that she was an ignoramus, and they would laugh at her.

So, just as she might have stepped into a cage of wild beasts, she stepped into the laboratory inhabited by monsters in blue coveralls.

The three vacuum specialists did indeed stalk around their pumps like caged animals; they had an urgent order to fill and they had not been allowed any sleep for forty-eight hours. But the middle one, a man over forty, with a bald spot, unkempt and unshaven, stopped, smiled and said, "Well, well! Reinforcements!"

All her fear disappeared. There was such winning simplicity in that exclamation that only by a great effort could Clara restrain an answering smile.

The youngest vacuum specialist, at the smallest of the pumps, also stopped his work. He was very young and had a gay, slightly mischievous face with big innocent eyes. His glance at Clara seemed to indicate that he had been caught by surprise.

The senior vacuum specialist, Dvoyetyosov, from whose enormous pump in the depths of the room issued a particularly loud roar, was a tall awkward man, wiry but with a bulging stomach. He looked contemptuously at Clara and disappeared behind the cabinets, as if to avoid the sight of such an abomination.

Later on, Clara learned that he was that way with all the free employees, and that when the chiefs entered the room he purposely turned on something that made a tremendous noise so they would have to shout over it. He was slovenly in appearance and might arrive with a trouser button hanging by a thread or with a hole in his clothes. When the girls were present, he would start scratching himself under his coveralls. He loved to say, "Here I am at home in my own country, so why should I worry?"

The middle vacuum specialist was known by the prisoners, including the younger ones, simply as Zemelya, and he took no offense at this at all. He was one of those people with what psychologists call "sunny natures." As she watched him in the subsequent weeks, Clara noticed that he never regretted anything that had been lost, whether it was a pencil or his whole wrecked life. He never got angry at anything or anyone, nor was he afraid of anyone. He was a good engineer, except that he was a specialist in airplane engines. He had been brought to Mavrino by mistake. Nonetheless, he had settled in and made no effort to be transferred anywhere else, rightly considering that he was better off where he was.

In the evening when the pumps were shut down, Zemelya loved to listen to stories and to talk.

"It used to be you could get a breakfast for a five-kopeck piece. And you could buy whatever you wanted. At every step they'd push things at you." He smiled broadly. "And no one sold shit either; they'd have spit in his face. Boots—those were real boots. They'd last ten years even if you didn't keep them repaired, fifteen if you mended them. The leather on the uppers wasn't cut like it is now, but came around under the foot. And then there were those—what did they call them? They were red, and were ornamented—they weren't boots, they were a second soul!" He broke into a smile as if the sun had suddenly come out. "Or, for example, at stations . . . You'd come a minute before the train, buy a ticket, and find a seat—there were always empty cars. They kept the trains running—didn't economize. Living was easy, very easy. . . ."

During these stories the senior vacuum specialist would emerge from his dark corner, where his writing desk was safely hidden from the bosses. He came slowly, his heavy body rocking from side to side, his hands shoved in his pockets, and he would stand there in the middle of the room, his drained eyes averted, his glasses falling forward on his nose.

"What are you talking about, Zemelya? Can you remember?"

"I remember it a little," Zemelya said, excusing himself with a smile.

"Too bad," Dvoyetyosov said, shaking his head. "Forget it. Let's stick to our pumping."

He stood there a while longer, dumbly, staring over the tops of his glasses. Then he shuffled back to his corner.

Clara's duties turned out to be simple: she was supposed

to come in the morning one day and be there till 6 P.M., and
on the next day to come after lunch and stay until 11 P.M. She
alternated with Tamara. The captain was always there from
morning on, because the chiefs might want him in the daytime. He never came in the evening because he had no ambition to advance in the service. The girls' main task was to
be on duty, in other words, to keep an eye on the prisoners.
Beyond this, "for their own development," the chief entrusted
them with petty work which wasn't urgent. Clara saw Tamara only a couple of hours each day. Tamara had worked
at the institute for more than a year and dealt rather curtly
with the prisoners. However, it seemed to Clara that she
brought books to one of them, and surreptitiously exchanged
them with him. Besides this, right there in the institute,
Tamara went to an English-language study group in which
the free employees were the students and the convicts the
teachers—without pay, of course. Tamara had quickly calmed
Clara's fears that these people were capable of doing them
some awful harm.

Finally, Clara herself had a conversation with one of
the prisoners. True, he was not a political criminal but an
ordinary prisoner, of whom there were very few in Mavrino.
It was Ivan the glass blower, who was, to his misfortune,
a great master of his art. His old mother-in-law had said of
him that he was a glorious workman—and an even more
glorious drunk. He had earned a great deal of money, drunk
a great deal of it away, beaten his wife whenever he was
drunk and roughed up the neighbors. But all that would
have been nothing had his path not crossed that of the MGB.
A comrade with an air of authority but no insignia had
called him in and proposed that he go to work for three
thousand a month. The salary was less where Ivan worked,
but he could earn more on piece rates. Forgetting whom he
was talking to, he asked for four thousand. The responsible
comrade added two hundred. Ivan stuck to his guns. They let
him go. The next pay day he got drunk and began to get
unruly in the courtyard. This time the police, who previously couldn't be reached, showed up quickly in force and
took Ivan off. The next day he was tried and given a year.
After the trial they took him to the same responsible comrade, who explained that Ivan would be working in the new
place designated for him but would not get paid. If these
conditions did not suit him, he could mine coal in the Arctic.

So Ivan was imprisoned and blew cathode ray tubes. His one-year term was coming to an end, but his conviction remained on his record. To avoid being sent away from Moscow because of that record, he was begging the administration to keep him on as a free employee, even at a salary of only fifteen hundred rubles.

Though no one in the sharashka would be troubled by such a simple story with such a happy ending—for there were people there who had waited fifty days at a time in death cells, and people who had personally known the Pope and Albert Einstein—nonetheless Clara was shocked by the story. It turned out, as Ivan said, that "what they want to do they do."

Her head, which had always been so squarely fixed on her shoulders, was suddenly filled with the suspicion that among those people in blue coveralls there might even be some who were not guilty at all. If that was so, then had not her father, too, at one time or another sentenced an innocent man?

Soon after that she went to the Maly Theater with Alexei Lansky, who was courting her.

The play was Gorky's *Vassa Zheleznova*. It made a dismal impression. The auditorium was less than half filled. Probably this threw the actors off. They came on stage bored, like employees showing up for work in an institution, and they were glad when they could leave. It was a disgrace to play in such an empty auditorium. Nothing about the performance seemed worth the attention of an adult. This ruined even the acting of the amazingly natural Pashennaya. One felt that if in the stillness of the auditorium some members of the audience were to say quietly, as if in an ordinary room, "Well, all right, friends, stop making faces!" the play would have fallen apart. The cast's humiliation was communicated to the audience. Everyone felt he was participating in something shameful, and it was awkward to look at one another. So in the intermissions it was just as quiet as during the performance. Couples talked in half-whispers or strolled silently through the foyer.

Clara and Lansky also wandered around quietly during the first intermission, and Lansky made excuses for Gorky and for the theater. He criticized Peoples' Artist Zharov, who was openly playing down to the audience, and he criticized even more the general bureaucratic atmosphere in the Ministry of Culture, which had undermined the confidence of the Soviet playgoer in the realist theater.

Alexei Lansky had a regular, oval face. His color was good because he found time for sports. His eyes were calm and intelligent from all the reading he had done in his twenty-seven years. As the holder of the graduate degree of Candidate of Philological Sciences, a candidate member of the Union of Soviet Writers, and a noted critic who was under the benign protection of Galakhov, Lansky did not so much write himself as reject other writers.

In the second intermission Clara asked to remain in the box. There was no one either in the neighboring boxes or below them in the orchestra. She said, "That's why I'm bored with seeing Ostrovsky and Gorky—because I'm tired of these exposés of the power of money, of family disapproval when an old man marries a young woman. I'm sick of this wrestling with ghosts. Fifty years, a hundred, have gone by, and we still act indignant about things which have long since ceased to exist. You never see a play about things that go on now."

"Like what, for example?" Lansky looked at Clara with curiosity, smiling. He had not been wrong about her. He thought: this girl might not impress you with her appearance, but you would never be bored with her. "Like what?"

Clara, trying not to reveal too much of the secret of her involvement, told him that she was working with prisoners who had been described to her as the bloodhounds of imperialism, but that on getting to know them better they had turned out to be quite different. And one question kept bothering her, and she let Lansky answer it: were there, after all, innocent men among them?

Lansky listened carefully and replied calmly, "Of course, there are. That is inevitable in any penal system."

"But, Alexei! That would mean that they can do whatever they want! That's terrible."

With tender care Lansky placed his long-fingered, pinkish hand on Clara's, which was clenched in a fist on the red velvet.

"No," he said softly but convincingly, "not 'whatever they want.' Who 'wants' anything? Who 'does' anything? History. To you and me that sometimes seems terrible, but, Clara, it's time to get used to the fact that there is a law of big numbers. The bigger the scope of an historical event, the greater the probability of individual errors, be they judicial, tactical, ideological, economic. We grasp the process only in its basic, determining forms, and the essential thing is to be convinced that this process is inevitable and necessary. Yes, sometimes someone suffers. Not always deservedly. What about those killed at the front? And those who died meaninglessly in the Ashkhabad earthquake? And traffic fatalities? As traffic increases, so will the number of traffic victims. Wisdom lies in accepting the process as it develops, with its inevitable increment of victims."

But Clara shook her head indignantly.

"Increment!" she exclaimed, in a whisper, since the bell had already rung twice and people were re-entering the hall. "The law of big numbers should be tried out on you! Everything is going well for you, and you say everything very smoothly, but don't you see that not everything is the way you write it?"

"You mean we are hypocrites?" Lansky countered. He loved to argue.

"No, I don't say that." The third bell rang. The lights went down. With a feminine urge to have the last word, she whispered quickly into his ear, "You're sincere, but in order not to upset your views you avoid talking with people who think differently. You pick your thoughts from conversations with people like yourself, from books written by people like yourself. In physics they call it resonance," she hurriedly finished just as the curtain had begun to open. "You start out with modest opinions, but they match and build each other up to a scale. . . ."

She fell silent, regretting her incomprehensible passion. She had spoiled the whole third act for Lansky as well as for herself.

As it happened, in the third act the actress Royek played with bell-like clarity the role of Vassa's younger daughter, and she began to lift the performance out of its doldrums. Pashennaya, too, recovered her divine form.

Clara herself failed to realize that she was interested not in some innocent person somewhere, who had perhaps long since been rotting beyond the Arctic Circle, but in the youngest vacuum specialist, blue-eyed, with a play of golden color in his cheeks, still a boy in spite of his twenty-three years. From their very first encounter his look had revealed

his fascination with Clara, an unconcealed and joyful fascination like nothing she had ever known in her Moscow admirers. The fact was that Clara did not understand that her
suitors who lived in freedom were surrounded by women,
saw many who were more beautiful than she, and knew
their own value, while Ruska had come from camp, where
for two years he had not heard the click of a woman's
heel; and Clara, like Tamara before her, had seemed to him
an unfading miracle.

But in the seclusion of the sharashka this fascination
with Clara did not obsess him entirely. Almost all night
long under the electric light in the half-dark laboratory, this
youth lived his own full, fast-moving life. On occasion, hiding from the bosses, he would construct something. Now he
would secretly study English during working hours. Now he
would phone his friends in other laboratories and rush off
to meet them in the corridor. He always moved impetuously
and always, every moment, especially at that particular moment, was totally absorbed in something intensely interesting. And his fascination with Clara was just one of his
intensely interesting preoccupations.

In all this activity he did not forget to look after his
personal appearance. At the neck of his coveralls, under
his multicolored necktie, he always wore faultlessly white
linen. Clara did not know that this was, in fact, the dickey
that was Ruska's own invention and consisted of one-thirty-
second of a government-issue sheet.

The young people Clara encountered in freedom had already done themselves credit in official advancement, dressed
well, moved and conversed circumspectly, so as not to demean themselves. With Ruska, Clara felt she was growing
younger, that she, too, wished to be mischievous. Secretly
she observed him with increasing sympathy. She did not believe that he and good-natured Zemelya were those dangerous dogs against whom Major Shikin had warned her. She
wanted especially to learn about Ruska, about the evil deed
he had been punished for, whether he had a long sentence
to serve. That he was not married was already clear. She
could not bring herself to ask him the other questions; she
imagined they must be very painful since they would remind him of the abominable past he wished to cast off in
order to reform.

Two more months passed. Clara had become fully accustomed to all of them. They often talked in her presence about all sorts of nonsense which had nothing to do with work. Ruska watched for those moments during her evening duty period, during the prisoners' dinnertime, when Clara was alone in the laboratory. And he invariably began to turn up then, sometimes with the excuse that he had left his things behind, sometimes to work in quiet.

During these evening visits Clara forgot all the warnings of the security officer.

Last night, somehow, that intense conversation had, like a flood, swept away the wretched barriers of convention between them.

The youth had no abominable past to cast off. He had only a youth which had been destroyed for no reason and a passionate thirst to learn and explore.

He had lived with his mother in a village near Moscow. He had just finished high school when Americans from the embassy rented a house in their village. Ruska and his comrades were careless enough—and curious enough as well—to go fishing a couple of times with the Americans. Everything had apparently turned out all right. Ruska entered Moscow University. But they arrested him in September. They grabbed him secretly, on the highway, so that his mother had no idea where he had disappeared to. Ruska explained to Clara that they always tried to arrest a person in such a way that he could not hide anything he was carrying, and would not be able to give anyone a secret password or sign. They put him in the Lubyanka. Clara had not even heard the name of that prison until she was in Mavrino. Interrogations began. They wanted Ruska to tell them what assignment he had received from the American intelligence service. What secret apartment was he supposed to bring information to? Ruska was, in his own words, still a calf and simply failed to understand and wept. Then, suddenly, a miracle happened. Ruska was allowed to leave that place which no one is allowed to leave.

That was in 1945.

And that was where he had stopped his story the day before.

All night Clara was stirred by the story he had begun. The next day, disregarding the most elementary security regulations and even the bounds of propriety, she had openly sat down next to Ruska at his rumbling little pump and they had resumed their conversation.

By lunchtime they were fast friends, like children taking turns biting into one big apple. It already seemed strange to them that for so many months they had said nothing. They were hardly able to express the thoughts which filled them. Interrupting her in his impatience to talk, he had touched her hands, and she saw nothing bad in that. When everyone went out for lunch, leaving them alone, suddenly there was a new meaning in the brush of a shoulder or the touch of a hand. And Clara saw his clear blue eyes taking delight in her.

Ruska in a voice that barely passed his lips said, "Clara, who knows when we will be sitting like this again? For me this is a miracle. I don't believe it. I am prepared to die, here, now!" He pressed and caressed her hands. "Clara, perhaps I am destined to waste away my life in prisons. Make me happy, so that wherever I am I can remember this moment. Just once—let me kiss you!"

Clara felt like a goddess who had descended underground to a prisoner. It was not an oridinary kiss. Ruska pulled her to him and kissed her with violent force, the kiss of a prisoner, tortured by deprivation. And she answered it.

He wanted to kiss her again, but Clara pulled away, dizzy and shaken.

"Please go," she said.

He hesitated.

"For now—go!" Clara ordered.

He obeyed then. At the doorway he turned to Clara beseechingly, pitifully, then left the room.

Soon everyone returned from lunch.

Clara did not dare look up at Ruska or at anyone else. There was a burning feeling inside her, but it was not shame. Yet, if it was happiness, it was not a peaceful happiness.

Then she heard that the prisoners would be permitted to have a New Year's tree.

She sat still for three hours, only her fingers moving; she was weaving a little basket from colored vinyl-covered wires, a gift for the New Year's tree.

And Ivan the glass blower, returning from his visit, blew two amusing little glass devils who appeared to be carrying rifles, and he wove a cage out of glass rods, and inside it, on a silvery thread, he hung a glass moon which made a sad little ringing sound.

42

THE CASTLE OF THE HOLY GRAIL

For half the day a low, murky sky covered Moscow. It was not cold. But before the lunch period, when the seven returning prisoners stepped out of the blue bus in the exercise yard of the sharashka, the first impatient snowflakes were flying.

Just such a snowflake, a six-sided star, fell on the sleeve of Nerzhin's old front-line overcoat, which had turned rusty-brown. He stopped in the middle of the yard and inhaled the air.

Senior Lieutenant Shusterman, who happened to be there, warned him that this was not an exercise period and that he must go inside.

He did not want to go inside. He did not want to tell anyone about his visit—in fact, he could not. He did not want to share it with anyone or have anyone participate in it. He did not want to talk or to listen to anyone. He wanted to be alone and experience slowly all he had brought back with him, before it disintegrated, before it became merely a memory.

But solitude was precisely what was lacking in the sharashka, as it was in every camp.

Entering the building by the prisoners' entrance, a wooden ramp leading down to a cellar corridor, Nerzhin stopped and considered where he could go.

Then he thought of a place.

He went to the back staircase, which hardly anyone used any more, past a heap of broken chairs, and started up to the closed-off landing on the third floor.

This space was assigned to the zek painter Kondrashev-Ivanov as a studio. He had nothing at all to do with the basic work of the sharashka but was maintained there in the capacity, one might say, of a court painter. There were extensive lobbies and hallways in the section of the ministry to which the sharashka belonged, which needed to be decorated with paintings. Less extensive, but more numerous, were the private apartments of the Deputy Minister, of Foma Guryanovich Oskolupov, and of other officials close to them, and there was an even more pressing need to decorate all these apartments with big, beautiful pictures at no cost.

True, Kondrashev-Ivanov hardly satisfied these artistic demands. He painted big paintings, but though they cost nothing, they were not beautiful. The customers who came to his studio tried in vain to show him how to paint, and with what colors; then, sighing, took what there was. However, when they were put in gold frames, the paintings improved.

On the way up, Nerzhin passed a large and already completed order for the lobby of the ministry section—entitled "A. S. Popov Showing Admiral Makarov the First Radiotelegraph"—then started up the last flight of stairs and saw on the wall above him a six-foot-tall painting entitled "The Maimed Oak." It, too, had been completed, but no customer had wanted to take it.

It showed a solitary oak which grew with mysterious power on the naked face of a cliff, where a perilous trail wound upward along the crag. What hurricanes had blown here! How they had bent that oak! And the skies behind the tree and all around were eternally storm-swept. These skies could never have known the sun. This stubborn, angular tree with its clawing roots, with its branches broken and twisted, deformed by combat with the tireless winds trying to tear it from the cliff, refused to quit the battle and perilously clung to its place over the abyss.

On the walls of the stairwell hung smaller canvases. On the landing others stood on easels. The light came from two windows, one facing north, the other west. The Iron Mask's small window opened on this landing, with its grille and pink curtain, a window which daylight did not reach.

There was nothing else, not even a chair. Instead of a chair, there was a low block of wood.

Although the stairway was hardly heated at all and the cold dampness penetrated even here, Kondrashev-Ivanov's padded jacket lay on the floor. The artist, his arms and legs

protruding comically from coveralls which were too small
for him, stood motionless, tall, straight, apparently not uncomfortably cold. His great eyeglasses, which made his face
larger and more severe, and gripped firmly behind his ears
and on his nose, suited his abrupt movements. He was staring at a place in a painting, holding his brush and palette at
his side.

Hearing steps, he turned around.

The two men's eyes met. Each was still thinking his own
thoughts.

The artist was not pleased to have a visitor. At this moment he needed silence and solitude.

Yet, in another way, he was glad to see him. Without being in the least hypocritical, indeed with his customary excess of enthusiasm, he exclaimed, "Gleb Vikentich! Welcome!" And he waved the brush and palette in a gesture of
hospitality.

Openheartedness is a two-edged quality in an artist: it
feeds his imagination, but it ruins his daily routine.

Nerzhin hesitated on the next to last step. He said almost
in a whisper, as if he were afraid of awakening some third
person, "No, no, Hippolyte Mikhailich. I came, if it's all
right, just—to be quiet here."

"Ah, yes. Ah, yes. Of course," the artist answered just
as quietly, seeing in his visitor's eyes, or perhaps remembering, that Nerzhin had just seen his wife. He backed away,
indicating with his brush and palette the block of wood.

Picking up the long flaps of the overcoat (he had managed
to keep them from being trimmed off in camp), Nerzhin
sat down on the block and leaned back against the banister.
Though he wanted very much to smoke, he did not.

The artist concentrated on the painting.

They were both silent.

Nerzhin's aroused feelings ached pleasantly inside him.
Once more he wanted to place his fingers where, saying
good-bye, he had touched his wife's hands, her arms, her
neck, her hair.

You lived for years without the one thing men were put
on earth for.

You are left whatever intelligence you might have had,
your convictions if you were mature enough to possess any,
and, above all, your readiness for sacrifice and your concern

for public welfare. You would appear to be an Athenian citizen, humanity's ideal.

But there is no core to it.

The love of a woman, of which you are deprived, seems worth more than anything in the world.

The simple words "Do you love me?" and "I love you," said with glances or with murmuring lips, fill the soul with quiet rejoicing.

It was too bad he had not decided to kiss her at the very beginning of their visit. For now he could not get that extra kiss by any means.

His wife's lips were not as they used to be. They felt weak. And how tired she had seemed. How tormented and persecuted she had sounded when she had spoken of divorce.

A legal divorce—what did it matter? Gleb would have no regrets about tearing up the official document.

But he had been knocked around by life enough to know that events have their own implacable logic. People never dream that from their ordinary actions consequences will follow which are the opposite of what they intend. So it would be with Nadya. She would get divorced so as to escape harassment. Once divorced she would not even notice anything strange when she remarried.

Somehow, from that last wave of her ringless hand he had known with a tightening of his heart that this was how people say good-bye to one another forever.

Nerzhin sat there a long time in silence, then recovered himself. The excess of joy he had felt after the visit had subsided, displaced by somber considerations; his thoughts had settled, and he was a convict again.

"It suits you here," she had said.

In other words, prison.

There was some truth in it. Sometimes he was not at all sorry to have spent five years in prison. Those years had come to mean something in themselves.

Where could one learn about people better than here?

And what better place to reflect about oneself?

How many youthful hesitations, how many wrong starts, had he been saved from by the iron path of prison?

As Spiridon said: "Your will is a treasure, but the devils keep watch over it."

Or take this dreamer here, so unreceptive to the mockeries

of the age—what had he lost by being imprisoned? Of course, he could not wander about the hills and woods with a box of paints. But exhibitions? He could never have arranged for one; in half a hundred years he had not exhibited a single painting in a respectable hall. Money? He had not received anything for his paintings out there either. Admirers of his work? Well, he had more here than he had ever had there. A studio? In freedom he had not even had this cold landing. He had had to live and paint in the same place: a narrow, long room like a hallway. To have space to work in, he had put one chair on top of the other and rolled up the mattress; visitors had asked him if he was moving. There was only one table, and when a still life was set out, he and his wife had to eat off the chairs until the painting was finished.

During the war there was no oil for painting. He painted with the sunflower-seed oil from his rations. He had to have a job to get ration cards, and he was sent to a Chemical Warfare division to do portraits of distinguished women in the political and military branches. He was expected to paint ten portraits, but he worked on only one, driving his model out of her mind with endless sittings. But he portrayed her not at all the way the commanding officers had in mind, and afterward no one wanted the portrait, which was called "Moscow 1941."

Yet the portrait had caught the feeling of 1941. It showed a girl in the uniform of a gas-warfare unit. Her luxuriant hair was coppery-chestnut and streamed out wildly from under her forage cap. Her head was thrown back, her insane eyes were witnessing something horrible, something unforgettable. They were filled with tears of rage, but her body was not relaxed by weeping. Her hands, tense and ready for battle, held the straps of her gas mask, and her dark-gray anti-mustard-gas uniform, ridged with hard silvery folds, gleamed like medieval armor. Cruelty and nobility joined in the face of this dedicated Kaluga Komsomol girl, who was not beautiful but in whom Kondrashev-Ivanov saw the Maid of Orleans.

One would have thought that the portrait resembled the well-known painting called "We Shall Not Forget! We Shall Not Forgive!" Yet they were frightened by it, they did not accept it, did not exhibit it anywhere, and for years it stood, like a madonna of wrath and vengeance, turned against the wall in his tiny room; it stayed there until the day of his arrest.

It so happened that a certain unrecognized and unpublished writer wrote a novel and invited a couple of dozen friends to listen to it. It was a literary Thursday in the style of the nineteenth century. This novel cost every one of those present a twenty-five-year sentence in corrective labor camps. Kondrashev-Ivanov was one of those who listened to the seditious novel. (He was a grand-grandson of the Decembrist Kondrashev, who had been exiled for twenty years and had been visited in exile by a French governess who was in love with him.)

Kondrashev-Ivanov did not actually go to a camp. After he had signed the decree of the special court, he was taken directly to Mavrino and put to work painting, at the rate of one painting a month, the production norm set for him by Oskolupov. In the past year, he had painted the paintings which hung here and others which had been taken away. And what difference did it make? He was a man of fifty with a twenty-five-year term ahead of him, and he did not live but flew through that calm prison year, not knowing whether he would ever have another like it. He paid no attention to what he was being fed, or noticed when they counted him among the rest.

He worked on several paintings at once, leaving and returning to a canvas many times. He had not yet brought any of them to that level which gives the master a sense of perfection. He was not even certain whether any such level existed. He left them when he stopped seeing anything in them, when his eye became accustomed to them. He left them when he was able to improve them less and less, when he noticed that he was spoiling them instead.

He left them, turned them to the wall, covered them. He became detached, far removed from them. And when he looked at them again with fresh eyes, before giving them away to hang forever amid pretentious luxury, the artist felt a sense of triumph. Even if no one ever saw them again— still, he had painted them.

Attentive now, Nerzhin began to examine Kondrashev's latest painting—a canvas in the proportions of the Egyptian quadrangle, four to five. It was entitled "Autumn Stream," or, as the artist privately called it, "Largo in D Minor."

A still stream occupied the center of the canvas. It seemed

not to be flowing at all, and its surface was about to ice over. Where the stream was shallow, brown shadows of fallen leaves laced the bottom. The left bank was a cape and the right bank curved into the distance. The first snow lay in patches on both shores, and yellowish-brown grass sprouted where it had melted. Two white willow brushes grew beside the shore, faintly smoke-colored, wet from the melting snowflakes. But the focus of the painting did not lie there. In the background was a dense forest of olive-black firs, before which flamed a single rebellious crimson birch. Behind its lonely, tender fire the evergreen sentinels stood even gloomier, massed together, raising their sharp peaks to the sky. The sky was hopelessly skewbald, and the suffocating sun was sinking in the mottled overcast, powerless to break through with a single ray. But even that was not the most important element; rather it was the stagnant water of the settling stream. It had a feeling of being poured, a depth. It was leadlike and transparent and very cold. It held in itself the balance between the autumn and winter. And some other kind of equilibrium.

The artist was concentrating on this very painting.

There was a supreme law of creative activity which Kondrashev had known for a long time. He had tried to resist it, but once again he yielded helplessly. This law said that nothing he had done previously had any value, counted for anything, was any credit to the artist. Only the canvas being painted today held the essence of his whole life experience, marked the summit of his ability, the keystone of his talent.

And so often it was a failure!

Each previous painting, just as it was about to succeed, had failed also, but his former desperation would be forgotten, and now this one—the first he had really learned to paint—was failing too, and all his life had been lived in vain, and he had never had any talent at all!

The water in the stream had indeed the feeling of being poured; it was cold and deep and motionless—but all that was nothing if it failed to communicate the highest synthesis of nature. This synthesis—comprehension, peace, the unity of all things—Kondrashev had never found in himself, in his most intense feelings, but he recognized it and bowed to it in nature. Therefore, did the water in his picture communicate that supreme peace or not? He longed to understand, and he despaired of ever knowing.

"You know Hippolyte Mikhailich," Nerzhin said slowly, "I think I begin to agree with you: all these landscapes *are* Russia."

"Not the Caucasus?" Kondrashev-Ivanov said, turning around quickly. His glasses stayed in place, as if they were welded to him.

This question, though not the most important one, was not negligible either. Many people misunderstood Kondrashev's paintings. Either because they were too majestic or too exalted, they seemed to portray not Russia but the Caucasus.

"There may well be such places in Russia," Nerzhin agreed.

He stood up and walked around, looking at "Morning of an Unusual Day" and the other landscapes.

"Well, of course! Well, of course!" the artist insisted. "There not only *may* be such places in Russia, but there are. I'd like to take you to some places near Moscow—without an escort guard. What's more, they *can't* be the Caucasus. Understand one thing: the public has been fooled by Levitan. After Levitan we've come to think of our Russian nature as low-key, impoverished, pleasant in a modest way. But if that's all our nature is, then tell me where all those rebels in our history come from: the self-immolators, the mutineers, Peter the Great, the Decembrists, the 'People's Will' revolutionaries?"

"Zhelyabov! Lenin!" Nerzhin agreed excitedly. "It's true!"

But Kondrashev did not need support. He, too, was getting excited. He twisted his head and his glasses splashed lightning.

"Our Russian nature exults and rages and doesn't give way before the Tatar hoofs!"

"Yes, yes," said Nerzhin. "And that twisted oak there— what the hell kind of Caucasian oak is that? If even here, in the most enlightened place in GULAG, every one of us . . . ?" He gestured impatiently. "And in camp? In exchange for seven ounces of black bread they demand of us not only our spiritual harmony, but also the last remnants of conscience."

Kondrashev-Ivanov rose to his full height. "Never! Never!" He looked upward, like a man being led to execution. "No camp must break a man's spirit."

Nerzhin laughed coldly. "Perhaps it must not, but it does! You haven't been in camp yet, so don't judge. You don't know how they break us there. People go in, and when they come out—if they come out—they're unrecognizably different. Yes, it's well known: circumstances determine consciousness."

"No!" Kondrashev stretched out his long arms, ready at this moment to do combat with the whole world. "No! No! No! That would be degrading. What is one to live for then? And, tell me, why are people who love each other faithful when they're separated? After all, the circumstances dictate that they betray one another! And how do you explain the difference in people who have fallen into the same conditions, even the same camp?"

Nerzhin was confident of the advantage his experience gave him in comparison with the fantastic concepts of this ageless idealist. Yet he could not help but respect his objections.

"A human being," Kondrashev continued, "possesses from his birth a certain essence, the nucleus, as it were, of this human being. His 'I.' And it is still uncertain which forms which: whether life forms the man or man, with his strong spirit, forms his life! Because—" Kondrashev-Ivanov suddenly lowered his voice and leaned toward Nerzhin, who was again sitting on the block—"because he has something to measure himself against, something he can look to. Because he has in him an image of perfection which in rare moments suddenly emerges before his spiritual gaze."

Kondrashev moved very close to Nerzhin and asked in a conspiratorial whisper, his glasses gleaming as if with promise, "Shall I show you?"

This is the way all arguments with artists end. They have their own logic.

"Well, of course."

Kondrashev went off to a corner, pulled out a little canvas nailed to a frame, and brought it over, holding the gray, unpainted side toward Nerzhin.

"Do you know about Parsifal?" he asked in a strained voice.

"Something to do with Lohengrin?"

"His father. The keeper of the chalice of the Holy Grail."

"There's a Wagner opera, isn't there?"

"The moment I have portrayed is not to be found in either Wagner nor von Eschenbach, but it's the one that interests me. Every person can experience such a moment when he suddenly sees the image of perfection."

Kondrashev shut his eyes and bit his lips. He was concentrating.

Nerzhin wondered why the painting he was about to see was so small.

The artist opened his eyes. "It is only a study. A study for the principal painting of my life. I will probably never paint it. This is the moment when Parsifal first sees the castle! The castle of the Holy Grail!"

He placed the study on an easel before Nerzhin, keeping his own gaze fixed on it. Then he raised his hand to his eyes, as if he were shielding them from a light. And stepping back, he tripped on the first step of the stairway and almost fell.

The painting was twice as high as it was wide. It showed a wedgelike gorge between two mountain cliffs. On both cliffs, left and right, there was a forest, slumbering, primeval. Creeping ferns and clinging, hostile bushes had invaded the cliffs. At the top left, from out of the forest a light gray horse bore a rider in helmet and cloak. The steed was not frightened of the abyss, and had just raised its hoof, ready, at the will of his rider, to step back or to hurtle across.

But the horseman was not looking at the abyss. Amazed, he was looking into the distance where a reddish-gold light, coming perhaps from the sun, perhaps from something purer than the sun, flooded the sky behind a castle. It stood on the crest of the mountain—which piled up, ledge after ledge—rising in steps and turrets, visible from below the gorge through the ferns and the trees, spiring to the sky, unreal as if woven out of clouds, vibrant, vague yet visible in its unearthly perfection: the aureate-violet castle of the Holy Grail.

43

THE DOUBLE AGENT

Except for fat Gustav with his pink ears, Doronin was the youngest zek in the sharashka. Adolescent pimples still appeared on his face. His easygoing nature, his good luck, his

nimbleness endeared him to everyone. In the few minutes
the administration allowed for volleyball, Ruska devoted
himself to the game wholeheartedly. If the men at the net
let the ball past them, he would make a swan dive from the
rear to return it, even though he would fall and skin his
knees. Everyone liked his unusual nickname, Ruska, which
proved to be justified when, after two months in the sharashka, his hair, which had been shaved off in camp, grew
out curly and red.

He was brought in from a Vorkuta camp because he was
listed on his official GULAG record card as a milling-
machine operator. But he turned out to be a fake milling-
machine operator and was quickly replaced by a real one.
He was saved from being sent back to camp by Dvoyetyosov, who took him on to teach him how to run the small
vacuum pump. Being imitative, Ruska learned quickly. For
him the sharashka was like a rest home, and he wanted to
stay there. At the camp he had had to endure all sorts of
misfortunes, which he now related with gay ardor: how he
had almost died in a mine, how he had simulated a daily
fever by putting hot stones in his armpits. (When they tried
to catch him by using two thermometers, he found stones
of similar size so that the thermometers would never show a
difference of more than one-tenth of a degree.)

But recalling the past with laughter—a past which would
recur again and again over the next twenty-five years—
Ruska told only very few, and those in secret, of his principal feat: deceiving the all-Union wanted-persons hunters
for two years.

In the variegated crowd of sharashka inhabitants Ruska
was not particularly noteworthy until one September day.
That day, wearing a conspiratorial look, he went around to
twenty of the most influential zeks in the sharashka, those
who represented public opinion. He told each of them excitedly that that morning Major Shikin, the security officer,
had enlisted him as an informer and that he, Ruska, had
agreed, with the idea of making use of his status as an
informer for everyone's benefit.

In spite of the fact that the personnel file of Rostislav
Doronin was speckled with five aliases, check marks, letters
and coded symbols indicating that he was dangerous, pre-
disposed to escape, and must be handcuffed when moved
from place to place, Major Shikin, anxious to increase his
staff of informers, had decided that Doronin, being young,

was unstable, that he treasured being allowed to stay in the sharashka and would therefore be loyal to the security officer.

Secretly called to Shikin's office—people were first called to the secretariat and told, "Yes, yes, go see Major Shikin" —he was there for three hours. During this time, listening to the tedious instructions and explanations of their "protector," Ruska's sharp eyes studied not only the major's large head with hair grown gray from collecting denunciations and slanders, his dark face, his tiny hands, his boy's shoes, the marble desk set and the silk window blinds, but also read, upside down, from more than five feet away, the headings on files and on papers under the glass on Shikin's desk. And he noted which documents Shikin evidently kept in the safe and which he locked in the desk.

As he was observing these things, Ruska fixed his blue eyes on the major's and nodded in agreement. Behind this blue innocence, adventuresome plans were stirring, but the security officer, accustomed to the gray monotony of human submissiveness, could not guess this.

Ruska understood that Shikin could send him back to Vorkuta if he refused to become an informer.

Ruska and his whole generation had been taught to believe that "pity" was a shameful feeling, that "goodness" was to be laughed at, that "conscience" was priestly jargon. At the same time they were taught that informing was a patriotic duty, was the best thing one could do to help the person one denounced, and would improve the health of society. It wasn't that all this got to Ruska, but it did have an effect. The main question for him now was not how evil or unacceptable it was to be an informer but what it might lead to. Already enriched by turbulent experience, by many prison encounters, and by violent prison arguments, this young man could imagine all these archives being opened and all these Shikins turned over to courts of infamy.

Thus he realized that in the long run it would be as dangerous to cooperate with the "protector" as it would, in the short run, be dangerous to refuse.

But beyond these considerations, Ruska had a passion for gambling. As he read upside down the amusing papers under the glass on Shikin's desk, he trembled in anticipation of playing for high stakes. He had grown tired of the lack of activity in the coziness of the sharashka.

And when, for the sake of making it all seem real, he had ascertained how much he would be paid, he eagerly agreed.

After Ruska left, Shikin, pleased with his psychological acuteness, paced back and forth in his office wringing his tiny hands; such an enthusiastic informer promised a rich harvest of denunciations. At the same time Ruska, no less pleased, was going around to the trusted zeks acknowledging that he had agreed to be an informer out of his love of sport—and that he would study the security officer's methods and expose the real informers.

The zeks, even the older ones, could not recall any similar admission. Mistrustfully they asked Ruska why he was risking his neck by bragging about it. And he answered, "When the day arrives when that whole gang is tried, you'll testify in my favor."

Each of the twenty zeks who learned about it told one or two more, yet no one denounced Ruska to the "protector." Thus fifty people proved to be irreproachable.

This occurrence excited the sharashka for a long time. The zeks believed Ruska. They kept on believing him. But, as always, events run their own unique course. Shikin demanded material, which meant denunciations. Ruska had to give him something. He went around to his confidants and protested, "Gentlemen! Just think how much other informing there must be, since I've not yet been at it a month and Shikin is already pressing me hard. Please appreciate my situation. Give me some material."

Some would have nothing to do with him, and others helped him. It was decided to finish off a certain lady who worked there only out of greed, to add to the thousands of rubles her husband brought home. She was contemptuous of the zeks, and had expressed the opinion that they should all be shot. She said this among other free women employees, but the zeks soon heard about it. She had denounced two zeks herself, one for a liaison with one of the girls and the other for making a suitcase out of government-issue materials. Ruska slandered her unmercifully, reporting that she mailed letters for the zeks and stole condensers from the cabinets. And though he did not present Shikin with a single piece of evidence, and though the woman's husband, an MVD colonel, protested, still the power of the secret denunciation so irresistible in our

Fatherland did its work, and the lady was fired and departed in tears.

Sometimes Ruska informed on the zeks, too, about petty and harmless matters, warning them beforehand. Then he stopped warning them and said nothing. They did not ask him either. They understood instinctively that he was still informing—but about things he did not care to admit.

So Ruska suffered the usual fate of double agents. As before, no one informed on him or the game he was playing, but they began to avoid him. The fact that he told them how Shikin kept a special schedule under the glass on his desk showing the hours when informers could drop in without being summoned—which would have exposed them—did not compensate, somehow, for his own adherence to the priesthood of stool pigeons.

Nerzhin, who liked Ruska and admired his intrigues, did not suspect that it was Ruska who had denounced him for having a copy of Yesenin. Ruska could not have foreseen that the loss of the book would cause Nerzhin so much pain. He had reasoned that the book belonged to Nerzhin, that it would be discovered anyhow, that no one would take it away from him, and that instead Shikin would be side-tracked by the charge that the book in Nerzhin's suitcase had probably been brought to him by a free employee.

With the salty-sweet taste of Clara's kiss still on his lips, Ruska went out in the yard. The snow on the lindens reminded him of blossoms, and the air seemed as warm as spring. In his two years of underground wanderings, with all his youthful thoughts concentrated on deceiving the detectives looking for him, he had never sought a woman's love. He had gone to prison a virgin, and at night this fact weighed on him like a heavy burden.

But out in the yard, the sight of the long, low head-quarters building reminded him that on the following day, during the lunch period, he wanted to put on a show. The time had come to announce it; he could not have done so earlier because the project might have collapsed. Enveloped in Clara's admiration, which made him feel triply capable and intelligent, he looked around and saw Rubin and Nerzhin at the far end of the exercise yard, by a big double-trunked linden, and he started toward them with determination. His cap was shoved back to one side so that his curly hair was trustingly exposed to the mild day.

As he approached, Rubin's back was to him, Nerzhin was facing him. They were obviously not discussing trivial matters because Nerzhin seemed gloomy and very serious. As Ruska came up to them, Nerzhin did not look at him, did not change his expression in the slightest or break the rhythm of his speech, did not nod, but it was clear that the words Ruska heard were not part of their conversation:

"As a rule, if a composer writes too much, I'm always prejudiced against him. For example, Mozart turned out forty-one symphonies. Can anyone produce that much and avoid potboilers?"

No, they did not trust him. These words were, of course, a switch, because they told Rubin that someone was approaching, and he turned around. Seeing Ruska, he said, "Listen here, youngster. What do you think—are genius and villainy compatible?"

Ruska looked at Rubin without attempting to dissemble. His face radiated purity and mischief.

"In my opinion, no, Lev Grigorich. But for some time everyone has been avoiding me as if I combined those qualities myself. Gentlemen, I've come to make a proposal to you: would you like, during lunch tomorrow, to have me sell you all the Judases at the very moment they receive their thirty pieces of silver?"

"How can you do that?"

"Well, you know the general principle of a just society, that all labor must be paid for? Tomorrow each Judas will receive his pieces of silver for the third quarter of the year."

Nerzhin expressed mock indignation. "What inefficiency! It's already the fourth quarter and they're only paying for the third? Why the delay?"

"A lot of people have to approve the pay list," Ruska explained in an apologetic tone. "I'll receive mine, too."

"Why are they paying you for the third quarter?" Rubin asked in surprise. "After all, you only worked half of it."

"So what? I distinguished myself!" said Ruska, looking at both of them with a winning smile.

"Just like that, in cash?"

"God, no. A money order sent from a fictitious person for deposit in one's personal account. They asked me in whose name they should send it. They said, 'Would you like it from Ivan Ivanovich Ivanov?' The cliché jarred me. So I asked, 'Couldn't you send it from Klava Kudryavtseva?' After all, it's nice to think that a woman cares about you."

"And how much do you get for the third quarter?"

"That's the cleverest part of all! According to the pay list, the informer gets 150 rubles a quarter. But for decency's sake the money must be sent by mail. So the post office takes three rubles as its fee. All the 'protectors' are so greedy they don't want to add anything out of their own pocket and so lazy that they don't suggest increasing the informers' pay by three rubles. Since no normal person would ever send such an odd sum by mail, the missing three rubles are the mark of Judas. Tomorrow during lunch period you might all gather around staff headquarters and look at the money orders of all those who come out of the security office. This country ought to get to know its stool pigeons, don't you think, gentlemen?"

44

LIFE IS NO LOVE STORY

As scattered snowflakes began to fall, one by one, on the dark sidewalk of Sailors' Rest Street, from whose cobblestones car tires had licked off all traces of the past days' snow, the girls in Room 418 of the students' residence on Stromynka were preparing for Sunday evening.

Room 418 was on the third floor. The nine panes of its rectangular window looked down on Sailors' Rest Street. Against the right and left walls stood three cots in a row, wicker shelves with books, and night tables. Two desks occupied the middle of the room, leaving only two narrow aisles between them and the cots. The one nearer the window was called the "dissertation desk" and was cluttered with books, notebooks, drawings, and stacks of typewritten pages. At one corner of it Olenka, a pale blonde, sat reading the typewritten sheets. Farther on was the common table, at which Muza was writing a letter, and Lyuda, a mirror in front of her, was unrolling her curlpapers. The cots stopped just short of the doorway wall, leaving room for hangers on one side and a washstand hidden by a curtain on the other. The girls were supposed to wash at the end of the hall, but they found that too cold and uncomfortable.

The Hungarian, Erzhika, was lying on the cot nearest the washbasin, reading. She wore a dressing robe the girls called "the Brazilian flag." She possessed other intriguing robes which delighted her roommates. But when she went out in public, she dressed with great restraint, as if deliberately trying not to draw attention to herself. She had grown used to doing this during her years in the Hungarian underground.

The next cot in the row belonged to Lyuda and was in a mess. Lyuda had got out of bed only a short time before. The blanket and the sheet were trailing on the floor, while over the pillow a freshly ironed blue silk dress and stockings had been carefully laid out. At the desk Lyuda herself was loudly telling no one in particular—since no one was listening—how a Spanish poet, taken from his country while still a boy, had courted her. She remembered in detail a restaurant he had taken her to, what orchestra had been there, what entrees and side dishes they had been served, and what they had had to drink.

Resting her chin in her small round fists, Olenka tried to read and not listen to Lyuda. She could, of course, have cut her off, but, as Olenka's late mother had told her, "Avoid quarrelsome people; you'll never see the last of them." They had already found out that when anyone tried to stop Lyuda it only stirred her up. Lyuda was not really a graduate student. She had finished at the Financial Institute and had come to Moscow to take courses for teachers of political economy. She came from a family with money to spend, and she was attending these courses, it seemed, mostly to amuse herself.

Olenka found Lyuda's stories nauseating in their constant dwelling on the frivolous aspects of a life whose sole requirements were money, leisure, and an empty head; and she found even more repulsive Lyuda's primitive notion that the entire meaning of life consists of dates and relations with men.

It was Olenka's firm belief that their ill-fated generation

of women—she had been born in 1923—could simply not
afford to look at things this way. To accept such an idea
meant to hang one's whole life on a single cobweb, and
spend each day waiting for it to break or to find that it
had never been attached to anything in the first place.

True, just such a pearly strand had appeared in Olenka's
own life. It dangled before her like a swing. This evening
Olenka was to go to a concert with a man she liked very
much. The strand was there, and if she wanted, she could
take hold of it with both hands. But she was afraid to pull
on it for fear it might break.

Olenka had not yet begun to press her clothes for the
evening. She was finishing her reading not out of a sense of
obligation but with genuine fascination. She was reading
the third carbon of a poorly typed manuscript reporting on
the digs in Novgorod that autumn, after Olenka had left
there. She had transferred to archaeology late in her studies,
at the beginning of her fifth year. She wanted to work in
history with her own hands as much as possible, and since
her transfer had been delighted with her decision. That summer she had had the good fortune to dig up a birch-bark
letter—a living document from the twelfth century.

In it, in "her" letter, there were only a few words. A husband was writing his wife, asking her to send Sashka with
two horses to a certain place at a certain time. But for
Olenka these lines she had excavated were like a blare of
music warming the earth, and were far more important than
the exalted phrases of the chronicles. After all, this twelfth-
century Novgorod housewife had obviously been literate.
What kind of a woman had she been? And what kind of a
city was Novgorod then? Who was Sashka—a son, a
worker? And how had the horses looked as Sashka drove
off? This ordinary domestic letter drew Olenka more and
more into the ancient streets of Novgorod. She always
found it difficult to restrain her imagination. Sometimes,
even in the reading room, she would shut her eyes and
imagine herself on a winter evening, neither stormy nor
cold, driving up to Novgorod in a sleigh by way of Tver,
and from far away she would see a multitude of fires. (For
they did not yet use wooden-wick lamps.) And she dreamed
that she herself was a girl of ancient Novgorod, and that
her heart was pounding with happiness to be returning

after a long absence to her own dear, free, noisy, unique city of half a million people!

As for Lyuda, the most exciting thing about her story was not the external details of her affair with the poet. Back in her own Voronezh, where she had been married for three months and then had had a number of other men, Lyuda always considered that her virginity had somehow passed too quickly. So, here, from the beginning of her acquaintance with the Spanish poet, she had played the role of a chaste virgin, acting shy and trembling at his least touch. When the astonished poet begged her for her *first kiss*, she had shuddered and passed from delight to disappointment, which inspired the poet to write a poem twenty-four lines long, unfortunately not in Russian.

Muza, excessively plump, coarse-featured, and wearing glasses, appeared to be over thirty. Though she considered it improper to ask Lyuda to be quiet, she was attempting, while the intrusive and offensive story was going on, to write a letter to her elderly parents in a distant provincial city. Her mother and father still loved each other like newlyweds, and every morning when he went to work, her father would turn again and again and wave to her mother, who continued to wave to him through the little window in the door. Their daughter loved them the same way. No people in the world were closer to her than her parents. She loved to write them often and in detail about her experiences.

But at this moment she was not herself. For two days, since Friday evening, something had been happening to her which had overshadowed her tireless daily work on Turgenev, the work which had displaced every other interest in her life. She felt as if she had been smeared with something dirty and shameful, something which could not be washed off, hidden, or shown to anyone—and which it was also impossible to live with.

It had happened this way. Friday evening, when she had returned from the library and was about to go to bed, she had been called down to the office of the dormitory and told: "Into this room, please." Two men in civilian clothes were sitting there, at first very polite, introducing themselves as Nikolai Ivanovich and Sergei Ivanovich. Paying no attention to how late it was, they had kept her an hour, two

hours, three. They started with questions: with whom did
she live, with whom did she work—though they knew all
this, of course, as well as she did. They talked unhurriedly
about patriotism, about the social obligation of every schol-
arly and scientific worker not to shut himself up in his own
specialty, but to serve people with all his means and poten-
tialities. Muza found nothing to say against this; it was all
completely true. Then the brothers Ivanovich proposed that
she should help them; that is, meet with one of them here
in this office at a specified time, or at the university's political propaganda center, or in the clubrooms, or wherever in
the university buildings they agreed upon, and there answer
certain questions and communicate her observations.

With that began the whole long horrible thing. They
started speaking to her more and more rudely, shouting at
her, then addressing her insultingly, using the familiar pronoun: "Well, why are you so reluctant? It's not a foreign
intelligence service that's recruiting you." "What would a
foreign intelligence service do with her? She'd be like a fifth
leg on a horse." Then they declared that they would not
allow her to defend her dissertation, that they would wreck
her university career, because the country had no use for
such ninny scholars. This frightened her very much. She
would finish her studies in June. And her dissertation was
almost ready. She was fully prepared to believe they would
expel her from graduate school—it would be no trouble at
all for them. Then they took out a pistol, handed it back
and forth to one another and, as if by accident, pointed it
at Muza. When she saw the pistol, Muza's fear passed. For
in the end, to remain alive after being expelled with a bad
record was worse than anything. At 1 A.M. the Ivanoviches
let her go so that she could think it over until Tuesday,
until this Tuesday, the 27th of December. And they made
her sign a paper that she would reveal nothing that had
happened.

They assured her that *they knew everything*. And if she
told anyone about this conversation, she would be immediately arrested and sentenced on the basis of the paper
she had signed.

What miserable choice did they leave her? Now doomed,
she waited for Tuesday. She had no strength to study. She
remembered those days just past when she could think of

nothing but Turgenev, when no one oppressed her, and when she, foolishly, had no realization of her own happiness.

"And I said, 'You Spaniards, you make so much of a person's honor, but since you've kissed me on the lips I have been dishonored.'"

The attractive though hard face of the light-haired Lyuda communicated the despair of a violated girl.

Olenka sighed loudly and put aside the report. She wanted to say something cutting, but again she restrained herself. In such moments her chin thrust forward prettily, and her whole face acquired firm lines. Frowning, she got up on the chair and reached up to plug the iron into the "thief" socket on top of the hanging lamp, which had not yet been removed after Lyuda finished ironing. Irons and hot plates were strictly forbidden at Stromynka. The commandants hunted for "thief" sockets, and of course there were no floor sockets in any of the rooms.

Thin Erzhika was lying there all this time, reading the *Selected Works* of Galakhov. This book opened before her a world of high, bright personalities, a clear, beautiful world, where all suffering was easily conquered. Galakhov's characters were never shaken by doubts: whether to serve one's country or not, whether to sacrifice oneself or not. The depth and integrity of these people surprised Erzhika. She admitted to herself that in her years of underground work in Horthy's Hungary she would never have worried about not having paid her dues if, like Galakhov's young Komsomol, she had been blowing up trains in the enemy's rear.

Putting down the book and rolling over on her side, she, too, began to listen to Lyuda. Here in Room 418 she had come to learn surprising and conflicting things. For instance, an engineer who refused to go to an attractive Siberian construction project remained in Moscow—selling beer— while someone who had defended his dissertation still had no job. Erzhika's eyes had widened. "Are there really people without jobs in the Soviet Union?" Also, it appeared that to be registered in Moscow one had to give someone a big bribe. "But, after all, that's an instantaneous phenomenon, isn't it?" she had asked—meaning not "instantaneous" but "temporary."

Lyuda was concluding her story about the poet, saying that if she was to marry him, she now had no way out but to fake being a virgin. And she began to explain how she intended to accomplish this illusion on their first night.

A look of suffering crossed Muza's face. She could not restrain herself and pounded the table.

"But how can that be? How many heroines of world literature are there who because of that—"

"Because they were fools!" gaily retorted Lyuda, pleased that someone was listening to her. "Because they believed a lot of nonsense. It's all so simple!"

Olenka put a blanket on one end of the common table and tested the iron. Her new gray-brown jacket and matching skirt were everything to her. Olenka had been getting along on potatoes and kasha, and there had not been a time since the beginning of the war when she could remember having had really enough to eat. If she could get by without paying forty kopecks on the trolley-bus, she did. But this suit was first-rate; there was nothing about it that wasn't right. It would have been easier for her to scorch her own body with the iron than this suit.

All things considered, Lyuda had her doubts about whether to marry the poet: "He's not a member of the Union of Soviet Writers; he writes only in Spanish; and I just can't imagine how things are going to work out with his author's fees."

Erzhika was so astonished that she swung her feet to the floor and sat up.

"What?" she asked. "You in the Soviet Union also marry a man for material gain?"

"You'll get used to it and understand," Lyuda said, shaking her head from side to side in front of the mirror. She had taken off the curlpapers, and a profusion of blond curls trembled on her head. Just one such ringlet would have been enough to snare the youthful poet.

"Girls, I have come to the following conclusion—" Erzhika began, but she noticed Muza staring oddly at the floor beneath her, and she gasped and pulled up her legs.

"What? Did it run past?" she cried out in alarm.

The girls laughed. Nothing had run past.

In Room 418, sometimes even in daytime, and particularly at night, horrible Russian rats would scamper across the floor, squeaking. During all her years of underground struggle against Horthy, Erzhika had never feared anything so much as she now feared that these rats would jump on her cot and run across her. In daytime, amid the laughter of her girl friends, her terror passed, but at night she tucked in the blanket on all sides and over her head and swore that if she lived until morning she would leave Stromynka. Nadya, the chemist, brought poison and they scattered it around in the corners. The rats quieted down for a time but then came back. Two weeks before there had been a crisis. Of course, it had to be Erzhika who, while getting water from the pail in the morning, scooped up a little drowned rat in her cup. Shuddering with disgust and remembering its peaceful little face, Erzhika went that same day to the Hungarian Embassy and asked to be moved to a separate apartment. The embassy forwarded the request to the Ministry of Foreign Affairs of the U.S.S.R.; and the Ministry of Foreign Affairs forwarded it to the Ministry of Higher Education; and the Ministry of Higher Education passed it on to the rector of the university, who addressed an inquiry to the Administrative and Economic Sector; and the sector replied that there were no private apartments and that there had been no complaints about rats at Stromynka. The correspondence proceeded back through the same channels. Nevertheless the embassy gave Erzhika hopes of getting a room.

Now Erzhika, embracing her knees, sat there in her Brazilian flag like some exotic bird.

"Girls, girls," she said in a complaining singsong, "I like you all so much! I wouldn't leave you for anything—except *rats*."

This was only partly true. She did like the girls, but Erzhika could not tell any of them about her concern over the fate of Hungary, all alone on the European continent. Since the trial of László Rajk, something incomprehensible was happening in her homeland. There were rumors that Communists she had been with in the underground had been arrested. A relative of Rajk, who had also been studying at Moscow University, and other Hungarian students who were with him, had been called back to Hungary, and there had been no letters from any of them.

There was a special knock at the door, which meant, "You don't have to hide the iron, it's someone who belongs here." Muza got up and limped over—her knee ached from early rheumatism. She lifted the hook. Dasha came in quickly. She was a solid girl, with a large, slightly crooked mouth.

"Girls," she laughed, not forgetting to hook the door behind her. "I just managed to get away from an admirer. Guess who!"

"You have so many suitors?" Lyuda asked in surprise, as she searched through her suitcase.

Indeed, the university had groggily recovered from the war as from a dead faint. The men in graduate study were few, and all, one way or another, had something wrong with them.

"Wait a minute!" cried Olenka, entering into the spirit of the game and throwing up her hand. She looked questioningly at Dasha. "Was it 'Jaws'?"

"Jaws" had been a graduate student who had failed dialectical and historical materialism three times in a row and had been expelled from graduate school as a hopeless idiot.

"The 'Waiter'!" Dasha exclaimed, pulling her cap with ear flaps off her dark hair and hanging it on a hook. She did not take off her sheepskin-collared coat, bought with a coupon three years before at the university distribution center, but remained standing by the door.

"Ah—him!"

"I was riding in a streetcar and he got on," Dasha laughed. "He recognized me right away. 'What's your stop?' he asked. Well, after all, there was nowhere to hide. We got off together. 'You're not working at that bath any longer, are you? I've gone there so many times, and you're never there.'"

"Then you should have said—" Dasha's laughter was infectious and caught Olenka like a flame. "You should have said . . . you should have said . . . !" But she could not say what she wanted to and, giggling, sat down on the cot.

"What waiter? What bath?" Erzhika demanded.

"You should have said—" Olenka burst out, but new fits of laughter shook her. She gestured with her hands in an attempt to communicate what she could not manage to utter.

Lyuda laughed, too, and so did Erzhika, who still understood nothing. Even Muza's severe, homely face opened in a smile. She took off her glasses and cleaned them.

" 'Where are you going?' he said. 'Whom do you know

there in the students' residence?'" Dasha laughed, choking. "I said, 'I know a janitress there. And she's—she's knitting me some mittens—'"

"Mittens?"

"Knitting!"

"But tell me, I want to know! What waiter?" Erzhika pleaded.

They slapped Olenka on the back. She always laughed very easily. But her laughter was more than an expression of youthful vitality; she also believed that laughter is good for both the person who laughs and for the person who hears it, and that only someone able to laugh wholeheartedly has a real capacity for life.

They quieted down. The iron was ready. Olenka promptly began to sprinkle her jacket with water and adroitly covered it with a white cloth.

Dasha took off her coat. In her clinging gray sweater and plain skirt with a tight belt, one could see how supple and shapely she was, how she could work all day at anything physical without getting tired. Pulling back her colored spread, she carefully sat down on the edge of the bed, which had been made up with religious care—the pillows fluffed, with a lace pillow cover, and embroideries tacked on the wall above it. She told Erzhika:

"It happened last fall, in a warm spell before the cold came. After all, where can you find suitors? How can you make acquaintances? Lyuda advised me to take a walk in Sokolniki Park, but *alone!* She said girls spoil everything by going in pairs."

"It's the best way!" Lyuda said. She was carefully cleaning a spot from the toe of her shoe. "It's unusual to see a girl all by herself. Naturally a man wants to pick her up."

"So that's what I did," Dasha continued, but now without amusement in her voice. "I walked around and I sat down. I looked at the trees. And in fact someone nice-looking did sit down. Who was he? He turned out to be a waiter in a snack bar. And I? I was ashamed to say that I was a graduate student. A 'learned broad' is a horror to a man—"

"Oh, come on now—stop that kind of talk! Where will that attitude get you?" Olenka objected quickly in annoyance.

Here the world was so empty in the wake of the iron juggernaut of war. Black emptiness gaped where men of their age or five, ten, or fifteen years older should have been

walking and smiling. And with that crude and meaningless
term thought up by some unknown person, "a learned
broad," it was impossible to enjoy the one bright ray of light
that was left to them, and beckoned to them, and led them
on.

"... and I said I was working as a cashier in a bath-
house. He kept after me to find out which one and on what
shift. I could hardly get away...."

Dasha had lost all her animation. Her dark eyes looked
anguished.

She had been studying all day in the Lenin Library, then
had eaten a tasteless and unsatisfying meal in the dining
room and returned home weary to an empty Sunday evening
which promised nothing.

There had been a time in the middle grades, when she
was attending a spacious log schoolhouse in their village,
that she had enjoyed her achievement as a student. She was
glad, too, that using the institute as a reason she could get
a passport and be registered in the city. But now she was
getting older and had been studying uninterruptedly for
eighteen years. Studying gave her headaches. And why was
she studying anyway? Happiness for a woman was simple:
give birth to a child; but there was no one to have it by,
no one to have it for.

Thoughtfully, in the now silent room, Dasha uttered her
favorite saying: "No, girls, life is no love story."

It was true that in their Machinery and Tractor Station
there was an agronomist. He kept writing Dasha and asking
her to marry him. But she was about to get her degree and
the whole village would say, "What did the girl study for—
to marry an agronomist? Any woman field-gang leader on
the farm would have been just as good for him." On the
other hand, Dasha felt that even as a Candidate of Sciences
she still could not set foot in the society she wanted to be a
part of; she was not light-minded or carefree enough—and
brazen Lyuda was.

Looking at her jealously, Dasha said, "Lyuda, I'd advise
you to wash your feet."

Lyuda looked at her feet. "You think so?"

But the water could be warmed only on the hot plate,
which was now hidden away, and the iron was using the
"thief" socket.

Dasha wanted to drive away her sadness with work of

some kind. She remembered that she had bought underwear which was not the right size, but she had to take it while there was any available. Now she got it out and began to make alterations in it.

Everyone was silent. The desk wobbled under the ironing. Muza could concentrate fully on her letter. But no, it wasn't working out. Muza read over the last sentences she had written. She changed a word. She wrote over several unclear letters. No, the letter was not turning out right! The letter was a lie, and her mother and father would sense it at once. They would understand that things were going badly for their daughter, that something dreadful had happened. But why, they would wonder, didn't Muza write about it openly? Why for the first time was she telling a lie?

Had there been no one else in the room, Muza would have broken into sobs. She would simply have cried out loud, and perhaps it would have at least made things a little better. But, as it was, she threw down her pen and held her head in her hands, hiding her face from everyone. So that's how it happens! The decision of a lifetime, and no one to talk it over with. There was no one to turn to for help.

And so on Tuesday she would again face those two cocky men with their ready words, who were prepared for all eventualities. Just so does a shell fragment probably enter the body—alien, steely, seeming much bigger than it is. How good it would be to live without that steel fragment in one's chest. Yet now it could not be removed; everything had come to an end. Because they would not yield. And she would not yield either. She would not yield because how could she judge the human qualities of Hamlet and Don Quixote, remembering that she was an informer, that she had a code name, like "Daisy" or something, and that she had to gather information against these girls or against her own professor?

Trying to do it unnoticed, Muza wiped the tears from her eyes.

Olenka had already finished ironing the skirt. The cream-colored blouse with pink buttons was next.

"Where is Nadya?" Dasha asked.

No one answered. No one knew.

But Dasha, at her sewing, was determined to speak about Nadya: "How long can a woman go on that way? So he was missing in action. Well, it's five years since the war ended. You'd think it was time to break it off, wouldn't you? To look at life."

"What are you saying! What are you saying!" Muza exclaimed agonizingly, throwing up her hands. The broad sleeves of her gray-checked dress slid down to the elbows, revealing her flaccid white arms. "That's the only way to love! Real love reaches across the grave."

Olenka's full, moist lips expressed disapproval. "Across the grave? That's a transcendental idea, Muza. One can keep a grateful memory and tender recollections—but love?"

"During the war," Erzhika interrupted, "many people were taken far away, overseas. Maybe he's alive somewhere, too."

"He could be," Olenka agreed. "In that case she could hope. But Nadya is the kind of person who enjoys her own grief to the end. And only her own. People like that have to have grief in their lives."

Dasha stopped sewing, moving her needle idly along a seam, and waited until everyone had spoken. She knew, when she started the conversation, how she would surprise them.

"Listen to me, girls," she said. "Nadya is deceiving us, she has been telling us lies. She doesn't believe that her husband is dead at all, and she doesn't just hope that he is missing either. She knows her husband is alive. And she even knows where he is."

The girls were bewildered.

"Where did you learn that?"

Dasha looked at them triumphantly. Because of her unusual keenness of observation, the room had nicknamed her "The Investigator."

"All you have to do is know how to listen. Has she ever once spoken of him as dead? No. She even tries not to say 'he was,' and somehow tries to manage without saying either 'he was' or 'he is.' Well, if he is missing, then at least she might once have spoken of him as dead."

"Well, what happened to him then?"

"What!" Dasha cried, putting her sewing aside altogether. "Isn't it clear?"

No, it was not clear to them.

"He is alive, but he has *left* her. And she's ashamed to admit it! It's humiliating! So she thought up the idea of his being 'missing.'"

"I can believe it, I can believe it!" Lyuda agreed, rinsing her mouth behind the curtain.

"It means she is sacrificing herself in the name of her happiness with him!" exclaimed Muza. "It means that for some reason she feels she must keep silent and not get married."

"Yes, that's absolutely right; you're smart, Dashka!" said Lyuda, coming out from behind the curtain, without her robe, in only her chemise, her legs bare, which made her seem even taller and more shapely. "She's eating her heart out, and that's why she took up the role of a saint who is faithful to a corpse. She's not sacrificing a damn; she's trembling for someone to caress her, but no one wants her! After all, a girl can walk along the street and everyone turns around to look at her—but she could throw herself at someone and no one would want her."

She went back behind the curtain.

"But you certainly don't have to want people to turn around and look at you!" Olenka objected vigorously. "You have to be above that!"

"Ha, ha!" Lyuda retorted. "It's easy for you to think that because people do look at you."

"But Shchagov visits her," said Erzhika, pronouncing the Russian sound "shch" with difficulty.

"He visits her—that doesn't mean anything yet!" said the invisible Lyuda with conviction. "He has to nibble on the line!"

"What do you mean, 'nibble'?" said Erzhika, not understanding.

Everyone laughed.

"No, what you're saying," Dasha said, pressing her own point, "is that maybe she still hopes to get her husband back from the other woman."

At the door there was the agreed knock—"Don't hide the iron, it's a friend."

Everyone was silent. Dasha lifted the hook.

Nadya entered, with a dragging step, her face burdened and aging, as if she were confirming all Lyuda's worst mockeries. Strangely, she did not even greet those present, she did not even say, "Well, here I am" or "What's new, girls?" She hung up her coat and went over to her own bed.

The hardest thing in the world for her at this moment would have been to say a few polite, meaningless words.

Erzhika was reading. Olenka finished her ironing, and the ceiling lamp was turned on.

No one found anything to say. Then, wishing to end the awkward silence, Dasha took up her sewing and said again, "No, girls, life is no love story."

45

THE OLD MAID

After her visit with Gleb, Nadya wanted only to be with other people as miserable as she was, to talk only about prison and prisoners. From Lefortovo she went straight to Krasnaya Presnya, all the way across Moscow, to tell Sologdin's wife her husband's three sacred words.

But she did not find her at home, and no wonder: Sunday was the only day Sologdin's wife had to do all the week's errands, for herself and for her son. Nor could Nadya leave a note with the neighbors. Sologdin's wife had told her, and she could believe it, that her neighbors were against her and spied on her.

Nadya had climbed the steep, dark stairs quickly, excited at the thought of talking with this woman who shared her secret grief. She came back down not just disappointed but crushed. And as images slowly appear on blank paper in the photographer's darkroom, all the gloomy thoughts and presentiments which had started in the prison now emerged and began to weigh on Nadya's heart.

He had said—yes, he *had* said it—"Don't be surprised if they send me away from here, if my letters stop." He might be sent away! Then even these visits, once a year, would stop? What would she do?

And something about the lower reaches of the Angara.

And hadn't he said something about God—some phrase or other? Prison was crippling his spirit, leading him off into idealism, mysticism, teaching him submissiveness. He was changing; when he came back, she wouldn't know him any more.

But the worst thing had been his saying, almost threaten-ingly, "You should not hope too much for the end of my term. A term is a conditional thing." Nadya had cried out, "I don't want to believe you! It simply can't be!" Now, hours later, as she traveled all the way back across Moscow, from Krasnaya Presnya to Sokolniki, her heavy thoughts still burdened her; she could not shake them off.

If Gleb's prison term would never end, what was the use of waiting? Why go on living?

She arrived at Stromynka too late to go into the dining room, and this was all it took to push her into complete despair. She thought of the ten-ruble fine she had received two days before, for boarding the rear platform of a bus. Ten rubles! That was real money for her these days.

A pleasant, light snow was starting to fall. A small boy with a forage cap pulled down over his eyes stood selling Kazbek cigarettes. Nadya went up to him and bought two.

"Matches?" she said to herself, out loud.

"Here you are, Auntie! Have a light!" The boy handed her a box of matches. "We don't take money for a light."

Without thinking how it might look, Nadya managed to light the cigarette, crookedly, on one side, on the second match. She gave the boy back his matches, and, not wanting to go inside yet, began to walk slowly up and down. Though this was not her first cigarette, she was not used to smoking. The smoke was hot in her mouth, and made her feel nause-ated; and this took away a little of the ache in her heart.

When she had smoked half the cigarette, Nadya threw it away and went upstairs to Room 418.

She walked past Lyuda's unmade bed and lay down heavily on her own, wanting more than anything to be left alone.

There on her desk were the four reams of her dissertation, four typed copies. The endless troubles she had had with the thing—the drawings, the photocopies, the first revision, the second, and now here it was back for a third.

How hopelessly, illegally, it kept being held up. Right now she could give it that secret, *special* reworking which would bring her peace and a good salary. But that would mean filling out that terrible eight-page security questionnaire, and getting it to the Personnel Section by Tuesday.

To report everything as it really was—that would mean

expulsion by the end of the week, from the university, from the dormitory, from Moscow.

Or else she could get a divorce on the spot.

And Gleb had not advised her at all.

Her muddled, aching brain could find no way out.

Erzhika made her bed as best she could. She did not do very well at it; all her life servants had done that kind of work for her. Then she put on some rouge and went off to the Lenin Library.

Muza was trying to read, but she could not concentrate. She noticed Nadya's sadness, and watched her, worried, but could not bring herself to ask her about it.

Dasha wondered whether or not to do her ironing. She could never sit still long. "Yes," she said, "I heard today they're going to double our 'book' money this year."

Olenka gave a start. "You're joking!"

"That's what the dean told our girls."

"Just a minute. How much will it be?" Olenka's face burned with a joy which money can bring only to people unused to and not greedy for it. "Three hundred and three hundred is six hundred. Seventy and seventy is one hundred and forty. And five and five is—ha!" she shouted, clapping her hands. "Seven hundred and fifty! Now that's something!"

"Now you'll go buy yourself a full set of Soloviev," said Dasha.

"I don't know. I don't know," said Olenka with a smile. "Maybe a dress the color of pomegranates, made out of Georgette crepe? Can you imagine?" She picked up the edge of her skirt. "With double flounces."

There were many things Olenka did not have. She had only begun to care again this last year, since her mother's death. Since then Olenka had had no one of her own left alive. In one week in 1942 she and her mother had received funeral allowances for both her father and her brother. Just after that her mother had fallen seriously ill, and Olenka had had to drop out of the first year of her history course. A year later she had taken it up again through a correspondence school. She had worked nights in a hospital and during the day looked after things at home. She had had to search for firewood, and exchange her bread ration for milk.

None of all that showed at the moment on her sweet, plump twenty-six-year-old face.

She believed that one must surmount everything, and
never let one's troubles be a burden to others.

So she was annoyed at the sight of Nadya's open suffering, which could only depress everyone.

Olenka asked, "What's wrong with you, Nadya? You
were cheerful enough this morning."

The words were sympathetic, but they conveyed her irritation. Through its undertones and overtones the human
voice can reveal feelings which defy analysis.

Nadya became aware of Olenka's annoyance as she
watched her fasten a red, flower-shaped brooch in her jacket
lapel and then put perfume on.

And the perfume which gave Olenka an invisible air of
joy came to Nadya as the scent of loss itself.

Without changing her expression, and speaking with great
difficulty, Nadya said, "Am I disturbing you? Am I spoiling
your mood?"

Though on the surface her words contained no reproach,
there was a suggestion of reproach in the way she spoke
them.

Olenka straightened up. Her lips thinned and tightened,
and her jaw took on a firm, hard line.

The two women looked at each other across the cluttered
desk.

"Look here, Nadya," Olenka said, pronouncing each word
carefully. "I don't want to hurt you. But as our mutual
friend Aristotle said, a human being is a social animal. We
can share our joys, but we don't have the right to spread
gloom."

Nadya sat on her bed, bent over and still, like an old
woman.

"Do you have any idea," she said, in a quiet, dull voice,
"how sad one can be?"

"I can understand very well. You're sad. I believe it. But
you can't start thinking you're the only one suffering in this
world. Maybe others have lived through much more than
you. Think about it."

She did not go on to say, "Why is a missing husband, who
can be replaced, worse than a father and brother who have
been killed, and a dead mother, who can never be replaced?"

She stood very still, looking at Nadya.

Nadya knew Olenka was talking about her own losses.

Still, she thought: every death is irrevocable, but every death happens only once. It shakes you only once. Then, little by little, imperceptibly, that death recedes into the past. Gradually, grief lets go of you. And you put on a red flower pin, and perfume, and go out for a date.

But Nadya's grief was always with her, always held her; it was in the past, the present, and the future. No matter how she tried, or what she seized hold of, she could not get away from it.

But to give an acceptable explanation she would have to reveal her secret, and that was too dangerous.

So she gave in and lied, nodding her head toward her thesis. "Well, forgive me, I'm completely worn out. I don't have the strength to revise it again. How many times can you revise a thing?"

With this, Olenka's anger completely disappeared, and she said in a friendly way, "Oh, you've got to throw out the foreigners? Well, there, you're not the only one. Don't let it get you down."

"Throwing out the foreigners" meant going through the thesis and replacing every reference to a foreigner: "Lowe demonstrated," for instance, would have to read, "Scientists have succeeded in demonstrating"; "as Langmuir demonstrated" would become "as has been shown." Or if a Russian, or a Dane, or a German in the Russian service had done anything at all to distinguish himself, then you had to put in his full name and duly emphasize his high patriotism and immortal services to science.

"Not foreigners. I got rid of them long ago. Now I have to throw out Academician B——."

"Our own Soviet?"

"—and his whole theory. And I'd built the whole thing on that. And now it turns out that he—his—"

Academician B—— had fallen into the same abyss as Nadya's husband.

"Well, don't take things so hard!" Olenka was saying. "At least they're going to let you revise it. It could be worse. Muza was telling me—"

But Muza did not hear her. She was buried in her book now, and the room around her did not exist.

"—Muza was saying there was a girl in the literature department who defended her thesis on Zweig four years ago, and was made an assistant professor. Suddenly they discovered that she had said three times in the thesis that Zweig was 'a cosmopolitan,' and that the thesis supported it. So they called her in to the Highest Credentials Commission and took her degree away. Awful!"

"Phoo, Nadya, you're upset about chemistry," said Dasha. "What about us in political economy? Our necks are in the noose, but somehow we manage to survive. We breathe. Now I'm getting out of it all right, thanks to Stuzhaila-Olyabishkin."

Dasha was beginning her thesis for the third time. Her first subject had been "Problems of Food Distribution under Socialism." This subject had been very clear twenty years before, when every Pioneer, Dasha among them, would have known by heart that the family kitchen was a thing of the past, and that liberated women would get their breakfasts and lunches in collective dining rooms. But over the years the subject had become clouded and even dangerous. Certainly whoever ate in a collective dining room—Dasha herself, for instance—did so only out of bleak necessity.

Only two forms of collective dining were prospering: the expensive restaurants—where the expression of the socialist principle was not all it might have been—and the cheapest little bars, selling only vodka. In theory, there were still the collective dining rooms, because the Great Coryphaeus had been too busy for the last twenty years to speak out on the subject of food distribution. So it was dangerous to risk speaking out on one's own. Dasha worried over the thesis for a long time, and finally her sponsor changed her subject; but he took her new one from the wrong list: "Trade in Consumer Goods under Socialism." There did not seem to be much material on this theme. All the speeches and directives stated that consumer goods could be, even that they should be, produced. Still, practically speaking, these goods, compared to rolled steel and petroleum products, had begun to be held in disfavor, and whether light industry would develop or wither away, even the learned council did not know. So, in due time, they rejected that subject, too.

Then the good folk put their minds to work, and Dasha found herself with the subject, "The Russian Nineteenth-Century Economist Stuzhaila-Olyabishkin."

Laughing, Olenka asked, "Have you found his portrait yet, your benefactor?"

"That's just it. I can't find it."

"Cruel ingratitude!" Olenka was trying to cheer Nadya up, feeling very cheerful herself at the prospect of her evening out. "I'd have found it and hung it up over my bed. I can just picture him: a very handsome old estate-owner type, with unfulfilled spiritual longings. After a big breakfast he would sit in his dressing gown in front of the window, out there, you know, in that province in *Evgeni Onegin* where storms of history never blow; there he'd sit, watching the girl Palashka feeding the pigs, musing dreamily to himself:

> 'How the state grows wealthy,
> and what it lives on . . .'

Then in the evenings he would play cards." Olenka laughed and laughed.

Lyuda had put on her light-blue dress, which had been lying across her bed.

Nadya sighed and looked away from the messy bed. Lyuda was in front of the mirror, freshening up the makeup on her brows and lashes and painting her lips with great care in the shape of petals.

Suddenly Muza spoke up, as if she had been in the conversation all along: "Have you ever noticed what makes Russian literary heroes different from the heroes of Western novels? The heroes of Western literature are always after careers, money, fame. The Russians can get along without food and drink—it's justice and good they're after. Right?"

And she buried herself in her book again.

Lyuda had put on her overshoes and was reaching for her fur coat. Nadya nodded sharply in the direction of Lyuda's bed, and said with disgust, "You're going to leave that filth for us to pick up again?"

"So don't pick it up!" Lyuda said, flying into a rage, her eyes shining. "Don't you ever dare touch my bed again!" Her voice rose to a scream. "And don't preach to me!"

"It's time you understood!" Nadya burst out, letting loose all her pent-up feelings. "You're insulting us. You think we have nothing on our minds but your nights out?"

"You're jealous? No one's nibbling on your line."

Their faces were distorted, ugly, as women's faces in anger always are.

Olenka opened her mouth to snap at Lyuda, too, but she did not like the tone of the words "nights out."

Oh, they weren't such pure pleasure as they might seem, those nights out.

"There's nothing to be jealous of!" Nadya cried dully, in a broken voice.

"If you got lost on the way," Lyuda shouted even louder, sensing victory, "and instead of landing in a nunnery you turned up here doing graduate work, all right then, sit there in your corner, but don't act like such a stepmother. It makes me sick. Old maid!"

"Lyuda, don't you dare!" Olenka screamed.

"Then what's she doing sticking her nose into everyone else's business? The nun! The old maid! The flop!"

At this point Dasha joined in and started trying to prove something or other very energetically. And Muza roused herself, too, and, waving her book at Lyuda, began to scream, "Narrow-mindedness! And she's crowing about it!"

All five of them were shouting at once, no one listening to anyone, no one agreeing with anyone.

Not understanding anything, ashamed of her outburst and her uncontrollable sobs, Nadya, still dressed in her best for the prison visit, threw herself face down on her bed and covered her head with the pillow.

Lyuda powdered her face and brushed her blond curls once more, dropped her hat veil down just below her eyes, and, not making her bed but throwing her blanket over it as a concession, left the room.

The others spoke Nadya's name, but she did not move. Dasha took Nadya's shoes off and covered up her legs with the corners of the blanket.

There was a knock at the door. Olenka burst out into the hall, came back in like the wind, tucked her curls up under her hat, slipped into a dark-blue coat trimmed with yellow fur, and went to the door with a fresh step.

It was a step not toward happiness but into battle.

So it was that Room 418 sent out into the world, one after the other, two beautiful and elegantly dressed temptresses.

But, losing with them its liveliness and laughter, the room became even more dispirited.

Moscow was an enormous city, but there was nowhere to go in it.

Muza was not reading any more; she took off her glasses and hid her face in her large hands.

Dasha said, "Olenka's silly. He's only going to play with her and drop her. They say he has another girl somewhere. And maybe a child, too."

Muza looked into her hands. "But Olenka isn't tied to him. If he turns out that way, she can always leave him."

"What do you mean, not tied to him!" Dasha smiled ironically. "What kind of tie do you mean, if—"

"Oh, you always know everything! How can you know that?" Muza was indignant.

"Well, she spends the night at his place."

"Oh, that doesn't mean anything! That doesn't prove anything at all!" said Muza.

"And it's the only way now; otherwise you can't keep them at all."

The two girls were silent, each thinking her own thoughts.

The snow outside was falling more heavily. It was already dark.

The water gurgled quietly in the radiator under the window.

It was unbearable to think they were going to kill Sunday night in this hole of a place.

Dasha thought of the waiter she had thrown over, a strong, healthy man. Why had she given him up? All right, he had taken her to that club on the edge of town, where no one from the university ever went. What of it?

"Muza, let's go to the movies!" Dasha said.

"What's playing?"

"That German film, *The Indian Tomb*."

"Oh, that nonsense! Commercial nonsense!"

"But it's playing right here in the building, right next door."

Muza did not answer.

"Well, this is deadly dull!"

"I'm not going," said Muza. "Find some work to do."

Suddenly the electric light dimmed. Only a thin red filament burned in the bulb.

"That's all we needed!" Dasha groaned. "You could hang yourself in a place like this!"

Muza sat there like a statue.

Nadya lay on her bed, motionless.

"Muza, let's go to the movies."

There was a knock at the door.

Dasha looked out and came back. "Nadya! Shchagov is here! Are you going to get up?"

46

FIRE AND HAY

Nadya cried for a long time. She bit the blanket to try to stop herself. Her face was hot and wet; the pillow was stifling her.

She would have been glad to go out somewhere, to get out of the room until late at night. But there was nowhere in the whole enormous city of Moscow to go.

It was not the first time such names had been thrown at her: "stepmother," "grumbler," "nun," "old maid." The worst of it was that they were so untrue.

But is the fifth year of a lie ever easy? Your face becomes drawn and cramped under the constant mask, your voice becomes shrill, your judgments bloodless. Maybe by now she *had* become an unbearable old maid?

It's so hard to tell about oneself. In a dormitory where you can't, as you could at home, stamp your feet at Mama. In a dormitory, among your peers, you learn to see yourself as all bad.

Except for Gleb Nerzhin, there was no one, no one at all, who could understand her.

But Gleb couldn't understand her either. He had failed to tell her anything—what to do, how she should live. He had only said there would be no end to his term.

With a few quick, confident sentences, he had broken down all that had given her strength from day to day, all her faith, her expectations, all that had sustained her in her loneliness.

There would be no end to his term!

And that meant he didn't need her.

Oh, God, God!

Nadya lay stretched out flat. With open, unmoving eyes she stared between the pillow and the blanket at a bit of the wall in front of her—and she could not understand, and did not try to understand, what kind of light there was in the room. It seemed very dark, but she could still make out the blisters in the familiar ocher paint.

Suddenly through the pillow she heard the twelve special

drumlike rappings at the plywood door, like peas dropping into a pot: four fingers thrice over! And even before Dasha had told her, "Nadya! Shchagov is here! Are you going to get up?" Nadya had thrown aside the pillow, straightened out her skirt which was all wound around her waist, run a comb through her hair, and was feeling for her shoes with her feet.

In the lifeless, dim light of the half-normal voltage, Muza watched her rushing around, and withdrew.

Dasha hurried to make Lyuda's bed and pick up the things that had been thrown around the room.

They let the visitor in.

Shchagov came in with his old front-line overcoat thrown over his shoulders. He was tall, with a military bearing. He could bend down, but not hunch over. His movements were spare, thought out.

"Hello, gracious ladies," he said in a condescending tone, "I came to see how you're spending your time without enough light—and to do the same. One could die of boredom!"

What a relief, Nadya thought; in that light he would not be able to tell she had been crying.

"You mean if it weren't for the blackout you wouldn't have come?" Dasha took up Shchagov's tone, flirting unconsciously, as she did with every unmarried man she met.

"By no means, never. In bright light women's faces are deprived of all their charm; it reveals their spiteful expressions, their envious glances, their premature wrinkles, their heavy cosmetics."

Nadya shuddered at the words "envious glances"—it was as if he had overheard their argument.

Shchagov went on: "If I were a woman, I would make it a law that lights be kept low. Then everyone would soon have a husband."

Dasha looked disapprovingly at Shchagov. He always talked that way, and she didn't like it. All his phrases seemed memorized, insincere.

"May I sit down?"

"Please," Nadya replied, in an even voice that carried no trace of her recent fatigue, bitterness, tears.

Unlike Dasha, she liked Shchagov for his self-possession, his slow way of talking, his low, firm voice. Calm seemed to emanate from him. And his wit seemed pleasant enough to her.

"A group like this might not ask me a second time, so I'll sit down quickly. And what are you doing with yourselves, my young graduate students?"

Nadya was silent. She could not talk easily with him; they had quarreled the day before, and Nadya, with a sudden, impulsive movement, which implied an intimacy that had never existed between them, had struck him on the back with her briefcase and run away. It was silly, childish; and now the presence of others made things easier for her.

Dasha replied, "We're going to the movies. We don't know who with."

"And what is the movie?"

"*The Indian Tomb.*"

"Oh! You certainly must go. As one of the nurses said, 'There's lots of shooting, lots of killing, and in every way it's a wonderful picture.'"

Shchagov was sitting comfortably at the desk they all shared.

"Forgive me, gracious ladies, I thought I would find you dancing hand in hand, but there seems to be some sort of funeral going on instead. Problems with your parents? Are you unhappy about the Party Bureau's latest decision? After all, it doesn't seem to refer to graduate students."

"What decision?" Nadya asked almost soundlessly.

"What decision? About verification of students' social origins; whether they are telling the truth when they list their parents. Well, Muza Georgiyevna? Are you sure you haven't hidden something? There are all sorts of rich possibilities here—maybe someone trusted someone with something, or talked in his sleep, or read someone else's mail; oh, all sorts of things."

Nadya's heart skipped a beat. They were still looking and probing and digging! How sick she was of it all. Where could she possibly get away from it?

"What kind of vileness is that?" exclaimed Muza.

"You mean even that doesn't cheer you up? Well, shall I tell you a very amusing story about the secret vote taken yesterday at the council of the mathematics faculty?"

Shchagov talked to all of them, but kept looking at Nadya. He had been wondering for a long time what she wanted from him. Every new incident seemed to make it clearer.

She would stand beside the chessboard while he played chess with somebody, and ask him to play with her so she could learn the opening moves.

But, after all, chess helps one forget the passage of time.

Or she would ask him what he thought of her performance at a concert.

But that was natural! Anyone wants to be praised, and by someone not entirely indifferent.

Or once she happened to have an "extra" ticket to the movies and had asked him to come.

Oh, she just wanted to have the illusion, for one evening, of somebody taking her somewhere.

And then on his birthday she had given him a present, a notebook—but so awkwardly. She had shoved it into his jacket pocket and run away. Why did she act like that? Why run away?

Oh, it was only embarrassment.

He had caught up with her in the hall and struggled with her, pretending he was trying to give the notebook back, and in the struggle he had embraced her—and she let him hold her; for a minute she had not made a move to break away.

It had been so many years since anyone had held Nadya, the suddenness and sharpness of it must have overwhelmed her.

And then that playful blow with the briefcase.

As he did with everyone, Shchagov had kept himself under iron control with Nadya. Could she be simply a lonely woman begging for help? And if that was it, who would be so unbending, so hard, as to refuse her?

So this evening Shchagov had come from his room, 412, to Room 418, sure that he would find Nadya there, and filled with agitation at what might happen between them.

If the girls showed any amusement at his story about the curious vote taken by the mathematics council, it was out of politeness.

"Well, are the lights going to go on or not?" Muza finally cried out.

"I see my stories don't entertain you. Especially Nadezhda Ilinichna; her face is like a thundercloud. I know why, too: they fined her ten rubles the other day, and she can't get over it."

Nadya became furious. She grabbed her purse, tore open the clasp, pulled out a piece of paper, and tore it up hysterically. She threw the pieces down on the desk in front of Shchagov.

"Muza, for the last time, are you coming?" Dasha asked in a strained voice, picking up her light coat.

"I'm coming!" Muza replied in a monotone, and went to get her coat.

Shchagov and Nadya did not turn to watch the girls go.

But when the door closed behind them, Nadya felt awful.

Shchagov picked up the scraps of paper and held them up to the light. Another ten-ruble note.

He got up and went over to Nadya. He towered above her. He took her small hands in his.

"Nadya!" It was the first time he had called her that. He felt strangely agitated. "Forgive me! I'm to blame for a great deal. . . ."

She stood stock-still; her heart was pounding, and she felt weak. Her fury over the ten-ruble note had passed as quickly as it had come. A strange thought came over her: there was no guard there, leaning his bullish head toward them. They could say anything they wanted. They could decide for themselves when to say good night.

His face was very close, very strong, even-featured.

He clasped her elbows, warm under her batiste blouse.

"Nadya!" he said again, very quietly.

He was the one she could speak to about the special-theme problem and the new questionnaire—she could talk to him about everything.

"Let me go," she said at last in a tone of weary regret.

She had started it, and now she was saying, "Let me go."

"I don't understand you, Nadya," he said, moving his hands from her elbows to her shoulders, feeling her softness and warmth.

For the third time he had called her "Nadya," and she had not said anything.

"Understand—what?" she asked, but without moving away.

He drew her close to him.

The half-light hid the color that rushed to her face.

She pushed him away.

"Let me go! How could you think—"

She shook her head, and her braid fell down over her face, covering one eye.

"I'll be damned if I can figure you out, decide what to think of you!" He let her go and walked past her over to the window.

The water in the radiator flowed quietly back and forth.

Nadya straightened her hair with trembling hands.

Shchagov lit a cigarette. He was breathing hard. Impossible to know what the woman wanted!

"Do you know," he asked, pausing between each word, "how dry hay burns?"

"Yes, I know," she answered dully. "It blazes up to the sky, and then it's a pile of ashes."

"Up to the sky!" he repeated.

"A pile of ashes," she said again.

"Tell me then—why do you keep on throwing lighted matches into dry hay?"

Could she have been? How could he have misunderstood her? After all, everyone wants to please someone sometimes, even by fits and starts. "Let's go out!" she cried. "Somewhere!"

"We're not going anywhere. We're going to stay right here."

He was smoking calmly now, holding his cigarette holder in one corner of his mouth. She liked the way he smoked.

"No, please, let's go somewhere!" she said again.

"Either here or nowhere," he said, cutting her short pitilessly. "I must tell you: I have a fiancée. I can't promise you anything. And—I can't be seen with you in the city."

47

THE RESURRECTION OF THE DEAD

Nadya and Shchagov had common ground in the fact that neither of them had been born in Moscow. The natives of the city Nadya met in graduate school had a poisonous air of superiority; "Muscovite patriotism," they called it. They thought Nadya a second-rate person, and more so than most other provincials because she was so bad at hiding her feelings.

Shchagov was a provincial, too, but he had knifed his

way through the Moscow setup as easily as an icebreaker through still water. Once she had heard a young graduate student who was out to humiliate Shchagov ask him with a proud lift of the head, "What backwater are you from?"

Shchagov had looked down on the student with a sort of lazy regret. Rocking quietly back and forth on his heels, he had answered, "You never had the chance to go there. From a province called the Front. A village called Foxhole."

It has long been known that our life stories do not follow an even course over the years. In every human being's life there is one period when he manifests himself most fully, feels most profoundly himself, and acts with the deepest effect on himself and on others. And whatever happens to that person from that time on, no matter how outwardly significant, it is all a letdown. We remember, get drunk on, play over and over in many different keys, sing over and over to ourselves that snatch of a song that sounded just once within us. For some, that period comes in childhood, and they stay children all their lives. For others it comes with first love, and these are the people who spread the myth that love comes only once. Those for whom it was the period of their greatest wealth, honor, or power will still in old age be mumbling with toothless gums of their lost grandeur. For Nerzhin, prison was such a time. For Shchagov, it was the war.

Shchagov had entered the war with longing and terror. He had been called up in the first month, and not released until 1946. And for the entire four years of the war, each morning he doubted if he would live till evening. He did not serve on important staffs, and he only left the front to enter the hospital. He retreated in 1941 from Kiev, and in 1942 along the Don. Although the war was going better in 1943 and '44, he spent those years in retreat, too—in '44 below Kovel. In roadside ditches, in washed-out trenches, among the ruins of burned houses he learned the value of a can of soup, an hour of quiet, the meaning of true friendship, of life itself.

The sufferings of Captain of Combat Engineers Shchagov could not be assuaged now, not in whole decades. He could think of people in only one way: either they were soldiers or they were not. Even in the anonymity of the Moscow streets he maintained this distinction: among all human beings, only soldiers were bound to be sincere and friendly.

Experience had taught him not to trust anyone who had not been tried in the fire of war.

After the war Shchagov had been left with no family; the house he had lived in had been bombed. His worldly goods amounted to the pack on his back and a suitcase full of German loot. True, to soften their return to civilian life, all demobilized officers were given twelve months' pay at "salary according to their rank"—wages for no work.

When he came back from the war, Shchagov, like many front-liners, was stunned. They returned—for a little while —better people than when they had left. They returned cleansed by the closeness of death, and the change in their country struck them all the harder because of that—a change which had occurred far behind the front lines, a kind of hardheartedness and bitterness, often a total lack of conscience, a chasm between starving poverty and the insolence of fattening wealth.

To hell with it! And, indeed, these former soldiers were still around; they walked the streets and rode the subways. But they were dressed in different clothes and no longer recognized each other. Somehow they dropped the old rules of the front and took up the rules of home. It was something to think about.

Shchagov did not ask questions. He was not one of those indefatigable people always on the lookout for universal justice. He understood that everything moves along just as it pleases, and that no one can stop it. You can choose only to jump on board or not. It was clear now that a general's daughter was predestined to have clean hands all her life solely by virtue of her birth; she would not be found working in a factory. Even if the secretary of a local Party organization got fired, it was impossible to imagine him ever working at a lathe. The piecework norms in factories were not being filled by those who thought them up, just as the men going into battle were not the same as those who wrote the orders for an attack.

All this, in fact, was nothing new on our planet. But it hurt individual people: it hurt Captain Shchagov that he had no right, after his faithful service, to participate in that very way of life for which he had fought. Now he had to fight for that right all over again, in bloodless battle, without a gun, without hand grenades; he had to process that right to live here through the accountant's office, and make it official with a formal seal.

And do it cheerfully.

Shchagov had gone to war before finishing his fifth year and getting his diploma, so now he had to catch up and push his way through to a degree of Candidate of Sciences. His specialty was theoretical mechanics, and he had planned, even before the war, to go into it as a scientific field. It had been easier then. Now he found himself in the midst of a universal outburst of love for science—any science, all science—which followed the rise in salaries.

All right! He gathered his strength for one more long attack. Little by little he sold off his German "souvenirs" at the bazaar.

He did not go in for fashionable clothes but wore exactly what he had been demobilized in: army jackboots, army trousers, a field shirt made of English wool and decorated with four ribbons and two wound stripes. They reminded Nadya of another front-line captain—Nerzhin.

Sensitive to every failure and criticism, Nadya felt like a little girl in the face of Shchagov's iron common sense. She had asked his advice. But she had lied to him, with a little girl's stubbornness, saying that Gleb was missing at the front.

Nadya herself had not noticed how or when she had let herself in for all this—the "extra" movie ticket, the joking embrace over the birthday present. But the minute Shchagov had come in tonight, even while he was flirting with Dasha, she had known he had come to see her, and that something was going to happen.

A minute before, she had been weeping inconsolably for her wrecked life. But after she tore up the ten-ruble note she had stood up renewed, ripe, ready for a new life, now.

She was not conscious of any contradiction in this.

Now Shchagov had recovered his usual deliberate poise. He had clearly let this girl know that she could not hope to marry him.

After hearing about his fiancée, Nadya walked restlessly around the room a minute, then came over and stood at the window, too, and silently drew on the pane with her finger.

He was sorry for her. He wanted to break the silence and explain things simply, with a directness he had long ago abandoned: a poor graduate student, without connections, without a future—what could he give her? And he had his right to a fair piece of the pie. He wanted to explain to her that though his fiancée lived in leisure, she was not particularly spoiled. She had a fine apartment in a restricted apartment house, where only the best people lived. There was a doorman, there were carpets on the floor—where could you see that these days? The whole problem would be solved in one blow. What could be better?

But he only thought these things; he did not say them out loud.

And Nadya, leaning her forehead against the glass and staring out into the night, finally answered him flatly, "That's fine! You have a fiancée. And I have a husband."

Shchagov turned around, amazed. "A husband! Isn't he missing?"

"No, not missing," Nadya almost whispered. How rashly she was giving herself away!

"You think he's still alive?"

"I saw him—today."

She had given herself away, but she would not cling to his neck like a schoolgirl.

It did not take Shchagov long to realize what he had been told. He did not think, as a woman might have, that Nadya had been abandoned. He knew that "missing in action" almost always meant a displaced person, and that if such a person was displaced again, this time in an eastward direction, it usually meant behind bars.

He took Nadya's elbow. "Gleb?"

"Yes," she said tonelessly, almost soundlessly.

"What is it? Is he in prison?"

"Yes."

"Well, well, well," Shchagov said, greatly relieved. He thought a minute, then went quickly out of the room.

Nadya was so overcome with shame and hopelessness that she had not caught the change in his voice.

Let him go. It was enough that she had said it all. Now she was all alone again with her honest burden.

The lamp filament barely glowed.

She walked heavily across the room and found the second cigarette in her coat pocket. She found a match and lit it. There was a strange satisfaction in the bitter taste, even though the smoke made her cough.

There was Shchagov's overcoat, lying across one of the chairs. What a hurry he'd been in! So scared he'd forgotten his overcoat.

It was very quiet; someone in the next room was playing Liszt's Etude in F Minor.

She had played that once when she was young, but had she understood anything about it? Her fingers had played the notes, but she had known nothing then of that word "*disperato.*" Desperate.

Leaning her forehead against the middle pane, she reached out and touched the other cold panes with the palms of her hands.

She stood like someone crucified on the black cross of the window.

There had been one tiny little warm spot in her life, and it was gone. And in only a minute or two she had resigned herself to that loss. She was her husband's wife again.

She stared out into the darkness, trying to make out the chimney of the Sailors' Rest. "*Disperato!*" Desperate! That impotent desperation. Trying to rise, dropping again. That insistent high D-flat—a woman's voice, straining, finding no answer.

A series of street lights led off somewhere into the darkness, as if into the future—a future to be lived without the will to live.

The Etude ended. A voice announced the time: 6 P.M.

Nadya had forgotten all about Shchagov, and he came back in without knocking.

He had a bottle and two glasses with him.

"Well, soldier's wife," he said heartily, "don't lose heart! Here, take a glass! If you've got a good head on your shoulders, there'll be happiness yet. Let's drink—*to the resurrection of the dead!*"

48

THE ARK

On Sunday, even in the sharashka, there was universal rest after 6 P.M. It was absolutely impossible to avoid this regrettable interruption in the prisoners' work, because on Sunday the free employees had only one shift on duty. This was a reprehensible tradition, against which, however, the majors and lieutenant colonels were powerless to struggle, because they themselves did not care to work on Sunday evenings. Only Iron Mask Mamurin, horrified by those empty evenings when the free employees had left, when they had rounded up and locked in all the all-too-human zeks, was left to stalk the empty corridors alone past the sealed doors, or else to languish in his cell between the washstand, the wardrobe, and the cot. Mamurin tried to have Number Seven work on Sunday evenings, too, but he could not overcome the conservatism of the officials of the special prison, who did not want to double the number of guards inside the zone.

So it happened that fourteen score prisoners—all reasonable considerations and prisoners' labor codes to the contrary—brazenly rested on Sunday evenings.

This period of respose was such that a person not initiated into that life might think it was a torture devised by the devil. The outer darkness and the special vigilance necessary on Sundays prevented the prison administration from authorizing recreation in the yard or movies in the barn. After a year of correspondence with all superior jurisdictions it had been decided that even musical instruments such as the accordion, the guitar, the balalaika, and the harmonica, not to speak of larger instruments, could not be allowed at the sharashka, since their sounds in unison might cover the noise of digging an escape tunnel through the masonry foundation. The security officers, through their informers, were incessantly trying to discover whether the prisoners had any homemade flutes or musical pipes; and for playing on a comb zeks were summoned to the office and special reports prepared. Still less, of course, could there be any talk of permitting radio receivers, or even the most primitive phonograph, in the prison dormitory.

True, the prisoners were allowed to use the prison library. But the special prison had no funds for book purchases or bookcases. They simply appointed Rubin the prison librarian—a post he had requested, thinking thereby to get hold of the best books for himself—and issued him, just once, a hundred or so worn-out volumes such as Turgenev's *Mumu*, Stasov's *Letters*, and Mommsen's *History of Rome*, with instructions that they be distributed among the prisoners. The prisoners had either read all these books long ago or else did not want to read them, and they begged reading material from the free employees, thus opening to the security officers a rich field for investigation and search.

For their rest and recreation the prisoners were allotted ten rooms on two floors, two hallways, an upper and a lower one, a narrow wooden staircase connecting the floors, and a toilet under the stairs. Their recreation consisted in being permitted, without restriction, to lie in their bunks and even to sleep if they could fall asleep amid the uproar; to sit on their bunks, there being no chairs; to walk around the room and from one room to the other, even in their underwear; to smoke in the halls as much as they wished; to argue about politics in the presence of informers; and to make use of the toilet without interference or limitation. Incidentally, those who had been imprisoned for long periods and who had had to relieve themselves on command twice a day valued this aspect of immortal freedom. The feeling of plenitude during the Sunday rest came from the fact that time belonged to them, not to the government. Therefore the rest period was appreciated as something real.

During this period the prisoners were locked in from outside by heavy iron doors, which no one opened, and no one entered, no one summoned them or picked on them. During these short hours the outer world could not penetrate inside to disturb anyone. This was what the rest period meant: that the entire outside world—the universe with its stars, the planet with its continents, the capital with its glitter and banquets and increased production drives—all had sunk into nonexistence, had been transformed into a black ocean, almost indistinguishable through the barred windows, beyond the pallid yellowish illumination in the zone.

Filled with the perpetual electric light of the MGB, the two-story ark of the former estate church, with its walls four and a half bricks thick, floated aimlessly and indifferently, faintly glowing, through that black sea of human destinies and confusion.

On Sunday night the moon could split in two, new Alps could arise in the Ukraine, the ocean could swallow Japan, or the universal deluge begin, but the prisoners, locked in their ark, would learn nothing about it until the morning check. Nor could telegrams from relatives reach them, or bothersome telephone calls, or news of a dying child, or a nighttime arrest.

Those who floated in the ark were weightless and had

weightless thoughts. They were neither hungry nor satiated.
They had no happiness and no fear of losing it. Their heads
were not filled with petty official calculations, intrigues, pro-
motions, and their shoulders were not burdened with concerns about housing, fuel, bread, and clothes for their
children. Love, which from time immemorial has been the
delight and the torment of humanity, was powerless to communicate to them its thrill or its agony. Their prison terms
were so long that no one even thought of the time when he
would go out into freedom. Men with exceptional intellect,
education, and experience, but too devoted to their families
to have much of themselves left over for their friends,
here belonged only to friends.

The light of bright bulbs reflected from the white ceilings,
from the whitewashed walls, flooded their lucid minds.

From here, from the ark, confidently plowing its way
through the darkness, the whole tortuous flow of accursed
History could easily be surveyed, as from an enormous
height, and yet at the same time one could see every detail,
every pebble on the river bed, as if one were immersed in
the stream.

In these Sunday evening hours solid matter and flesh no
longer reminded people of their earthly existence. The spirit
of male friendship and philosophy filled the sail-like arches
overhead.

Perhaps this was, indeed, that bliss which all the philosophers of antiquity tried in vain to define and teach to
others.

49

THE COMEDY ACT

In the semicircular room on the second floor, under the high,
arched ceiling above the altar, the atmosphere was particularly lively and conducive to thought.

By 6 p.m., all twenty-five men who lived in the room had
gathered there in an amicable mood. Some stripped to their

underwear as quickly as possible, getting rid of the prison garb they were fed up with, and flopped down on their bunks or scrambled like monkeys to upper ones. Others fell into their bunks without taking off their coveralls. Someone was standing on a top bunk, waving his arms and shouting to a friend across the room. Others merely sat or drummed their feet and looked around, anticipating the pleasure of the free hours ahead, uncertain how to spend them as pleasantly as possible.

Among the latter was Isaak Moiseyevich Kagan, the short, dark, shaggy "director of the battery room," as he was called. He was in a particularly good mood for coming into this bright, spacious room, since the battery room where he was holed up like a gopher fourteen hours a day was in a dark cellar with poor ventilation. However, he was satisfied with his work in the cellar, saying that in a camp he would have been dead long ago. He was never like those who boasted that in camp they had lived better than in freedom.

In freedom Isaak Kagan, who had never completed his engineering course, had been head of a stockroom of materials and parts. He had tried to live an obscure life and pass through the Era of Great Accomplishments sideways. He knew it was more peaceful and profitable to be quietly in charge of a stockroom. In his seclusion he concealed an almost fiery passion for gain, and this was what occupied him. Yet at the same time, as far as possible, even in the stockroom, he observed the laws of the Sabbath. He was not drawn toward any sort of political activity. But for some reason State Security had selected precisely this Kagan to be hitched to its chariot, and they had dragged him to closed rooms and conspiratorial assignations, insisting that he become a secret informer. That proposal was repulsive to Kagan. He had neither the candor nor the boldness—who did? —to tell them to their faces that what they were suggesting was vile. But with inexhaustible patience he kept silent, mumbled, dragged things out, demurred, fidgeted on his chair—and never did sign an agreement to work for them. It was not that he was incapable of informing. Without a tremor he would have informed on anyone who had harmed or humiliated him. But it would have nauseated him to inform on people who had been good or even indifferent to him.

But because of this stubbornness he was in the bad books

of State Security. One cannot protect oneself against everything in this world. There was talk among the people in his own stockroom. Someone cursed out a tool. Someone complained about supplies, someone else about planning. Isaak said nothing and went on writing out his invoices with his indelible pencil. But it became known—indeed, it had probably all been prearranged anyway—and everyone told on everyone else, and all of them received, under Section 58, Paragraph 10, ten years each. Kagan underwent five confrontations, but no one proved that he had said a word. If Section 58 had been tighter, they would have had to let Kagan go. But the interrogator knew that he had a last resort, which was Paragraph 12 of the same section: *failure* to inform. So it was for failure to inform that they gave Kagan the same astronomical ten years as the others.

Kagan got into the sharashka from camp thanks to his own remarkable wits. At a difficult moment in his life, when they had evicted him from the post of "deputy head of the barracks" and driven him out for timbercutting, he wrote a letter addressed to Chairman of the Council of Ministers, Comrade Stalin, to the effect that if he, Isaak Kagan, was given the chance by the government, he would undertake to invent a system for radio-controlled torpedo boats.

His calculation had been correct. No one in the government would have missed a heartbeat if Kagan had written that things were very bad for him and that he was appealing to them to save him. But the prospect of an important military invention brought the inventor immediately to Moscow. Kagan was taken to Mavrino, and various dignitaries wearing light-blue and dark-blue insignia came to him and urged him to hurry and put his bold technical idea into the form of a working design. However, now that he was beginning to get white bread and butter, Kagan did not rush. With great coolness he replied that he was not a torpedo expert himself so that, naturally, he needed one. In two months they got him a torpedo specialist—a zek. But at this point Kagan objected, quite reasonably, that he was not himself a ship's mechanic and naturally needed such a specialist, too. In another two months they brought him a marine technician— also a zek. Kagan then sighed and said that radio did not happen to be his field either. There were many radio engineers in Mavrino, and one of them was immediately assigned to Kagan. Kagan gathered them all together and imperturbably, in such a way that no one could accuse him of levity, declared: "Now, my friends, since you all have been gathered together, you may now, entirely by your own efforts, invent a system for directing torpedo boats by radio. It's not for me to stick my nose into it and advise you people, who are specialists, how best to do it." And sure enough, the three of them were sent to a naval sharashka, while Kagan meanwhile got himself a spot in the battery section, and everyone had become used to his being around.

Now Kagan was pestering Rubin, but from far enough away so that Rubin, who was lying on his bunk, could not kick him.

"Lev Grigorich," he said in his slow, unctuous way of speaking, "you are obviously losing your sense of social responsibility. The masses await entertainment. Only you can provide it, and here you've buried your nose in a book."

"Isaak, go to hell," said Rubin. He was already lying on his stomach, reading, his padded camp jacket thrown over his shoulders on top of his coveralls. The window between him and Sologdin was opened one Mayakovsky, and there was a pleasant draft of snowy fresh air.

"No, seriously, Lev Grigorich!" protested Kagan. "Everyone is anxious to hear your admirable 'The Crow and the Fox' again."

"And who turned me in to the 'protector'? It was you, wasn't it?" Rubin snarled.

The previous Sunday evening, to amuse the public, Rubin had composed a parody of the Krylov fable "The Crow and the Fox," full of camp jargon and innuendoes unfit for female ears. He had had to give five encores and had been lifted up on the prisoners' shoulders, and on Monday Major Myshin had called him in and proceeded to make a case against him for corrupting the morals of the enemies of the people. Statements from witnesses were taken. Rubin had to produce the manuscript of the parody, along with an explanatory note.

Today after lunch, Rubin had worked for two hours in the new room set aside for him. He had selected speech patterns and formants typical of the unidentified criminal, had fed them into the visible-speech apparatus, and hung up the wet strips to dry. He had arrived at some guesses and suspicions, but he felt no inspiration as he watched Smolosidov putting a seal on the door when they left the room. After

this, he had returned to the semicircular room amid a
stream of zeks like a herd returning home to its village.

As always, under his pillow, under his mattress, under
his bunk, and with the food in his night stand, lay a half-
dozen or so of the most interesting books he had received
in parcels—interesting, that is, to him alone, which was why
they had not disappeared: Chinese-French, Latvian-Hungar-
ian, Russian-Sanskrit dictionaries, Capek's *War with the
Newts*, a collection of stories by extremely progressive Japanese writers, *For Whom the Bell Tolls* by Hemingway—
whom they had stopped translating in Russia because he
was no longer progressive—two monographs on the Encyclopedists, *Joseph Fouché* by Stefan Zweig in German, and
a novel by Upton Sinclair which had never been translated
into Russian. (The various foreign-language dictionaries reflected the fact that for two years Rubin had been at work
on the grandiose project, in the spirit of Engels and Marr, of
deriving all words of all languages from the concepts of
"hand" and "manual labor"—unaware that the previous
night the Coryphaeus of Philology had raised the ideological
guillotine over Marr's head.)

There was an incredibly large number of books in the
world, essential and important books, and the thirst to read
them all never left Rubin time to write one of his own.
Even now he was ready to read on and on till long after
midnight without a thought to the working day tomorrow.
But in the evenings his thirst for dispute and his wit and elo-
quence were especially intense, and little was needed to call
them into the service of society. There were prisoners in the
sharashka who did not trust Rubin, regarding him as an
informer because of his orthodox views, which he did not
hide; but there was no one who was not delighted by his
entertainments.

The recollection of "The Crow and the Fox," adapted into
underworld slang, was so alive that now, following Kagan's
example, many in the room began loudly demanding some
new comedy act of Rubin. And when Rubin sat up, gloomy
and bearded, and clambered out from under the shelter of the
bunk above him, almost all the zeks dropped what they were
doing and prepared to listen. Only Dvoyetyosov, on his upper
bunk, went on cutting his toenails in such a way that they
flew far and wide, and Adamson, under his blanket, went
on reading without turning around. Zeks from other rooms

crowded at the doors, among them the Tatar Bulatov, in horn-rimmed glasses, who cried out harshly, "Yes, please! Please!"

Rubin had no desire to amuse a crowd which included men who scorned everything dear to him. He knew, too, that a new comedy performance on his part would inevitably mean new unpleasantness on Monday: questioning by "Shishkin-Myshkin," intimidation. But being that proverbial hero who for the sake of a witticism would not spare his own father, Rubin pretended to frown, looked around solemnly, and said in the quiet which followed:

"Comrades! I am amazed by your frivolity. How can there be talk of a comedy act when among us there are blatant criminals still at large? No society can flourish without a fair system of justice. I consider it necessary to begin our evening with a small trial. As a drill."

"Right!"

"Whom are we going to try?"

"Doesn't matter—he's right anyway!" the voices resounded.

"Amusing! Very amusing!" Sologdin egged him on, settling himself more comfortably. Today, as never before, he had earned his rest, and he wanted his rest period to be entertaining.

Cautious Kagan, feeling that the fun he had initiated threatened to get out of hand, quietly moved back to the wall and sat on his bunk.

"You will find out whom we are going to try in the course of the judicial deliberations," explained Rubin, who had not yet thought it out himself. "I, if you please, shall be the prosecutor, inasmuch as the office of prosecutor has always aroused very special feelings in me." (Everyone in the sharashka knew that Rubin had had prosecutors who had hated him personally, and that for five years he had been single-handedly fighting both the General and the Military Prosecutors.) "Gleb! You be the court chairman. Choose a troika of judges, objective, without personal connections—in a word, completely subject to your will."

Nerzhin, dropping his shoes to the floor, sat up in his upper bunk. With every passing hour he became more detached from his morning's meeting and more a part of the ordinary prisoner's world. He could respond to Rubin's challenge. He moved to the wooden railing of the bed, put his

legs between the bars, and sat there as if on a tribune raised
above the room.

"Well, who will be my court assessors? Climb up here!"

There were many prisoners in the room, all of whom
wanted to hear the trial, but no one ventured to volunteer
as an assessor—either out of cautiousness or fear of appearing ridiculous. On the top bunk next to Nerzhin's the vacuum
specialist Zemelya lay reading the morning newspaper. Nerzhin grabbed the paper.

"Smiley! Enough enlightenment for you! If you're not
careful, you'll get involved in world domination. Sit up and
be an assessor."

There was applause from below.

"Come on, Zemelya, come on!"

Zemelya was easygoing and could not hold out for long.
Smiling awkwardly, he hung his balding head through the
bars of the upper bunk. "It's a great honor to be chosen
by the people! But, friends, I haven't studied, I am incapable—"

There was friendly laughter. "None of us is capable! None
of us has studied for it!" And that was his answer and his
election as an assessor.

On Nerzhin's other side lay Ruska Doronin. He had undressed and was entirely hidden under his blanket, with a
pillow over his head in addition. He was rapturously happy
and did not want to hear or see or be seen. He was there only
in body; his thoughts and his heart had followed Clara, who
had now gone home. Just before leaving she had finished
weaving her basket for the New Year's tree and had secretly
given it to Ruska. He was now holding this basket under the
blanket and kissing it.

Seeing that it was useless to bother Ruska, Nerzhin looked
around for a second candidate.

"Amantai! Amantai!" he called to Bulatov. "Come join
the court."

Bulatov beamed.

"I'd come, but there's nowhere to sit there! I'll be the
bailiff here at the door."

Khorobrov, who had already given Adamson and two
others haircuts, and who was giving a trim right now to a
new customer sitting naked to the waist in the middle of the
room, shouted out: "Why do you want any other assessor?

The verdict, after all, is settled, isn't it? Make do with just one."

Nerzhin agreed. "Right! Why keep a parasite? But where is the accused? Bailiff! Bring in the accused! I ask for quiet!"

He knocked his long cigarette holder on the bunk. Conversation ceased.

"Let's have the trial!" voices demanded. The public was sitting and standing.

Below the court chairman, Potapov's lugubrious voice intoned: "If I ascend to Heaven, You are there. If down to Hell, You are there. And if I should descend to the depths of the sea, there, too, Your right hand will reach me!" (Potapov had studied religion in school and his precise engineer's mind had retained the text of the Orthodox catechism.)

Underneath the assessor, there was the loud clinking of a spoon stirring sugar in a glass.

"Valentulya!" Nerzhin cried threateningly. "How many times have you been told not to clink your spoon?"

"Put him on trial!" Bulatov bellowed, and several ready hands dragged Pryanchikov out of the half-darkness of the lower bunk into the center of the room.

"Quit it!" said Pryanchikov, breaking away angrily. "I'm sick of prosecutors! I'm sick of your trials! What right does one person have to try another? Ha, ha! Very amusing! I despise you, my friend!" he shouted at the court chairman. "Go fuck yourself!"

By the time Nerzhin had assembled his court, Rubin had thought out the whole performance. His dark brown eyes shone with the light of discovery. With a broad gesture he took mercy on Pryanchikov.

"Let him go! Valentulya, with his love of world justice, can perfectly well be the government's lawyer. Give him a chair!"

In every joke there is an elusive moment when it either becomes banal and offensive or else catches on. Rubin, who had thrown a blanket over his shoulder like a mantle, climbed up on a night table in his stocking feet and directed his words to the chairman:

"State Counselor of Justice! The defendant has declined to appear in court, so we will judge him *in absentia*. I ask you to begin."

Among the crowd at the doors stood the red-mustached janitor Spiridon. His intelligent face, flabby in the cheeks, lined with many wrinkles, showed both severity and amusement. He glared sullenly at the court.

Behind Spiridon, his long, refined, waxen face crowned by a woolen cap, stood Professor Chelnov.

Nerzhin announced in an unnaturally shrill voice: "Attention, comrades! I declare the session of the military tribunal of the Mavrino sharashka to be open. We are hearing the case of—?"

"Olgovich, Igor Svyatoslavich," the prosecutor prompted.

Seizing the idea, Nerzhin in a monotonous nasal tone pretended to read:

"We are hearing the case of Olgovich, Igor Svyatoslavich, Prince of Novgorod-Seversky and Putivilsk, year of birth approximately—hell, Secretary, why approximately? Attention! In view of the absence of a written text, the indictment will be read aloud by the prosecutor."

50

THE TRAITOR PRINCE

Rubin began to speak with ease and fluency, as if he were really reading a sheet of paper. He had been tried four times, and the juridical phrases were imprinted in his memory.

"The concluding charge of the case under investigation, number five million slant three million six hundred fifty-one thousand nine hundred seventy-four, indicting Olgovich, Igor Svyatoslavich.

"Organs of State Security have arrested the accused in the said case, Olgovich, I. S. The investigation has established that Olgovich, who was a military leader of the brilliant Russian Army, with the rank of prince, in the post of troop commander, turned out to be a foul traitor to his country. His traitorous activities consisted of voluntarily surrendering and becoming a prisoner of the accursed enemy of our people, Khan Konchak. In addition, he surrendered his own son, Vladimir Igoryevich, as well as his brother and his nephew, and the whole troop with all its men, armaments, and inventoried material property.

"His traitorous activity was manifest from the very beginning, when, duped by an eclipse of the sun, a provocation arranged by the reactionary clergy, he failed to direct mass political propaganda work among his own troops, who were going off 'to drink out of their helmets from the River Don'— not to speak of the unhygienic state of the River Don in those days before the introduction of double chlorination. Instead, the accused limited himself, when he was already in sight of the enemy forces, to a completely irresponsible appeal to his armies:

> 'Brothers, this is what we sought, so let us attack!'
> (Indictment, Volume 1, Sheet 36.)

"The fatal significance to our country of the defeat of the united Novgorod-Seversky-Kursk-Putivilsk-Rylsk forces has best been characterized in the words of the Great Prince of Kiev, Svyatoslav:

> 'God let me exhaust the pagans, but I could not hold back that youth.'
> (Indictment, Volume 1, Sheet 88.)

"The mistake of the naïve Svyatoslav, a consequence of his class blindness, has been that he ascribes the bad organization of the whole campaign and the dispersal of the Russian military efforts only to 'the youth' of the accused, not realizing that we are concerned here with a far-reaching and calculated treason.

"The criminal himself succeeded in evading investigation and trial, but the witness Borodin, Aleksandr Porfiryevich, and a witness who wished to remain anonymous and who henceforth is herein named 'The Author of the Lay,' have by irrefutable testimony exposed the foul role of Prince I. S. Olgovich, first in the conduct of the battle itself, which was accepted under conditions unfavorable for the Russian command:

"Meteorological:

> 'The winds are blowing, carrying on them arrows,
> Strewing them on the regiments of Igor—'

"And tactical:

> 'From all sides the enemy approached,
> Surrounding our forces from every direction.'
> (*Ibid.*, Volume 1, Sheets 123, 124,
> testimony of the Author of the Lay.)

"Yet even more foul was his conduct and that of his princely scion in captivity. The living conditions in which both were maintained in so-called captivity show that they were in the highest good graces of Khan Konchak, which fact objectively constituted a reward to them from the Polovtsian command for the criminal surrender of their troops.

"Thus, for example, the testimony of the witness Borodin established that in captivity Prince Igor had his own horse, and undoubtedly other horses:

> 'If you wish, take any horse you like!'
> (*Ibid.*, Volume 1, Sheet 233.)

"Khan Konchak said, furthermore, to Prince Igor:

> 'You consider yourself a captive here.
> But are you really living as a captive,
> or are you rather my guest?'

"And further:

> 'Admit it—do captives live like this?'
> (*Ibid.*, Volume 1, Sheet 300.)

"The Polovtsian Khan discloses the cynicism underlying his relations with the traitor prince:

> 'For your courage and for your daring,
> You, my prince, are beloved by me.'
> (*Ibid.*, Volume 3, Sheet 5.)

"A more careful investigation has disclosed that these cynical relations existed long before the battle on the River Kayal:

> 'You have always been beloved by me.'
> (*Ibid.*, Sheet 14, evidence of the witness Borodin.)

"And further:

> 'Not your enemy, but your loyal ally,
> And reliable friend, and your brother,
> I would like to be. . . .'
> (*Ibid.*)

"All this objectively characterizes the accused as an active accomplice of Khan Konchak, as a long-time Polovtsian agent and spy.

"On the basis of the above, Olgovich, Igor Svyatoslavich, born 1151, a native of the city of Kiev, of Russian nationality, non-Party, previously unconvicted, a citizen of the U.S.S.R., by profession a military leader, serving in the position of troop commander with the rank of prince, decorated with the order of Viking in the First Degree, the Red Sun, and the medal of the Gold Shield, is accused of the following:

"That he willfully executed vile treason against his country, combined with sabotage, espionage, and collaboration over a period of many years with the Polovtsian Khanate.

"In other words he is guilty of crimes provided for in Sections 58-1B, 58-6, 58-9, and 58-11 of the Criminal Code of the Russian Socialist Federated Soviet Republic.

"To the accusations herewith presented Olgovich has confessed his guilt, and has been exposed by testimony of witnesses, and also in a poem and an opera.

"Guided by Section 268 of the Criminal Procedural Code of the Russian Socialist Federated Soviet Republic, the said case has been sent to the prosecutor for trial of the accused."

Rubin took a breath and solemnly looked at the zeks. Carried by a torrent of imagination, he had been unable to stop. Laughter rolled through the room and to the doors, urging him on. He had already said more and sharper things than he would have cared to in the presence of several informers and other spiteful individuals.

Spiridon, with his coarse grayish-red hair which, uncut and uncombed, grew down on his forehead, around his ears and the back of his neck, did not smile once. Frowning, he examined the court. A fifty-year-old Russian, he was hearing for the first time about that prince of long ago who had been taken prisoner; yet in the familiar environment of the court and the unassailable self-assurance of the prosecutor he relived once more everything that he had felt himself. He sensed all the injustice of the prosecutor's conclusions, and all the anguish of this wretched prince.

"In view of the absence of the accused and of the inconvenience of questioning the witnesses," Nerzhin interrupted in the same measured, nasal tone, "let us proceed to the summations of the opposing sides. The prosecutor again has the floor."

Nerzhin looked to Zemelya for confirmation.

"Of course, of course," nodded the assessor, who was agreeable to anything.

"Comrade judges," Rubin intoned gloomily, "I have but little to add to that chain of dreadful accusations, to that dirty jumble of crimes, which has been revealed before your eyes. In the first place, I would like to reject once and for all the widespread rotten opinion that a wounded man has the moral right to let himself be taken prisoner. That's basically not our view, comrades! And all the more so in the case of Prince Igor. They tell us that he was wounded on the battlefield. But who can prove this now, 765 years later? Has there been preserved any official evidence of a wound, signed by his divisional military surgeon? In any case, there is no such official attestation in the indictment file, comrade judges!"

Amantai Bulatov took off his glasses, and without their mischievous gleam his eyes were utterly sad.

He, Pryanchikov, Potapov, and many others among those present had been imprisoned for this very same "treason to the country": "voluntary" surrender.

"And furthermore," thundered the prosecutor, "I would like to point out the repulsive conduct of the accused in the Polovtsian camp. Prince Igor thought nothing at all about his country, only about his wife:

> 'You are alone, my dearest dove,
> You are alone. . . .'

"Upon analysis this is entirely comprehensible to us, for his Yaroslavna was a young wife, his second, and he couldn't trust such a woman very far. In fact, Prince Igor appears to us a self-seeking opportunist! Whom did the Polovtsian dancers dance for? I ask you. For him, naturally. And his repulsive offspring promptly entered into sexual union with Konchak's daughter, even though marriage with foreigners has been categorically forbidden to our citizens by the appropriate competent authorities! And this at a time of extreme tension in Soviet-Polovtsian relations, when—"

"Wait a minute!" said shaggy Kagan from his bed. "How does the prosecutor know there was Soviet authority in Russia in those years?"

"Bailiff! Remove that bribed agent!" Nerzhin ordered. But before Bulatov could make a move, Rubin accepted the challenge lightly.

"If you don't mind, I will reply! Dialectical analysis of the texts provides conclusive proof of that. Read what the Author of the Lay writes: 'Red banners wave in Putivl.'

"That seems clear enough, doesn't it? The noble Prince Vladimir Galitsky, Chief of the Putivl District Military Commissariat, was assembling a people's home guard, led by Skula and Yeroshka, for the defense of his native city. Prince Igor at this time was contemplating the naked legs of the Polovtsian women. I qualify this by stating that we all sympathize with this preoccupation of his, but after all Konchak offered him the choice of 'any one of the beauties'— so why didn't the bastard take one? Who among us will believe that a man would refuse a woman? And then the ultimate cynicism of the accused is revealed in his so-called escape from captivity and his *voluntary* return to his homeland. Who will believe that a man who has been offered 'the horse of his choice and gold' and also 'any one of the beauties' would voluntarily return to his homeland and give up all that? How could that be?"

This was precisely the question which prisoners who returned had been asked at investigations. Spiridon, too, had been asked, "Why did you return to your country if you were not recruited by the enemy?"

"Here there can be one and only one interpretation: Prince Igor was recruited by Polovtsian intelligence and sent back to assist in the disintegration of the Kievan state! Comrade judges! In me, as in you, noble indignation boils. I demand in the name of humanity that the son-of-a-bitch be hanged! But since capital punishment has been abolished, let him stew for twenty-five and give him five more on the horns! And let the court's further determination be to remove the opera *Prince Igor* from the stage as being totally amoral, popularizing treasonable attitudes among our youth! And let there be brought to justice the witness in the said trial, Borodin, A. P., who must be arrested as a preventive measure. And let there also be brought to justice those aris-

tocrats: (1) Rimsky and (2) Korsakov. Because if they had
not completed the said opera it would never have reached
the stage. I am done!" Rubin jumped down heavily from the
night table. The burlesque had suddenly gone stale.

No one laughed.

Pryanchikov, not waiting to be invited, rose from his
chair and in the deep silence said vaguely, "*Tant pis*, gentlemen! *Tant pis!* Are we living in the twentieth century or the
Stone Age? What is the meaning of treason? In the age of
atomic disintegration! Of semiconductors! Of electronic
brains! Who has the right to judge another human being,
gentlemen? Who has the right to deprive him of freedom?"

"Pardon me, is that the defense?" Professor Chelnov
politely spoke out, as everyone turned in his direction. "I
would like first of all to add to the prosecutor's arguments
certain facts which my colleague has kept out of sight,
and—"

"Of course, of course, Vladimir Erastovich!" agreed Nerzhin. "We are always for the prosecution and against the
defense, and we are ready to permit any violation of judicial
rules. Proceed!"

A restrained smile appeared on the professor's lips. He
spoke quietly, yet he could be readily heard because his
audience listened to him with respect. His faded eyes seemed
to stare past those present, as if he were seeing before him
the pages of the chronicles. The wool ball on his cap emphasized the sharpness of his face and gave him an air of
watchfulness.

"I would like to say," said the mathematics professor,
"that, even before he was named a military leader, Prince
Igor would have been exposed the first time he filled out
our special security questionnaire. His mother was a Polovtsian, the daughter of a Polovtsian prince. He himself was
half-Polovtsian by blood. He had been in alliance with the
Polovtsians for many years. He had already been 'an ally
true and a reliable friend' to Konchak before this campaign! In 1180, when he was defeated by the Monomakh
family, he escaped from them in the same boat as Khan
Konchak. Later on, Svyatoslav and Ryurik Rostislavich
called on Igor to join the all-Russian campaigns against the
Polovtsians, but Igor declined under the pretext of ice—'The
earth will be covered with ice.' Perhaps because at that time
Svoboda Konchakovna, Konchak's daughter, was already
engaged to Vladimir Igoryevich? In the year 1185, which

we are considering now, who was it, after all, who helped Igor escape from captivity? A Polovtsian! The Polovtsian Ovlur, whom Igor later 'made a nobleman.' And Konchak's daughter eventually gave Igor a grandson. For concealing these facts I propose that the Author of the Lay also be brought to justice, and also the musical critic, Stasov, who overlooked the treasonable tendencies in Borodin's opera, and then, finally, Count Musin-Pushkin, since he was undoubtedly an accomplice in the burning of the only manuscript of the Lay. It is clear that someone covered the tracks for someone else's advantage."

Having finished, Chelnov stepped back. That same faint smile was still on his lips.

They were silent.

"But isn't there someone to defend the accused? After all, the man certainly needs a defense!" Isaak Kagan demanded indignantly.

"He doesn't deserve a defense, the bastard!" Dvoyetyosov shouted.

"This comes under Section 1B. Up against the wall with him!"

Sologdin frowned. What Rubin had said was very amusing, and he respected Chelnov's knowledge. But Prince Igor was the pride of Russian history, a representative of the knighthood of a most glorious period; therefore he should not, even indirectly, be ridiculed. Sologdin had a bad taste in his mouth.

"No, no, if you don't mind, I'm going to speak in his defense anyway!" said the emboldened Isaak, circling the room with a sly look. "Comrade judges! As an honorable government lawyer I concur without reservation in all the conclusions of the state prosecutor." He drawled his words. "My conscience tells me that Prince Igor ought to be not only hanged but also quartered. True, this is the third year there has been no death penalty in our humane legislation, and we are forced to substitute something else in its place. However, it is incomprehensible why the prosecutor is so suspiciously lenient. Obviously the prosecutor ought to be investigated himself. Why has he stopped two steps short of the maximum penalty and settled for twenty-five years of hard labor? After all, there is a punishment in our Criminal Code which is the final penalty, a punishment far more dreadful than twenty-five years of hard labor."

Isaak paused, so as to make as big an impression as possible.

"What is it, Isaak?" they shouted at him impatiently. And unhurriedly, with mock innocence, he replied: "Section 20-Z, Paragraph a."

Of all those present, for all their great prison experience, no one had ever heard of such a section. How did this legalist know a thing like that?

"And what does it say?" They screamed indecent suggestions at him from all sides: "Castrate him?"

"Almost, almost," Isaak confirmed imperturbably. "It is, in fact, spiritual castration. Section 20-Z, Paragraph a, provides that one is declared an enemy of the workers and expelled from the boundaries of the U.S.S.R.! He can die in the West as far as we are concerned. I have nothing more to say."

Modestly, with his head to one side, small and shaggy, he went back to his bunk.

An explosion of laughter shook the room.

"What? What?" roared Khorobrov, choking, and his customer jumped from the pull of the clippers. "Expelled? Exiled? Is there really such a section?"

"Have them give him the maximum punishment! Have them give him the maximum punishment!" they shouted.

Spiridon smiled shrewdly.

They all talked at once and then dispersed.

Rubin again lay on his stomach, trying to concentrate on a Mongolian-Finnish dictionary. He cursed his foolish way of becoming the center of attention, and he was ashamed of the role he had played.

51

WINDING UP THE TWENTIETH YEAR

Adamson, propped on his rumpled pillow, was still devouring *The Count of Monte Cristo*. He lay with his back to what was going on in the room. No courtroom comedy could amuse him now. He only turned his head slightly when Chelnov was speaking, because what he said was new to him.

In twenty years of exile, investigation prisons, solitary cells, camps, and sharashkas, Adamson, who had once been a forceful and responsive orator, had become unfeeling, indifferent to his own sufferings and those of people around him.

The trial just enacted in the room was dedicated to the fate of prisoners of war—Soviet soldiers first ineptly led into captivity by their generals and then coldheartedly abandoned by Stalin to be ravaged by hunger, POWs of the wave of 1945 and 1946. Adamson could admit the tragedy of what had happened to them, and yet this was only one wave of prisoners, one of many and not the most remarkable. The POWs were interesting because they had seen many foreign countries, and were therefore automatically "living false witnesses," as Potapov jokingly called them. But nonetheless their wave was gray, drab. They were hapless victims of war and not men who had voluntarily chosen political struggle as their battleground in life.

Every zek wave arrested by the NKVD, like every human generation on earth, had its history, its heroes.

It was difficult for one generation to understand another.

It seemed to Adamson that these people who were in the room were not to be compared with those giants who, like himself, had voluntarily chosen exile on the Yenisei instead of retracting what they had said at Party meetings, thereby holding onto comfort and prosperity. Every one of them had had that choice. They had not accepted the perverting and disgracing of the Revolution but were ready to sacrifice themselves for its purification. But this tribe of young strangers, thirty years after the October Revolution, had come into the cell with peasant oaths and openly said blasphemous things for which they would have been shot during the Civil War.

So Adamson, who was not personally hostile to any of the ex-POWs, in general did not recognize the species.

Furthermore, as he assured himself, he had long since lost interest in prisoners' arguments, confessions, and eyewitness stories. He had lost whatever curiosity he might have had as a youth about what was being said in the other corner of the cell. He had lost interest in work, too. He was not in touch with his family because he was not a native of Moscow, never had visits, and the censored letters which reached him at the sharashka had involuntarily been drained of all spontaneity as they were being written. He did not waste his time on newspapers—their contents became clear to him after a glance at their headlines. He could not listen to musical broadcasts more than an hour a day, and his nerves could not stand the spoken word on the radio, any more than books which told lies. And though somewhere deep inside him he maintained a lively and indeed an acutely sensitive interest in the world and in the fate of that doctrine to which he had dedicated his life, outwardly he had trained himself to be totally indifferent to everything around him. And so it happened that Adamson, who had not been shot in good time, or starved to death, or poisoned, now loved not those books which burned with truth but those which amused him and helped shorten his endless prison terms.

No, they had not read *Monte Cristo* in the Yenisei taiga in 1929, just twenty years ago. On the Angara, in the distant village of Doshchany, to which a two-hundred-mile sleigh road cut through the taiga, they had gathered other exiles from settlements seventy miles beyond—under the pretext of a New Year's party—for a conference to discuss the international situation and internal state of the country. The temperature went to 58 below Fahrenheit. The temporary iron stove in the corner, which had been given to the exiles because the regular stove was wrecked, could by no means heat the spacious Siberian hut. The walls of the cabin were frozen through. Now and then in the quiet of the night the wall logs cracked like rifle shots.

The conference was opened by Satanevich with a report on Party policy in the village. He took off his cap, freeing his wavy black hair, but he kept on his sheepskin coat with his English phrase book forever sticking out of the pocket. "One must understand the enemy," he would explain. Satanevich always played at being the leader. He was later shot, it appeared, during the strike at the Vorkuta camps. But, alas, the more passionately his and other reports were discussed, the more the unity of this frail gathering of exiles disintegrated. Not just two and three opinions emerged, but as many as there were people. In the morning, wearily, the official part of the conference ended without reaching a resolution.

Then they ate and drank from government-issue crockery, and there were pine branches for decoration, covering the gouges in the table and the torn cloth. The thawing sprigs smelled of snow and tar and pricked the hands. They drank home-distilled vodka.

During the toasts they took an oath that no one present would ever sign a renunciation or a capitulation.

They sang glorious revolutionary songs: "Varshavyanka," "Over the World Our Banner Is Floating," "The Black Baron."

And they went on arguing about anything they happened to think of.

Rosa, a worker from the Kharkhov Tobacco Factory, had sat on a feather comforter. She had brought it from the Ukraine to Siberia, and she was very proud of it. She smoked one cigarette after another and contemptuously brushed back her bobbed curls. "I can't stand the intelligentsia! It disgusts me with all its fine points and complexities. Human psychology is much simpler than prerevolutionary writers liked to imagine it. Our problem is to free humanity from its spiritual overload!"

Somehow they got on the subject of jewelry for women. One of the exiles, Patrushev, a former Odessa prosecutor whose bride, as it happened, had recently come from Russia, inquired challengingly, "Why do you want to keep our future society poor? Why shouldn't I dream of the time every girl can wear pearls? When every man can adorn his beloved's head with a tiara?"

What an uproar there had been! With what outrage they had lashed out with quotations from Marx and Plekhanov, from Campanella and Feuerbach!

Our future society! They spoke of it so easily!

The sun of the new year 1930 rose, and everyone went out to admire it. It was a bracing, frosty morning with the pillars of pink smoke rising straight up to the skies. On the white expanses of the Angara the peasant women drove the cattle to drink at a hole in the ice near a bank of fir trees. There were no male peasants or horses; they had all been driven out for timbering work.

Two decades passed. The timeliness and relevance of those toasts had bloomed and faded. They had shot those who held firm, and they had shot those who capitulated. Only in Adamson's lonely head, intact within the greenhouse shelter of the sharashka, did there still grow, like an invisible tree, a consciousness of those years.

Adamson looked at the book but did not read it.

Then Nerzhin sat down on the edge of his bunk.

Nerzhin and Adamson had become acquainted three years before in the Butyrskaya cell in which Potapov was also imprisoned. Adamson was then finishing his first ten-year term, and he astonished the other prisoners in the cell with his icy authority, his deep-rooted prison skepticism, while he himself was secretly living in the insane hope of returning soon to his family.

They had gone their different ways. Adamson, through negligence, had become freed, but only long enough for his family to move and settle in Sterlitamak where the police had agreed to register him. As soon as his family had moved, they arrested him again and subjected him to a single interrogation: had he really been in exile from 1929 to 1934 and imprisoned since then? Having established that this was the case, that he had already served his term, had even served more than his full sentence, the Special Session thereupon handed him another ten years. The leadership of the sharashkas had learned through the big all-Union prisoners' card file about the incarceration of their former employee and promptly pulled him out again and thrust him into the sharashkas. Adamson had been brought to Mavrino, where, as everywhere in the prisoners' world, he immediately met old acquaintances, including Nerzhin and Potapov. And when all three had stood and smoked on the staircase, it seemed to Adamson that he had never returned to freedom for a year, that he had not seen his family, that he had not rewarded his wife with another daughter during that period, that this all had been a pitiless dream, and that the only firm reality in the world was prison.

Now Nerzhin sat down to invite Adamson to his birthday party, for it had been decided to celebrate his birthday. Adamson belatedly congratulated Nerzhin and, looking at him sideways, asked who would be there. Adamson was not at all pleased to have to pull on his coveralls and ruin a Sunday which was being spent so marvelously, in just his underwear, to have to put down his diverting book and go to some sort of birthday party. The main thing was that he had no hope of passing the time agreeably because it was almost certain that a political argument would break out, and that it would be, as always, fruitless and unrewarding, yet impossible not to get involved in. At the same time it would be impossible really to be involved in it, because he could as easily display his wife naked to the "young" prisoners as disclose to them his own deeply held and so often outraged thoughts.

Nerzhin told him who would be there. In the sharashka only Rubin was truly close to Adamson, yet Adamson still had the task of dressing him down for today's farce, which was unworthy of a true Communist. On the other hand, Adamson did not like Sologdin or Pryanchikov.

Still, there was nothing else to do. Adamson accepted. Nerzhin told him that the celebration would begin between Potapov's and Pryanchikov's bunks in half an hour, as soon as Potapov finished preparing the pudding.

As they talked, Nerzhin found out what Adamson was reading and said, "I had a chance to read *Monte Cristo* in prison once, too, but not to the end. I observed that while Dumas tries to create a feeling of horror, he portrays the Château d'If as a rather benevolent prison. Not to mention his missing such nice details as the carrying of the latrine bucket from the cell daily, about which Dumas with the ignorance of a free person says nothing. You can figure out why Dantès could escape. For years no one searched the cell, whereas cells are supposed to be searched every week. So the tunnel was not discovered. And then they never changed the guard detail, whereas experience tells us that guards should be changed every two hours so one can check on the other. At the Château d'If they didn't enter the cells and look around for days at a time. They didn't even have any peepholes, so d'If wasn't a prison at all, it was a seaside resort. They even left a metal bowl in the cell, with which Dantès could dig through the floor. Then, finally, they trustingly sewed a dead man up in a bag without burning his flesh with a red-hot iron in the morgue and without running him through with a bayonet at the guardhouse. Dumas ought to have tightened up his premises instead of darkening the atmosphere."

Nerzhin never read a book simply for entertainment. He was looking for allies or enemies and would deliver a precise judgment of every book he read, which he then tried to force on others.

Adamson knew this oppressive habit of his. He listened to him without raising his head from the pillow, looking at him calmly through his rectangular spectacles.

"All right, I'll come," he said and, stretching out more comfortably, he went back to his reading.

52

PETTY PRISON MATTERS

Nerzhin went to help Potapov prepare the pudding. During his hungry years in German captivity and Soviet prisons, Potapov had learned that eating is not something shameful, to be despised, but one of life's most delectable experiences, revealing the very essence of our existence.

> "I love to tell the hours
> By lunch and tea
> And dinner"

recited this remarkable Russian high-voltage engineer, who had devoted his life to transformers with capacities of thousands of kilowatts.

And since Potapov was one of those engineers whose hands are as quick as their heads, he soon became an excellent cook: in the *Kriegsgefangenlageren* he used to bake an orange cake out of nothing but potato peels, and at the sharashka he specialized in desserts and confections.

Right now he was fussing over two night tables that had been pushed together in the aisle between his own bunk and Pryanchikov's. The upper mattresses cut off the ceiling light to create a pleasant twilight. Because of the semicircular shape of the room, with bunks set along the radii, the aisle was narrow at the hub, then broadened out toward the window. The massive window sill, four and a half bricks thick, was also being put to use by Potapov. Cans, plastic boxes, and bowls were laid out everywhere. Potapov was solemnly, ritually, beating condensed milk, chocolate, and two eggs (some of these ingredients having come from Rubin, who often received parcels from home and always shared them) into something which had no name in human language. He muttered at Nerzhin for being late and ordered him to improvise two "goblets," having already collected a thermos top, two small chemical beakers, and two containers, like those used for ice cream on the outside, which he had glued together out of waxed paper. Nerzhin proposed to borrow two shaving mugs and rinse them out with hot water.

A serene Sunday repose had settled over the semicircular room. Some zeks sat chatting with comrades lying in their bunks; others read, while around them scraps of conversation flew back and forth. Others lay silently, their hands behind their heads, staring up at the white ceiling.

All sounds united in a single dissonance.

The vacuum specialist, Zemelya, luxuriated on his upper bunk: he lay in his shorts, stroking his hairy chest, smiling his invariably good-natured smile, as he told a story to Mishka Mordvin two aisles away.

"If you want to know the truth, it all began with a half-kopeck."

"How was that?"

"Well, before, in 1926, in 1928—when you were little—there was a sign over every cashier's window: 'Demand your change down to the half-kopeck!' There was a real coin, too—a half-kopeck piece. Cashiers handed it out without a word. This was the NEP time, just like peacetime."

"There was no war?"

"That's right, no war—can you imagine? That was before all the wars. Peacetime. Yes. During the NEP, people in state institutions worked six hours, not like now. And everything went all right. People got their jobs done. If they kept you for fifteen minutes extra, they had to put it down as overtime. So what do you think disappeared first? The half-kopeck! That's how it all began. Then copper coins disappeared. And in 1930 silver, too. There wasn't any more change. They wouldn't give you change for anything in the world. Ever since then nothing has gone right. There is no small change, and sometimes they don't even bother giving you your change in rubles. No beggar asks for a kopeck for alms; he says, 'Citizen, give me a ruble!' And when you get your pay in a state institution, don't bother to ask for the kopecks shown on the pay lists—they'll laugh at you, call you a small-changer! They are the ones who are fools! A half-kopeck means respect for a man, and they don't even give you back sixty-kopecks change from a ruble. In other words, they shit on your head. No one stood for the half-kopeck—so there you are: we lost half a life."

On the other side, another prisoner on an upper bunk, who had been distracted from his book, said to the man next to him, "The czarist government was rotten! Listen, a woman revolutionary went on a hunger strike for eight days to force the prison head to apologize to her. And the fool apologized. Just try to get the head of Krasnaya Presnya to apologize!"

"Nowadays they would have started feeding her through the intestine on the third day. Yes, and they'd hang a second term on her for provocation. Where did you read that?"

"In Gorky."

Dvoyetyosov, who was lying not far away, roused himself. "Who is reading Gorky?" he asked in an awesome bass.

"I am."

"What the hell for?"

"Well, here, for example, are some details about the Nizhny Novgorod prison: you could put a ladder up to the wall and climb over it and no one would stop you. Can you imagine that? And the prison guards, the author says, had revolvers which were so rusty the only thing they could use them for was driving nails into the wall. That's a very useful thing to know."

Below them, one of those age-old prison arguments was in progress: *When is it best to be imprisoned?* The way the question was put presupposed that no one was ever destined to avoid prison. Prisoners were inclined to exaggerate the number of other prisoners. When, in fact, there were only twelve to fifteen million human beings in captivity, the zeks believed there were twenty or even thirty million. They believed that hardly any males were still free. "When is it best to be imprisoned?" simply meant was it better in one's youth or in one's declining years. Some zeks, usually the young ones, cheerfully insisted that it was better to be imprisoned in one's youth. Then one had a chance to learn what it meant to live, what really mattered and what was crap; then at the age of thirty-five, having knocked off a ten-year term, a man could build his life on intelligent foundations. A man who'd been imprisoned in old age could only suffer because he hadn't lived right, because his life had been a chain of mistakes, and because those mistakes could no longer be corrected. Others—usually the older men—would maintain no less optimistically that being imprisoned in old age is, on the contrary, like going on a modest pension or into a monastery, that one had already drawn everything from life in his best years. (In a prisoner's vocabulary, "everything" narrowed down to the possession of a female body, good clothes, good food, and liquor.) They went on to prove that in camp you couldn't take much hide off an old man, whereas they could wear down and cripple a young man, so that afterward he "wouldn't even want to get on a woman."

That was the substance of the argument in the semicircular room. That's how prisoners always argue. Some were reassuring themselves. Some were tormenting themselves. But the truth became no clearer from their arguments and illustrations from life. On Sunday evening it was always a good thing to be imprisoned, but when they got up on Monday morning, it was always bad.

Yet even that was not quite true. . . .

Arguing about "when it was best to be imprisoned" did not, however, inflame the disputants but, rather, drew them together in philosophic melancholy. The argument led nowhere, certainly not to angry outbursts.

Thomas Hobbes said somewhere that blood would only be shed over the theorem that "The sum of the angles of a triangle equals 180 degrees" if it injured somebody's interests.

But Hobbes knew nothing about prisoners.

An argument was in progress on the end bunk beside the doors that could have led to a fight and bloodshed, although it damaged no one's interests. The lathe operator had come over to chat with the electrician, and they happened to get on the subject of Sestroretsk; from there they moved on to the stoves that heat the houses in Sestroretsk. The lathe operator had lived in Sestroretsk one winter and remembered clearly what kind of stoves they had there. The electrician had never been there himself, but his brother-in-law had been a stove maker, a first-class stove maker, and had made stoves in Sestroretsk in particular. The electrician described a stove which was just the opposite of what the lathe operator remembered. Their dispute, which had begun as an ordinary argument, had already advanced to the stage of unsteady voices and personal insults. By now it drowned out all other conversations in the room. Each of the disputants suffered from the indignity of being unable to prove himself in the right. They sought in vain for a court of arbitration, then each suddenly remembered that the janitor Spiridon was familiar with stoves, and that he would at least tell the

other that such absurd stoves as he imagined did not exist
either in Sestroretsk or anywhere else. And almost at a run,
to the satisfaction of the whole room, they went off to find
the janitor.

But in their haste they forgot to shut the door behind
them, and another, no less explosive quarrel burst from the
corridor: Did one greet the second half of the twentieth
century on January 1, 1950, or on January 1, 1951? The
argument had evidently been going on for some time and
had foundered on the question: On the twenty-fifth of what
year was Christ born, or supposed to have been born?

The door was slammed shut. The head-splitting noise
abated. The room became quiet, and now Khorobrov could
be heard telling the bald designer above him:

"When our people start on the first flight to the moon,
there will naturally be one final session right beside the
rocket just before take-off. The crew will agree to economize on fuel, beat the cosmic speed record, not to stop
the space ship for repairs in flight, and to carry out the
landing on the moon with a rating of 'good' or 'excellent.'
One of the three crew members will be a political guidance
officer. During flight he will instruct the pilot and the navi-
gator in the political uses of cosmic journeys, and demand
statements from them for the newspapers."

Pryanchikov heard this prediction as he was running
through the room with a towel and soap. With a ballet
movement he leaped toward Khorobrov and, frowning
oddly, said, "Ilya Terentich! Let me assure you, it won't
be that way."

"And how will it be?"

Pryanchikov put his fingers to his lips mysteriously, as in
a detective film. "Americans will be on the moon first."

He burst into clear, childish laughter and ran off.

The engraver was sitting next to Sologdin on his bunk.
They were in the middle of a long-drawn-out conversation
about women. The engraver was forty, but though his face
was still youthful, his hair was almost completely gray. It
became him.

Today the engraver was in an excellent mood. True, he
had made a mistake that morning and eaten the short story
he had wadded up, and, as it turned out, he could have
taken it through the search and given it to his wife. But he
had learned that his wife had shown his earlier short stories
to several trusted individuals who were all delighted with

them. Of course, the praise of relatives and acquaintances could be exaggerated and distorted, but where in heaven could one find an unbiased opinion? Whether he was doing it well or badly, the engraver was preserving for all time the truth of what Stalin did with millions of Russian war prisoners, their souls' cry. He was proud, glad of this, and he had firmly decided to continue writing stories. Yes, and the visit itself had gone very well today. His faithful wife had been waiting for him, had petitioned for his liberation, and they would soon get word of the successful outcome of her intercessions.

Seeking an outlet for his exultation, he was telling a long story to Sologdin, whom he regarded as a not stupid but entirely mediocre person with nothing either ahead of or behind him so brilliant as what he himself enjoyed.

Sologdin lay stretched out on his back, with a trashy book lying open on his chest, listening to the storyteller with a slight twinkle in his eyes. With his curly little blond beard, clear eyes, high forehead, and the symmetrical features of an ancient Russian Viking, Sologdin was unnaturally, almost indecently handsome.

Today he was full of joy. His heart sang of victory over the absolute encoder. His liberation was now one year away —that is, it would be if he decided to give the encoder to Yakonov. A breath-taking career awaited him. Moreover, today his body was not, as usual, languishing for a woman, but had been soothed, freed. Though he had jotted down penalty marks on his pink sheet of paper, though he had made an effort to push Larisa away, tonight, stretched out on his bunk, Sologdin admitted that she had given him precisely what he had wanted from her.

Now he was amusing himself by idly following the twists and turns of a story to which he was indifferent, told by a person who, though not stupid, was completely ordinary, and had nothing either ahead of or behind him so brilliant as what Sologdin himself enjoyed.

Sologdin never tired of telling everyone that he had a weak memory, limited abilities, and a total lack of will. But one could guess what he really thought about himself from the way he listened to people: patronizingly, as if trying to conceal that he was listening only out of politeness.

First the engraver told about his two wives in Russia; then he began to recall his life in Germany and the lovely German women he had been intimate with. He made a com-

parison between Russian and German women which was new
to Sologdin: he said that Russian women are too independent, too self-reliant, too uncompromising in love; they study
the man they love, learn his weaknesses, find him at times
insufficiently courageous. You always feel the Russian woman you love is your equal. On the contrary, a German woman bends like a reed in the hands of her beloved. Her man is
her god. He is the first and the finest on earth. She subjects
herself entirely to his will. She dreams only of how to please
him. Therefore the engraver felt himself more of a man,
more a lord and master, with German women.

Rubin had been careless enough to go into the corridor
to smoke. But there was nowhere in the sharashka he could
escape being bothered.

Now, to get away from the pointless argument in the corridor, he cut across the room, hurrying to his books, but
someone on a lower bunk caught him by the trousers and
asked, "Lev Grigorich! Is it true that in China 'informers''
letters are delivered postage free?"

Rubin tore himself away. But the electrical engineer, who
was hanging from the upper bunk, caught him by the collar
and insistently tried to go on with their earlier argument:
"Lev Grigorich! One has to rebuild man's conscience so
that people will be proud only of the work of their own
hands and will be ashamed to be overseers, commanders,
prattlers. It should be a disgrace to her whole family when
a girl marries an official—I'd be willing to live under that
kind of socialism."

Rubin shook himself free, pushed through to his own
bunk, and lay down on his stomach, once again alone with
his dictionaries.

53

THE BANQUET TABLE

Seven were seated at the birthday table, consisting of three
night tables of different heights, pushed together and covered
with a piece of bright green paper. Sologdin and Rubin sat
with Potapov on his bunk, Adamson and Kondrashev-Ivanov

were with Pryanchikov on his, and the birthday celebrant sat at the head of the table on the broad window sill. Above them Zemelya was already asleep, and there was no one else near them. The double-decked bunks shut off their compartment from the rest of the room.

In the center of the table, in a plastic bowl, they had set out Nadya's pastry—consisting of thin noodle-shaped strips of dough cooked in fat until they were dry and crunchy. This was something never before seen at the sharashka. For seven men the treat seemed absurdly small. But there were also plain cookies and cookies spread with pudding and, therefore, called cream puffs. And there was taffy prepared by boiling an unopened can of condensed milk. And hidden behind Nerzhin's back, in a dark quart can, was that enticing beverage for which the "goblets" were intended: a little alcohol the zeks in the chemical laboratory had bartered for a piece of hard-to-get insulating material. The spirits had been diluted with water in the proportion of one to four, then colored with chocolate. The result was a brown liquid containing very little alcohol, which, nevertheless, was impatiently awaited.

"Well, gentlemen," declared Sologdin, leaning back dramatically, his eyes shining in the half-darkness. "Let's think back to the last time each of us sat at a banquet table."

"I did yesterday, with the Germans," blurted out Rubin, who disliked emotionalism.

In Rubin's view, the fact that Sologdin always addressed a group as "gentlemen" was a consequence of the trauma of twelve years in prison. As a result of the same trauma, Sologdin's ideas were distorted in many other respects, and Rubin tried always to keep this in mind and not to explode in anger, even though he was forced to listen to some outrageous things.

"No, no!" Sologdin insisted. "I have in mind a *real* table, gentlemen! It has a heavy, pale tablecloth, liquor and wine in crystal decanters, and, of course, well-dressed women."

He wanted to savor this vision and delay the beginning of the feast, but Potapov, looking over the table and the guests with the proprietary, anxiously observant glance of the mistress of the house, interrupted in his peevish voice: "You must understand, boys, that before 'the thunder of the midnight patrols' catches us with this potion we'd better proceed with the official formalities."

He gave a sign to Nerzhin to pour.

While the liquor was being poured they were silent, and each, in spite of himself, remembered something from the past.

"It was a long time ago," Nerzhin sighed.

"I don't remember!" Potapov said impatiently. Until the war he had been caught up in the mad vortex of work, and though he did remember something about a marriage celebration, he could not say now whether the marriage had been his own or someone else's.

"Why not?" said Pryanchikov, coming to life. "*Avec plaisir!* I will tell you right now. In 1945 in Paris I—"

"Just a minute, Valentulya," Potapov stopped him. "A toast?"

"To the person responsible for our getting together!" Kondrashev-Ivanov pronounced louder than was necessary, and he straightened up, although he was already sitting very straight. "And may there be—"

But the guests had not had time to reach for their "goblets" when Nerzhin stood up in the little space at the window and said quietly, "My friends, I am violating a tradition! I—"

He was moved. The men's warm feelings, showing in their eyes, had stirred something inside him. He went on without stopping for breath.

"Let's be fair! Not everything in our lives is so black! This happiness we have right now—a free banquet, an exchange of free thoughts without fear, without concealment —we didn't have that in freedom."

"Yes, as a matter of fact, freedom itself was quite often lacking in freedom," Adamson said, smiling ironically. Since childhood he had spent less than half his life in freedom.

"Friends!" Nerzhin said earnestly. "I am thirty-one years old. Over these years life has both blessed and degraded me. According to the sinusoidal principle, I could still look forward to further peaks of vain success, of false grandeur; but, I swear to you, I will never forget the genuine grandeur; of human beings as I have come to know them in prison! I am proud that my modest anniversary today has drawn together such a select company. Let's not burden ourselves with ceremony. Let's raise a toast to the friendship which thrives in prison vaults!"

Paper cups touched glass and plastic soundlessly. Potapov

grinned self-consciously, adjusted his spectacles and recited:

> "Famous for sharp eloquence,
> The members of this family gathered
> At restless Nikita's,
> At cautious Ilya's."

They drank down the brown liquor slowly, trying to savor the aroma.

"It has proof!" said Rubin approvingly. "Bravo, Andreich!"

"Yes, it does," Sologdin agreed. He was in a mood to praise everything today.

Nerzhin laughed. "It's an unusual event when Lev and Dmitri agree about something! I can't remember that ever happening before."

"No, Gleb? Don't you remember once at New Year's when Lev and I agreed that a wife who has been unfaithful can't be forgiven, but that a husband can be?"

Adamson laughed wearily. "What man wouldn't agree with that?"

"That fellow over there," said Rubin pointing at Nerzhin, "declared on that occasion that one can forgive a woman, too, that there's no difference."

"Did you say that?" Kondrashev-Ivanov asked quickly.

"Oh, wonderful!" Pryanchikov laughed ringingly. "How come there's no difference?"

"The structure of the body and the mode of union prove there's an enormous difference!" Sologdin exclaimed.

"Don't blame me, my friends," Nerzhin said. "After all, when I was growing up, a red banner with golden lettering fluttered over our heads—equality! Since then, of course, life has beaten *this* simpleton over the head quite enough. But it seemed then that if nations were equal, and people were equal, then men and women must be equal—in everything."

"No one is blaming you!" Kondrashev-Ivanov said, just as quickly. "Don't give in so easily."

"We can forgive you that sort of nonsense only because of your youth," Sologdin pronounced. (He was five years older.)

"Theoretically Gleb is right," Rubin said, embarrassed. "I, too, am prepared to break a lance for equality between men and women. But to make love to my wife after someone else has? Brrr! Biologically I couldn't do it."

"But, gentlemen, it's too ridiculous to discuss!" Pryanchikov cried out, but, as always, they didn't let him speak.

"Lev Grigorich, there's a simple way to achieve equality," Potapov said firmly. "Don't *you* make love to anyone except your wife!"

"Now, listen here—" protested Rubin, drowning his broad smile in his pirate's beard.

The door opened noisily and someone came in. Potapov and Adamson looked around. It was not a guard.

"Carthage must be destroyed," said Adamson, nodding at the quart can.

"The quicker, the better. Who wants to sit in solitary? Gleb, pour the rest of it."

Nerzhin poured what was left into their cups, dividing it accurately.

"Well, this time will you let us drink to the person whose birthday it is?" Adamson asked.

"No, brothers. I am waiving my traditional right so as to—I—saw my wife today. I saw that she was—all of our wives—worn down, frightened, persecuted. We can bear it because we have nowhere to hide, but what about them? Let's drink to them, who have bound themselves to—"

"Yes, indeed! What a blessed thing their constancy is!" Kondrashev-Ivanov exclaimed.

They drank.

Then they were silent for a time.

"Look at the snow," Adamson remarked.

Everyone looked past Nerzhin to the fogged-up windows. The snow itself couldn't be seen, but the lamps and the searchlights of the zone cast the black shadows of falling snowflakes on the windowpanes.

Somewhere beyond that curtain of heavy snow was Nadya Nerzhin.

"Even the snow we see is black," Kondrashev-Ivanov said.

They drank to friendship. They drank to love. Rubin praised it: "I have never had any doubts about love. But to tell you the truth, until the front and prison I didn't believe in friendship, especially the 'give-up-your-life-for-your-friend' kind. In ordinary life you have your family, and somehow there's no place for friendship, is there?"

"That's a widespread opinion," Adamson replied. "After

all, the song called 'In the Valley' has been popular in Russia for a hundred and fifty years, and today people often ask for it on the radio, but if you listen to the words, it's a repulsive whine, the complaint of a petty soul:

> All your friends, all your comrades,
> Last till the first black day."

"That's outrageous!" the painter said. "How can anyone live one day with such a thought? One would have to hang oneself!"

"It would be truer to put it the other way: it's only on a black day that you begin to have friends."

"Who wrote it?"

"Merzlyakov."

"What a name! Lev, who was Merzlyakov?"

"A poet, twenty years older than Pushkin."

"You know his biography, of course?"

"A professor at the university in Moscow. He translated *Jerusalem Delivered*."

"Tell me, what doesn't Lev know? Only higher mathematics."

"Lower, too."

"But he is always saying, 'Let's simplify and find the common factor.'"

"Gentlemen! I must cite an example of a time Merzlyakov was right!" said Pryanchikov, choking and hurrying like a child sitting at the table with grown-ups. He was not inferior to the others in any way; he understood things quickly; he was bright; and his frankness was attractive. But he lacked the look of masculine command, of outward dignity, and therefore he appeared fifteen years younger than he was and the others treated him like an adolescent. "After all, it's a proved fact. The very one who eats out of the same bowl with us is the one who betrays us. I had a close friend I escaped with from a Nazi concentration camp. We hid together. And—imagine it!—he was the one who betrayed me."

"What a rotten thing to do!" the artist exclaimed.

"Here's how it happened. To be frank, I didn't want to come back. I was already working. I had money. And there were girls."

Almost all of them had heard the story. To Rubin it was

perfectly clear that the gay, likable Valentine Pryanchikov, with whom it was all right to be friends at the sharashka, had been, objectively, in Europe in 1945, a reactionary, and what he called his friend's betrayal—that is, helping to have Pryanchikov returned to his country against his will—was not betrayal at all but a patriotic act.

Adamson dozed behind his spectacles. He had known there would be these empty conversations. But he recognized that this whole crowd would somehow have to return to the fold, whereas he. . . .

Rubin and Nerzhin, in the counterintelligence centers and prisons of the first postwar year, had been so much a part of the wave of POWs flowing in from Europe that it was as though they had themselves spent four years as war prisoners. They weren't interested in stories of repatriation, and so at their end of the table they urged Kondrashev-Ivanov into a conversation about art. On the whole Rubin did not regard Kondrashev as a very important artist, or a very serious person, and felt that his affirmations were ideologically unfounded. But in talking with him, without knowing it he learned a great deal.

Art for Kondrashev-Ivanov was not an occupation, nor a branch of knowledge. Art for him was the only possible way of life. Everything around him—a landscape, an object, a human personality, or a shade of color—had the resonance of one of twenty-four tonalities, and without hesitation Kondrashev-Ivanov could identify the tonality in question. He called Rubin, for instance, C minor. Every tonality had its corresponding color—a human voice, a passing mood, a novel of the same tonality had the same color—and without hesitation Kondrashev-Ivanov could name it. For instance, F-sharp major was dark blue and gold.

The one state Kondrashev-Ivanov never experienced was indifference. He was known for his extreme likes and dislikes, his absolute judgments. He was an admirer of Rembrandt and a detractor of Raphael. He was a worshiper of Valentine Serov and a violent enemy of the *Peredvizhniki*, the populist Russian artists who preceded the Socialist Realists. He could not accept anything halfheartedly but could only delight in something or loathe it. He refused even to hear Chekhov's name, he recoiled from Tchaikovsky, declaring, "He suffocates me! He takes away hope and life!" But he was so close to the Bach chorals and the Beethoven concertos that it was as though he personally had first set them down on paper.

And now Kondrashev-Ivanov was involved in discussing whether or not art had to follow nature.

"For example, you want to depict a window that opens on a garden on a summer morning," he was saying. His voice was youthful and full of enthusiasm, and if one closed one's eyes, one would think a young man was speaking. "If one honestly follows nature, and represents everything as he sees it, will that really be *everything*? What about the singing of the birds? And the freshness of the morning? And that invisible cleanness and purity which pour through you? After all, you, as you paint, perceive these things; they are part of your perception of the summer morning. How can they be captured in the painting? How can you preserve them for the viewer? They obviously have to be included! By composition, by color . . . you have nothing else at your disposal."

"In other words, the painter doesn't simply copy?"

"Of course not! In fact, with every landscape," Kondrashev-Ivanov went on excitedly, "every landscape, and every portrait, too, you begin by feasting your eyes on nature and thinking, 'How wonderful! How perfect! If I could only succeed in getting it just as it is!' But as you go more deeply into your work, you suddenly notice in nature a sort of ungainliness, nonsense, incongruity! Right there, and there too! And it *ought* to be that way! So that's the way you paint it!" Kondrashev-Ivanov looked triumphantly at the others.

"But, my dear fellow," Rubin objected, " 'ought to be' is a most dangerous path! You will go on from there to turn living people into angels and devils, making them wear the buskins of classical tragedy. After all, if you paint a portrait of Andrei Andreich Potapov, it must show Potapov as he is."

"And what does that mean, show him as he is?" the artist demanded. "Externally, yes. There must be some resemblance in the proportions of the face, the shape of the eyes, the color of the hair. But isn't it rash to believe that one can see and know reality precisely as it is? Particularly *spiritual* reality? Who sees and knows it? And if, in looking at the model, I see something nobler than what he has up to now displayed in his life, then why shouldn't I portray it?

Why shouldn't one help a man find himself and try to be better?"

"Well then, you're a hundred percent Socialist Realist!" said Nerzhin, clapping his hands. "Foma simply doesn't know whom he has here."

"Why must I undervalue his soul?" Kondrashev-Ivanov glared balefully through his spectacles, which never moved on his nose. "I will tell you something else: it is a major responsibility not only of portraiture but of all human communication for each of us to help everyone else discover the best that is in him."

"What you mean," Rubin said, "is that there can be no such thing as objectivity in art."

"Yes, I am nonobjective, and I am proud of it!" roared Kondrashev-Ivanov.

"What? How is that?" Rubin asked in astonishment.

"Just that! Just that! I am proud of my nonobjectivity!" declared Kondrashev-Ivanov, his words falling like blows. He started to stand up. "And you, Lev Grigorich? You are not objective either, but you think you're objective, and that's much worse! At least I am nonobjective and know it! I cite it as a merit! It is my 'I'!"

"I am not objective?" Rubin demanded. "Me? Then who is objective?"

"No one, of course!" the artist exulted. "No one! No one ever was, and no one ever will be! Every act of perception has an emotional coloring. The truth is supposed to be the final result of long investigation, but don't we perceive a sort of twilight truth before any investigation has begun? We pick up a book and right away the author seems unpleasant, and we know on the first page that we will not like it, and, of course, we are right! You have studied a hundred languages, you have buried yourself in dictionaries, you have forty years of work ahead of you, but you are already convinced that you will prove successfully that all words derive from the word 'hand.' Is that objectivity?"

Nerzhin, delighted, was laughing hard at Rubin. Rubin laughed, too—how could anyone get angry at this pure spirit!

"Doesn't the same thing happen in social science?" Nerzhin added.

"My child," Rubin reasoned with him, "if it were impossible to predict results, then there could hardly be any 'progress,' could there?"

"Progress!" Nerzhin growled. "The hell with progress. I like art because there can't be any 'progress' in it."

"What do you mean?"

"Just that! In the seventeenth century there was Rembrandt, and there is Rembrandt today. Just try to improve on him. And yet the technology of the seventeenth century now seems primitive to us. Or take the technological innovations of the 1870's. For us they're child's play. But that was when *Anna Karenina* was written. What can you name that's superior?"

"Your argument, Gleb Vikentich," Adamson interrupted, turning away from Pryanchikov, "can have another interpretation. It could mean that scientists and engineers have been creating great works all these centuries, and have made real progress, while the art snobs have obviously been clowning around. The parasites have—"

"Sold out!" Sologdin exclaimed, with unaccountable satisfaction.

And such opposites as he and Adamson were united in a single thought.

"Bravo! Bravo!" Pryanchikov joined in. "Fellows, that's wonderful! That's exactly what I said to you last night in Acoustics!"

On that occasion he had been advocating the superiority of jazz, but it seemed to him now that Adamson was expressing his very idea.

"I believe I can reconcile your positions," said Potapov, grinning slyly. "In this century there was an actual case in which a certain electrical engineer and a certain mathematician, concerned about their country's literature gap, collaborated on a short story. Alas, it remained unwritten because neither of them had a pencil."

"Andreich!" Nerzhin exclaimed. "Could you remember it?"

"Well, I'll try, with your help. After all, it was the only opus of my life. I ought to be able to remember it."

"Very amusing, very amusing, gentlemen!" Sologdin said, coming to life and settling himself more comfortably. He was fond of such prison diversions.

"But of course you realize, as Lev Grigorich teaches us, that no artistic creation can be understood without knowing how it came to be created and the *social justification for it.*"

"You are making progress, Andreich."

"You guests, finish up your pastry—it was prepared especially for you! The history of this creative event is as follows: In the summer of 1946 in a certain outrageously overcrowded cell in the Bu-Tyur sanatorium—so named after the monogram stamped on the bowls at the Butyrskaya-Tyurma—Gleb Vikentich and I were close neighbors, first under the plank beds and then on top of them, suffocating from the lack of air, groaning a bit from hunger now and then, and we had nothing to do but talk and comment on social mores. One of us said first, 'And what if . . . ?'"

"It was you, Andreich, who first said, 'And what if . . .?' The basic idea, which was also the title, was yours in any case."

"'And what if . . . ?' Gleb Vikentich and I said. 'And what if suddenly in our cell—'"

"Oh, don't drag it out! What was the title?"

"Indeed, 'setting out to entertain the proud world,' let's both try to remember that story, eh?" Potapov's cracked monotone droned in the manner of a confirmed reader of dusty volumes. "The title was 'Buddha's Smile.'"

54

BUDDHA'S SMILE

"The action of our extraordinary tale takes place during that blazing heat wave of 1945, when prisoners numbering considerably more than the legendary forty thieves were languishing half naked in the dead air behind the muzzled windows of a cell in the world-famous Butyrskaya Prison.

"What can one say about that serviceable institution? It traced its origin back to a barracks in the time of Catherine the Great. In that cruel age, the Empress did not spare bricks for its fortified walls and vaulted ceilings.

> The venerable castle was built
> As all castles ought to be.

"After the death of Voltaire's enlightened correspondent, those resonant chambers, where the rough tramp of carabineers' boots had once echoed, fell into ruin. But, years later, as progress advanced in our homeland, the reigning descendants of the aforementioned powerful lady found it convenient to house there, on an equal footing, heretics who were shaking the orthodox throne and obscurantists who were opposing progress.

"The mason's trowel and the plasterer's blade divided those vaults into hundreds of spacious and agreeable cells. The unsurpassed artistry of Russian smiths forged unyielding gratings on the windows and tubular frames for bunks which were let down at night and raised during the day. The best craftsmen from among our talented serfs made invaluable contributions to the deathless glory of the Butyrskaya castle: weavers wove canvas to stretch over the bunk frames; plumbers installed a clever system of sewage disposal; tinkers made latrine barrels in two generous sizes, complete with handles and tops; carpenters cut 'food openings' in the doors; glaziers installed peepholes; locksmiths fitted locks; and, during the ultra-modern era of People's Commissar Yezhov, specialists poured nontransparent molten glass over steel reinforcing-bars and installed these unique 'muzzles' in the windows, cutting the vicious prisoners off from any glimpse of the prison courtyard, the jail church (also used as a prison), or a patch of blue sky.

"Practical considerations prompted the wardens of the Butyrskaya sanatorium to set twenty-five bunk frames in the walls of each cell, thereby providing a basis for simple arithmetical reckoning (since few of the guards had graduated from higher educational institutions): four cells equaled one hundred heads; one corridor of eight cells equaled two hundred heads.

"And so for long decades this health resort flourished, arousing neither the censure of society nor complaints from the prisoners. We can deduce that there were virtually no objections on the part of society from the fact that very few appeared in the pages of the *Stock Exchange News* and none at all in *Izvestiya*, 'The News of the Workers and Peasants' Deputies.'

"But time was not working in favor of the major general who was the head of Butyrskaya Prison. By the first days of the war it was necessary to violate the established norm of twenty-five heads per cell and admit extra inhabitants, for whom there were no bunks. When the surplus reached awesome proportions, the bunks were permanently lowered, the canvas removed, planking was placed on top of them, and the exultant major general and his comrades shoved fifty persons into each cell. After the war the number reached seventy-five. This, however, did not make things more difficult for the guards, who now knew that there were six hundred heads in each corridor. Also, they were paid bonuses for the extra ones.

"In such crowded conditions there was no point in giving out books, chess sets, or dominoes, since there would have been no space for them anyway. In time, the bread ration was reduced for these enemies of the people, and fish was replaced by the flesh of amphibians and hymenoptera, cabbage and nettles with cattle silage. And the terrifying Pugachev Tower, where the Empress had kept the folk hero bound in chains, did peacetime duty as a silo.

"People poured in. New ones kept arriving, and the local legends grew dim and distorted. People didn't know that their predecessors had lolled on canvas and read forbidden books (which could only be found in prison libraries). Ichthyosaur bouillon or fodder soup was brought into the cell in a steaming barrel. Due to the crowding the prisoners crouched on the planks like dogs, their legs pressed against their chests, bracing themselves with their hands. They watched with bared teeth to see that the liquid was poured into the bowls equally. The bowls were passed in a spiral 'from the latrine barrel to the window' and 'from the window to the radiator'; then the occupants of the plank beds and the kennels under the planks lapped up the life-giving gruel, and only the sound of their lapping disturbed the philosophic silence of the cell.

"Everyone was satisfied. There were no complaints in the trade-union paper, *Trud*, or in the Moscow *Patriarchate Herald*.

"Among the cells was No. 72, in no way distinguishable from the rest. It had been already singled out and specially fated, but the prisoners who dozed peacefully under its plank beds and were cursing foully on top of them knew nothing of what awaited them. On the fateful day they lay, as usual, on the cement floor near the latrine barrel; they lay in loincloths on the planks, fanning themselves in the stagnant heat—the cell was never aired from one year to the next. They killed flies and told each other about how good it had been in the war, in Norway, Iceland, and Greenland. Their inner sense of time told them there were less than five minutes before the jailer on duty would bellow through the 'food opening': 'Come on, lie down. Lights out.'

"But suddenly the prisoners' hearts trembled at the sound of locks opening. The door swung open, and in the doorway appeared a slender, springy captain in white gloves. He was extremely excited. Behind him hummed a whole pack of lieutenants and sergeants. In the funereal silence the zeks were led out into the corridor *with their gear*. At once the whispered rumor circulated that they were being taken out to be shot. In the corridor fifty were counted off into five groups of ten each and were shoved into adjacent rooms, where each, as it happened, managed to get some sleeping space.

"These lucky individuals were spared the awesome fate of the others. The last the remaining twenty-five saw of their dear Cell 72, some kind of hellish machine with an atomizer was being brought through the door. Then they were ordered to face right and, to the sound of the guards' keys clanking against their belt buckles and the snapping of fingers, which was the Butyrskaya signal for 'I am conducting a prisoner,' they were led through a number of steel doors and down a number of staircases and into a hall which was neither the execution cellar nor the torture dungeon but was well known among the zeks as the outer room of the famous Butyrskaya baths. This room had a deceptively harmless, everyday appearance: walls, benches, and floor were tiled in chocolate, red, and green; trolleys rolled thunderously on rails from the 'roaster'—the sterilization room—with hellish hooks to hang the prisoners' lousy clothing on. Bumping one another —the prisoners' third commandment states, 'If they give it, grab it!'—the zeks disentangled the hot hooks and hung on them their beat-up clothes, scorched, and in places burned through, by the sterilization they underwent every ten days. And the two heat-flushed crones, servants of Hell, contemptuous of the prisoners' nakedness which was repulsive to them, pushed the rumbling trolleys into Tartarus and clanged the steel doors shut behind them.

"The twenty-five prisoners were locked in on all sides. They kept only their handkerchiefs or bits of torn-up sheeting. Those who, however emaciated, had still a thin layer of tanned meat on that undemanding part of the body with which nature accords us the happy faculty of sitting down—those fortunate individuals sat on the warm stone benches, inlaid with emerald, raspberry, and brown tiles. In the luxury of their appointments the Butyrskaya baths leave the Sandunovsky baths far behind and, they say, many inquisitive foreigners purposely turned themselves in to the Cheka just in order to bathe there.

"The prisoners who had grown so thin that they could not sit on anything hard paced from one end of the room to the other, not bothering to cover their private parts. They tried, in heated argument, to penetrate the mystery of what was taking place.

> Long had their imagination
> Craved the food of knowledge.

"However, they were kept there so many hours that the arguments ended in silence, bodies were covered with goose flesh and stomachs that were used to being asleep from 10 P.M. on called longingly to be filled. Among the disputants, victory had gone to the pessimists who maintained that poison gas was already pouring in through the gratings in the walls and floor and that they would all die immediately. Several of them already felt ill from the obvious smell of gas.

"But the door clanged open, and everything was suddenly transformed! There was no sign of the two guards in dirty robes who usually appeared with dirty clippers to shear the prisoner-sheep; no one came in to break their nails with two of the world's dullest pairs of scissors. No. Four journeymen barbers wheeled in four mirror stands with eau de cologne, hair cream, fingernail polish . . . even theatrical wigs. And four very venerable and portly master barbers, two of them Armenian, followed. In the barbershop set up behind the door, the prisoners not only did not have their pubic hair shaved with the flat edge of the clippers pressed against the tender areas, but they actually had it powdered with pink powder. Razors glided lightly over their emaciated cheeks, and their ears were tickled by the whisper, 'Does that bother you?' Not only were their heads not shaved bare, but they were offered wigs. Not only were their chins not scraped, but, at the customer's request, incipient beards and sideburns were allowed to remain. At the same time the journeymen barbers, lying flat on the floor, trimmed their toenails. Last but not least, no one stood at the entrance to the bath to pour half an ounce of dripping, stinking soap into their palms. Instead, a sergeant stood there and, in exchange for a receipt, gave each one of them a sponge from the coral isles and a full-size piece of toilet soap called 'Fairy Lilac.'

"Then, as always, they locked them in the bath and let them bathe to their hearts' content. But the prisoners were not interested in bathing. Their arguments were hotter than the steaming Butyrskaya water. At this point the optimists among them were prevailing. They declared that Stalin and Beria had fled to China, that Molotov and Kaganovich had become Roman Catholics, that there was a provisional Social Democratic government in Russia and that the elections to the Constituent Assembly were already under way.

"Just then the door to the bath opened with a cannon-like rumble, and in the violet hall outside, the most improbable events awaited them. Each was given a fluffy pink towel and one full bowl of oatmeal—six days' rations for a working camp prisoner. The prisoners threw the towels on the floor and, with astonishing speed, without spoons or other implements, gulped down the oatmeal. Even the old prison major was surprised, and he ordered one more bowl of oatmeal for each zek. They ate that, too. What happened next no one could possibly have guessed! They brought in ordinary edible potatoes—not frozen, not rotten, not black —simply edible."

"That's impossible!" the listeners protested. "That's not true to life."

"But that, in fact, was exactly the way it was. True, the potatoes were the kind meant for pigs; they were small and unpeeled; and zeks with full stomachs might not have eaten them. But the fiendish cleverness of the thing was that they brought them not in portions but in one common bucket. With a violent yell, pummeling one another and crawling over each other's backs, the zeks rushed to the bucket and in one minute it was rolling and rattling empty on the stone

floor. At that moment salt was brought in, but by then
there was nothing left to salt.

"By that time their naked bodies had dried. The old major
ordered the zeks to pick up the fluffy towels from the floor
and proceeded to address them:

" 'Dear brothers,' he said, 'you are all honest Soviet citizens, only temporarily separated from society, some for ten,
some for twenty-five years, because of your minor missteps.
Up to now, in spite of frequent directives from Comrade
Stalin himself, the leadership of Butyrskaya Prison has been
guilty of grave mistakes and deviations which are at present
being corrected.' ('They're going to let us go home,' the
prisoners decided brazenly.) The major continued: 'From
now on we are going to see to it that you enjoy sanatorium
conditions.' ('We stay in prison,' they realized.) 'In addition to everything you have been allowed in the past you
will now be permitted: (1) to worship your own God;
(2) to lie on your bunks, day or night; (3) to leave the cell
to go to the toilet without interference; (4) to write your
memoirs.

" 'In addition to what you have hitherto been forbidden,
now you will also be forbidden: (1) to blow your noses in
government-issue sheets and curtains; (2) to ask for a second plate of food; (3) to contradict the prison administration or to make complaints against it when high-ranking
visitors enter your cell; (4) to take Kazbek cigarettes without asking permission.

" 'Anyone who violates any of these rules will be subject
to fifteen days in strict solitary confinement and be exiled
to a remote camp without the right of correspondence. Is
all that clear?'

"And hardly had the major finished his speech than the
clanking trolleys rolled out from the 'roaster'—but not with
the prisoners' underwear and tattered padded jackets—not
at all. Hades, having swallowed up those rags, did not dis-
gorge them. Instead, four young linen attendants entered,
their eyes downcast, blushing; their lovely smiles encouraged the prisoners to feel that all was not lost to them as
men; and they began handing out blue silk underwear, cotton shirts, modestly colored neckties, bright yellow American shoes received under Lend-Lease, and suits made from
synthetic twill.

"Mute from terror and delight, the prisoners were marched

back in a double column to their Cell 72. But, good Lord, how it had changed!

"Even in the corridor their feet had sunk into a thick-napped carpet runner, leading invitingly to the toilet. And when they entered the cell, they were enveloped in streams of fresh air, and the immortal sun shone directly in their eyes. (The frantic work had taken all night, and it was now morning.) They found that the bars had been painted light blue, the 'muzzles' had been removed from the windows, and on the former Butyrskaya church which stood inside the courtyard an adjustable mirror had been mounted. A guard was specially stationed there to regulate it so that reflected sunlight poured constantly through the window of Cell 72. The walls of the cell, which the evening before had been dark olive, were now gleaming with off-white paint, decorated here and there with doves and ribbons bearing the slogans: 'We are for Peace!' and 'Peace to the World!'

"Not a trace was left of the plank beds and the bedbugs. Canvas was stretched on the bunk frames, and on the canvas lay feather-stuffed comforters and feather pillows; the coquettishly folded-back blankets revealed the whiteness of sheets. At each of the twenty-five cots stood night tables. Along the walls were shelves containing the works of Marx, Engels, St. Augustine, and St. Thomas Aquinas. In the middle of the room stood a table with a starched tablecloth; on it were an ashtray and an unopened box of Kazbek cigarettes. All the opulence created in that magic night had been successfully worked out through the accounting office, and only the box of Kazbek cigarettes could not be allocated to any expense category. So the head of the prison had decided to dress things up with Kazbeks out of his own pocket, which was why so severe a punishment had been imposed for the unauthorized use of them.

"But what had changed most was the corner where the latrine bucket had stood. The wall had been washed clean and painted. High up, a large icon lamp burned before an icon of the Virgin Mary with the Child. The frame glittered on another icon, of the miracle worker St. Nikolai Mirliki-ski. On the shelves stood a white statue of the Roman Catholic Madonna, and in a shallow niche, left there by the builders, lay a Bible, the Koran, and the Talmud. The niche also held a small bronze statue of Buddha. Buddha's eyes were almost closed, the corners of his lips were drawn back, and it looked as if Buddha were smiling.

"The zeks, sated with oatmeal and potatoes and astounded by the overwhelming multitude of new impressions, undressed and went to sleep immediately. A gentle Aeolus wafted the lace curtains over the windows, which kept out the flies. A guard stood in the half-open doors and watched to be sure that no one stole a Kazbek.

"Thus they luxuriated in peace until midday, when an extremely agitated captain in white gloves ran in and announced reveille. The zeks dressed swiftly and made up their bunks. A round table with a white cover was hurriedly pushed into the cell, and on it were spread copies of the magazines *Ogonyek*, *The U.S.S.R. in Construction*, and *Amerika*. Two old armchairs, with slip covers, were rolled in. A sinister, intolerable silence descended. The captain tiptoed between the bunks and with a handsome white rod rapped on the fingers of those who reached for the magazine *Amerika*.

"In the enervating silence the prisoners listened. As you know from your own experience, hearing is a prisoner's most important sense. His sight is usually limited by walls and 'muzzles.' His sense of smell is numbed by bad odors. There are no new objects to touch. But his hearing is abnormally developed. He immediately recognizes every sound, even at the far end of the corridor; it tells him what's going on in the prison and keeps track of time for him: hot water is being brought in; prisoners are being led out for their walk; a parcel is being delivered to someone.

"Listening gave them the clue to the solution of the riddle. A steel door rattled from the direction of Cell 75, and many people entered the corridor all at once. Restrained conversation could be heard, then steps muffled by the carpets, then women's voices, the rustle of skirts, and at the door of Cell 72 the voice of the head of Butyrskaya Prison saying cordially:

"'And now, Mrs. R——, perhaps it would be interesting for you to visit one of our cells. Which one? Shall we say the first we happen to come to? Cell 72 here, for example. Open it up, Sergeant!'

"And Mrs. R—— came into the cell, accompanied by a secretary, a translator, two venerable Quaker matrons, the head of the prison, several people in civilian clothes and others in MVD uniforms. The widow of the well-known statesman, a perspicacious woman prominent in many good causes, who had done much to defend the rights of man, Mrs. R—— had undertaken the task of visiting America's brilliant ally and seeing with her own eyes how UNRRA aid was being used. Rumors had reached America that UNRRA food was not being distributed to ordinary people. And she also wished to see whether freedom of conscience was being violated in the Soviet Union. She had already been shown ordinary Soviet citizens—officials who had changed out of uniform for the occasion—and in their rude work clothes they had thanked the United Nations for its unselfish help. Now Mrs. R—— had insisted that she be shown a prison. Her wish had been granted. She sat down in one of the armchairs, her suite arranged itself around her, and a conversation began through the interpreter.

"The rays of the sun shone into the room, reflected from the mirror. Aeolus' breath rustled the curtains.

"Mrs. R—— was very pleased that the cell which had been chosen at random and which they had entered unexpectedly was so amazingly clean and free of flies, and that the icon lamp was burning in the right-hand corner even though it was a weekday.

"At first the prisoners were shy and did not stir, but when the distinguished guest asked through the interpreter whether the prisoners weren't smoking because they wanted to keep the air clean, one of them rose nonchalantly, opened the box of Kazbeks, lit up, and offered a cigarette to his comrade.

"The major general's face darkened.

"'We are struggling to give up smoking,' he said expressively, 'because tobacco is a poison.'

"Another prisoner sat down at the table and began to look through the magazine *Amerika*—very hurriedly, for some reason.

"'What are these people being punished for? For example, that gentleman who is reading the magazine?' the distinguished guest asked.

"('That gentleman' had received ten years for a careless acquaintance with an American tourist.)

"The major general replied, 'That man was an active Hitlerite. He worked for the Gestapo. He personally burned down a Russian village, and, if you'll forgive my speaking of such things, raped three Russian peasant girls. The number of children he killed will probably never be known.'

" 'Has he been condemned to death?' Mrs. R—— exclaimed.

" 'No, we hope he will reform. He has been sentenced to ten years of honest labor.'

"The prisoner's face showed pain, but he did not interrupt and went on reading the magazine with trembling haste.

"At this moment, a Russian Orthodox priest entered the cell as if by accident. He wore a large mother-of-pearl cross on his breast. He was obviously on his regular rounds and was very embarrassed at finding the prison authorities and foreign guests in the cell.

"He wanted to leave, but Mrs. R—— liked his modesty and asked him to carry on with his duties. The priest thereupon shoved a pocket gospel at one startled prisoner. He sat down on the bunk next to another, who was rigid with surprise, and said, 'My son, last time you asked me to tell you about the sufferings of our Lord, Jesus Christ.'

"Mrs. R—— then asked the major general to ask the prisoners a question: did any of them wish to complain to the United Nations?

"The major general said in a threatening voice, 'Attention, prisoners! What did I say about the Kazbeks? You want strict solitary?'

"The prisoners, who had been spellbound up to then, answered indignantly, several of them speaking at once:

" 'Citizen Major General, there isn't anything else to smoke.'

" 'I left my tobacco in my other trousers.'

" 'We didn't know!'

"The famous lady saw the genuine indignation of the prisoners, heard their sincere outcries, and listened to the translation with great interest:

" 'They unanimously protest against the serious predicament of Negroes in America and demand that the Negro question be submitted to the United Nations.'

"Thus about fifteen minutes passed in pleasant conversation. Then the duty officer in the corridor reported to the head of the prison that lunch had arrived. The guests asked them not to stand on ceremony but to have lunch served in their presence. The door swung open and pretty young

waitresses—the linen attendants had changed clothes—
brought in ordinary chicken noodle soup and began to pour
it into bowls. At once a rush of primitive passion overwhelmed the docile prisoners. They jumped up on their
bunks with their shoes on, crouched there with their legs
against their chests, their hands beside their feet, and in that
canine stance watched with bared teeth to make sure the
soup was equally distributed. The lady guests were shocked,
but the interpreter explained that it was a Russian national
custom.

"It wasn't possible to persuade the prisoners to sit at the
table and eat with the German-silver spoons. They had already brought out their cherished wooden spoons, and hardly
had the priest blessed the table and the waitresses distributed
the dishes around the bunks, with the warning that there
was a dish for the bones on the table, than an awesome
sucking sound was heard and then a crunching of chicken
bones in unison—and everything that had been poured into
the dishes had completely disappeared. The dish for bones
hadn't been necessary.

"'Are they hungry?' The alarmed guest voiced the awkward possibility. 'Maybe they would like more?'

"'Does anyone want more?' the general asked hoarsely.

"No one did; they all knew the wise camp saying: 'The
prosecutor will hand out more.'

"With the same indescribable speed the zeks gobbled down
some meatballs with rice.

"Stewed fruit for dessert was not on the menu that day—
it was a weekday.

"Having convinced herself of the falsity of the innuendoes
spread by hostile people in the West, Mrs. R—— and her
whole suite went out into the corridor. There she said, 'But
how crude their manners are! And how low the develop-
mental level of these unfortunates! One must hope, however, that in the course of ten years here they will become
accustomed to culture. You have a magnificent prison!'

"The priest leaped out of the cell into the midst of the
suite, hurrying before they shut the door.

"When the guests had left the corridor, the captain in
white gloves ran into the cell.

"'Up!' he shouted. 'Line up by twos. Into the corridor!'

"And noticing that not everyone understood his words,

he offered the slow ones additional explanations with the sole of his shoe.

"Only then was it discovered that one clever zek had taken literally the permission to write his memoirs. That morning, while everyone else had been asleep, he had managed to write two chapters entitled 'How I Was Tortured' and 'My Lefortovo Encounters.'

"The memoirs were taken away from him on the spot and a new case begun against the eager author, charging him with foul slander against the State Security organs.

"And once again, with finger-snapping and key-clanking, they were led through a multitude of steel doors into the room at the entrance to the baths, which was still gleaming in its eternal ruby-malachite beauty. There everything was taken from them, including the sky-blue silk underwear, and an especially careful body search was carried out. In the course of it, the Sermon on the Mount, which had been torn out of the pocket gospel, was discovered inside a zek's cheek. For this offense he was forthwith beaten, first on the right cheek and then on the left. They also took the sponges and the 'Fairy Lilac' soap, and made the zeks sign for them again.

"Two guards in dirty robes came in; with dull and dirty clippers they began to clip the prisoners' pubic hair, and then used the same instruments to shave their faces and the crowns of their heads. Finally, they poured half an ounce of stinking synthetic liquid soap into each palm and locked them all in the bath. There was nothing else to do, so the prisoners all washed themselves again.

"Then with a cannon-like roar the exit door opened, and they went out into the dark purple of the lobby. Two old women, servants of Hell, trundled out the trolleys from the 'roaster'; there on hot hooks the rags familiar to our heroes were hanging.

"Downcast, they returned to Cell 72, where their fifty comrades were lying on the bedbug-ridden planks, burning with curiosity to learn everything that had happened. Once again 'muzzles' covered the windows and the doves had been painted over with dark olive-colored paint. In the corner stood a four-pail latrine.

"In the niche, forgotten, the little bronze Buddha smiled mysteriously."

55

YOU HAVE ONLY ONE CONSCIENCE

At the very same time this story was being told, Shchagov, in another part of Moscow, polished up his boots, which were old but still in good shape, put on his freshly ironed uniform, with its ribbons and wound stripes, and went off to the other end of the city. He had been invited through Alexei Lansky, his friend from the front, to a party at prosecutor Makarygin's. (Unfortunately for Shchagov, military dress was going out of fashion in Moscow, and soon he would have to join in the harsh competition for suits and shoes.)

The party was for the young people, and for the Makarygin family in general, to celebrate the prosecutor's second Order of Lenin. Actually, the young people who turned up were not at all close to the family, and not at all interested in the prosecutor's new honor. But Papa had been generous about the expense, and that was reason enough for a party. Liza was going to be there, too—the girl Shchagov had told Nadya he was engaged to, although nothing had yet been finally decided or formally announced. It was because of Liza that he had asked Lansky to get him invited.

And now, with several opening remarks all prepared, he climbed the same stairway on which Clara kept seeing the woman scrubbing the steps; climbed to the very same apartment where, four years before, the man whose wife he had almost taken away just a little while ago had crawled on his knees laying the parquet floor.

Buildings, too, have their stories.

Shchagov rang the bell, and Clara opened the door to him. They did not know each other, but each guessed who the other was.

Clara was wearing a dress of green woolen crepe, gathered at the waist into a full skirt. Shiny green embroidery wound around the collar, down across her breast like a chain, and around her sleeves like bracelets.

A number of fur coats were already hanging in the close little hall. Before Clara could ask Shchagov to take his coat off, the telephone rang. She picked up the phone and started talking, at the same time gesturing to Shchagov to hang up his coat.

"Innokenty? Hello—what? You haven't left yet? Come right away! Innokenty, what do you mean you're not in the mood? Papa will be so hurt. Yes, your voice does sound tired, but you must try! Well, wait a minute then, I'll call Dotty. Dotty!" she shouted into the other room. "Your true love is calling. Come here! Take your coat off!" Shchagov had taken off his military overcoat. "Take off your rubbers!" He was not wearing rubbers. "Listen, he doesn't want to come. What's wrong with him?"

Clara's sister, Dotnara—the "diplomat's wife," in Lansky's phrase describing her to Shchagov—came into the hall and took the phone. She stood blocking Shchagov's way into the other room, and he was in no hurry to get past this perfumed creature in her light, cherry-colored dress. He dropped his eyes a bit and looked her over. One thing about her dress surprised him: the sleeves were not part of the dress itself, but part of a little cape she wore over it. Something about her—and Shchagov didn't know whether it was the absence of the crude padded shoulders everyone was wearing or the lovely natural line of her arms, from her rounded shoulders down to her hands—something made Dotnara seem utterly feminine, unlike anyone else.

None of the people gathered in the cozy little entrance hall could have imagined that in that harmless black telephone, in that light conversation about coming to a party, the ruin lay hidden which lies in wait for us all, even, as Pushkin says, in the bones of a dead steed.

Earlier the same day Rubin had called for additional tapes of the telephone voice of each suspect. This was the first time since then that Volodin had used his phone. Over in the central telephone station the tape rustled, recording his voice.

It had crossed Innokenty's mind that it would be best not to use the telephone now; but his wife had gone out, leaving a note saying he must come to her father's that night.

So he phoned to say he would not be there.

Undoubtedly it would have been easier for Innokenty if,

after that frightening night, today had been a weekday, not
Sunday. Then he could have assessed his situation by various signs, for instance, by the progress or cancellation of
his assignment to Paris. But he could not tell anything on a
Sunday, whether peace or danger hung over the quiet of the
day.

For the past twenty-four hours he had felt that his phone
call had been madness, suicidal, and had probably not
done any good either. He remembered with irritation Dobroumov's dunce of a wife; although, of course, she was not
really to blame, and mistrust did not begin or end with her.

Nothing indicated that Innokenty had been found out,
but some inner premonition gnawed at him, one of those
strange signs we are sometimes mysteriously given. A sense
of approaching disaster rose in him, and he did not want
to go to the party.

He tried to explain this now to his wife, drawing out his
words, as people always do when they are saying something
unpleasant. His wife insisted—and the precise "formants"
of his "individual speech pattern" were etched on the narrow brown magnetic tape, to be converted into a voice
print which would be spread out in front of Rubin by nine
the next morning.

Dotty was not talking in the categorical tone she had
adopted in the past few months; touched by the fatigue in
her husband's voice, she asked very gently if he wouldn't
come, just for an hour.

Innokenty felt sorry for her and agreed to come.

But as he put the phone down, he stood still for a moment,
his hand still on the receiver, as if he had not finished
what he wanted to say.

He felt sorry, not for the wife he lived with and yet did
not live with these days, the wife he was going to leave
again soon, but for the blond girl with curls hanging down
to her shoulders, the girl he had known in tenth grade, when
together they had begun to learn what life is. The passion
between them in those days overrode all arguments; they
would not hear of postponing their marriage, even for one
year. Thanks to the instinct that guides us past surface illusions and false impressions, they were truly aware of one
another, and they did not want to let each other go. Innokenty's mother, already seriously ill, opposed the marriage.
(But then what mother doesn't oppose her son's marriage?)

The prosecutor was opposed, too. (But what father is likely to give away gladly a lovely eighteen-year-old daughter?) But everyone had to give in. The young people married, and their happiness together became a legend among their friends.

Their married life began under the best auspices. They belonged to that circle of society in which people do not know what it means to walk or take the subway, that group who even before the war preferred planes to sleeping cars, who never even had to concern themselves with furnishing an apartment. Wherever they went—Moscow, Teheran, the Syrian coast, Switzerland—a furnished house, villa, or apartment awaited the young couple. And their philosophies of life were the same: "We have only one life!" So take everything life can give, except one thing: the birth of a child. For a child is an idol who sucks dry the juices of your being without any return for your sacrifices, not even ordinary gratitude.

With such views, they were very much in tune with the circumstances they lived in, and the circumstances were in tune with them. They tried every new and strange fruit. They learned the taste of every fine cognac, learned to tell Rhône wines from the wines of Corsica, to know all the wines from all the vineyards of the earth. To wear clothes of every kind. To dance every dance. To swim at every resort. To play tennis and to sail a boat. To attend an act or two of every unusual play. To leaf through every sensational book.

For six years, the best of their youth, they gave each other everything. Those were the years when mankind was racked by partings, dying in the front lines and under the ruins of cities, when adults gone mad were grabbing crumbs of black bread from the hands of children. But none of the world's grief had touched Innokenty and Dotnara.

After all, we have only one life!

Nonetheless, as Russians used to say, the ways of the Lord are unfathomable. By the end of the sixth year of their marriage, when all the bombers had stopped flying and the guns had fallen silent, when green things, forgotten in the smoke of war, began to stir in a renewal of growth, when people everywhere began to remember that they had only one life —in those very months Innokenty suddenly began to become acutely dissatisfied with his and his wife's way of life.

He was frightened by this. He struggled against it; he

waited for it to pass like an illness; but it did not pass. He could not understand it. Everything seemed to be at his fingertips—except the one most important thing.

His lively friends, whom he had felt so close to, began for some reason to please him less and less. One seemed rather stupid, another somehow crude, another too wrapped up in himself.

Not only had he grown apart from his friends, but also from his blond Dotty—as he had long ago nicknamed Dotnara, in the European manner—his own wife, with whom he had formerly felt so much in harmony.

At times her opinions seemed too sharp. Or her voice would sound too assured. In one situation after another he found her behavior distasteful, and at the same time she seemed more and more convinced she was right about everything.

Their chic life began to oppress Innokenty, but Dotty wouldn't hear of changing any part of it. Even worse, she used to run through things, abandoning each new possession for the next; now she felt she must hang onto all the things in all their apartments forever. For two years she had been sending huge packages to Moscow from Paris, fabrics, shoes, dresses, hats—Innokenty found it awful. And had she always chewed her food this way, chomping, smacking her lips, especially when she was eating fruit?

But the heart of the matter was a change not in his friends or in his wife, but in Innokenty himself: the lack of something, he didn't know what.

Innokenty had been known for a long time as an epicurean. That was what they called him, and he accepted the appellation gladly, though he himself did not know exactly what it meant. Then one day, at home in Moscow with nothing else to do, it occurred to him to look up the teacher's work and find out exactly what he had taught. He began looking through his dead mother's bookcases. In one of the three he thought he would find a book about Epicurus; he remembered seeing it somewhere there in his boyhood.

He started the search with cramped, laborious movements, as if he were pushing very heavy objects from place to place. The air was full of dust. He was not used to work like this, and he got very tried. But he kept at it—and a breeze of renewal seemed to breathe on him from the depths of the old bookcases, with their peculiar musty smell. He did find

the book about Epicurus, among other things, and later he
got around to reading it. But the great discovery was finding
his mother's letters. He had never understood her, and had
been close to her only in his childhood. He had accepted
her death almost with indifference, and he had not come
home from Beirut for her funeral.

From early childhood his picture of his father had been
mixed in with the long silver bugles that thrust up toward
the sculptured plaster ceiling, and the call of "Rise in Bonfires, O Blue Nights!" Innokenty did not remember his
father himself; he had died in 1921 in the Tambov District. But people everywhere loved to tell him about his
father—the celebrated hero of the Civil War, the sailors'
leader. Hearing his praises sung by everyone, everywhere,
Innokenty used to feel very proud of his father, and of his
struggle for the ordinary people against the few who lived
steeped in luxury. At the same time, he was almost condescending toward his mother, who was always ill, always
suffering from something, grieving over something, always
surrounded by her books and her hot-water bottles. Like
most sons, he never thought of his mother as having a life
of her own apart from him, his childhood, his needs; or
that her illness and her suffering were real; or that she had
died at the age of forty-seven.

His parents had lived together very rarely, almost never.
But Innokenty had never wondered much about this as a
boy, and he had never thought to ask his mother about it.

And now it was all laid open to him, in his mother's
letters and diaries. Their marriage had not been a marriage
but more like the passage of a hurricane, like everything in
those years. Sudden circumstances had thrown them together,
circumstances kept them from seeing each other often, and
circumstances parted them. In these diaries, his mother
turned out not just to be a supplement to his father, as the
son believed, but to inhabit a whole separate sphere of her
own. Innokenty learned that his mother had always loved
another man, and that she had never been able to share his
life.

There were bundles of letters, tied up with various colored
ribbons, from women friends, men friends, acquaintances;
actors and actresses, artists and poets, whose names were
now completely forgotten, or remembered only to be dismissed. Her diaries, the daily entries in Russian and in

French, were kept in old notebooks with dark-blue morocco bindings: page after page of her strange handwriting, which looked as though a wounded bird had fluttered back and forth, scratching a crooked and fanciful trail with its claws. Many pages were filled with recollections of literary gatherings and plays. His heart was seized by his mother's description of the night—one of the white nights of June—when she and some of her young friends had met the troupe of the Moscow Art Theater at the Petersburg Station, and she had wept with happiness. An unselfish love of art glowed joyously in those pages, and the freshness of it reached Innokenty. He did not know of any such troupe these days, and he could not imagine anyone going the whole night without sleep to meet it, unless they had been sent by the Cultural Section, with bouquets paid for by the accounting office. And certainly no one would think of weeping.

The diaries carried him on and on. He came to some pages headed "Notes on Ethics."

"Pity is the first action of a good soul."

Innokenty frowned. Pity? A shameful and humiliating emotion, both for the person who pitied and for the one who was pitied—at least that was what he had learned in school.

"Never consider yourself more in the right than others. Respect other opinions, even those opposed to yours."

That was rather old-fashioned. If my view of the world is the right one, how can I respect those who disagree with me?

The son felt not as if he were reading, but as if he were listening to his mother speaking in her brittle voice.

"What is the most precious thing in the world? Not to participate in injustices. They are stronger than you. They have existed in the past and they will exist in the future. But let them not come about through *you*."

Yes, his mother had been a weak creature. It was impossible to picture Mama fighting, struggling, impossible to reconcile images of Mama and struggle.

If Innokenty had opened her diaries six years before, he would never even have noticed all these passages. Now he read them slowly, and was astonished. There was nothing very mysterious in them, and there were things that were simply not correct, but he was surprised. The very words in which his mother and her women friends had expressed

themselves were old-fashioned. They wrote, in dead seriousness, with capital letters: "Truth, Beauty, Good, Evil: ethical imperatives." In the language Innokenty and his friends
used, words were more concrete, and therefore more comprehensible: moral intelligence, humaneness, loyalty, pur-
posefulness.

But even though Innokenty was beyond doubt morally
intelligent, humane, loyal, and purposeful—it was being
purposeful that everyone of his generation valued most of
all in themselves and worked at hardest—still, sitting there
on a low bench in front of those bookcases, he felt he had
found something of what he lacked.

There were albums there, too, with the pure clarity of
old photographs. And there were several packets of Petersburg and Moscow theater programs. And the daily theatrical paper *The Spectator*. And the *Cinematographic Herald*
—was that around in those days? Had they all belonged to
that time? And piles and piles of different magazines, whose
names were only colored spots before his eyes: *Apollo, The
Golden Fleece, The Scales, The World of Art, The Russian
Sun, The Awakening, Pegasus*. There were reproductions of
unknown paintings and sculptures and theatrical décors—
not a trace of them now in the Tretyakov Gallery. Verses
by unknown poets. Innumerable issues of magazine supple-
ments filled with the names of European writers Innokenty
had never heard of. And dozens of unknown publishers, as
forgotten as if they had dropped into Hell: Griffon, Haw-
thorne, Scorpion, Musaget, Halcyon, Spolokhi, Logos, Pro-
metheus, Social Service.

For several days he would come and sit on that bench in
front of the open bookcases, breathing it all in, poisoning
himself with the air of his mother's world, that world into
which, long ago, his father, in a black raincoat, his belt hung
with grenades, had entered with a search warrant.

While he was there, Dotty had come in to ask him to go
to a party of some sort. Innokenty had looked at her
blankly, and then had frowned, imagining the pretentious
gathering where everyone would thoroughly agree with
everyone else, where they would leap to their feet for the
initial toast to Comrade Stalin, and then eat and drink a
great deal, oblivious of Comrade Stalin, and then play cards
stupidly.

He looked at Dotty across an inarticulate distance and asked her to go alone.

Dotty found it barbarous that anyone would rather poke through old albums than go to a good party. Stirring the vague but never dead recollections of childhood, everything he found in those bookcases spoke deeply to Innokenty, but not at all to his wife.

His mother had finally done what she wanted: rising from her grave, she had taken her son away from his bride.

It was through all this that Innokenty came to understand her; just as the essence of food cannot be conveyed in calories, the essence of life will never be captured by even the greatest formulas.

Having begun, Innokenty could not stop. In recent years he had grown lazy; he no longer cared about learning. He had learned from his mother in his youth the fluent French which had carried him along in his career. Now he threw himself into reading.

It turned out that you have to know how to read. It is not just a matter of letting your eyes run down the pages. Since Innokenty, from youth on, had been shielded from erroneous or outcast books, and had read only the clearly established classics, he had grown used to believing every word he read, giving himself up completely to the author's will. Now, reading writers whose opinions contradicted one another, he was unable for a while to rebel, but could only submit to one author, then to another, then to a third.

Then he had gone to Paris and worked for UNESCO. While he was there he had read a lot after work. And he had reached a point where he felt less tossed about from one writer's ideas to another's, felt that he himself had his hand on the helm.

He had not discovered very much in those years, but he had discovered something.

Up to then the truth for Innokenty had been: you have only one life.

Now he came to sense a new law, in himself and in the world: you also have only one conscience.

And just as you cannot recover a lost life, you cannot recover a wrecked conscience.

Innokenty was beginning to realize it when, on that Saturday, several days before his planned trip to Paris, he learned

to his misfortune about the trap being prepared for that
simpleton Dobroumov. He already knew enough to understand that such an affair would not end with Dobroumov,
that it would be the beginning of a long campaign. But
Dobroumov was especially dear to him as someone who
figured in his memories of his mother.

For several hours he had paced his office in indecision—
the diplomat who shared the office was off on an official
trip. He had rocked back and forth, started to tremble,
held his head in his hands. Finally he had decided to call,
even though he knew that Dobroumov's phone might well
be under surveillance and that there were only a few men
in the ministry who knew the secret.

Now, all that seemed ages ago—though it had only been
the day before.

All day today Innokenty had been violently perturbed.
He had left home so that they could not come and arrest
him there. All day his feelings shifted back and forth, from
cruel regret to contemptible fear, to an indifferent "come
what may" and back to fear again. The day before, he had
not expected this terrible nervousness. He had not known
he could be so afraid for himself.

Now the taxi was taking him along Bolshaya Kaluzhskaya,
bright with lights. A heavy snow was falling, and the wind-
shield wipers swept back and forth.

He thought about Dotty. Their estrangement had gone so
far this past spring that he had arranged not to take her
with him when he had gone to Rome.

And in return, when he had come back in August, he
learned she had taken up with an officer on the General
Staff. With stubborn female conviction, she had not even
denied her unfaithfulness, but had put all the blame on
Innokenty: why had he left her all alone?

But he had not even felt the pain of loss, only relief. He
had not felt vengeful or jealous. He had simply stopped going to her room, and had maintained a contemptuous silence
for the past four months. Of course, there could not even
be talk of divorce. In his branch of the service a divorce
would be fatal to his career.

But now, in these last days before his departure—before
his arrest!—he wanted to be gentle with Dotty. He remembered not the bad, but all that was good about her.

If he was to be arrested, she would be knocked around enough and terrified enough because of him.

On the right, past the iron fence that ran around the Neskuchny Gardens, the black trunks and branches of the trees flashed by, white with snow.

The thick snowfall brought peace and forgetfulness.

56

THE DINNER PARTY

The prosecutor's apartment, which aroused the envy of the whole Entry No. 2, but which the Makarygin family itself found too small, was made up of two adjoining apartments, whose connecting walls had been taken down. Therefore it had two front doors, one of which was nailed shut, two baths, two toilets, two hallways, two kitchens, and five other rooms, in the most spacious of which dinner was now being served.

There were twenty-five in all, guests and hosts, and the two Bashkir maids were barely able to cope with serving everyone. One of them was their own servant, and the other had been borrowed from neighbors for the evening. Both girls were quite young; both came from the same village; and last summer they had completed the course at the same secondary school in Chekmagush. Their faces, strained and reddened from the heat of the kitchen, expressed seriousness and effort. The prosecutor's wife, a tall, heavy woman in vigorous middle age, watched them approvingly.

The prosecutor's first wife was dead. She had gone through the Civil War with her husband; she had known how to fire a machine gun, had worn a leather coat, and had lived by every last decree of the Party cell. But she could never have lifted the Makarygin household to its present style, and in fact it was hard to imagine what her later life would have been if she had not died when Clara was born.

But Alevtina Nikanorovna, Makarygin's present wife,

knew that a good family cannot prosper without a good
kitchen, that carpets and tablecloths are important tokens
of prosperity, and that crystal is the proper service for a
banquet. She had been collecting crystal for years, and not
the current crude, lopsided crystal, passed down the assembly line through many indifferent hands, with no trace
in it of a master craftsman's soul. She collected antique
crystal, crystal confiscated by court order in the twenties
and thirties and sold in the distribution centers open only
to officials of the courts; every bowl and cup bore the special
quality of its maker. She had added a great deal to her
stock in Latvia during the two postwar years the prosecutor
had worked in Riga; in the commission stores and on the
open market, she had acquired furniture, china, even single
silver spoons.

Now at the two large tables the bright light cast multicolored sparkles from the cut crystal facets and ridges.
There were shades of ruby (dark golden red), copper (a
chocolate red), selenium (a red with a breath of yellow).
There were a dark heavy green, a cadmium green with a
hint of gold, and a cobalt blue. And there was milky white.
And iridescent crystal with oxide tints. And crystal that
looked like ivory. There were double-throated carafes with
round, cut-glass stoppers. And triple-tiered bowls made of
ordinary white crystal, packed to their rims with fruits,
nuts, and candies. And plain little lead glass vases, goblets,
and glasses. All of it varied tremendously; there were rarely
more than six of the same color or with the same monogram.

In the midst of this brilliance, at the table for the older
generation, the object responsible for all the festivity—the
prosecutor's new Order of Lenin—blazed out among his
previous orders, now grown dull and tarnished.

The young people's table stretched the whole length of
the room. The two tables were joined, but at right angles, so
that some guests could not see each other, and no one could
hear much of anything; there were many separate conversations. The talk rose in a lively, happy hum, and over it
sounded the ring of young laughter and clinking glasses.

They had long ago got through the formal toasts: to Comrade Stalin, to officials of the judiciary, and to the host—
that this honor might not be his last. By ten-thirty many
dishes had been brought in and taken away—salted, salt and

sweet, sharp, sour, smoked, lean, fat, frozen, vitamin-packed. Many of the dishes had been marvelous, but no one ate with concentrated attention and pleasure, as they would have by themselves. The dinner was doomed, as it always is at formal parties: rare dishes were prepared and set out in huge quantities; the guests were seated too close together and got in each other's way; they were caught up in their social duties, talking, joking, and showing a careful lack of interest in the food.

But Shchagov, who had been wasting away in the students' dining room for years, and Clara's two friends from the institute went at every dish with real feeling, though they tried to appear decently indifferent. Another guest who ate heartily was a protégée of the hostess, sitting next to her. She was a girlhood friend, a lower-class girl who had married a Party instructor in the distant Zarechensky District. She was unhappy; she would never make her way in good society with that doltish husband of hers. She was here in Moscow on a shopping expedition. In a way, the hostess was pleased that her friend ate everything, praised it, asked for the recipe, and was so openly delighted with the décor of the house and the whole milieu of the prosecutor's family. But she was ashamed, too, of this woman friend who was barely a friend, especially in front of her unexpected guest, Major General Slovuta. And she was ashamed of Dushan Radovich, an old friend of the prosecutor's; he, too, was hardly a friend any more. Both had been invited because the party had originally been planned as a family gathering. Now Slovuta might think the Makarygins were in the habit of taking in beggars. ("Beggar" was Alevtina Nikanorovna's word for anyone unable to set himself up well in life and earn a high salary.) This poisoned the party for her. So she had seated her friend as far as possible from Slovuta, and hushed her as much as she could.

Dotty moved up to their end of the table because she had caught part of what sounded like a fascinating story about a servant. (They had all been liberated from serfdom and educated so rapidly that no one wanted to help cook, wash dishes or clothes.) In Zarechensky District people would help a girl leave a collective farm, and in return she would work for them for two years. Then they would get her a passport, and she could go off to the city. At the epidemiology station there, wages were budgeted for two

fictitious women orderlies; instead, the wages actually went
to girls working as household servants for the head of the
station and the head of the District Health Administration.
Dotty wrinkled her brow; in the districts everything was
simpler. But here in Moscow?

Dinera, a quick, dark-haired woman who rarely finished
a complete thought herself, and certainly never let anyone
else do so, got bored with the "table of honor" and went
over to join the young people. She was dressed all in black;
imported satin covered her like a thin, sleek skin, all but
her arms, which were white as alabaster.

She waved at Lansky from across the room.

"Alexei! I'm coming to join you! Were you at *Unforgettable 1919*?"

With the same even smile with which he greeted everyone,
Lansky answered, "Yesterday."

"Why not at the premiere? I hunted for you with my opera
glasses; I wanted to follow your blazing trail!"

Lansky, sitting next to Clara and waiting for an important
answer from her, prepared himself, without much enthusiasm, for an argument—it was impossible not to argue with
Dinera. Time after time, at literary gatherings, editorial offices, the Central Writers' Club restaurant, arguments arose
between them. Dinera, who was not tied down by a Party
or literary position, attacked harshly, though always just
within the bounds. Dramatists, scenario writers, directors—
no one was spared, not even her own husband, Nikolai Galakhov. The daring of her judgments suited her perfectly,
along with the daring of her dress and her life, which was
well known to everyone; they were a breath of fresh air in
the vapid atmosphere of literary criticism turned out not by
men but by the official positions they occupied. She attacked literary criticism in general, and the essays of Alexei
Lansky in particular. Smiling and restrained, Lansky never
tired of explaining to Dinera her anarchical errors, her petty-
bourgeois deviations. He was willing to go along with this
half-joking dialogue, part intimacy, part anger, because his
own literary fate was to a great extent in Galakhov's hands.

Unforgettable 1919 was a play by Vishnevsky, ostensibly
the story of revolutionary Petrograd and the Baltic sailors,
but in fact about Stalin: how Stalin had saved Petrograd,
saved the entire Revolution, saved all Russia. The play,
written for the seventieth birthday of the Father and Teach-

er, revealed how, under Stalin's guidance, Lenin had some-how managed to cope.

"You see," said Dinera, with a dreamy swoop of her hand, as she sat down across the table from Lansky, "there must be imagination, sharp imagination, in a play; mischief, in-solence. Do you remember Vishnevsky's *An Optimistic Tragedy?* Where he had the chorus of two sailors exchang-ing wisecracks: 'Isn't there too much blood in this tragedy?' 'No more than in Shakespeare.' Now that's original! And then you go to Vishnevsky's new play, and what is it? Realistic, of course; historically accurate; a stirring image of the Leader; but that's all."

"What?" demanded the very young man who had given Dinera the chair next to his. In his buttonhole he wore, a little carelessly, a little crookedly, a ribbon of the Order of Lenin. "Isn't that enough for you? I can't remember when we've been given a more touching portrayal of Iosif Vis-sarionovich! The audience was full of people weeping."

"I myself had tears in my eyes!" Dinera said, dismissing him. "I'm not talking about that!" She went on to Lansky: "But hardly anyone in the play even has a name! For characters you have three Party secretaries with no personali-ties at all, seven commanders, four commissars—like a table of organization! And those sailors again, dashing around— 'little brothers' migrating from Belotserkovsky's plays to Lavrenev's, from Lavrenev's to Vishnevsky's, from Vishne-vsky's to Sobolev's." Dinera shook her head as she named the playwrights, then narrowed her eyes and continued: "You know ahead of time who's good, who's bad, and how it will all come out—"

"And why don't you like that?" asked Lansky, seeming surprised. "Why do you insist on false and superficial enter-tainment? What about real life? Do you think that in real life our fathers had any doubt how the Civil War would end? Did we have any doubt how the War of the Father-land would end, even when the enemy was in the suburbs of Moscow?"

"Does the playwright have any doubt how his play will be received? Tell me, Alexei, why is it that our premieres never *flop*? Why is that something our playwrights never have to worry about? I promise you, someday I won't hold myself back, I'll put two fingers in my mouth and give such a whis-tle—"

She pursed her lips very daintily to show how, from which it was clear that she didn't know how to whistle.

The young man beside her, bearing himself with great importance, poured her some wine, but she did not touch it.

"I will explain," Lansky answered, unperturbed. "Plays never fail here, and can't fail, because the playwrights and the public share the same vision, both artistically and in their general view of the world."

"Oh, Alexei," Dinera said, frowning. "Save that for an article. I know that thesis: the people are not interested in your *personal* perceptions; as a critic you must express the truth, and there is only one truth—"

"Of course," said Lansky, smiling calmly. "The critic is duty-bound not to give in to ordinary impulses of feeling, but to adapt such feelings to the general task—"

He went on explaining, but he did not forget to look at Clara, to touch her fingertips with his beneath the rim of her plate, as if to say that, although he was talking, he was really waiting for her answer.

Clara could not be jealous of Dinera, and in fact it was Dinera who had first brought Lansky into the Makarygin home, just to meet Clara. But she was annoyed at this literary conversation which took Alexei away from her. As she watched Dinera cross her white arms, she regretted her own long sleeves. She had nice arms, too.

But she was really pleased with the way she looked. This brief annoyance could not spoil the gaiety she had felt today, a lightheartedness she was not used to. She did not think about it, but that was how things were working out—she was destined to be gay today. The extraordinary day was ending with an extraordinary evening. This morning—though it seemed ages ago—she had not yet had that wonderful talk with Rostislav. His tender kiss. The basket she had woven for the New Year's tree. And then when she had dashed home, it was almost time for the party. The whole evening, really, was for her. What a pleasure to put on her new green dress with its gleaming fretwork embroidery, to meet all the guests as they came in. Her youth, which had stretched on too long, was blossoming a second time at the age of twenty-four. This was her time—now, this moment. She had even, it seemed, in the ecstasy of that morning, promised Rostislav that she would wait for

him. She, who had always shunned any physical contact—
she, the very same person—that night when she met Alexei
in the hallway had let him take her hand in his. Was it she?
There had been a coolness between them this past month,
and then, there in the hall, Alexei had said:

"Clara! I don't know what you'll think of me—I've ordered
two seats at the Aurora Restaurant for New Year's Eve.
Shall we go? I know it's not our style, but shall we go, just
for the fun of it?"

She had not said no. She had hesitated, and then that
fat young Zhenka had come running in, asking her to find
some record for him. Since then they had not been left
alone for a minute, and the unfinished conversation hung
between them half the night.

Zhenka and the girls who had been students with Clara
at the Communications Institute still felt like students here
tonight and, in spite of all the high-ranking guests, were very
relaxed. Zhenka was drinking like a trooper, and regaling the
girl next to him with one joke after another, until finally,
blushing and choking with laughter, she exclaimed, "Oh! I
can't hear any more!" and jumped up and left the table. A
young lieutenant in the MVD, a nephew of the prosecutor's
wife, came up to her and slapped her on the back to stop
her choking. Everyone called him a border guard, because
his cap had a green band and piping; but, in fact, he lived in
Moscow, and his job was checking people's documents on
trains.

Shchagov was at the young people's table, too, sitting next
to his Liza. He served her with food and drink, and talked
to her, but his mind wasn't on what he was saying. He was
thinking about everything he saw around him. Behind the
calm, courteous expression on his face, he was taking everything in: everything displayed, hung, and arranged there,
and the guests who partook of it all so casually. From the
braided epaulets of the jurists, who held the rank of generals,
to the diplomatic shield in another part of the room, to the
ribbon of the Order of Lenin pinned so carelessly in his very
young neighbor's lapel (and to think that he had hoped to
look distinguished here with his own modest orders and
decorations!), Shchagov could not find in all this grand
company one front-line soldier, one brother from the mine
fields, one companion from the jog-trot over plowed ground,

that vile little trot so resoundingly called "Attack." At the beginning of the party he had summoned up the faces of comrades who had been killed in the fields of flax, under the walls of sheds, in attacks, and he had felt like seizing the tablecloth, tearing it off, and shouting, "You sons-of-bitches, where were you?"

But the party went on. Shchagov drank, not so much that he got drunk, but just enough so that his booted feet no longer felt the full weight of his body. And as the floor began to feel lighter, he began to feel more open to all the warmth and brightness around him. It no longer repelled him; now Shchagov could enter into the party, mind and body, for all his gnawing wounds and the burning dryness of his stomach.

Wasn't it out of date, that old distinction he made between soldiers and those who had not been soldiers? Most people nowadays felt shy about wearing their decorations won at the front, which had cost them so much and had shone so brightly for a time. You couldn't go around these days shaking everyone by the shoulder and asking, "Where were you?" Who fought, who hid? You couldn't tell now, it was all mixed up. There is a law of time, a law of oblivion: glory to the dead, life to the living.

He alone in this company knew the price of well-being, and he alone here was really worthy of it. This was his first entrance into this world, but he felt he had arrived once and for all. He looked around the room and thought to himself, "This is my future! This is my future!"

Shchagov's young neighbor, the one with the ribbon, looked around at everything with his eyes half closed. He was wearing a light-blue and yellow necktie, and his pale, smoothed-down hair was already thinning. He was twenty-four years old and trying to act at least thirty, moving his hands very deliberately and bearing his lower lip with enormous dignity. In spite of his youth, he was already one of the most prized reference consultants in the Reception Office of the Presidium of the Supreme Soviet. This reference consultant knew that the prosecutor's wife hoped to marry him to Clara, but Clara was already much too small a fish for him. He had good reason to take his time about getting married. Dinera, now, was quite a different matter—she exuded something, something that made him feel good just to be near her. Aside from anything else, it raised him very much in his own esteem just to be flirting with such a famous writer's wife. He paid court to her now, trying to touch her now and then, and he would gladly have sided with her in the argument, but it turned out that she wanted no support—it was impossible to show her where she was mistaken.

"But then you disagree with Gorky! You're disputing Gorky himself!" Lansky was saying.

"Gorky was the founder of Socialist Realism!" the reference consultant reminded her. "To cast doubt on Gorky, after all, is just as criminal as—" He hesitated to make a comparison. As—?

Lansky nodded at him seriously. Dinera smiled.

"Mama!" Clara called out, loudly, impatiently. "Can't our table have an intermission till tea?"

The prosecutor's wife had been in the kitchen giving orders; she returned to find that her tedious friend had attached herself to Dotty, and was telling her at great length how all the children of the Party activists in Zarechensky District were on a special list, so that there was always enough milk for them, and all the penicillin shots they needed. This led the conversation to medicine. Dotty, young as she was, had already begun to suffer various ailments, and any talk of illness was fascinating to her.

Alevtina Nikanorovna looked at it this way: Whoever had status was assured of good health. All you had to do was telephone some famous professor, best of all some Laureate of the Stalin Prize; he would write out a prescription and any coronary occlusion would instantly disappear. You could always afford to go to the best sanitarium. She and her husband were not afraid of illness.

She answered Clara's outcry reproachfully: "Now, hostess! Serve your guests! Don't drive them from the table!"

"No, we want to dance! We want to dance!" the border guard shouted.

Zhenka quickly poured himself another glass and drank it down.

"Dance! Dance!" shouted the others.

And the young people scattered.

Loud music poured in from the next room. They were playing a tango called "Autumn Leaves."

57

TWO SONS-IN-LAW

Dotty went off to dance, too, and the hostess got her friend to help her clear the table. This left five men at the older people's table: Makarygin himself; his old and dear friend from Civil War days, the Serb Dushan Radovich, who had been a professor at the Institute of the Red Professoriate, long since abolished; a more recent acquaintance, Slovuta, who had completed the Higher Jurisprudence courses with Makarygin and was also a prosecutor, as well as a major general; and Makarygin's two sons-in-law—Innokenty Volodin, wearing, on Makarygin's insistence, his mouse-gray uniform with its golden palm branches; and the famous writer Nikolai Galakhov, Laureate of the Stalin Prize.

Makarygin had already celebrated his new order at a banquet for his colleagues, and he had wanted this party to be for the young people, and more *en famille*. But Slovuta, an important colleague, had missed the first party, having just come back from the Far East the day before; he had been one of the chief prosecutors in the notorious case of the Japanese military men who worked on bacteriological weapons. So Makarygin had had to invite him to come tonight. Yet he had already asked Radovich, who was almost *persona non grata* officially. It was awkward to have Radovich there with the prosecutor's present colleague; Makarygin had originally invited him to the family party simply for the pleasure of talking over old times. He could have put Radovich off at the last minute, but it irritated him to have to think of doing something so cowardly. So he had decided to balance Radovich's dubious presence with his two sons-in-law: the diplomat in his gold braid and the writer with his laureate's medal.

Now, with only the five of them left at table, Makarygin was afraid that Radovich would come up with some barbed remark. He was an intelligent man but apt to say wild things when he lost his temper. So Makarygin was trying to get the conversation onto some safe, shallow plane. Subduing his usual hearty voice, he proceeded to chide Innokenty in a good-humored way for not having comforted his old age with grandchildren.

"After all, what are they, these two?" he complained. "That's a pair for you—a ram and a ewe with no lambs. They live for themselves, put on fat, and have no worries at all. They've got things all worked out. Burning their lives away! Ask him—it seems the fellow is an epicurean. Well, Innokenty? Admit it—you're a follower of Epicurus."

No one, even as a joke, could call a member of the all-Union Communist Party a Neo-Hegelian, a Neo-Kantian, a Subjectivist, an Agnostic, or, God forbid, a Revisionist. But "epicurean" sounded so harmless it could not possibly imply that one was not an orthodox Marxist.

At that point Radovich, who cherished every detail of the lives of the Founders, put in: "Well, Epicurus was a good person, a materialist. Karl Marx himself wrote a dissertation on Epicurus."

Radovich was thin and dry, the dark parchment of his skin stretched tight over his bones.

Innokenty felt a surge of well-being. Here, in this room humming with lively talk, laughter, and vivid colors, the idea of being arrested seemed impossible. The last fears stirring in the depths of his heart dissolved. He drank quickly, warmed up, and looked gaily around him at these people who knew nothing of his anxiety. He felt like the favorite of the gods. Makarygin, even Slovuta, who on another occasion might have inspired his contempt, seemed human and dear to him now, as though they were taking a hand in protecting him.

"Epicurus?" He answered the challenge with shining eyes. "Yes, I am a follower of his. I don't deny it. But I'd probably surprise you if I told you that 'epicurean' is a word that is usually misunderstood. When people want to say someone is too greedy for life, a voluptuary, lascivious—in short, a pig—they call him an 'epicurean.' No, wait a minute, I'm serious," he said, warding off Makarygin's interruption; he was speaking excitedly now, tipping his tall wine glass back and forth in his thin, sensitive fingers. "Actually, Epicurus stands for just the opposite of what people think. He includes *insatiable desires* among the basic evils that hinder human happiness. He says, in fact, that a human being needs very *little*, and therefore his happiness

doesn't depend on fate. He doesn't at all urge us on to orgies.
It's true he thinks of ordinary human pleasure as the highest
good. But he goes on to say that all pleasures don't appear
the minute they're wanted; they must be preceded by periods
of unsatisfied desire; in other words, the absence of pleasure.
So he finds it best to renounce all striving except the humb-
lest. His teachings free us from our fear of fate, of its blows.
And therefore he's a great optimist, Epicurus!"

"You don't say!" said Galakhov in surprise, and pulled
out a notebook with a tiny white ivory pencil. For all his
meteoric fame, Galakhov had no pretensions; he could jest
and clap people on the back with as much good fellowship
as anyone. Some streaks of white hair already shone at-
tractively above his rather swarthy, plump face.

"Give him some more!" Slovuta said to Makarygin, pointing to Innokenty's empty glass. "More, or he'll talk our
heads off."

Makarygin poured him more wine, and Innokenty drank
it with pleasure. It was only now, when he had so adroitly
defended it, that Epicurus' philosophy really seemed like
something to live by.

Radovich smiled at the extraordinary credo. He drank no
alcohol—he was forbidden to. For most of the evening he
had sat immobile, somber, wearing a sort of military-looking
field jacket, and severe spectacles in cheap frames. Until
very recently, whenever he went for a walk in Sterlitamak
he would wear a cap shaped like a Budënny helmet, rising
to a tall thin peak, just as he had in Civil War or NEP times.
But nowadays the cap made passers-by laugh and dogs bark.
It was simply impossible to wear it in Moscow—the police
would not allow it.

Slovuta, whose face was puffy but not old, adopted a
slightly condescending manner with Makarygin. His promotion to lieutenant general had already been signed. However,
he was altogether satisfied to find himself sitting here with
Galakhov, and he imagined how, after leaving the party for
another one he was going to still later, he would casually
remark that he had just been drinking with Kolya Galakhov,
who had told him . . . Actually, Galakhov had not told him
anything, and was quite reserved, probably thinking up a new
novel. So Slovuta, concluding there was nothing more for
him here, was about to leave.

That was just when all the young people were rushing

off to dance. Makarygin said everything he could think of to persuade Slovuta to stay a while longer, and finally insisted that his guest come and see his "tobacco altar." Makarygin kept a collection of tobaccos in his study, and he was very proud of it. He himself ordinarily smoked a Bulgarian pipe tobacco which he managed to get hold of through friends, and in the evening, when he had smoked his pipe to his heart's content, he would switch to cigars. But he loved to astonish his guests, treating them to each variety in turn.

The door to the study was just behind him, and he opened it now and invited Slovuta and his sons-in-law to join him. But Innokenty and Galakhov declined, excusing themselves from the company of their elders on the ground that they had to go and keep an eye on their wives. The prosecutor was offended; more than that, he was afraid Dushan would say something awkward. Letting Slovuta go into the study ahead of them, he turned back to his friend and wagged a warning finger at him.

The sons-in-law did not hurry to find their wives. They were at that fortunate age—Galakhov was older than Innokenty by a few years—when they were still considered young but no one dragged them off to dance. They could give themselves over to the satisfaction of a man-to-man talk surrounded by unfinished bottles and the beat of distant music.

Galakhov had just this past week begun to consider writing something about the plotting of the imperialists and the Soviet diplomats' struggle for peace. He thought of it not as a novel this time, but as a play—that way he could get around a lot of things he knew nothing about, such as the details of building interiors and clothes. So he seized on this chance to talk to his brother-in-law, hoping to pick up both traits typical of a Soviet diplomat and characteristic details about Western life. The action of the play was supposed to take place in the West, but Galakhov himself had been there only very briefly, at one of the progressive congresses. He realized it was not altogether a good idea to write about a way of life he knew nothing about. But in recent years it had seemed to him that fantasies about the inhabitants of the moon would come more easily than stories of the real life around him, where every theme was loaded with its own perils.

They talked, leaning their heads close across the table.

The servant rattled the dishes as she took them away. Music came from the next room, and then the TV set began to mutter metallically.

"It's a writer's privilege to ask questions," agreed Innokenty, his eyes still gleaming as they had when he was defending Epicurus.

"Perhaps it's his misfortune," Galakhov countered.

His flat white ivory pencil lay ready on the tablecloth.

"In any case, writers always remind me of investigators, but investigators who never take a vacation, never rest: on trains or at the tea table, in a bazaar or in bed, they are always investigating crimes, real and imaginary."

"In other words, they remind us that we have consciences?"

"Well, reading your magazines, I'd say, not always."

"But it's not a man's crimes we're investigating, but his worth, his qualities."

"It is just there that your work is the opposite of the work undertaken by the conscience. Well, I take it you want to write a book about diplomats?"

Galakhov smiled. It was a manly smile, suited to his large features, so unlike the delicate features of his brother-in-law.

"What you want, Innokenty, and what you don't want, isn't decided as simply as it sounds in New Year's interviews. You store up material ahead of time; you can't ask just any diplomat. I'm lucky you're a relative."

"You're wise. A diplomat who was a stranger to you would tell you all kinds of lies. After all, we have things to cover up."

They looked directly into each other's eyes.

"I understand. But I wouldn't have to know that side of your work. For me, it—"

"Ah! So you're mostly interested in embassy life, an ordinary working day, receptions, presenting credentials."

"No, deeper than that! How the work he does affects the soul of a Soviet diplomat."

"Ah! His soul! Well, I understand. I see. And by the end of the evening I'll tell you everything. But first you must tell me something. Why have you abandoned the theme of war? Have you exhausted it?"

Galakhov shook his head. "It's impossible to exhaust it."

"It's true, you were lucky with that war. That conflict, those tragedies—where else could you have found them?"

Innokenty looked at him cheerfully.

The writer frowned and said with a sigh, "The theme of war is etched on my heart."

"Well, you've written masterpieces on that theme."

"And it's eternal for me. I will return to it until I die."

"Maybe you shouldn't?" Innokenty asked, very quietly, carefully.

"I have to!" Galakhov answered, with strong feeling. "War lifts up a man's heart."

"His heart? Yes," Innokenty quickly agreed, "but just look at what has happened to literature on the war. The loftiest subjects are descriptions of how to take up battle positions, how to direct annihilating fire; 'We will not forget, we will not forgive'; the commander's order is law. But that's all set forth in the military statutes much more effectively than in literature. And, of course, you have also shown how exhausting it is for those poor military commanders to read their maps."

Galakhov frowned again.

Innokenty quickly reached across the table and put his hand on Galakhov's. He said, with no mockery now, "Nikolai, does literature really have to repeat the military statutes? Or the newspapers? Or the slogans? Mayakovsky, for instance, considered it an honor to use a newspaper clipping as an epigraph for a poem. In other words, he considered it an honor not to rise above the newspaper! But then why have literature at all? After all, the writer is a teacher of the people; surely that's what we've always understood? And a greater writer—forgive me, perhaps I shouldn't say this, I'll lower my voice—a greater writer is, so to speak, a second government. That's why no regime anywhere has ever loved its great writers, only its minor ones."

The brothers-in-law seldom met, and they did not know each other well. Galakhov answered carefully, "What you are saying is true only of a bourgeois regime."

"Well, of course, of course," Innokenty said easily. "We have completely different laws. We have the fascinating example of a literature created not for readers but for writers."

"You mean we aren't read very much?" Galakhov could listen to and make quite bitter remarks about literature and about his own books, but there was one belief he could never give up: that he was read, and read widely. In the same way Lansky believed that his critical essays formed the taste, and even the character, of a great many people. "You're wrong there. We're read, perhaps more than we deserve."

Innokenty made a quick gesture of denial.

"No, that's not what I meant. Oh, what nonsense! Dotty's father gave me too much wine, and that's why I'm being so inconsistent. Kolya, believe me. I'm not saying this because we're related, I really wish you well. There's something about you I like very much and so I'm bound to ask you in my own way: Have you thought about it? How do you understand your own place in Russian literature? After all, there could be a six-volume edition of your work by now. You're thirty-seven—at that age Pushkin had already been finished off. You're in no such danger. But all the same, you can't escape the question of who you are. What ideas have you brought to this tortured age of ours? Other than those unquestioned ideas, of course, that Socialist Realism provides for you?"

Little waves, the movement of small rippling muscles, passed over Galakhov's forehead and cheek.

"You're touching a tender spot," he answered, staring at the tablecloth. "What Russian writer hasn't secretly measured himself for Pushkin's dinner jacket? Or Tolstoi's shirt?" He turned his pencil over twice on the tablecloth, and looked at Innokenty with eyes that now concealed nothing. He was longing to speak out, to say what he could not say in literary circles.

"When I was a boy, at the beginning of the Five-Year Plan, it seemed to me I would die of happiness if I could see my name printed over some poems. It seemed to me that would be immortality, but here—"

Bending over to move aside some chairs, Dotty came up to them.

"Innokenty! Kolya! You won't send me away? Are you having a very intelligent conversation?" She held her lips in a pretty O.

Innokenty looked at her radiantly. Her blond hair fell freely to her shoulders just as it had nine years ago. She played with the ends of her belt while she waited for them to answer. Her cherry-red dress brought out the rosy color in her cheeks.

Innokenty had not seen her like this for a long time. For the last few months she had been insisting on her independence, the difference between her own views of life and his. But then something had broken in her—or was it a premonition of their separation that had entered her heart? She had become so submissive, so affectionate. And though he could not forgive her that long period of misunderstanding and alienation, and knew that she could not set the clock back, still her sweetness brought waves of warmth into his soul. Now he pulled her down to sit beside him, even though it was an untimely interruption of their talk. How lithe and trim she still was; sitting so close to him there, everyone could see that she loved her husband and loved to be with him. It flashed through Innokenty's mind that for the sake of her future they should not make a show of an intimacy that did not exist. But he caressed her arm gently.

The ivory pencil lay there unused.

Leaning on his elbows, Galakhov stared past the husband and wife through a big window lit up by the lights of Kaluga Gates. It was impossible for him to talk frankly about himself in the presence of a woman.

But out there—out there—they were starting to print his complete narrative poems. Hundreds of theaters around the country, taking their cue from the capital, were putting on his plays. Young girls copied out his verses by hand and memorized them. During the war the most important newspapers had gladly given him space. He had tried his hand at essays, short stories, and criticism. And finally his novel had appeared, and he had become a Laureate of the Stalin Prize. What next? It was strange: He had fame but not immortality.

He himself had not noticed when or how the flight of his immortality had faltered and finally collapsed. Perhaps its only moment of true freedom had been in those few verses that the young girls now learned by heart. His plays, his stories, and his novel had died on their feet before he was thirty-seven.

But why should one necessarily seek immortality? Most of Galakhov's colleagues didn't; their present situations were what mattered, how things went for them during their lives. The hell with immortality, they said; isn't it more important to influence the course of events in the present? And they had their influence. Their books served the people; were published in huge editions; were supplied by a system of automatic mass distribution to all libraries; and months of

promotion were devoted to them. Of course, they couldn't
write much of the truth. But they consoled themselves with
the thought that someday things would change, and then
they would return to these times and these events, and record them truthfully, revising and reprinting their old books.
Right now they must concentrate on that quarter, eighth,
sixteenth—oh, all right, that thirty-second—part of the truth
that was possible. Even that little bit was better than nothing.

But what oppressed Galakhov was that it was getting
harder and harder to write each new page. He made himself
write on a schedule. He fought against yawning, against his
lazy brain, against distracting thoughts, against listening for
the mailman or settling down to read the newspapers. He
tried for months not to look into Tolstoi, because the insistent Tolstoyan style kept taking him over. He made sure
his study was well ventilated and was kept at exactly 64
degrees; that the table was always clean. Otherwise he could
not write.

Whenever he began some big new work, he would be
fired up, he would swear to his friends and to himself that
this time he would not make any concessions to anyone,
this time he would write a real book. For the first few
pages he would work away with enthusiasm. But soon he
would notice that he was not writing alone; that the presence
of the person he was writing for always loomed over him;
that he was involuntarily rereading every paragraph with
that person's eyes. That person was not the reader, fellow
man, or friend; not even the critical fraternity in general—
it was always that most important critic, the celebrated Zhabov.

Galakhov imagined Zhabov reading his new work and
writing a long essay against it, taking up a whole column of
the *Literary Gazette*—and that had actually happened. The
title of the essay would be "Through What Gate Do These
Breezes Blow?" or "More About Certain Fashionable Trends
Along a Well-Beaten Path." He would not begin his attack
directly, but with some sacrosanct words from Belinsky or
Nekrasov, with which only a scoundrel could disagree. Then
he would carefully turn those words inside out, presenting
them in some completely different light, so that Belinsky or
Nekrasov would serve to prove that Galakhov was an anti-
social, antihuman creature, and on shaky philosophical
ground to boot.

So, paragraph after paragraph, Galakhov would try to anticipate Zhabov's objections and adapt himself to them; and the book would roll out, duller and duller, falling obediently into place.

By the time he was halfway through, Galakhov would see that his book had quietly changed, that once again it wasn't working out.

"As for the traits of our diplomat?" Innokenty said with a sad smile, stroking his wife's wrist. "Well, what can I say? You can imagine for yourself. A high level of ideological orientation. High principles. Deep loyalty to our cause. Deep personal devotion to Iosif Vissarionovich. Unwavering obedience to instructions from Moscow. Some with a strong knowledge of foreign languages, some not. And some—well, a few—with a great attachment to physical pleasures. Because, as they say, we only live once. But that's not typical any more."

58

THE DIE-HARD

Radovich was a confirmed and thoroughgoing loser. His lectures had been canceled in the thirties; not one of his books had been published; and on top of it all he was victimized by various ailments. He had shrapnel from a Kolchak shell in his chest. A duodenal ulcer had dragged on for fifteen years. And for a number of years he had had to go through a painful operation every morning without which he could not eat and live—that of irrigating his stomach through the esophagus.

But fate, who knows moderation in her tyranny as in her bounty, was protecting Radovich by means of these very ailments. Though a well-known figure in Comintern circles, Radovich remained untouched during the most critical years simply because he never crept out of the hospital. Again, just a year ago, when all the Serbs left in the Soviet Union had been either imprisoned or herded into the anti-Tito

movement, Radovich, out of circulation for reasons of ill
health, was once more overlooked.

Understanding the equivocal nature of his situation, Radovich made an extraordinary effort to restrain himself, never
speaking out, never allowing himself to be excited into fanatical argument; he did his best to live the dull life of an
invalid.

He was restraining himself at the present moment, too,
aided in this endeavor by the tobacco table. An oval table
of carved ebony, it had a special place in the study. Long
cardboard tubes, a small machine for filling them, a collection of pipes arranged on a rack, and a large mother-of-
pearl ashtray were set out. Close by was a cabinet, a Karelian
birch cabinet, resembling a miniature pharmacy with its
many drawers, each of which contained a special type of
cigarette, cigar, pipe tobacco, even snuff. Together, table and
cabinet composed what Makarygin called "the tobacco altar."

Listening in silence to Slovuta's discourse on the preparations for bacteriological warfare, followed by his judgment
of the heinous crimes perpetrated against mankind by the
Japanese officers (based on his study of official materials
collected during the pretrial investigation), Radovich examined and sniffed voluptuously the contents of the tobacco
drawers without deciding which he would choose. It was
suicidal for him to smoke. He had been categorically forbidden to by all his doctors. But since he had also been forbidden to eat and drink—and, in fact, he had eaten hardly
anything at all at dinner—his senses of taste and smell were
particularly sensitive to various kinds of tobacco. Life without smoking seemed to him utterly pedestrian. To all in-
junctions against his favorite diversion he had a single reply: "*Fumo, ergo sum*," whereupon he would roll up some
leaves of the crudest cheap tobacco on the market, which,
in his present financial straits, he preferred. In Sterlitamak,
during the evacuation, he used to buy leaf from old men in
the fields and dry and cut it himself. Now, in the leisure of
his bachelorhood, he found that handling tobacco was benefi-
cial to his thought processes.

In actual fact, even if Radovich had let himself go, he
had nothing so terrible to say. He was a Marxist, flesh of
their flesh, blood of their blood, and he held orthodox views
about everything. However, Stalin's entourage was more violently allergic to minute differences of tone and shading than

to completely contrasting colors, and for the slight deviations that distinguished Radovich from the others he could have been immediately liquidated.

So he had kept silent, fortunately, and the conversation shifted from the Japanese to a comparison of cigars—about which Slovuta understood nothing, and, in fact, almost choked from an awkward draw. Then from cigars the subject again changed, this time to prosecutors. Not only was their work load not decreasing with the years, but even though there were more prosecutors, their burden was growing heavier.

"And what do the crime statistics say?" asked Radovich, outwardly impassive, sealed in the armor of his parchment skin.

Statistics said nothing at all. Mute and invisible, no one even knew whether they still existed.

But Slovuta answered, "Statistics say that the number of crimes is decreasing in our country."

He had not read the statistics themselves, but what had been said about them in a magazine.

And he added in the same sincere tone: "Nevertheless there are still a lot of crimes. A heritage from the old regime. People are very depraved because of bourgeois ideology."

Three-quarters of those who passed through the courts today had grown up after 1917, but that fact never occurred to Slovuta. He had not read *that* in any of his magazines.

Makarygin nodded in agreement—he needed no persuading in that regard.

"When Vladimir Ilyich told us that the *cultural* revolution would be much more difficult than the October Revolution, we couldn't even imagine what he meant! Only now do we understand how foresighted he was."

Makarygin had a high square forehead and protruding ears.

Puffing together, they filled the study with smoke.

Makarygin's study was furnished with a number of diverse objects. There was the desk, somebody's old antique, supported on eight round and stubby columns, and there was the desk set, in the latest style, with a foot-and-a-half-tall model of the Spasskaya Tower with the Kremlin clock and a Red Star. In the two massive inkwells, shaped like the turrets of the Kremlin wall, there was no ink.

Makarygin had long ago stopped writing at home; the time

he spent at the office was sufficient for everything, and the inkwells were useless in any case since he wrote his letters with a fountain pen. Behind the glass windows of the bookcases were ranked law digests and several bound volumes of the magazine *State and Law*. There were also the old *Great Soviet Encyclopedia* (which contained errors and included enemies of the people), and the new *Great Soviet Encyclopedia* (still including enemies of the people), and the small edition, the *Shorter Encyclopedia* (also containing both errors and enemies of the people).

Makarygin had not consulted any one of these works for a long time, not even the hopelessly antiquated, though still valid, 1926 code of criminal law. They had all been ever so successfully replaced by a set of more or less secret fundamental instructions, each one of which was known to him by a number—083 or 005 slash 2742. These instructions, the quintessence of wisdom in judicial procedures, were bound together in a small file kept at Makarygin's place of work. The books in his study were meant not to be read but to impress visitors. The books that Makarygin did read, at night, or in trains, or on vacation, were hidden in a locked cabinet. They were detective stories.

Above the prosecutor's desk hung a huge portrait of Stalin in his Generalissimo's uniform. A small bust of Lenin stood on the shelf.

Slovuta, big-bellied, the flesh distending his uniform and pouring over the edge of his high collar, surveyed the study with approval.

"You live well, Makarygin! Your elder son-in-law has received the Stalin Prize twice, if I'm not mistaken?"

"Twice," the prosecutor repeated with satisfaction.

"And the younger is a first counselor?"

"Still second as yet."

"Don't worry, he's a clever boy, and before you know it he'll be an ambassador! And whom are you marrying off your youngest to?"

"My youngest? I've tried several times, but she's a stubborn girl and won't have anything to do with marriage. If you ask me, she's already waited too long."

"Does that mean she's educated? Looking for an engineer?"

When Slovuta laughed, his belly shook and his whole body puffed out. "For only eight hundred rubles a month? Marry her off to a Chekist—that's it, marry her off to a Chekist, that's a solid investment! Well, Makarygin, thanks a lot for remembering me, I'll be on my way, you mustn't keep me, you know, I've got people waiting and it's getting on to eleven o'clock. Stay healthy, Professor, don't get sick."

"Good-bye, Comrade General."

Radovich got up to say good-bye, but Slovuta did not offer his hand to him. Radovich's offended and contemptuous glance followed the round, broad back of Slovuta as, accompanied by Makarygin, he went out the door and downstairs to the waiting car.

Alone with the books, Radovich immediately turned to them. Running his hands over the shelves, he finally picked out, after some hesitation, a volume of Plekhanov. He was about to settle into an armchair with it when his eye was caught by a small book in a gaudy black and red binding on Makarygin's desk, and he picked that one up, too. But this second book burned in his lifeless, parchment hands. It was a newly published short book entitled *Tito, the Traitors' Marshal* by somebody called Renaud de Jouvenel. The first edition of one million copies had just rolled off the presses.

During the past twelve years or so a huge quantity of dishonest literature had passed through Radovich's hands—infamous, sycophantic, thoroughly false books—but never, he thought, had he held such foul, such vile stuff as this. With the experienced eye of a man who knows books he scanned its pages, and within a few minutes he saw who needed it and why, what kind of a bastard its author was, and how much new bile it would raise in the public's soul against Yugoslavia, which of course deserved none of it. His eyes focused on one sentence; he read it over twice: "There is no need to dwell in detail on the motives which led László Rajk to confess; *the fact that he confessed meant he was guilty.*"

Of course, there was no need to dwell in detail on his motives! Superfluous to add that Rajk had been beaten by his interrogators and executioners. Of no interest to mention that he had been tortured by starvation and lack of sleep. And for all we know, they may have laid him out flat on the floor and trampled his genitals with their boots. In Sterlitamak, the old-time prisoner Adamson, whom he had been close to from their very first words, had told Radovich about some of the favorite methods they used *there.* No need to dwell in detail. The fact that he confessed meant he was guilty!

The *summa summarum* of Stalinist justice!

But Yugoslavia was a sore too deep, too painful to touch on in conversation with Makarygin. So when the latter returned, throwing an involuntary loving glance at the new ribbon he was wearing ("It's not the medal itself, but the fact that they haven't forgotten you"), Dushan was leaning forward in the armchair, smoldering, staring at the Plekhanov volume.

"Thanks, Dushan, for not blurting anything out. I was afraid you might!" Makarygin said, pulling out a cigar and flopping down heavily on the divan with a sigh of relief.

"And what do you think I would have blurted out?" Radovich asked, a little surprised.

"What could you have blurted out? Oh, I don't know." The prosecutor cut the end of his cigar, "It might have been anything. You can't keep anything from slipping out." He lit up. "When he was talking about the Japanese, I could tell by the way your mouth was twitching you were just dying to object."

Radovich straightened up. "Because it's a frame-up, and you can smell it seven thousand miles away."

"Are you out of your mind, Dushan? It's a Party matter! How can you call it a frame-up?"

"It doesn't have anything to do with the Party! Do you call Slovuta the Party? Figure it out for yourself. Why is it that we've just now, in 1949, discovered the preparations they were making in 1943? After all, they've been our prisoners for four years now. And if you follow that line of reasoning, show me the country in the midst of a war that isn't making plans to step it up! How can you be so gullible? I suppose you believe the Americans are dropping potato bugs from airplanes?"

Makarygin's prominent ears reddened.

"Well, they just might be, and even if they aren't, what's the difference? It's government policy—you have to carry on as though you were on the stage: talk a little louder and put on a bit of makeup. Otherwise the audience won't get the point."

Parchment-faced Radovich continued to leaf through the volume of Plekhanov. Makarygin smoked on in silence, pursuing a fugitive thought.

Before long he came upon it. It was about his daughter Clara. On the surface, everything was all right with Makarygin's daughters, but there was something wrong with Clara, the youngest, his favorite, the one most like her mother. For a long time now, something unfortunate had been going on, and in recent months it had grown worse. At mealtimes together, the three of them no longer enjoyed the warmth and family feeling they had in the past, but somehow always ended up fighting like cats and dogs. Clara rejected any subject that was simple and human and could be discussed in a manner that would not disturb one's digestion. Instead, she worked every conversation around to the subject of the "unfortunates" with whom she worked and with whom she had obviously dropped all caution and vigilance. She had fallen prey to sentimentality; she claimed there were innocents among the prisoners; she insulted her father and laid the blame on him, implying that it was he in particular who was responsible for condemning innocent men. She would get absolutely furious and half the time storm away from the table, leaving her meal unfinished.

A few days ago, Makarygin had come upon his daughter in the dining room. She was standing by the sideboard, banging a nail into her shoe with a candlestick and chanting some weird, incomprehensible words like "Drumbeat, drumbeat" to a tune her father recognized all too well as that of an old revolutionary song.

Trying his best to appear calm, he remarked, " 'The Boundless World Is Filled with Tears'—you might choose a different song for mending a shoe. People died with that song on their lips, went into exile, hard labor!"

Out of stubbornness or the devil knows what, she bristled and spoke out angrily: "Think of that! The noble heroes! They *went* into exile and hard labor! Well, they're still going *now!*"

"What?" The prosecutor was completely taken aback by such an impudent and unjustified comparison. How could anybody lose her sense of historical perspective to such an extent? He could hardly contain himself, and in an effort to avoid striking his daughter, he tore the shoe from her hands and threw it violently on the floor.

"How dare you compare the Party of the working class and those Fascist dregs!"

She was hardheaded; even if you hit her, she wouldn't

cry. She just stood there, motionless, one foot in a shoe, the other in a stocking.

"Never mind the speeches, Papa! You call yourself the working class! You were a worker for two years, ages ago, and for thirty years since you have been a prosecutor. Some worker you are, you don't even have a hammer in the house. A worker who won't go near a car without a chauffeur! Existence determines consciousness—that's what we were taught, isn't it?"

"Yes, *social* existence, you little fool! And *social* consciousness!"

"Well, what do you call being *socially* conscious then? Some have mansions and others live in huts. Some have cars and others walk to work with holes in their shoes. Which of the two is *social?*"

Her father choked with rage and impotence. Again the eternal impossibility of explaining the wisdom of the older generation logically and clearly to the foolish young.

"You're a fool! You don't understand anything and you don't learn anything!"

"Well, teach me! Go on and teach me! What money are you living on? They wouldn't be paying you thousands if you weren't giving them something in return!"

A flash of angry lightning passed over her darkened face.

"Accumulated labor, little idiot! Read Marx. You have an education, a profession—that's accumulated labor, and you get more pay for it. And what about the eighteen hundred rubles you get from your institute? What do you do for it?"

Just then his wife burst in because of the commotion and started reprimanding Clara for trying to mend a shoe by herself. She should pay a shoemaker to do it. That's what shoemakers were for; there was no need to ruin the candlestick and the sideboard.

Now, sitting there on the divan, Makarygin closed his eyes and saw his daughter, his beloved and hated daughter, skillfully showering him with insults; he saw her pick up the shoe he had thrown down, stare at him a minute, and limp off to her own room.

"Dushan, Dushan," sighed Makarygin softly. "What can I do about my daughter?"

"Which daughter?" Radovich was surprised. He continued to leaf through his Plekhanov.

Makarygin's face was hardly any narrower at the chin

line than at the temples. A broad, rectangular face suited the severe social responsibility of a prosecutor. His big ears stuck out like the wings of a sphinx. It was disturbing to see confusion on that face.

"How did it happen, Dushan? When we were pursuing Kolchak, who would have imagined we would receive such gratitude from our children?"

He told the story of the shoe.

Radovich pulled out a dirty piece of suède from his pocket and, with emotion, wiped his glasses. He was nearsighted without them. He said:

"A wonderful young man lives next door to me, a demobilized officer. He talks to me sometimes. Once he told me that when he was in the army he used the same dugouts as the enlisted men. Whenever any of his superiors came by, they always said, 'Why don't you get yourself a separate dugout? Why don't you get the orderly to cook for you? You don't respect yourself! Why do you think you're getting an officer's ration?' Now this fellow had our kind of upbringing, our Leninist training—a person simply couldn't do that. It would be offensive. So the commanding officer simply gave him an order: 'Don't disgrace your officer's rank!' And he turned to some soldiers and said, 'Build me a dugout! Take my furniture over to it!' His superiors praised him: 'You should have done that long ago.' "

"Well, what do you expect?" the prosecutor frowned. Old Dushan had become disagreeable over the years. He was jealous because he had got nowhere, and so he had to stick pins in others.

"What do I expect?" Radovich put his glasses back on and stood up, lean and erect. "The girl is absolutely right, and we've been warned about it. One has to be able to learn from one's enemies."

"Are you suggesting we learn from anarchists?" demanded the prosecutor in astonishment.

"Not at all, Pyotr. I am only making an appeal to the Party conscience!" exclaimed Dushan, raising his hand and pointing a long finger. " 'The Boundless World Is Filled with Tears'—and accumulated labor? And maybe a few extra handouts? You make eight thousand rubles, don't you? And a cleaning woman gets about 250?"

Makarygin's face settled into a perfect rectangle. On one side his cheek twitched.

"You've gone crazy in that cave of yours! You've lost all ties with reality! What am I supposed to do? Go up to them tomorrow and ask for 250 rubles? How would I live? They would think I was insane and throw me out! After all, the others don't object!"

To reinforce his answer, Radovich, pointing his finger like a spear, punctuated his words with stabbing gestures.

"What we need is to purge ourselves of this bourgeois rot. A thorough clean-up job is what we need! Look at yourself and the ideas you're encrusted with. Pyotr! Look at what you've become!"

Makarygin put out a hand as though to defend himself.

"So what is there left to live for? What have we fought for? Don't you remember Engels? 'Equality does not mean the equality of everything with zero! We are moving toward a condition in which everyone will succeed and flourish!' "

"Don't hide behind Engels! The example you set is more like Feuerbach: 'Your first responsibility is to yourself. If you are happy, you will make others happy too.' "

"Be-eau-ti-fully put!" said Makarygin, clapping his hands together in approval. "There you are, I never even read that. Show me where you found it."

" 'Be-eau-ti-fully put!' " Radovich laughed, and his whole frame shook with dreadful coughing laughter. "That's the moral of Wilde's miller, Hugh! No. Anyone who hasn't suffered in twenty years shouldn't be allowed to dabble in philosophy."

"You are a dried-up fanatic! A mummy! A prehistoric Communist!"

"And haven't *you* become historical a little too fast?" Radovich seized from the desk a framed photograph of a white-haired woman wearing a leather jacket and holding a Mauser. "Lena was on Shlyapnikov's side. Don't you remember? You should be glad she died. If she hadn't, they certainly wouldn't have put you on the Shakhtinsky case."

"Put that down!" ordered Makarygin, suddenly grown pale. "Don't disturb her memory. Die-hard! Die-hard!"

"I am *not* a die-hard! All I ask for is Leninist purity!" Radovich lowered his voice. "No one writes a word about it here. In Yugoslavia the workers control production. There—"

Makarygin smiled ironically and with hostility. "You are a Serb. It's difficult for a Serb to be objective. I understand that and forgive you. Remember what Marx said about 'Balkan provincialism'? The Balkans are not the whole world."

"Nevertheless—" exclaimed Radovich, but cut himself short. This was the line beyond which even a friendship that began in a Red Guard detachment thirty years ago could break apart. This was the line beyond which Pyotr Makarygin could be nothing but a prosecutor.

Radovich crumpled into a small parchment-faced man again.

"Well, go on and finish what you had to say, die-hard!" insisted Makarygin in a hostile voice. "You mean the semi-Fascist regime in Yugoslavia is a socialist government? You mean that what we have here is an aberration? The end of the Revolution? These are old accusations. We heard them long ago, and those who dared utter them are now in the other world. The only thing you forgot to say is that we are destined to perish in the struggle with the capitalist world. Is that what you mean?"

"No, no, of course not!" Radovich burst forth with renewed conviction, his face illuminated by insight into the future. "That will never happen. The capitalist world is doomed by incomparably worse contradictions. And as everyone in the Comintern predicted, I believe firmly that we will soon witness an armed conflict between America and England for world markets!"

59

THEY ENTERED THE CITY FIRST

In the living room they were dancing to the record player, a huge new combination radio-phonograph. Makarygin had a cabinet full of records, including speeches by the Father of the Peoples, with his drawl, his mooing, and his accent. These records were to be found in all socially orthodox homes, but the Makarygins, like anyone in his right mind, never listened to them. There were also songs like "The

Dearest Beloved," and songs about airplanes, which "came
first," and girls, who "came afterward." However, it would
have been as out of place to listen to these songs in this house
as to talk seriously about Biblical miracles in an aristocrat's
drawing room. The records being played at the moment
came from abroad, records which were neither available in
the stores nor played on the radio. Among them were a
few émigré records of Leschenko.

In the room next to the living room the overhead light
was off. Clara had turned on the television set. That room
was also equipped with a piano which had not been played
since the day it was bought, and the gay cloth on its lid was
never removed. TV sets had just put in their appearance,
and the screen was no bigger than an envelope. The image
was spotty and refused to stand still. As a radio engineer,
Clara should have been able to solve the problem herself,
but she preferred to call in Zhenka, who, though quite
drunk at the moment, knew his business. His regular job
was running a multi-megawatt foreign broadcast jammer.
Wavering a little, he still had enough control over himself
to adjust the set before he got even more under the weather.

From the living room, a glass door opened onto the balcony. The dark silk curtains were drawn back, and there
was an animated view of the bustle of Kaluga Gates—automobile headlights, red and green traffic lights, red braking
signals, all beneath the snow that kept on falling and falling.

There was too much furniture in the room for eight
couples to dance at the same time, so they took turns. Conspicuous in contrast to the lively faces of the girls and the
eager-to-please expression of the MVD lieutenant was the
apologetic smile of Lansky, who looked as if he wished to be
excused for indulging in such a trivial pastime. The young
reference consultant with the Order of Lenin who worked
in the reception room of the Presidium of the Supreme
Soviet danced with Dinera until finally, taking advantage of
his embarrassment, she insisted that he go off and find another partner. Throughout the whole evening, a thinnish,
pleasant-looking girl, one of Clara's fellow students, had not
taken her eyes off the young Supreme Soviet official. He
usually kept away from run-of-the-mill people; nevertheless,
wearily flattered by her attention, he decided to reward this

skinny girl with a dance. A two-step began playing. And soon there was a general demand for an intermission.

One of the Bashkir maids began to pass around ice cream.

The young reference consultant led his partner over to a balcony window where two armchairs were pushed back; he brought her ice cream and complimented her on her dancing. She smiled and seemed anxious to say something. He observed her nervous neck and the rather flat chest under her thin blouse and, taking advantage of the fact that the curtains partially concealed them, in a gesture to reassure her, he touched the hand that lay on her knee. The girl began talking in a nervous and excited way.

"Vitaly Yevgenyevich, what a piece of luck to meet you here! Please don't be angry with me for being so bold as to bring up a business matter when you're off duty, but it is impossible to get hold of you at the Supreme Soviet." Vitaly removed his hand from the girl's. "For half a year my father's papers have been lying in your secretariat. He is stricken with paralysis. His camp certification is there, and my request for his pardon." The reference consultant withdrew defensively into his armchair and drilled out a little ball of ice cream with his spoon. The girl had already forgotten about her own ice cream and brushed her hand awkwardly against the spoon. It somersaulted, spotted her dress, and fell to the floor near the balcony door. Neither made an effort to pick it up. "He has lost the use of his whole right side! One more stroke and he's finished! He is already doomed. Why do you need him in prison now?"

The young official's lips twisted in an unpleasant grimace. "Come now, it's tactless of you to speak to me here. Our office phone number is no secret. Call me at work and I will make an appointment to see you. Incidentally, what section does your father come under—58?"

"Oh, no, no, he doesn't!" the girl exclaimed with relief. "Do you think I would have dared ask you if he were political? He comes under the law of August 7!"

"In the case of August 7 sentences, petition for reprieve has also been rejected."

"But that's horrible. He is going to die in a camp. Why must a person who is certain to die be kept in a camp?"

The young official, his eyes wide and staring, looked at the girl.

"If we reason that way, what is left of the law?" He smiled ironically. "After all, he was sentenced by a court. Can't you understand? And what does it mean anyway, 'to die in a camp'? People have to die—they die even in camps. People have to die somewhere. *When the time comes to die, does it make any difference where?*"

He got up in annoyance and left.

His words rang with that conviction and simplicity that leave even the cleverest orator powerless to retort.

The tactless girl silently crossed the living room into the dining room, where tea and cakes had been set out, and, without being noticed by Clara, put on her coat in the entrance hall and left.

Clara fiddled with the TV set, making the image even worse. As for Zhenka, he was coming around.

After the thin, troubled girl went past them, Galakhov, Innokenty, and Dotnara advanced into the living room. Lansky came toward them.

We particularly like people who value us highly. Lansky esteemed what Galakhov had written and expected more from each succeeding book. It was therefore with all the more satisfaction that Galakhov cooperated with Lansky and advanced his career.

Alexei Lansky was now in that gay party mood in which one can even say something a little impertinent without making a bad impression.

"Nikolai Arkadevich!" he exclaimed, brightening. "Halt!" he said in English. "Admit that at the bottom of your heart you're not a writer at all. Do you know what you really are?" This sounded like a repetition of Innokenty's question, and Galakhov was a little embarrassed. "You are a soldier!"

"A soldier, of course!" And Galakhov smiled a manly smile.

He also squinted as if gazing off into the distance. Even the greatest days of his literary career had not left with him such a feeling of pride, and above all such a sense of purity, as he had experienced on that day when a daredevil spirit led him, his head full of glory, to make his way to the command post of an all but surrounded battalion. There he underwent artillery and mortar fire, and then, late at night, in the dugout that was being rocked and shaken by bombing, he ate out of one pot with four of the battalion staff, and he felt on equal terms with those battle-singed warriors.

"Then, let me introduce you to a comrade in arms from the front, Captain Shchagov."

Shchagov stood erect, not deigning to assume a posture of respect. His large, straight nose and broad face endowed him with a forthright appearance.

The famous writer, on the other hand, when he saw the decorations and medals, and the two ribbons awarded for being wounded in battle, enthusiastically offered a hearty handshake. "Captain Shchagov," he smiled. "Where did you fight? Come, sit down and tell us about it."

They sat down on the ottoman, crowding Innokenty and Dotty. They wanted Lansky to sit down, too, but he made a secretive gesture and disappeared—certainly front-line veterans could hardly meet without a drink. Shchagov explained that he had become friends with Lansky on one hell of a crazy day in Poland, the fifth of September, 1944, when the Russian forces on the run broke through to the Narew and crossed it—God knows how—on logs! They knew it would be easy the first day, but there'd be hell to pay if they waited. Afterward they had pushed through the Germans like daredevils, opening a corridor only a half-mile wide; whereupon the Germans rushed to cut them off with three hundred tanks from the north and two hundred from the south.

Almost as soon as the war stories began, Shchagov abandoned the language he spoke every day at the university, and Galakhov the habitual speech of editorial offices, meetings and, especially, the deliberate calculated language in which books are written. And they both dropped the language of the living room, for it became impossible to use such a threadbare and cautious medium to communicate the spirit and smoke of the front. After a few words they were sorely at a loss without profanity, but that, alas, was unthinkable here.

At that moment, Lansky appeared with three shot glasses and an unfinished bottle of cognac. He pulled up a chair to be able to see the other two. Each took a glass, and he poured out the first round.

"To soldiers' friendship!" Galakhov pronounced, blinking. They drank it down.

"There's still some more in here!" Lansky held the bottle

up to the light and shook it reproachfully. He poured out the rest.

"To those who didn't come back!" Shchagov raised his glass.

They drank down the second round. Lansky looked around to see if anybody was watching, then hid the empty bottle behind the ottoman.

The fresh intoxication mingled with the old.

Lansky maneuvered the story to his own part in the events. He told how, on 'hat memorable day, as a fledgling war correspondent two months out of the university, he was off to the front for the first time, how he hitched a ride on a truck, a truck carrying antitank mines to Shchagov, how they made their way under German mortar fire from Dlugo-sedlo to Kabat through a corridor so narrow that the "northern" Germans were lobbing mortar shells into the positions of the "southern" Germans; how on that very day and at that very spot a Russian general returning to the front after home leave drove his jeep right into the Germans and was never seen again.

Innokenty, who had been listening to their conversation, asked them how they mastered the fear of death. Lansky was excited by now and answered without hesitating that in such desperate moments death is not terrible because you forget about it. Shchagov raised an eyebrow and offered his own view.

"You don't fear death until it comes over you. At first you're not afraid of anything, then you get a taste of it and are afraid of everything. But the comfort lies in the fact that death doesn't really concern you. You exist, death doesn't; death comes, and you're no longer there."

Somebody had put on the record, "Bring Me Back My Baby."

For Galakhov the reminiscences of Shchagov and Lansky were uninteresting. For one thing, he had not been in on the operation they were talking about, he did not know Dlugosedlo, Kabat, and Nove-Myasto, and, for another, he had not been a minor war correspondent like Lansky but a "strategic" correspondent. He did not view battles in terms of one rotten plank bridge or the backyard hemp fields of some village, but in broad terms, with a general's or a marshal's concept of their strategic function.

Galakhov interrupted the conversation.

"Yes, that's war! We go into it as stumbling city-dwellers and come out with steely hearts. Alexei, did they use to sing 'The Song of the Front-Line Correspondents' where you were?"

"Of course we did!" said Lansky and began to hum.

"Nera, Nera!" Galakhov called out. "Come give us a hand. We're going to sing 'The Song of the Front-Line Correspondents.'"

When his even white teeth flashed, the heavy-set look of his swarthy face disappeared.

Dinera rushed over to join them.

"Of course!" she said proudly, tossing her head, "I'm a front-line veteran myself!"

The record player was turned off and the three of them sang, making up in sincerity for their lack of musicianship:

> "From Moscow all the way to Brest,
> On the front line going West,
> Tramping the country, wandering in dust,
> With Leica and with notepad,
> Sometimes even guns we had,
> Through blaze and cold, to victory go we must!"

Everyone gathered around to listen. The young people observed with curiosity the famous man one didn't see every day in the week.

> "Winds and vodka our throats did parch,
> But we kept on through the toughest march.
> If any reproach us, say no more;
> Come along with us,
> Spend the nights with us,
> Help your correspondents fight the war!"

No sooner had they broken into song than Shchagov, though he kept the same smile on his lips, grew inwardly cold. A feeling of guilt came over him for his inappropriate enthusiasm, guilt toward those who, of course, were not here—who back in '41 were swallowing the waves of the Dnieper, who in '42 were gnawing pine needles in the forest of Novgorod. Alexei Lansky was a pleasant chap and Galakhov a highly respected writer, but they knew very little about the front which they had now transformed into something holy. Even the most daring correspondents, those who had crawled into the hottest hell—and these were not in the majority—were as different from the rank and file of the front as a count who plows the soil is different from a born peasant. Correspondents were not subject to military regulations and orders, nor to battle discipline. No one could forbid them behavior which amounted to treason if committed by a soldier: panic, saving their own lives, flight from the battle area. Hence the abyss between the psychology of the rank-and-file front-line soldier, whose feet had grown roots in the ground no matter how far advanced his position, for whom there was no place to hide and who was likely to perish on the field, and the correspondent with his little wings who in two days' time could be back in his Moscow apartment.

> "And to get our story over the wire,
> We weren't covered by tank fire,
> No matter if reporters got the worst.
> In an old Emka with nothing more,
> It's in the annals of this war,
> We entered the city first!"

The line about entering the city first echoed several anecdotes about some correspondents who, having misread their position on a topographic map, drove through no-man's land on a good road—since an Emka couldn't make it on a bad one—right into a city in no-man's land, only to turn round again and hurry out as if they had been scalded.

Playing distractedly with his wife's fingers, Innokenty listened; he too, had his own idea of what the song meant. He had no experience of the war, but he knew about the situation of the correspondent. The correspondent was not at all the tramp reporter they were singing about—a reporter whose life was supposedly of little value, who could lose his job if he was slow in reporting sensational events. In truth, all the correspondent had to do was flash his press pass and he was received like an important dignitary, from whom you try to hide the shortcomings of your organization while showing off its merits. Wherever he visited he was regarded almost as though he had the right to issue commands. And the success of the correspondent depended not on the speed and accuracy with which he conveyed his reports but on his presenting them in the correct light, according to the right philosophy. Having the right outlook on things, the correspondent obviously didn't need to push ahead to such-and-such a bridgehead, such-and-such a hot spot; the correct interpretation of events can be formulated equally well in the rear.

Having somehow adjusted the TV set so that it worked reasonably well, and feeling proud of her accomplishment, Clara stepped from the half-dark room into the living room. Lansky saw her. He looked her over and thought she was nice—yes, and she had a pretty good figure and in general he really did like her. He smiled, looking at her with his clear eyes as he sang the last verse, in which the original threesome had now been joined by half the company:

> "Let us drink to victory!
> Let us drink to our newspaper!
> And if we don't survive, my dear,
> Someone will know,
> Someone will show
> What the war was we fought here!"

The last words had just rung out when from somewhere close by came a hissing sound and the whole apartment was plunged into darkness.

"An explosion," cried a voice, and the young people rocked with laughter. When it had quieted down a little, somebody joked in the darkness: "Mika! What are you up to? It's not Lyusya, it's me!"

They all started laughing and talking again without doing anything about the lights. Here and there a match was lit. They blew them out or dropped them on the floor still burning.

Light was coming in through the windows. From the hallway, the Bashkir girl reported to her mistress: "The stairway lights are on!"

"Where's Zhenka? Zhenka! Come fix the lights!"

"Zhenka can't come fix the lights," somebody replied in an assured, morose voice.

"Call the repairman!" the prosecutor's wife ordered from the dining room. "Clara, call the electricity people!"

"Keep Clara here! Why do we need a repairman? She can fix it herself."

"What kind of nonsense is this, you young people?" the prosecutor's wife demanded severely from the darkness. "Do you want my daughter to be electrocuted? Please, whoever wants to fix it may do so. Otherwise we will have to telephone."

There was an unpleasant silence.

Somebody said the trouble was in the TV set. Or else it might have been in one of the fuses located in the ceiling. But none of those present, those useful members of society, those natives of the twentieth century, offered any help. Neither the diplomat, the writer, the literary critic, nor the young official of an important state institution. Neither the actor, the "border guard" of the MVD, nor the law student. It was the front-line soldier in boots, whose presence had seemed superfluous to some, who spoke up.

"Allow me to help, Clara Petrovna. Just unplug the TV set."

Shchagov made his way into the entryway; the Bashkir girls, trying to hold in their giggles, lit his way with the stub of a paraffin candle. The girls had been praised today by the lady of the house and promised ten rubles more than had been agreed. They were very happy with their job here and hoped that by the following spring they would have saved enough money to buy some pretty clothes, find husbands in the city, and not have to go back home.

When the lights went on again, Clara was no longer among the guests. Taking advantage of the darkness, Lansky had led her into a dead-end hallway where nobody could see them. There they stood conferring, hidden by a wardrobe. Lansky had already made her agree to a New Year's Eve date at the Aurora Restaurant. He was delighted that this mocking, restless girl would undoubtedly become his wife. She would be his critic and companion, too demanding to let him falter or fail. He bent down and kissed her hands and the embroidered cuffs of her long sleeves.

Clara looked down at her companion's bowed head; emotion choked her. It was not her fault that the other man and this man were not one and the same but were two different people. Nor was it her fault that the time of her fullest ripening had come and that she was destined by the implacable laws of nature to fall, like a September apple, into the hands of whoever reached for her.

60

A DUEL NOT ACCORDING
TO THE RULES

Alone on his upper bunk, with the arched ceiling over-head like the dome of heaven, burying his face in the warm pillow he imagined to be Clara's breast, Ruska burned with happiness. Half a day had passed since the kiss which had overcome him, and he was still reluctant to soil his happy lips with food or empty talk.

"After all, you wouldn't be able to wait for me!" he had said to her.

And she had replied, "Why not? *I could*—"

"There you go again—avoiding an honest man-to-man argument!" sounded a hearty young voice almost directly below him. "As usual, you're more interested in tossing out bird words!"

"And as usual you aren't saying a thing—you're handing down riddles! The Oracle! The Oracle of Mavrino! What makes you think I'm so anxious to argue with you? Perhaps it's as boring for me as to try pounding the fact that the sun doesn't circle the earth into the head of some old peasant. He'll never learn no matter how long he lives."

"Prison is the place to argue! Where else? On the outside you'd be put away for it soon enough. But here you meet real debaters! And you decline the opportunity? Is that it?"

Sologdin and Rubin, absorbed in their eternal disagree-ments, each reluctant to leave the battlefield lest he seem to be admitting defeat, were still seated at the scene of the birthday party, which the others had left. Adamson had gone back to reading *Monte Cristo*. Pryanchikov had run off to leaf through an old copy of *Ogonyek* which had turned up from somewhere. Nerzhin had gone with Kon-drashev-Ivanov to see the janitor Spiridon. Potapov, fulfill-ing his duties as host to the end, had washed the dishes, put back the night tables, and was lying on his bed with a pillow over his face to shut out the noise and light. Many in the room were asleep. Others were quietly reading or chatting. The hour had come when people were wondering whether the officer of the day might have forgotten to turn off the white light bulb and turn on the blue one. Sologdin and Rubin were still sitting on Pryanchikov's empty bunk.

Sologdin said softly, "I can tell you from experience that a real debate is carried out like a duel. We agree on a mediator. We could even invite Gleb right now. We take a sheet of paper and draw a line down the middle of it. Across the top we state the argument. Then, each expresses his views on the question as clearly and concisely as he can on his own half of the page. The time allowed for writing is unlimited, so there won't be accidental mistakes."

"You're kidding me," Rubin objected sleepily, his wrinkled eyelids sagging. Above his beard, his face showed extreme fatigue. "What are we going to do, argue till morning?"

"Quite the contrary!" Sologdin exclaimed, his eyes agleam. "That is, in fact, the remarkable thing about a real man-to-man debate. Beating the air with empty words can go on for weeks. But a debate *on paper* is sometimes over and done with in ten minutes: it immediately becomes obvious that the opponents are talking about totally different things or that they don't disagree at all. If it turns out that there is any point in continuing the debate, then they proceed, in turn, to write down their arguments on their respective halves of the page. Just as in a duel: A thrust! A reply! A shot! A return shot! There is no possibility of evasion, of denying what has been said, of changing words. And after two or three statements, the victory of one and the defeat of the other becomes clear."

"There's no time limit?"

"For upholding the truth? No!"

"And we won't actually come to blows about it?"

Sologdin's flaming face darkened. "I knew that's how it would be. You're attacking me first."

"In my opinion, you're the one who's attacking first!"

"You pin all kinds of labels on me, and you've got plenty of them, too: obscurantist! backslider!—" (he avoided the incomprehensible foreign word, "reactionary")—"professional bootlicker!—" (avoiding the term "official lackey") —"priest-lover! You've got more abusive words than you have scientific concepts. But whenever I propose an *honest argument*, you're too busy, you don't feel like it, you're too tired!"

Sologdin was tempted into argument, as always, on Sunday evening, a time which according to his schedule was reserved for amusement. Moreover, this particular day had been, in many respects, a day of triumph.

Rubin was, in fact, tired. A new, difficult, not particularly pleasant job awaited him. Tomorrow morning he had to begin creating, singlehanded, a whole new scientific field, and he had to conserve his strength. There were letters he had to write. His Mongolian-Finnish, Spanish-Arabic, and other dictionaries were waiting for him. And Capek, Hemingway, Upton Sinclair. Beyond that, because of the mock trial, because of the petty goadings of his neighbors, because of the birthday party, he had been unable all evening to finish working on a certain project of civic importance.

But he was bound by the unwritten laws of prison controversy. Rubin couldn't allow himself to lose even one argument, because he was the spokesman for progressive ideology in the sharashka.

"But what can we argue about?" Rubin asked, spreading his hands. "We've already said everything there is to say."

"What about? I leave the choice to you!" Sologdin replied with a gallant gesture, as if leaving to his opponent the selection of weapons and the dueling ground.

"All right, I choose: *about nothing!*"

"That's not according to the rules."

Rubin tugged irritably at his black beard. "According to what rules? What rules are they? What kind of an inquisition is this? Understand one thing: to argue usefully there has to be some common ground. There must, in a general way, be at least some agreement—"

"So that's it! That's what you're used to! You can only hold your own with people who think the same way you do. You don't know how to argue like a man."

"And what about your arguing with me? After all, no matter where we dig in, whatever we start with . . . For instance, do you think that duels are still the best way of settling quarrels?"

"Try to prove the contrary!" Sologdin responded, glowing with delight. "Who would slander anyone if duels still took place? Who would push weaker people around?"

"There you go again with your ridiculous knights! In your eyes, the murk of the Middle Ages, their stupid, supercilious chivalry, the Crusades—they're the high point of history!"

"That was when the human spirit reached its peak!" Sologdin insisted, straightening up. "A magnificent triumph of spirit over flesh! An incessant striving, sword in hand, toward sacred goals!"

"And the pillage, the pack trains of stolen wealth? You are nothing but a conquistador, do you realize that?"

"You flatter me!" Sologdin replied with an air of self-satisfaction.

"I flatter you? How appalling of me!" And Rubin, to convey his horror, shoved the fingers of both hands into the sparse hair on top of his head. "You are a boring *hidalgo*!"

"And you are a *Biblical fanatic*! In other words, a man who is possessed!" Sologdin countered.

"Well, you can see for yourself: what can we argue about? About the qualities of the Slavic soul according to Khomyakov? About the restoration of icons?"

"All right," Sologdin agreed. "It's late and I don't insist that we choose any major topic. But let's run through the dueling procedure with some nice, simple question. I'll give you several to choose from. Would you care to debate some subject in the field of literature? That's your field, not mine."

"For example?"

"Well, for example, how ought one to interpret Stavrogin?"

"There are already a dozen critical essays—"

"They're not worth a kopeck! I've read them. Stavrogin! Svidrigailov! Kirillov! Can one really understand them? They are as complex and incomprehensible as people in real life! How seldom do we understand another human being right from the start, and we never do completely! Something unexpected always turns up. That's why Dostoyevsky is so great. And literary scholars imagine they can illuminate a human being fully. It's amusing."

But observing that Rubin was about to leave—for the moment had come when one could break off without suffering disgrace—Sologdin said quickly, "All right. A moral theme: the significance of pride in a man's life."

Rubin shrugged his shoulders. Looking bored, he said, "Are we back to being high school students again?"

He got up. It was the moment when one could leave with honor.

"Very good. Now, this subject—" Sologdin said, taking him by the shoulder.

"Oh, go on," Rubin waved him off, though not angrily. "I haven't any time for banter. And as for arguing seriously! You're a savage! A cave dweller! Everything in your head is turned upside down! You're the only person left on the whole planet who doesn't recognize the three laws of dialectics. And everything else depends on them!"

Sologdin brushed the accusation aside with a wave of his pink palm. "I don't accept them? I accept them now."

"What? You accept dialectics?" Rubin's thick, meaty lips set in a pout, and he lisped deliberately, "My little chick! Come here and let me kiss you! You've accepted dialectics?"

"I've not only accepted it—I have also thought about it! I have thought about it every morning for two months. And you haven't!"

"You have even been *thinking*? My dear fellow! My *comme il faut* lad!" Rubin continued to pout. "And perhaps —I hardly dare ask—you have also accepted gnosiology?"

Sologdin frowned. "The ability to apply theoretical conclusions in practice? Well, that's what material knowledge is."

"Ah, so you're an elemental materialist!" Rubin said. "That's a bit on the primitive side. But then what do we have to argue about?"

"What do you mean?" Sologdin demanded indignantly.

"If we have no common ground, we have nothing to argue about. And if we do have a common ground, we have nothing to argue about! Look here! If you don't mind, now it's up to you to argue."

"What kind of obligation is that? What shall we argue about?"

Sologdin stood up, too, and waved his arms energetically.

"You listen! I accept battle on the most disadvantageous terms. I will vanquish you with a weapon torn from your own hands! We will debate the premise that you yourself don't understand the three great laws! You've learned them by heart, like a parrot, and you've never thought about their real meaning. I can trip you up over and over again."

"Well, all right, trip me up!" Rubin couldn't help crying

out. He was angry at himself, but he was again caught up
in the argument.

"Please," said Sologdin, sitting down. "Be seated."

Rubin remained standing, still hoping to be able to get
away.

"Well, let's start with something easy," said Sologdin with
satisfaction. "Do the laws of dialectics show us the *direction*
of development or not?"

"The direction?"

"Yes! Where development leads us," he said. "The process."

"Of course."

"And just where do you find this? Where in particular?"
Sologdin demanded coldly.

"Well, in the laws themselves. They embody motion."

Now Rubin sat down, too. They began to speak more
quietly, more seriously.

"Which law in particular embodies motion?"

"Well, not the first, of course. The second? Let's say the
third."

"Hmm. The third? And how can we define it?"

"Define what?"

"The direction of the motion, of course."

Rubin frowned. "Listen, why all this scholasticism, after
all?"

"You call it scholasticism? You know nothing about the
exact sciences. If a law doesn't give us numerical correla-
tions, and if we don't know the direction development is
moving in, then we know nothing whatsoever. All right.
Let's start from the other end. You often use the phrase,
'a negation of a negation.' What do you understand those
words to mean? For example, can you tell me if a negation
of a negation *always* occurs in the course of development, or
does it not occur always?"

Rubin thought about this a moment. The question was
unexpected. It wasn't usually put in those terms. But, as
one does during an argument, he concealed his hesitation
and hastened to reply, "Basically, yes. For the most part."

"There!" roared Sologdin, satisfied. "You have the whole
jargon—'basically,' 'for the most part'! You mix things up so
that you can't find the beginning or the end. If someone says
'a negation of a negation,' you have a mental picture of a
seed, a stalk springing out of it, and ten new seeds coming

from the stalk. What a bore! It makes me sick!" It was as if he were flourishing a sword, cutting into a mob of Saracens. "Answer me directly: when does 'a negation of a negation' occur and when does it *not* occur? When is it inevitable and when is it impossible?"

No trace remained of Rubin's lassitude. He brought his wandering thoughts to bear on the argument; it was of no use to anyone, yet it was important.

"What is the practical significance of asking, 'When does it occur?' and 'When does it not occur?' "

"Well, well! What is the practical significance of the one basic law from which the other two are derived? How can anyone talk to you?"

"You're putting the cart before the horse!" Rubin said indignantly.

"Jargon again! Jargon! In other words—"

"The cart before the horse!" Rubin insisted. "We would consider it inexcusable to deduce an analysis of concrete phenomena from the ready-made laws of dialectics. And we therefore don't have to know 'when it occurs' and 'when it does not occur.' "

"Well, I'll tell you! But you'll immediately say you knew it all the time, that it was taken for granted, obvious. Listen: If the return to a previous qualitative state is possible through reversing the direction of quantitative change, you do not have the negation of a negation. For example, if a nut is screwed on tight and has to be unscrewed, you unscrew it. It's the reversal of a process, a case of a quantitative change giving rise to a qualitative change, and not the negation of a negation at all! If, however, by reversing the direction of movement it is not possible to reproduce or return to a previous qualitative state, then development can take place through a negation, but only if repetitions are permissible within it. Otherwise, irreversible changes will be a negation only in those cases in which negations of these negations themselves are possible."

"Logistic games," muttered Rubin. "Intellectual acrobatics."

"To go on with the nut. If you spoil its thread when you screw it on, then you can no longer return it to its former condition when you unscrew it. This condition can only be recovered by throwing the nut into a vat of molten steel, running it through a rolling mill, getting a six-sided rod, drilling and tapping it, and, finally, cutting a new nut."

"Listen, Dmitri," Rubin stopped him in a placating tone, "you can't seriously expound dialectics on the basis of a nut."

"Why not? Why is a nut any worse than a seed? Not a single machine would hold together without nuts. So there you are, each successive state is irreversible. It negates the preceding, and in relation to the old nut which you've spoiled the new nut is a negation of a negation. Simple?" And he thrust his goateed chin forward.

"Wait a minute!" Rubin said. "Where did you refute me? What you've just said proves that the third law does give the direction of development."

With his hand over his heart, Sologdin bowed.

"If you didn't have a quick mind, Lev, I would hardly be so eager for the honor of conversing with you! Yes, the third law does give the direction! But one must learn to use what a law offers. Are you able to work with that law and not just to worship it? You have deduced that it does supply the direction. But let's ask: does it always? In nature, in organic life, yes, it always does: birth, growth, death. But what about the inanimate world? It doesn't always, by any means."

"But we're principally interested in society."

"Who do you mean by 'we'? Society is not my subject. I am an engineer. Society? The only kind of society I recognize is the society of beautiful ladies." He smoothed his mustache comically and laughed.

"Well," Rubin declared thoughtfully. "Perhaps there is some rational core in all this. But in general it has the smell of high-flown, empty verbiage. No enrichment of dialectics emerges from it."

"The high-flown, empty verbiage is all yours!" said Sologdin in a new outburst of vehemence, cutting him off with a wave of his hand. "If you deduce everything from those three laws—"

"But I've told you—we *don't*."

"You don't?" Sologdin asked in surprise.

"No!"

"Well then, what are the laws good for?"

"Listen," Rubin began to pound at Sologdin insistently, almost in a sing-song. "What are you, a block of wood or a human being? We decide all questions on the basis of the concrete analysis of specific information, do you understand that? All economic doctrine is derived from production figures. The solution of every social question is based on an analysis of the class situation."

"Then what do you need the three laws for?" Sologdin raged, oblivious of the quiet in the room. "You mean you don't need them?"

"Oh, yes, we need them very much," Rubin said quickly.

"But why? If nothing is deduced from them? If even the direction of development can't be ascertained through them, if it's high-flown empty verbiage? If all that's necessary is to repeat like a parrot, 'negation of a negation,' then what the hell are they for?"

Potapov had been trying vainly to shut out the increasing uproar with his pillow. Finally, he tore the pillow angrily from over his head and raised himself up in bed.

"Listen, my friends, if you don't want to sleep, at least respect other people's sleep." And he pointed meaningfully to Ruska lying diagonally across the upper bunk. "That is, if you can't find a better place."

Sensible people would have quieted down in response to the outraged cry of Potapov, who loved order, and the hush which had settled over the semicircular room, which Rubin and Sologdin finally noticed, and the presence of informers among them (though Rubin, of course, had no reason to refrain from shouting out *his* convictions).

But these two went on almost as before. Their long argument, certainly not their first, had only begun. They realized they must leave the room, since they were unable either to quiet down or to break it off. They went out, hurling words back and forth on the way until the door into the hallway closed behind them.

Almost immediately after they left the white light was extinguished and the blue night light turned on.

Ruska Doronin, who had paid close attention to their argument, was actually the last person in the world to collect "material" for the purpose of informing on them. He had heard Potapov's unspoken warning and understood it, even though he hadn't seen Potapov's finger pointing at him. And he experienced the intolerable hurt we feel when we are accused by someone whose opinion we respect.

When he had begun his double game with the security

officer he had foreseen everything; he had tricked Shikin; he was on the eve of unmasking the informers who would receive 147 rubles. But he was defenseless against his friends' suspicions. His solitary scheme, precisely because it was so unusual and so secret, doomed him to ignominy and contempt. He was astonished that these mature, efficient, experienced men were not generous enough to understand him, believe in him, realize that he was not a traitor.

And, as always happens when we forfeit our friends' goodwill, the one person who does continue to love us becomes doubly precious.

And when the person is also a woman . . . !

Clara—she would understand! He would tell her about his dangerous enterprise tomorrow—she would understand.

With no hope of sleeping, nor, indeed, the desire to sleep, he twisted in his feverish bunk, remembering Clara's questioning eyes, and working out ever more confidently a plan to escape under the barbed wire along the ridge to the highway, and from there by bus to the heart of the city.

Clara would help him from there on.

It was harder to find one person among the seven million people in Moscow than in the whole barren Vorkuta region. Moscow was the place to escape to.

61

GOING TO THE PEOPLE

Nerzhin's friendship with the janitor Spiridon was referred to by Rubin and Sologdin as "going to the people." In their view, Nerzhin was seeking that same great homespun truth which before his time had been sought in vain by Gogol, Nekrasov, Herzen, the Slavophiles, the "People's Will" revolutionaries, Dostoyevsky, Lev Tolstoi, and, last of all, Vasisualy Lokhankin.

Rubin and Sologdin didn't bother looking for this homespun truth themselves because they were in firm possession of absolute truth.

Rubin knew perfectly well that the concept of "the people" is artificial, an illegal generalization; that every people is divided into *classes*, and that even classes change in time. To look for life's loftiest meaning in the peasant class was a squalid and fruitless occupation, because only the proletariat was consistently purposeful to the end, and to it alone the future belonged. Only through the collectivism and unselfishness of the proletariat could life achieve its highest significance.

And Sologdin knew equally well that "the people" is an over-all term for a totality of persons of slight interest, gray, crude, preoccupied in their unenlightened way with daily existence. Their multitudes do not constitute the foundation of the colossus of the human spirit. Only unique personalities, shining and separate, like singing stars strewn through the dark heaven of existence, carry within them supreme understanding.

Both were convinced that Nerzhin would outgrow this interest, would become more mature, reconsider.

Nerzhin had, in fact, already tried out both Rubin's and Sologdin's extreme positions.

Nineteenth-century Russian literature, swooning with compassion for the *suffering brother*, had created for Nerzhin, and for everyone reading it for the first time, the image of a haloed, silvery-haired People, embodying all wisdom, moral purity, and spiritual grandeur.

But that was far away, on bookshelves; it was somewhere else, in villages and fields at the crossroads of the nineteenth century. The heavens unfolded, the twentieth century came, and those places had long since ceased to exist under Russian skies.

There was no old Russia, but the Soviet Union instead; in it there was a great city. Young Gleb had grown up in that city. From the cornucopia of science, success showered upon him. He found out that his mind worked quickly but that there were others whose minds worked even faster, whose wealth of knowledge oppressed him. The People remained on the bookshelves; he was convinced that the only people who matter are those who carry in their heads the accumulated culture of the world, encyclopedists, connoisseurs of antiquity, men who value beauty; highly educated, manysided men. One must belong to that elite. And leave failure to itself.

But the war began, and Nerzhin was first sent out as a driver on transport wagons. Clumsy, choking with shame, he rounded up horses in the pasture, bridled them, jumped on their backs. He did not know how to ride, how to harness a horse, how to pitch hay, and every nail he hit invariably bent, as if to mock the inept workman. And the more bitter Nerzhin's lot, the louder the laughter of the unshaven, profane, pitiless, and extremely disagreeable People around him.

Then Nerzhin worked up to the rank of artillery officer. He became young and capable again; he walked around wearing a tight belt and flourishing a switch he had picked up on the way, because he had nothing else to carry. He rode recklessly on the running boards of speeding trucks, cursed heatedly at river crossings, was ready to attack at midnight or in the rain, and he led the obedient, loyal, industrious, and, consequently, pleasant People. And they, his own small personal People, listened agreeably to his propaganda talks about that big People which had risen as one man.

Then Nerzhin had been arrested. During his very first interrogation, in his first transit prison, in his first camp, struck dumb by these deadly blows, he had been horrified by seeing the other side of certain members of the "elite": in circumstances where firmness of character, strength of will, and loyalty to one's friends were vital to a prisoner and could determine the fate of his comrades, these delicate, sensitive, highly educated persons who valued beauty often turned out to be cowards, quick to cave in, adroit in excusing their own vileness. They soon degenerated into traitors, beggars, and hypocrites. And Nerzhin had just barely escaped becoming like them. He turned away from men he used to think it an honor to be with. He began to ridicule and mock what he had once worshiped. He strove for simplicity, to rid himself of the intelligentsia's habits of extreme politeness and intellectual extravagance. In a time of hopeless failure, amid the wreckage of his shattered life, Nerzhin believed that the only people who mattered were those who planed wood, worked metal, plowed land, and cast iron with their own hands. He tried to acquire from simple working people the wisdom of capable hands and their philosophy of life. And so he came full circle back to the fashion of the previous century: the creed that one must "go to the people."

Yet it was not quite full circle. Nerzhin, the educated zek, had one advantage over our grandparents. Unlike those cultivated nineteenth-century aristocrats, he did not have to change his clothes and feel his way down the staircase to go to the people. Instead, he was tossed down among the people, in his tattered cotton-padded trousers and soiled pea jacket, and ordered to work his *norm.* Nerzhin shared the life of the people not as a condescending and therefore alien gentleman, but as one of them, no different from them, an equal among equals.

He had to learn to drive a nail straight home, to fit one board to another, not in order to ingratiate himself with the peasants but to earn his soggy chunk of daily bread. And after the harsh appenticeship of camp, one more of Nerzhin's illusions disappeared. He realized there was *nowhere to go any more.* It turned out that the People had no homespun superiority to him. Sitting down in the snow with them at the guards' command, hiding with them from the foreman in the dark corners of a construction project, hauling barrows together in the cold, drying footcloths with them in the barracks, Nerzhin saw clearly that these people were of no greater stature than he. They did not endure hunger and thirst any more stoically. They were no more firm of spirit as they faced the stone wall of a ten-year term. They were no more foresighted or adroit than he during the difficult moments of transports and body searches. They were blinder and more trusting about informers. They were more prone to believe the crude deception of the bosses. They awaited amnesties—which Stalin would have rather died than give them. If some camp martinet happened to be feeling good and smiled, they hastened to smile back at him. And they were also greedier for petty things: for the "supplementary" three ounces of soured millet cake, for the ugly camp trousers, as long as they were a bit newer or a brighter color.

What was lacking in most of them was that personal *point of view* which becomes more precious than life itself.

There was only one thing left for Nerzhin to do—be himself.

Having got over one more bout of enthusiasm, Nerzhin—whether definitively or not—understood the people in a new

way, a way he had not read about anywhere: the people is
not everyone who speaks our language, nor yet the elect
marked by the fiery stamp of genius. Not by birth, not by
the work of one's hands, not by the wings of education is
one elected into the people.

But by one's inner self.

Everyone forges his inner self year after year.

One must try to temper, to cut, to polish one's soul so as
to become *a human being*.

And thereby become a tiny particle of one's own people.

62

SPIRIDON

As soon as he had arrived at the sharashka, Nerzhin had
singled out redhaired Spiridon, on whose round face it was
impossible to distinguish respect from derision unless one
knew him well. There were other carpenters, turners, and
milling-lathe operators, but Spiridon's surprising vigor set
him apart, and there could be no doubt that he was that
very representative of the People from whom one should
seek inspiration.

However, Nerzhin could not find any pretext for getting
better acquainted with Spiridon; he had nothing to talk to
him about; they did not meet at work; they lived in separate
areas. The small labor force occupied a separate room at
the sharashka, and they spent their off-duty hours separately.
So when Nerzhin started dropping in on Spiridon, Spiridon
and his bunkmates unanimously agreed that Nerzhin was an
informer and was seeking prey for the "protector."

In Spiridon's opinion, his standing at the sharashka was
at the bottom of the ladder, and he could not imagine why
the security officer might be trying to trap him. Nevertheless,
since the authorities weren't squeamish about gathering up
any kind of carrion, one had to be cautious. Whenever Nerzhin entered the room, Spiridon acted as though he were
delighted and made room for him on his bunk. With a stupid

expression on his face, he would start talking about something a hundred miles from politics: how a spawning fish is hooked by the gills with a forked stick and then netted; how he used to hunt elk and red bear, and how one should beware of a black bear with a white stripe around his neck. How snakes were driven away with clover. How red clover is the best for hay. And he told a long story about courting his Marfa Ustinovna in the twenties. She was performing in the drama circle in the village club and was destined to marry a rich miller. But out of love she agreed to run off with Spiridon, and he had married her in secret on St. Peter's Day.

And all the time Spiridon's sick eyes, unwavering under his thick reddish brows, said, "Why did you come, informer? There's nothing for you here."

Indeed, any informer would have been discouraged long ago and let the unyielding victim go. No one would have remained curious long enough to visit Spiridon every Sunday evening to hear his hunting tales. But Nerzhin, who went to see Spiridon at first with a certain shyness, Nerzhin, with his insatiable desire to resolve in prison everything he had not been able to decide about in freedom, month after month never tired of Spiridon's stories. They refreshed him, they carried the breath of the damp river dawn, of the day breeze from the fields, they carried him back to that unique seven-year period in the life of Russia, the seven-year period of the NEP, which had no equal in the history of rural Russia, from its first beginnings in the primeval forest, before the Viking Ryurik, to the latest division of the enlarged collective farms into smaller units. Nerzhin had known this seven-year period only as a boy who didn't understand anything, and he wished he had been born earlier.

Listening to the warm grate of Spiridon's voice, Nerzhin never tried to change the subject to politics with a sly question. And Spiridon gradually came to trust him. He, too, became engrossed in the past. He relaxed. The deep furrows on his brow eased. His reddish face was softly alight.

Only his ruined eyesight prevented Spiridon from reading books at the sharashka. Adapting himself to Nerzhin, he now and then ventured such learned words as "analogous," usually not in the right place. In the days when Marfa Ustinovna had acted in the village drama circle he had heard from the stage, and remembered, the name of Yesenin.

"Yesenin?" said Nerzhin, who had not expected this. "Wonderful! I have him here in the sharashka! It's a rarity now." And he brought the little book in its paper cover with a pattern of autumn maple leaves. He was intrigued: would a miracle occur? Would the semiliterate Spiridon understand and appreciate the poetry of Yesenin?

The miracle did not take place. Spiridon did not remember a single line of what he had heard long ago, although he did like "Tanyusha Was Pretty" and "The Threshing."

Two days later Major Shikin called Nerzhin in and ordered him to turn over his copy of Yesenin for the censor's approval. Nerzhin did not know who had squealed on him. But having suffered publicly at the hands of the "protector," and having lost Yesenin indirectly because of Spiridon, Nerzhin finally won his trust, and Spiridon began to use the familiar pronoun with him. From then on they conversed not in the room but under the arch of the stairway in the prison itself, where no one could overhear them.

Since then, for the last five of six Sundays, Spiridon's stories had shone with the folk profundity Nerzhin had been yearning to hear. Evening after evening he reviewed the life of a Russian peasant who was seventeen in the year of the Revolution and over forty when the war with Hitler began.

What tumult he had known! What waves had battered him! At fourteen he became the head of the family. His father had been killed in the war against Germany. And he had gone out to the mowing with the old men. "I learned to scythe in half a day," he said. At sixteen he went to work in a glass factory and marched to meetings under red banners. When the government declared that the land belonged to the peasants, he rushed to the village and took an allotment. That year he, his mother, and his brothers and sisters worked the land, and by October, on Pokrov Day, they had some wheat. But after Christmas the authorities began to requisition the wheat for the city: deliver some, then deliver some more. And after Easter, Spiridon, who was eighteen, was ordered into the Red Army. But he had no intention of going into the army and leaving his bit of land behind and so he went off into the woods with other young men, where they joined the "Greens." The slogan was: "Don't touch us and we won't touch you." But then it got crowded even in the forest, and they found themselves among the Whites, who were there for only a short time. The Whites asked whether there were any commissars among them. There weren't, but the Whites shot their leader just to frighten them, ordered the rest to put on tricolor cockades, and issued them rifles. On the whole, the Whites maintained the old order, as it had been under the czar. They fought a while for the Whites and were taken prisoner by the Reds— in fact, they made no attempt to avoid capture, but surrendered voluntarily. And the Reds shot the officers and ordered the soldiers to remove the cockades from their hats and to put on red arm bands. Thus Spiridon was with the Reds until the end of the Civil War. He marched off to Poland, and after Poland their army was a work force and they still weren't allowed to go home. Afterward they were taken to Petrograd during the first week of the Lenten fast and sent right out across the ice, and they captured some sort of fort. Only then did Spiridon get home.

He returned to the village in the spring and threw himself into working the bit of land he had won. He didn't return from the war like some—spoiled, a good-for-nothing. He quickly established himself, got married, acquired horses. As the proverb says: "Where there's a good householder, you can walk through the yard and you'll find a ruble."

Of course, power was based on the poor peasants, but by then people didn't want to be poor but to get rich, and the poor peasants, like Spiridon—those, at least, who liked to work—were also inclined toward acquisition. There was a term current at that time: "an intensive farmer." It referred to a person who wanted to have a good, prosperous farm that didn't depend on landless hired laborers, who wanted to do it scientifically, with knowhow. (With landless hired men, one didn't need a brain to get rich.) So Spiridon Yegorov and his wife became intensive farmers.

"To marry well is half of life," Spiridon always said. Marfa Ustinovna was his chief happiness and his greatest success. Because of her he didn't drink and he kept away from bad company. She gave him a child each year, two sons, then a daughter, yet their births did not separate her one inch from her husband. She pulled her weight. She put together a household. She was literate, and she read the magazine *Be Your Own Agronomist*—that was how Spiridon became an intensive farmer.

The intensive farmers were favored; they were given loans and seed. Success followed success, and there was plenty of money. He and Marfa got ready to build themselves a brick house, not realizing that the time of such openhandedness was ending. Spiridon was respected. He sat in the "prisidim" as he called it. He was a hero of the Civil War and, by now, a Communist.

But then and there they were burned out. They barely saved the children from the fire. They were left hungry, with nothing.

But they had little time to grieve. Hardly had they begun to work their way up from the ruin of the fire, than from far-off Moscow thundered the slogan, "Dekulakization." And all those intensive farmers who had been encouraged for no reason were reclassified as kulaks for no reason and exterminated. Marfa and Spiridon were glad they had not managed to build themselves a brick house.

For the millionth time fate showered riddles on them, and misfortune turned into luck.

Instead of going off in a GPU convoy to die in the tundra, Spiridon Yegorov was given the assignment of "Commissar for Collectivization": to drive people into the collective farms. He wore a frightening revolver on his hip; he personally expelled people from their homes and sent them off under arrest, stripped of their possessions, one after the other, kulaks or anyone else, whomever he had to.

No easy explanation or class analysis was available to Spiridon to help him understand this or the other sudden changes in his life. Nerzhin did not reproach or question him, but he could tell that Spiridon's spirit had been troubled. He had begun to drink at that time, and though once he had been master of the whole village, he now drank on such a scale that everything fell into ruin. He had the rank of commissar, but he was inept at giving orders. He didn't notice that the peasants were killing their cattle and joining the collective farms without a living horn or hoof.

Because of all this, Spiridon was dismissed as commissar. Nor did they stop there. He was immediately ordered to put his hands behind his back, and with one policeman in front and another behind, revolvers at the ready, they took him off to prison. They tried him quickly. As he said, "Where we were, they never wasted time sentencing people." They gave him ten years for "economic counterrevolution" and sent him off to work on the White Sea Canal and, when that was finished, to the Moscow-Volga Canal. There Spiridon worked as a ditchdigger and as a carpenter. He received an ample ration, and the only thing his heart pined for was Marfa, who had been left with the three children.

Then Spiridon got a retrial. They changed the charge from "economic counterrevolution" to "abuse of authority." He was thereby switched from the category of "socially hostile" to "socially friendly." Then they summoned him and told him that they would entrust a rifle to him and make him a prisoner guard. And though just the day before, Spiridon, like a decent zek, had been cursing the guards with the foulest language, and the prisoner guards with even worse, he took up the rifle they offered him and served as a guard in charge of his former comrades because to do so would reduce his term and give him forty rubles a month to send home.

Soon after that, the head of the camp, who wore the insignia of a Commissar of State Security, congratulated him on his liberation. Spiridon was given papers assigning him not to a collective farm but to a factory. He took Marfa and the children there, and soon he was listed on the honor roll on the factory's red bulletin board as one of the best glass blowers. He worked overtime to make up for everything they had lost since the fire. They were already thinking of a little one-family cabin with a vegetable garden and of the children's further education. When the war broke out, the children were fifteen, fourteen, and thirteen. Soon the front had almost reached their town.

At every turning point in Spiridon's life Nerzhin waited in silence to hear what Spiridon would do next. He now supposed that out of spite for having been sent to camp Spiridon would wait to welcome the Germans. But no. Spiridon behaved at first like a character in the best patriotic novels. What possessions they had, he buried in the ground. As soon as the factory equipment had been sent off on freight cars, and the workers had been provided with carts, he put his wife and three children in a cart, and, pushing on "with someone else's horse and someone else's whip, without stopping," he retreated from Pochep to Kaluga with thousands of others.

But below Kaluga somthing cracked; their column was broken somewhere, and suddenly there were not thousands of them but merely hundreds, and the men were to be taken into the army at the nearest military registration office while their families were to go on alone.

As soon as it was clear that he would have to say farewell to his family, Spiridon, without the least doubt as to the correctness of his course of action, hid in the woods until the front passed him. Then, in that same cart, with that same horse—no longer government issue, to be treated carelessly, but his own property to be carefully tended—he pushed his family back from Kaluga to Pochep, returned to his own village, and settled in someone's empty hut. There he was told to take as much of the former collective farm land as he could work. Spiridon took it and began to plow and sow with not a pang of conscience, paying little attention to the war communiqués, working hard and steadily, exactly as if these were the long-gone years when there were no collective farms and no war.

The partisans came to him and told him not to plow but to gather up his things and join them. "Someone has to plow," Spiridon said, and he refused to leave the land.

Then the partisans managed to kill a German motorcyclist, not outside the village but right in the middle of it. The partisans knew the German orders. The Germans came in, drove everyone out, and burned the whole village to the ground.

Now Spiridon no longer doubted that the time had come to pay the Germans back. He took Marfa and the children to her mother, and he went straight to those partisans in the woods. They gave him an automatic pistol and grenades. And he, conscientiously, wholeheartedly, just as he had worked in the factory or on the land, shot German patrols, drove transports, helped blow up bridges. On holidays he left to visit his family. Thus it turned out that after all he was with his family one way or another.

But the front overtook them again. The partisans had been bragging that Spiridon would be given a medal as soon as the Soviet forces arrived. And it was rumored that they would be taken into the Soviet Army, that their hiding in the woods would end.

The Germans herded to the west all the inhabitants from the village where Marfa was living. A boy ran to Spiridon with the news.

So, without waiting for our forces, without waiting for

anything, telling no one, Spiridon dropped his automatic pistol and two drums of ammunition and ran after his family. He managed to make his way into their column as a civilian, and, once again whipping the same horse ahead of the same cart, acting on this new decision which seemed somehow right to him, he marched west along the jammed road from Pochep to Slutsk.

When Nerzhin heard this, he put his hands to his head and rocked back and forth in bewilderment. He could no longer understand. But since it was not up to him to educate Spiridon in the philosophy of social experiment, he still did not reproach him. Instead, he asked, "And what next, Danilich?"

What next? He could, of course, have gone back to the woods, and he did once, but they had a wild encounter with some bandits, and he barely saved his daughter from them. So he went on with the river of people. He began to suspect that our own forces wouldn't believe him, that they would remember his not having gone with the partisans at the beginning and his having run away from them. Then, there being nothing else to do in any case, he arrived at Slutsk. There they were put aboard a train for the Rhineland and were given food coupons. At first there was a rumor that they wouldn't take children, and Spiridon was already figuring out what to do next. But they took all of them. He abandoned the horse and cart, and they left. Near Mainz he and the boys were assigned to a factory and his wife and daguhter were sent to work on German farms.

Once a German foreman in the factory struck Spiridon's younger son. Spiridon didn't stop to think, but jumped forward with an ax. Under the laws of the German Reich, the regular, peacetime laws, such an act meant the firing squad. But the foreman held himself in check, approached the rebel, and said, "I am myself a V*ater*. I *verstehe* you."

He did not report the incident. Spiridon learned later that that very morning the foreman had received word of his son's death in Russia.

And Spiridon, half-blind now and sick, remembering that Rhenish foreman, wiped away a tear with his sleeve. "After that I wasn't angry at the Germans. Not even for having burned our house or anything else—that 'V*ater*' wiped out all the evil. After all, the human being in him shone through, German or not."

But that was one of the rare, very rare times when his opinion was shaken, and it jarred the soul of the stubborn redheaded peasant. Throughout the rest of the difficult years, in all the cruel sinkings and surfacings, no second thoughts weakened Spiridon in moments of crisis. His instinctive actions challenged the most rational pages of Montaigne and Charron.

Despite Spiridon Yegorov's shocking ignorance of the highest attainments of man and society, his behavior was distinguished by a steady sobriety. If he knew that the village dogs were being hunted down by the Germans, he would put out a severed cow's head in the light snow for any possible survivors. And though he of course had never studied either geography or German, when bad luck landed him and his older son in Alsace to build trenches, and the Americans were pouring in on them from the air, he and his son ran away and, without asking directions, without being able to read the German signs, hiding in the daytime, traveling by night, in an unknown land, without roads, straight as the crow flies, he covered more than fifty miles to reach the house of the peasant farmer near Mainz where his wife was working. There they sat in a shelter in the orchard until the Americans came.

Not one of the eternal questions about the validity of our sensory perceptions and the inadequacy of our knowledge of our inner lives tormented Spiridon. He knew unshakably what he saw, heard, smelled, and understood.

In the same way, everything about his concept of virtue fitted together without forcing. He did not slander anyone. He never lied about anyone. He used profanity only when it was necessary. He killed only in war. He fought only because of his fiancée. He would not steal a rag or a crumb from anyone. And if, before his marriage, he had, as he himself said, "played around with the skirts," well, had not the supreme authority, Aleksandr Pushkin, confessed that "Thou shall not covet thy neighbor's wife" was particularly hard on him?

Now at the age of fifty, nearly blind, a prisoner evidently doomed to die in prison, Spiridon did not seem to be moving toward sanctity, or fatigue, or repentance, much less toward the reform implicit in the term "corrective camps." Every day from dawn till dusk he swept the court with his busy broom and in this way defended himself against the commandant and the security officers.

What Spiridon loved was the land.

What Spiridon had was a family.

The concepts of "country" and "religion" and "socialism," which seldom turn up in everyday conversation, were evidently unknown to Spiridon. His ears were closed to them; his tongue would not speak them.

His country was—family.

His religion was—family.

Socialism was—family.

Therefore he was obliged to say to all the kings, priests, and promulgators of the good, the reasonable, and the eternal, all the writers and orators, all the scribblers and critics, all the prosecutors and judges who made Spiridon their business:

"Why don't you go to hell?"

63

SPIRIDON'S STANDARDS

Above their heads the wooden stairs rumbled and creaked under the tramping and shuffling of many feet. Now and then dust and debris sifted down, but Spiridon and Nerzhin hardly noticed.

They were sitting on the unswept floor, the seats of their dirty, worn-out coveralls stiff with grime. It was uncomfortable without any logs to lean against. Hands clasped around their knees, they leaned back against the planks nailed crookedly to the bottom of the staircase. They stared straight ahead, their eyes fixed on the peeling wall of the toilet.

Nerzhin was smoking a lot, as he always did when he had to think something through. He lined up the stamped-out cigarette butts along the half-rotten baseboard of the staircase wall, a dirty triangle of crumbling plaster.

Like everyone else Spiridon received the Belomorkanal cigarettes, which reminded him of deadly work in a deadly region where he had almost laid his bones to rest. But he was firm about not smoking, obedient to the warning of the German doctors who had given him back 30 percent of the sight of one eye, who had given him back the light.

Spiridon felt gratitude and esteem toward those German doctors. He was already blind when they had driven a big needle into his spine, kept him a long time with ointment on his bandaged eyes, and then taken off the bandages in a half-darkened room and told him: "Look!" And the world started to grow light. By a dim night light, which seemed to Spiridon like a bright sun, he had been able to make out with one eye the dark shape which was the head of the man who had saved his sight and, pressing against the doctor's hand, he kissed it.

Nerzhin always pictured to himself the intent and, at that moment, gentle face of the ophthalmologist from the Rhine. Yes, and the man freed from his bandages whose warm voice and choking gratitude were in such contrast to the heedless folly which had landed him in the hospital—he must have seemed like a redheaded barbarian to that doctor.

That happened after the end of the war. Spiridon and his whole family were living in the American camp for displaced persons. And a man from his native village ran into him there, an in-law whom Spiridon called his "bastard in-law" because of certain incidents having to do with collectivization. They had traveled to Slutsk with this "bastard in-law" and been separated from him in Germany. And so, of course, they had to drink to their lucky encounter, and, since there was nothing else available, his in-law produced a bottle of spirits. It was not sealed, and they could not read the German label. But he had got it for nothing. And indeed the cautious, suspicious Spiridon, who had escaped a thousand dangers, was not proof against that Russian failing. All right, open it up, in-law! Spiridon downed a whole glass, and the "bastard in-law" drank down the rest of it. Fortunately, his sons were not there, too, or they would have had a glass also. When he awoke after midday, Spiridon was frightened because it was dark so early, and he stuck his head out the window. But it was not very light there either, and he couldn't understand for a long time why the upper half of the guard post and the American headquarters across the street didn't exist, but the lower did. He wanted to hide his misfortune from Marfa, but by evening the mantle of blindness had covered his eyes completely.

His "bastard in-law" had died.

After the first operation the ophthalmologists told him that if he lived quietly for a year and they then performed another operation, his left eye would recover 100 percent of its sight and the right eye 50 percent. They guaranteed it, and he should have waited, but the Yegorov family decided to return home.

Nerzhin looked attentively at Spiridon.

"But, Danilich, did you realize what awaited you here?"

Spiridon's face broke into fine wrinkles and he smiled ironically.

"Me? I knew they'd make us pay. Sure, our pamphlets kept saying just the opposite . . . you couldn't get away from them: everything will be forgiven you, your brothers and sisters are waiting for you, the bells are ringing, and there will be freedom even in the collective farms and only those who choose to go there will go. Run home just as fast as you can. But I didn't believe those pamphlets and I knew I wouldn't escape prison."

His short, coarse, reddish mustaches trembled as he remembered.

"I said to Marfa Ustinovna right away, 'My girl, they're offering us a whole lake, but all we'll get'll be a mud puddle.' And she patted my head and said to me, 'Old fellow, if you had your eyes back, then we could see what to do. Let them do the second operation.' Well, but all three children were saying, 'Papa, Mama, let's go home. Let's go back to our own country! Why should we wait here for an operation? Do you think we don't have eye doctors in Russia? After all, we beat the Germans and we can heal the wounded! We want to finish school in Russia.' The eldest had only two years left to go. My daughter, Vera, wouldn't stop crying, 'Do you want me to marry a German?' She felt she would never find a suitable husband. Well, I scratched my head. 'Children, children, there are doctors in Russia, but what makes you think we'll ever get to those doctors?' But I thought they would put all the blame on me: why should they bother the children? They would imprison me—so let the children live."

So they went. At the border station the men and the

women were separated right away and sent on in separate trains. The Yegorov family, which had kept together through the whole war, now fell apart. No one asked whether they came from Bryansk or Saratov. Without any trial at all, Spiridon's wife and daughter were sent to the Perm region, where the girl was put to work running a gasoline-powered saw in a lumber camp. Spiridon and his sons were thrown behind barbed wire, and all three were given ten years apiece for treason. Spiridon and his younger son had landed in the camp in Solikamsk, which meant he could at least bring the boy up for another two years. The elder son had been sent to a Kolyma camp.

This was home. This was the daughter's husband and the sons' schooling.

The strain of the interrogation and the years of hunger—in the camp Spiridon gave half his daily ration to his son—had not improved Spiridon's eyesight; in fact, his remaining eye, the left, had dimmed. In the midst of the unending wolf fight in that far-off forest hole, to ask the doctors to restore one's eyesight was like praying to ascend living into heaven. The wretched camp clinic could not even have figured out where to send him to be cured, much less cure him.

Hands pressed to his head, Nerzhin considered the riddle of his friend. He did not look down or look up at this peasant whom events had overtaken, but he felt as one with him. For some time all their conversations had been leading Nerzhin more and more urgently toward one question. The whole fabric of Spiridon's life was bound up with it. And today it seemed that the time had come to ask it.

Spiridon's complex life, his crossing and recrossing from one warring side to another, wasn't there more to it than simple self-preservation? Didn't it somehow relate to the Tolstoyan teaching that no one in the world is just and no one guilty? Wasn't there a whole system of philosophical skepticism in the almost instinctive acts of the redheaded peasant?

Today, under the staircase, the social experiment undertaken by Nerzhin promised to produce a completely unexpected and brilliant result.

"I feel bad, Gleb," Spiridon was saying, and he rubbed his callused palm roughly along his unshaven face, as if he wanted to rub off the skin. "After all, I've had no letter from home for four months."

"You said the Snake has a letter?"

Spiridon looked at him reproachfully (his eyes were gone, but they never looked glassy, like those of people blind from birth, and they were full of expression).

"What can that letter say after four months?"

"When you get it tomorrow, bring it here and I'll read it."

"Sure I'll bring it."

"Maybe some letters got lost in the mail. Maybe the 'protectors' have been keeping them. There's no use worrying, Danilich."

"What do you mean, when my heart is all in a knot? I am anxious about Vera. The girl is only twenty-one, and she has no father, no brothers, and her mother isn't with her."

Nerzhin had seen a photograph of Vera Yegorova which had been taken last spring. A big plump girl with big trusting eyes. Her father had managed to bring her unscathed through a world war. He had used a hand grenade to save her from evil men who tried to rape her at fifteen. But what could he do from prison?

Nerzhin imagined the dense Perm forest, the machine-gun clatter of the gasoline saw, the abominable roar of the tractors, the dragging tree trunks, the trucks with their rear ends mired in swamps and their radiators raised skyward imploringly, the dark, angry tractor drivers who could no longer differentiate between vile oaths and ordinary words—and among them a girl in work clothes, in trousers, her feminine figure temptingly setting her apart. She sleeps at bonfires with them. No one who passes her misses the chance to paw her. Indeed, it was not for nothing that Spiridon's heart ached.

To try to reassure him would be pitifully futile. It would be better, Nerzhin felt, to divert his mind, and, at the same time, try to discover an alternative to the wisdom of his intellectual friends. He felt he was on the verge of hearing a confirmation of skepticism as the people understood it, and that later, perhaps, he might make use of it himself.

"I've wanted to ask you something for a long time, Spiridon Danilich, while I've been listening to all your adventures. Your life has been torn up, yes, and so have many many others', too, not just yours. You've gone back and forth, seeking something impossible. Why? I mean, what standards—" he almost said "criteria"—"what standards are we to use in trying to understand life? For example, are there really people on earth who consciously want to do evil? Who think, 'I'm going to do those men real harm.

I'll squeeze them so they won't have a chance to live.'
Probably not, don't you think? Maybe everyone wants to
do good or *thinks* he wants to, but not everyone is free of
guilt or error, and some are totally conscienceless, and they
do each other so much harm. They convince themselves
they are doing good, but in fact it turns out to be evil. As
you might say, they sow rye and grow weeds."

Evidently he had not expressed himself clearly. Spiridon
looked at him, squinting and frowning, as if he suspected a
trap.

"Let's say you make a mistake and I want to correct you.
I speak to you about it, and you don't listen to me, you even
shut me up. Well, what am I supposed to do? Beat you over
the head? It's fine if I'm right, but what if I only think I
am, if I have merely convinced myself that I'm right? Or
maybe I used to be right, but now I am wrong. After all,
life changes, doesn't it? I mean, if a person can't always be
sure that he is right then how can he act? Is it conceivable
that any human being on earth can really tell who is right
and who is wrong? Who can be sure about that?"

"Well, I can tell you!" Spiridon, alight with sudden understanding, replied readily, as if he had been asked which officer would have the morning duty. "I'll tell you: the wolfhound is right and the cannibal is wrong!"

"What? What?" Nerzhin said, struck by the simplicity
and force of the answer.

"That's how it is," Spiridon repeated with harsh conviction, turning directly toward Nerzhin and breathing hotly into his face:

"The wolfhound is right and the cannibal is wrong."

64

CLENCHED FISTS

After lights-out the slender young lieutenant with square
mustaches who had come on duty Sunday evening went
personally through the upper and lower hallways of the spe-

cial prison, chasing prisoners back to their rooms. On Sunday they were always reluctant to go to bed. He would have made the rounds a second time, but he could not tear himself away from the plump young medical assistant in the dispensary. She had a husband in Moscow who couldn't get to see her for days on end when she was assigned to the restricted area. And the lieutenant was counting on getting something for himself that night. She would pull away from him, laughing coarsely and repeating the same thing over and over, "Stop acting like that!"

Therefore he sent his sergeant around the second time. The sergeant understood that the lieutenant wouldn't be leaving the medical office before morning and wouldn't be checking up on him, so he made no special effort to send everyone to bed. He didn't bother because being a bastard had become a bore to him after many years and also because he knew very well that adults who had to work the next day would eventually go to sleep.

The lights on the staircase and in the hallways of the special prison were never turned off at night because that might contribute to an escape or rebellion.

That was why no one had chased Rubin and Sologdin to bed during the two inspections. They were still standing against the wall in the big main hallway. It was past midnight, but they had forgotten about sleep.

This was one of those endless, angry arguments with which, like actual fights, Russian celebrations frequently conclude.

The debate on paper hadn't worked out. During the past hour or two Rubin and Sologdin had covered the two other laws of dialectics, disturbing the shades of Hegel and Feuerbach. But their argument could not keep its footing on those cold, lofty heights, and with each blow that was exchanged it slipped further into the abyss.

"You are a fossil, a dinosaur!" Rubin raged. "How do you think you'll be able to live in freedom with such wild ideas? Do you really think society will accept you?"

"What society?" Sologdin demanded, looking astonished. "I've been in prison for as long as I can remember, with nothing but barbed wire and guards around me. I am already cut off from that *society* beyond the zone, cut off, as a matter of fact, forever. So why should I prepare myself for it?"

They had already argued about the way young people were growing up.

"How dare you pass judgment on the young?" Rubin stormed. "I fought with young people at the front, went on scouting missions with them across the lines, and all you know about them is what you heard from some drip at a transit camp. For twelve years you've done nothing but grow sour in some camp. How much of the country have you seen? Patriarch's Ponds? Kolomenskoye on Sundays?"

"The *country*? You take it on yourself to talk about the country?" Sologdin cried, in a stifled shout, as if he were being choked. "Shame! Shame on you! How many people went through Butyrskaya? Do you remember Gromov, Ivanteyev, Yashin, Blokhin? They told you real things about the country. They told you everything about their lives. Are you going to tell me you didn't listen to them? And what about Vartapetov, and then that what's-his-name?"

"Who? Why should I listen to them? Blind people . . . yelping like an animal whose paw has been crushed. They talk as if the failure of their own lives means the world is collapsing. Their observatory is a latrine bucket. They view the world from the stump of a tree; they haven't got a real point of view!"

They went on and on, losing track of their arguments, unable to follow their own trains of thought, unaware of the hallway where, besides themselves, there were only two half-witted chess players sitting at a chess board and the blacksmith, an inveterate smoker. All they were conscious of were their own angry gestures, their inflamed faces, a big black beard confronting a precise blond goatee.

Each was trying for one thing only: to hit a sore spot that would make the other wince.

Sologdin glared at Rubin with such passion that if eyes could melt in a blaze of feeling, his eyes would have been molten.

"How can anyone talk to you? You can't be reached by reason! It costs you absolutely nothing to switch from black to white. And what really enrages me is the fact that inside you, you really believe in the motto—" in his frenzy he had used a word of non-Russian origin, but at least it belonged to the age of chivalry—"that 'the ends justify the means.' Yet if anyone asks you to your face if you believe in it, you deny it! I'm sure you deny it."

"No, why?" Suddenly Rubin spoke with soothing coolness. "I don't believe in it for myself. But it's different in a social sense. Our ends are the first in all human history which are so lofty that we can say they justify the means by which they've been attained."

"Ah, so it comes to that," said Sologdin, seeing an unguarded target for his rapier, and dealing a formidable and resounding blow. "Just remember: *the higher the ends, the higher must be the means!* Dishonest means destroy the ends themselves."

"What do you mean by dishonest? Who uses dishonest means? Perhaps you deny the morality of revolutionary means? Perhaps you also deny the necessity of dictatorship?"

"Don't try to drag me into politics!" Sologdin said, shaking his finger rapidly in front of Rubin's nose. "I was imprisoned under Section 58, but I have never had anything to do with politics, and I don't now. The blacksmith sitting over there—he's here under Section 58, too, and he's illiterate."

"Answer the question!" insisted Rubin. "Do you recognize the dictatorship of the proletariat?"

"I haven't said a word about the rule of the workers. I asked you a purely ethical question: do the ends justify the means or don't they? And you've given me your answer! You have exposed yourself."

"I didn't say they do in one's personal life!"

"What of it?" Sologdin said, hardly able to suppress a shout. "Morality shouldn't lose its force as it increases its scope! That would mean that it's villainy if you personally kill or betray someone; but if the One-and-Only and Infallible knocks off five or ten million, then that's according to natural law and must be appraised in a progressive sense."

"The two things cannot be compared! They are qualitatively different."

"Stop pretending! You're too intelligent to believe that filth! No right-thinking person can think that way! You're simply lying!"

"You're the one who is lying! Everything with you is just a big act! Your idiotic 'Language of Maximum Clarity'! And your playing at chivalry and knighthood! And getting yourself up to look like Aleksandr Nevsky! Everything is an act with you, because you're a failure. Your sawing fire

"For some reason you've stopped coming out there! You have to work with your hands there, not with your tongue!"

"What do you mean stopped? Three days?"

Their argument plunged nonstop through the dark and lighted places of their memories, like a night express rushing past whistle stops and signal lights, across the empty steppes and through the twinkling cities; and from the world flashing by outside, a fleeting light gleamed, or a transient roar sounded, without effect on the headlong rush of their coupled thoughts.

"You might first apply morality to yourself!" Rubin said indignantly. "What about ends and means in your case? *In one's personal life!* Just remember what you dreamed about when you started out to be an engineer! You were determined to make a million."

"You might recall that you taught village children to inform against their parents!"

They had known each other for two years. And now they were trying to turn against each other in the most damaging and painful way everything they had learned in their most intimate conversations. Everything they remembered became an accusation, a weapon. Far from rising to abstract questions, their duel was descending lower and lower to the most personal and painful details.

"There are your fellow thinkers! There are your best friends!" Sologdin stormed. "Shishkin-Myshkin! I can't understand why you keep away from them? What kind of hypocrisy is that?"

"What? What are you saying?" Rubin choked. "Do you mean that seriously?"

No. Sologdin knew very well that Rubin was not an informer and would never be one. But at the moment the temptation was great to lump him with the security officers.

"After all," Sologdin insisted, "it would be much more consistent with your point of view. Since our jailers are in the right, it's your duty to help them as much as you can. And why shouldn't you play the informer? Shikin will write a favorable report, and your case will be reconsidered—"

"That smells of blood!" Rubin clenched his big fists and lifted them as though he meant to fight. "Faces get smashed for saying things like that."

"I only said," Sologdin parried with as much restraint as

he could manage, "that it would show more consistency on
your part. If the ends justify the means."

Rubin unclenched his fists and glared with contempt at
his opponent.

"One must have *principles!* You haven't any. All that
abstract chatter about Good and Evil—"

Sologdin clarified his point: "What do you expect! Figure
it out yourself. Since all of us have been imprisoned justly,
and you're the only exception, that means our jailers are in
the right. Every year you write a petition asking for a pardon—"

"You lie! Not asking for a pardon, but for a review of my
case."

"What's the difference?"

"A very big difference indeed."

"They turn you down, and you keep on begging. You're
the one who didn't want to argue about the significance of
pride in a man's life, but you ought to be thinking very
hard about pride! You're willing to demean yourself just for
the sake of superficial freedom. You're like a puppy on a
chain: whoever has the chain in his hand has you in his
power."

"And you're not in anybody's power?" said Rubin, furious. "And you wouldn't beg?"

"No!"

"Well, you haven't the slightest chance of getting your
freedom! But if you did, you wouldn't just beg, you would—"

"Never," Sologdin said.

"How noble of you! You make fun of all the confusion
in Number Seven, but if you could do something spectacular
to clear it up, you'd crawl on your belly."

"Never!" Sologdin repeated, trembling.

"But I tell you!" Rubin crowed. "You just don't have the
talent. Nothing but sour grapes! Still, if you could produce
something—if they were to call on you—you'd crawl on
your belly!"

"Prove it!" Now it was Sologdin who clenched his fists.
"We'll see whose face gets smashed!"

"Give me time, and I'll prove it! Give me . . . a year!
Will you give me a year?"

"Take ten."

"But I know you! You'll hide behind dialectics, say that 'everything flows, everything changes.' "

"It's for people like you that 'everything flows, everything changes'! Don't judge others by yourself."

65

DOTTY

Relations between a man and a woman are always strange: nothing can be foreseen, they have no predictable direction, no law. Sometimes you come to a dead end, where there is nothing to do but sit down and weep; all the words have been said, and to no purpose; all the arguments have been thought of, and shattered. But then sometimes, at a chance look or word, the wall doesn't start to crack, but simply melts away. And where there was nothing but darkness, a clear path appears again, where two people can walk.

Just a path—perhaps only for a minute.

Innokenty had decided long ago that everything was finished between him and Dotty. It had to be, with this remoteness, this pettiness, of hers. But she had been so gentle at his father-in-law's party that he had felt a great warmth toward her. He still felt it, driving home with her and chatting about the party. He listened while Dotty went on about Clara's marriage, and, without thinking, he put his arm around her and took her hand.

Suddenly he thought: if this woman had never been either his wife or his mistress, and he had put his arm around her in the same way, what would he be feeling? It was clear enough: he would give anything to make love to her.

Then why, when she was his own wife, did it depress him to want her?

It was degraded, contemptible. Just exactly as she was now—spoiled, soiled by other hands—now, this moment, she excited him terribly . . . terribly. As if he were driven to prove something. What? To whom?

Back in their living room, saying good night, Dotty laid

her head on Innokenty's chest, kissed his neck awkwardly, and left without looking at him. Innokenty went on to his own room and undressed for bed. Suddenly he felt he had to see her.

It was partly that he had felt safe from arrest at the party; the crowd of people drinking, talking, and laughing had been like armor around him. Now, in the loneliness of his study, he was afraid again.

He stood at his wife's door in his bathrobe and slippers. Still undecided whether to knock or not, he pushed the door lightly with his hand. Dotty had always locked her door at night. But now it opened at his touch.

Without knocking, Innokenty went in. Dotty was lying in bed under a soft, silvery-violet blanket.

She should have started, but she did not move.

A small lamp on the bedside table shone on her tender face, her fair hair, her apricot satin nightgown, delicately trimmed with lace, through which her shoulders, arms and breasts gleamed alluringly.

It was rather hot in the bedroom, but Innokenty welcomed the warmth; he seemed to have some sort of chill. There was a scent of perfume.

He went up to a small table covered with a smoky-gray cloth. Picking up a seashell, turning it over and over, he said angrily, without looking at her, "I can't understand why I'm here. I can't imagine there being anything between us again." (He did not speak or even think about his own infidelity in Rome.) "But just now I thought to myself: 'What if I do go to her?'"

Nervously, he turned the seashell over, and looked at Dotty.

He despised himself.

She turned her head on the pillow and looked up at him, attentively and tenderly, though she could hardly make out his face in the half-darkness. Her arms looked bare and helpless beneath the lovely folds of her nightgown. She held a book lightly in one hand.

"Just lie down beside me for a while, anyway," she said touchingly.

Just lie down? Why not? To forgive her for everything that had happened was another matter.

It was easier to talk lying down—for some reason he could say much more, the most intimate things, if they were

lying in each other's arms under the blanket rather than
sitting opposite each other in armchairs.

He took a couple of steps toward the bed, then hesitated.
She lifted the edge of the blanket for him to come under it.

Unaware that he'd stepped on the book that had slipped
from her fingers, Innokenty lay down, and everything closed
behind him.

66

THE DAMASCENE SWORD

At last the sharashka slept.

Two hundred and eighty zeks slept under the blue light
bulbs, their heads thrown back or shoved into their pillows,
breathing silently or snoring obnoxiously or crying out,
curled up to get warm or sprawled out because they were
too hot. They slept on two floors of the building, on two
tiers of bunks on each floor, seeing different things in their
dreams: old men saw their loved ones; young men saw wom-
en; some saw what they had lost, some a train, some a
church, some their judges. But however their dreams differed,
in all of them the sleepers were wearily aware that they
were prisoners; if they were wandering about on the green
grass or in the city, it meant they had escaped, deceived
their jailers, there had been a misunderstanding and they
were being pursued. That happy, complete oblivion which
Longfellow had envisioned in "The Slave's Dream" was not
their lot. The shock of undeserved arrest, the sentence of
ten or twenty-five years, the barking police dogs, the hammering boots of the escort guards, and the rending sound of
camp reveille had penetrated every level of their beings, all
secondary and even primary instincts, into their very bones.
Had there been a fire, the suddenly awakened prisoner
would have first remembered he was in prison and only then
sensed the flames and the smoke.

The deposed executive Mamurin slept in his solitary cell.
The off-duty shift of guards slept. The guards who were on

duty slept. The medical assistant, after resisting the lieutenant with square mustaches all evening, had recently given in, and now they, too, were asleep on the narrow divan in the dispensary. And, finally, the little gray guard posted at the bolted iron doors that led into the prison from the main stair landing, seeing that nobody was coming to check on him, and having received no response when he buzzed his field telephone, had gone to sleep, too, his head resting on the stand, no longer watching the prison corridor through the window, as he was supposed to do.

And resolutely choosing that hour in the depths of night when the Mavrino prison rules had ceased to function, prisoner No. 281 quietly left the semicircular room, squinting at the bright light, his boots trampling the thickly strewn cigarette butts. He had somehow pulled his boots on without footcloths inside them, and thrown on his well-worn frontline overcoat over his underwear. His black beard was tousled. His sparse hair hung on each side of his head, and his face showed suffering.

He had tried in vain to go to sleep. Now he had gotten up to pace the hallway. He had done this more than once. It relieved his irritation and eased the sharp pain in the back of his head and the throbbing ache near his liver.

But though he had left the room in order to walk, he was, as usual, carrying a couple of books, in one of which was folded a manuscript draft of a "Project for Civic Temples." Also, a badly sharpened pencil. Having placed books, pencil, a box of light-colored tobacco and a pipe on a long, dirty table, Rubin began to pace the hallway steadily, back and forth, holding his coat closed.

He admitted that things were difficult for all the prisoners, both those imprisoned for no reason and those who had been imprisoned because they were enemies of the state. But his own situation seemed to him tragic in the Aristotelian sense. He had been dealt the blow by the hands of those he loved the most. He had been imprisoned by unfeeling bureaucrats because he loved the common cause to an improper degree. And as a result of that tragic contradiction, in order to defend his own dignity and that of his comrades, Rubin found himself compelled to stand up daily against the prison officers and guards whose actions, according to his view of the world, were determined by a totally true, correct, and progressive law. His comrades, on the other hand, were for

the most part not comrades at all. Throughout the prison
they reproached him, cursed him, almost attacked him, because they were unable to look beyond their own grief and
see the great Conformity to Natural Law behind it all. In
every cell, in every new encounter, in every argument, he
was forced to prove to them—tirelessly, disdainfully disregarding their insults—that according to comprehensive
statistics and in the over-all view everything was going as
it should, industry was flourishing, agriculture was producing
a surplus, science was progressing by leaps and bounds,
culture was shining like a rainbow.

His opponents, being in the majority, acted as if they
were the people and as if he, Rubin, spoke for a small
minority. But everything told him this was a lie. The *people*
were outside prison, outside barbed wire. The people had
taken Berlin, had met the Americans on the Elbe, had
poured eastward in the demobilization trains, had gone to
reconstruct Dneproges, put life into the Donbass, rebuild
Stalingrad. The sense of unity with millions saved him from
feeling alone in his battle against dozens.

Often they taunted him not for truth's sake but to avenge
their wrongs, as they could not against their jailers. They
persecuted him, not caring that each such conflict destroyed
him and brought him closer to the grave.

But he had to argue. On the Mavrino sharashka sector
of the front, there were few who could defend socialism as
he could.

Rubin knocked on the little glass window in the iron door,
once, twice, the third time very hard. The third time the gray
face of the sleepy guard appeared at the window.

"I feel sick," Rubin said. "I need medicine. Take me to
the medical assistant."

The guard thought for a moment.

"All right. I'll ring up."

Rubin continued to pace.

He was, all in all, a tragic figure.

He had been imprisoned before anyone else here.

His grown-up cousin, whom sixteen-year-old Lev had worshiped, had asked him to hide some fonts of type. Lev had
carried out the order exultantly. But he neglected to evade
the neighbor boy who sneaked a look, and turned him in.

Lev did not turn in his cousin; he made up a story about finding the fonts under a staircase.

As he walked up and down the hallway with his heavy, measured pace, Rubin remembered solitary in the Kharkov inner prison, twenty years earlier.

The inner prison had been built along American lines—an open, multistory well with iron landings and stairs, and a guard with signal flags directing traffic at the bottom. Lev could hear the rumble as they dragged someone along the iron staircase—and suddenly a heart-rending yell would shake the prison:

"Comrades! Greetings from the freezing punishment cell! Down with the Stalinist executioners!"

They were beating him—there was that special sound of blows on soft flesh. Then they must have held his mouth shut; the yell became intermittent until it ceased entirely. But three hundred prisoners in three hundred solitary cells rushed to their doors, hammered on them, and roared:

"Down with the bloody dogs!"

"They're drinking the workers' blood!"

"We've another czar on our backs."

"Long live Leninism!"

And suddenly in some of the cells frenzied voices rose:

"Arise, ye prisoners of starvation . . ."

And the invisible mass of prisoners, unmindful of their own condition, thundered out:

"This is our last
And decisive battle. . . ."

They were unseen, but, like Lev, many of those who sang surely had tears of triumph in their eyes.

The prison hummed like an angry hive. Clutching their keys, the jailers huddled together on the stairs, terrified by the deathless hymn of the proletariat.

What waves of pain in the back of his head! What pressure in his lower right side!

Rubin tapped at the little window again. At his second knock the sleepy face of the same guard loomed up. Moving back the glass, he muttered, "I rang. They don't answer."

He wanted to close the glass. But Rubin grabbed it and
didn't let him.

"Well, go there!" he cried out in pain-racked irritation. "I
am sick, do you understand? I can't sleep! Call the medical
assistant."

"Well, all right," agreed the guard. He shut the window.

Once more Rubin began to pace back and forth, hopelessly measuring off the bespattered stretch of smoke-filled,
rubbish-strewn hallway. Time seemed to move as slowly as
his steps.

And beyond the image of the Kharkov inner prison—
which he always remembered with pride, even though those
two weeks in solitary were a blot on his security questionnaires and his whole life, and had contributed to his present
sentence—other, hidden recollections entered his mind, sear-
ing him with shame.

One day he had been called into the Party office of the
tractor factory. Lev considered himself one of the corner-
stones of the factory. He worked on the editorial staff of the
newspaper, went through the shops to inspire the young
workers and pump energy into the older ones, and posted
bulletins on the triumphs of the elite brigades and examples
of special initiative or slovenly work.

The twenty-year-old boy in his Ukrainian peasant shirt
walked into the Party office as unself-consciously as, on an
earlier day, he had strolled into the office of Pavel Petrovich Postyshev, Secretary of the Central Committee of the
Ukraine. And just as on that occasion he had simply said,
"Hello, Comrade Postyshev!" and been the first to offer his
hand, this time he said to the forty-year-old woman whose
short hair was covered by a red triangular scarf, "Hello,
Comrade Bakhtina! You wanted me?"

"Hello, Comrade Rubin," she shook his hand. "Sit down."

He sat down.

There was a third person in the room, but he was not a
worker. He wore a necktie, a suit, yellow oxfords. He was
sitting to one side, looking through some papers but not paying any attention to them.

The Party office was stark as a confessional, decorated in
flaming red and sober black.

In a constrained, somehow lifeless manner, the woman
had talked with Lev about factory affairs, which they had

always discussed fervently before. Then suddenly, leaning back, she had said firmly, "Comrade Rubin! You must confess your shortcomings to the Party."

Lev was astonished. What was wrong? Wasn't he giving the Party all his strength, all his health, night and day?

"No! That's not enough."

"But what else is there?"

Now the stranger intervened. He addressed Rubin with the formal pronoun, which hurt his proletarian ear. He said that Rubin must tell the Party truthfully everything he knew about his married cousin—the whole story. Was it true that his cousin had been active in an opposition organization and had kept this fact a secret from the Party?

He had to say something instantly. They were both staring at him.

It had been through the eyes of this very cousin that Lev had learned to see the Revolution. He had learned from him, too, that everything was not so fine and untroubled as it seemed in the May Day demonstrations. Indeed, the Revolution was springtime—but that meant there was a lot of mud to squelch through before one found the firm path.

But four years had passed, and disputes within the Party had ceased. They had already begun to forget the opposition. They had built, for better or worse, the ocean liner of collectivization out of thousands of fragile little peasant boats. The blast furnaces of Magnitogorsk were belching smoke, and tractors from the first four tractor factories were turning furrows in collective-farm fields. And "518" and "1040" were right behind them. Objectively, everything was being done for the greater glory of the world revolution— was there any point in battling now because one particular person's name would be given to all these great deeds? Lev had forced himself to love even that name. Yes, he had come to love him. Why, then, should people be arrested now? Why take vengeance against those who had once disagreed?

"I don't know. He was never a member of the opposition," Lev found himself answering. Yet he realized that were he to speak like a grown man without any youthful romanticism, denials were already pointless.

Comrade Bakhtina's gestures were brusque and forceful. The Party! Can there be anything higher than the Party? How can one answer the Party with denials? How can one hesitate to confess to the Party? The Party does not punish; it is our conscience. Remember what Lenin said.

Ten pistols pointed at his head would not have frightened Rubin. Neither a cold punishment cell nor exile to Solovki would have torn the truth from him. But he could not, in that red and black confessional, lie to the Party.

He told them when and where his cousin had belonged to the opposition organization, and what he had done.

The woman-confessor fell silent.

The polite guest in yellow oxfords said, "So, if I understand you correctly—" and he read what he had written down on a sheet of paper. "And now, sign. Right here."

Rubin recoiled.

"Who are you? You are not the Party."

"Why not?" asked the guest, offended. "I am a member of the Party, too. I am a GPU investigator."

Again Rubin knocked at the little window. The guard, who had obviously just waked up again, said in annoyance, "Look here, why are you knocking? I've rung up I don't know how many times, and they don't answer."

Rubin's eyes burned with indignation. "I asked you to go *there*, not to phone! My heart is bad! Perhaps I'll die."

"You won't die," the guard drawled placatingly, even sympathetically. "You'll last till morning. Now judge for yourself: how can I go away and abandon my post?"

"What idiot is going to take over your *post?*" Rubin cried.

"It's not that someone will take it, but regulations forbid it. Didn't you serve in the army?"

Rubin's head was throbbing so hard he almost believed he would indeed die that minute. Seeing his contorted face, the guard decided, "Well, all right, go away from the window and don't knock. I'll run down there."

He had apparently gone. It seemed to Rubin that his pain had lessened a bit.

Again he began to pace the corridor.

And through his mind flashed further recollections, which he had no wish to awaken. To forget them meant to be freed from them.

Soon after prison, anxious to expiate his guilt in the eyes of the Komsomols, and to prove his usefulness both to himself and the revolutionary class, Rubin, a Mauser on his hip, had gone off to collectivize a village.

When he was running barefoot two whole miles, exchanging gunfire with enraged peasants, what had he thought he was doing? "At last I am fighting in the Civil War!" Just that.

It all seemed perfectly natural: to dig up pits filled with buried grain, to keep the owners from milling their grain or baked bread, to prevent their getting water from the wells. And if a peasant child died—die, you starving devils, and your children with you, but you'll not bake bread! It evoked no pity in him but became as ordinary as a city streetcar when at dawn the solitary cart drawn by an exhausted horse went through the stifled, deathly village.

A whiplash at a shutter: "Any corpses? Bring them out."

And at the next shutter: "Any corpses? Bring them out."

And soon it was: "Hey! Anyone still alive?"

... He felt a burning pressure in his head. Seared with a red-hot brand. And sometimes he had the feeling that his wounds were retribution, prison was retribution, his illnesses were retribution.

Therefore his imprisonment was just. But since he now understood that what he had done was dreadful, and would never do it again, and had atoned for it. ... How could he purge himself of it? To whom could he say that it had never happened? From now on let us consider that it never happened! We shall act as if it never happened!

What will one sleepless night not drain from the miserable soul of the man who has erred?

This time the guard pushed back the glass. He had decided after all to leave his post and go to headquarters. It turned out that everyone was asleep, and there was no one to pick up the phone when it buzzed. The sergeant he had awakened listened to his report and reprimanded him for leaving his post; knowing that the medical assistant was asleep with the lieutenant, he was afraid to wake them.

"It's impossible," the guard said through the peephole window. "I went there myself and reported. They say it's impossible. It will have to wait till morning."

"I'm dying. I'm dying!" Rubin wheezed at him through the opening. "I am going to break the window! Call the duty officer right now! I'm declaring a hunger strike!"

"What kind of a hunger strike? Who's feeding you now?" the guard objected reasonably. "In the morning there'll be breakfast and you can declare your hunger strike then. Come on now, run along. I'll ring up the sergeant once more."

Rubin had to master himself. Overcoming his nausea and pain, he tried to pace up and down the hallway again. He remembered Krylov's fable "The Sword." Out in freedom the sense of that fable had somehow escaped him, but in prison it struck home.

> The sharp-bladed damascene sword,
> Was thrown on a heap of iron scrap
> And taken off to the market
> And sold to a peasant for nothing.

The peasant used the sword to strip bark off trees, to split wooden wicks for his lamp. The sword was hardly more than jagged edges and rust. And a hedgehog asked the sword on a shelf in the hut:

> Tell me, what kind of life are you leading?
> Isn't it shameful to split wicks
> And plane stakes?

And the sword replied to the hedgehog just as Rubin had answered himself hundreds of times:

> In a warrior's hands I'd dismay the foe!
> But here my talent is wasted.
> Yet it is not I who am to blame,
> But the one who could not use me.

67

CIVIC TEMPLES

Rubin's legs felt weak and he sat down at the table, his chest resting against it.

No matter how violently he refuted Sologdin's statements they hurt because he knew there was some justice in them. Yes, the foundations of virtue had been shaken, especially among the younger generation; people had lost their feeling for beautiful moral action.

In old societies they knew that a church and an authoritative priest were needed to maintain morality. Even now, what Polish peasant woman would undertake a serious step without the counsel of her priest?

Maybe at present it was more important for the Soviet Union to improve public morality than to build the Volga-Don Canal or Angarastroi.

How could it be done? That was the subject of Rubin's "Project for Civic Temples," already in rough draft. Tonight, since he had insomnia anyway, he must add the finishing touches. Then, when he was next allowed a visit, he could try to transmit it to the outside. It could be typed and sent onto the Central Committee. He couldn't send it over his own name—the Central Committee would be offended at such advice coming from a political prisoner—but it could not be done anonymously either. Let one of his front-line friends sign it; for the sake of a good cause, Rubin would gladly sacrifice the glory of having originated it.

Forcing himself to disregard the waves of pain in his head, Rubin packed his pipe with Golden Fleece tobacco—out of sheer habit; he had no real desire to smoke at this moment and, in fact, found it nauseating. Still, he smoked and began to look over the project.

Sitting in his overcoat and underwear at the rough table strewn with bread crumbs and ashes, breathing the stuffy air of the unswept hallway, through which, now and then, sleepy zeks hurried to the toilet, the anonymous author studied the selfless proposal he had scrawled across many sheets of paper.

The preamble set forth the necessity of raising still higher the already high morality of the population, of giving greater meaning to revolutionary and state holidays and lending ceremonial dignity to acts of marriage, naming the new-born, entering adulthood, and mourning the dead. The author noted in passing that birth, marriage, and death are observed among us in a routine way, so that the citizen feels his family and social ties are of the weakest.

As a solution, the proposal called for the establishment of Civil Temples, so majestically designed as to dominate their surroundings.

Then, in separate sections, which were, in turn, broken

into paragraphs, the organizational plan was carefully outlined: In population centers of what size or on the basis of
what territorial unit the Civic Temples were to be built.
What particular dates would be celebrated in the presence of
all the inhabitants of the area. The approximate duration of
individual rituals: Marriage would be preceded by betrothal
and announcement of the marriage two weeks in advance.
Those entering adulthood would be presented in groups
and, in the presence of the whole community assembled in
the temple, would take a special oath to fulfill their obligations to the country and to their parents, and would also take
an oath of a general ethical nature.

The proposal emphasized that the ritual aspect of all these
observances was not to be treated casually. The clothes of
the temple attendants must be out of the ordinary, distinguished by high decorations and stressing the snow-white
purity of those who wore them. The rituals must be developed rhythmically and emotionally. No opportunity was to
be overlooked of playing on every physical sense of the
audience: a special scent in the air, melodious music and
singing, the use of colored glass, stage lights, and wall paintings, all should further the development of people's aesthe-
tic tastes—indeed, the whole architectural ensemble of the
temple must breathe majesty and eternity.

Every word of the project had to be painstakingly, delicately chosen from among many possible words. Otherwise, shallow, superficial readers might conclude from some slight
carelessness that the author was simply proposing to revive
Christian temples without Christ. But in the most profound
sense this was not true! Someone who liked to draw historical analogies might also accuse the author of copying
Robespierre's cult of the Supreme Being. But of course that,
too, was not the same thing at all!

The author considered the most original part of the project to be the section on the new—no, not priests, but
temple attendants, as he called them. He considered that the
key to the success of the whole project lay in establishing
throughout the nation a corps of authoritative attendants
who enjoyed the love and trust of the people because of
their own irreproachable, unselfish, and worthy lives. He
proposed to the Party that the selection of candidates for
the courses that would prepare them to become temple at-

tendants should be made according to the principles of morality, and that they be taken off any other jobs they might be engaged in. After the initial heavy demand had been supplied, this program of courses could with the years become much more extensive and more profound, and could provide the attendants with a broad and brilliant education, including, in particular, rhetoric. (The proposal fearlessly declared that the art of oratory in the country had declined, perhaps because there was no need of persuasiveness where the entire population unconditionally supports its beloved state without it.)

The revision of his proposal so absorbed his attention that if he couldn't altogether forget his pain, it at least no longer seemed to concern him directly.

The fact that no one came to take a look at a prisoner who might be dying at an odd hour did not surprise Rubin. He had seen enough instances of this in counterintelligence prisons and at transit camps.

Thus when the key rattled in the door, Rubin, at the first throb of his heart, was afraid he would be discovered in the middle of the night engaged in an activity that was against the rules, and that he would have to undergo some boring, stupid punishment. He gathered up his papers, his book, his tobacco, and started back into the semicircular room, but he was too late. The tough, heavy-set master sergeant spotted him through the little window and called him from behind the closed doors.

Immediately, Rubin felt all over again his loneliness, his painful helplessness, his wounded dignity.

"Sergeant," he said, slowly approaching the duty officer's deputy, "I have been asking for the medical assistant for more than two hours. I am going to file complaints with the MGB prison administration against the medical assistant and against you."

But the master sergeant said in a conciliatory tone, "Rubin, I couldn't do anything before. It wasn't my fault. Let's go."

The fact was that as soon as he learned it wasn't someone just raising a minor fuss but one of the most troublesome zeks, he tried to rouse the lieutenant. There had been no answer for a long time; then the medical assistant peered out for a moment and disappeared. Finally, the lieutenant left the dispensary frowning and gave the master sergeant permission to bring Rubin in.

So Rubin put his arms in the sleeves of his coat and buttoned it up over his underwear. The master sergeant led him through the cellar corridor, and they went up into the prison court by the stairs on which a thick layer of powdery snow had fallen. The night was as still as a painting, the snow piled in white pillars against the dark, as the master sergeant and Rubin crossed the court, leaving deep tracks in the fluffy snow.

Here, under the lovely cloudy night sky, smoky brown from the lights, feeling the innocent touch of cold little hexagonal stars on his warm face and beard, Rubin stopped and shut his eyes. He was filled with a sense of peace that was all the keener for being so brief—all the power of existence, all the delight of going nowhere, of asking nothing, desiring nothing, just to stand there the whole night long, blessedly, blissfully, as trees stand, catching the snowflakes.

And at that very moment he heard a long, piercing locomotive whistle from the railroad which passed a half-mile from Mavrino, that special, lonely-in-the-night, soul-seizing whistle which in our later years recalls our childhood because in childhood it promised so much.

If one could stand like this for half an hour, everything would go away, body and soul would become whole again, and he could compose tender verses about locomotive whistles in the night.

If only he did not have to follow the guard!

But the guard was already looking back suspiciously—was he perhaps planning a night escape?

Rubin's legs took him where he was supposed to go.

The young medical assistant was pink from sleep, the blood suffusing her cheeks. She wore a white robe, not, obviously, over her field shirt and skirt but over very little. At any other time Rubin, liked every other prisoner, would have noticed this and tried to look at her body, but just now his thoughts were not concerned with this coarse creature who had been the cause of his torment all night long.

"I need a 'three-in-one' pill and also something for insomnia, but not Luminal. I have to go to sleep immediately."

"There isn't anything for insomnia," she said, automatically refusing.

"I need it!" Rubin repeated insistently. "I have crucial work to do for the minister from early morning on. And I can't get to sleep."

The mention of the minister, and the possibility that Rubin might continue to stand there, insisting on the pills, as well as the fact that something told her the lieutenant would be returning right away, convinced the medical assistant that she ought to give him the medicine.

She got the pills out of the cabinet and made Rubin swallow every one in her presence, because, according to prison rules, every medication was regarded as a weapon and could be issued not to the prisoner but only to his mouth.

Rubin asked the time and learned it was already half-past three; he went out. He returned through the court, looking fondly at the lindens, which were lit from below by the beams of the 200- and 500-watt searchlights in the zone; he breathed in the air which smelled of snow, bent down and grabbed a fistful of starry snowflakes and rubbed his face and neck and filled his mouth with the weightless, bodiless, icy substance.

And his soul was at one with the freshness of the world.

68

THE ROOTLESS COSMOPOLITE

The door from the dining room to the bedroom was not quite shut, and a single, heavy stroke of the wall clock could be clearly heard, reverberating in harmonic waves before dying away.

Half-past what hour? Adam Roitman wanted to look at his wristwatch, cozily ticking on the night table, but he was afraid the sudden flash of light would disturb his wife. His wife slept in a particularly graceful position, curved toward him on her side, her face tucked against her husband's shoulder, and Adam felt her breast at his elbow.

They had been married for five years, but even half asleep he was aware of a flood of tender gratitude for her being beside him, for the funny way she slept, warming her small, always icy feet between his legs.

He had just wakened from an incoherent dream. He wanted to go back to sleep, but he began remembering the evening news bulletins and problems at the sharashka, and as thoughts piled on thoughts, his eyes opened and stared. He found himself prey to that nighttime lucidity which renders useless all efforts to get to sleep.

The tramping around and furniture moving which had gone on for most of the evening in the Makarygins' apartments upstairs had long since ceased.

Through a narrow space between the drawn curtains came the faint, grayish glow of night.

Sleepless, lying there in his pajamas, Adam Veniaminovich Roitman felt none of the self-assurance and superiority imparted to him during the day by the shoulder boards of an MGB major and a Stalin Prize medal. He lay flat on his back in bed and, like all other mortals, felt that the world was full of people, that it was cruel, that it was not an easy place to live in.

That evening, while the Makarygins' quarters had been bubbling with gaiety, one of his oldest friends had come to see him. He, too, was a Jew. He had come without his wife; he was worried, and what he had told Roitman was depressing.

It was nothing new. It had first begun the previous spring in the field of theatrical criticism. At the beginning, it seemed innocent enough to print the critics' real names, which were Jewish, in parentheses after their Russian-sounding pen names. Then it started to infect the literary world. In a certain second-rate newspaper that dealt with everything under the sun but its own business, somebody slipped in the venomous word "cosmopolite." Thus the word was discovered. The beautiful, proud word that united all worlds of the universe, that had crowned the noblest geniuses of all the ages—Dante, Goethe, Byron—that word had been distorted and made ugly on the pages of that worthless rag and came to mean "kike."

Then it crawled further on, hiding shamefully in document files behind closed doors.

And now the chill, warning breath was reaching even the technical sphere. Roitman, steadily and brilliantly advancing toward fame, had in the past month felt his own position being undermined.

Could his memory be playing him false? During the Revolution, and for a long time afterward, the word "Jew" had had a connotation of greater reliability than the word "Russian." A Russian had to be checked up on more than a Jew: Who were his parents? What had been his source of income before 1917? This wasn't necessary with a Jew. To a man, the Jews were in favor of the Revolution that had rid them of pogroms, of settlement restrictions.

And now, imperceptibly, Iosif Stalin, hiding behind a screen of second-rank figures, was grasping the whip of the persecutor of Israelites.

When a group of people is hounded because they exploited others, or have been members of a dominant caste, or hold certain political views or have certain acquaintances, there are always reasonable (or pseudo-reasonable) grounds for taking action against them. At least one would know he had chosen his lot himself, that he could have chosen otherwise. But nationality?

Roitman's inner self, his nighttime self, objected: people didn't choose their social origin either. Yet they were certainly persecuted for it.

But in Roitman's case, the real hurt lay in the fact that at bottom one wants to belong, wants to be the same as everyone else. But they don't want you, they reject you, they say you are an alien. You have no roots. You're a "kike."

Slowly, with great solemnity, the wall clock in the dining room struck four times and stopped. Roitman waited for the fifth chime; he was glad to hear only four. He still had time to go back to sleep.

He moved slightly. His wife murmured in her sleep, turning to face the other way and pressing her back against her husband. He changed his position, fitting the contour of his body to hers, and put an arm around her. Gratefully she fell silent.

In the dining room his son slept quietly, ever so quietly. He never woke during the night, never cried, never called out.

This quick-witted three-year-old was the pride of his young

parents. Adam Veniaminovich described all his habits and accomplishments with delight, even to the zeks in Acoustics. With the happy person's usual insensitivity, he didn't realize how painful this was to men deprived of fatherhood. His son could prattle on fluently, but his pronunciation was still uncertain. During the day, he imitated his mother—you could tell she came from the Volga by the way she pronounced an unaccented "o." In the evening he talked like his father—Adam not only sounded his "r's" in the back of his throat, but had some unfortunate speech defects as well.

It happens in life that if and when happiness does finally come, it comes unstintingly. Love and marriage, followed by the birth of his son, had coincided in Roitman's history with the end of the war and his Stalin Prize. Not that he had been badly off during the war. In quiet Bashkir, granted generous food rations, he and his present colleagues at the Mavrino Institute had designed the first system for telephonic encoding. Such a system seemed utterly primitive now, but in those days it had made them laureates.

How feverishly they had worked at it! What had become of their enthusiasm, their steadfast spirit of inquiry, the flame that rose within them?

With the penetration that comes of lying wakeful in the dark, when one's vision is undistracted and turns inward, Roitman suddenly understood what he had been missing these past years. Surely it was the fact that everything he was doing he was not doing himself.

He had not even noticed when and how he had slipped from being a creator into the role of boss of other creators.

He moved his arm away from his wife as if he had been burned, propped the pillow higher, and turned on his back again.

Yes, yes, yes! It was deceptive. It was easy to say, starting home Saturday evening, and already drawn into the coziness of home and family plans for Sunday: "Valentine Martynich! You must figure out tomorrow how we can get rid of the nonlinear distortions! Lev Grigorich, would you run through this article from *Proceedings* and jot down the basic ideas?" And on Monday morning he would return to work, feeling fresh and rested, and on his desk—as in a fairy tale —he would find a résumé of the article from *Proceedings* and Pryanchikov would explain how they could get rid of the nonlinear distortions—if he hadn't already done it himself on Sunday.

Very convenient!

And the zeks were never resentful of Roitman. On the contrary, they liked him because he didn't act like a jailer but like a decent human being.

But creativity—the joy of a successful brain storm and the bitterness of unexpected defeat—had abandoned him.

What had kept him so busy all these years? Intrigue. The power struggle within the institute. He and his friends had done everything they could to discredit and topple Yakonov, because he overshadowed them with his seniority and his aplomb. They were afraid he personally would get the Stalin Prize all to himself. Taking advantage of the fact that, despite all his efforts, Yakonov had not been taken into the Party because of the black marks on his record, the "Young Turks" had used Party meetings to mount their attack against him. They would put a report he had prepared on the agenda and ask him to leave while they discussed it, or else they would discuss it right in his presence ("only Party members voting") and pass a resolution. According to these Party resolutions, Yakonov was always in the wrong. At times Roitman even felt sorry for him. But there was nothing he could do.

Now everything had turned the other way. In their persecution of Yakonov, the "Young Turks" had lost sight of the fact that among the five of them four were Jews. And these days Yakonov never tired of proclaiming from every platform that cosmopolitanism is the most vicious enemy of the Socialist fatherland.

Yesterday, after the ministerial wrath, a crucial day for the Mavrino Institute, the prisoner Markushev had proposed combining the clipper and the vocoder. Such an idea was probably total nonsense, but it could be presented to the ministry as a fundamental improvement. So Yakonov ordered the construction of the vocoder transferred to Number Seven immediately and ordered Pryanchikov to be transferred with it. In the presence of Sevastyanov, Roitman impetuously raised several objections and began to argue. Whereupon Yakonov, patronizingly, like an overly forthright friend, slapped him on the back.

"Adam Veniaminovich! Don't force the deputy minister to think you put your personal interests above those of the Special Technical Section."

Therein lay the tragedy of their present situation: they hit you in the face and you couldn't even weep! They strangled you in broad daylight and you were supposed to stand up and applaud!

Five o'clock struck—he had not heard the half-hour.

He no longer wanted to sleep, and he felt hemmed in by the bed.

Slowly and carefully, he slipped out and pushed his feet into his slippers. Soundlessly he avoided the chair in his path and went over to the window, parting the silk curtains.

How much snow had fallen!

Across the yard was the farthest and most forgotten corner of Neskuchny Gardens, a steep ravine covered with snow and overgrown with solemn white pines. The window sill was hidden under a fluffy little snowdrift that clung to the glass panes.

The snow had almost stopped falling.

The radiators under the window made his knees hot.

Another reason he hadn't accomplished anything in his field during the last few years was that he was continually plagued by meetings and paper work. There were political indoctrination every Monday and technical instruction every Friday; Party meetings twice a month; meetings of the Party Bureau for the institute twice a month, too; and two or three times a month he was called to the ministry; once a month there was a special session on security and vigilance; every month he had to work up a plan for new scientific projects, and every three months he had to send in a report on its fulfillment; then, for some reason, every three months he also had to write individual reports on each prisoner—a whole day's work. And on top of it all, his subordinates interrupted him every half-hour with requisitions; every condenser the size of a gumdrop, every yard of wire and every electronic tube had to be requested on a requisition signed by the head of the laboratory before it could be issued at the warehouse.

Oh, if only he could get free of all the red tape and the cutthroat struggle to come out on top! If only he himself could pore over diagrams, take the soldering iron in his own hand, sit in front of the green window of the oscilloscope and try to catch a particular curve, then he, like Pryanchikov, could hum a carefree boogie-woogie. What bliss it had been to be thirty-one, without the weight of those oppressive shoulder boards, unconcerned with external appearances, and, like a boy, to dream of building something.

He had said to himself "like a boy," and, through a trick of memory, he remembered himself as a boy. In his nighttime mind, a deeply buried episode, forgotten for many years, surfaced with merciless clarity. Twelve-year-old Adam in his red Pioneer's tie, his voice trembling with hurt and dignity, stood before the General Pioneer Assembly at school, demanding the expulsion from the Young Pioneers, and from the Soviet school system, of an agent of the class enemy. Mitka Shtitelman had spoken before him and Mishka Lyuksemburg after him, and they had all denounced their fellow student, Oleg Rozhdestensky, on grounds of anti-Semitism, attending church, and having an alien class origin. As they spoke, they cast annihilating glances on the trembling boy who was being judged.

The twenties were coming to an end, and boys at that time were still living on politics, newspapers posted on walls and windows, self-government, and debates. It was a southern city, and Jews made up half the group. Although the boys were sons of lawyers, dentists, and even small merchants, all considered themselves, with frenzied conviction, members of the proletariat.

Oleg was pale, thin, the best student in the class. He avoided political subjects, and he had joined the Pioneers with an obvious lack of zeal. The young enthusiasts suspected an alien element in him. They watched him, waiting to catch him in a misstep. One day Oleg said, "Every person has the right to say anything he thinks." Shtitelman jumped on him: "What do you mean, anything? Nikola called me a 'kike face'—is that all right, too?" "To *say* it?" Oleg stretched his thin neck and did not back down. "Everyone has a right to *say* whatever he wants."

The case against Oleg was launched. Friends were found to inform on him; Shurik Burikov and Shurik Vorozhbit saw the accused enter a church with his mother and saw him come to school one day with a cross around his neck. Meetings were held, sessions of the pupils' committee, the group committee, Young Pioneer musters, Pioneer parades; and at all of them the twelve-year-old Robespierres denounced to the student masses the accomplice of anti-Semites and the peddler of religious opium, who hadn't eaten for two weeks out of terror and had concealed from his family the fact that he had already been expelled from the Pioneers and would soon be expelled from school.

Adam Roitman had not been the instigator. He had been dragged into it. But even now, the vileness of it all made him flush with shame.

A circle of wrongs, a circle of wrongs! And no way to break the vicious ring. No exit. Just as there was no way out of the contest with Yakonov.

Where should one begin to set the world aright? With others? Or with oneself?

That heaviness had settled in his head and that emptiness in his breast which are the indispensable preliminaries to falling asleep.

He went over and lay down quietly under the blanket. He had to get some sleep before the clock struck six.

In the morning he would go ahead with the phonoscopy! That was the big trump up his sleeve! In case of success, the enterprise might even grow into a separate scientific . . .

69

MONDAY DAWN

Reveille at the sharashka was at 7 A.M.

But on Monday, long before reveille, a guard entered the room where the workers lived and shook the janitor's shoulder. Spiridon snorted, woke up, and looked at the guard in the light of the blue bulb.

"Put your clothes on, Yegorov. The lieutenant wants you," the guard said quietly.

But Spiridon lay there with his eyes open, not moving.

"Do you hear? I told you the lieutenant wants you."

"What for? Did he crap in his pants?" Spiridon inquired, still not moving.

"Get up, get up," the guard persisted. "I don't know why."

"Bah!" Spiridon sighed heavily, putting his hairy red arms behind his head and yawning. "The day will come when I won't get up. What time is it?"

"Almost six."

"Not six yet? Well, go along, it's all right."

And he continued to lie there.

The guard looked sideways at him and went out.

Half in the blue light, half in the shadow of the upper bunk, Spiridon lay on his pillow with his hands behind his head, not moving.

He was sorry he had not finished his dream.

He had been traveling on a cart piled high with dry branches, and under the dry branches were some logs hidden from the forester. He seemed to be going from the forest he knew to his home in the village, but by an unfamiliar road. Yet even though the road was unfamiliar, Spiridon saw every detail of it clearly with his two eyes—which in the dream were both good: the swollen roots across the road, trees splintered by old lightning, pine woods, and deep sand the wheels sank into. In his sleep Spiridon smelled all the forest scents of early spring and breathed them in eagerly. He breathed them in eagerly because he remembered clearly in his dream that he was a zek, and that his term was ten years plus five, that he had escaped from the sharashka, that they must have missed him by now, and that he had to hurry to take these pieces of firewood to his wife and daughter before they sent the dogs after him.

But the chief joy of his dream was that the horse was not just any horse but the favorite of all he had ever had, the three-year-old mare Grivna, the first horse he had bought for his farm after the Civil War. She was all gray; the gray had an even, reddish cast, and they had called her color "rosy." With Grivna's help, he had managed to get on his feet in his farming, and she was in the shafts when he stole off to marry Marfa Ustinovna. And now Spiridon was riding along, happily surprised that Grivna was still alive and still young, and that she still hauled the load uphill and through the sand without having to be whipped. All Grivna's brains showed in her long, gray, sensitive ears, whose movements told her master that she understood what he required of her and that she would manage. To have given Grivna even a glimpse of the whip from far off would have insulted her. When he drove Grivna, Spiridon never took a whip with him.

He was so glad that Grivna was young and would apparently still be there when his term was ended that in his dream he wanted to climb down and kiss her on the nose. But on a slope leading to a stream Spiridon suddenly noticed that his cart was loaded badly and that the branches were slipping, and might fall off entirely at the ford.

Just then a big shove threw him from the cart to the ground—it was the guard waking him up.

Spiridon lay there and remembered not only Grivna but dozens of horses he had driven and worked, each one fixed in his memory like a living person. He remembered, too, thousands of other horses he had seen, and he was sad that these first servants of man had been driven out of existence for no reason, some starved, others worked to death, others sold to the Tatars for meat. Spiridon could understand reasonable decisions. But it was impossible to understand why they had destroyed the horses. They had claimed at the time that tractors would replace them. But what happened was that the work had all fallen on the women's shoulders.

And was it only horses? Had not Spiridon himself cut down orchards on individual farms so that there would be nothing left for people to lose, and they would then submit more easily to being herded together?

"Yegorov!" the guard cried loudly at the door, waking up two other zeks.

"I'm coming, Mother of God!" Spiridon quickly responded, setting his bare feet on the floor. And he went to the radiator to get his dried footcloths.

The door shut behind the guard. His neighbor, the smith, asked, "Where are you going, Spiridon?"

"The lords are calling me. I have to work for my rations," the janitor said in a burst of anger.

In his own house Spiridon was a peasant who did not lie late in bed, but in prison he hated to get up in the dark. To get up before dawn with a club over one's head was the worst part of being a prisoner.

In SevUrallag they got them up at five.

At the sharashka it was worthwhile giving in.

Winding the bottoms of his padded cotton pants around his shoe tops and lacing high soldier-like puttees over them, Spiridon climbed into the blue skin of his coveralls, pulled on his black pea jacket and fur cap with ear flaps, fastened his well-worn canvas belt, and went out. They let him through the bolted door of the prison, but beyond that point no one escorted him. Spiridon went down an underground corridor, shuffling along the cement floor in his iron-shod shoes, and climbed the stairway to the yard.

Seeing nothing in the snowy half-darkness, Spiridon felt with his feet that the snowfall was about ten inches deep. That meant it had been snowing all night long, that it was a big snow. Pushing through the snow, he went toward the light at the headquarters door.

At that moment the duty officer, the lieutenant with the dreadful mustaches, stepped out the door. Having just left the nurse and discovered that everything was a mess, that a lot of snow had fallen, he had summoned the janitor.

Placing both hands in his belt, the lieutenant said, "Come on, Yegorov, come on! Clean up from the main entrance to the guardhouse, and from headquarters to the kitchen. Also in the exercise yard. Come on!"

"Come, come! If you keep coming, there'll be none left for your wife," muttered Spiridon, going off through the new snow for a shovel.

"What? What did you say?" the lieutenant demanded threateningly.

Spiridon looked back at him. "I said *'Jawohl,'* chief, *'Jawohl!'* " The Germans used to say things too, and Spiridon would say *"Jawohl"* to them. "Tell them to save some potatoes for me in the kitchen."

"All right. Get going!"

Spiridon had always behaved sensibly, had not quarreled with the authorities. But today he was in a very bitter mood —because it was Monday morning, because he had to start work without even a chance to rub his eyes, because of the proximity of the letter from home and his premonition of disaster about it. The bitterness of all his fifty years of marching in line gathered into a burning in his chest.

No more snow was falling. The lindens stood motionless.

They were white, not with yesterday's frost, but with the new snow. The dark sky, the stillness, told Spiridon this snow would not last long.

Spiridon set to work grimly, but once he got going, after the first fifty shovelfuls, he worked smoothly and even cheerfully. Both he and his wife were the kind who found release in work from everything that burdened their hearts. And things became easier.

Spiridon began his task not by clearing a path from the guardhouse for the chiefs, as he had been told, but according to his own understanding: first the path to the kitchen, and then a circular path in the exercise area, three plywood-shovel widths across, for his brother zeks.

Meanwhile his thoughts dwelled on his daughter. His wife and he had already lived their share. His sons, though they, too, were behind barbed wire, were men after all. The harder life is for a man when he is young, the easier it will be in the future. But what about his daughter?

Though Spiridon saw nothing with one eye and the other had only partial vision, he went around the whole exercise yard in a perfect oval. It was not yet light, just seven, when the first fresh-air enthusiasts, Potapov and Khorobrov, who had got up and washed before reveille, were climbing the stairway to the yard.

Air was rationed and was valuable.

"What happened, Danilich," asked Khorobrov, turning up the collar of the worn black civilian coat he had been arrested in. "Didn't you go to bed at all?"

"You think the bastards would let a person sleep?" Spiridon said. But his early morning anger had left him. During the hour of silent work all his dark thoughts about his jailers vanished, and he was left with the bright determination of a man accustomed to suffering. Without putting it in words in his mind, Spiridon had decided in his heart that if his daughter had gone wrong one way or another, things would be hard enough for her as it was, and he must answer her gently, without cursing her.

But even this important thought about his daughter, which had come to him from the motionless, predawn lindens, was now being pushed aside by the petty problems of the day: two boards which were buried somewhere under the snow; the broom which must be fastened more securely to the broomstick.

Also, he had to clear the road to the guardhouse for passenger cars and for the free employees. Spiridon tossed the shovel onto his shoulder, rounded the sharashka building and disappeared.

Sologdin came out to cut wood, light, slender, his padded jacket thrown carelessly around his shoulders, which stood the cold well. After yesterday's pointless fight with Rubin, and all the irritating accusations, he had slept badly for the first time in his two years at the sharashka. Now he wanted air, solitude, and space to think things over. There were sawed logs; all he had to do was split them.

Potapov was walking slowly with Khorobrov, his injured leg throwing him a bit off stride. He wore the Red Army overcoat which had been given him when he'd been sent in on a tank as an assault trooper in the taking of Berlin. (He had been an officer, but they didn't recognize officer ranks among POWs.)

Khorobrov had just barely got up and washed, but his ever-alert mind was already vigilant. The words which burst from him seemed to describe an aimless arc in the dark air and return to tear at him:

"Do you remember how, long ago, we read that the Ford assembly line turns the worker into a machine, that the assembly line is the most inhuman aspect of capitalist exploitation? But fifteen years have passed and now we acclaim that same assembly line, renamed the 'flow line,' as the best and newest form of production. What we should have now is another baptism of all Russia—and Stalin could immediately fit it right in with atheism."

Potapov was always melancholy in the morning. It was the only time he could think about his ruined life, his son growing up without him, his wife wasting away without him. Later in the day the work absorbed him, and there was no time to think.

Potapov heard too much discontent in Khorobrov's words, which could lead to its own errors. Therefore he walked on silently, awkwardly throwing forward his injured leg, and tried to breathe deeper and more regularly.

They completed one circle after another.

Others joined them. They walked singly or in twos and threes. For various reasons they kept their conversations to themselves and tried not to come too near or overtake each other unnecessarily.

It was just dawn. Obscured by snowy clouds, the sky was late with its morning rays. The lamps still cast yellow circles on the snow.

The air was fresh; the new-fallen snow did not crunch underfoot but packed down softly.

Erect and tall, wearing a felt hat (he had never been in a camp), Kondrashev-Ivanov walked with his bunkmate, the puny Gerasimovich. Gerasimovich, who wore a visored cap, did not reach to Kondrashev's shoulder.

Gerasimovich, overwhelmed by his visit, had stayed in bed like an invalid all through Sunday. His wife's parting cry had shaken him. This morning he had mustered all his strength to go outdoors for a walk. Bundled up and shivering, he had immediately wanted to go back inside the prison. But he ran into Kondrashev-Ivanov, and after one circle of the yard he forgot his troubles for the rest of the hour.

"What? You know nothing about Pavel Dmitrievich Korin?" Kondrashev-Ivanov demanded in astonishment, as if every schoolboy had heard of him. "Oh! He has—they say, though I've never seen it—an amazing painting called 'Vanishing Russia'! Some say it's six yards long, some say twelve. And in that painting . . ."

It had begun to grow gray.

The guard walked through the court, shouting that the exercise hour was over.

Going back through the underground corridor, the zeks, refreshed, met a gloomy, bearded, pale, exhausted Rubin, who was hurrying outside. He had not only slept through the woodcutting—to which in any case it was unthinkable for him to go after his quarrel with Sologdin—but he had missed the morning stroll. After his brief, drugged sleep, his body felt heavy and numb. He was also experiencing oxygen starvation, which is unknown to anyone who can breathe fresh air whenever he wants. He tried to break through to the court for a swallow of air and a handful of snow to rub himself down.

But the guard at the top of the stairs would not let him out.

Rubin stood in the cement hole at the bottom of the stairs, where some snow had drifted, and breathed the fresh air. He made three slow circular motions with his arms, breathing deeply, then picked up some snow, rubbed his face with it, and went back into the prison.

Energetically, Spiridon went in, too, having cleared the automobile road from the gates to the guardhouse.

In the prison headquarters, two lieutenants—the one with the square mustaches who was going off duty and the new duty officer, Zhvakun—were studying the orders left by Major Myshin.

Lieutenant Zhvakun was a coarse, broad-featured, impenetrable fellow. During the war he had served, with the rank of master sergeant, as "executioner attached to a divisional military tribunal," and he had acted in that capacity throughout his stay in the service. He was very attached to his position in the special prison, and, not being excessively literate, he always read Myshin's orders twice so as not to get anything mixed up.

At ten to nine they went through the rooms to carry out a check and to read out an announcement, as they had been instructed:

"In the course of the next three days all prisoners are to submit to Major Myshin a list of their close relatives as follows: surname, given name, patronymic, relationship, place of work, and home address.

"Close relatives are considered to be the following: mother, father, wife in a registered marriage, sons and daughters of a registered marriage. All others—brothers, sisters, aunts, cousins, grandchildren, and grandparents—are not considered close relatives.

"From January 1, correspondence and visits will be allowed only with the close relatives listed by the prisoner.

"In addition, from January 1, the size of the monthly letter will be limited to not more than one folded notebook sheet."

This was so bad and so implacable that the mind could not grasp it. Therefore there was at first neither desperation nor revolt; only a few derisive outcries followed Zhvakun:

"Happy New Year!"

"We wish you happiness!"

"Hoo, hoo!"

"Write denunciations of your own relatives!"

"Can't they find out for themselves?"

"Why not tell us what size our handwriting has to be?"

Zhvakun was counting the prisoners and, simultaneously, trying to remember who was shouting what, so as to tell the major later.

Anyway, prisoners were always dissatisfied whether you did them a good turn or a bad one.

The zeks went off to their work in a stupor.

Even those who had been in prison a long time were astounded at the cruelty of the new measure. The cruelty was double-edged. On the one hand, it meant that the thin thread of communication with a wife or child or parent could be maintained only at the cost of a police denunciation of them. After all, many outside still managed to hide the fact that they had relatives behind bars, and this secrecy was all that protected their jobs and their housing. On the other hand, it meant that unregistered wives and children were cut off from all contact—also brothers, sisters, and first cousins. Yet after the war, after the bombings, the evacuation, the famine, many zeks had no other relatives. And because people didn't anticipate being arrested and make their confessions, take Communion, and settle their accounts with life, many a loyal girl was left without the black stamp of the ZAGS marriage-registration office in her passport. So now these faithful girls were to become strangers.

Even those who were usually impatient to get to work were disconsolate. When the bell rang, the zeks went out slowly, their arms at their sides, milled through the corridors, smoked and talked. Sitting at their desks, they lit up again and continued to talk. The question which chiefly occupied them was: how could it be that the information about their relatives was not already collected and correlated in the central card catalogue? The newcomers and innocents believed it was. But the old, hardened zeks shook their heads firmly. They explained that the card files were in a state of disorder, that behind the black leather doors they often "don't catch the mice"—they don't pick up the information from the innumerable questionnaires; the prison officials don't bring their records up to date from the ledgers in which visits and parcels are registered; and the list which Klimentiev and Myshin were demanding was therefore the best-aimed death blow one could strike at one's relatives.

That was what the zeks were saying, and no one wanted to work.

But the last week of the year began that very morning, and, according to the projections of the institute administration, it was to witness a heroic push forward, in order to fulfill the plan for 1949 and the plan for December, as well as to work out and adopt the annual plan for 1950, the quarterly plan for January through March, and the plan for the first ten days of January. Everything which had to do with *paper* was to be carried out by the administration itself. Everything which had to do with *work* was to be executed by the zeks. Therefore enthusiasm on the part of the prisoners was particularly essential today.

The institute administration knew nothing about the annihilating morning announcement which the prison administration had made in accordance with its *own* annual plan.

No one could accuse the Ministry of State Security of evangelical behavior. But it had one evangelical trait: the right hand knew not what the left hand was doing.

Major Roitman, on whose fresh-shaven face not a trace of nocturnal anxiety remained, had assembled all the zeks and free employees of the Acoustics Laboratory to brief them about the program. From his long intelligent countenance, Roitman's lips protruded like a Negro's. Over his field shirt, across his thin chest, hung a shoulder belt which he did not need, and which was particularly unsuited to him. He wanted to brace up and infuse energy into his subordinates, but the breath of failure already had permeated the space beneath the arches; without the vocoder installation, which had already been removed, the middle of the room looked empty and abandoned. Pryanchikov, pearl of Acoustics' crown, was not there; Rubin was absent, too, locked up with Smolosidov on the third floor; and Roitman himself was hurrying to get it over with here and go on upstairs.

Simochka was not there either. She was to be on duty after lunch in place of someone else. So be it, thought Nerzhin; she was not there. It was the one thing that relieved him right now. He would not have to try to explain matters to her by signs and notes.

In the assembled circle, Nerzhin sat leaning against the springy back of his chair with his feet on the lower rung of another chair. Most of the time he looked out the window.

Outside a moist west wind was rising and the cloudy sky was leaden. The fallen snow was beginning to crumble and pack down. One more senseless, rotten thaw!

Nerzhin sat there lax, not having slept enough, his wrinkles sharply etched in the gray light, the corners of his mouth drooping. He was experiencing a Monday morning feeling familiar to many prisoners, when one seems not to have the strength to move or live. His narrowed eyes stared without seeing at the dark fence, and the watchtower with the guard standing in it, directly across from his own window.

What was one visit a year? He had had a visit only yesterday. As recently as that, it had seemed that the most urgent, most necessary things had all been said. And now today. . . !

When could he speak to her now? When could he write to her? How could he write to her? Get in touch with her at work? After yesterday it was clear that that was impossible.

How could he explain to her that to keep them from finding out where she worked, he could no longer write? The address on the envelope would be a denunciation in itself.

And if he just didn't write at all? What would she think? "Just yesterday I smiled; after today will I be silent forever?"

The sensation of being caught in a vise—not a poetical, figurative vise but an enormous locksmith's vise with teeth milled into it, with jaws for squeezing a man's neck—the sensation of having that vise close around him took Nerzhin's breath away.

It was impossible to find a way out. Every course was fatal.

Polite and myopic, Roitman peered through his anastigmatic glasses with gentle eyes, and he spoke of plans, plans, plans in a voice which was not the voice of a boss but carried a hint of fatigue and supplication.

However, he was sowing his seed on stony ground.

70

THE BARREL IN THE YARD

That Monday morning there was also a meeting in the Design Office. The free employees and the zeks sat together at several tables.

Though the room was on the upper story and the windows faced south, the gray morning gave little light, and here and there electric lamps were turned on at the drawing boards.

The head of the office, a lieutenant colonel, did not stand up to address them but spoke without much insistence of the fulfillment of the plan, of new plans, and of "Socialist obligations" in response to challenges. He said, though he did not believe it himself, that by the end of the coming year they would deliver the technical solution of the absolute encoder project. He phrased his statements so as to leave his designers an escape hatch.

Sologdin sat in the last row and stared past the others at the wall. His gaze was clear, his face was smooth and fresh, and it was impossible to suppose he had anything on his mind or that he was worried. Rather, one would have imagined that he was making use of the meeting to relax.

But this was not so. He was thinking intensely. He had several hours or perhaps only several minutes left, he did not know how much time, and he had to solve the problem of his whole life without making a mistake. All morning, as he had split wood, he had not been conscious of a single log or a single blow—he had been thinking. And as in optical devices many-faceted mirrors whirl, their various facets catching and reflecting rays of light, so all this time, on beams which did not intersect and were not parallel, flashes of thought revolved and sparkled within him.

He had heard the morning announcement with an ironic smile. He had foreseen such a measure for a long time. He had been the first to prepare for it: he had broken off his correspondence himself. The announcement only confirmed his judgment that the prison regime would become harsher and harsher, that the road back to freedom called the "end of the term" would be closed.

His chief bitterness and regret arose from the awkward turn the argument had taken the night before, and the fact that Rubin seemed to have assumed the right to judge his actions. He could cross Lev Rubin from his list of friends and try to forget him, but he could not forget the challenge he had thrown down. It remained. It was an ulcer.

The meeting ended, and they all went to their places.

Larisa's desk was empty. She had the day off in exchange for the Sunday she had worked.

It was just as well. After all, a woman won yesterday would be in the way today.

Standing up, Sologdin unpinned an old, dirty sheet of paper from his drawing board, and under it appeared the heart of the encoder.

Leaning on the back of his chair, he stood for a long time in front of the drawing.

The more he studied and absorbed his creation, the more he calmed down. The mirrors inside him whirled more and more slowly. The axes of light seemed to fall parallel with each other.

Two of the women draftsmen, as the rules required once a week, went among the designers to collect old, unneeded sheets that were to be destroyed. They were not supposed to be torn up and tossed into wastebaskets; instead, they were counted, their total was recorded, and they were burned in the yard.

Sologdin took a fat soft pencil and casually drew several lines through his drawing; then he spotted and smudged it.

Untacking it, he took it off the board, put the dirty top sheet over it, put another sheet under it, rolled them all together and handed them to one of the women. "Three sheets, please."

Then he sat down, opened a reference book, and looked up to see what would happen to his drawing next.

The two women counted what they had collected and wrote down the total.

Sologdin watched to be certain that none of the designers checked the sheets.

No one approached the woman who had taken his.

This was sheer laxity on the part of Shishkin-Myshkin:

they were too trustful. Why had they not created in the Design Office a Design Office Security Office which would inspect all drawings to be destroyed by the Design Office?

There was no one to tell his witticism to, and Sologdin laughed to himself.

At last, having gathered all the unwanted sheets into several rolls and taken a box of matches from one of the habitual smokers, the women went out.

Sologdin made rhythmical strokes on a piece of paper, counting the seconds: they must now be going down the stairs . . . now putting on their coats . . . now coming out into the yard.

He stood behind his raised drawing board in such a way that almost no one in the room could see him. But he could see outside to that part of the yard where a sooty iron barrel stood, to which the resourceful Spiridon had that morning shoveled a path. The snow had apparently packed down, and both women, wearing boots, got to the barrel easily.

But they were a long time trying to set fire to the first sheet. They lit one match after another, then several at once, but either the wind put them out, or the matches broke, or the burning sulphur leaped onto the women and they had to brush it off frantically. Now there were almost no matches left in their box, and it looked as if they might have to come back for more.

Time was dragging on—Sologdin might be summoned to Yakonov at any moment.

But the women shouted something, motioning with their arms, and Spiridon, in his fur cap with the big ear flaps, came over to them, carrying his broom.

He took off his cap so it would not get singed, put it down on the snow beside him, stuck the sheet of paper and his red head into the barrel, rooted about there, pulled out his head—and the sheet of paper was red. It had caught and flamed. Spiridon left it in the barrel and began to throw all the other sheets in with it. The flames flared up out of the barrel, and the sheets were burned to black cinders.

Just then someone at the head desk of the Design Office called out Sologdin's name.

The lieutenant colonel wanted to see him.

Someone from the Filtration Laboratory was complaining

about not receiving a drawing for two brackets which they had ordered.

The lieutenant colonel was not a rough man. He only said, with a furrowed brow, "Look here, Dmitri Aleksandrovich, what's so complicated about it? It was ordered on Thursday."

Sologdin drew himself up. "Excuse me. I am finishing it now. It will be ready in an hour."

He had not yet begun it, but he could not very well admit that the entire job would take him only an hour.

71

HIS FAVORITE PROFESSION

The operational Chekist sector (security and counterintelligence) at Mavrino was divided between Major Myshin, the prison "protector," and Major Shikin, the institute "protector." Active in different departments and receiving their pay from different cashiers, they were not in competition with each other. Yet a sort of inertia prevented them from working together; their offices were in different buildings and on different floors; counterintelligence and security affairs could not be discussed on the telephone; and because they were of equal rank each considered it humiliating to go to see the other, as if to do so would be kowtowing. So they worked, one during the night, the other during the day, without running into one another for months on end, even though both stressed in their quarterly reports the need for close coordination of all security and counterintelligence functions at Mavrino.

Once when reading an article in *Pravda* Major Shikin had been struck by its title: "His Favorite Profession." The article was about a propagandist who loved explaining things more than anything else in the world. He would explain to workers the importance of increasing productivity, to soldiers the necessity of sacrificing oneself, to voters the correctness of the policy of the "Communist and non-Party bloc." Shikin liked the title. He drew the conclusion that he, too, had made no mistake in choosing his life work. He had never been attracted to any other profession. He loved his own, and it loved him.

In his day Shikin had finished the GPU school, and had then taken graduate courses in interrogation and investigation. But he had spent little time actually working as an interrogator and could therefore not call himself one. He had worked as a security officer in the GPU transportation section; during the war he had been the head of an army military censorship department; then he had been on the commission for repatriation; then in a verification and classification camp; then a special instructor in the techniques of deporting Greeks from the Kuban to Kazakhstan; and finally security officer of the Mavrino Research Institute.

There were many positive aspects to Shikin's profession. In the first place, after the Civil War it had ceased to be dangerous. In every operation there was an overwhelming superiority of forces—two or three armed men against one disarmed, unwarned enemy who was often just waking up.

Then, too, it was highly paid, gave one access to the best of the special distribution centers, to the best apartments taken over from people who had been arrested and sentenced, to pensions higher than those paid the military, and to first-class sanatoria.

It didn't exhaust one; there were no work norms for it. True, friends had told Shikin that in 1937 and 1945 security officers had been driven like horses, but Shikin had never personally fallen into that kind of situation and did not really believe it. In good times one could doze for months at one's desk. The work was characterized by deliberation. The naturally deliberate manner of every well-fed man was joined with a deliberation of method calculated to work on the prisoner's psyche and elicit testimony—the slow sharpening of a pencil, selecting a pen, choosing a sheet of paper, the patient recording of all kinds of procedural nonsense and circumstantial data. This pervasive deliberation was excellent for the nerves and contributed to a long life.

No less precious to Shikin was the system basic to his job. It consisted essentially of record-keeping, of absolute, all-encompassing record-keeping. No conversation could end simply as a conversation; it had to end in the writing of a denunciation, or the signing of a statement or an agreement —not to give false testimony, not to reveal secrets, not to leave the area, gather information, or transmit information. What was especially required was that patient attentiveness and that tidiness which distinguished Shikin's character; he did not let papers fall into chaos, but sorted them out, had them filed, and was always able to find any particular one. As an officer, Shikin himself could not do the physical work of filing; this was done by a part-time assistant, a thin, awkward girl with bad eyesight and a special security clearance, who had come over for the purpose from the secretarial staff.

Above all, security and counterintelligence work were pleasing to Shikin because they gave him power over people and a feeling of omnipotence, and surrounded him with mystery.

Shikin was flattered by that esteem, that timidity in his presence, which he encountered even in fellow workers who were also Chekists, though not "operational" Chekists in security and counterintelligence. All of them—including Colonel of Engineers Yakonov—were required, the moment Shikin asked, to give him a report on their activities. Shikin, on the other hand, was not required to account for anything to any of them. When, swarthy-faced, with close-cropped gray hair, his big briefcase under his arm, he climbed the broad, carpeted staircase, and the girl lieutenants of the MGB shyly made way for him, each hurrying to be the first to say hello to him, Shikin was proudly conscious of his special worth.

If anyone had said to Shikin (as no one ever did) that he inspired hatred, that he tortured other people, he would have been genuinely outraged. For him torturing people had never been a gratification or an end in itself. True, such people did exist, he had seen them in the theater, in movies; they were the sadists, the passionate devotees of torture, people who had nothing human about them—but they were always White Guards or Fascists. Shikin only carried out his duty, and his sole purpose was that no one should think or do anything harmful.

Once, on the main staircase of the sharashka, used by both free employees and zeks, a package had been found containing 150 rubles. The two lieutenants who found it could neither hide it nor secretly locate the owner because they had found it together. Therefore they turned the package over to Major Shikin.

Money on the staircase the prisoners used . . . money lying beneath the feet of men who were strictly forbidden to have any—this was after all an extraordinary event, affecting the state! However, Shikin did not try to make a big case out of it; he merely hung an announcement on the staircase wall:

WHOEVER LOST 150 RUBLES IN CASH ON THE STAIRCASE
CAN RECLAIM IT FROM MAJOR SHIKIN AT ANY TIME.

This was no small amount of money. But such was the universal esteem in which Shikin was held and the diffidence toward him that days and weeks passed and no one claimed the lost money. The announcement began to fade, got dusty, a corner was torn off. Finally someone printed on it with a blue pencil:

EAT IT, YOU SON-OF-A-BITCH!

The duty officer tore off the announcement and took it to the major. For a long time after this Shikin walked the laboratories comparing the shades of blue in all the blue pencils. The crude, gratuitous profanity offended Shikin. He had no intention of taking someone else's money. He would have much preferred that the owner come to claim it; he could then work up an edifying case against him, work him over at security meetings, and, to be sure, give him back his money.

Of course, he had no intention of throwing it away either. After two months he presented it as a gift to the girl with the walleye who came in once a week to file his papers.

A model family man until then, Shikin devilishly got involved with that secretary with coarse, fat legs, neglected for all her thirty-eight years. He barely came up to her shoulder, but he discovered something untried in her. He could hardly wait for the days she came to work, and he so abandoned caution that while his office was being repaired and he was in temporary quarters, he was found out. Two prisoners, a carpenter and a plasterer, not only heard them but watched them through a crack. The story got around quickly, and the zeks made a laughingstock of their spiritual pastor and wanted to write a letter to his wife, but they did not know the address. So instead they reported it to the heads of the institute.

Yet they did not manage to destroy the security officer. On this occasion Major General Oskolupov reprimanded Shikin, not for his relations with the file clerk—since that was a question of her moral principles—and not for the fact that his relations with her took place during working hours —since Shikin had no fixed schedule—but only because the prisoners had found out about them.

On Monday, December 26, having allowed himself a day off on Sunday, Major Shikin came to work shortly after nine in the morning, although even if he hadn't arrived until lunchtime there was no one to rebuke him for it.

On the third floor, opposite Yakonov's office, there was a short blind corridor which was never lit by electric light; off this corridor two doors opened, one into Shikin's office and the other into the Party Committee room. Both doors were covered with black leather and neither bore any name or sign. The proximity of the two doors in the dark corridor was convenient for Shikin. It was impossible to see from the hallway exactly which office people entered.

Today, on his way to his office, Shikin met Stepanov, the secretary of the Party Committee, a thin, ailing man who wore gleaming, lead-colored glasses. They shook hands. Stepanov quietly proposed, "Comrade Shikin—" he never called anyone by name and patronymic—"come on in and knock some balls around."

What he referred to was the Party Committee's pool table. Shikin sometimes went in to play, but today he had many important matters to attend to, and he shook his silvering head with dignity.

Stepanov sighed and went in to knock the balls around by himself.

Entering his office, Shikin set his briefcase carefully on his desk. All Shikin's papers were Secret and Top Secret and were kept in the safe and never taken anywhere, but if he had gone around without a briefcase, he would have made no impression. Therefore he carried *Ogonyek*, *Krokodil*, and *Vokrug* home in his briefcase, though it would have cost him only a few kopecks to subscribe to them himself. He crossed the rug to the window, stood there, then went back to the door. Important matters seemed to have been lurking in the office, awaiting him—behind the safe, behind the cabinet, behind the couch. Now suddenly they were crowding around him clamoring for his attention.

He had things to do.

He rubbed his hand over his short, graying crew cut.

In the first place he had to check on an important project, which he had worked out during the course of many months, and which had recently been authorized by Yakonov, adopted by the administration, explained to the laboratories, but not yet put into effect. It was a new system of using secret daybooks. Carefully analyzing the security situation at the Mavrino Institute, Major Shikin had discovered—and he was very proud that he had—that genuine security still did not exist. It was true that steel fireproof safes as tall as a man stood in every room, fifty of which had been brought from some plundered German firm. It was also true that all papers which were secret, semisecret, or lying near any which were secret were locked up in these safes in the presence of special duty officers during the lunch break, the dinner break, and overnight. But the tragic oversight was that only complete projects and work in progress were locked up. The first glimmers of an idea, the first concepts, vague hypotheses—indeed, everything from which the projects for the following year would emerge, in other words, the most promising material—none of that was locked up in the steel safes. An adroit spy who knew his way around in technology could simply make his way through the barbed wire, find a piece of blotting paper with a drawing or diagram in some wastebasket, and then go back the way he had come—and at once the American intelligence service would understand what the institute was up to.

Being a conscientious officer, Major Shikin had once made Spiridon sort out in his presence all the contents of the

wastebasket in the yard. When he did this, he found two
pieces of paper, crusted with frozen snow and ash, on which
it was evident that diagrams had at one time been drawn.
Shikin was not loath to pick up these scraps, holding them
carefully by the corners, and put them on Yakonov's desk.
And there was nothing for Yakonov to say. Thus Shikin's
project for individually labeled secret daybooks was adopted. Suitable ledgers were immediately acquired from the
MGB's stationery warehouse. They contained two hundred
large pages each, were numbered and bound, and could
be sealed. The plan was to distribute the daybooks to
everyone except the lathe operators and the janitor. Writing anything down anywhere but in the pages of one's own
daybook was to be strictly forbidden. Besides keeping
rough drafts out of enemy hands, this plan had the additional
feature of providing a means of keeping an eye on the prisoners' thought production. Since the date had to be entered
in the daybook every day, Major Shikin would be able to
check on any zek to see how much he had thought on
Wednesday and whether he had dreamed up a lot that was
new on Friday. Two hundred and fifty such daybooks would
mean another two hundred and fifty Shikins, hanging over
each prisoner's head. The prisoners were always sly and
lazy. They were always trying to avoid work whenever possible. It was routine to check on the performance of an
ordinary worker. Now they would have a means of checking on an engineer, a scientist—that was what Major Shikin's invention amounted to. And it was too bad that security
and counterintelligence officers were not given Stalin Prizes.
Today he would have to verify whether the daybooks had
been given out to the zeks who should get them and also
whether they had begun to use them.

Another job for Shikin that day was to complete the list of
prisoners for the transport scheduled to take place some-
time soon, and to learn precisely when it had been promised.

In addition, Shikin was absorbed in the affair he had
begun so grandly but had so far failed to carry any
further—the "Case of the Broken Lathe." While ten prisoners had been moving a lathe from Laboratory Number
Three to the repair shop, the lathe had acquired a crack

in its bedplate. After a week's investigation, an eighty-page report had been written, but the truth had not come to light: none of the prisoners involved was a newcomer.

He also had to find out where a book by Dickens had appeared from. Doronin had given information to the effect that it was being read in the semicircular room, by Adamson in particular. Calling in a second-termer like Adamson for questioning would have been a waste of time. That meant he had to call in the free employees who worked near Adamson and frighten them by announcing that everything had been found out.

Shikin had so much to do today. And he didn't even know the new things his informers would tell him. He did not yet know that he would be investigating a mockery of Soviet justice—the performance of something called "The Trial of Prince Igor." In desperation he rubbed his temples and forehead so that the whole great swarm of problems would settle down.

Uncertain where to begin, Shikin decided to go among the masses, in other words to walk down the hall in the hope of meeting some informer who would indicate by raising his eyebrow that he had an urgent denunciation to make which could not be put off until his scheduled appointment.

But no sooner had he reached the duty officer's table than he heard the officer talking on the phone about some new group that had been created.

What was this? How could things move so quickly? How could a new group have been created at the institute on Sunday, when Shikin had not been there?

The duty officer told him about it.

It was a heavy blow! The deputy minister had come, and generals, too, and Shikin had been absent. He was overcome with remorse. He could have given the deputy minister ample reason for believing that he was on the alert in matters of security. And they hadn't warned him or asked his advice in time; it was impossible to include that damnable Rubin in so responsible a group—that double-dealer, false through and through! He swore he believed in the victory of Communism but refused to become an informer. And, besides, he wore that provocative beard, the filthy dog, the Vasco da Gama! It should be shaved off him!

Making deliberate haste, his small feet in boy's shoes taking careful little steps, round-headed Shikin headed toward Room 21.

There was a way to get even with Rubin. Recently he had submitted a petition for reconsideration of his case (he submitted them twice each year). Shikin could decide whether to send the petition on with a favorable recommendation or—like all the other times—a nasty negative comment.

Door No. 21 was solid, without glass panes. The major pushed on it. It was locked. He knocked. He heard no steps. Then, suddenly, the door opened slightly. In the crack of the door stood Smolosidov with his menacing black forelock. Seeing Shikin, he did not move, nor did he open the door wider.

"Good morning," Shikin said uncertainly, unaccustomed to this kind of reception. Smolosidov was even more of an "operational Chekist" than Shikin himself.

Smolosidov stood poised like a boxer, his arms bent and drawn back slightly. He said nothing.

"That is, I . . ." Shikin said in confusion. "Let me in. I have to get acquainted with your group."

Smolosidov stepped back half a step and, still guarding the room with his body, beckoned to Shikin. Shikin pushed through the narrow slit of the door and followed Smolosidov's finger with his eyes. On the inside of the door hung a sheet of paper:

> List of persons permitted in Room 21:
> 1. Deputy Minister MGB—Sevastyanov
> 2. Section Chief—Major General Bulbanyuk
> 3. Section Chief—Major General Oskolupov
> 4. Group Chief—Major of Engineers Roitman
> 5. Lieutenant Smolosidov
> 6. Prisoner Rubin
>   Confirmed by:
>   MINISTER OF STATE SECURITY ABAKUMOV

With a reverent shudder Shikin retreated into the hall.

"I have to . . . get hold of Rubin," he said in a whisper.

"Can't be done!" said Smolosidov also in a whisper.

And he locked the door.

72

THE PARTY SECRETARY

At one time the trade union had played a large and significant role in the lives of the Mavrino free employees. But then a highly placed comrade—so highly placed that it was awkward to call him "comrade"—had heard about it. He had said, "What's all this about?" And he did not add the word "comrade," believing he should not pamper his subordinates. "After all, Mavrino is a military unit. What do they want with a trade union? You know what that smells of?"

That day the trade union at Mavrino had been abolished. Its disappearance did not cause any upheaval.

Then followed an extraordinary increase in the importance of the Party organization at the institute, which had been of considerable importance before. The District Party Committee considered it necessary for the Party organization at Mavrino to have a full-time paid secretary who would be free of all other work. After examining several questionnaires submitted by the personnel section, the District Party Committee recommended for the position:

> Stepanov, Boris Sergeyevich; born 1900; native of the village of Lupachi, Bobrovsk District; social origin: landless farm laborers; after the Revolution a rural policeman; no profession; social situation: employee; education: four grades of elementary school, two years of Party schooling; member of the Party from 1921 on; active in Party work since 1923; no hesitation in carrying out the Party line; never participated in the opposition; never served in the armies or institutions of the White governments; was never on occupied territory; has never been abroad; knows no foreign languages; knows none of the national languages of the U.S.S.R.; shell-shocked; awarded the order of the "Red Star" and the medal "For Victory in the Patriotic War Against Germany."

At the time the District Party Committee recommended

Stepanov, he had been working as a propagandist at the harvest in Volokolamsk District. He made use of every minute when the farmers of the collective weren't actually at work in the fields. Whether they were sitting down to lunch or simply taking a moment for a smoke, he immediately assembled them at a field camp, or, in the evening, summoned them to the administration building. Relentlessly he explained the importance of sowing the land each year with good-quality seed; told them the yield should exceed the amount of seed sown; that it should be harvested without waste or pilferage and as quickly as possible turned over to the state. Without pausing, he would then go to the tractor drivers and explain the importance of economizing on fuel and of not abusing their equipment; and the absolute inadmissibility of a moment's idleness; he also reluctantly answered questions about slapdash repairs and the shortage of work clothes.

By then the general assembly of the Mavrino Party organization had warmly accepted the district committee's recommendation and unanimously elected Stepanov as its salaried secretary—without ever having seen him. A new propagandist was selected and sent to Volokolamsk District— an official who had been removed from his post in the cooperatives in Yegoryevsk District because large quantities of goods kept disappearing. In Mavrino, Stepanov was provided with an office next to the security officer's and he took over the management of Party affairs.

He began by checking into the Party work performed by the former secretary, who had *not* been salaried nor excused from other work.

The ex-secretary was Lieutenant Klykachev. He was thin, no doubt because he was very active and never rested. He managed to direct the Decoding Laboratory and the cryptographic and statistical groups, and also to conduct a Komsomol seminar; he was the soul of the "Young Turks," in other words the Roitman clique, and, in addition to all this, he had been the secretary of the Party Committee. And while the administration considered Lieutenant Klykachev too demanding, and his subordinates considered him a stickler, the new secretary suspected that Party affairs at the Mavrino Institute would turn out to have been neglected.

And so it did turn out.

Stepanov's researches into Party affairs went on for one week. Without once emerging from his office, he examined every last paper and got to know every Party member from his personnel file and his photograph before meeting them in the flesh. Klykachev felt the heavy hand of the new secretary upon him.

One shortcoming after another turned up. Leaving aside the incomplete data on questionnaires, the inadequate certifications and recommendations in personnel files, the absence of detailed characterizations of each member and candidate for membership, a generally unfortunate tendency appeared in regard to all procedures: a tendency to carry them out in fact, but to neglect to document them, so that the procedures became, so to speak, illusory.

"But who is going to believe it? Who is going to believe that those measures were actually carried out?" Stepanov demanded, his palm pressed down on his bald head, a smoking cigarette between his fingers.

And patiently he explained to Klykachev that everything had been done on *paper* only (because verbal testimony alone confirmed it) and not in *actual fact* (because it was not recorded on paper).

For example, what good was it for the athletes of the institute—not including the prisoners, obviously—to play volleyball every lunch period (even taking a little time from work for it)? Maybe it was true. Maybe they really did play. There was obviously no point in Stepanov or Klykachev or anyone else checking up on this by going out into the yard to see whether the ball was bouncing back and forth. But why shouldn't these volleyball players, after they'd played so many games and acquired so much experience, why shouldn't they have shared this experience and produced a special athletic newspaper for the bulletin board: "Red Volleyball" or "The Honor of the Dynamo Team Member"? And if thereafter Klykachev had neatly removed such a newspaper from the bulletin board and put it in the Party documentation file, then in no subsequent inspection could there be the slightest doubt that the "volleyball playing" had actually taken place, and that the Party had supervised it. But who now was going to take Klykachev at his word?

So it was with everything. "You can't prove deeds by

words!"—and with that profound utterance Stepanov assumed his duties.

Just as a priest would never believe that anyone could lie in confession, Stepanov never imagined that written documentation could lie.

Klykachev, with his narrow head and long neck, did not attempt to argue with Stepanov; with undisguised gratitude in his eyes he agreed with him and learned from him. And Stepanov quickly softened toward Klykachev, thereby showing that he was not a malicious person. He listened attentively to Klykachev's misgivings about a person who not only had a doubtful questionnaire but was purely and simply a former enemy—Colonel of Engineers Yakonov—heading such an important secret institute as Mavrino. Stepanov himself became extremely watchful. He made Klykachev his right-hand man, told him to visit the Party Committee more often, and benignly instructed him from the treasure house of his own experience.

And so Klykachev came to know the new Party organizer sooner and more intimately than anyone else. Because Klykachev had christened him "the Shepherd," the "Young Turks" began calling him that. And precisely because of Klykachev's relationship with "the Shepherd," things worked out rather well for the "Young Turks." They quickly understood that it was greatly to their advantage to have a Party organizer who was not openly in their camp, an objective letter-of-the-law man, who would stay on the sidelines.

And Stepanov was a letter-of-the-law man. At any suggestion that someone deserved to be pitied, that the full severity of the law should not be brought to bear against him, that mercy should be shown, furrows of pain etched themselves upon Stepanov's forehead(which was high because he had no hair at his temples), and Stepanov's shoulders bowed as if under a new burden. But, with flaming conviction, he would find the strength to straighten up, and would turn abruptly to one member after another, the little white-squared reflections of the windows flashing back and forth in his glasses.

"Comrades! Comrades! What do I hear? How can you say such things? Remember: always uphold the law! Uphold the law with all your strength! That's the only way of really helping this person you wish to violate the law for. Because the law is set up solely to serve society and mankind. Yet how often we don't understand that and, in our blindness, want to get around the law."

For his part, Stepanov was satisfied with the "Young Turks" and their eagerness for Party meetings and Party criticism. In them he saw the nucleus of the *healthy collective*, which he tried to create in every new place he worked. If the collective did not disclose to the leaders the lawbreakers in its midst, if the collective kept silent at meetings, Stepanov rightly considered that collective *unhealthy*. If the collective as one man attacked one of its members, especially one it was necessary to attack, that collective—according to the notion shared by people even higher than Stepanov—was *healthy*.

Stepanov had many such fixed ideas which it was impossible for him to abandon. For example, he could not imagine a meeting which didn't close with the adoption of a thunderous resolution, lashing individual members and mobilizing the entire collective for new production victories. He especially loved this sort of thing in the "open" Party meetings where all the non-Party people appeared, too, and where one could smash them to pieces. They had no right to vote or to defend themselves. Sometimes offended or even indignant voices could be heard before the voting: "What is this? A meeting or a trial?"

"Please, comrades, please!" Stepanov would in such cases use his authority to interrupt any speaker, even the chairman of the meeting. Quickly popping a pill into his mouth with a trembling hand—after his shell shock his head ached very badly from any kind of nervous strain, and it always made him nervous when truth was under attack—he would advance to the middle of the room under the ceiling lights, so that big drops of sweat shone on his bald head. "What is this? Are you, after all, against criticism and self-criticism?" And hammering the air with his fist, as if he were nailing his ideas into his listeners' heads, he would explain: "Self-criticism is the foremost motivating force in our society, the prime power behind its progress! It is time you understood that when we criticize the members of our collective it is not to put them on trial, but to keep each worker at every moment in constant creative stress. And there can be no two opinions about this, comrades! Of course, we don't want just any kind of criticism, that's true. We

need *businesslike criticism*, criticism which does not impugn
our experienced leaders. We must not confuse the freedom
to criticize with the freedom of petty-bourgeois anarchism."

Then he would return to the decanter of water and swallow
another pill.

It always turned out that the entire healthy collective voted
for the resolution unanimously, including those members the
resolution lashed and destroyed with charges of a "criminally careless attitude toward work" or "failure to fulfill the
plan, bordering on sabotage."

Sometimes it even happened that Stepanov, who loved
elaborate, full-scale resolutions, Stepanov, who in the most
felicitous way always knew beforehand what speeches would
be made and the final consensus of the meeting, did not
manage to compose the whole resolution *before* the meeting.
Then when the chairman declared, "Comrade Stepanov has
the floor for the statement of the resolution!" Stepanov wiped
the sweat from his brow and his bald head and spoke as follows:

"Comrades! I have been very busy and therefore I did
not manage to find out fully and accurately, before drafting
the resolution, certain circumstances, certain names and
facts," or:

"Comrades! Today I was called to the administration, and
I have not yet prepared the draft of the resolution."

Then in either case:

"So I ask you to vote for the resolution *as a whole*, and
when I have time tomorrow, I will complete the details."

And the Mavrino collective turned out to be so healthy
that hands were raised without a murmur, although no one
knew, or would find out, who would be reviled and who
would be praised in that resolution.

The position of the new Party organizer was greatly
strengthened by the fact that he did not permit himself the
frailty of intimacy with anyone. Everyone respectfully called
him "Boris Sergeyich." Accepting this as his due, he did
not in turn address anyone in the installation by first name
and patronymic. Even in the excitement at the pool table,
whose cloth glowed green in the Party Committee room, he
would exclaim, "Put out the ball, Comrade Shikin!"

"Off the side, Comrade Klykachev!"

Generally, Stepanov disliked having people appeal to his

noblest feelings. And he himself did not inspire such feelings in others. Therefore, as soon as he sensed any kind of dissatisfaction or resistance to his measures, without a lot of talk or attempts at persuasion, he took a big sheet of clean paper and wrote in large letters across the top: "It Is Proposed That the Comrades Named Below Must Fulfill . . ." this or that by such and such a date. Then he divided the sheet into numbered columns: "Surname," "First Name," "Signature Acknowledging Receipt of Notice." And he instructed his secretary to take the sheet around. The designated comrades read it, took out their bitterness as they pleased against the indifferent piece of paper, but had to sign. Having signed, they could not fail to carry out the extra duties.

Stepanov was a Party secretary free not only of ordinary work but also of doubts and any tendency to wander in the dark. It was enough for him to hear on the radio that there was no longer a heroic Yugoslavia but a Tito clique. Within five minutes he would be explaining this decision with such insistence, such conviction, that one might have thought that he personally had been working it out for years. If someone cautiously directed Stepanov's attention to a discrepancy between today's instructions and yesterday's, to the bad state of supply at the institute, the poor quality of Soviet-made equipment, or difficulties with housing, the salaried secretary smiled as if anticipating the words he would then pronounce:

"Well, what do you expect, comrades? That's just departmental confusion. But there is no doubt that we're making progress in that area, as I trust you agree."

Nevertheless Stepanov did have certain human failings, though only on a very limited scale. For instance, he liked having higher-ups praise him, and he liked impressing ordinary Party members with his experience. He liked these responses because they were thoroughly justified.

He also drank vodka, but only if someone treated him to it or if it was put on the table, and he always complained that vodka was ruinous to his health. For this reason he never bought it himself or treated anyone to it. And those were his only faults.

The "Young Turks" sometimes argued among themselves about "the Shepherd." Roitman said, "My friends! He is a prophet of the bottomless inkwell. He has the soul of a page of typescript. You inevitably have such people in a period of transition."

But Klykachev smiled crookedly and said, "Suckers—he's got us—he's going to push our faces in crap. Don't think he's stupid. In fifty years he's learned how to get along! You think it's for nothing that there's a denunciation at every meeting? He's writing the history of Mavrino with them. He is piling up anticipatory data: no matter what happens, an inspection will show the secretary warned everyone about the situation beforehand."

In Klykachev's prejudiced view, Stepanov was a furtive slanderer who would go to any lengths to fix things for his three sons.

Stepanov actually did have three sons, and they were forever asking their father for money. He had placed all three of them in the history department at the university. His calculation had seemed right at the time, but he had not taken into account the increasing oversupply of historians in all schools, technical institutes, and short-term courses, first in the city of Moscow, then in the Moscow district, and then on into the Urals. The first son finished his schooling, but instead of staying home to feed his parents, he went off to Khanty-Mansiysk in western Siberia. The second son's mandatory assignment was in Ulan Ude, east of Lake Baikal, and when the third finished his studies, it seemed unlikely he would find a job nearer than the island of Borneo.

All the more tenaciously did their father hold on to his own job and to the little cottage on the outskirts of Moscow with a third of an acre of vegetable garden, casks of sauerkraut, and three fattening pigs. To his wife, a sober woman who was even, perhaps, a shade backward in matters of ideology, fattening the pigs was her basic interest, and she considered it the mainstay of the family budget. She had set aside this past Sunday for an obligatory trip into the country to buy a piglet. Because of that undertaking—successful, as it turned out—Stepanov had not come to work yesterday, even though a certain conversation on Saturday had alarmed him, and he was eager to be at Mavrino.

On Saturday, in the Political Section, Stepanov had suffered a blow. A certain official, very highly placed, but also very well fed despite his cares and responsibilities, weighing, in fact, something around two hundred and fifty pounds, had stared at Stepanov's thin nose, marked by the glasses he wore, and asked in a lazy baritone, "So, Stepanov, what about the Judeans at your place?"

"The Ju— Who?" said Stepanov, cocking his head to hear better.

"The Judeans." And then observing the secretary's total lack of understanding, the official made himself clear: "All right, the kikes, I mean."

Taken by surprise and afraid to repeat that double-edged word, the use of which had so recently earned an immediate ten-year sentence for anti-Soviet propaganda, Stepanov muttered vaguely, "Yes, there are some."

"Well, what are you planning on doing with them?"

Just then the phone rang and the highly placed comrade picked it up and said nothing further to Stepanov.

Perplexed, Stepanov read through the whole pile of instructions and directives at the administration, but the black letters on the white paper cunningly skipped over the Judean question.

All day Sunday, on the trip in search of the piglet, he thought and thought, and scratched his chest in desperation. Obviously his intuition was dulling with old age! But how could he have guessed? During his years of work Stepanov had come to believe that Jewish comrades were particularly dedicated to the cause. And now—disgrace! Stepanov, the experienced official, had failed to detect some important new drive and had even been indirectly implicated in the intrigues of enemies. After all, that whole Roitman-Klykachev faction . . .

On Monday morning Stepanov came to work in a state of confusion. After Shikin's refusal to play a round of pool —during which Stepanov had hoped to learn something from him—and breathing with difficulty because he had received no instructions, the salaried Party secretary locked himself up in the Party Committee office and for two solid hours knocked the balls about wildly, sometimes even sending them over the edge of the table. The huge bronze bas-relief on the wall witnessed several brilliant strokes when two or three balls landed in pockets simultaneously. But the profiles on the bas-relief gave Stepanov no hint of how to avoid destroying his healthy collective, let alone strengthen it in the new situation.

Worn out, he at last heard a telephone ringing and dashed to pick it up.

They said that a car had already left for Mavrino with two comrades who would provide the necessary instructions in respect to the struggle against toadyism.

The salaried secretary immediately cheered up, even became gay, caromed a ball off the inner edge and sank it, then put cue and balls away in a cabinet.

It also put him in a good mood to remember that the pink-eared piglet he had bought yesterday had eaten its mash both evening and morning without fussing. This gave promise that it could be fattened cheaply and easily.

73

TWO ENGINEERS

Major Shikin was in the office of Colonel of Engineers Yakonov.

They sat and talked as equals, amicably, even though each despised and loathed the other.

Yakonov loved to say at meetings, "We Chekists." But as far as Shikin was concerned, Yakonov was still that enemy of the people who had gone abroad, served out his term, been forgiven and taken into the bosom of State Security, but who was *not* innocent! Inevitably, inevitably, the day would come when the security organizations would expose Yakonov and arrest him again. How Shikin would enjoy ripping off his shoulder boards! The splendid condescension of the colonel of engineers, the gentlemanly self-assurance with which he bore his authority irritated the diligent little major with the big head. Shikin therefore tried always to emphasize his own significance and that of "operational" work, whose value the colonel of engineers consistently underestimated.

Now he was proposing to place on the agenda at the next

security meeting a report by Yakonov on security at the institute, which would be harshly critical of all shortcomings. Such a meeting might well be tied to a transport of uncooperative zeks and the introduction of the new secret daybooks.

Colonel of Engineers Yakonov, worn out after yesterday's attack, with bluish circles under his eyes, his features nonetheless retaining their pleasant plumpness, nodded at the major's words. In his innermost depths, behind walls and moats where no eye could penetrate except perhaps his wife's, he was thinking what a vile louse this Major Shikin was, grown gray poring over denunciations . . . what lunatic nonsense his occupation . . . what idiocy all his proposals.

Yakonov had been given one month. In one month his head might be lying on the executioner's block. He ought to throw off his armor, walk away from his high post, sit himself down in front of the diagrams and think in solitude.

But the oversized leather-upholstered armchair in which the colonel of engineers was sitting carried its own negation: responsible for everything, the colonel could not touch a thing himself, but only lift his phone and sign papers.

And then that petty war with Roitman's crowd was still sapping his mental energies. He had to carry it on as before. He was not in a position to force them out of the institute, and all he wanted was their unconditional surrender. They, after all, wanted to have him expelled, and they were capable of destroying him.

Shikin was still talking. Yakonov looked just past him. His eyes remained open but, leaving his languid body, he returned in thought to his home.

"My home! My home is my castle!" Like the wise Englishmen who were the first to understand that truth. On your own little territory only your laws exist. Four walls and a roof separate you from a world that is continually oppressing you, turning you upside down, squeezing something out of you. Attentive eyes with a quiet glow meet you in the doorway of your home. Droll little children, always up to something new (it's good that they're not yet going to school), comfort and refresh you, however fatigued you may be from persecution, from being pulled this way and that. Your wife has already taught both of them to chatter in English. Sitting down at the piano, she plays a pleasant waltz by Waldteufel. Lunch hours are brief, and when your evening's work has ended, it is almost night, but in your own home there are no inflated fools or young leeches.

In Yakonov's work there were so many torments, so many humiliating situations, so many violent frustrations, so much administrative pressure; and Yakonov felt so old that he would have gladly given up that work if he could, and stayed in his own home, his own cozy little private world.

This didn't mean that the external world did not interest him—it interested him profoundly. It would be hard to find a more absorbing time in all history. He saw world politics as a sort of chess game. But Yakonov did not pretend to play the game himself or even to be a pawn in it . . . or part of a pawn . . . or the lining on the bottom of a pawn. Yakonov wanted to observe it from the sidelines, to enjoy it as he lounged in comfortable pajamas in his old rocking chair, among his many bookshelves.

Yakonov had all the qualifications and the means for this pursuit. He had mastered two languages, and foreign radio stations vied with each other in offering him information. The ministry received foreign technical and military journals, and sent them at once to its restricted institutes. The editors of these journals loved now and then to include an essay on politics, or the future global war, or the future political structure of the planet. Also, moving as he did in high circles, Yakonov from time to time heard about details not available to the press. Nor did he disdain translations of books on diplomacy and intelligence. And beyond all that information, he had his own penetrating thoughts. In particular, he followed from his rocking chair the game of East versus West, and tried to guess the outcome from the moves that were made.

Whose side was he on? When things went well for him at work, he was, of course, for the East. When they put the squeeze on too hard, he was rather more for the West. His own superior view was that whoever was strongest and cruelest would win. In this, unfortunately, all history and its prophets concurred.

Early in his youth he had adopted the popular phrase: "People are all bastards!" And the longer he lived, the more this insight was confirmed and reconfirmed. He found more proof of it the deeper he probed; thus the easier it became for him to live. For if people are all bastards, then one need never do anything "for people" but only for oneself. There is no "social altar," and no one need waste time demanding sacrifices of you. Long ago all this had been very simply expressed by the people themselves: "Your own shirt is closer to your body."

The watchdogs of questionnaires and souls had therefore no reason to worry about his past. Thinking about life, Yakonov had realized that the only people who go to prison are those who, at some moment in their lives, fail in intelligence. Really intelligent people look ahead; they may twist and dodge, but they always stay in one piece and in freedom. Why spend behind bars the existence which is ours only as long as we breathe? No! Yakonov had renounced the world of zeks not for appearances only but out of inner conviction. From whose hands would he otherwise have received four spacious rooms with a balcony and seven thousand a month? At least he would not have received these things so soon. They injured him, they treated him capriciously, often stupidly, always cruelly—but in cruelty, after all, was strength, its truest manifestation.

Shikin now was handing him the list of the zeks to be transported the following day. The list already agreed on had run to sixteen names, and now Shikin added with approval the two names on Yakonov's desk pad. Twenty had been the total fixed on with the prison administration, so they had to "work up" two more, and inform Lieutenant Colonel Klimentiev not later than 5 P.M.

However, no candidates came to mind immediately. Somehow it always turned out that Yakonov's best specialists and workers were unreliable in the security area, while the security officer's pets were good-for-nothings and slackers. This made it difficult to agree on names for the outbound transports.

Yakonov put the list down on his desk and gestured reassuringly with his hands.

"Leave the list with me. I'll think it over. And you think about it. We'll talk on the phone."

Shikin got up slowly and—he should not have said anything but he did—complained to this person who was unworthy of hearing his complaint about the minister's action in admitting Rubin and Roitman into Room 21, while he,

Shikin, and Colonel Yakonov as well were not allowed in. Their own installation! How could that happen?

Yakonov raised his brows and let his lids close so that his face was blank for a moment. It was as if he were saying, "Yes, Major, yes, my friend, it's painful to me, very painful, but I cannot raise my eyes and look at the sun!"

Yakonov considered Room 21 a doubtful affair, and Roitman an overeager boy who might break his neck this time.

Shikin went out, and Yakonov remembered the most pleasant of the duties which awaited him today—for yesterday he had not had time for it. If he could make definite progress on the absolute encoder, it would save him with Abakumov when their month was up.

He telephoned the Design Office and ordered Sologdin to bring along his new project.

In two minutes Sologdin knocked and entered, empty-handed, in soiled coveralls.

Yakonov and Sologdin had hardly ever spoken to each other before; there had never been any reason to summon Sologdin to this office. In the Design Office or when they met accidentally, the colonel of engineers paid no attention to this insignificant personality. But now, glancing at the list of names and patronymics under the glass, Yakonov, with all the cordiality of a hospitable gentleman, looked approvingly at the prisoner who had entered and spoke expansively, "Sit down, Dmitri Aleksandrovich, it is very good to see you."

Holding his arms firmly at his sides, Sologdin came closer, bowed silently, and remained standing, erect and rigid.

"It appears you have prepared a secret surprise for us," Yakonov rumbled. "Just a few days ago—on Saturday, wasn't it?—I saw your drawing of the main section of the absolute encoder at Vladimir Erastovich's. Why don't you sit down? I glanced over it quickly, and I am extremely anxious to talk about it in greater detail."

Without averting his eyes from Yakonov's gaze, which was full of sympathetic feeling, Sologdin continued to stand half turned away and motionless, as if a duel had begun and he was waiting for the shot. He replied distinctly, "You are mistaken, Anton Nikolayevich. I did, as much as I was able, work on the encoder. But all I succeeded in doing, and what you saw, was a grotesque and imperfect creation consistent with my very mediocre abilities."

Yakonov leaned back in his chair and protested genially, "Now look here, my friend, please let's do without false modesty! Even though I glanced over your project hurriedly, I did form a most favorable impression of it. And Vladimir Erastovich, who can judge better than either of us, definitely praised it. Right now I am going to give instructions to admit no one. Go get your drawing and your calculations, and we'll go over it. Would you like me to call Vladimir Erastovich?"

Yakonov was not a stupid administrator interested only in the outcome of the productive process. He was an engineer and at one time he had even been an adventurous engineer, and right now he felt something of that delicate satisfaction which human invention long in development can grant us. This was the one and only satisfaction his work still gave him. He looked questioningly, smiling in a kindly way.

Sologdin was an engineer, too, and had been for fourteen years. He had been a prisoner for twelve.

Dryness tightened his throat, and it was difficult for him to speak.

"Anton Nikolayevich, you are absolutely mistaken. That was just a sketch not worthy of your attention."

Yakonov frowned, now getting a bit angry, and said, "Well, all right, we'll see, we'll see. Go get it."

On his shoulder boards, gold with light-blue edging, there were three stars, three large imposing stars set in a triangle. Senior Lieutenant Kamyashan, the security officer at Gornaya Zakrytka, had also acquired a triangle of three gold stars with blue edging during the months he was beating up Sologdin. But his were smaller ones.

"The sketch doesn't exist any more," said Sologdin in an unsteady voice. "Because I found profound and irreparable mistakes in it, I—burned it."

The colonel turned pale. In the sinister silence his heavy breathing was audible. Sologdin tried to breathe soundlessly.

"What do you mean? You burned it yourself?"

"No. I turned it in to be burned. According to regulations." His voice was muffled and unclear. There was no trace of his former self-assurance.

"So perhaps it is still intact?" said Yakonov, moving forward with sudden hope.

"It burned. I watched from the window," Sologdin answered with heavy insistence.

With one hand gripping the arm of the chair and the other seizing a marble paperweight, as if he intended to crack Sologdin's skull, the colonel raised his big body and stood leaning forward over the desk.

Throwing his head slightly back, Sologdin stood there like a statue in blue coveralls.

Between the two engineers no further questions or explanations were necessary. Through their locked stares passed an unendurable current of insane frequency.

"I will destroy you," declared the eyes of the colonel.

"Go ahead and hang a third term on me, you bastard!" shouted the prisoner's eyes.

There had to be a roaring explosion.

But Yakonov, covering his eyes with one hand, as if the light hurt them, turned away and went over to the window.

Seizing the back of the nearest chair, Sologdin, exhausted, dropped his eyes.

"A month. One month. Am I really done for?" Everything down to the smallest detail appeared clear to the colonel.

"A third term. I couldn't survive it," Sologdin told himself, swept by horror.

Again Yakonov turned to Sologdin. "Engineer! How could you do it?" his stare demanded.

Sologdin's eyes flashed back: "Prisoner! You've forgotten it all!"

With fascinated loathing, each seeing himself as he might have become, they glared at each other and could not look away.

Now Yakonov would start shouting and pounding the table; he would pick up the phone, jail him. Sologdin was prepared for this to happen.

But Yakonov pulled out a soft, clean, white handkerchief and wiped his eyes with it. He looked steadily at Sologdin.

Sologdin tried to keep his composure.

With one hand the colonel of engineers leaned on the window sill, and with the other he quietly motioned the prisoner to come over to him.

In three firm steps Sologdin came up to him.

Hunched slightly, like an old man, Yakonov asked, "Sologdin, are you a Muscovite?"

"Yes," said Sologdin, still looking directly at him.

"Look down there," Yakonov told him. "Do you see the bus stop there on the highway?"

The bus stop could be clearly seen from the window.

Sologdin looked at it.

"From here it's just half an hour's ride to the center of Moscow," Yakonov said quietly.

Sologdin turned to him again.

And suddenly, as if he were falling, Yakonov placed both his hands on Sologdin's shoulders.

"Sologdin!" he said in an urgent, plaintive voice. "You could have been getting on that bus yourself one day next June or July. And you don't want to. I would think that in August you might have got your first leave—gone to the Black Sea. To bathe in the sea, can you imagine that? How many years is it since you were in the water, Sologdin? After all, prisoners aren't ever allowed that!"

"Why not? At timbering," protested Sologdin.

"Some bathing!" Yakonov still kept holding on to Sologdin's shoulders. "But you're going to end up there in the north, Sologdin, where rivers never thaw. . . . Listen, I can't believe there's a human being on earth who doesn't desire the good things of life. Explain to me why you burned the drawing."

Dmitri Sologdin's sky-blue eyes remained imperturbable, incorruptible, immaculate. In their black pupils Yakonov saw his own portly head reflected.

Sky-blue circles with black holes in the center, and behind them the whole astounding world of an individual human being.

"Why do you suppose?" Sologdin answered the question with another. Between his mustache and his little beard the corners of his moist lips lifted slightly, as if in derision.

"I don't understand." Yakonov removed his hands and started to walk away. "It's suicide—I don't understand."

And behind him he heard a resonant, assured voice: "Citizen Colonel! I am too unimportant, no one knows me. I didn't want to give my freedom away for nothing—"

Yakonov turned around sharply.

"If I had not burned my drawing, if I had put it in front
of you all complete, then our lieutenant colonel, you, Oskolupov, whoever cared to, could have shoved me off on a
transport tomorrow and signed any name at all to the drawing. These things have happened. And I can tell you, it's
quite inconvenient to complain from a transit camp; they
take your pencil away, they don't give you any paper, petitions are not sent on."

Yakonov listened to Sologdin almost with delight. He
had liked this man the moment he had come in.

"So you will undertake to reconstruct your drawing?"
This was not the colonel of engineers speaking, but a desperate, worn-out, powerless being.

"Exactly what was on my sheet—in three days!" said
Sologdin, his eyes shining. "And in five weeks I'll give you
a complete draft of the whole project, with detailed calculations of its technical aspects. Does that suit you?"

"One month! One month! We need it in a month!" Yakonov's hands on the desk moved toward this diabolical
engineer.

"All right, you'll have it in a month," Sologdin agreed
coldly.

But Yakonov became suspicious.

"Just a minute," he said. "You just told me this was a
worthless sketch, that you found profound and irreparable
mistakes in it."

"Oh, ho!" Sologdin laughed openly. "Sometimes the
lack of phosphorus and oxygen and the lack of new impressions from real life play tricks on me, and I have a sort of
mental blackout. But at the moment I agree with Professor
Chelnov: everything in it was quite all right."

Yakonov smiled, too, yawning from relief, and sat down
in his armchair. He was fascinated by the way Sologdin
controlled himself, by the way he had managed the interview.

"You played a risky game, my friend. After all, it could
have ended otherwise."

Sologdin spread his hands lightly. "Hardly, Anton Nikolayevich. It seems that I estimated the institute's position
and your own quite accurately. Of course, you know French.
Sa Majesté le Cas! His Majesty Opportunity! Opportunity

rarely passes close to us; one has to jump on its back in time, and squarely in the middle of its back!"

Sologdin spoke and acted as simply as if he were cutting wood with Nerzhin. Now he, too, sat down, continuing to watch Yakonov with amusement.

"So what shall we do?" the colonel of engineers asked amicably.

Sologdin replied as if he were reading from a printed page, as if it had long since been decided: "As a first step, I would like to avoid dealing with Oskolupov. He happens to be the sort of person who loves to be a co-inventor. I don't expect such a trick from you. I'm not wrong, am I?"

Yakonov nodded happily. Oh, how relieved he was, and had been even before Sologdin's last words.

"Also, I must remind you that the drawing is still—so far —burned. Now, if you really want to go ahead with my project, you will find a way to inform the minister about me directly. If that is absolutely impossible, the deputy minister. Let him personally sign an order naming me the chief designer. That will be my guarantee and I will set to work. I'll need the minister's signature particularly because I'm going to establish a quite unprecedented system with my group. I don't approve of night work, Sunday heroics, and the transformation of scientific personnel into zombies. Experts should approach their work as eagerly as if they were going to meet their mistress." Sologdin spoke more and more cheerfully, and freely, as if he and Yakonov had known each other si e childhood. "And so let them get their sleep, let them relax. Let whoever wants to saw firewood for the kitchen. We have to think of the kitchen, too, don't you agree?"

Suddenly the door of the office swung open. Bald, thin Stepanov entered without knocking, the lenses of his glasses gleaming deathlike.

"Anton Nikolayevich," he said solemnly, "I have something important to discuss."

Stepanov had addressed someone with his name and patronymic! It was unbelievable.

"And so I will await the order?" asked Sologdin, getting up.

The colonel of engineers nodded. Sologdin went out with a light, firm step.

Yakonov did not gather at first what the Party organizer was talking about so energetically.

"Comrade Yakonov! Some comrades from the Political Section just came to see me, and they gave me a good dressing down. I have permitted serious mistakes to be made. I have allowed a group of, shall we say, rootless cosmopolites to build their nest in our Party organization. And I have shown political nearsightedness. I did not support you when they tried to persecute you. But we must be fearless in acknowledging our errors. And right now you and I will work out a resolution together, and then we will call an open Party meeting—and we will deal a heavy blow at toadyism."

Yakonov's affairs, which had been so hopeless just the day before, had made an about-face.

74

ONE HUNDRED AND FORTY-SEVEN RUBLES

Before the lunch break the duty officer Zhvakun posted in the hallway a list of the zeks Major Myshin wanted to see in his office during the break. It was understood that these zeks were being called in to receive letters and to be notified of money orders deposited in their personal accounts.

The procedure of delivering letters to a zek was carried out in secret in the special prisons. It could not, of course, be handled in such a routine way as in freedom—by entrusting the letter to just any irresponsible postman. The "protector," who had already read the letter and decided that it was neither criminal nor incendiary, gave it to the prisoner behind a thick door, accompanying the action with a sermon. The letter was handed over with no attempt to conceal the fact that it had been opened, thereby destroying the last vestige of intimacy between two people dear to one another. By that time the letter had passed through many hands, passages had been excerpted which were inserted in the prisoner's dossier, been stamped with the black, blotted seal of the censor, and has lost its minor personal meaning and acquired the larger significance of a state document. Indeed, at some sharashkas this significance was so well understood that letters were seldom turned over to the prisoner; he was only permitted to read them, rarely to read them twice, and in the "protector's" presence he had to put his signature at the bottom of the letter as evidence that he had read it. If, reading a letter from his wife or mother, the zek tried to write down extracts in order to remember them, this aroused as much suspicion as if he had tried to copy a General Staff document. The zek in such sharashkas also signed any photographs sent from home, and, after he had seen them, they were put in his prison file.

So the list was posted, and the zeks stood in line for their letters. Those who wanted to send their own letters for the month of December stood in the same line—outgoing letters, too, had to be submitted personally to the "protector." These operations gave Major Myshin the chance to talk freely with his informers, and to call them to his office outside their regular schedules. But to protect the identity of any informer he was spending a long time with, the prison "protector" sometimes detained honest zeks in his office, too.

Therefore the zeks standing in line suspected each other. Sometimes they knew exactly which of their number held their lives in his hands, but nevertheless they smiled at him ingratiatingly so as not to antagonize him.

At the lunch bell the zeks ran out of the cellar into the yard and, crossing it without coats or caps in the damp wind, darted into the door of the prison headquarters. Because of the new rules about correspondence that had been announced, the line was particularly long—forty men. There was not enough room in the corridor for all of them. The duty officer's assistant, an officious master sergeant, zealously devoted his full strength to issuing commands. He counted off twenty-five men and ordered the rest to go take a walk and come back at the dinner break. He placed those who had been allowed into the corridor along the wall at a distance from the bosses' offices, and he paced back and forth seeing to it that regulations were observed. The zek whose turn it was went past several doors, knocked at the door of Myshin's office and, on receiving permission, entered. When he left, the next was admitted. Throughout the entire lunch break the fuss-budget master sergeant directed traffic.

Despite Spiridon's morning-long importunities about his letter, Myshin had said firmly he would not get it before the break when all the rest got theirs. But half an hour before lunch Spiridon was summoned by Major Shikin for questioning. If Spiridon had given the evidence demanded from him, if he had admitted everything, he would probably have got his letter. But he denied everything, was stubborn, and Major Shikin could not let him go in such an unrepentant state. Therefore, sacrificing his own lunch break (though, to avoid being jostled, he never went to the free employees' dining room at that hour anyway), Shikin continued to question Spiridon.

The first in line was Dyrsin, an emaciated, overworked engineer from Number Seven, one of the regular workers there. He had not received any letters for more than three months. In vain had he inquired of Myshin. The answer was always: "No" or "They don't write." In vain had he asked Mamurin to order a search to be made. No search was made. Today he saw his name on the list, and, despite the pain in his chest, he managed to get in line first. Of his whole family, only his wife remained, worn out like himself by ten years of waiting.

The master sergeant motioned Dyrsin to go in. Next in line was the mischievously beaming Ruska Doronin, with his loose, wavy hair. The Latvian Hugo, one of those he trusted, was standing next to him, and Ruska tossed his head and whispered with a wink, "I'm going to get the money. What I've earned."

"Go on in!" the master sergeant commanded.

Doronin rushed ahead, meeting Dyrsin face to face as he came out looking wilted.

Out in the courtyard Amantai Bulatov asked Dyrsin, his friend, what had happened.

Dyrsin's face, always unshaven, always fatigued, was gloomier than ever. "I don't know. They say there's a letter, but that I should go in after the break, that we have to discuss it."

"They're whores!" Bulatov said with assurance. Then he

added, his eyes flashing over his horn-rimmed glasses, "I've
been telling you for a long time—they're using that letter to
squeeze you dry. Refuse to work!"

"They'll hang a second term on me," Dyrsin said with a
sigh. He had always been stoop-shouldered, and his head
sank into his shoulders, as if he had once been hit hard
with something heavy.

Bulatov sighed, too. He was so belligerent because he
had a long, long time to serve yet. However, a zek's com-
bativeness declines as he approaches liberation. Dyrsin was
"putting in" his last year.

The lowering sky was an even gray; no dark or bright
patches showed; it wasn't a great, vaulted dome—it was just
a dirty tarpaulin cover spread over the earth. Driven by the
cutting wet wind, the snow had settled, become spongy; little
by little its morning whiteness turned reddish-brown. Underfoot, it packed down into slippery mounds.

The exercise period proceeded as usual. It was impossible
to imagine the sort of weather which would make sharashka
zeks, withering from lack of air, decide to stay indoors.
After long hours of confinement, even these sharp gusts of
damp wind were pleasant—they blew the stagnant air and
stagnant thoughts out of a man.

Among those strolling outside was the engraver. He took
one zek after another by the arm and walked around the
circle with him a couple of times. He needed advice. His
situation was particularly dreadful, as he saw it. Being in
prison, he could not legally marry the woman he had lived
with, and because she wasn't his lawful wife, he no longer
had the right to correspond with her. Since he had already
used up his letter quota for December, he couldn't even write
her that he wouldn't be writing. The others sympathized
with him. His situation was in truth awkward. But one's own
pain blots out anyone else's.

Inclined at all times to extreme feelings, Kondrashev-
Ivanov, as tall and erect as if he had a pole inside his coat,
was staring over the heads of the strollers. He went over to
Professor Chelnov, and announced with gloomy rapture that
it was humiliating to go on living at a time when human
dignity was so flouted. Every courageous human being had
a simple way out of this endless succession of mockeries.

Professor Chelnov, wearing his knit cap, his plaid shawl

thrown over his shoulders, answered in a reserved manner with a quotation from Boethius' *The Consolation of Philosophy.*

Outside the headquarters door a group of volunteer stool-pigeon hunters had gathered: Bulatov, whose voice resounded through the whole yard; Khorobrov; the good-natured vacuum specialist, Zemelya; Dvoyetyosov, who wore a torn camp pea jacket out of principle; the mercurial Pryanchikov, who involved himself in everything; Max, from among the Germans; and one of the Latvians.

"The country must know who its stool pigeons are!" Bulatov repeated, to reinforce their intention of staying together.

"Well, after all, essentially we know them anyway," answered Khorobrov, standing on the doorstep and scanning the straggling mail line. He could say for certain that some in the line were standing there for their thirty pieces of silver. But those whom the zeks suspected were, of course, the least skillful of the informers.

Ruska came out of the office exultant, hardly able to refrain from waving his money order over his head. Shoving their heads together, they all inspected the money order from the mythical Klava Kudryavtseva to Rostislav Doronin in the amount of 147 rubles.

Having finished lunch, the superinformer, the king of stool pigeons, Arthur Siromakha, joined the end of the mail line. He observed the circle around Ruska with a sinister gaze. He observed it because it was his habit to notice everything, but he did not yet see any significance in it.

Ruska took back his money order and, as they had arranged earlier, left the group.

The third to go in to see the "protector" was an electrical engineer, a man of forty who had exasperated Rubin the night before in the locked-up "ark" with his new projects for socialism and had then childishly engaged in a pillow fight on the upper bunks.

The fourth to go in, with a swift, light stride, was Victor Lyubimichev, known as "a regular guy." When he smiled, he displayed large, even teeth, and he addressed all prisoners, young or old, with the winning salutation of "brother." His pure soul shone through this simple form of address.

The electrical engineer came out on the doorstep, reading

his letter. Deeply absorbed, he didn't feel the edge of the step and lost his balance. The informer-hunters didn't bother with him. Without outdoor coat or cap, the wind ruffling his hair, he was still young-looking despite all he had suffered. He was reading his first letter from his daughter Ariadna after eight years of separation. When he had left in 1941 for the front, where he had been taken prisoner by the Germans —and gone from there into a Soviet prison—she had been a blond six-year-old who had clung to his neck. And when they walked along in the POW barracks, crunching beneath their feet a layer of typhus-infected lice, and when they stood in line four hours at a time for a ladle of smelly, turbid gruel, he held on to the memory of Ariadna's dear, blond head as if it had been the thread of the Cretan Ariadne, and somehow it enabled him to live through it all and return. But when he had returned to his homeland, he went straight to prison, and he never saw his daughter. She and her mother had remained in Chelyabinsk, to which they had been evacuated. And Ariadna's mother, who had apparently found herself another man, was unwilling for a long time to tell his daughter that her father was still alive.

In a careful, sloping, schoolgirl handwriting, without any crossings-out or corrections, Ariadna had written:

HELLO, DEAR PAPA!

I did not answer because I did not know how to begin or what to write. This is forgivable, since I had not seen you for a very long time and had grown used to my father being dead. It even seems strange to me that now, all of a sudden, I have a father.

You ask how I am getting along. I am getting along like everyone else. You can congratulate me—I have joined the Komsomols. You ask me to write you what I need. I want, of course, a lot. Right now I am saving my money for overshoes and to have a spring coat made. Papa! You ask me to come to see you. But is there really such a hurry? To take such a long journey to find you wouldn't be very pleasant, you'll agree. When you can, you will come here yourself. I wish you success in your work. Good-bye for now.

I kiss you.

ARIADNA

Papa, did you see the picture, *The Boxing Gloves*? It is very good! I don't miss a single movie.

"Are we going to check on Lyubimichev?" Khorobrov asked as they waited for him to come out.

"Look here, Terentich! Lyubimichev is one of us!" they answered.

But Khorobrov, with his deep perceptions, had sensed something wrong about the man. And Lyubimichev was staying in there with the "protector" a long time.

Victor Lyubimichev had the candid eyes of a deer. Nature had equipped him with the supple body of an athlete, a soldier, a lover. Suddenly, life had torn him from the stadium and thrown him into a concentration camp in Bavaria. In this crowded death trap, into which the enemy drove Russian soldiers and Stalin did not permit the Red Cross to enter, in this small, overcrowded pit of horror, the only ones who survived were those who went furthest in abandoning comparative ideas of good and the obligations of conscience; those who, acting as interpreters, could sell out their fellow men; those who, as camp guards, could club their countrymen in the face; those who, as bread cutters and cooks, could eat the bread of others who were starving. There were two other roads to survival: to work as a gravedigger or as a "golddigger"—in other words, a latrine orderly. The Nazis gave an extra ladle of gruel for gravedigging and for latrine cleaning. Two men could take care of the latrines, but every day fifty went out to dig. Every day a dozen wagons were loaded with corpses to be dumped in the graves. By the summer of '42 it was the gravediggers' turn to be buried.

With all the yearning of his young body, Victor Lyubimichev wanted to live. He resolved that if he had to die he would be the last. He had already agreed to become a guard when his opportunity dawned. A fellow with a nasal twang turned up in the camp. He had been a political officer in the Red Army, but now he urged the POWs to fight against the Soviets. They signed up. Even the Komsomols. Outside the camp gates was a German military kitchen, and the volunteers filled their bellies then and there. After that, Lyubimichev fought in France as a member of the Vlasov legion; he hunted down resistance fighters in the Vosges, and later defended himself against the Allies on the Atlantic Wall. In 1945—the time of the great "catch"—he somehow managed to make his way through the net, reached home and married a girl with eyes as bright and clear, and a body as young and lithe, as his own. A few weeks later he was arrested. The Russians who had fought in the resistance movement in the Vosges—Lyubimichev's former prey—were passing through the same prisons at the same time. In Butyrskaya they all played dominoes while they waited for parcels from home, and the "resistance" Russians and Lyubimichev together recalled the days and battles in France. Then all of them, impartially, received ten-year sentences. Thus all his life Lyubimichev had the chance to learn that no one ever had or ever could have "convictions"—including, of course, his judges.

Unsuspecting, his eyes innocent, holding a piece of paper that looked like a money order, Victor made no effort to slip past the group of "hunters." In fact, he went up to them and asked, "Brothers! Who's had lunch? What was the second course? Is it worth going?"

Khorobrov nodded at the money order in Lyubimichev's hand. "You just got a lot of money, didn't you? You can buy your own lunch."

"What do you mean, a lot?" Lyubimichev asked casually, and was about to put the money order in his pocket. He hadn't bothered to hide it before because he thought no one would dare ask to see it, since they all had a healthy respect for his strength.

But while he was talking with Khorobrov, Bulatov, as if playing around, bent down and read, "Phew! One thousand four hundred seventy rubles! You can spit on Anton's chow from now on!"

If it had been any other zek, Lyubimichev would have jokingly punched him in the head and refused to show him the money order. But he couldn't with Bulatov, because Bulatov had promised, and was trying, to get Lyubimichev into Number Seven. It would have been striking a blow against destiny and the chance of freedom. So Lyubimichev answered, "Where do you see any thousands? Just look!"

And everyone saw: "147.00 rubles."

"Now that's a funny thing! Why couldn't they send 150?" Bulatov observed imperturbably. "All right, run along; there's a cutlet for the second course."

But before Bulatov had finished speaking and before Lyubimichev could move away, Khorobrov began to tremble. He was no longer able to play his role. He forgot that

one must control oneself, smile, and then fish further. He
had forgotten that the only important thing was to identify
the informers. They couldn't be destroyed. But, having suffered at their hands himself, and having seen many lives
wrecked by them, he hated these sneaky squealers more than
anything else. Lyubimichev was young enough to have been
Khorobrov's son, he was handsome enough to pose for a
statue, and he had turned out to be such a willing rat!

"Son-of-a-bitch!" Khorobrov blurted out with trembling
lips. "Trying to get out ahead of time through our blood!
What more do you need?"

A scrapper, always ready for a fight, Lyubimichev jumped
back and cocked his fist.

"You Vyatka carrion!" he warned.

"Now look out, Terentich!" said Bulatov, jumping even
more quickly to get Khorobrov away.

Huge, awkward Dvoyetyosov in his ragged pea jacket
seized Lyubimichev's fist and held it.

"Easy, boy!" he said with a disdainful grin, with that
almost caressing quietness transmitted by the springlike tension of the entire body.

Lyubimichev spun around sharply, and his open, deerlike
eyes met the bulging, nearsighted gaze of Dvoyetyosov.

Lyubimichev did not draw back his other arm to strike.
He understood from the peasant's stare and that grip on his
arm that one of them was going to be killed.

"Easy, boy!" Dvoyetyosov repeated insistently. "The second course is cutlet. Run along and eat your cutlet."

Lyubimichev jerked away. With a proud toss of his head
he went over to the stairs. His full, satiny cheeks flamed. He
wanted some way to get even with Khorobrov. He did not
yet understand that he had been skewered. He was ready to
assure anyone that he understood life, but it had turned out
that he didn't.

How could they have guessed? Where could they have
found out?

Bulatov watched him go, then put his hands to his head.
"Good Lord! Whom are we going to trust now?"

The whole scene had been played quietly, and no one in
the yard noticed it, neither the strolling zeks nor the two
guards who stood motionless at the edge of the exercise
area. Only Siromakha, his heavy, tired eyes half-closed, had

seen the whole thing from just inside the door. Remembering the group gathered around Ruska a little earlier, he understood exactly what had happened.

He rushed to the head of the line.

"Listen, boys!" he said to those in front. "I left my circuit on. How about letting me in ahead of my turn? It will just take a few seconds."

"All of us left our circuits on."

"We all have our problems," they answered, and laughed. They wouldn't let him get in ahead.

"Then I'll have to go and turn it off!" Siromakha exclaimed in concern, and he ran past the "hunters" and disappeared into the main building. Without stopping for breath he ran up to the third floor. Major Shikin's office was locked from the inside, and the key was in the keyhole. An interrogation could be going on. Or a rendezvous with his tall, thin secretary. Siromakha stepped back helplessly.

With every minute that passed, the network of informers was being exposed, and there was nothing he could do.

He knew he should go back and stand in line again, but the sensation of being a hunted animal was stronger than his desire to curry favor with Myshin. It was terrible to think of going past that angry, evil pack again. They might even grab him. They knew him all too well in the sharashka.

Meanwhile, in the yard, Doctor of Chemical Sciences Orobintsev, a small man in glasses, wearing the rich fur coat and cap he had worn in freedom—for he had not been taken to a transit prison, and they had not got around to cleaning him out yet—had gathered around him other simpletons like himself, including the bald designer, and was according them an interview. It is well known that a person believes, for the most part, only what he wants to believe. Those zeks who wanted to believe that the list of relatives they had just submitted was not a denunciation but an intelligent regulatory measure now clustered around Orobintsev. Orobintsev had just handed in his list, neatly divided into columns. He had spoken personally to Major Myshin and was now repeating authoritatively the security officer's explanations: where one should enter the names of minor children, and what to do if one's father was not one's real father. Only once had Major Myshin abused Orobintsev's courtesy. Orobintsev had said that he didn't remember his

wife's birthplace, and Myshin opened his mouth wide and
started to laugh. "What do you mean, you don't remember?
Did you find her in a whorehouse?"

Now the trusting sheep were listening to Orobintsev. Another group stood in the shelter of three linden trunks, while
Adamson addressed them.

Adamson, after a filling meal, was smoking lazily and
informing his audience that all these restrictions relating to
correspondence were not new, that things had been even
worse, and that this prohibition would not last forever but
only until some minister or general was replaced, and that
they should therefore not lose heart. They should delay
handing in their lists as long as possible, and the whole
thing would blow over. Adamson's eyes were long and narrow, and when he took off his glasses, the impression that he
viewed the prisoners' world with boredom grew stronger.
Everything repeated itself; the archipelago of GULAG could
not surprise him with anything new. Adamson had seen so
much that he seemed to have unlearned how to feel; he
accepted what struck others as tragedy as no more than a
piece of petty news about domestic affairs.

Meanwhile the "hunters," more numerous than before,
had caught another informer. They had jokingly pulled out
of Isaak Kagan's pocket a money order for 147 rubles. They
had first asked him what he had received from the "protector," and he had answered that he received nothing, and
was surprised that he had been called in by mistake. When
they took the money order from him by force, Kagan didn't
blush, didn't hurry to leave. He swore insistently, importun-
ing them, clutching their clothes, swore to all his tormentors
in turn that it was pure misunderstanding, that he would
show them a letter from his wife saying she had not had
the three rubles to pay for the money order and so had to
send him just 147. He urged them to go with him to the
Battery Laboratory right away; he would get the letter and
show it to them. And then, shaking his shaggy head, unaware that his muffler had slipped off his neck and was
dragging on the ground, he explained quite convincingly
why he had at first denied that he had received a money
order. Kagan had been born with a remarkable tenacity.
Once he started talking, it was impossible to get away from

him except by admitting that he was absolutely right and leaving him the last word.

Khorobrov, his bunkmate, who knew he had been imprisoned for refusing to inform, could no longer find the strength to be angry with him. He only said, "Oh, Isaak, you're a pig, just a pig! In freedom you turned down their offer of thousands, and here you went along with them for hundreds."

Or had they scared him by threatening him with the prospect of camp?

But Isaak Kagan, not in the least put out of countenance, continued to explain and would have ended by convincing them all if they had not caught still another informer, this time a Latvian. Their attention was distracted, and Kagan left.

The second shift was called to lunch, and the first shift went out to stroll in the yard. Nerzhin climbed up the ramp. At once he saw Ruska Doronin, standing by the exercise yard. With a bright triumphant gaze Ruska was watching the hunt he had organized. Then he turned to look along the path to the free employees' yard and, beyond it, to the place on the highway where Clara—on duty this evening—would soon be getting off the bus.

"Well?" He grinned at Nerzhin and nodded in the direction of the hunt. "Did you hear about Lyubimichev?"

Nerzhin came up to him and took him lightly by the shoulders.

"You should be tossed in the air in triumph. But I'm worried about you."

"Ho! I'm just getting started; just wait, this is nothing."

Nerzhin shook his head, gave a laugh, and moved on. He met Pryanchikov, who was hurrying to lunch, all aglow after having shouted to his heart's content among the hunters.

"Ha, fellow!" Pryanchikov greeted him. "You missed the whole show! Where is Lev?"

"He has urgent work. He didn't come out for the break."

"What? More urgent than Number Seven? Ha, ha! There's no such thing. Screw you! Screw all of you!" And he ran off.

Farther on in the yard Nerzhin met Gerasimovich, wearing a bedraggled little cap on his small head and a short coat with the collar turned up. They nodded to each other sadly. Gerasimovich stood with his hands in his side pockets, hunched against the wind, looking puny as a sparrow.

The sparrow in the folk saying whose heart was as brave as the cat's.

75

INDOCTRINATION IN OPTIMISM

In comparison with the work of Major Shikin the work of Major Myshin had its pluses and its minuses. The main plus was reading letters and deciding whether or not to let them be sent on. There were minuses, too: the fact, for instance, that Myshin wasn't the one who decided about such things as the prisoner transports, withholding wages, determining food categories, how long visits with relatives could last, and various other important matters. Major Myshin found much to envy in the rival organization of Major Shikin, who got word of prison affairs before he did. Therefore he relied a good deal on peering through the transparent curtain in his office to see what was going on in the exercise yard. Shikin was deprived of this opportunity because of the unfortunate location of his window.

Watching the prisoners in their day-to-day life also gave Myshin a certain amount of material. Observing from his ambush who walked with whom, and whether he spoke vehemently or casually, he could supplement the information he received from the informers. Then later, handing over a letter or accepting one to be sent out, he would suddenly ask, "Incidentally, what was it you and Petrov were talking about yesterday during the lunch break?"

Sometimes this resulted in his eliciting useful information from the confused prisoner.

Today, during the lunch break, Myshin told the next zek in the mail line to wait while he peered out into the yard.

But he missed seeing the hunt for informers. It was going on at the other end of the building.

At three o'clock, when the lunch break ended and the officious master sergeant had dismissed all the zeks who were still waiting to get into Myshin's office, the major gave orders to admit Dyrsin.

Ivan Selivanovich Dyrsin had been endowed by nature with a sunken face, prominent cheekbones, and indistinct speech; even his surname—suggesting "hole"—seemed to have been given him in a spirit of mockery. He had at one time been taken into a training institute, going straight from his lathe via the evening workers' school, where he had studied inconspicuously and hard. He had certain abilities, but he had never been able to use them to advantage, and all his life he had been pushed aside and badly treated. In Number Seven anyone who wanted to exploited him. And because his ten-year term, slightly reduced, was coming to an end, he was particularly timid these days in front of the authorities. More than anything he dreaded getting a second term. He had seen many prisoners get them during the war years.

Even the way he was first sentenced was absurd. He was imprisoned at the beginning of the war for "anti-Soviet propaganda," the result of a denunciation cooked up by some neighbors who wanted his apartment and afterward got it. It became clear subsequently that he had not engaged in any such propaganda, though he could have, since he listened to the German radio. Then it turned out that he didn't listen to the German radio, but he *could* have listened to it since he had a forbidden radio receiver at home. And when it appeared that he didn't have any such radio receiver, it was still true that he *could* have had one since he was a radio engineer by profession. Also, following the denunciation, they found two radio tubes in a box in his apartment.

Dyrsin had had his full share of wartime camps, both those where the zeks ate wet grain stolen from the horses and those where they mixed their flour with snow beneath a sign saying "Camp Site"—the sign had been nailed years before to a pine tree at the edge of the taiga. In the eight years Dyrsin had spent in the land of GULAG his wife had become a bony old woman and their two children had died. Then they remembered that he was an engineer and brought him to the sharashka and issued him butter—yes, and he could even send a hundred rubles a month to his wife.

Then, unaccountably, his wife's letters stopped coming. She could have died.

Major Myshin sat with his arms folded on his desk. The desk before him was free of papers, the inkwell closed, the pen dry, and there was no expression, as indeed there never had been, on his plump face, which was lilac with a touch of red. His forehead was so plump that neither the wrinkles of age nor the creases of meditation could engrave themselves there. His cheeks were plump, too. Myshin's face was like that of an idol made of fired clay to which rose and violet tints had been added. His eyes were lifeless, with a peculiar arrogant vacuity.

It had never happened before: Myshin asked him to sit down. Dyrsin tried to guess what misfortune would be his lot, what the report against him would say. The major kept silent, according to instructions.

Finally, he said, "So you've been complaining, coming here and complaining, about not getting any letters for two months."

"More than three, Citizen Major!" Dyrsin shyly interjected.

"Well, three—what's the difference? And have you thought at all about the kind of person your wife is?"

Myshin spoke unhurriedly, pronouncing his words distinctly and pausing lengthily between phrases.

"What kind of person is your wife, eh?" he prompted.

"I don't understand," Dyrsin mumbled.

"What don't you understand? What are her politics?"

Dyrsin grew pale. He had not got used to everything, after all. His wife must have written something in a letter and now just before his liberation she . . .

And he secretly prayed for his wife. He had learned to pray in camp.

"She's a whiner, and we don't need whiners," the major explained firmly. "And she has some strange sort of blind spot: she doesn't see the good side of our life, just the bad."

"For God's sake, what has happened to her?" Dyrsin cried pleadingly, his head wobbling in his anguish.

"To her?" And Myshin paused even longer. "To her? Nothing." Dyrsin sighed. "So far."

Proceeding very deliberately, the major took a letter from a box and handed it to Dyrsin.

"Thank you!" said Dyrsin, choking. "Can I go now?"

"No. Read it here. I can't let you take a letter like that back to the dormitory. What will the other prisoners think of freedom on the basis of such letters? Read it."

And he fell silent, like a stone idol, prepared to accept the full weight of his responsibilities.

Dyrsin took the letter out of the envelope. He was not aware of it, but an outsider's eye would have been unpleasantly impressed by its appearance. It seemed to reflect the image of the woman who had written it: it was on rough paper, almost wrapping paper, and not a single line stayed horizontal. Each line slid downhill toward the right margin. The letter was dated September 18:

> DEAR VANYA! I just sat down to write but I really want to go to sleep. I can't. I come home from work and go out to the garden right away. Manyushka and I are digging potatoes. We only got little ones. In vacation I didn't go anywhere, had nothing to wear, everything was rags. I wanted to save up some money, yes, and go to see you—but nothing works out. Then Nika went to see you and they told her that there was no one of that name there, and her mother and father scolded her—"Why did you go? Now they've got your name down too, and they'll keep an eye on you." In general our relations with them are strained, and they and L.V. don't speak at all.
>
> We live badly. Grandmother has been sick in bed for three years now, doesn't get up, she's all dried up, she doesn't die and she doesn't get well, and she's worn us all out. There's an awful stink from her and there are quarrels all the time. I am not speaking to L.V., Manyushka has separated from her husband for good, her health is bad, her children don't obey her, when we come home from work it's awful, all you can hear are curses, where is there to run away to, when is it going to end?
>
> Well, I kiss you. Keep in good health.

There was not any signature or even the word "yours."

Waiting patiently till Dyrsin had read and reread this letter, Major Myshin twitched his white eyebrows and his violet lips and said, "I didn't give you that letter when it came. I thought this was just a passing mood of hers, and you have to keep up your spirits for your work. I waited for her to send a proper letter. But here's the one she sent last month."

Silently Dyrsin looked up at the major, but his clumsy face did not express reproach, just pain. He took the second unsealed envelope, opened it with trembling fingers, and took out a letter with the same depressed, uneven lines. This time it was on a page torn from a notebook:

October 30

DEAR VANYA! You are offended because I seldom write. But I come back from work late and almost every day go into the woods for sticks, and then it's evening and I am so tired that I simply fall into bed. I sleep badly at night, Grandmother doesn't let me. I get up early, at five in the morning, and by eight I must be at work. It's still, thank God, a warm autumn, but winter is coming soon! You can't get any coal at the warehouse, only the bosses or people with connections. Not long ago a pile of wood fell off my back, I dragged it right on the ground behind me, I didn't have the strength to lift it up, and I thought to myself: "An old woman dragging a load of sticks!" I got myself a hernia from the weight. Nika came for the holidays, she is becoming an attractive woman, and she didn't even drop by to see us. I can't think of you without pain. I've no one to count on. I will work while I have strength, and I am only afraid that I'll fall sick like Grandmother. Grandmother has completely lost the use of her legs. She is all swollen up, can't lie down by herself or get up. And they don't take people as sick as that into the hospital, it's not worth their while. L.V. and I have to lift her up every time, she goes under herself in bed, we have an awful stink, it's not a life but prison labor. Of course she is not to blame, but I have no strength to last out any longer. In spite of your advice not to curse we curse every day, from L.V. all I hear is bastard and bitch. And Manyushka at her children, too. Would ours really have grown up like that too? You know, often I'm glad they're not here. Valerik entered school this year, he needs lots of things but there's no money. True, they pay Manyushka alimony from Pavel's salary, by decree. Well, so far there's nothing to write. I wish you good health. I kiss you.

If there were even a chance to sleep over the holidays— but we have to drag ourselves to the demonstration. . . .

Dyrsin froze as he read this letter. He put his palm to his forehead and rubbed it as if he were trying to wash himself.

"Well? Have you read it? You don't look like you're reading. Now you're an adult person. Literate. You have been in prison, you understand what kind of letter that is. During the war they handed out sentences for letters like that. A demonstration—it's a joy for everyone else, and for her? Coal? Coal doesn't go to the bosses but to all citizens; they stand in line for it, of course. Everything considered, I didn't know whether to give you that letter or not, but then a third one came which is just the same kind. And I decided this whole thing has to be stopped. You have to stop it yourself. Write her something in an optimistic tone—you know, encouraging, give the woman some support. Tell her she shouldn't complain, that everything will work out. You'll see, they got rich, received an inheritance. Read."

The letters were in chronological order. The third was dated December 8.

DEAR VANYA! I am informing you of some sad news. On November 26, 1949, at 12:05 P.M. Grandmother died. She died and we didn't have a kopeck. Luckily Misha gave 200 rubles, and everything was cheap, but, of course, the funeral was a mean one. No priest. No music. The coffin was just carried on a cart to the cemetery and dropped in the grave. Now things are a little more quiet at home, but there's a kind of emptiness. I am sick myself, have awful sweats at night, and the pillows and sheets are soaked. A gypsy foretold that I will die this winter, and I will be glad to be rid of such a life. It seems that L.V. has tuberculosis. She coughs and there's blood in her throat. When she comes from work the cursing starts—she's as spiteful as a witch. She and Manyushka are driving me mad. I am a wretched person—another four teeth have spoiled and two have fallen out. I ought to have some put in but I have no money and then one has to sit in line too.

Your wages for three months, 300 rubles, came just when we needed it, we were freezing, our turn at the warehouse was coming up—I was No. 4,576—and they only give out coal dust. Well, why take it at all? Manyushka added 200 of her own to your 300 and we paid a driver ourselves and he brought some coal in big lumps. But our potatoes aren't going to last till spring. Two gardens, can you imagine, and we got nothing. No rains. No harvest.

There are constant quarrels with the children. Valery gets failing grades at school—two's and one's—and after school he fools around God knows where. The director called in Manyushka—what kind of a mother are you that you can't cope with your children? And Zhenka, six years old, and they both swear foul oaths, in a word they're trash. All my money goes for them, and Valery not long ago cursed me out and called me a bitch, and I have to hear that from some rubbish of a boy, what are they going to be like when they grow up? In May, they say, we come into the inheritance, and it's going to cost 2,000, and where are we going to get it? Yelena and Misha are going to court—they want to take the room away from L.V. How many times in her lifetime Grandmother told her she didn't want to decide who got what. Misha and Yelena are also sick.

I wrote you in the fall, yes, I think even twice, can it be you don't get the letters? Where are they going astray?

I am sending you a forty-kopeck stamp. Well, what do you hear there? Are they going to free you or not?

There's some very pretty kitchenware being sold in the store, aluminum pans, bowls.

I kiss you. I wish you good health.

A wet spot spread on the paper, dissolving some ink.

Again it was impossible to tell whether Dyrsin was still reading or whether he had already finished.

"So," asked Myshin, "is it all clear?"

Dyrsin did not move.

"Write an answer. A cheerful answer. I'll let it run more than four pages. You wrote her once that she should believe in God. Well, it's better she should believe in God—why not? Otherwise what is all this? Where is it leading? Calm her down, tell her you'll be coming soon. That you'll be getting big wages."

"But are they really going to let me go home? They aren't going to exile me?"

"That's up to the authorities. It's your obligation to help your wife. After all, she is your lifetime companion." The major was silent for a moment. "Or maybe you want a young one now?" he suggested sympathetically.

He would not have been sitting there so calmly had he known that out in the corridor, wild with impatience to see him, jumping from one foot to the other, was his favorite informer, Siromakha.

76

THE KING OF STOOL PIGEONS

In those rare moments when Arthur Siromakha was not occupied with the struggle for existence, when he was not making an effort to please the authorities or to work, when he relaxed his constant leopard-like tension, he became a wilted young man with a slim body, the face of a worn-out actor, and gray cloudy-blue eyes, moist with apparent sadness.

Two men had lost their tempers and called Siromakha an informer. Both had soon been sent away in prisoner transports, and no one said anything to him again. The zeks were afraid of him. After all, no one was ever allowed to confront and challenge the informer who had accused him, perhaps, of preparing to escape . . . of terrorism . . . revolt. The zek doesn't know; they tell him to get his things together. Are they sending him to a camp? Or are they taking him to a special prison to be investigated?

It is a human characteristic, which has been richly exploited in every era, that while hope of survival is still alive in a man, while he still believes his troubles will have a favorable outcome, and while he still has the chance to unmask treason or to save someone else by sacrificing himself, he continues to cling to the pitiful remnants of comfort and remains silent and submissive. When he has been taken and destroyed, when he has nothing more to lose, and is, in consequence, ready and eager for heroic action, his belated rage can only spend itself against the stone walls of solitary confinement. Or the breath of the death sentence makes him indifferent to earthly affairs.

Thus certain zeks, not doubting that Siromakha was an informer, considered it less dangerous to be friends with him, to play volleyball, to talk about "broads" with him, than to try to unmask him publicly, or to catch him while he was making a denunciation. That was the way they got along with the other informers, too. As a result, life at the sharashka appeared peaceful when, in fact, an underground death struggle was going on all the time.

But Arthur could talk about more than women. *The Forsyte Saga* was one of his favorite books, and he could discuss it very intelligently. He could also without embarrassment turn from Galsworthy to that tired old detective story, *The House Without a Key.* Arthur also had an ear for music, and he loved Spanish and Italian melodies. He could whistle Verdi and Rossini accurately, and in freedom he had felt something was missing from his life if he did not attend a concert at the Conservatory once a year.

The Siromakhas had been a noble family, though poor. At the beginning of the century one Siromakha had been a composer, another had been exiled to hard labor on a criminal charge, while still another had unequivocally joined the Revolution and served in the Cheka.

When Arthur came of age, his inclinations and requirements left no doubt that he needed to have permanent independent means. Not for him a regular, grimy little life, sweating daily from morning till night, carefully counting twice a month what was left of his pay after deductions for taxes and loans. When he went to the movies, he seriously weighed his chances of captivating all the female stars. He could easily imagine himself running off to the Argentine with Deanna Durbin.

Of course, no career either in an institute or in any other branch of teaching was the path to such a life. Arthur looked into another area of government service, which involved lots of scurrying around and darting here and there. And although that particular sphere of action did not provide all the funds he would have liked, it did save him from military service during the war; that is, it saved his life. While fools out there were rotting in muddy trenches, Arthur, his cheeks glowing with health, was blithely entering the Savoy Restaurant. Oh, that moment when you first came into the restaurant, when the warm air laden with kitchen odors and the music hit you all at once, and you saw the brilliant room, and the room could see you, and you picked your table!

Everything inside Arthur had sung, telling him he was on the right track. He was indignant that people considered his occupation vile. It could only be due to lack of understanding or envy. His branch of the service called for gifted people. It required powers of observation, memory, resourcefulness, a talent for pretending, acting—one had to be an artist. And it had to be kept secret. It could not exist without secrecy—for technological reasons, just as a welder needs a protective shield when he works. Otherwise Arthur would never have concealed what he did for a living—there was nothing shameful in it.

Once, having failed to stay within his budget, Arthur got in with a crowd that was tempted by state property. He was caught and imprisoned. But he was in no sense offended. He had only himself to blame; he should never have let himself get caught. From his first days behind barbed wire he quite naturally felt that he was practicing his former profession, and that his prison term was only a new phase of it.

The security officers did not abandon him; he was not sent north to a timbering project, nor to the mines, but was assigned to a cultural-educational section. This was the only bright spot in a camp, the only corner where prisoners could drop in for half an hour before lights-out and feel human again—leaf through a newspaper, take a guitar in their hands, recall poems or their own unreal, unlikely lives. The "Dill Tomatoes," as the thieves called the incorrigible intellectuals, flocked there, and Arthur felt very much at home, with his artistic soul, his understanding eyes, his recollections of the capital, and his ability to talk lightly and casually about anything at all.

Arthur worked up his cases quickly: against several individual *propagandists*; one anti-Soviet-oriented *group*; two alleged plots to escape; and a *doctors' case*, in which the camp doctors were accused of delays in curing their patients for the purpose of sabotage—in other words, permitting prisoners to rest up in the hospital. All these sheep received second terms and Arthur, through Third Section channels, had two years taken off his term.

When he landed in Mavrino, Arthur did not neglect his tried and true activities. He became the favorite of both "protector" majors, and the most awesome stool pigeon at the sharashka.

But, while the majors made use of his denunciations, they did not in turn disclose their secrets to him, and now Siromakha did not know to which of the two it was more important to give the news about Doronin; he did not know *whose* informer Doronin was.

Much has been written to prove that people on the whole are ungrateful and disloyal. But the opposite turns out to be the case, too. With an insane lack of caution, with a prodigious lack of judgment, Ruska Doronin had confided his intention of becoming a double agent not just to one or two or three zeks but to more than twenty. Everyone who knew about it had told several others, and Doronin's secret had become the property of almost half the population of the sharashka. It was talked about almost openly in the rooms; and although one out of every five or six in the sharashka was an informer, not one of these zeks learned about it; or, if any of them did, no one reported it. Even the most observant, the most sensitive, the king of stool pigeons, Arthur Siromakha, had not known of it until today.

It was an affront to his honor as an informer: what did it matter if the security officers in their offices had missed the whole thing—how could *he* have missed it? And what about his personal safety? They might have caught him with the money order just as they had caught the others! For Siromakha, Doronin's treason was a shot that had barely missed his head. Doronin had turned out to be a powerful enemy; therefore he had to be struck powerfully in return. However, Arthur still did not realize the extent of the disaster. He thought that Doronin had only that morning revealed himself to the others as an informer.

Siromakha could not break through into the offices. He must not lose his head, must not try to smash through Shikin's locked door or even run upstairs to it too often. And at Myshin's there was a line! It had been dismissed at the three o'clock bell, but for a while the most tenacious and stubborn of the zeks stood arguing with the duty officer in the hallway. Siromakha, clutching his stomach with a look of suffering, approached them as if he were going to the medical assistant and stood there expecting the group to scatter. Dyrsin had already been called in to see Myshin. According to Siromakha's terms of reference, there was no reason for Dyrsin to linger in the "protector's" office. And he stood there and stood there. Risking Mamurin's displeasure over his prolonged absence from Number Seven, from the smoking soldering irons and rosin, Siromakha waited in vain for Myshin to let Dyrsin go.

But he could not afford to make his situation clear even to the guards who were watching the hallway. Losing patience, Siromakha again went up to the third floor to find Shikin. At last he was in luck: hiding in the dark alcove near Shikin's door, he heard through the wood the unique creaking voice of the janitor, the only such voice in the sharashka.

He gave the special knock. The door was unlocked and Shikin appeared in the narrow opening.

"Very urgent!" Siromakha said with a whisper.

"One minute," Shikin answered.

With a light step Siromakha went far down the long hallway so as not to encounter the janitor on his way out. Then he returned in a businesslike way and pushed open Shikin's door without knocking.

77

AS FOR SHOOTING...

After a week's investigation of the "Case of the Broken Lathe" the essence of the accident remained a riddle to Major Shikin. All that had been established was that this lathe, with an open, stepped pulley, and a manual feed, a lathe produced by Russian industry in 1916, in the heat of the First World War, had been disconnected from its electric motor on Yakonov's orders and transferred from Laboratory Number Three to the repair shop. Since there was no agreement as to who was to move it, the laboratory personnel were ordered to take the lathe as far as the cellar corridor, and from there the repair shop personnel were to hand-tow it up the ramp and deliver it to the repair shop across the yard. There was, in fact, a shorter route, which would have eliminated taking it down to the cellar, but in that case the zeks would have had to cross the main yard, which had an open view of the highway and the park, and that, of course, could not be permitted from the security point of view.

When the irreparable had already happened, Shikin could reproach himself, too: he had not recognized the importance of this vital link in the chain of production and had therefore not supervised it personally. But, after all, in historical perspective, the mistakes of public figures are always the most apparent—and how can they be avoided?

Laboratory Number Three—whose staff consisted of one boss, one man, one invalid, and one girl—was unable to move the lathe itself. Therefore, with a total lack of responsibility, auxiliaries—ten zeks—were assembled from various rooms on a random basis, and nobody made a list of who they were. The result was that later on, after half a month, Major Shikin had to devote a great deal of effort to comparing testimony in order to re-create the full roster of those under suspicion. The ten zeks had taken the heavy lathe down the stairs from the first floor to the cellar. However, since the man in charge of the repair shop did not wish to take custody of this lathe for technical reasons, his staff failed not only to get their work force to the cellar in time to take over, but even failed to send anyone to the rendezvous to take formal charge of the lathe. Nobody was directing the ten zeks who had dragged the lathe down to the cellar, and they scattered. So the lathe stood in the cellar corridor for several days, blocking the passageway. Shikin had, in fact, tripped over it personally. The people from the repair shop came for it finally, but they found a crack in the bedplate, complained about it, and refused to take the lathe until they were compelled to do so three days later.

Now that fateful crack in the bedplate was the basis for initiating the "case." Perhaps the crack was not the reason the lathe wasn't in use. Shikin had heard that opinion expressed. But the significance of the crack was much broader than the crack itself. The crack meant that undiscovered hostile forces were operating within the institute. The crack meant also that the leadership of the institute was blindly credulous and criminally negligent. A successful investigation, resulting in the exposure of the criminal and the true motives behind the crime, would make it possible to punish someone, deliver a warning to someone else, and, even further, undertake large-scale indoctrination within the collective. Last but not least, Major Shikin's professional honor demanded that this foul web be unraveled!

But it was not easy. Too much time had passed. The prisoners who had carried the lathe had evolved the successful technique of vouching for one another—criminal collusion. Not one free employee—a horrible instance of negligence—had been present while it was being moved. Among the ten lathe-movers there had been only one informer, who was, moreover, incompetent, his greatest coup having been his report about the sheet which was cut up into dickeys. In this case the only way he had been of help was in reconstructing the full list of ten men. In everything else, all the zeks involved, insolently confident that they were immune to punishment, swore they had delivered the lathe to the basement intact and undamaged, and that they had not slid or bumped the bedplate down the stairs. According to their testimony, no one had been holding the lathe where the crack had subsequently developed, at the back of the bedplate under the rear mandrel. Everyone had been supporting it under the pulleys and spindle. In pursuit of the truth, the major had drawn several diagrams of the lathe and the relative positions of the zeks carrying it. But it would have been easier to become a qualified lathe operator than to find the person to blame for the crack. The only person who could be accused, if not of sabotage, at least of intention to commit sabotage, was Potapov. Angered by the three-hour interrogation, he had let the cat out of the bag:

"Come on, if I had wanted to wreck that lathe, I would have simply poured a handful of sand into the bearings and that would be that! What's the point of cracking the bedplate?"

Shikin immediately wrote down this typical utterance of the inveterate saboteur, but Potapov refused to sign it.

What made the present investigation particularly difficult was that Shikin did not have at his disposal the ordinary means of getting at the truth: solitary cells, punishment cells, beatings, punishment cell rations, night interrogations, or even the elementary precaution of placing those under investigation in different cells. Here things had to be done in such a way that the suspected criminals could go on working at full capacity and, to that end, eat and sleep normally.

Nevertheless, on Saturday Shikin had managed to learn from one zek that when they were going down the last steps and had jammed the lathe in the narrow doorway, the janitor Spiridon had come toward them, and shouting, "Wait a minute, friends, I'll help!" had grabbed hold and helped carry it to where they left it. From the diagram it turned out that the only place he could have taken hold of it was at the bedplate under the mandrel.

Shikin had decided to unwind this rich new thread today, Monday, neglecting the two denunciations which had been delivered that morning about the trial of Prince Igor. He had summoned the red-haired janitor before lunch, and Spiridon had come in from the yard just as he was, in his pea jacket, belted with a worn canvas belt. He had taken off his big-eared cap and crushed it guiltily in his hands, like the classic Russian peasant come to beg some bit of land from the landowner. And he had been careful not to dirty the carpet by stepping off the rubber runner. Casting a disapproving eye at the janitor's wet overshoes, and looking at him severely, Shikin let him stand there while he sat down in an armchair and silently looked over various papers. From time to time, as if he was astonished by what he was reading about Yegorov's criminal nature, he looked up at him in amazement, as one might look at a man-eating beast that has finally been caged. All this was done according to the system and was meant to have an annihilating impact on the prisoner's psyche. A half-hour passed in the locked office in inviolate silence. The lunch bell rang out clearly. Spiridon hoped to receive his letter from home, but Shikin did not even hear the bell; he riffled silently through thick files, he took something out of a box and put it in another box, he leafed, frowning, through various papers and again glanced up briefly in surprise at the dispirited, guilty Spiridon.

All the water from Spiridon's overshoes had dripped on the rubber runner, and they had dried when Shikin finally spoke:

"All right, move closer!" Spiridon moved closer. "Stop. Do you know him?" And he pushed toward him the photograph of a young man in German uniform, without a cap.

Spiridon bent over, squinted, examined it, and said apologetically, "You see, Citizen Major, I am a little blind. Let me look at it closer."

Shikin let him look. Still holding his shaggy fur cap in one hand, Spiridon took the photograph by the edge and, holding it toward the light from the window, he passed it in front of his left eye, as if to examine it section by section.

"No," he said with a sigh of relief, "I never saw him."

Shikin took the photograph back.

"Very bad, Yegorov," he said crushingly. "Denying it is only going to make things worse for you. Well, what the hell, sit down," and he pointed out a chair farther off. "We have a long conversation ahead of us; you wouldn't last on your feet."

Again he fell silent, busying himself with his papers.

Spiridon backed up and sat down. He put his cap on a chair next to him, but, observing how clean the soft leather chair was, he moved the cap to his knees. He hunched his round head into his shoulders and bent forward, his whole appearance expressing repentance and submissiveness.

Quite calmly he thought to himself, "You snake! You dog! When am I going to get my letter now? And you're the one who's holding it up."

Spiridon had undergone in his lifetime two investigations and one reinvestigation, and had known thousands of prisoners who had been through investigations. He could see through Shikin's game perfectly, but he knew he had to pretend to believe in it.

"New material against you has just come in," said Shikin, sighing heavily. "You seem to have played some tricks in Germany!"

"Maybe it wasn't me!" Spiridon told him. "Us Yegorovs were like flies in Germany. They say there was even a general named Yegorov!"

"What do you mean it wasn't you? Not you! Spiridon Danilovich is the name here," said Shikin and jabbed his finger at one of the files. "And the year of birth's right, and everything else."

"Year of birth? Then it wasn't me!" Spiridon said with conviction. "Because just to make things easier with the Germans I added three years."

"Oh, yes," Shikin remembered. Then his face lit up, and the burdensome necessity of conducting an investigation faded from his voice. He pushed aside the papers. "Before

I forget. Do you remember, Yegorov, ten days ago when you were helping carry a lathe? Down the stairs to the cellar."

"Well?" said Spiridon.

"Well, now, where did the banging occur? Was it on the stairs or when you were already in the corridor?"

"Banging?" Spiridon said in astonishment. "I didn't bang anybody."

"The lathe!"

"Good God, Citizen Major, why should I hit a lathe? Do you mean it hurt someone or something?"

"That's what surprises me, too—why did they break it? Maybe they dropped it?"

"What do you mean, dropped it? We held it by its feet, carefully, like a little baby."

"And you personally, where did you hold it?"

"Where? From here."

"Where?"

"From my side."

"Yes, but you took hold of it where—under the rear mandrel or under the spindle?"

"Citizen Major, I don't understand spindles and mandrels. I'll show you how!" He clapped his cap down on the nearby chair, got up and turned as if he were lugging a lathe through the door into the office. "I was coming down, this way. Backwards. And two of them got stuck in the door—see?"

"Which two?"

"How should I know. I never went to their christening. I was puffing. 'Stop!' I shouted. 'Let me get a new grip!' And there was the sardine!"

"What do you mean, the sardine?"

"Why can't you understand?" asked Spiridon over his shoulder, growing angry. "What do you think we were carrying?"

"You mean the lathe?"

"Sure, the lathe! And quick I got a new grip!" He demonstrated, straining, squatting.

"Then one of them pushed himself through sideways and the other shoved through and the third—why shouldn't we have kept holding it up? Hell!" He straightened up. "In the country we hauled around bigger loads than that. Six women on your lathe—fine, they'd carry it a whole half-mile. Where is that lathe? Let's go right now and lift it up for the hell of it!"

"You mean you didn't drop it?" the major asked threateningly.

"That's what I'm telling you. No!"

"So who did drop it?"

"Someone did?" Spiridon asked in surprise. "I see." He had stopped demonstrating how he had carried the lathe, and he sat down again in his chair, all attention.

"Was it all right when they picked it up?"

"Now that's what I didn't see. I couldn't say, maybe it was broken then."

"Well, when you set it down, what condition was it in?"

"Oh, then it was all right!"

"But there was a crack in the bedplate?"

"There was no crack," said Spiridon with conviction.

"How could you see it, you blind devil? You *are blind*?"

"Citizen Major, I am blind when it comes to papers, true—but as for things around the place, I see everything. You, for instance, you and the other citizen officers toss your butts away when you walk through the yard, and I rake them up, even off the white snow. Ask the chief."

"So what are you trying to say now, that you set the lathe down and made a special point of inspecting it?"

"Of course, what do you think? After our work we had a smoke, we couldn't get along without that. Then we slapped the lathe."

"You *slapped* it? With what?"

"Well, with our hands, like this, on the side, like a warm horse. One engineer said: 'What a good lathe! My grandfather was a lathe operator—he used to work on one like this.'"

Shikin sighed and took up a clean sheet of paper.

"It's too bad you aren't willing to confess, Yegorov. We shall write a report. It's clear you were the one who broke the lathe. If it hadn't been you, you would have come right out with the name of the one who did it."

He said this with conviction, but inwardly he no longer felt any. He was the master of the situation; he had conducted the interrogation; the janitor had answered willingly and had provided additional details. Nevertheless the whole careful build-up had been to no purpose: his long silence, the photograph, the play of his voice, and the rapid conversation about the lathe had all been wasted. Since this redheaded prisoner, whose face still wore an obliging smile, whose shoulders were still hunched forward, had not given in right away, there was no chance that he would give in now.

When Spiridon had mentioned there being a General Yegorov, he had already guessed that he had not been called in because of any German tricks, that the photograph was a blind, that the "protector" was bluffing, and that the lathe was the reason he was there. It would have been surprising if he hadn't been questioned about it, since the ten other zeks had been shaken like pear trees all week. With his lifelong habit of deceiving the authorities, he entered easily into the bitter game. But this pointless fencing grated on him. He was distressed because he had again not received his letter. Also, although he was sitting warm and dry in Shikin's office, his work in the yard was not getting done, but was piling up for the next day.

So time passed, and the bell ending the lunch break had rung long ago, and Shikin had written down his questions and, to the best of his ability, distorted Spiridon's answers, and had instructed Spiridon to sign, as stipulated in Clause 95, for giving false testimony.

Just then there was a precise knock at the door.

Shikin got rid of Yegorov, whose muddle-headedness had bored him, and admitted the snaky, businesslike Siromakha, who always got the main points across in the shortest way.

Siromakha entered with soft, swift steps. The astounding news he brought, added to his pre-eminence among the sharashka informers, made him the major's equal. He shut the door behind him and, without giving Shikin time to lock it, stepped back dramatically. He was acting.

Distinctly, but so softly that he could not possibly be heard through the door, he reported, "Doronin is going around showing a money order for 147 rubles. Lyubimichev, Kagan and five others have been caught. They got together and caught them in the yard. Is Doronin yours?"

Shikin put his finger in his collar and pulled it, to give his neck more room. His eyes looked as if they'd been squeezed from their sockets. His thick neck turned brown. He jumped for the phone. His face, always so superior and self-satisfied, looked insane.

Bounding softly across the room, Siromakha headed Shikin off before he could pick up the telephone.

"Comrade Major!" he reminded him. As a prisoner he did not dare call him "comrade," but he had to say it as a friend. "Not directly! Don't let him prepare himself!"

It was an elementary prison rule, but Shikin had to be reminded of it.

Stepping back as adroitly as if he could see the furniture behind him, Siromakha retreated to the door. He did not take his eyes off the major.

Shikin drank some water.

"May I go, Comrade Major?" Siromakha asked perfunctorily. "Whenever I find out more, I'll be back—this evening or in the morning."

Reason was slowly returning to Shikin's eyes; they looked almost normal again.

"Nine grams of lead for him, the viper!" his words erupted with a hiss. "I'll fix that!"

Siromakha left silently, as if he were leaving a sickroom. He had done what was expected of him, according to his own convictions, and he was in no hurry to ask for a reward.

He was not entirely convinced that Shikin would be a major in the MGB very much longer.

This was an extraordinary case, not only at the Mavrino sharashka but in the entire history of the ministry.

The call to the head of the Vacuum Laboratory was not made by Shikin personally but by the duty officer whose table was in the hallway. Doronin was ordered to report immediately to the office of Colonel of Engineers Yakonov.

Although it was 4 P.M., the overhead light in the Vacuum Laboratory, which was almost always dark, had been on for some time. The head of the lab was absent, and Clara picked up the phone. Later than usual, she had just come into the laboratory for her duty period—she had stopped to speak with Tamara and was still wearing her fur cap and coat. Ruska had not once averted his blazing stare, but she had not looked at him. She had picked up the phone, her hand in a scarlet glove, and had answered it with her eyes downcast. Ruska had stood at his pump, three steps away from her, looking steadily at her face. He was thinking that this evening when everyone else was at dinner he would clasp that dear head in his hands. Clara's closeness made him forget where he was.

She looked up, sensing he was there, and said, "Rostislav Vadimovich! An urgent summons to Anton Nikolayevich."

People could see and hear them; it was impossible for her to speak to him in any other way—but her eyes were no longer the same eyes. A sort of dead dullness veiled them.

Obeying mechanically, without even trying to guess what the unexpected summons could mean, Ruska went out. He could think of nothing but Clara's expression. At the door he glanced back, and he saw that she was watching him leave. She immediately looked away.

Disloyal eyes. She had shifted them as though she were frightened.

What could have happened to her?

Thinking only about her, he went upstairs to the duty officer, without a trace of his ordinary caution, forgetting completely to get ready for unexpected questions, for an attack, as a prisoner's cunning required. The duty officer, blocking Yakonov's door, motioned him toward the rear of the dark alcove, to Major Shikin's office.

Had it not been for Siromakha's advice, and had Shikin called the Vacuum Laboratory himself, Ruska would have expected the worst right away. He would have run to a dozen friends and warned them. Then at the last moment he would somehow have found a chance to talk to Clara and find out what was wrong. And he would have taken away with him either a triumphant faith in her, or else he himself would have been released from his loyalty to her. Now, in front of the "protector's" door, he guessed too late what it was all about. In the presence of the duty officer it was impossible to hesitate, to turn back; it was madness to arouse suspicion if there still was none. Yet Ruska did turn, with the idea of running down the stairs. Just then on the top step the prison duty officer appeared, Lieutenant Zhvakun, the former executioner, who had been summoned by phone.

Ruska went into Shikin's office.

He had taken only a few steps before he recovered control of himself and changed the expression on his face. With the experience gained from being hunted for two years, and with his special gambler's talent, he instantly quelled the storm inside him, forced himself to concentrate on a whole new set of considerations and dangers, and with a look of boyish openness, of carefree readiness, said as he entered, "May I come in? I am at your service, Citizen Major."

Shikin was sitting in an odd position, his chest slumped against his desk, one hand hanging down, dangling like a noose. He stood up, facing Doronin, and brought that noose-like hand upward and struck him in the face.

Then he swung with the other. But Doronin ran back to the door, and stood there, poised to defend himself. Blood seeped from his mouth, and a tangle of blond hair hung down on his forehead.

Unable now to reach his face, the short major stood facing him with bared teeth, splattering saliva.

"You bastard! Selling us out! Say good-bye to life, Judas! We'll shoot you like a dog! We'll shoot you in the cellar."

It had been two and a half years since the Most Humane of Statesmen had abolished capital punishment for all eternity. But neither the major nor his former informer had any illusions: what could be done with an objectionable person except to shoot him?

Ruska glared savagely, blood flowing down his chin; his lip was swelling.

Yet he straightened up and answered brazenly, "As for shooting—we'll have to see about that, Citizen Major. *I'll have you in prison yet!* For four months now, everybody's been laughing at you, and you've been sitting there picking up your wages. They'll tear off your little shoulder boards! As for shooting—we'll have to see about that!"

78

EPICURUS' PUPIL

The ability to carry through some extraordinary act is partly a matter of will, and partly, it seems, given the individual at birth. The hardest act is the one that calls for an effort of

will when the will is unused to effort. It is far easier if the
act is the consequence of years of steady discipline. And
easiest of all is the act which comes as naturally as breathing.

That was how Ruska Doronin had lived under the shadow
of arrest—with simplicity and a childlike smile. He seemed
born to take risks; gambling was in his blood.

But for the upright, prosperous Innokenty, the idea of
living under a false name, of running from hiding place to
hiding place all over the country was unthinkable. It would
not occur to him to try to avoid arrest, if his arrest was
ordered.

He had acted in the heat of strong emotions, and he was
left devastated, exhausted. When he had made that call, he
had never imagined how fear would grow in him, how it
could burn him out. If he had, he could never have called.

Only at Makarygin's party had he found any rest. Suddenly, there, he had felt unburdened, almost ready to enjoy
the dangerous game.

He had spent that night with his wife, forgetting everything.

The fear was all the worse when it came back. Monday
morning it took all his strength to start again, to live, to go
to work, alert for any sign of change in the voices around
him.

He bore himself, as far as he could, with dignity, but
inwardly he felt already destroyed, and all his resistance,
all his will to save himself, was gone.

A little before eleven Innokenty went to see his chief, but
the secretary wouldn't let him go in. She said she had heard
that Volodin's Paris assignment had been held up by the
deputy minister.

This rumor shook him so deeply that he did not have the
strength to ask for an appointment and find out the truth.
Nothing else could be behind this delay! He had been
caught. . . .

Feeling dizzy and drained, he went back to his office; he
had just strength enough to lock the door and remove the
key, to make them think he had gone out.

He felt nauseated. He waited for the knock. It was awful,
heart-breaking, to think that any minute they might come to

arrest him. It crossed his mind that he must not open the door—let them break it down.

Or should he hang himself before they came?

Or jump out the window? From the third floor. Right to the street. Two seconds of flight—and everything would explode . . . and consciousness be shut off.

On his desk lay a fat pile of papers from the accounting office—Innokenty's office expenses. They had to be audited before he left. But it made him sick just to look at them.

The heated office seemed terribly cold.

He was sick at his own mental impotence. Just to sit waiting to die . . .

Innokenty stretched out on the leather sofa and lay there without moving. It was as if he hoped to draw support from the sofa, some sort of reassurance along the whole length of his body.

Was all this really happening? Was it he? Had he really telephoned Dobroumov day before yesterday? How had he dared? Where had he found such desperate courage?

And why had he done it? That stupid woman! *And who are you? How can you prove you're telling the truth?*

He should never have phoned. He was swept with self-pity. To die at thirty.

No, he was not sorry he'd phoned. He had had to. It was as if someone had guided his hand.

No, that wasn't it—he hadn't enough will left to be either sorry or not. He lay there, hardly breathing, hoping only that it would all be over quickly.

No one knocked; no one tried the door. The telephone did not ring.

Innokenty drifted into a light sleep. Then urgent, absurd dreams came to wake him, and he woke feeling unrefreshed, even more oppressed than before, tortured by the sense that they had come to arrest him, or had arrested him already. He had no strength to get up, to shake off his nightmares, even to move. The dreadful, somnolent impotence overcame him again, and he fell at last into a deep sleep. He was wakened by the sounds of the tea break in the corridor, and was unpleasantly aware of the wetness of the sofa where his open mouth had lain against it.

He got up, unlocked his office, and went off to wash. Tea and sandwiches were brought around.

No one came to arrest him. His colleagues greeted him in the corridor as they always did. No one had changed toward him.

Not that that proved anything. None of them would know.

But he drew strength from their familiar faces and voices. He asked the girl for stronger, hotter tea, and drank down two glasses; that made him feel even better.

Still, he was not up to getting in to see his chief and finding out.

To put an end to himself would be the wisest course, simply out of a sense of self-preservation, out of compassion for himself. But he had to know definitely that they were going to arrest him.

And if not?

Suddenly the phone rang. Innokenty began to tremble, and he could hear his heart pounding.

It was Dotty. Her voice was affectionate; she sounded like a wife again. She asked how things were going, and proposed that they go out somewhere that night.

Again Innokenty felt a wave of warmth and gratitude toward her. Whether she was a good wife or a bad wife, she was closer to him than anyone else on earth.

He said nothing about his assignment being put off. He imagined relaxing in the safety of the theater that night—after all, they don't arrest you in an auditorium full of people.

"Well, get tickets for something cheerful," he said.

"An operetta?" asked Dotty. "There's something called *Akulina* playing. Nothing else. At the Red Army Theater there's *The Law of Lycurgus* on the small stage, a premiere, and *The Voice of America* on the big stage. At the Art Theater, *Unforgettable 1919*."

"*The Law of Lycurgus* sounds too attractive. The worst plays always have the best names. Better get tickets for *Akulina*, I guess. Then we'll go on to a restaurant afterward."

"O.K., O.K.!" Dotty laughingly agreed.

He would spend the whole night out so they would not find him at home. They always come at night.

Slowly Innokenty's will was returning. All right, suppose he was under suspicion? What about Shchevronok and Zavarzin? They were directly involved in all the details; suspicion must have fallen on them even sooner. Suspicion is not proof.

Suppose his arrest had been ordered? There was no way of escaping it, no use in hiding. So there was no point in worrying.

He was already strong enough to think reasonably again.

And what if they did arrest him? It might not be today, or even this week. Should he therefore put an end to his life? Or live out his last days as intensely as he could?

Why had he been so terrified? Damn it, he had defended Epicurus so high-mindedly last night—why not put some of his teachings to use? He had said some wise things.

Remembering that he had copied out some Epicurus once, and thinking he ought to look through his old notebook anyway, to see if there was anything he ought to destroy, he began to leaf through it. The first thing he found was: "Inner feelings of satisfaction and dissatisfaction are the highest criteria of good and evil."

Innokenty's distraught mind could not take this in, and he went on: "They fear death only because they fear sufferings beyond the grave."

What nonsense! People fear death because they hate saying good-bye to life. A strained interpretation, Teacher!

Innokenty pictured the park in Athens: Epicurus, seventy years old, dark-skinned, speaking from the marble steps; Innokenty himself, in his ordinary clothes, lounging casually against a pedestal, like an American, listening to him.

"But one should know," he read on, "that there is no immortality. There is no immortality, and therefore death for us is not an evil; it simply does not concern us: while we exist, there is no death, and when death comes, we are gone."

"How good that is," Innokenty thought, settling back. Who was it who had said the same thing just lately? Oh, yes, that fellow who had been a front-line soldier, at the party yesterday.

"Faith in immortality was born of the greed of unsatisfied people who make unwise use of the time that nature has allotted us. But the wise man finds his life span sufficient to complete the full circle of attainable pleasures, and when the time of death comes, he will leave the table of life, satisfied, freeing a place for other guests. For the wise man one human life is sufficient, and a stupid man will not know what to do with eternity."

Beautifully said! The only trouble is: what if it is not nature that pushes you away from the table at the age of seventy, but people with pistols at the age of thirty?

"One must not fear physical suffering. Whoever knows the limit of suffering is immune from fear. Protracted suffering never matters; the suffering which does matter is always brief. The wise man will not lose his spiritual calm even during torture. Memory will recall to him his former feelings and spiritual satisfactions and, in contrast to today's bodily suffering, reestablish the equilibrium of the soul."

Innokenty began to pace grimly around his office.

Yes, that was what he was afraid of: not just death, but that they would torture him.

Epicurus said one can overcome torture. Oh, if he had that strength!

But he did not find it in himself.

And to die? He might not mind dying so much if people knew about it—if they knew why, and if his death could inspire them.

But no, no one would know. No one would see his death. They would shoot him in the cellar like a dog, and his "case" would be filed away somewhere behind a thousand locks.

Yet with these thoughts there came a sort of calm. The cruelest despair seemed to be over.

Before closing his notebook, he read what he had noted down at the very end: "Epicurus influenced his pupils against participating in public life."

Yes, how easy. To philosophize. In gardens . . .

Innokenty threw back his head, just as a bird tilts back its head so that water will flow down its throat.

No! No!

The fretwork hands of the bronze clock pointed to five of four.

It was getting dark outside.

79

THAT'S NOT MY FIELD

At twilight the long black Zim entered the guardhouse gates, which had swung open for it. It picked up speed along the asphalt curves through the Mavrino yard, cleared by Spiridon's broad shovel and now thawed down to the black pavement. It passed Yakonov's Pobeda, parked beside the building, and came to an abrupt stop at the formal stone entrance.

The major general's aide jumped out and quickly opened the back door. Corpulent Foma Oskolupov, in a gray coat that was too small for him and a tall gray astrakhan hat, climbed out and straightened up. His aide opened the first and the second doors into the building, and he proceeded upstairs, preoccupied. On the first landing, beyond two old-fashioned standing lamps, was a cloakroom. The attendant ran out, ready to take the general's coat, but knowing that he would not check it. The general did not check the coat, did not take off his hat, and continued up one side of the divided staircase. Several zeks and some of the minor free employees, passing him on the stairs, hurried out of the way. The general in his astrakhan hat climbed the stairs in a stately manner but—since circumstances demanded it—hurriedly. The aide, who had checked his things at the coatroom, caught up with him.

"Go find Roitman," Oskolupov told him over his shoulder. "Warn him that in half an hour I'm going to visit the new group and check on the results."

On the third-floor landing he did not turn toward Yakonov's office but went in the opposite direction, toward Number Seven. The institute duty officer who saw his disappearing back immediately got on the phone to locate and warn Yakonov.

There was disorganization in Number Seven. One did not have to be a specialist—and Oskolupov was not a specialist—to understand that *nothing was in working order*, that all the systems which had been set up over the course of long months were now disconnected, ripped apart, broken up. The marriage of the clipper with the vocoder had begun by both newlyweds being taken apart by units, by components, almost condenser by condenser. Here and there smoke rose from soldering irons, from cigarettes; one heard the whine of a hand drill, the cursing of men at work, and Mamurin shouting hysterically into the telephone.

But even in that smoke and din, Siromakha immediately noticed the major general. The entrance door was always under his vigilant eye. He threw his soldering iron on the stand and rushed off to warn Mamurin, standing at the phone; then he picked up Mamurin's upholstered chair and took it over to the major general, waiting to be told where to put it. Had it been anyone else, this performance might have seemed mere fawning, but Siromakha lent it the aspect of an honorable service performed by a youth for an elderly, respected person. He stood rigidly, awaiting instructions.

Siromakha was neither an engineer nor a technician, and he was only an electrical assembly worker in Number Seven; but because of his speed, his loyalty, his readiness to work twenty-four hours a day and to listen patiently to all the deliberations and doubts of the officials in charge, he was highly regarded and was allowed to sit in when the heads of Number Seven conferred. He believed that all this would be more useful to him in the long run than his work as an informer, and might provide him with a chance of winning his freedom.

Foma Guryanovich Oskolupov sat down, without taking off his hat and unbuttoning his coat only part way.

The laboratory fell silent. The electric drill stopped drilling. Cigarettes were extinguished and voices stilled. Only Bobynin, not leaving his own back corner, continued giving instructions to the electrical assembly workers in his bass voice; and Pryanchikov, in a state of distraction, continued to walk around the ruined stand of his vocoder with a hot soldering iron in his hand. The rest watched and waited to hear what the boss was going to say.

After his trying telephone conversation—during which he had quarreled with the head of the repair shop who had spoiled the framework panels—Mamurin, exhausted, wiped the sweat from his face and went over to greet the former colleague who was now an inaccessibly high-ranking boss.

Oskolupov extended three fingers to him. Mamurin had reached that pallid, moribund state at which it seems a crime to allow a person to get out of bed. He had suffered much more acutely than his high-ranking colleagues from the blows of the past days: the minister's wrath and the dismantling of the clipper. If the sinews under his skin could have got any stringier, they would have. If human bones could lose weight, his would have. For more than a year Mamurin had lived for the clipper, in the belief that the clipper, like the Little Hunchback Horse in the Russian fairy tale, would carry him out of misfortune. No compensation, such as Pryanchikov's transfer to Number Seven with the vocoder, could make up for the impending catastrophe.

Foma Guryanovich Oskolupov was a capable director, though he had never mastered the knowledge and skills of the field he directed. He had learned long ago that all a leader has to do is bring together the opinions of knowledgeable subordinates and then direct. That was what he was doing now.

He frowned and asked, "Well, what's going on? How are things?"

He was forcing his subordinates to speak up.

A discussion began which was both boring and futile and only took people away from their work. They spoke reluctantly, sighing; if two of them started to say something at the same time, each yielded to the other instantly.

There were two themes: "It is essential" and "It is difficult." "It is essential" was the line adopted by the frantic Markushev, backed by Siromakha. The small, pimply, bustling Markushev tried feverishly day and night to discover a path to glory and be freed ahead of time. He had proposed combining the clipper and the vocoder not because he was convinced it would succeed from an engineering point of view, but because the combination would diminish the individual importance of Bobynin and Pryanchikov and increase his own. And though he himself disliked working for "uncle" —in other words, without any share in the fruits of his labor—he was indignant because his comrades in Number Seven had become so dispirited. In Oskolupov's presence he complained, obliquely, about the listlessness of the engineers.

He was a human being of that common species from which oppressors create others in their own likeness.

Siromakha's face reflected endurance and faith.

With his lemony-limpid face sunk in his weightless palms, Mamurin, for the first time since he had been in charge of Number Seven, was silent.

Khorobrov could hardly hide the gleam of malicious pleasure in his eyes. He, more than anyone else, had objected to Markushev's proposal and had emphasized the difficulties it entailed.

Oskolupov was especially hard on Dyrsin, accusing him of lack of zeal. When Dyrsin was excited or was wounded by some injustice, his voice almost disappeared. Because of this failing he always seemed to be apathetic.

In the midst of the discussion, which was meaningless to Oskolupov, Yakonov came in, and, out of politeness, entered into it. Finally, he called over Markushev, who sat down next to him, and together they began to sketch a new variation of the diagram.

Oskolupov would have preferred to handle the situation by reprimand and recrimination—a technique with which he was familiar and which, during his years of leadership, he had perfected down to the last nuances of intonation. It was what worked best for him. But he saw that at the present time this approach would not help matters.

Whether Oskolupov felt that his contributions to the conversation were unimportant or whether he wished to breathe different, easier air before the fateful month of grace had ended, without listening to Bulatov's final remarks, he rose and somberly went out the door, leaving the entire staff of Number Seven to suffer pangs of conscience over the pain their remissness had caused the section head.

As protocol required, Yakonov rose and projected his heavy body in pursuit of the man in the tall hat who only came up to his shoulder.

In silence, side by side, they proceeded down the hallway. The section head did not like having his chief engineer walking beside him, because of Yakonov's powerful physique and the fact that he was at least a head taller.

Yakonov might have chosen this moment to announce their surprising and unforeseen progress with the encoder, and indeed this would have had its advantages. It would have immediately dissolved the bullish displeasure Oskolu-

)ov had exhibited toward him ever since Abakumov's night-
ime conference.

But he didn't have the drawing. Sologdin's astounding
self-control, evidenced by his being prepared to die rather
han give his drawing away for nothing, had convinced
Yakonov that he should keep his promise and report tonight
to Sevastyanov, by-passing Oskolupov. Oskolupov, of course,
would be enraged, but he would have to calm down quickly.
Victors are not judged, as they say. And Yakonov could tell
him later that he hadn't been sure Sologdin could really
work it out, that it was an experiment.

This simple-minded calculation was not the only one
Yakonov had arrived at. He had seen how gloomy Oskolupov was, how frightened about his fate; and it pleased
Yakonov to leave him in torment for another few days.
Anton Nikolayevich Yakonov felt an engineer's outrage over
the encoder project, as if he had created it himself. Sologdin
had been right in foreseeing that Oskolupov would undoubtedly try to force his way in as co-inventor. And when he did
find out, he wouldn't even look at the drawing of the central
section but would immediately order Sologdin isolated in a
separate room, and would interfere with their letting in
those who were to work with him, and would call in Sologdin and threaten him and give him drastic deadlines, and
would phone from the ministry every two hours to harass
Yakonov, and in the end he would give himself airs and say
that it was thanks only to his supervision that the encoder
worked effectively.

Because all this was nauseatingly familiar to him, Yakonov was quite content to keep silent for the moment. However, on entering his office he did something he never would
have done in the presence of outsiders: he helped Oskolupov
off with his coat.

"What does Gerasimovich do here?" Foma Guryanovich
asked and sat down in Yakonov's armchair, without taking
off his hat.

Yakonov sat down to one side.

"Gerasimovich? Let's see, when did he come from
Streshnevka? October, I guess. Well, since then he made the
TV set for Comrade Stalin."

"Call him in."

Yakonov phoned.

Streshnevka was another of the Moscow sharashkas. Recently, under the leadership of engineer Bobyer, an extremely clever and useful device had been created at Streshnevka—an attachment for an ordinary city telephone. The ingenuity of this apparatus was that it went into action only when the telephone was *not* being used, when it was lying quietly in its cradle. The device was approved and put into production.

The pioneering ideas of the authorities (their ideas being, by definition, pioneering) had now turned to other devices.

The duty officer looked in the door.

"Prisoner Gerasimovich."

"Have him come in," said Yakonov, nodding. He was sitting in a small chair some distance from his desk and almost spilling over it on both sides.

Gerasimovich came in, adjusted his pince-nez, and tripped on the carpet runner. In comparison with the two fat dignitaries he seemed very narrow in the shoulders and very small.

"You summoned me?" he said dryly as he approached, staring at the wall between Oskolupov and Yakonov.

"Uh-huh," Oskolupov replied. "Sit down."

Gerasimovich sat down. He took up half the chair.

"You . . . that . . ." recalled Oskolupov. "You are a specialist in optics, Gerasimovich? Not the ear department, but the eye, is that right?"

"Yes."

"And you . . . that . . ." Oskolupov twisted his tongue as if he were wiping his teeth. "You're well thought of. Aren't you?"

He fell silent. Screwing up one eye, he peered at Gerasimovich with the other.

"Are you familiar with Bobyer's most recent work?"

"I've heard about it."

"Uh-huh. And the fact that we have recommended that Bobyer be freed ahead of time?"

"I didn't know."

"So now you know. How much longer have you?"

"Three years."

"Oh, what a long time!" said Oskolupov as if he were surprised, as if all his prisoners were serving sentences that were counted in months. "Oh, what a long time!"

(Recently, trying to cheer up a newcomer, he had said

"Ten years? Nonsense! People stay in prison for twenty-five.")

He went on: "It wouldn't be bad for you to earn your parole ahead of time, too, would it?"

How strangely the question coincided with the plea Natasha had made yesterday.

Exerting all his self-control, since he refused to show any good humor or make any concessions in talking with the bosses, Gerasimovich grinned ironically.

"How would I do that? I haven't seen any paroles lying around."

Oskolupov rocked back and forth in his chair.

"Ha! Of course, you won't get it by making TV sets! But I'm going to transfer you to Streshnevka in a few days, and I'm going to make you the head of a project. If you can finish it in six months, you'll be home by autumn."

"What kind of work is it, may I ask?"

"Well, there's a lot of work lined up, there for the asking. I'll tell you right out: the assignment comes from Beria himself. There's one idea, for example: to build microphones into park benches. People talk freely in the parks, and one might hear almost anything. But that's not in your professional field?"

"No, not my field."

"Well, there's something for you, too, as it happens. There are two projects; one is fairly important and the other is urgent. And they're both in your field. Isn't that right, Anton Nikolayevich?" Yakonov agreed with a nod. "One of them is a camera that can be used at night. It works on those . . . what are they called? Ultra-red rays. You take a picture of a person at night, on the street, you find out who he's with, and he'll never know as long as he lives. There are already rough versions of it abroad, and all that has to be done is to imitate them creatively. The camera has to be easy to operate. Our agents aren't as smart as you are. And here's the second one. I'm sure you can work it out as quick as you can spit, but we need it badly. All it is is a simple camera, but so tiny it can be installed in the frame of a door. And whenever the door is opened, it automatically takes a picture of whoever goes through. At least it does in the daytime, or when the lights are on. You don't have to worry about its working in the dark. We want to put an apparatus

like that into mass production. Well, how about it? Will
you do it?"

Gerasimovich had turned his thin, dried-up face to the
windows and was not looking at the major general.

In Oskolupov's vocabulary there was no such word as
"mournful." Therefore he could not have named the expression on Gerasimovich's face. Indeed, he did not intend to
name it. He was waiting for a reply.

Here was the answer to Natasha's plea.

Gerasimovich saw her withered face, and her glassy frozen tears.

For the first time in many years, the actual possibility, the
imminence, the warmth of returning home stirred in his
heart.

All he had to do was what Bobyer had done: fix it so that
a few hundred unsuspecting, stupid people were put behind
bars.

Hesitating, embarrassed, Gerasimovich asked, "But
couldn't I stay—with television?"

"You refuse?" Oskolupov asked indignantly. He frowned.
His face easily took on a look of anger. "Why?"

Every law of the cruel land of the zeks told Gerasimovich that it was just as ridiculous to take pity on the thriving,
myopic, unbroken, unwhipped people outside as to refuse to
slaughter a pig for bacon. Those who were free lacked the
immortal soul the zeks had earned in their endless prison
terms. They made stupid and greedy use of the freedom
they were allowed to enjoy. They besmirched themselves
with petty schemes, base acts.

Natasha was his one lifetime companion. Natasha was
waiting for his second term to end. Natasha was on the
threshold of extinction, and when her life flickered out, his,
too, would be over.

"My reasons? Why do you ask? I can't do it. I wouldn't
be able to cope with it," Gerasimovich replied very quietly,
his voice almost inaudible.

Yakonov, inattentive up to this moment, now stared at
Gerasimovich with curiosity. Here evidently was another
case that verged on madness. But the universal law that
"your own shirt is closer to your body" had to prevail this
time, too.

"You've just got out of the habit of doing important
work, that's why you're timid," Oskolupov said, trying to

persuade him. "Who else but you is there? Very well, I'll let you think it over."

Gerasimovich kept silent, his small hand pressed against his forehead.

"But what is there to think over? It's right in your field."

Gerasimovich could have remained silent. He could have bluffed. He could have accepted the assignment and then failed to do it, according to the zek rule. But Gerasimovich stood up. He glared contemptuously at the fat, double-chinned, stupid mug in a general's astrakhan hat.

"No! That's *not* my field!" he said in a clear high voice. "Putting people in prison is not my field! I don't set traps for human beings! It's bad enough that they put *us* in prison. . . ."

80

AT THE FOUNTAINHEAD
OF SCIENCE

In the morning Rubin was still obsessed by the dispute with Sologdin. He thought of new arguments he had failed to marshal the night before. But as the day went on he was lucky enough to become immersed in his great task and the controversy faded from his mind.

He was working on the third floor, in the quiet little Top Secret room. It had heavy curtains at the window and door, an old couch and a worn carpet. The fabrics deadened sound, but there was hardly any sound to disturb him anyway. He was listening to the tapes through earphones, and Smolosidov had been silent the whole day, his heavily furrowed face glaring at Rubin as if he were an enemy and not a comrade engaged in the same work. Rubin in turn paid no attention to Smolosidov, except as a machine for changing the tape cartridges.

Through the earphones Rubin listened over and over again to the fateful conversation, and then to the five tapes of the suspects' voices which had been made for him. Sometimes he trusted his ears; at others, he lost faith in them and turned to the violet tracings on the voice prints. The yards of paper were too long even for the big desk and fell in white streamers to the floor, left and right. From time to time he took up his album of specimen voice prints, some classified by sounds—by phonemes—others by the "basic tone" of various male voices. With a red and blue pencil worn blunt at each end—the act of sharpening a pencil being a task which Rubin had to work up to over a long period—he marked off places on the prints which caught his attention.

Rubin was absorbed. His jet-black eyes were afire. His big, uncombed, black beard fell in tangled tufts, and gray ash from his pipe and cigarettes was scattered over it and on the sleeves of his soiled coveralls—a button was torn off the cuff—on the table, the voice prints, the voice-print album, and the armchair.

He was launched on that mysterious flight of the soul which physiologists have never explained. Forgetting his liver, his hypertension pains, feeling refreshed after the exhausting night, not hungry although he had eaten nothing since the birthday party cookies the night before, Rubin was soaring aloft on the wings of the spirit, a state of being in which one's vision can distinguish single grains in the sand, when memory easily retrieves everything stored in it.

Not once did he ask what time it was. On arriving he had wanted to open the window to make up for having missed his chance of fresh air earlier, but Smolosidov had said, frowning, "You can't; I have a cold," and Rubin had yielded. Not once had he risen from his chair thereafter, throughout the entire day, not even to look out the window to see how the snow had softened and turned gray under the damp west wind. He had not heard Shikin knock or noticed that Smolosidov had refused to admit him. He had seen Roitman come and go as through a mist; although he had not turned around, it had vaguely entered his consciousness. He was unaware that the lunch hour bell had rung, and, after it, the work bell. The zek's instinct, which holds the ritual of mealtime sacred, barely stirred in him when Roitman shook him by the shoulder and indicated an omelet, fruit dumplings with sour cream, and some stewed fruit set out on a separate table. Rubin's nostrils quivered and surprise lengthened his face, but even then his consciousness was not fully engaged. He stared in astonishment at that food fit for the gods, as if trying to understand why it was there, changed seats and began to eat hurriedly, not really tasting what he ate, anxious only to get back to work.

Rubin may not have appreciated to the full what he was eating, but it had cost Roitman far more than if he had paid for it out of his own pocket. He had been on the telephone for two hours, calling first one place and then another, coordinating that lunch: first he had talked with the Special Equipment Section, then with General Bulbanyuk, then with the prison administration, then with the Supply Section and, last, with Lieutenant Colonel Klimentiev. The officials he had talked to had in their turn cleared the matter with the accounting office and with still other officials. The difficulty lay in the fact that Rubin's regular rations were in the "third category," but in view of his particularly important task Roitman was trying to arrange for him to get "first category" meals for several days, and also a special diet. After all the coordinating had been done, the prison authorities began to advance organizational objections: the foods requisitioned weren't in the prison warehouse; they needed a voucher in order to pay the cook extra for preparing a separate menu.

Now Roitman sat opposite Rubin and watched him, not as a master sits, awaiting the fruits of a slave's labor, but with a caressing smile, like that of an admiring child, envying Rubin's inspiration and looking forward to the moment when he could grasp the meaning of the work and thus share in it.

As Rubin ate, an awareness of his surroundings returned, and his face softened. For the first time that day he smiled.

"You shouldn't have fed me, Adam Veniaminovich. '*Satur venter non studet libenter*.' The traveler must cover most of his day's journey before he stops for lunch."

"Come now, you've been working for hours, Lev Grigorich! After all, it's three-fifteen."

"What! I didn't think it was noon yet."

"Lev Grigorich! I'm besieged by curiosity—what have you discovered?"

It was not the command of a superior. He spoke apologetically, as if he were afraid Rubin would refuse to share what he'd found out. In those moments when Roitman bared his soul he could be very nice, despite his unfortunate appearance; his thick lips always parted for breath because of the polyps in his nose.

"Only the beginning! Only the most tentative deductions, Adam Veniaminovich!"

"And what are they?"

"They're open to dispute, but one thing is incontrovertible. The science of phonoscopy, born today, December 26, 1949, does have a rational core."

"Aren't you getting carried away, Lev Grigorich?" Roitman warned. No less than Rubin he desired this to be true, but, trained in the exact sciences, he knew that the specialist in the humanities might let his scientific objectivity get swamped by enthusiasm.

"When have you known me to get carried away?" Rubin asked, close to being offended. He stroked his tangled beard. "Nearly two years of gathering material, all those sound and syllable analyses of Russian speech, our study of voice prints, the classification of voices, of national, group, and individual *speech patterns*, everything Anton Nikolayevich considered an empty waste of time—yes, and which you, too, for that matter, sometimes had doubts about—all that is now bearing real fruit. We ought to get Nerzhin into this, too. What do you say?"

"If the operation develops, why not? But so far we still have to prove our effectiveness and bring off our first assignment."

"Our first assignment! The first assignment is a good half of the entire science! Not so fast."

"But—what do you mean, Lev Grigorich? Don't you really understand how urgently it's needed?"

Oh, how could he help but understand! "Needed" and "urgent" were words which Komsomol member Lev Rubin had been raised on. Those were the supreme slogans of the thirties. They had no steel, no electricity, no bread, no cloth —but they had "needed" and "urgently needed." Blast furnaces were built, and iron smelting plants put into operation. Later, just before the war, comfortably concerned with scholarship, absorbed in the unhurried eighteenth century, Rubin became spoiled. But, of course, "urgently needed" stayed with him, disrupting his efforts to carry any one piece of work through to completion.

Now the scanty daylight was fading. They turned on the overhead light, sat down at the work table, examined the specimen voice prints, and outlined in blue and red pencil the characteristic sounds, the linkings of consonants, the lines of intonation. They did all this together, paying no attention to Smolosidov, while he, who had not once left the room, sat beside the magnetic tape, guarding it like a grim black dog, and looked at the backs of their heads. His heavy, unrelenting stare drove into their skulls like a nail and pressed against their brains. Smolosidov thus deprived them of that elusive factor which was also the essential factor— freedom from constraint: he was a witness to their hesitations; he would still be present when they delivered their enthusiastic report to the chief.

As if by turns, one would incline toward doubt and the other toward conviction; then the doubter would become convinced and his colleague would begin to have doubts. Roitman was restrained by his training in mathematics, but his official position spurred him forward. The disinterested wish to assist at the birth of a genuinely new science acted as a moderating force, but the lessons of the Five-Year Plans urged him on.

They both felt that the sample conversations of the five suspects were all they needed. They did not ask for tapes of the four men picked up at the Arbat Metro Station. The men had been apprehended too late anyway. Nor did they ask to listen to the recorded voices of the other employees of the ministry which Bulbanyuk had promised in case of extreme need. They rejected the hypothesis that the man who had phoned was not one who had access to firsthand information about Dobroumov, but was an outsider who had been asked to make the call.

It was hard enough to cope with the five! They compared the five voices with the criminal's by ear. They compared the five voice prints with the criminal's, line by violet line.

"Just see how much the voice-print analysis gives us!" Rubin pointed out with enthusiasm. "You can hear on the tape that at first the criminal was speaking in a different voice, trying to disguise it. But what change does the voice print show? Only the intensity of the frequencies—the individual speech pattern has not changed in the slightest! That's our main discovery—that there is such a thing as a speech pattern! Even if the criminal kept changing his voice all the time he was speaking, he could not conceal his specific characteristics."

"But we don't so far know much about the limits of voice modification," Roitman objected. "Perhaps in microintonations. The limits are very broad."

It was easy for the ear to be unsure whether a voice was the same one or a different one, but on voice prints the variations in the amplitude-frequency patterns made the difference clear and precise. True, their voice-print machine was unfortunately a crude one. It could discriminate among only a few frequencies, and it indicated amplitude by indecipherable blots. But it had never been intended for such vitally important work.

Of the five under suspicion, Zavarzin and Syagovity could be eliminated without the slightest doubt; that is, if the future science would allow any conclusion at all on the basis of a single conversation. They decided after some hesitation that Petrov could be eliminated also—and indeed Rubin, in his enthusiasm, definitely eliminated Petrov from the beginning. On the other hand, the voices of Volodin and Shchevronok resembled the voice of the criminal in basic tone frequency, had certain phonemes in common with it, such as "o," "r," "l," and "sh," and were similar in individual speech pattern.

Right there, with those similar voices, the science of phonoscopy should have been properly developed and its techniques refined. Only on the basis of such fine differences could a sensitive apparatus eventually be perfected. Rubin and Roitman leaned back in their chairs with the triumph of inventors. They envisioned the system, like fingerprinting, which would someday be adopted: a consolidated audio-library with voice prints of everyone who had at one time or another been under suspicion. Any criminal conversation would be recorded, compared, and the criminal would be caught straight off, like a thief who had left his fingerprints on the safe door.

But then Oskolupov's aide opened the door a crack and warned them that his boss was approaching.

Both men came out of their reveries. Science was science,

but it was necessary now to work out a general conclusion and together defend it to the section head.

As a matter of fact, Roitman believed they had already achieved a good deal. And, aware that the chiefs did not like hypotheses, but did like certainties, he gave in to Rubin and agreed to consider Petrov's voice above suspicion, and to inform the major general firmly that only Shchevronok and Volodin were still under consideration, and that additional recordings should be made of their voices in the next day or so.

"All in all, Lev Grigorich," Roitman said reflectively, "we ought not, you and I, to neglect psychology. We must picture to ourselves the kind of person who would decide to make such a telephone call. What could motivate him? And then compare our conclusion with what we can learn about the actual suspects. We must ask the right questions so that, looking ahead, we phonoscopists will be given not only the suspect's voice and his surname but also concise information about his circumstances, his occupation, his way of life, maybe even his biography. It seems to me that even now I could build some sort of psychological portrait of our criminal."

But Rubin, who had insisted to Kondrashev-Ivanov only the previous night that objective knowledge has no emotional content, had already come to favor one of the two suspects, and he protested.

"I have gone into the psychological considerations, Adam Veniaminovich, and they would have weighed the scales in favor of Volodin's being the criminal. In his conversation with his wife he sounds listless, oppressed, even apathetic, and that would be quite typical of a criminal afraid of being caught. And I admit there's nothing like that at all in Shchevronok's cheerful Sunday prattling. But we would be fine fellows indeed if at the very start we were to base an opinion not on the objective materials of our science but on outside considerations. I have already had quite a little experience working with voice prints, and you must believe me: a good many indefinable signs absolutely convince me that Shchevronok is the criminal. I didn't have time to measure all those indications on the print and *translate them into numerical terms.*" (The philologist never had enough time for that.) "But if I were taken by the throat right now and ordered to name one man and guarantee that he is the criminal, I could name Shchevronok almost without hesitation."

"But we are not going to do so, Lev Grigorich," Roitman objected gently. "Let's work out the measurements, let's translate them into numerical terms—then we will name a name."

"But think how much time that will take! After all, *this is urgent!*"

"But if truth demands it?"

"Well, just look yourself, look here!" And picking up the voice prints again, and dropping more and more ashes on them, Rubin proceeded ardently to prove Shchevronok's guilt.

It was at this occupation that Major General Oskolupov found them, bearing down on them with slow, powerful strides of his short legs. They all knew him well enough to tell from the forward jut of his hat and the twist of his upper lip that he was acutely dissatisfied.

They jumped to their feet; he sat down on one end of the couch and shoved his hands deep in his pockets. "Well!" he barked as though it were an order.

Rubin courteously kept silence, allowing Roitman to report.

During Roitman's report, Oskolupov's saggy-jowled face was absorbed in profound thought, his eyelids drooped sleepily, and he did not even deign to examine the sample prints offered him.

Rubin was troubled during Roitman's report. Despite the precise words of that intelligent man, he felt that the obsession, the inspiration, which had started him on the investigation had been lost from view. Roitman concluded by saying that Shchevronok and Volodin were under suspicion, but that new recordings of both men's voices were required before a final judgment could be made. Then he looked at Rubin and said, "But it seems that Lev Grigorich would like to add or correct something?"

To Rubin, Foma Oskolupov was a dolt, an out-and-out dolt. But he was also a high government official and as such a representative of those progressive forces to which Rubin had dedicated himself. Therefore he spoke out energetically, brandishing the voice prints and the album. He asked the general to understand that although a twofold possibility still existed, such ambiguity was by no means typical of the science of phonoscopy, and that there had simply been too little time to deliver a final judgment, that more recordings were necessary, but if Rubin's own personal guess were in question, then—

The boss no longer looked sleepy. He frowned disdainfully. Without waiting for Rubin to finish, he said, "Old women tell fortunes with beans! What do I need with your 'science'? I have to catch the criminal. Give me a responsible answer. Is the criminal here, on the table, do you have him, is that definite? Are you sure he's not walking around free? Someone else besides these five?"

He peered at them. They stood erect in front of him, arms at their sides. The paper prints streamed down on the floor from Rubin's lowered hands. Behind their backs Smolosidov crouched over the tape recorder like a black dragon.

Rubin crumpled. He had intended to speak in a general sense, not in these terms.

Roitman, more used to the ways of bosses, spoke out—as courageously as he could.

"Yes, Foma Guryanovich. I, to be sure . . . we certainly . . . we are convinced that he is among these five."

What else could he say?

Oskolupov squinted one eye.

"Will you *answer* for what you say?"

"Yes, we . . . yes . . . we will answer."

Oskolupov rose heavily from the couch.

"Listen here, I didn't force you to talk. I'm going now and report to the minister. We'll arrest both the sons-of-bitches!"

He said this in such a way, glaring hostilely, that they might well have taken it to mean that they themselves were the ones who were going to be arrested.

"Wait a minute," Rubin objected. "Give us one day more. Give us the chance to establish complete proof!"

"When the interrogation begins, then you can go ahead and put a microphone on the interrogator's desk and record them for three hours at a time if you feel like it."

"But one of them is not guilty!" Rubin exclaimed.

"What do you mean, not guilty?" Oskolupov asked in astonishment, opening his green eyes wide. "Not guilty of anything at all? The security organizations will find something; they'll sort it all out."

He left without a single good word for the adepts of the new science.

Oskolupov had that style of leadership: to make his subordinates try harder, he never praised them. It was not even his personal style; it descended directly from *Him.*

Still, it was painful.

They sat down again on the chairs where they had recently dreamed of the great future of the new-born science. And they fell silent.

It was as though everything they had so delicately constructed had been trampled on. It was as though phonoscopy wasn't essential in the least. If they could arrest two instead of one, then why not arrest all five and be absolutely sure?

Roitman felt acutely the precariousness of the new group's future, and, recollecting that half the Acoustics Laboratory had been dispersed, the sense he had had last night of the world's cold hostility and his own loneliness returned to him. Rubin, released from the momentum of the work, felt an indirect relief: the speed of Oskolupov's decision proved that all the men would have been arrested without Rubin's complicity and without phonoscopy. So, in fact, he had saved three men.

The passion of dedication which had burned for so many hours was extinguished. He remembered that his liver and his head ached, that his hair was falling out, that his wife was growing old, that he had another five years to serve, and that all this time they kept pressing on and on in a wrong direction. Now they had defamed Yugoslavia.

But neither man spoke his thoughts. They sat there in silence.

Behind them Smolosidov was silent.

Rubin's map of China was pinned up on the wall, the Communist areas colored with a red pencil.

This map was the one thing that cheered him. Despite everything, despite everything, we are going to conquer. . . .

A knock at the door; Roitman was called out to see to it that the free employees of the Acoustics Laboratory showed up to listen to a visiting lecturer. After all, it was Monday, the one day of political indoctrination.

81

NO, NOT YOU

Everyone attending the lecture had been buoyed up by the simple hope of getting out soon. They had all left home at seven or eight in the morning on streetcars, buses, or trains. By now there wasn't the faintest chance of getting back home before 9:30 P.M.

Simochka was more anxious than the others for the lecture to be over, even though she had to stay on as duty officer and wasn't concerned about getting home. Warm waves of fear and joyful expectation in turn swept through her, and her knees were as weak as if she had been drinking champagne. Her Monday rendezvous with Nerzhin would take place in a few hours. She could not let this high and solemn moment of her life happen casually, and that was the reason she had felt unready two days ago. But she had spent yesterday and half of today as if she were on the eve of a great holiday. She had sat with her seamstress, urging her on to finish a new dress, and it had turned out to be very becoming. She had bathed thoroughly, in a tin tub in the Muscovite confinement of her room. She had spent hours putting up her hair at night, and hours unwinding the curlers in the morning; she had preened endlessly in front of the mirror, turning her head this way and that, trying to convince herself that from a certain angle she really was attractive.

She had been supposed to see Nerzhin at three in the afternoon, right after the break, but Gleb was late coming back from lunch, openly flouting the rules (she must speak to him about that today; he had to be careful!), and in the meantime Simochka had been sent off with another group for a long siege of counting and collecting spare parts. She had returned to Acoustics just before six, and again Gleb had not been there, though his desk was piled high with magazines and file folders and the light was on. So she had gone off to the lecture without seeing him, but also without hearing the dreadful news that he had been allowed a visit yesterday with the wife he had not seen for a year.

Thanks to being so small, Simochka easily found a seat in one of the crowded rows where, surrounded by the others, she was invisible. She felt her cheeks getting hotter and hotter as she followed the hands of a large electric clock. She would be alone with Gleb soon after eight. . . .

When the lecture was over and everybody poured out past the coatroom on the second floor, Simochka went along to see her friends off. There were noise and confusion, the men hurrying into their coats and lighting up cigarettes for the road, the girls leaning against the wall, balancing first on one foot and then the other as they pulled on their overshoes. But despite their rush to get away, all the girls found time to examine Simochka's new dress admiringly and discuss every detail of it.

The brown dress had been designed and executed with full understanding of the virtues and drawbacks of her figure; the top, cut like a jacket, was tight around her narrow waist and loosely pleated over the bust. Below the waist, to broaden her hips, the skirt had two flounces, one shiny and one dull, that fluttered as she walked. Her thin arms were almost ethereal in the sheer sleeves, full at the shoulders and snug at the wrists. And at the throat, there was a charming and naïve little invention: a wide strip of the same material was sewn on like a long scarf, and the loose ends were tied in a bow whose graceful loops resembled the wings of a silvery-brown butterfly.

Someone in this milieu might have been made suspicious by Simochka's wearing a brand-new New Year's dress on duty. So she told the girls that after finishing work she was going to a birthday celebration at her uncle's, where there was to be a party with a lot of young people.

Her friends warmly approved the dress and said she was "simply lovely" in it, and wanted to know where she had bought the satin crepe.

At the last moment, Simochka's resolution deserted her, and she put off going back to the lab.

Finally, at two minutes to eight, her heart pounding— though her friends' compliments had helped to give her courage—she entered Acoustics. The prisoners were already turning in their classified materials to be locked up in the steel safe. Beyond the empty space in the middle, which looked abandoned after the transfer of the vocoder, she saw Nerzhin's desk.

He had gone. (Couldn't he have waited?) His light was off, the roll top of his desk had been locked, his classified materials turned in. But one thing was unusual: the middle of his desk was not cleared off, as it generally was when Gleb left for breaks. A dictionary and a big American magazine lay open on it. Perhaps this was a secret signal meaning, "I'm coming back soon."

Roitman's deputy turned over to Simochka the keys to the lab and the seal (the laboratories were sealed every night). Simochka was afraid Roitman might want to see Rubin again, in which case he might drop in on Acoustics at any time. But no, Roitman was right there, with his hat on, pulling on his leather gloves, hurrying his deputy to get ready to go. He was in a dark mood.

"Well, Serafima Vitalyevna, you're in charge," he said to her as he left.

The long clanging of the electric bell resounded through the hallways and rooms of the institute. The prisoners were on their way to dinner. Simochka, her face serious, paced the lab, watching the last of them go. When she wasn't smiling, she looked very severe and rather unattractive—mainly because of her sharp, longish nose.

She was all alone.

Now he could come!

But she walked around the laboratory, wringing her hands. What an awful coincidence! The curtains that always hung over the windows had been taken down to be laundered, and three windows were left defenselessly bare. The whole room—except at the very back—could be seen by anyone hiding in the darkness of the yard. And not far away was the wall surrounding the yard, and directly opposite the window beside which she and Gleb worked stood the watchtower. The sentry there could look right in and see everything.

Should she put out all the lights? The door was locked, so everyone would think the duty officer had gone out.

But what if they tried to force the door or found a key to open it?

Simochka went over to the acoustical booth, not consciously connecting her action with the fact that the sentry couldn't see inside it. At the entrance to this tiny cubicle, she leaned against the heavy, solid door and closed her eyes. She would not go in without him. She wanted him to bring, drag, carry her in himself.

She knew from her friends how it all was supposed to happen, but the picture in her mind was vague. Her nervousness kept mounting, and her cheeks burned hotter and hotter.

What she had guarded for so long had by now become a burden.

Yes! She wished fervently to have a child that she could raise by herself until Gleb was released. It would be a mere five years.

She went over to his comfortable revolving chair and embraced the back of it as if it were a living person.

She glanced out the window, sensing the presence of the watchtower in the dark and atop it, like the black embodiment of everything inimical to love, the sentry with his rifle.

Gleb's firm, swift steps sounded in the hall outside. Simochka fluttered over to her desk, sat down, turned a three-stage amplifier on its side, its tubes exposed, and began to study it, a screw driver in her hand. She could feel the pounding of her heart inside her head.

Nerzhin shut the door quietly, so that the sound would not carry down the silent hallway. Across the space that had housed Pryanchikov's installation, he saw Simochka from a distance, huddling behind her desk like a quail behind a hummock.

"Little quail" was his name for her.

He went up to her quickly, to say what he had to say, to kill her mercifully with one shot.

Simochka looked up at Gleb with shining eyes—and froze instantly. His expression was dark and forbidding.

Until he came in, she had been convinced that the first thing he would do would be to kiss her, and that she would stop him—after all, the windows were uncovered and the sentry on the alert.

But he did not rush to her as she sat behind the desk, and instead it was he who was the first to say, sternly and sadly, "There are no curtains, Simochka. I won't come nearer. How are you?"

He stood there beside his own desk, leaning on it with his hands, looking down at her like a prosecutor. "If nobody comes to disturb us, we have something important to discuss."

"To discuss?"

"Exactly."

He unlocked his desk. The slats of the roll top rattled as he opened it. Without looking at her, he took out various books, magazines, and files—the camouflage she knew so well. He moved quickly and precisely.

Simochka sat motionless, the screw driver in her hand, her eyes fixed on his expressionless face. She decided that Gleb's summons to see Yakonov on Saturday must have borne evil fruit, that he was being harassed, or was to be sent away soon. But if that was it, why didn't he come over and kiss her?

"Something has happened? What has happened?" she asked him in a choking voice.

He sat down, his elbows on an open magazine, his head between his hands, his spread fingers capping his skull. He looked at the girl, straight and hard.

There was dead silence. Not a sound reached them from outside.

They were separated by two desks—two desks lit by four ceiling lamps and two table lamps, and in direct line with the staring sentry atop the watchtower.

The sentry's gaze was like a curtain of barbed wire slowly descending between them.

Gleb said, "Simochka, it would be a terrible thing if I didn't confess something to you."

She waited.

"Somehow I behaved too carelessly. I didn't think it through."

She said nothing.

"Yesterday I—I saw my wife. I was allowed a visit."

A visit?

Simochka sank down in her chair. She became even smaller. The butterfly wings on her dress fell limply on the aluminum amplifier chassis.

"Why didn't you tell me on Saturday?" she said in a cracked voice.

"Come now, Simochka!" Gleb asked, horrified. "Do you really think I would have hidden it from you?"

"And why not?" she thought.

"I only found out yesterday morning. It was unexpected.

We hadn't seen each other for a whole year—as you know. But now we have seen each other again—after our meeting—" His voice sounded tormented, and he understood how hard it was for her to listen. "I—I love only her! You know when I was in the camps she saved my life. And above all she has killed her youth for my sake. You said you would wait for me, but it's impossible. I must go back to her alone. I couldn't bear to cause her . . ."

Nerzhin could have stopped there. The shot he had fired in a voice hoarse with strain had already found its mark. Simochka did not look at him. She collapsed, collapsed utterly; her head fell forward against the tubes and condensers of the amplifier.

Gleb stopped talking. He heard sobs quiet as breathing.

"Simochka, don't cry! Please don't cry, my little quail!" he said to her tenderly, two desks away, without stirring from his place.

She wept almost soundlessly, her bowed head, the straight part in her hair, directly opposite him.

Had he met resistance, wrath, an accusation, he would have answered firmly and gone away relieved. But her defenselessness stabbed his heart with remorse.

"My little quail!" he murmured, leaning forward across the desk. "Please don't cry! Please don't! It's my fault, I've hurt you so much! But what other way is there? What else can I do?"

He, too, was almost moved to tears by the weeping girl he was leaving to suffer alone. But it was totally, totally inconceivable that he might make Nadya weep like that!

His lips and hands were pure after yesterday's visit, and it was unthinkable to go over to Simochka now, to hold her in his arms, to kiss her.

What a blessing that the curtains had been taken down!

He went on and on with his appeals to Simochka to stop crying.

But she went right on.

Finally, he gave up trying to quiet her and lit a cigarette, the last resort of a man who finds himself in an intolerably stupid position.

Inside him the reassuring conviction arose that none of this really mattered, that it would all pass.

He turned away and walked to the window, pressing his face to the glass and looking toward the sentry. Blinded by the yard lights, he could not make out the watchtower, but here and there in the distance beyond gleamed single lights that seemed to dissolve into vague stars still further away and higher, taking up a third of the sky, the reflected, whitish glow of the capital.

He could see it was thawing in the yard below.

Simochka lifted her face.

Gleb turned to her, openly, ready to go to her.

Her tears had left wet trails down her cheeks, and she did not dry them. Her eyes widened, radiant with suffering, and they were beautiful.

She looked at Gleb, a single insistent question in her shining eyes.

But she said nothing.

He felt awkward. He said, "She has given up her whole life to me! Who else could have done that? Are you sure *you* could have?"

"You and she are not divorced?" Simochka asked quietly, distinctly.

Intuitively she had grasped the main point. But he didn't want to admit to her what he'd learned yesterday.

"No."

"Is she beautiful?" Simochka asked, then fell silent. The tears were still undried on her numbed cheeks.

"Yes, to me, yes . . ."

Simochka sighed. She nodded silently to herself, seeing gleaming spots in the mirror-like surfaces of the radio tubes.

"Well, if she's beautiful, she isn't going to wait for you," she declared in a clear sad voice.

That woman—who turned out not to be a ghost, not just an empty name—why had she insisted on the visit? What insatiable greed made her reach out for someone who could never belong to her?

Simochka was unable to concede to that invisible woman any of a wife's prerogatives. For a short while, once upon a time, she had lived with Gleb, but that was eight years ago. Since then, Gleb had fought in the war, had been in prison, and she, of course, must have lived with other men. No beautiful young woman without children would wait for eight years. And after all, neither at yesterday's visit nor after a year nor after two years could he belong to her. But he could belong to Simochka. Simochka could have become his wife today!

"She isn't going to wait for you," Simochka repeated.

Her prediction stung him.

"She has already waited for eight years," he objected. But his analytical mind forced him to add: "Of course, the last years will be more difficult."

"She isn't going to wait for you," Simochka reiterated in a whisper. With the back of her hand she wiped away the drying tears.

Nerzhin shrugged. Looking out the window at the scattered lights, he answered, "Well, so she won't! Suppose she doesn't? Whatever happens I don't want her to have any reason to reproach me."

He put out his cigarette.

Simochka sighed deeply again.

She was no longer crying. Nor did she feel any desire to go on living.

Caught up in his train of thought, Nerzhin went on, "Simochka, I don't consider myself a good person. When I think of the things I—like everyone else—did at the front in Germany, I realize I am not a good man. And now with you . . . But this is how I learned to behave in so-called normal life. I had no idea what good and evil were, and whatever was allowed seemed fine to me. But the lower I sink into this inhumanly cruel world, the more I respond to those who, even in such a world, speak to my conscience. She won't wait for me? So be it! So be it! Let me die uselessly in the Krasnoyarsk taiga. But if you know when you die that you haven't been a complete bastard, that's at least some satisfaction."

He had happened onto one of his favorite lines of thought. He could have pursued it a long time, especially since there was nothing else to say.

But she was scarcely listening to his sermon. It seemed to her he was still talking only about himself. But what would happen to her? With horror, she saw herself going home, mumbling something to her nagging mother, throwing herself on her bed—her bed, where for months she had gone to sleep each night thinking of him. What humiliating shame! And to think how she had prepared for this evening, how she had bathed and perfumed herself!

But if a prison visit, under surveillance and lasting a half-hour, counted more than their sitting next to each other for months, what could she do?

The conversation ended. Everything had happened so suddenly, without warning, and there was no way to soften the shock of it. She had nothing to hope for. All she could do was go into the booth, cry some more, and then pull herself together.

But she hadn't the strength to send him away or to leave herself. This was the last time they would be linked to one another, even by a thread as thin as a spider web.

Nerzhin stopped talking when he saw she was not listening, that she had no need for his exalted explanations.

They sat for a while in silence.

Then Nerzhin began to feel annoyed at their sitting there, saying nothing.

For many years now, he had lived among men who, when they had to have something out, got it over with quickly. Once everything had been said and the subject exhausted, why should they just sit there not speaking? Senseless female stubbornness! So that she wouldn't notice, he glanced at the wall clock without moving his head. It was only twenty-five minutes to nine.

But it would be unspeakably insensitive to get up and go for a walk for the remainder of the break. Somehow he had to sit there until the bell rang for the prison check.

Who would be on duty this evening? Shusterman, he thought. And tomorrow morning the junior lieutenant.

Simochka sat, bending forward over her amplifier, senselessly removing tube after tube from its socket, jiggling it in her hands, then putting it back in place.

She had understood nothing about this amplifier before, and right now she understood even less.

However, Nerzhin's active mind needed to be busy, to be engaged in some kind of forward motion. Every morning he noted the radio programs for the day on a narrow strip of paper he slipped under the inkwell. Looking down now, he read:

20:30—Rs.s and b. (Obkh)

That meant Russian songs and ballads performed by Obukhova.

What a rare event! And at a time of day when there wouldn't be any songs about the Father and Leader or the Simple Man.

On Nerzhin's left, in reach, was a radio with a station

selector limited to the three Moscow programs, a gift from Valentulya. Should he turn it on? The concert had already started. By the end of the century, Obukhova would be remembered as Chaliapin is today. And we are her contemporaries. Nerzhin glanced at Simochka and with a furtive movement turned on the set, adjusting it to the lowest volume.

As soon as the tubes warmed up, the music of stringed instruments sounded, and then the low passionate voice of Obukhova flowed into the quiet room:

> "No, it's not you whom I love so passionately,
> Not for me the radiance of your beauty. . . ."

It had to be that song—as though on purpose! Nerzhin fumbled for the knob, trying to turn off the set without being observed. Simochka trembled and stared at the radio in astonishment.

> ". . . And youth,
> And youth,
> My wasted youth!"

Obukhova's inimitable low notes quavered ardently.

"Don't turn it off," Simochka suddenly said. "Make it louder."

Obukhova sang those "you-ou-ou-ou-th's" with a long, sustained modulation. Then her voice broke off and there was a short burst of despair from the strings. Then she sang out again, in mournful three-quarter time:

> "When at times I look upon you . . ."

Nerzhin would not have turned up the volume for anything, but he had not been quick enough in turning it off. How pathetically it had happened! By what law of probability had these particular words come over the radio just then?

Simochka rested her hands on the amplifier, and looking at the radio, began to weep again, easily, abundantly, neither sobbing nor trembling.

Only when the song came to an end did Nerzhin increase the volume. But the next one was no better:

> "You will forget me quickly. . . ."

And Simochka wept.

Nerzhin was being punished: now he had to hear Obukhova sing all the reproaches Simochka had not expressed.

When that song was over, the fateful, mysterious voice came back one more, returning to the same open wound:

> "When you say farewell to me,
> Tie my shawl around me tight."

"Forgive me," said Gleb, shaken.

"I'll be all right," Simochka said, smiling wanly. But her weeping continued.

Strangely, the longer Obukhova sang, the more relief they both felt. Ten minutes before, they had been so far apart they could not even have found the will to say good-bye. Now someone gentle and refreshing was with them, had reached them.

At that moment, Simochka was sitting in such a way, with the light shining on her, that—a woman's looks being unpredictable—she seemed genuinely attractive.

Nine out of ten men would have ridiculed Nerzhin for his renunciation—after so many years of deprivation. Who would have compelled him to marry her afterward? What was to stop him from seducing her right now?

But he was happy he had acted as he had. He was moved . . . as if it were someone else who had made the great decision.

Obukhova kept on singing, tormenting the heart:

> "All is unpleasant, all is repulsive,
> I keep on suffering for him. . . ."

Ah, there was no law of probability involved! It was simply that all songs—a thousand years ago, a hundred years ago, or three hundred years in the future—were, and would be, about one and the same thing. Parting requires songs; when you meet, there are better things to do!

Nerzhin got up, walked over to Simochka, and without giving the sentry a thought, took her head in his hands, bent down, and kissed her forehead.

The minute hand on the wall clock jumped forward one more notch.

"Simochka, darling! Go wash your face. They'll all be here any time now for the prisoner check."

She gave a start, looked at her watch, understood. Then she raised her light, narrow brows, as if at just that moment she had finally realized what had happened during the evening—and obediently, sadly, she went over to the sink in the corner.

Once again Nerzhin pressed his forehead against the glass and peered out into the blackness of the night. And, as often happens when one gazes long and hard at widely scattered lights in the night sky, and thinks his own thoughts, the lights he saw were no longer the lights of the Moscow suburbs. He forgot what they were, and they took on other meanings and other forms.

82

ABANDON HOPE, ALL YE
WHO ENTER HERE

The day had gone well. Though Innokenty still felt some anxiety—which he knew would get worse at night—he clung to the equilibrium he had reached after midday. But he felt he had to hide in the theater this evening, so as to stop being afraid of every ring at the door.

Then the telephone rang. It was shortly before they were to leave for the theater, and Dotty, flushed and lovely, was coming out of the bathroom in a rubber bath cap, fluffy robe, and slippers.

Innokenty stood there staring warily at the telephone like a dog at a hedgehog. Then he said, "Dotty, get the phone! I'm not here and you don't know when I'll be back. The hell with them, they'll spoil the evening."

Holding her robe closed with one hand, Dotty went to the phone.

"Hello? . . . He's not home. . . . Who? Who?" And suddenly her expression became friendly. "Hello, Comrade General! . . . Yes, I'll find out." She covered the mouthpiece and said, "It's the general. He sounds in a good mood."

Innokenty was seized with doubt. The general calling personally at night and in a good mood . . .

His wife noticed his hesitation. "Just a moment—I heard the door open and maybe it's he. Yes, it is! Ini! Don't take your coat off, come quickly, the general is on the phone."

Even though Dotnara had never studied to be an actress, as her sister Dinera had, she was a natural actress in real life. No matter how stubbornly suspicious the person at the other end of the line might have been, Dotnara's voice would have made him see Innokenty pausing at the door, wondering whether to take off his overshoes, then crossing the carpet and picking up the phone.

The general's voice was benevolent. He reported that Innokenty's assignment had just been finally approved; he would fly to Paris on Wednesday; tomorrow he would have to delegate his official duties; and right now he must come for half an hour to coordinate certain details. A car had already been sent for him.

Innokenty hung up the phone. He breathed in deeply, deliberately, contentedly, and when he let out his breath, it was as if he had been emptied of his burden of doubt and fear.

"Think of it, Dotty, I'm flying on Wednesday! And right now I'm—"

But Dotty had put her ear to the receiver and had already heard everything.

"What do you think?" she asked, tilting her head to one side. "Those 'certain details'—am I one of them?"

"Perhaps . . ."

"But what have you said about me?" She pouted. "Would Ini really go to Paris without his little nanny goat? His little nanny goat wants to go very much."

"Of course, you'll go, but not right away. First I'll introduce myself, get acquainted with things, get settled—"

"But little nanny goat wants to go right now!"

Innokenty smiled and squeezed her shoulders.

"Well, I'll try. Nothing has been said about it yet, and I'll see what can be worked out. But in the meantime don't hurry getting dressed. We won't make the first act—we don't have to see all of *Akulina* anyway, do we? We might make the second. I'll give you a ring from the ministry."

He had hardly got into his uniform when the driver rang at the apartment. It was not Victor, who usually drove him, nor was it Kostya. This driver was thin, quick-moving, with a pleasant, cultivated face. He was cheerful as he descended the staircase, walking close to Innokenty, twirling the ignition key on a chain.

"I don't seem to remember you," said Innokenty, buttoning his overcoat as they went.

"But I can even remember your stairway. I've been to get you twice." The driver's smile was at once candid and mischievous. He was the sort of lively fellow it would be pleasant to have driving one's car.

They drove off, and Innokenty settled himself in the rear seat. Twice the driver tried to joke with him over his shoulder, but he was not listening. Then suddenly the car turned sharply toward the curb and stopped tight up against it. A young man wearing a soft hat and an overcoat pinched in at the waist was standing on the sidewalk with his finger raised.

"It's our mechanic from the garage," the amiable chauffeur explained, and he started to open the right front door for the man. But the door refused to open. The lock seemed to be stuck.

The chauffeur cursed mildly and asked, "Comrade Counselor, could he possibly ride in back with you? He's my boss —I'm in a spot."

"Yes, of course," Innokenty agreed readily, moving over. He was in a state of elation; he saw himself receiving his travel documents and his visa, leaving danger behind.

The mechanic, a long cigarette in the corner of his mouth, bent down and got into the car, and in a half-restrained, half-familiar manner asked, "You don't mind?" and he flopped down beside Innokenty.

The automobile surged forward.

For a moment Innokenty squirmed with contempt, thinking "Boor!" but he soon retreated into his own thoughts and paid little attention to where they were going.

Puffing on his cigarette, the mechanic had already half-filled the car with smoke.

"You might at least open the window!" Innokenty said to him, raising an eyebrow.

But the mechanic did not understand irony and did not open the window. Instead, slouching in the seat, he pulled a sheet of paper from his inside pocket, unfolded it, and handed it to Innokenty.

"Here, Comrade Chief, read this for me. I'll put some light on it for you."

The car turned up a steep, dark street, which might have

been Pushechnaya. The mechanic had turned on a pocket flashlight, and its beam lit the sheet of green paper. Innokenty shrugged, took the paper with a feeling of disgust, and began to read it carelessly, almost to himself:

"I, Deputy Prosecutor General of the U.S.S.R., confirm—"

He was still, as before, in the world of his own thoughts, and he could not understand what was the matter with the mechanic. Was he illiterate or couldn't he make out the meaning of the paper, or was he drunk and eager for a soulful conversation?

"—the warrant for the arrest—" he read, still not realizing what he was reading—"of Volodin, Innokenty Artemyevich, born 1919—"

And only then was he pierced, as by a single long needle, through the entire length of his body. He felt he had suddenly been drenched in burning pitch. He opened his mouth, but no sound came. His hands, still holding the green sheet, fell to his lap, and the "mechanic" grabbed his shoulder near the back of his neck and shouted, "All right, take it easy, take it easy! Don't move or I'll kill you right here!"

He blinded Innokenty with the flashlight and blew cigarette smoke in his face.

And though Innokenty had just read that he was under arrest, and though it meant the destruction of his life, for that brief moment what was unbearable were the insolence, the clawlike fingers, the smoke, and the light in his face.

"Let go of me!" he cried, trying with faltering fingers to break the grip on his shoulder. By now his mind had grasped that the warrant for his arrest was genuine, but it still seemed to him that an unfortunate set of circumstances had landed him in this car, setting down this "mechanic" beside him, and that what he must do was escape and get to his chief in the ministry and that the arrest would then be called off.

Trembling, he jerked at the handle of the left door, but that door wouldn't open either. Its lock, too, was stuck.

"Driver!" he shouted angrily. "Answer me! What kind of provocation is this?"

"I serve the Soviet Union, Counselor!" the driver snapped aggressively over his shoulder.

Obeying traffic rules, the car went all the way around brightly lit Lubyanka Square, as though making a farewell circle to give Innokenty a last glimpse not only of the world he was leaving but also of the Old and the New Lubyankas, five stories high, where he was destined to end his life.

Files of automobiles stopped and started up at the traffic lights. Trolleybuses swayed from side to side. Buses honked. People went by in dense crowds, oblivious of the victim being taken to his doom under their very eyes.

A red flag, brightly lit by a concealed searchlight, could be seen fluttering through a gap in the pillared turret on top of the Old Lubyanka building. Two half-recumbent stone naiads gazed down contemptuously on the tiny citizens below.

The car passed the façade of the world-famous building and turned into Bolshaya Lubyanskaya Street.

"Let go of me!" Innokenty said, trying to pull away from the "mechanic's" grip.

Black iron gates opened the instant the car approached and closed as soon as it had passed through.

Beneath a black archway the car moved silently into a courtyard.

Once the car entered the archway, the "mechanic's" hold relaxed. In the courtyard he let go of Innokenty entirely. Getting out the door on his side, he said in a businesslike manner, "All right, let's get out!"

It was clear now that he was altogether sober.

The driver got out also; the lock on his door was evidently working now.

"Get out! Hands behind your back!" he ordered. Who would have recognized the recent jester in that icy command?

Innokenty climbed out of the car he had been trapped in through the right-hand door, straightened up and obeyed, although he could not understand why he was obeying. He put his hands behind his back.

They had treated him harshly, but being arrested was by no means as fearsome as he had imagined it would be while waiting for it. There was even a feeling of relief. There was nothing more to fear, nothing more to fight against, no more need to pretend. He had the numbing and pleasant relief which takes possession of the body of a wounded soldier.

Innokenty looked around the little courtyard, unevenly lit by one or two lamps and by an occasional lighted window. The courtyard was the bottom of a well, walled in by the buildings rising around it.

"Don't look around!" shouted the driver. "March!"

They proceeded in file, Innokenty in the middle, past impassive men in MGB uniforms, through a low arch, down some steps into another small court—roofed and dark—and then turned left. The driver opened a rather elegant-looking door, like the door to an eminent doctor's waiting room.

It led into a small, tidy hallway flooded with electric light. Its floor was freshly painted and scrubbed clean, and a carpet ran the full length.

The driver began to click his tongue oddly, as if he were calling a dog. But there was no dog to be seen.

The hall ended at a glass door with faded curtains on the other side. The glass was reinforced with diagonal grating like the fences near railroad stations. On the door, instead of a doctor's name plate, hung the sign: RECEPTION OF ARRESTED PERSONS.

They turned the knob of an ancient doorbell. A moment later a long-faced guard, with sky-blue shoulder boards and white sergeant's stripes, peered out impassively from behind the curtain and opened the door. The driver took the green warrant from the mechanic and shoved it at the guard. The latter glanced at it with a bored look, like a drowsy pharmacist reading a prescription, and the two went inside, shutting the door behind them.

Innokenty and the mechanic stood in front of the closed door in profound silence.

The sign, RECEPTION OF ARRESTED PERSONS, was the sort of sign that might have said MORTUARY—and the meaning was the same. And Innokenty did not even have the spirit to challenge the insolent fellow in the pinched-in coat who had played out the comedy with him. Perhaps he should have protested, shouted, demanded justice. But he had forgotten even that he had put his hands behind his back and that he still held them there. His mind had stopped, and he stared, hypnotized, at the sign: RECEPTION OF ARRESTED PERSONS.

The lock in the door turned softly. The long-faced guard called to them to enter and went on ahead of them, making the same dog-calling clicking sound with his tongue.

But there were no dogs here either.

This hallway was also brightly lit and hospital-clean.

There were two doors, painted olive. The sergeant opened one and said, "Go in."

Innokenty went in. He hardly had time to look around

and see that the room was windowless and contained only a large rough table and a pair of stools, when the driver came up beside him and the mechanic seized him from behind and, while they held him, deftly searched his pockets.

"What kind of gangsterism is this?" Innokenty cried out weakly. "Who gave you the right?" He tried feebly to fight back, but the awareness that it wasn't gangsterism at all and that the two men were performing their assigned duty drained his strength and robbed his voice of conviction.

They took his gold watch and pulled from his pockets two notebooks, a gold fountain pen, and a handkerchief. He saw in their hands the narrow silver shoulder boards of the diplomatic service, and he could not realize that they were his own. The crude embraces continued. The mechanic handed him his handkerchief.

"Take it."

"After you've had your dirty hands on it?" Innokenty cried out shrilly and drew back.

The handkerchief fell to the floor.

"You'll get a receipt for the valuables," said the driver, and both hurried out of the room.

The long-faced sergeant, on the contrary, was in no hurry. Looking at the floor, he advised, "I'd pick up the handkerchief."

But Innokenty did not bend down to get it.

"What have they done? They've torn off my shoulder boards!" He was in a rage. Only at that moment, reaching in under his overcoat, had he realized what had happened.

"Hands behind your back," said the sergeant, bored. "Move along!"

And he clicked his tongue.

The corridor curved and opened into another, flanked on both sides by narrow olive-colored doors side by side. Each door had an oval number plate. As they came around the turn, a worn, elderly woman in a military skirt and field shirt, wearing those sky-blue shoulder boards and white sergeant's stripes, was looking through the peephole in one of the doors. At their approach she calmly let drop the pivoted lid that covered the peephole and looked at Innokenty as if he had passed her a hundred times that day and there was nothing surprising in his going by once again. Her features were morose. She put a long key in the steel lock on the door marked "8," shoved open the door, and motioned to him.

"Go in."

Innokenty went through the doorway. Before he could turn around and ask for an explanation, the door was shut behind him and locked.

So this was where he was destined to live now! One day? A month? Years? It was impossible to call this place a room, or even a cell, because, as we know from books, a cell must have a window even if it's very small, and it must have space for pacing back and forth. Here it was not only impossible to walk around or lie down, but one hardly had room to sit. A little table and a stool occupied almost the entire floor space. Sitting on the stool, it was impossible to stretch out one's legs.

There was nothing else in the cubicle. Above the chest-high, oily, olive paneling, the walls and ceiling were bright white, lit dazzlingly by a two-hundred-watt bulb hanging from the ceiling in a wire cage.

Innokenty sat down. Twenty minutes ago he had been picturing how he would arrive in Paris and take up his impressive new post. Twenty minutes ago his past life had appeared to him as a single harmonious whole, every event evenly illuminated by the light of other events, all of them well ordered and linked up by brilliant bursts of success. But those twenty minutes had passed, and here in this narrow little trap his past life seemed to him, just as convincingly, a clutter of mistakes, a black heap of refuse.

No sound came from the corridor, except that once or twice a door opened and shut somewhere nearby. Once every minute the lid of the peephole was lifted and a single, searching eye observed Innokenty through the glass. The door was about three inches thick, and the peephole was a cone opening into the cubicle. There was nowhere for the prisoner inside to hide from the guard looking in.

Innokenty began to feel stifled and hot. He took off his warm winter coat, sadly observing the torn threads where the shoulder boards had been ripped from his uniform. There was no nail in the wall, nor any ledge, so he put his coat and cap on the little table.

Strangely enough, now that his life had been struck by the thunderbolt, Innokenty was not conscious of any paralyzing fear. In fact, his mind had begun to work again, focusing on the mistakes he had made.

Why hadn't he read the entire warrant? Had it been legally drawn up? Was there an official stamp on it? Was it signed by a prosecutor? Yes, the prosecutor's signature had been right at the top. On what date had it been signed? What was the charge? Had the general known of it when he telephoned? Of course, he must have known. Did that mean the phone call was part of the trick? And why that strange performance with the "driver" and the "mechanic"?

He felt something small and hard in one of his pockets and took it out. It was a slender pencil that had fallen out of his notebook. Innokenty was delighted to find it. It might be very useful. What sloppy work! Even in the Lubyanka they were unprofessional! They didn't know how to carry out a search! After considering the best place to hide the pencil, Innokenty broke it in two, and shoved the halves into his shoes, under the arches of his feet.

Oh, what a blunder not to have read the charge against him! Perhaps his arrest had nothing to do with that ill-fated phone call. Perhaps it was a mistake, a coincidence. How ought he to act?

Only a short time had passed, but he had heard more than once the whine of some sort of machine behind the wall opposite the door. The machine would start up, run, then stop. Innokenty became obsessed by trying to figure out what kind of machine it was. This was a prison, not a factory. Why would they have a machine? To a person of the forties, who had heard a lot of talk about mechanical means of destroying people, the idea of a machine immediately suggested something very horrible. The thought crossed Innokenty's mind—absurd, but at the same time striking him as somehow probable—that what he was hearing was a machine for grinding up the bones of prisoners who had already been killed. He became terrified.

At the same time another thought stung him deeply: that it had been a dreadful oversight, an awful mistake, not only to have failed to read the warrant to the end, but, worse, to have neglected to protest—no, insist—that he was innocent. He had submitted to arrest so spinelessly that they must have been convinced of his guilt! How had that happened? How could he possibly have let them take him without declaring his innocence? It must have seemed obvious to them that he had expected to be arrested, that he had been prepared for it!

He was stunned by this fatal omission. His first thought was to jump up, beat the door with his fists, kick it, and shout at the top of his lungs that he was innocent, that they must open the door. But then he was overcome by another, more sober thought: that such behavior would not surprise anyone here, that many others before him had hammered on the door and shouted like that, and that his silence in the first minutes had already spoiled his case.

Oh, how could he have let himself fall into their hands so easily? With no sign of resistance and without a sound a highly placed diplomat had let himself be led off from his own apartment, from the streets of Moscow, and locked up in this torture chamber.

There was no escape. From here there was no escape.

Maybe his chief was waiting for him at the ministry after all. How could he get to him—even under escort? How could he clear things up?

No. Things weren't clearing up, they were getting more complicated, more mixed up.

The machine on the other side of the wall whined again and then stopped.

Innokenty's eyes, aching from the light which was so much too bright for the high, narrow room only four cubic yards in size, had been resting for some time on the single dark area in the ceiling. This small grilled square was evidently an air vent, although it was not clear where it led.

Suddenly it seemed obvious to him that it was not an air vent at all, but that poison gas was slowly seeping through it, produced perhaps by that whining machine, and that the gas had been coming in from the moment the door had closed on him, and that such a remote, sealed-off cubicle, its door tightly fitted to the sill, could be intended for nothing else.

That was why they kept looking at him through the peephole: to see whether he was still conscious or whether he had already succumbed.

No wonder his thoughts were confused! He was losing consciousness! That was why he was short of breath! That was why there was such a pounding in his head!

Gas was pouring in—colorless, odorless.

Terror, pure animal terror, the terror that drives both predators and prey in panicked flight from a forest fire, seized Innokenty, and, heedless of all other thoughts and calculations, he began beating the door with his fists, kicking it, and calling to anyone: "Open up, open up! I'm suffocating! Air!"

Here was another reason why the peephole had been made in the form of a cone—so that a battering fist could not reach it and break the glass.

A wild, unwinking eye, pressed against the tiny hole on the other side, watched the demise of Innokenty with malicious pleasure.

What a sight: the disembodied eye, the eye without a face, the eye containing all expression in itself, staring in on your death!

There was no way out.

Innokenty slumped down on the stool.

The gas was choking him.

83

KEEP FOREVER

Suddenly and, though it had shut with a crash, in absolute silence, the door opened.

The long-faced guard entered through the narrow doorway. Once inside, he asked in a soft, menacing voice, "Why are you banging?"

Innokenty felt relieved. If the guard was not afraid to come in, it meant there was no gas yet.

"I feel sick," he said, feeling his assurance ebb. "Give me some water."

"Remember this—you mustn't bang for any reason," the guard warned him sternly. "Otherwise you will be punished."

"But if I feel sick? If I have to call someone?"

"And don't shout. If you need to call someone," the guard explained with the same dour dispassion, "wait till the peephole opens and hold up your finger."

He backed out the door and locked it.

The machine behind the wall ran for a while and then stopped.

The door opened, this time noisily. Innokenty began to

understand that the guards were trained to open the door either quietly or with a lot of noise, as the occasion required.

The guard handed Innokenty a cup of water.

"Listen," Innokenty said as he took the cup. "I feel sick. I have to lie down."

"That's not allowed in a 'box.'"

"Where? In a what?" He wanted to talk with someone, even with this wooden-faced guard.

But the guard had already stepped back outside and closed the door.

"Listen, call the head of the prison! Why was I arrested?" Only at that moment had Innokenty remembered to ask.

The lock clicked.

He had said "in a 'box.'" Apparently they used the English word "box"—and it was an exact description of the tiny cell.

Innokenty drank a little water, and he wanted more to drink right away. There were about ten ounces in the cup, which was of green enamel and had a curious decoration on it: a cat wearing glasses pretended to be reading a book, but out of the corner of its eye it was watching a little bird hopping boldly near him.

The decoration had, of course, not been chosen intentionally for the Lubyanka. But how appropriate! The little book was the written law, and the tiny swaggering sparrow was Innokenty—yesterday.

He even smiled, and suddenly his own wry smile made him realize the whole abysmal catastrophe. Yet his smile also held a strange kind of joy—the joy of feeling a throb of life inside himself.

He would never have believed that anyone could smile during his first half-hour in the Lubyanka.

(Shchevronok in the "box" next to his was worse off—he could not have smiled at the cat at this moment.)

Moving the overcoat on the little table, Innokenty put the cup next to it.

The lock rattled. The door opened. A lieutenant came in with a paper in his hand. Behind him appeared the morose face of the sergeant.

In his gray diplomatic uniform, embroidered with gold palms, Innokenty rose to meet him.

"Look here, Lieutenant," he said in a familiar manner,

"what's all this about? What kind of a misunderstanding is this? Let me see that warrant. I haven't even read it."

"Last name?" the lieutenant asked tonelessly, staring glassy-eyed at Innokenty.

"Volodin," he replied readily, more than willing to clarify the situation.

"First name and patronymic?"

"Innokenty Artemyevich."

"Year of birth?" The lieutenant was checking his replies against the sheet of paper.

"Nineteen-nineteen."

"Place of birth?"

"Leningrad."

Then, just when the moment had arrived to straighten things out, and the counselor second rank was expecting an explanation, the lieutenant went out and the door was shut in the counselor's face.

Innokenty sat down and closed his eyes. He was beginning to feel the massive power of the system's mechanical jaws.

The machine behind the wall began to drone. Then it was silent.

Various things he had been supposed to do, important and petty, came to his mind—things so urgent an hour ago that his legs still strained to run and do them.

But there was no space in the "box" to take even a full step, let alone run.

The peephole cover moved. Innokenty held up his finger. The old woman in sky-blue shoulder boards, with her dull, heavy face, opened the door.

"I have to—"

"Hands behind your back! Move!" the woman ordered. Obeying her, Innokenty stepped into the corridor. After the closeness of the "box," it seemed pleasantly cool.

Having led Innokenty a short way down the corridor, the woman motioned with her head toward a door. "There."

Innokenty entered. The door was locked behind him.

Except for the hole in the floor and the knobbed iron foot stands, the floor and the walls of the little closet were set with reddish Metlach tile. Water splashed in the hole.

Gratified that here at least he could escape the constant surveillance, Innokenty squatted on his haunches.

But something scraped on the other side of the door. He

looked up and saw the conical peephole and the implacable eye observing him without interruption.

Disagreeably embarrassed, Innokenty straightened up. He had not even raised his finger to indicate he was ready when the door opened.

"Hands behind your back. Move!" the woman said imperturbably.

Back in the "box" Innokenty wanted to know what time it was. Without thinking, he pushed back his cuff, but the "time" was not there any more.

He sighed and began to study the cat on the cup. But he was given no chance to fall into meditation. The door opened. A new, large-featured, broad-shouldered man, wearing a gray smock over his field shirt, asked, "Last name?"

"I've already given my name!" Innokenty said indignantly.

"Your name?" the newcomer repeated with no expression in his voice, like a radio operator calling another station.

"All right—Volodin."

"Take your things. Get moving," Gray Smock said impassively.

Innokenty took his overcoat and his cap off the table and went out. He was led to the same room where they had torn off his shoulder boards and taken his wristwatch and notebooks.

His handkerchief was no longer on the floor.

"Look here, they took my things away!" Innokenty complained.

"Undress," said the guard in the gray smock.

"Why?" demanded Innokenty in astonishment.

The guard stared directly into his eyes.

"Are you a Russian?" he asked sternly.

"Yes." Innokenty, who had always been so resourceful, found nothing else to say.

"Undress!"

"Why? Non-Russians don't have to?" he joked dolefully.

The guard kept a stony silence, waiting.

With a contemptuously ironic smile and a shrug of his shoulders, Innokenty sat down on the stool, took off first his shoes, then his uniform, and handed the latter to the guard. Though he did not attach any ritual significance to the uniform, Innokenty nevertheless respected the gold-embroidered clothing.

"Throw it on the floor," said Gray Robe.

Innokenty hesitated. The guard tore the uniform from his hands, hurled it to the floor, and added abruptly, "Strip!"

"What do you mean?"

"Everything!"

"But that's quite impossible, Comrade! After all, it's cold here."

"You'll be stripped by force," the guard warned.

Innokenty thought it over. They had man-handled him once, and it was clear they would do it again. Shivering from cold and revulsion, he took off his silk underwear and docilely tossed it on the pile.

"Take off your socks!"

With his socks off, Innokenty now stood on the wooden floor, his hairless white legs as bare as the rest of his submissive body.

"Open your mouth. Wider. Say 'Ah.' Again. Hold it: 'Ahhhhh!' Now lift your tongue."

Having pulled back Innokenty's cheeks with dirty hands, as if he were a horse up for auction, and having looked under his eyelids, and thus determined that nothing had been hidden under his tongue, in his cheeks, or in his eyes, the guard forced Innokenty's head back hard, in order to see inside his nostrils. Then after checking both ears, pulling them by the lobes, he ordered Innokenty to spread open his fingers, in case he was hiding something between them, and to wave his arms to make sure there was nothing in his armpits.

Then, in the same mechanical, unanswerable voice, he ordered: "Take your penis in your hands. Turn back the foreskin. Farther. That's enough. Move your penis to the right and up . . . to the left and up. Good. Let go of it. Stand with your back to me. Put your feet wide apart. Wider. Lean over to the floor. Spread your feet wider! Pull your buttocks apart with your hands. That's it. Good. Now sit down on your heels. Quick! Again!"

When in the past Innokenty had considered the possibility of being arrested, he had imagined a violent psychological struggle. He had tensed inwardly, prepared to offer some lofty defense of his convictions and his habits. He had never imagined it would be so simple, so senseless, so relentless. The people he'd been turned over to in the Lubyanka, low-ranking subordinates, limited in intelligence, were indifferent to his existence as an individual and to whatever actions had brought him here. At the same time, they were vigilantly attentive to petty details Innokenty had not anticipated, and against which he could not struggle. Even if he could, what would such resistance mean, what good would it do? Each time, and always for a different reason, they asked him to do something that seemed inconsequential compared with the major battle that lay ahead—and each time it seemed not worth being stubborn about something so trivial. But the total effect of this procedure was to break the prisoner's will completely.

Dispirited, Innokenty endured all these humiliations in silence.

The guard in the gray smock ordered Innokenty to sit on a stool near the door. It seemed unthinkable to touch his naked body to that cold object, but he sat down, and was grateful to find that the wooden stool seemed to warm him.

He had known many varieties of intense gratification in his life, but this was a new one. Crossing his arms and drawing up his knees, he felt even warmer.

He sat that way while the guard stood over the pile of clothes and began to shake each garment, feeling it over thoroughly and looking at it against the light. Considerately, he spent little time on the undershorts and socks, though he carefully kneaded the seams and hems of the shorts. He threw them at Innokenty's feet, then he unfastened the socks from the elastic garters, turned them inside out, and threw them to Innokenty. After inspecting the undershirt, he threw that over, too, and Innokenty was able to start dressing and warm up.

Then the guard took out a big pocket knife with a rough wooden handle, opened it and went to work on the shoes. Contemptuously shaking out the two halves of pencil, he took the shoes out of their rubber overshoes and began to bend them back and forth, with a look of deep concentration, to discover if there was anything hard inside them. Cutting open the inner lining with his knife, he yanked some sort of steel strip out of each shoe and put them to one side on the table. Then he reached for an awl and pierced one heel.

As Innokenty watched him work, he thought how boring it must be, year after year, to feel through other people's underwear, cut up shoes, and look into anal orifices. Small wonder that the guard's face wore such a disagreeably glum expression.

But Innokenty's glimmers of irony soon gave way to melancholy apprehension. The guard began to remove all the gold embroidery from his uniform, as well as the buttons and tabs. Then he took out the felt lining. He spent as much time on the pleats and seams of the trousers. He was even more diligent with the overcoat because he heard a rustle in the depths of the padding. Was a note sewn in there? A list of addresses? A vial of poison? Opening the lining, he searched the padding for a long time, never losing his deeply concentrated, concerned expression, as though he were performing an operation on a human heart.

The whole thing went on a long time, somewhat more than half an hour. Finally, having established that the overshoes really did consist of only a single layer of rubber and that nothing was stuffed inside—when he bent them, they obediently moved both ways—the guard threw them at Innokenty's feet and began to gather up his trophies: the suspenders and the garters. Both items, as he had already told Innokenty, were prohibited in the prison, as were the necktie, the tie clip, the cuff links, the steel strips, the pieces of pencil, the gold braid, all the insignia of rank and the decorations on his uniform, and most of the buttons. It was only then that Innokenty understood and respected the work of destruction the guard had carried out. It was not the cuts in his shoes, nor the ripped-out lining, nor the padding sticking out of the sleeves of his coat, but being deprived of his suspenders and nearly all his buttons which, for some reason affected Innokenty more than any other of the night's ignominies.

"Why did you cut the buttons off?" he demanded.

"They are forbidden," said the guard.

"What do you mean? How am I supposed to keep my clothes on?"

"Tie them with string," he replied sullenly, already at the door.

"What kind of nonsense is that? What string? Where am I supposed to get string?"

But the door slammed shut and was locked.

Innokenty did not pound on the door or plead. He realized that a few buttons had been left on his coat, and that in itself was something to be thankful for.

He was learning quickly.

Holding up his trousers, he had hardly gone once around
his new room enjoying its spaciousness and stretching his
legs, when a key rattled in the door again and a new guard
came in, wearing a dirty white smock. He looked at Innokenty as at a familiar object that had always been in this
room and abruptly ordered, "Strip!"

Innokenty wanted to reply indignantly, menacingly. But
all that came from his throat, constricted by shock, was a
shrill unconvincing complaint: "But I just got through undressing! Why couldn't they let me know?"

Obviously they couldn't, because the new guard watched
with a bored, blank look to see how soon his order would be
carried out. What impressed Innokenty about everyone here
was their ability to keep silent when a normal person would
say something.

So, falling into the rhythm of unqualified compliance, Innokenty undressed and took off his shoes.

"Sit down!" said the guard, pointing to the stool on which
Innokenty had been sitting before.

The naked prisoner sat down submissively, without thinking why. The free person's habit of thinking his actions
through before carrying them out was rapidly ebbing in him,
since others were thinking so effectively for him. The guard
grabbed him roughly by the nape of the neck. Cold clippers
were pressed hard against his skull.

"What are you doing?" said Innokenty with a shudder,
trying with a feeble effort to free his head. "Who gave you
the right? I have not been arrested yet!" He had meant to
say that he had not been convicted yet.

But the barber, his grip as tight as ever, continued to clip.
The spurt of resistance which had flared up in Innokenty
was quenched. The proud young diplomat, so carefree and
independent, so accustomed to strolling down the steps of
transcontinental planes, so unimpressed with the gleam and
bustle of European capitals, was now a frail, naked, bony
male with his head half shorn to the scalp.

Innokenty's chestnut hair fell soft as snow in sad, soundless handfuls. He caught a tuft and rubbed it tenderly between his fingers. He felt that he loved himself and the life
that was retreating from him.

He remembered his conviction that capitulation would
be interpreted as guilt. He remembered his determination

to resist, to object, to argue, to ask to see his prosecutor; bu
contrary to his reason his will was being destroyed. He wa
experiencing the sweet indifference of a man slowly freezin
to death in the snow.

When the barber had clipped his head, he ordered Inno
kenty to stand up and raise one arm and then the othe
while he clipped his armpits. Then he squatted down an
with the same clippers began to clip Innokenty's pubic hai
This was a surprise to Innokenty, and it tickled. Involun
tarily he shivered, and the barber reprimanded him.

"May I get dressed?" asked Innokenty, when the busi
ness was finished.

The barber said nothing, but went out and locked th
door.

This time a measure of cunning warned Innokenty no
to hurry getting dressed. He felt an unpleasant pricklin
Passing his hand over his newly cropped head, he felt fo
the first time in his life the strange short bristles and uneve
patches on his scalp. He could not remember ever havin
been close-shorn even as a child.

He put on his underwear. As he was starting to pull o
his trousers, the lock clattered. Another guard came in, th
one with a meaty purple nose. In his hand he held a larg
card.

"Last name?"

"Volodin," the prisoner replied submissively, even thoug
he was sickened by the endless repetitions.

"Name and patronymic?"

"Innokenty Artemyevich."

"Year of birth?"

"Nineteen-nineteen."

"Place of birth?"

"Leningrad."

"Strip."

Understanding only dimly what was happening, Innokent
undressed again. As he did, his undershirt fell off the tab
onto the dirty floor, but he watched it fall without disgu
and did not bend over to pick it up.

The guard with the purple nose began to look carefully a
Innokenty from all sides, and he wrote down his observa
tions on the card. From the amount of attention he wa
paying to birthmarks and facial details, Innokenty realize
he was compiling a complete physical description for a
identification file.

Then this guard, too, went out.

Innokenty sat passively on the stool without getting essed.

The door rattled again. A big black-haired woman in a ow-white smock came in. She had a crude, arrogant face d the cultivated manner of an intellectual.

Innokenty was startled and quickly reached for his underorts to cover himself. But the woman glared at him with a ntemptuous, quite unfeminine look and, jutting out her ver lip, she asked, "Do you have lice?"

"I am a diplomat," Innokenty said, offended, looking nly into her black Armenian eyes and holding his underorts in front of him.

"What of it? What complaints do you have?"

"Why was I arrested? Let me read the warrant. Where is e prosecutor?" Coming to life, Innokenty spoke with a sh.

"No one is asking you about that," said the woman, •wning wearily. "You deny having VD?"

"What?"

"You've never had syphilis, gonorrhea, soft chancre? prosy? TB? No other complaints?"

She left without waiting for his answer.

The first guard, the one with the long face, entered. Innonty felt a surge of warmth when he saw him, because this e had neither taunted nor hurt him.

"Why aren't you dressing?" the guard asked harshly. "Get essed quickly."

It was not so easy. The guard left him locked in the om, and Innokenty tried to figure out how to keep his users on without suspenders and without most of the ttons. Having had no chance to profit from the experience dozens of earlier generations of prisoners, Innokenty puzd a while and then solved the problem alone, just as llions before him had solved it. He discovered where to a belt: he tied his trousers with his shoe laces. Only then he notice that the metal tips had been torn from the es. He didn't know that Lubyanka regulations assumed risoner could manufacture a file from those tips and saw ough the bars.

He had not yet worked out how to keep his jacket closed. The guard, having observed through the peephole that e prisoner was dressed, unlocked the door, ordered him put his hands behind him and took him to another room.

Waiting there was the guard with the purple nose, wh
Innokenty already knew.

"Take off your shoes," he said in greeting.

This presented no difficulty because they had no la
and came off by themselves. And of course his socks, n
garterless, fell to his ankles.

Against the wall stood a doctor's scale with a vert
white rod to measure height. Purple Nose pushed In
kenty's back against it, lowered the crossbar on the rod
the crown of his head and wrote down his height.

"You can put your shoes on," he said.

And Long Face in the doorway warned, "Hands beh
your back!"

Hands behind his back, even though "box" No. 8
only two steps across the corridor.

Once again Innokenty was locked up in his "box."

On the other side of the wall, the machine kept humm
and shutting down.

Holding his coat closed, Innokenty sat down wearily
the stool. Since he had arrived in the Lubyanka he had s
only blinding light, walls pressing in on him and blank-fac
silent jailers. The procedures they had gone through, e
more absurd than the last, struck him as mockeries.
failed to see that they constituted a logical and meanin
chain of events: preliminary search by the operatives
had arrested him; the establishment of the prisoner's id
tity; the registration of the arrested person by the pr
administration upon receipt; the basic search on arrival;
first hygienic processing; the notation of identifying ma
the medical inspection. These procedures threw the pris
off balance and deprived him of his ability to reason
his capacity to resist. Now Innokenty's single torment
desire was to sleep. Having concluded that they were lea
him alone for the moment, and not seeing how to arra
things otherwise, he put the stool on top of the table, spr
his fine woolen coat with its gray astrakhan collar on
floor, and lay down on it diagonally across the "box." I
first three Lubyanka hours he had acquired a new un
standing of life. His back was on the floor and his n
was bent steeply upward in one corner; his legs, crooke
the knees, squirmed in the other corner. For the first li
while, before his limbs became numb, he felt a blissful re

But he had not yet escaped into deep sleep when the c
opened with a particularly purposeful crash.

"Get up!" ordered the woman.

Innokenty barely moved his eyelids.

"Get up! Get up!" He heard the incantation over him.

"But what if I want to sleep?"

"Get up!" the woman shouted, bending over him like a Medusa in a dream.

With difficulty Innokenty wormed out of his cramped position and got to his feet.

"Please take me somewhere where I can lie down and sleep," he said feebly.

"That's forbidden!" said the Medusa in sky-blue shoulder boards and slammed the door.

Innokenty leaned against the wall and waited while she studied him through the peephole for a long time, left, returned again, then left again.

Once more he sank down on his coat, taking advantage of her absence.

And once more he had just lost consciousness when the door crashed open.

A new man, tall and strong enough to be a blacksmith or rock crusher, stood in the doorway in a white smock.

"Last name?" he asked.

"Volodin."

"Bring your things."

Innokenty gathered up his coat and hat, and, with lusterless eyes, staggered after the guard. He was in a state of extreme exhaustion, and his feet could hardly tell whether they were walking on one level or going up or down. He scarcely had the strength to move and was ready to lie down right in the corridor.

He was taken through some sort of narrow passageway but through a thick wall, then into another corridor, less well kept, where a door opened into the anteroom to a bath. There, giving him a piece of laundry soap smaller than a matchbox, the guard ordered him to take a shower.

Innokenty was slow to respond. He was accustomed to the mirror-like cleanliness of tiled bathrooms. And this wooden bath, which to an ordinary person would have seemed quite clean, appeared to him repulsively dirty. He managed to find a dry place on the bench, and he undressed here; squeamishly he walked along wet wooden gratings which showed the smudges of bare feet and the marks of toes. He would have welcomed not having to undress and

bathe, but the door opened and the blacksmith in the whit
smock ordered him to step under the shower.

The shower room lay behind a thin plain door with tw
unglazed apertures—untypical of the prison. Above fou
gratings, which Innokenty discovered to be dirty also, wer
four shower heads that poured forth first-rate hot and col
water, but Innokenty failed to appreciate it. Four showe
heads for one person—yet Innokenty derived no joy from
that fact either. Had he known that in the zek world it wa
more usual for four zeks to wash under one shower head
he might have been grateful for his sixteenfold advantag
He had already tossed aside with disgust the repulsiv
smelly soap. In all his thirty years he had never held a piec
of soap like that; he had not even known such a thin
existed. In a couple of minutes he managed to rinse himse
off, principally washing the stubble of pubic hair that wa
itchy and irritated after the clipping; then, with the feelin
that he had not washed at all but had simply picked up mo
dirt, he returned to put on his clothes.

But in vain. The benches of the anteroom were empt
all his magnificent, if mutilated, clothing had been take
away, and only his rubber overshoes with his shoes thru
inside them were still under the bench. The outer do
was locked, and the peephole shut from the other sid
There was nothing for Innokenty to do but sit down on th
bench like a naked statue, like Rodin's "Thinker," and thi
things over while he dried off.

Then they issued him rough, much-laundered priso
underwear with black letters spelling "Inner Prison
stamped on it back and front, and a square rag folded
four which Innokenty did not immediately recognize as
towel. The buttons on the underwear were made of car
board, and some of them were missing. There were string
but those, too, were torn off in some places. The undershor
were short and tight for Innokenty and chafed at the crotc
The undershirt on the other hand was much too large, a
the sleeves hung down to his fingers. They refused to e
change them because he had soiled them by putting them o

Clad in this ungainly underwear, Innokenty sat in th
anteroom for a long time. They told him his outer clothin
was in the "roaster." The word was new to Innokenty. A
through the war, when the country was dotted with "roas
ers," he had never encountered one. But the senseless moc

eries of this night made it seem perfectly appropriate that there should be a clothing "roaster." In his mind the word evoked a picture of a huge diabolical frying pan.

Innokenty tried soberly to think his situation through and to decide what he might conceivably do, but his thoughts grew confused and settled on such trivial subjects as the tight underwear or the frying pan where his coat now was, or the intent eye behind the peephole when the cover was moved aside.

The bath had driven away sleep, but the weakness that weighed him down now possessed him utterly. He wanted to lie down on something dry and warm, lie motionless, and recover his failing strength. He had, however, no desire to stretch out on the damp, sharp-edged planks of the bench.

The door opened, but his clothing was not being brought in from the "roaster." A ruddy, broad-faced girl in civilian clothes stood beside the bath guard. Shamefacedly covering the gaps in his underwear, Innokenty went to the doorway. The girl gave him a pink receipt—one copy of which she ordered him to sign—attesting that today, December 26, the Inner Prison of the MGB of the U.S.S.R. had received from Volodin, I. A., for safekeeping: one yellow metal watch with cover; one fountain pen with decorative work of yellow metal and a pen point of the same metal; one tie pin with a red stone in a setting; one pair of cuff links of blue stone.

Again Innokenty waited, his head sagging forward. At last they brought him his clothes. The coat was returned cold and fully intact. The tunic, trousers, and shirt were rumpled, faded and still hot.

"Couldn't you have taken as good care of the uniform as you did of the coat?" Innokenty asked indignantly.

"The coat has fur. You should understand that!" the blacksmith answered sententiously.

Even his own clothes had become unfamiliar and repulsive after being in the "roaster," and in this now alien and uncomfortable attire Innokenty was again led off to "box" No. 8.

He asked for two cups of water and greedily drank them down. The cups were decorated with the same cat.

Then another girl arrived and, when he had signed one copy, gave him a light-blue receipt signifying that today, December 27, the Inner Prison of the MGB of the U.S.S.R.

had received from Volodin, I. A., one silk undershirt, one pair of silk undershorts, suspenders, and one necktie. Was it already the 27th?

The machine kept humming in its sinister way.

Locked up once more, Innokenty folded his arms on the little table, put his head down and attempted to fall asleep sitting up.

"That's forbidden!" said a new guard who had opened the door.

"What's forbidden?"

"It's forbidden to put your head down."

Innokenty waited, his mind hopelessly confused.

Again they brought a receipt, this time on white paper, to the effect that the Inner Prison of the MGB of the U.S.S.R. had received from Volodin, I. A., 123 rubles.

Someone else came, another new person, a man wearing a dark-blue smock over an expensive brown suit.

Each time they brought a receipt they asked his last name. And now they were asking all over again: Last name? First name and patronymic? Year of birth? Place of birth?

Then the newcomer ordered: "Easy now!"

"What?" Innokenty asked in bewilderment.

"Come easy; leave your things here! Hands behind your back!" In the corridor all orders were given in a lowered voice, so that other "boxes" could not hear.

Clicking his tongue to the same invisible dog, the man in the brown suit led Innokenty through the main exit and down a corridor into a big room unlike a prison room: blinds were pulled down at the windows, and there was upholstered furniture, desks. They put Innokenty in a chair in the middle of the room. He was convinced they would begin to question him now.

But instead, they rolled out from behind a portiere a camera of brown polished wood and turned bright lights on Innokenty from both sides. They photographed him once head on and once in profile.

The man in the blue smock who had led Innokenty there took each finger of his right hand in turn and rolled it on a sticky black cylinder which seemed to be smeared with ink, blackening the tips of all five fingers. Then, holding Innokenty's fingers firmly, he pressed them on a sheet of paper and lifted them up quickly. Five black prints with white whorls remained on the paper.

Then he did the same with the left hand.

Over the fingerprints was written: "Volodin, Innokenty Artemyevich, 1919, Leningrad," and over that in thick black type:

KEEP FOREVER

Reading the two words, Innokenty shuddered. There was something mystical about them, something superhuman, supernatural.

They let him scrub his fingers at a basin with soap, brush, and cold water. The sticky ink was hard to remove and the cold water rolled off it. Innokenty scrubbed at his fingertips with the soapy brush without questioning the logic of having to bathe before being fingerprinted.

His acquiescent and tormented mind was mesmerized by those crushing, cosmic words:

KEEP FOREVER

84

SECOND WIND

Never in Innokenty's life had there been such an endless night. He had not slept at all, and more thoughts had crowded through his head than would have stirred in a month of ordinary existence. There had been ample time to think while they stripped the gold braid from his diplomat's uniform, and while he sat half naked after his shower and in the many "boxes" he had been locked into in the course of the night.

He was struck again by the significance of the words "Keep Forever."

Indeed, whether or not they could prove he was the one who had telephoned—and it was at least clear that the conversation had been overheard—once they had arrested him they were not going to let him out. He knew Stalin—he would let no one come back to life. He would be lucky if he was only sentenced to a camp; in his situation he might well be sent to one of the converted monasteries where they would forbid him ever to sit down during the daytime or to speak for years. No one would know anything about him, and he would know nothing about the world, even if whole continents changed flags or people landed on the moon. And voiceless prisoners could be shot in solitary cells. It had happened. . . .

But was he really afraid of death?

At first, Innokenty had welcomed any petty occurrence, any opening of the door, anything that interrupted his solitude, his unfamiliar new existence in the trap. But now he wanted to think his way through to some important, yet unperceived thought; and he was glad they had taken him back to his former "box" and left him there alone a long time, even though they watched him constantly through the peephole.

Suddenly it was as though a film had been removed from his brain, and what he had read and thought about during the office day emerged with full clarity:

"Faith in immortality was born of the greed of unsatisfied people. . . . The wise man finds his life span sufficient to complete the full circle of attainable pleasures. . . ."

But was it really a matter of pleasures? He had had money, good clothes, esteem, women, wine, travel, but at this moment he would have hurled all those pleasures into the nether world for justice and truth . . . and nothing more.

And how many others like himself, unknown by face or name, were enclosed in the brick compartments of this building? How maddening to die without any exchange of mind and spirit with them!

It was all very well to contrive a philosophy under leafy branches in stagnant periods of peace and order when nothing was going on.

Now, when he lacked both pencil and notebook, everything that floated up from the shadows of his memory seemed all the more precious. He remembered distinctly:

"One must not fear physical suffering. Protracted suffering never matters; the suffering which does matter is always brief."

Now, for instance: to sit sleepless, without air, for days at a time in a "box" in which it was impossible to straighten out one's legs, what kind of suffering was that—protracted or brief? Did it matter or not? What about ten years in solitary without hearing a single word?

In the photography and fingerprint room Innokenty had noticed it was after one in the morning. It might now be after two. A nonsensical thought stuck in his head, crowding out more serious ones: his watch had been put in the checkroom, and it would go on ticking away until it ran down and stopped. No one would ever wind it again, and until its owner died or his property was confiscated it would continue to tell the time—the hour and minute—when its hands had stopped. What time would the watch tell?

And was Dotty waiting for him to go to the operetta? Had she phoned the ministry? Probably not; they would have come to search the apartment. It was an enormous apartment. Five people would have to rummage there all night long. What would the fools find?

Dotty would get a divorce and remarry.

His father-in-law's career would be ruined—this would be a blotch on his record. And he would be the one to spill out everything and denounce Innokenty.

Everyone who had known Counselor Volodin would loyally erase him from memory.

The silent leviathan would crush him, and no one on the face of the earth would ever know what had become of him.

And he did want to live to see what the world would be like! Eventually everything on earth would merge. "Tribal hostilities" would cease. State boundaries would disappear, as well as armies. A world parliament would be convened. They would elect a president of the planet. He would bare his head before mankind and say—

"Bring your things!"

"What?"

"Bring your things!"

"What things?"

"Those rags of yours, of course."

Innokenty stood up, holding his coat and cap, which were particularly precious to him now because they had not been ruined in the "roaster." In the doorway, brushing past the corridor guard, appeared a swarthy, insolent master sergeant with sky-blue shoulder boards. Innokenty wondered where they found these types. And what tasks they gave them.

Checking against a sheet of paper, the sergeant asked, "Last name?"

"Volodin."

"First name and patronymic?"

"How often do you have to ask?"

"First name and patronymic?"

"Innokenty Artemyevich."

"Year of birth?"

"Nineteen-nineteen."

"Place of birth?"

"Leningrad."

"Bring your things. Move!"

And he walked ahead, clicking his tongue.

This time they went out into a courtyard and down a few steps into the darkness of that other, covered court. The thought crossed his mind: were they taking him to be shot? They said that executions always occurred in cellars at night.

Then, in that difficult moment, Innokenty asked himself: why would they have given him receipts for his possessions if they meant to shoot him? No, he would not be shot.

Innokenty still believed in a rational, intelligent coordination of all the monster's tentacles.

Still clicking his tongue, the swarthy sergeant led him into another building and through a dark entrance hall to an elevator. A woman with a bale of freshly ironed yellow-gray linen was standing to one side, and she watched Innokenty as he was taken into the elevator. And although this young laundress was not beautiful and her social level was low, and although she looked at Innokenty with the same impervious, stonily indifferent stare as did all the other mechanical dolls of the Lubyanka, still Innokenty was distressed in her presence, as he had been when the other girls had brought his pink, blue, and white receipts. The laundress was seeing him in so wretched and shattered a state that she might regard him with humiliating pity.

However, this thought, too, disappeared as quickly as it came. What difference did it make, after all? "Keep Forever!"

The master sergeant shut the elevator door and pressed an unnumbered floor button.

The moment the elevator motor began to hum, Innokenty recognized the sound of that secret machine he had thought might be grinding up bones beyond the wall of his "box."

He smiled sadly; this agreeable mistake raised his spirits.

The elevator stopped. The master sergeant led Innokenty

onto the landing and directly into a broad hallway where he noticed many guards with sky-blue shoulder boards and white stripes. One of them locked Innokenty in a "box" with no number. It was a roomier "box," with perhaps a dozen square yards of floor space, dimly lit, its walls painted olive-drab from floor to ceiling. This "box" was quite bare, but it did not appear to be very clean. It had a worn cement floor and there was a narrow wooden bench built into one wall, long enough for three people to sit on at once. It was chilly in the "box," and the cold made it seem more forbidding. There was a peephole here, too, but its cover did not slide back very often.

From outside came muffled sounds of boots shuffling on the floor. Evidently guards were continually coming and going. The Inner Prison had an active night life.

Innokenty had thought at first that he would be kept in the hot, cramped, blindingly bright "box" No. 8, and was tormented because there was no room to stretch out his legs, the light hurt his eyes, it was hard to breathe. Now he realized his mistake and understood that he was to live in this spacious, inhospitable, numberless "box." He suffered in the knowledge that the cement floor would freeze his legs, that the constant scurrying and shuffling would disturb him, and that the lack of light would oppress him. How badly he needed a window! Just a very small one, like a dungeon window in the set for an opera, but there was not even that.

One could listen to any number of tales and read countless memoirs about it, but one could never imagine it: corridors, staircases, innumerable doors, officers coming and going, sergeants, service personnel. The Big Lubyanka bustling with nightly activity, and yet no other prisoners anywhere in sight. It was impossible even to glimpse another like oneself; it was impossible to hear a single unofficial word, and very few official words were spoken. It seemed that the whole enormous ministry was awake that night because of him, was occupied with him and his crime alone.

The destructive intent of the first hours of prison is to isolate the new prisoner from his fellows, so that there is no one to offer him any encouragement, so that the weight of the whole elaborate apparatus bears down on him alone.

Innokenty's thoughts took an unfortunate turn. The telephone call, which only the day before had impressed him as a noble gesture, now seemed as rash and futile as suicide.

He now had space to walk back and forth, but he was exhausted, worn out by the processing he had undergone, and he had no strength to walk. After a couple of turns he sat down on the bench and let his arms hang limply alongside his legs.

How many great intentions were entombed in these walls, sealed in these "boxes" and unknown to posterity?

That cursed, double-cursed sensitivity. Today or tomorrow Innokenty would have flown off to Paris, where he could have forgotten all about that poor fellow he had wanted to save . . . whom, in spite of his efforts, he had failed to save.

When he pictured to himself his trip to Paris, especially the first few days there, he gasped at the dizzying unattainability of freedom. He wanted to claw the walls to give vent to his frustration.

But the opening of the door saved him from committing that infraction of prison regulations. Again they verified his identity, Innokenty replying as if out of a deep sleep. He was ordered to come out "with his things." Since he had become rather cold in the "box," he was wearing his cap, and his overcoat was thrown over his shoulders. He started to walk out of the "box" that way, not realizing that this would have enabled him to carry a pair of daggers or loaded pistols under the coat. He was ordered to put his arms in the coat sleeves and only then to put his bare hands behind his back.

He was led, once more with tongue-clickings, to the stairway next to the elevator and down the stairs. It would have been interesting to remember how many turns he made, how many steps, and then at leisure to learn the plan of the prison. But his perceptions of the world had so altered that he moved in a state of insensibility, and he was not aware how far down they had gone when suddenly, from some other corridor, another tall guard approached them, tongue-clicking as intently as the one leading Innokenty. Innokenty's guard suddenly opened the door of a green plywood booth obstructing a cramped landing, pushed him inside it and leaned against the door to keep it shut. Inside there was barely room to stand, and there was reflected light overhead; the booth had no ceiling, and the light came from the stair landing.

It would have been a natural human impulse to protest

loudly, but Innokenty, already accustomed to incomprehensible trials and to the silence of the Lubyanka, submitted quietly; he did what the prison required of him.

But he finally understood why Lubyanka guards clicked their tongues! It was their way of warning other guards that they were escorting a prisoner. The guards were forbidden to allow the prisoners to meet one another, lest they draw encouragement from one another's eyes.

One prisoner and then a second were taken past, and then Innokenty was let out of the booth and led farther down.

There, on the last stage of the march downstairs, Innokenty noticed how worn the steps were. He had seen nothing like it in his life. They were worn in oval hollows half a step deep, from the sides to the center.

He shuddered. In thirty years how many feet must have shuffled here to wear down the stone that way! And of every two people who passed, one was a guard and the other a prisoner.

On the landing there was a locked door with a small, barred window, tightly shut. Here Innokenty had a new experience: standing with his face to the wall. Still, out of the corner of his eye, he was able to see that his guard rang an electric bell, and that the barred window was cautiously opened and then closed. Suddenly, with the loud rattle of a key turning, the door opened. Someone, invisible to Innokenty, came out and asked, "Last name?"

Instinctively Innokenty turned around to look at the person who had spoken to him, and he glimpsed a face which was neither male nor female, swollen, flabby, with a big red scar from a burn, and he saw, lower down, a lieutenant's gold shoulder boards.

The lieutenant shouted, "Don't turn around!"

And he proceeded with the same monotonous questions, which Innokenty answered, speaking to a patch of white plaster in front of him.

Having ascertained that the prisoner gave the same description as that listed in the card file, and that he still remembered the year and place of his birth, the flabby lieutenant rang the bell at the door he had been careful to lock behind him. Again the bolt of the barred window was cautiously drawn back, and someone looked through the opening; the window was shut and the key rattled again, unlocking the door.

"Forward!" said the flabby lieutenant with the burned face.

They stepped inside, and the door was loudly locked behind them.

Innokenty had just time to see his escorts separate—one ahead, one to the right, one to the left—and to notice the dark corridor with its many doors, and a desk, a pigeonhole cabinet, and more guards by the entrance, when, in the silence, the lieutenant quietly but distinctly ordered, "Face to the wall! Don't move!"

It was a stupid situation: to be staring at the junction of olive-colored paneling and white plaster and feel several pairs of hostile eyes fixed on the back of his head.

Evidently they were examining his card; then the lieutenant issued an order almost in a whisper, but clear in the deep silence: "Into the third 'box.'"

Innokenty's guard moved away from the desk and, without letting his keys clank, started down the carpeted corridor on the right.

"Hands behind your back! Move!" he said very quietly.

Farther on, the corridor turned; then there were two more turns beyond. Along one side ran that same neutral olive-colored wall, and along the other were several doors with oval glass numbers:

$$47 \qquad 48 \qquad 49$$

Under the numbers there were peephole covers. Feeling warmed by the near presence of friends, Innokenty wanted to lift one of the covers and glue his eye for a second to a peephole, to look in at the sequestered life of the cell. But the guard drew him quickly forward; moreover, Innokenty was already infected with the passivity of prison—though what, in fact, did a lost man still have to fear?

Unfortunately for people—and fortunately for their rulers—a human being is so constituted that as long as he lives there is always something more that can be taken away from him. Even a person imprisoned for life, deprived of movement, of the sky, of family, of property, can, for instance, be transferred to a damp punishment cell, deprived of hot food, beaten with clubs, and he will feel these petty extra punishments as intensely as his earlier downfall from the heights of freedom and affluence. To avoid these final torments, the prisoner follows obediently the humiliating and hateful prison regime, which slowly kills the human being within him.

The doors beyond the last turn were close together, and the glass ovals on them read:

1 2 3

The guard opened the door of the third "box" with a broad, welcoming gesture, which in this place was rather comical. Innokenty noticed the humor of it and looked closely at the guard. He was a short, broad-shouldered lad, with smooth black hair and eyes slanted like saber cuts. He looked fairly evil, and neither his eyes nor his lips smiled, but after the dozens of stolid Lubyanka employees Innokenty had seen that night, the malign face of this last one struck him as rather pleasant.

Locked in his "box," Innokenty looked around. After tonight he could consider himself an expert on "boxes," having had the opportunity to compare several. This new one was superb: three and a half feet wide, seven and a half in length, a parquet floor, almost all the space taken up by a long and not too narrow wooden bench built into the wall. Beside the door stood a small hexagonal wooden table which was not built in. The "box" was, of course, completely sealed and windowless; there was only a black, grated vent above. Its ceiling was very high—ten feet. The walls were whitewashed and glaring from the two-hundred-watt bulb in the wire cage over the door. The powerful light warmed the "box," but it also hurt his eyes.

The science of being a prisoner is quickly and definitively mastered. This time Innokenty did not entertain false hopes of remaining very long in the comfortable new "box." When he saw the long bare bench, the former novice, who was less of a novice with every passing hour, knew that his immediate problem was to get some sleep. As a young forest creature who has been left motherless learns how to stay alive on its own, Innokenty quickly set about making a pallet of his coat, bunching the astrakhan collar and the sleeves to make a pillow. He lay down on the bench at once. It seemed very comfortable. He shut his eyes and prepared to go to sleep.

But sleep evaded him. He had twice been able to drowse off when there was no chance of sleeping. He had gone through all the stages of fatigue. But here, where he might have slept, he was wide-awake. The continual excitement kept him on edge and would not subside. Struggling to avoid regrets and speculations, Innokenty tried to breathe regularly and to count up to . . . It is terribly distressing not to be able to sleep when one's whole body is warm and one's legs can be stretched out full length and the guard for some reason doesn't fling the door open noisily.

He lay there for half an hour, and at last he began to lose his train of thought and a viscous heaviness spread through his body.

But at that moment Innokenty felt it was impossible to fall asleep with that insane light on. It not only irradiated the dusk behind his closed lids with an orange glow, but it seemed to press on his eyeballs with unbearable force. This pressure of light, which Innokenty had never experienced before, was driving him out of his mind. After twisting from side to side, vainly trying to find a position in which to escape the heavy pressure of the light, Innokenty gave up in despair, sat up and dropped his feet to the floor.

The peephole cover was often moved; now, hearing its scrape, he quickly raised his finger.

The door opened soundlessly. The slant-eyed guard looked in silence at Innokenty.

"Please, I beg you. Turn off the light!" Innokenty said.

"That's forbidden," the guard replied imperturbably.

"Well, then put in a smaller bulb. Why do you need such a big bulb for such a small . . . 'box'?"

"Don't talk so loud," said the guard quietly. And, indeed, behind him the big hallway and the whole prison were as silent as the grave. "The one that's there is the one that has to be there."

Still there was something alive in his blank face. Having exhausted the topic and realizing that the door would now be closed, Innokenty asked, "Give me a drink of water."

The slant-eyed guard nodded and silently locked the door. Inaudibly he moved away from the "box" along the sackcloth carpeting. When he returned, the key barely clicked, and he stood in the doorway with a cup of water in his hands. The cup, like the one on the first floor, had a picture of a cat, but this one wasn't wearing glasses, didn't have a book, and there was no little bird.

Innokenty drank the water, enjoying it. Between sips he looked at the guard, who did not leave but closed the door lightly, as much as his shoulders permitted, and, against all regulations, winked and asked softly, "Who were you?"

How strange it sounded to be addressed by a human being for the first time in the entire night! Astounded by the lively tone of the question, however furtively murmured, and fascinated by the inadvertently pitiless "were," Innokenty, conspiring, so to speak, with the guard, told him in a whisper: "A diplomat. A state counselor."

The guard nodded sympathetically and said, "And I was a sailor with the Baltic Fleet." Then he added more slowly: "What are you here for?"

"I don't know myself," Innokenty said, suddenly cautious. "Nothing in particular."

Again the guard nodded sympathetically.

"That's what they all say at first," he declared. And, with an indecent expression on his face, he added: "Do you want to go piss?"

"Not now," Innokenty said, with the blindness of a newcomer, not knowing that the offer was the greatest favor in a guard's power, and one of the greatest privileges on earth, unattainable to prisoners except on schedule.

After this fruitful conversation, the door was shut and Innokenty again stretched out on the bench, struggling against the pressure of the light through his defenseless lids. He tried to cover his eyes with his hand, but his hand grew numb. He could have folded his handkerchief into a pad and covered his eyes with that, but where was his handkerchief? Oh, why hadn't he picked it up from the floor? What a fool he had been yesterday evening!

Small things—a handkerchief, an empty matchbox, a piece of coarse thread, a plastic button—these are the prisoner's dearest treasures. The moment will always come when one of them will prove indispensable and save the day.

Suddenly the door opened. The slant-eyed guard shoved a red-striped mattress into Innokenty's arms. What a miracle! Not only did the Lubyanka not keep prisoners from sleeping; it concerned itself with their comforts. Rolled inside the mattress was a small feather pillow, a pillowcase and sheet—both stamped "Inner Prison"—and a gray blanket.

Bliss! Now he would sleep! His first impressions of the prison had been too dismal. With a foretaste of enjoyment, and for the first time in his life, he put the pillowcase on the

pillow with his own hands, and stretched out the sheet; the
mattress turned out to hang slightly over the edge of the
bench. He undressed, lay down, and covered his eyes with
the sleeve of his tunic—now the light did not bother him
at all. He began to slip into a deep, deep sleep.

But the door crashed open and the guard said, "Take
your hands out from under the blanket."

"What do you mean?" Innokenty cried out, close to tears.
"Why did you wake me up? It was so hard for me to get
to sleep."

"Take your hands out," the guard repeated coldly. "Hands
must be out in the open."

Innokenty obeyed. But it was not so simple to fall asleep
again with his hands on top of the blanket. It was a diabolical rule. It is a natural, deep-rooted, unnoticed human habit
to hide one's hands while asleep, to hold them against one's
body.

Innokenty tossed and turned for a long time, adapting to
one more humiliation. But at long last sleep started to win
out. The sweetly drugged haze was already invading his
consciousness.

Suddenly a noise in the hallway reached him; it was
coming nearer and nearer. They were pounding on the
doors. They were repeating something over and over. Then
it was—at the next door. Then Innokenty's own door
opened.

"Reveille!" the sailor from the Baltic Fleet announced
inexorably.

"What do you mean? Why?" Innokenty roared. "I haven't
slept all night."

"Six o'clock reveille is the rule!" said the sailor and moved
on.

At that instant Innokenty felt the need of sleep with particular intensity. He lay down again on his bed and went
sound asleep immediately.

But almost at once the slant-eyed guard banged the door
open and repeated: "Reveille! Reveille! Roll up your mattress."

Innokenty rose on one elbow and looked hazily at his
tormentor, who an hour ago had seemed to him a decent
human being.

"But I haven't slept, do you understand?"

"I don't know anything about that."

"But if I roll up the mattress and get up, what do I do then?"

"Nothing. Sit there."

"But why?"

"Because it's 6 A.M., I told you."

"I'll sleep sitting up."

"Not in the daytime. I'll wake you."

Innokenty held his head and rocked back and forth. A trace of pity seemed to show on the face of the slant-eyed guard.

"Would you like to wash?"

"Well—yes, I would," Innokenty said, changing his mind. And he reached for his clothes.

"Hands behind your back! Move."

The lavatory was around the corner. Having given up all hope of sleeping in the hours ahead, Innokenty took off his shirt and began washing in cold water to his waist. He splashed freely on the cement floor of the vast cold lavatory; the door was closed; the guard didn't bother him.

Maybe he was a human being after all, but why then had he maliciously failed to warn Innokenty that reveille was at six?

The cold water washed away his toxic fatigue. In the corridor he tried to ask about breakfast. The guard stopped him from talking, but in the "box" he replied, "There won't be breakfast."

"What do you mean? What will there be?"

"At eight there will be rations and sugar and tea."

"What are rations?"

"That means bread."

"And when will breakfast be?"

"There isn't any. Lunch is next."

"And must I sit up the whole time?"

"That's enough talk."

He had already shut the door to a slit when Innokenty raised his finger.

"Well, what else do you want?" asked the Baltic sailor, opening it again.

"They cut off my buttons, and ripped open the lining of my tunic. Who will sew it up?"

"How many buttons?"

They counted the missing ones.

The door was shut, but soon it opened again. The guard

handed him a needle, a dozen pieces of thread, and several
bone, plastic, and wooden buttons of various sizes.

"What use are these? These aren't the ones they cut off."

"Take them! There aren't any more, even of these!"
the guard shouted.

And for the first time in his life Innokenty began to sew.
He did not understand at first how to wet the end of the
thread in order to get it through the needle's eye, or how to
make a knot when he had finished. Unable to draw on
thousands of years of experience, he then invented sewing
for himself. He pricked himself often, and the sensitive tips
of his fingers began to hurt. It took him a long time to sew
back the uniform lining, and straighten out the padding
of the overcoat. And he sewed on some of the buttons in
the wrong places, so that his uniform pulled sideways when
he buttoned it.

But this deliberate, concentrated work not only killed time
but also quieted Innokenty completely. His emotions fell into
place, and he no longer felt either afraid or despondent. He
could perceive that even this legendary pit of horror, the
Bolshaya Lubyanka Prison, was not totally fearsome, that
there were people of flesh and blood here, too. Oh, how he
would like to meet them!

Here was a man who had not slept all night, who had not
eaten, whose life had been shattered in a dozen hours, and
he was suddenly getting that *second wind* thanks to which
an athlete's straining body feels refreshed and tireless.

A new guard took the needle away from him.

Then they brought him a one-pound piece of moist black
bread—with an additional wedge-shaped piece to make the
full ration weight—and two broken pieces of hard sugar.

They poured hot tea into the cup with the cat on it, and
promised him more later.

All this meant that it was 8 A.M., December 27.

Innokenty threw a whole day's sugar ration into the cup,
and started to stir it with his finger. But his finger couldn't
stand the hot water. Then he mixed it by swirling the cup,
drank it down, and raised his hand to ask for more. He had
no desire for food.

With a shudder of happiness Innokenty drank the second
cup, without sugar but sensing sharply the aroma of the tea.

His thoughts brightened to a clarity he had never known.

He began to pace the narrow passage between the bench

and the opposite wall in expectation of battle—three short steps forward and three short steps back.

Another of Epicurus' thoughts—unrefuted and difficult to grasp yesterday in freedom—floated into his mind:

"Inner feelings of satisfaction and dissatisfaction are the highest criteria of good and evil."

That meant, according to Epicurus, that what one liked was good and that what one didn't like was evil.

The philosophy of a savage.

Stalin enjoyed killing—did that mean that for him killing was a virtue? And since being imprisoned for trying to save somebody did not, after all, produce satisfaction, did that mean it was evil?

No! Good and evil had now been substantively defined for Innokenty, and visibly distinguished from one another, by that bright gray door, by those olive walls, by that first prison night.

From those heights of struggle and suffering to which he had been lifted, the wisdom of the ancient philosopher seemed like the babbling of a child.

The door rattled.

"Last name?" abruptly asked another new guard, with an Asiatic face.

"Volodin."

"For questioning! Hands behind your back!"

Innokenty put his hands behind him, and with his head held high, like a bird drinking water, he left the "box."

85

THE MORNING OF THE EXECUTION OF THE STRELTZI

At the sharashka, too, it was time for breakfast and morning tea.

This day, whose early morning hours presaged nothing special, was at first notable only for the faultfinding of Senior Lieutenant Shusterman; as he was about to hand over his shift, he tried to prevent the prisoners from sleeping after reveille. Outdoors it was unpleasant; after yesterday's thaw a frost had set in during the night, and the path was covered with ice. Many of the zeks went out, made one slippery circuit, and returned to the prison. In the rooms some zeks were sitting on the lower bunks; others sat on the upper ones with their legs hanging down or folded under them. They were in no hurry to get up; they scratched their chests, yawned, and began earlier than usual moodily making fun of each other and their unfortunate fate. They told their dreams—a favorite pastime of prisoners.

But while these dreams included the usual ones of crossing a small bridge over a misty flood and pulling on high boots, there was none that clearly forecast the transport out.

That morning Sologdin went out to saw wood as usual. During the night he had kept the window partly opened, and before he went out to the woodpile he opened it still wider.

Rubin, whose bunk was against the same window, did not say a word to Sologdin. He had gone to bed late and had again suffered from insomnia. He felt the cold draft from the window, but he did not protest his antagonist's action. Instead, he put on his padded jacket and fur cap with the ear flaps down and, dressed in this way, covered his head with his blanket and lay curled up, not getting up for breakfast, paying no attention to Shusterman's admonitions and the general noise in the room, trying desperately to lengthen out the scheduled hours of sleep.

Potapov, who had climbed down from his upper bunk and gone for a walk, was one of the first to eat breakfast. He had already drunk his tea, made his bed in a tight parallelepiped, and was sitting on it reading his newspaper. But in his heart he was anxious to get to work. Today he was to calibrate an interesting piece of equipment he had built himself.

The hot cereal was millet gruel, and for that reason many zeks did not go to breakfast.

Gerasimovich, however, sat in the dining room a long time, carefully and deliberately lifting small spoonfuls of cereal into his mouth.

From the opposite corner of the half-empty dining room, Nerzhin nodded to him, sat down at a table by himself, and ate halfheartedly.

Having breakfasted, Nerzhin climbed up to his own bunk for the last fifteen minutes of free time, lay there and looked up at the domed ceiling.

The room buzzed with discussions of Ruska's fate. He had not returned last night, and the zeks knew he had been arrested and locked up in the small dark cage in the headquarters building.

They did not talk openly, they did not call him a double agent out loud, but it was understood. In view of the fact that his term could not be increased and that he couldn't be sentenced to a new term on top of it, they debated whether his twenty-five years of "Corrective Labor Camps" might not be reclassified and changed to twenty-five years of solitary confinement. Special prisons consisting entirely of solitary cells were being built that year, and solitary confinement was increasingly coming into fashion. Of course, Shikin would not set up the case against Ruska on the basis of his being a double agent. But what a person was guilty of and what he was charged with did not necessarily have to be identical. A towhead, for instance, could be charged with having black hair, and thus given the same sentence dark-haired people were supposed to get.

Nerzhin did not know the extent of Ruska's intimacy with Clara, and so he was unsure whether he should talk to her and try to reassure her or whether he should even dare to attempt it. And how could he manage it?

Amid general laughter, Rubin threw off his blanket and sat up in his fur cap and padded jacket. (He was always good-natured about laughter directed at him personally.) Taking off his cap but keeping on the jacket, and without standing up to get dressed—which would have made no sense now that the periods for walking, washing, and breakfast were already past—he asked someone to pour him a glass of tea. Sitting there with his tangled beard, he shoved white bread and butter into his mouth and poured the hot liquid after it without being conscious of any of it. Before he had even rubbed the sleep out of his eyes, he had become absorbed in an Upton Sinclair novel, which he held in the hand that wasn't holding the glass. He was in the gloomiest possible mood.

Throughout the sharashka the morning rounds were in progress. The junior lieutenant had come in. He was counting heads, and Shusterman was making the announcements. Entering the semicircular room, Shusterman proclaimed:

"Attention! Prisoners are hereby notified that after dinner no one will be admitted to the kitchen for hot water. Therefore do not interrupt the duty officer for this purpose!"

"*Whose* order is that?" Pryanchikov screamed madly, jumping out of the cave of double-decked bunks.

"The chief's," answered Shusterman weightily.

"When was it issued?"

"Yesterday."

Pryanchikov clenched his fists and shook his thin arms over his head, as if he were calling all heaven and earth to witness.

"That's not possible!" he protested in a rage. "On Saturday evening Minister Abakumov himself promised me there would be boiling water for tea at night. It's not even logical! After all, we work till midnight."

A wave of laughter from the zeks was his reply.

"So don't work till midnight, you craphead," boomed out Dvoyetyosov.

"There's no allowance for a night cook," Shusterman explained soberly.

Then Shusterman took a typed list from the junior lieutenant. "Attention!" he announced in an oppressive voice. Everyone instantly fell silent. "The following will not report for work this morning but will get ready for transport. From this room: Khorobrov, Mikhailov, Nerzhin, Syemushkin! Get together all items of government issue to be turned in."

Then the two officers went out.

As by a whirlwind, the four whose names had been spoken were surrounded by everyone in the room.

The zeks left their tea, left their uneaten sandwiches, and clustered together. Four out of twenty-five was an unusually large harvest of victims. Everyone talked at once; spirited voices mingled with depressed voices and with voices that were noisily aggressive. Some stood on the upper bunks and waved their arms about; others held their heads; others argued, beating their chests; still others shook the pillows out of state-owned pillowcases. And the whole room turned into such a bedlam of grief, submissiveness, anger, defiance, complaints, calculations, that Rubin rose from his bunk just as he was, in his padded jacket and underpants, and bellowed above the pandemonium in a stentorian voice:

"A historical day at the sharashka! *The morning of the execution of the Streltzi!*"

And he spread his arms above the general scene.

His performance in no way meant that he was cheerful about the prisoner transport. He would have joked just as boisterously about his own departure. Nothing was so sacred as to restrain him from his own brand of commentary.

A transport is a turning point in a prisoner's life, as fateful as a wound is to a soldier. A wound may be light or serious; it may heal or prove fatal; the final destination of a transport can be near or far, a diversion or death.

When one reads what Dostoyevsky says about the horrors of existence in a hard-labor prison, it is surprising how peacefully those prisoners served their time. Not one single transport in ten years!

A zek lives in one place; he gets used to his comrades, to his work, to the authorities over him. No matter how alien to him the concept of acquisitiveness may be, he does inevitably collect things: he has a fiber suitcase that was sent to him from freedom, or a plywood one made in camp; a frame for the photograph of his wife or daughter; carpet slippers he wears to walk about the barracks and hides from searches in the daytime; he may have picked up an extra pair of cotton pants or failed to turn in some old shoes; and he manages to hide it all away, tuck it behind something else, from one inventory check to the next. He even has his own needle, his own buttons that he has sewed on firmly; he may even have one or two extra. There is some tobacco in his pouch.

If he is fastidious, he has some tooth powder and occasionally cleans his teeth. He collects a packet of letters from his family, acquires a book of his own; by trading it he gets to read all the books in the prison.

But the transport strikes the fragile structure of his life like a thunderbolt—always without warning, always catching him off guard, the announcement postponed until the last possible minute. He hurries to tear up the letters from his family and throw the scraps of paper down the toilet. If the transport is scheduled to be carried out in red cattle cars, the convoy guard cuts off all his buttons and throws his tobacco and tooth powder to the wind, because the guard could be blinded by them in an escape attempt on the way. If Stolypin cars are to be used, the guard furiously crushes the suitcase, which won't fit inside the narrow baggage space, and in doing so breaks the picture frame. In either case, they take away the book, which is forbidden on a transport, the needle, which might be used to file through the bars and stab the guard; and they throw out the carpet slippers as trash and take away the extra pair of trousers.

Thus cleansed of the sin of ownership, of any inclination for a settled life, or longing for the bourgeois comforts justly condemned even by Chekhov, and cleansed, too, of friends and of the past, the zek puts his hands behind his back and, four abreast (one step to the right or left and the guard will open fire without warning), surrounded by dogs and guards, he goes off to his railroad car.

You have all seen him at the railway station at that moment, but in your cowardly submissiveness you have averted your eyes and turned away. Otherwise the lieutenant in charge might suspect you of something and take you into custody.

The zek enters the railroad car, which is then hooked behind the mail car. Tightly barred on both sides, impenetrable to anyone on the station platform who might try to look inside, it moves according to regular railroad schedules, walled in, stifling, carrying its tight-packed freight, together with hundreds of memories, hopes, and fears.

Where are they being taken? They are not told. What awaits the zek at his destination? A copper mine? A timbering enterprise? Or some remote agricultural operation, where at times it may be possible to bake potatoes and one can eat a bellyful of cattle turnips? Will the zek get scurvy and dystrophy from the first months of "general assignment" work? Or will he be lucky enough to get a helping hand from an acquaintance, and grab a job as a barracks assistant, a hospital orderly, or even perhaps assistant to a checkroom attendant? Will they allow correspondence where he is going? Or will his family be deprived of letters for long years and believe him dead?

Perhaps he will not arrive at his destination. In a cattle car he may die either of dysentery or of hunger, because the zeks will be hauled along for six days without bread. Or the guard may beat him with a hammer because someone has tried to escape. Or, at the end of the journey in an unheated car, they may toss out the frozen corpses of the zeks like logs.

The red transports take a month to reach Sovetskaya Gavan.

May they rest in peace, O Lord, those who did not arrive!

Though the sharashka authorities would be easy on them when they left, even letting them keep their own razors until they reached the first prison, these questions weighed like eternal doom on the hearts of those twenty zeks who were told to get ready for transport that Tuesday morning.

For them the half-free, unpersecuted life of the sharashka zeks had ended.

86

FAREWELL, SHARASHKA!

Although Nerzhin was absorbed in the immediate concerns occasioned by his leaving, the conviction flared in him—and became more intense by the minute—that he must, in farewell, give Major Shikin a really bad time. So when the bell rang for work, despite the command to stay in the dormitory, he, like the rest of the zeks on the transport roster, rushed through the doors of the sharashka. He flew up to the third floor and knocked on Shikin's door. He was told to come in.

Shikin sat grim and dark behind his desk. Since yesterday something inside him had snapped. One foot was already over the abyss, and he knew how it feels to have nothing to stand on.

His hatred for that boy could find no direct or quick release. The most Shikin could do—the least dangerous course for himself—was to knock Doronin around in a punishment cell, dirty up his record, and then send him back to Vorkuta. There, with the record he'd have when Shikin got through with it, he would land in a special brigade and soon kick off. The result would be the same as if he'd been tried and shot.

Now, as the morning began, he put off calling Doronin in for questioning because he expected protests and difficulties from the men who were scheduled for the transport.

He was not wrong. Nerzhin came in.

Major Shikin had never been able to stand this thin, unpleasant zek with his rigid manner and meticulous knowledge of all the laws. Shikin had been urging Yakonov to pack Nerzhin off on a transport for a long time, and he noticed Nerzhin's hostile expression with malicious satisfaction, assuming he had come to demand the reason he was being shipped out.

Nerzhin had a natural gift for framing a complaint in a few striking words, and for uttering it fervently in that brief second when the food slot in the cell door was open, or for writing it on the soft toilet paper that was provided in prisons for written declarations. After five years in prison he had worked out, too, a particularly determined manner of talking with higher-ups—known, in zek language, as the unobjectionable taunt. His words were courteous, but his tone was lofty and ironic—the tone elders adopt when conversing with their juniors. It was impossible, however, to object to it.

"Citizen Major," he said from the doorway, "I have come to get the book illegally taken from me. I have grounds for supposing that six weeks are long enough, considering the state of communications in Moscow, to find out that it is not prohibited by the censors."

"Book?" Shikin exclaimed, because he could not at first find anything more intelligent to say. "What book?"

"I am equally certain," Nerzhin went on, "that you know what book I am talking about. The selected works of Sergei Yesenin in 'The Library of Poets—Pocket Edition.'"

"Ye-se-nin?" exclaimed Major Shikin, pushing back in his chair, as if he had only then recalled that disgraceful name and was shocked by it. His gray, close-cropped scalp expressed indignation and revulsion. "How can you bring yourself to ask for Ye-se-nin?"

"And why not? He was published here in the Soviet Union."

"That's not a reason."

"Besides, he was published in 1940—in other words, not in the forbidden period between 1917 and 1938."

Shikin frowned. "Where did you hear about any such period?"

Nerzhin replied succinctly, as if he had learned the answer by heart: "One of the camp censors very kindly explained it to me. During a pre-holiday search, Dahl's *Dictionary* was taken from me, on the grounds that it had been published in 1935 and was therefore subject to the most careful verification. But when I showed the censor that my copy was a facsimile of the 1881 edition, he readily returned the book to me, and explained that there were no objections to prerevolutionary editions because 'enemies of the people were not active at that time.' Unfortunately for you, this Yesenin was published in 1940."

Shikin maintained a dignified silence. Then he said insistently, "Very good. But have you read the book? Have you read it all? Can you confirm that in writing?"

"Under Section 95 of the Criminal Code of the U.S.S.R. you have no grounds for requiring my signature in the present case. I confirm it orally: I have the unfortunate habit of *reading* those books that are my property, and, conversely, of keeping only those books that I read."

Shikin spread his hands in a warning gesture. "So much the worse for you!"

He intended to pause meaningfully, but Nerzhin swiftly brushed the pause aside.

"So, to sum up, I repeat my request. In accordance with item seven of Section B of the prison rules, kindly return the book which was illegally taken from me."

Twitching under this flow of words, Shikin stood up. When he was sitting behind the desk, his large head led one to expect a big man; when he got up, he seemed to shrink, because his arms and legs were very short. Glowering, he approached the cabinet, unlocked it, and took out the lovely little volume of Yesenin, with yellow maple leaves on the dust jacket.

He had marked several places. He sat down comfortably in his armchair as before, without inviting Nerzhin to be seated, and began unhurriedly looking over the places he had marked. Nerzhin sat down calmly, his hands on his knees; he watched Shikin with a heavy, relentless stare.

"Well, here, listen to this," the major said with a sigh, and began to read without feeling, pounding the rhythm of the poetry like dough:

> "In a lifeless and alien grip
> My poems will die too.
> Only nodding oats
> Will mourn for their old master.

What master is he talking about? Whose grip?"

The prisoner looked at the security officer's fat white hands.

"In a class sense Yesenin was a limited person, and there was a lot he didn't altogether understand," Nerzhin said soothingly, pursing his lips. "Like Pushkin and like Gogol . . ."

There was something new in Nerzhin's voice which made Shikin look at him apprehensively. In the presence of zeks who weren't afraid of him, Shikin himself felt a secret fear, the usual fear of well-dressed, well-to-do people when they confront people who are badly dressed and worse than badly off. His authority at this moment was an inadequate defense. Just in case, he rose and half-opened the door.

"And what do you make of this?" he demanded, returning to his armchair and reading:

> "A white rose and a black toad
> I wanted to wed on earth. . . .

There. What's he hinting at there?"

A slight spasm shook the prisoner's tense throat. "Very simple," he replied. "One should not try to reconcile the white rose of truth with the black toad of villainy."

Like a black toad, the short-armed, big-headed, dark-faced "protector" sat facing him.

"However, Citizen Major," Nerzhin's words poured swiftly on, "I don't have time to go into literary interpretations with you. The guard is waiting for me. Six weeks ago you said you would ask the censorship—GLAVLIT—about it. Did you?"

Shikin's shoulders jerked, and he clapped the yellow book shut.

"I don't have to give you an accounting! I am not going to return the book to you. In any case, you won't be allowed to take it with you."

Nerzhin stood up angrily, without taking his eyes off the

Yesenin. He was remembering how his wife's kind hands had once held the small book and how she had written in it:

And so it will be that everything lost will return to you!

The words shot from his lips without the least effort: "Citizen Major! I hope you haven't forgotten that for two years I demanded from the Ministry of State Security the Polish zlotys which had been taken from me—they'd cut the sum in half maybe twenty times; it was down to kopecks —and I got them back through the Supreme Soviet. I hope you haven't forgotten my demand that the one-fifth ounce of sifted flour allotted by law should be actually included in my ration. They laughed at me, but I got it! And there are other cases. I warn you: I will not give up that book to you. I will die in the Kolyma—but from the other side of death I'll tear it away from you! I will fill the mailboxes of all the Central Committee and the Council of Ministers with complaints against you. Give it back without all that unpleasantness."

And the major of State Security yielded to this doomed, helpless zek, being sent to a slow death. He had, in fact, inquired of GLAVLIT, and been informed, to his surprise, that the book was not formally prohibited. Formally! His keen sense of smell told Shikin that this was negligence, that the book ought beyond a doubt to be forbidden. But it followed that he had to protect himself from the accusations of this indefatigable troublemaker.

"Very good," agreed the major. "I will return it to you. But we will not let you take it with you."

Nerzhin went out to the stairway triumphantly, holding the precious book in its shiny yellow dust jacket. It was a symbol of success at a moment when everything was in ruins.

On the landing he passed a group of prisoners discussing the latest events. Siromakha was among them, orating, but too quietly for his words to reach the authorities:

"What are they doing? Sending such fellows on the transport! Why? And Ruska Doronin? Who's the rat who squealed on him?"

Holding the volume of Yesenin tightly, Nerzhin hurried to Acoustics. He was wondering how he could destroy his notes on history before the guard came for him. The men scheduled for transport were not supposed to be running around loose in the sharashka.

Nerzhin owed this last brief freedom to the large number of zeks being sent out in the transport and also, perhaps, to the gentleness of the junior lieutenant, with his everlasting professional shortcomings.

He opened the door of Acoustics. Before him the doors of the steel cabinet stood open, and standing between them was Simochka, once more wearing an unbecoming striped dress and a gray shawl around her shoulders.

There had been no word or glance between them since yesterday's cruel exchange.

She did not see but rather felt Nerzhin come in, and she was confused; she stood stock-still, as if she were trying to decide what to take out of the cabinet.

He did not reflect, he did not consider; he went over to the steel doors of the cabinet and said in a whisper, "Serafima Vitalyevna! After yesterday it is merciless to appeal to you. But my work of many years is about to be destroyed. Should I burn it? Will you take it?"

She already knew of his departure, and she did not stir when he referred to it. But in answer to his question she raised her sad, sleepless eyes and said, "Give it to me."

Someone was approaching, and Nerzhin hurriedly went on to his own desk. There he encountered Major Roitman.

Roitman's face was distressed. With an awkward smile he said, "Gleb Vikentich! How unfortunate this is! I was not warned. . . . I had no idea. . . . And now it's too late to fix things."

Nerzhin looked up and stared with cold pity at this person whom he had hitherto believed to be sincere.

"Come, Adam Veniaminovich! After all, it's not my first day here. Such things aren't done without consulting the head of the laboratory."

He began clearing out his desk drawers.

Pain showed on Roitman's face. "But, believe me, Gleb Vikentich, I was *not* asked, not warned. . . ."

He said it aloud in the presence of the whole staff. He chose to lose face with the rest rather than look like a scoundrel in the eyes of the man who was leaving.

Beads of sweat appeared on his forehead. Numbly he watched Nerzhin cleaning out his desk.

They had not, in fact, asked his advice—one more blow the colonel of engineers had dealt him.

"Am I to turn in my materials on articulation to Serafima Vitalyevna?" Nerzhin asked indifferently.

Roitman, distracted, did not reply but went slowly out of the room.

"Take my work materials, Serafima Vitalyevna," said Nerzhin and began carrying over to her desk his files, papers stapled together, charts, tables.

He had put his three notebooks in one of the files. But some sort of inner counselor was urging him not to do it.

Nerzhin swiftly studied Simochka's long, impenetrable face. And suddenly he thought: Was it a trap? A woman's vengeance? The duty of an MGB lieutenant?

Even if her waiting hands were warm, would her virginal loyalty last for long? A dandelion head lasts until the first wind; a virgin lasts until the first man. She would say to her husband, "Here is something that was left with me, darling."

He shifted the notebooks to his pocket and gave the file folders to Simochka.

The great library at Alexandria burned. In the monasteries they did not surrender but burned the chronicles. And the soot of the Lubyanka chimneys—soot from burned papers and more and more burned papers—fell upon the zeks led out to stroll in the boxlike area on the prison roof.

Perhaps more great thoughts have been burned than have been published.

If he managed to survive, he could probably do it all over again from memory anyway.

Nerzhin seized his box of matches, then ran out and locked himself in the toilet.

Ten minutes later he returned, pale and indifferent.

By this time Pryanchikov had come into the lab.

"Just how can this be possible?" he was demanding. "We aren't outraged! We are numb! Shipping prisoners! Baggage can be shipped, but who has the right to ship *people*?"

Valentulya's heated sermon found a response in the zeks' hearts. Disturbed by the transport, all the laboratory zeks stopped work. Each time, a transport meant a moment of remembrance, a moment signifying, "We'll all be there." The prisoner transport compelled each zek, even those not touched by it directly, to reflect on the uncertainty of his fate, and the fact that his whole existence was at the mercy of the GULAG ax. Even a zek who had never stepped out of line was certain to be sent away from the sharashka a couple of years before the end of his sentence, so that every thing he knew would be out of date or forgotten. Among them all, only the twenty-five-year prisoners had no fore seeable end to their terms, and therefore the operationa sector liked to have them in the sharashkas.

Slack-bodied zeks surrounded Nerzhin. Some sat on desk instead of chairs, as if to indicate the seriousness of the moment. They were pensive and melancholy.

Just as at funerals people remember everything good the deceased ever did, so now they remembered, in praise o Nerzhin, how he would stand up for their rights, and how often he had defended the prisoners' interests. There wa the famous story of the sifted flour, when he had inundated the prison administration and the Ministry of Internal Af fairs with complaints because he was not given a fifth o an ounce of sifted flour each day *in person*. According t prison regulations, collective complaints and complaints o behalf of others were both prohibited. Even though the ide: was that the prisoner was to be retrained in the direction o socialism, he was forbidden to be concerned with the com mon cause. In those days the zeks of the sharashka had no yet eaten their fill, and the struggle for the fifth of an ounc of flour aroused far keener interest than international affairs The fascinating epic ended with Nerzhin's victory: the "cap tain in charge of underdrawers," as they then called him the assistant to the prison supply officer, was fired from hi job. From the sifted flour each man in the sharashka go each day they cooked extra noodles twice a week. The zek also remembered Nerzhin's struggle to extend the Sunda exercise periods. That, however, had ended in defeat: if th prisoners were allowed to stroll about freely on Sunday who would work?

Nerzhin himself hardly listened to all these eulogies. Fo him the moment of action had come and energy was erupt ing in him. Now that the worst had happened, any improve ment depended on him alone. Having turned the articulatio materials over to Simochka, having turned in his classifie material to Roitman's assistant, having burned or shredde all his personal papers, having stacked up several reams o books and magazines belonging to the library, he now dug out his last possessions from his drawers and presented them to his friends. They had decided who would get his yellow swivel chair, who his German roll-top desk, who the inkwell, who the roll of imported marbled paper. The dying man personally distributed his legacy with a cheerful smile, and each of his heirs brought him two or three packs of cigarettes. That was the sharashka rule: in this world cigarettes were in abundance; in the other they were more precious than bread.

Rubin came in from the Top Secret group. His eyes were sad and the lower lids sagged.

Sorting out his books, Nerzhin said to him, "If you cared for Yesenin, I would give it to you right now."

"Would you really?" Rubin asked in astonishment.

"But you like Bagritsky better, so there's no way I can help you there."

"You have no shaving brush," Rubin said and took from his pocket a shaving brush with a polished plastic handle. By zek standards it was luxurious. "After all, I made a vow not to shave until the day I'm acquitted—so take it."

Rubin never said "the day I'm freed," because that would refer to the natural end of his term. He always said "the day I'm acquitted," and continued to petition incessantly for a review of his case.

"Thank you, old man, but you've grown so used to the sharashka that you've forgotten camp rules. Who would let me shave myself in camp? Will you help me turn in my books?"

They began collecting and arranging the books and magazines. The men around them went off in their different directions.

Each carrying a large stack, the two of them left the laboratory and went up the main staircase. In an alcove off the upper hallway they stopped to catch their breath and to rearrange the armloads which were collapsing.

Nerzhin's eyes, which had burned with morbid excitement during all the preparations, had now become dull and lethargic.

"Listen, friend," he said, "for three years we haven't agreed once, we've argued all the time, ridiculed each other, but now that I'm losing you, maybe forever, I feel so strongly that you are one of my most—most—"

His voice broke.

Rubin's big black eyes, so often sparkling with anger were warm with tenderness and shyness.

"So that's all in the past," he nodded. "Let's kiss, beast." And he took Nerzhin's face into his black pirate's beard.

A moment later, just as they entered the library, Sologdin caught up with them. He looked concerned. Without thinking, he slammed the glass door too hard and the librarian looked around at them.

"So, Gleb!" said Sologdin. "It's happened. You're going away."

Not paying the slightest attention to the "Biblical fanatic" standing beside him, Sologdin looked only at Nerzhin.

Neither did Rubin feel like having a reconciliation with the "boring hidalgo," and he looked away from Sologdin.

"Yes, you are going. It's bad. Very bad."

It didn't matter how much they had talked together during woodcutting or how much they had argued during their walks. Now there was no time nor was this the place for Sologdin to share with Nerzhin, as he had hoped, his rules of thought and life.

"Listen here," he said. "Time is money. It's still not too late. If you'll agree to stay as a specialist on project computations, perhaps I can have you kept on here . . . in a certain group. . . . But it's going to be very hard work, I warn you frankly."

Rubin looked at Sologdin in surprise.

Nerzhin sighed. "Thank you, Dmitri. I had that chance. But for some reason I'm in a mood to try an experiment for myself. The proverb says: *'It's not the sea that drowns you, it's the puddle.'* I want to try launching myself into the sea."

"Yes? Well, it's up to you, up to you." Sologdin spoke swiftly, in a businesslike manner. "I'm very sorry, very sorry, Gleb."

His face showed deep concern. He was hurrying but forcing himself not to hurry.

Thus they stood, the three prisoners, and waited for the woman librarian, a lieutenant out of uniform, with dyed hair, overpainted lips, and heavily powdered face, to check Nerzhin's library list lazily.

Troubled by the ill will between his companions, Gleb

said quietly in the total silence of the library, "Friends. You must make it up."

Neither Rubin nor Sologdin moved.

"Dmitri," Gleb insisted.

Sologdin raised the cold blue flame of his gaze. "Why do you direct your remarks *to me?*" he said, acting surprised.

"Lev!" Gleb repeated.

Rubin looked at him vacantly. "Do you know," he asked, "why horses live a long time?" After a pause he explained: "Because they never go around clarifying their relationships."

Having disposed of his official property and his official business, and having been ordered by the guard to go to the prison and get his things together, Nerzhin, carrying a pile of cigarette packages in his cupped hands, met Potapov in the hallway, hurrying along with a box under his arm. Potapov going to work was not like Potapov walking in the yard: despite his limp he walked briskly, his head thrust forward and then pulled back, squinting intently at something far off, as if with his head and his stare he were trying to outdistance his short legs. Potapov had wanted to say good-bye to Nerzhin and to the others who were leaving, but hardly had he entered the laboratory that morning than the inner logic of work took hold of him, suppressing all other feelings and thoughts. This capacity to devote himself wholly to his work, to forget about life, had been the basis of his engineering triumphs on the outside, and in prison it helped him bear his misfortunes.

"This is it, Andreich," Nerzhin said, stopping him. "The corpse was happy and smiling."

Potapov made an effort to collect himself. Understanding returned to his eyes. He raised his free arm to the back of his head, as if he wanted to scratch it.

"Hello," he said.

"I would give you my Yesenin, Andreich, but for you there's no one but Pushkin."

"We'll be there ourselves," Potapov said sadly.

Nerzhin sighed. "Where shall we meet again? At the Kotlas transit prison? At the Indigirka mines? I can hardly believe we'll run into each other strolling along a city sidewalk, can you?"

With a slight squint at the corners of his eyes, Potapov
recited:

> "I've closed my eyes to ghosts;
> Only far-distant hopes
> Sometimes stir my heart."

At the door of Number Seven Markushev's head appeared, flushed with endeavor.

"Well, Andreich! Where are the filters? The work is waiting!" he shouted in an irritated voice.

The co-authors of "Buddha's Smile" embraced awkwardly. Packages of Belomor cigarettes scattered on the
floor.

"You have to understand," said Potapov. "We're *spawning*, and there's no time."

"Spawning" was Potapov's word for that hustling, shouting, slipshod style of work which prevailed at the Mavrino
Institute—and not only there: it was the style of work which
the newspapers describe as being done in a "last-minute
rush" or "by fits and starts."

"Write me!" Potapov added, and they both laughed.
There was nothing more natural to say in parting, but in
prison this request was a mockery. Correspondence between
the islands of GULAG did not exist.

Holding his box of filters under his arm, and throwing
back his head, Potapov dashed off down the corridor, seeming hardly to limp at all.

Nerzhin hurried off to the semicircular room, where he
started gathering his things together, foreseeing with sharpened insight the painful surprises of the searches ahead, first
at Mavrino and then at Butyrskaya.

The guard had come in twice to hurry him up. The
others had already left or been herded off to the prison
headquarters. As Nerzhin was finishing his packing, Spiridon,
breathing the freshness of outdoors, came into the room in
his black pea jacket, belted twice around. Taking off his
big-eared, reddish-brown cap and carefully turning back a
corner of someone's bed to avoid soiling the white sheet, he
sat down on the steel springs in his dirty padded-cotton
pants.

"Spiridon Danilich! Look!" said Nerzhin, holding out the
book to him. "Yesenin is here!"

"He gave it back, the rat?" A ray of light flitted across

Spiridon's gloomy face, which was particularly wrinkled today.

"It's not so much the book, Danilich," Nerzhin explained, "as the principle: they must not beat us down."

"That's right," nodded Spiridon.

"Take it, take the book. It's to remember me by."

"You aren't taking it with you?" Spiridon asked absent-mindedly.

"Wait a minute," Nerzhin said, taking back the book and opening it, looking for a page. "I'll find it for you, right here you can read . . ."

"Well, go on, Gleb," Spiridon said gloomily in farewell. "You know how life is in camp: your heart aches for the work, and your legs keep dragging you toward the clinic."

"I'm not a novice any more, so don't worry about me, Danilich. I want to try to work. You know what they say: 'It's not the sea that drowns you, it's the puddle.' "

Then, looking carefully at Spiridon, Nerzhin noticed that he was not himself, not himself at all, and that his distress could not be attributed merely to his parting with his friend. Then he remembered that yesterday, after the announcement of the new restrictions, the exposure of the informers, Ruska's arrest, and the conversation with Simochka, he had completely forgotten that Spiridon was to have received a letter from home. He put the book aside.

"The letter. Did you get your letter, Danilich?"

Spiridon's hand was in his pocket, holding the letter.

He brought it out; the envelope, folded in two, was already worn at the fold.

"Here . . . But you haven't time," Spiridon said, his lips trembling.

The envelope had indeed been folded and unfolded many times since yesterday. The address was written in the large round trusting hand of Spiridon's daughter, the scrawl she had preserved from the fifth grade, beyond which she had not had the chance to go.

According to his and Spiridon's custom, Nerzhin began reading the letter aloud:

MY DEAR FATHER!
    It's not fair to write to you, but I don't dare live any longer. What bad people there are in the world. What they promise—and how they deceive . . .

Nerzhin's voice fell. He looked up at Spiridon and met his wide, almost blind eyes staring from beneath his tangled red brows. But there wasn't a second to find any genuine words of comfort. The door swung open, and Nadelashin burst in angrily.

"Nerzhin!" he shouted. "When someone's decent to you, you treat them like this! Everyone is out there—you're the last!"

The guards were hurrying to get the zeks destined for the transport into the headquarters building before lunch began, so they wouldn't meet anyone else.

Nerzhin embraced Spiridon, one hand clasping the thick hair at his neck.

"Get moving! Get moving! Not a minute more!" cried the junior lieutenant.

"Danilich, Danilich!" said Nerzhin, embracing the red-haired janitor.

Spiridon sighed, wheezing in his chest, and waved his hand.

"Good-bye, Gleb."

"Good-bye forever, Spiridon Danilich!"

They kissed each other's cheeks. Nerzhin took up his things and went out in a rush, accompanied by the duty officer.

Spiridon took the open book in unwashed hands scored with years of dirt, put his daughter's letter inside the maple leaf cover, and went off to his own room.

He did not notice that he had knocked his matted fur cap off the bed with his knee, and that he had left it lying there on the floor.

87

MEAT

As the zeks scheduled for the transport came into the prison headquarters, they were searched. When the search was completed, they were taken into a room containing two bare tables and one rough bench. Major Myshin was present throughout the search, and from time to time Lieutenant Colonel Klimentiev came in, too. The plump, lilac-colored major did not deign to bend down to the sacks and suitcases —it would not have befitted his rank in any event—but his presence could only inspire the guards who were doing the actual searching. They eagerly undid all the prisoners' clothes, bundles, and rags and made a particular fuss about anything that contained writing. There was a rule that those leaving the special prison could not take with them a scrap of anything written, drawn, or printed. Therefore most of the zeks had burned all letters beforehand, destroyed their notes on their work, and given away their books.

One prisoner, Engineer Romashev, who had only six months left before the end of his term, having already served some nineteen and a half years, was openly taking with him a big file of clippings covering a long period, notes and calculations for the installation of hydroelectric power stations. He was expecting to go to Krasnoyarsk Province and was counting on working at his profession there. Although this file had already been reviewed personally by Colonel of Engineers Yakonov, who had put his visa on it so that it could be removed from the sharashka, and although Major Shikin had sent it to the section, where another visa had been issued, all Romashev's months of frenzied determination and planning turned out to be in vain. Major Myshin declared that he knew nothing about the file, and he ordered it to be taken away. It was carried off, and Engineer Romashev, his weary eyes accustomed to everything, watched it go. He had survived a death sentence and a prisoner transport in a cattle car from Moscow to Sovetskaya Gavan. In a mine in the Kolyma he had put his leg under an ore car to break his shinbone. Lying in the hospital, he had escaped the fearful death of the Arctic "general work assignments." Even the destruction of ten years' work was not worth crying over.

Another prisoner on the transport was the short, bald designer, Syemushkin, who on Sunday had invested so much effort in darning his socks. He was by contrast a newcomer, having served about two years altogether, and those only in prisons and the sharashka. He was extremely frightened about going to a camp. But despite his fright and his despair he tried to keep a small volume of Lermontov, who was a cult with him and his wife. He begged Major Myshin to return the book, and wrung his hands childishly. Affronting the sensibilities of the veteran zeks, he tried to get into the lieutenant colonel's office, but was not admitted. Suddenly he grabbed the Lermontov from the hands of the "protector," who jumped back to the door in alarm, regarding the action as a signal for revolt. Syemushkin, with a strength no one suspected he possessed, tore the green covers from the book, hurled them aside, and proceeded to tear out the pages, weeping and shouting as he threw them about the room, "Take them! Devour them. Swallow them down!"

The search went on.

By the time it was over, the zeks hardly recognized each other. On command they had thrown their blue coveralls onto one pile, their government-issue, stamped underwear onto another, and their overcoats—unless they were completely worn out—onto a third. Now they were all dressed in their own clothes, or in makeshift replacements of their own clothes. In the years of their service at the sharashka they had not earned any new clothes. It was not a question of spite or miserliness on the part of the authorities. The authorities were under the eye of the accountant.

Therefore some of them, in spite of the fact that it was midwinter, were left without underwear. Or else they had pulled on shorts and undershirts which were exactly the same ones they had worn the day of their arrival from camp and which, unlaundered for years, had been gathering mold in bags in the storeroom. Others wore clumsy camp shoes, for anyone who had camp shoes in his bundle had his regular shoes with their rubber overshoes taken away. Others had on canvas boots with hard soles, and the really fortunate ones wore felt boots.

Felt boots are the prisoner's second soul. The most deprived of all creatures on earth, less forewarned of his future than a frog, a mole, or a field mouse, the zek is defenseless against the reversals of fate. In the warmest, deepest den, the zek can never be free of the fear that in the night to come he will be thrust forth into the horrors of winter, that an arm with a sky-blue stripe will seize him and drag him off to the North Pole. It is a misery, then, if one's feet aren't shod in felt boots; he will throw them into the Kolyma from the back of a truck, like two lumps of ice. A zek with out his own felt boots will live all winter in hiding, will lie, dissimulate, endure any insults or persecute anyone else, in order to avoid a winter transport. But the zek who has his own felt boots is fearless! He looks boldly into the authorities' eyes and receives his travel orders with the smile of Marcus Aurelius.

Though there was a thaw outside, all those who had their own felt boots, including Khorobrov and Nerzhin, put them on and walked proudly around the room in them. They did this partly to cut down their load, but mainly to feel their reassuring warmth, even though today they were only going to Butyrskaya Prison, where it was no colder than at the sharashka. Only the fearless Gerasimovich, who had refused to help them trap people, had nothing of his own, and the checkroom had issued him, "as replacements," a long-sleeved pea jacket which wouldn't fasten in the front and had "been in use" and stubby canvas shoes, which had also "been in use."

Thanks to his pince-nez, he looked particularly comical in these clothes.

The search was over. All twenty zeks were herded into an empty waiting room with the things they had been allowed to keep. The door was shut behind them, and a guard was posted at the door while they waited for the Black Maria. Another guard was sent out to patrol the slippery ice beneath the windows, in order to chase away anyone who might come to see them off during the lunch break.

In this way all contact was broken off between the twenty who were leaving and the 261 remaining.

Those awaiting transport were still in the sharashka, and yet they were not there.

They found places to sit wherever they could, on their bundles or on the benches, and at first they were all silent.

Each reviewed the search: what had been taken from him and what he had left. And thought about the sharashka: the advantages he was losing by leaving it, and how much of his term had been spent there and how much was left. As prisoners will, they would count the months and years over and over: the time already lost and the time that remained to lose.

They thought about their families, whom they would be cut off from for who knew how long? And of the fact that they would have to ask them for help again. For GULAG was a land in which an adult man, working twelve hours a day, was unable to keep himself fed.

They thought about their unintentional blunders or the deliberate decisions which had led them to this transport.

They thought about where they would be sent, and what awaited them there, and how they would set themselves up.

Each kept his thoughts to himself, but the thoughts of all were gloomy.

Each wanted reassurance and hope.

Therefore, when they began to talk among themselves, and someone said that perhaps they wouldn't be sent to a camp after all but to another sharashka, even those who didn't believe it listened.

Even Christ in the Garden of Gethsemane, knowing his bitter fate full well, nonetheless prayed and hoped.

Khorobrov was trying to repair the handle of his suitcase which kept pulling off. He cursed loudly: "Oh, the sons-of-bitches! They can't even make a simple suitcase. Some bastard had an idea for economizing, God damn his hide, so they bent the ends of a steel arc and shoved it into the handle holes. It holds as long as the suitcase is empty. But just try to fill it up!"

Some bricks had fallen from the side of the stove (they had been laid according to the same principle of economy), and Khorobrov was angrily using a piece of one to beat the steel arc back into the holes.

Nerzhin understood Khorobrov. Each time he encountered humiliation, neglect, mockery, shoddiness, Khorobrov was outraged. And how, indeed, could one stay calm about such things? Could refined speech convey the animal cry of someone who has been hurt? On the threshold of sinking back into camp life, Nerzhin felt that important element of male freedom returning: every fifth word would be a mother oath.

Romashev was quietly telling the newcomers which railroads were usually used to transport prisoners to Siberia and describing the superiority of the Kuibyshev transit prison over those at Gorky and Kirov.

Khorobrov stopped pounding; in a rage he hurled the brick to the floor, where it burst into red fragments.

Then Nerzhin, feeling as though he were drawing energy from his camp clothes, got up, demanded that the guard call Nadelashin, and declared in a loud voice, "Junior Lieutenant! We can see through the window that lunch has been going on for half an hour. Why aren't we being brought any?"

The junior lieutenant shuffled his feet awkwardly and replied apologetically, "You have been taken off rations as of today."

"What do you mean, taken off?" And hearing a drone of supporting discontent behind him, Nerzhin pressed his point: "Go tell the head of the prison we're not going anywhere without lunch! And we won't let ourselves be loaded on by force either."

"Very good, I'll report that!" said the junior lieutenant, giving in at once. He hurried off guiltily to the authorities.

No one in the room kept quiet out of politeness; they all protested loudly. The squeamish and gratuitous good manners of people thriving in freedom seemed insane to a zek.

"You're right!"

"Work on them!"

"The rats are squeezing us."

"The misers! Three years of work and they're stingy about one lunch."

"We won't go! It's that simple! What can they do to us now?"

Even those who had been quiet and submissive to the authorities in the daily routine became bold now. The free wind of the transit prison was in their faces. This last chance to eat meat meant not only the last full stomach before months and years of thin gruel; it also meant their human dignity. And even those whose throats were dry with apprehension and who were incapable of eating anything at that moment, even they, forgetting their anguish, demanded lunch.

From the window they could see the path from headquarters to the kitchen. They could see a truck backing up to the woodpile, with a big fir tree in the rear, its branches and tip sticking out over the truck bed. The prison supply officer got out of the cab and a guard jumped off the back.

The lieutenant colonel had kept his word. Tomorrow or the day after, the fir tree would be set up in the semicircular room, and the zeks—fathers deprived of their children— would become children again themselves, would hang decorations on it, having been prodigal of government time in making them. Clara's little basket and the bright moon in its glass cage would be hung on it, and the mustached and bearded men would form a circle and, howling the wolf cry of their fate, would dance around the tree with bitter laughter:

> "In the forest grew a fir tree,
> In the forest it did grow. . . ."

They could see the guard beneath the window driving off Pryanchikov, who was trying to break through to the besieged zeks, and who was shouting something, raising his arms to the sky.

They could see Junior Lieutenant Nadelashin hurrying anxiously to the kitchen, then to headquarters, back to the kitchen, and back to headquarters.

And they could see, too, that Spiridon had been dragged away from his lunch to unload the fir tree from the truck. On the way, he wiped off his mustache and shifted his belt.

The junior lieutenant finally ran to the kitchen once again, and soon he was leading out two cooks who were carrying a milk can with a dipper between them. A third woman came behind them with a stack of bowls. Afraid of slipping, she stopped near the door. The junior lieutenant returned and took some of the bowls from her.

There was a stir of victory in the room.

Lunch appeared in the doorway. They began ladling out the soup at the table, and the zeks took their bowls and carried them off to their own corners, sitting on window sills and on suitcases. Some managed to eat standing up leaning against the high table where there were no benches.

The junior lieutenant and the servers left. In the room that real silence fell which should always accompany eating. They thought: "Here is a fat rich soup, a little thin to be sure, but with a meat flavor that one can taste; I am putting into my mouth this spoonful, and this one, and this one with the speck of fat and the white fibers of meat; the warm liquid will pass down my esophagus into my stomach; and my blood and muscles are already celebrating in anticipation of new reinforcements and new strength."

Nerzhin remembered the proverb: "For meat marry a man, for fine stew marry a woman." He understood the saying to mean that a man will provide the meat, but it takes a woman to cook it. Common people never attribute lofty motives to themselves in their proverbs. In their thousand of proverbs the Russian people were more candid about themselves than Tolstoi and Dostoyevsky in their confessions.

When there was almost no more soup and the aluminum spoons were scraping the bowls, someone drawled, "Yes. Yes."

From a corner came the reply: "Get ready for the fast, brothers!"

Some critic or other commented, "They scraped the bottom of the pot, and it's not thick enough. Maybe they fished out the meat for themselves."

Still another voice joined in wearily: "Yes, but we won't be having soup like this soon again!"

Then Khorobrov struck his spoon on his empty bowl and said distinctly, protest rising in his throat, "No, my friends! 'Better bread with water than pie with trouble.'"

No one answered him.

Nerzhin began to pound on the table and demand the main course.

The junior lieutenant appeared immediately.

"Have you eaten?" He looked around at the transportees with a cordial smile. And discovering in their faces the good humor brought on by satiety, he said what his prison experience had taught him not to say before: "There wasn't any of the main course left. They're washing out the pot. I'm sorry."

Nerzhin looked around at the zeks to see if they would raise a row. But with their Russian trait of being easily appeased, they had all calmed down.

"What was the main course?" a bass voice boomed out.

"Stew," said the junior lieutenant, smiling shyly.

They sighed.

For some reason they didn't think about dessert.

Outside the wall they heard an engine. The junior lieutenant was summoned, and was thus able to get away.

In the corridor they heard the harsh voice of Lieutenant Colonel Klimentiev.

Then they were called out one at a time.

Their names weren't checked off against a list because their own sharashka guard was to accompany the zeks to Butyrskaya and turn them over at that point. They counted each one as he took the step which was at once so familiar and so fateful, the step from the earth up into the Black

Maria. Each zek bent his head so as not to hit the top of the steel door, crouching under the weight of his bundles and banging them awkwardly against the sides of the door.

There was no one to see them off. The lunch break had ended, and the other zeks had been chased from the exercise yard into the building.

The Black Maria had been backed all the way up to the door. While loading the zeks on, even though there was no wild barking of police dogs, there was that crush, that tense bustle, caused by everyone trying to help the guard, which inevitably disturbed the prisoners, preventing them from looking around and seeing where they were.

Eighteen of them embarked this way, and not one raised his head in farewell to the tall, calm lindens which had shaded them in happy and in tragic moments throughout their long years.

The two—Khorobrov and Nerzhin—who did manage to look around didn't look at the lindens either, but at the side of the van, to see what color it was painted.

Their curiosity was rewarded.

The time had long since passed when lead-gray or black prison vans poked through city streets, creating horror among the citizens. After the war, the idea of building Black Marias exactly like grocery vans had been born in some genius' mind, and they were painted the same orange and light blue, with a sign lettered on the side in four languages:

KHLEB

    PAIN

        BROT

            BREAD

MYASO

    VIANDE

        FLEISCH

            MEAT

Just before getting into the Black Maria, Nerzhin managed to move to one side and read: "Meat."

Then he pushed through the narrow entrance door and the still narrower door beyond it, stepped on someone's feet, dragged his suitcase and bag past someone's knees, and sat down.

The space inside this three-ton Black Maria was not

"boxed"—in other words, not divided into ten steel "boxes," one to a prisoner. This van was one of the "general" variety, designed not to carry prisoners under investigation but those already sentenced; therefore its live-load capacity was much greater. In the rear, two steel doors with small gratings that served as air vents closed off a cramped vestibule where the two guards escorting the prisoners, having locked the inner door from the outside and the outer door from the inside, and having communicated with the driver and the guard beside him through a special speaking tube, sat jammed in with their legs crossed beneath them. This rear vestibule contained one small "box" for a possible rebel. The rest of the space behind the driver's cab was a single communal mousetrap, a low metal box into which, according to the norm, exactly twenty persons could be put. But if the steel door was forced shut with four jackboots, more than twenty could be jammed in.

A bench was built around three walls of this mousetrap, leaving very little room in the middle. Those who found places sat down. But they were not the most fortunate. When the Black Maria was full, other people and other people's possessions pressed against their wedged-in knees and their cramped, numb feet, and in this crush there was no sense in being either offended or apologetic: it would be impossible to move or to change places for a full hour. Having shoved in the last prisoner, the guards leaned on the door and clicked the lock.

But they didn't slam the rear outside door, and suddenly someone was banging against the back step and a new shadow blocked the gratings in the vestibule doors.

"Brothers!" resounded Ruska's voice. "I'm off to Butyrskaya for interrogation! Who's there? Who's being sent off?"

A burst of voices exploded instantly. All twenty zeks cried out in answer. Both guards shouted for Ruska to be quiet; and from the doorway of his headquarters Klimentiev shouted to the guards not to be lax and let the prisoners communicate.

"Quiet, you motherfucker!" someone in the Black Maria roared.

Things quieted down, and the zeks could hear the guards struggling, falling over their own feet as they tried to shove Ruska into the "box."

"Who turned you in, Ruska?" shouted Nerzhin.

"Siromakha!"

"The bastard!"

"How many of you are there?" Ruska shouted.

"Twenty."

"Who?"

But the guards had finally got him into the "box" and locked it.

"Don't be afraid, Ruska!" they shouted to him. "We'll meet in camp."

As long as the rear door was open, a little light leaked into the van, but now it was slammed shut and the guards' heads blocked the last uncertain rays coming through the double gratings. The motor roared, the van shuddered, moved, and now, as it rocked, only an occasional flicker of reflected light flashed across the faces of the zeks.

This fierce calling back and forth from cell to cell, this flashing spark arcing through stones and iron, always aroused the zeks.

After a while the Black Maria stopped. It was clear they were at the gates.

"Ruska!" a zek shouted. "Are they beating you?"

The reply didn't come right away; when it did, it sounded far-off: "Yes, they're beating me."

"God damn Shishkin-Myshkin!" shouted Nerzhin. "Don't give in, Ruska!"

Again various voices cried out and there was more confusion.

They moved on, passing through the gates; then the cargo shifted sharply to the right as the van made a left turn onto the highway.

The turn threw Nerzhin and Gerasimovich hard against one another. Each stared, trying to recognize the other in the darkness. Something more than the jam in the Black Maria was pushing them toward each other.

Ilya Khorobrov, his spirits reviving a little, spoke up: "Don't worry, boys, don't be sorry we're going away. Can you call that life in the sharashka a life? You go down the hall and trip over a Siromakha. Every fifth person is an informer. You barely have time to fart in the toilet before the 'protector' hears about it. They've given us no Sundays off for two years, the sons-of-bitches. We work twelve hours a day! You give them all your brains and get three-quarters of an ounce of butter in exchange. Now you can't even write home. The hell with them. And the work? It's a kind of hell!"

Khorobrov fell silent, filled with indignation.

In the ensuing silence, over the sound of the motor running smoothly over the asphalt highway, came Nerzhin's reply:

"No, Ilya Terentich, that's not hell. That's not hell at all! We are going into hell now. We are returning to hell. The sharashka is the highest, the best, the first circle of hell. It was almost paradise."

He did not say anything more, feeling it was not necessary. Everyone knew that what awaited them was incomparably worse than the sharashka, that in the camp the sharashka would be remembered as a golden dream. But right now, to keep up their courage and their sense of the rightness of their cause, they had to curse the sharashka . . . so that no one would have any regrets . . . so that no one would reproach himself for an ill-considered step.

And Khorobrov insisted, "No, boys! 'Better bread with water than pie with trouble.'"

Concentrating on the turns the van was making, the zeks fell silent.

Yes, the taiga and the tundra awaited them, the record cold of Oymyakon and the copper excavations of Dzhezkazgan; pick and barrow; starvation rations of soggy bread; the hospital; death. The very worst.

But there was peace in their hearts.

They were filled with the fearlessness of those who have lost *everything*, the fearlessness which is not easy to come by but which endures.

Tossing about its cargo of crowded bodies, the gay orange and blue van moved through the city streets, passed a railroad station, and stopped at an intersection. A shiny maroon automobile was waiting for the same red light to change. In it rode the correspondent of the progressive French paper *Libération*, who was on his way to a hockey match at the Dynamo Stadium. The correspondent read the legend on the side of the van:

MYASO

VIANDE

FLEISCH

MEAT

He remembered that he'd already seen more than one

such van today, in various parts of Moscow. And he took out his notebook and wrote in red ink:

"On the streets of Moscow one often sees vans filled with foodstuffs, very neat and hygienically impeccable. One can only conclude that the provisioning of the capital is excellent."

1955–1964